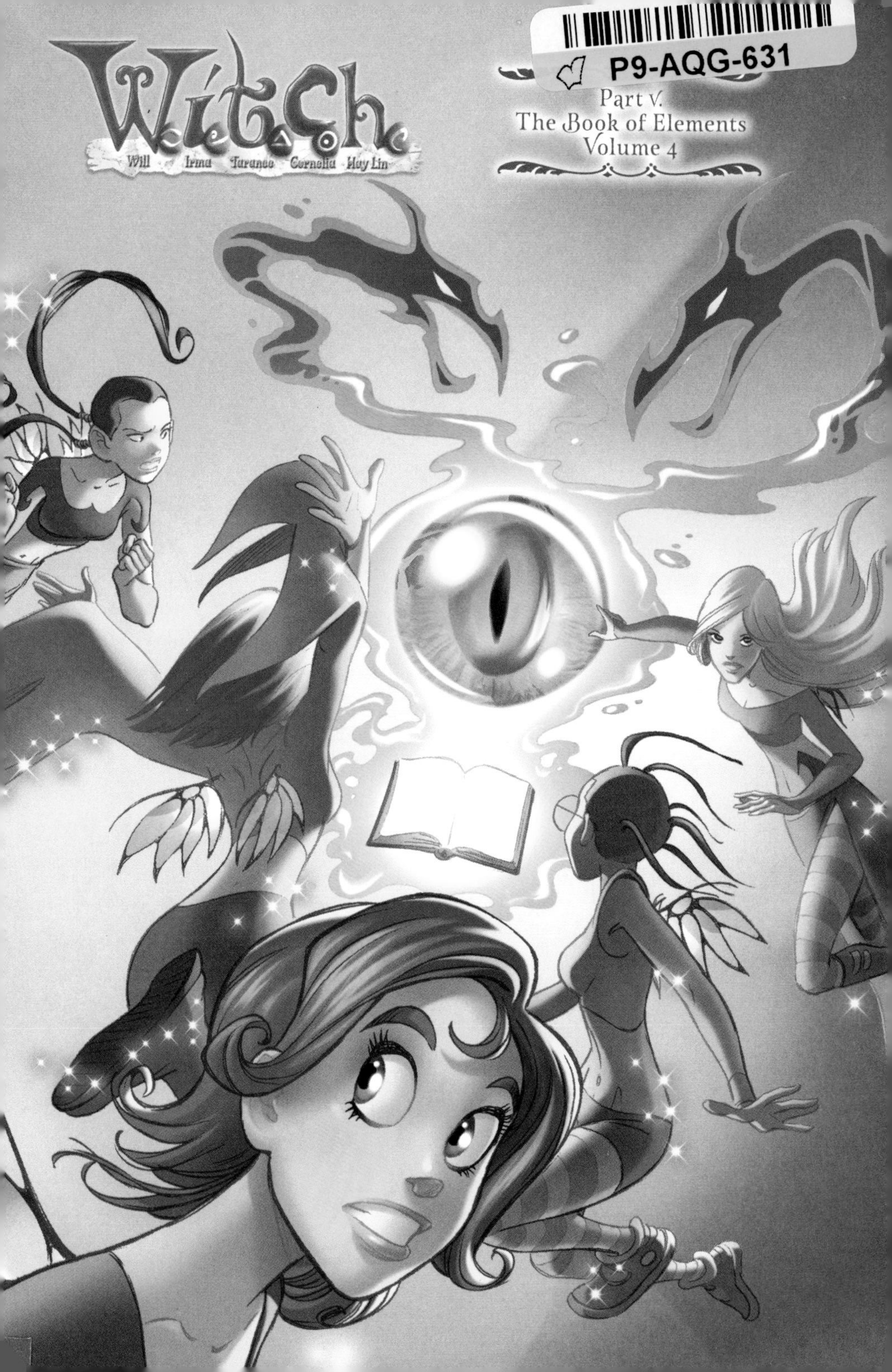
W.i.t.c.h.
Will Irma Taranee Cornelia Hay Lin
Part V.
The Book of Elements
Volume 4
P9-AQG-631

W.i.t.c.h.

Will · Irma · Taranee · Cornelia · Hay Lin

Part V.
The Book of Elements
Volume 4

CONTENTS

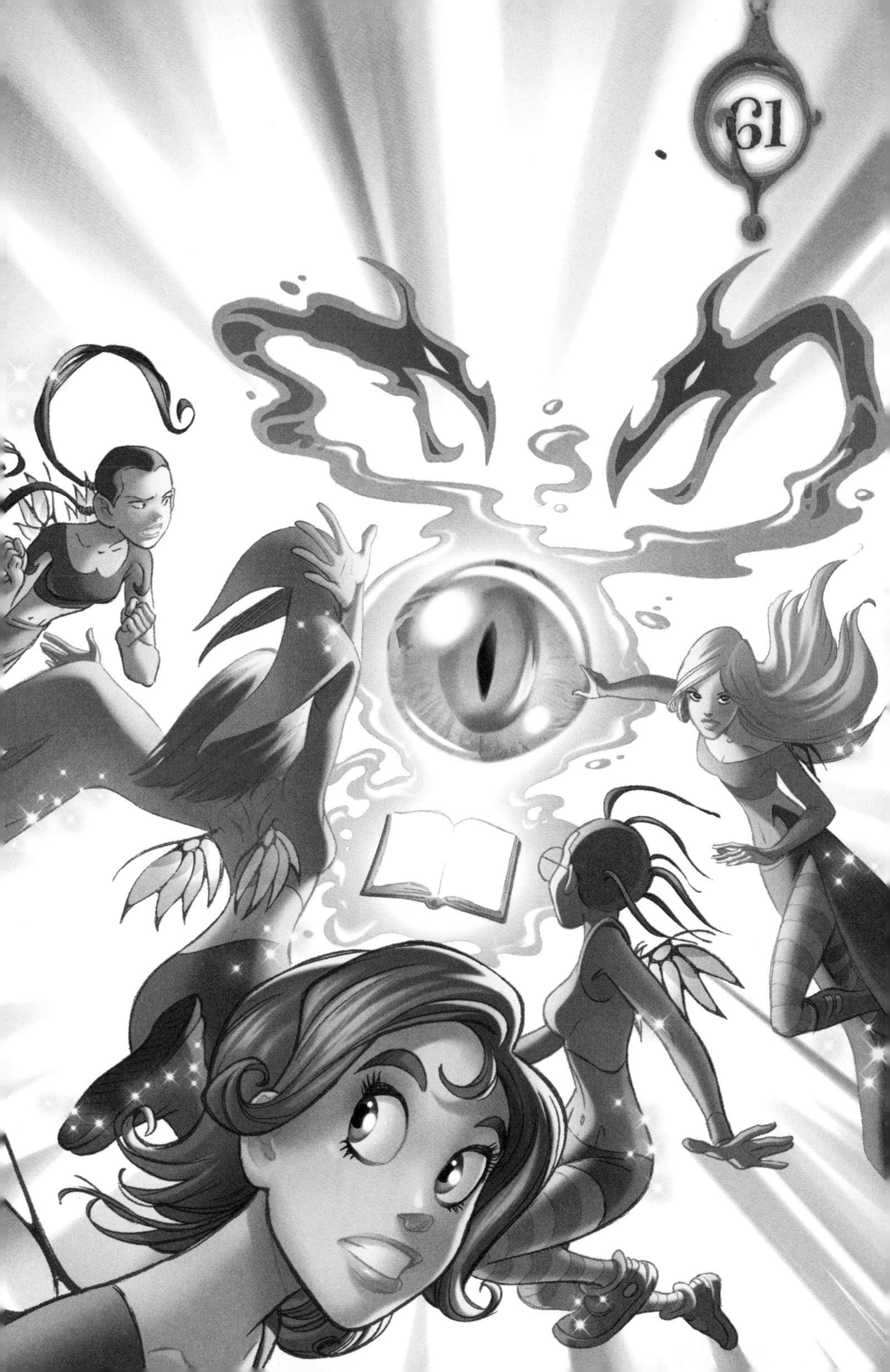
61

The World Inside the Book

"I invoke the power of the five elements."

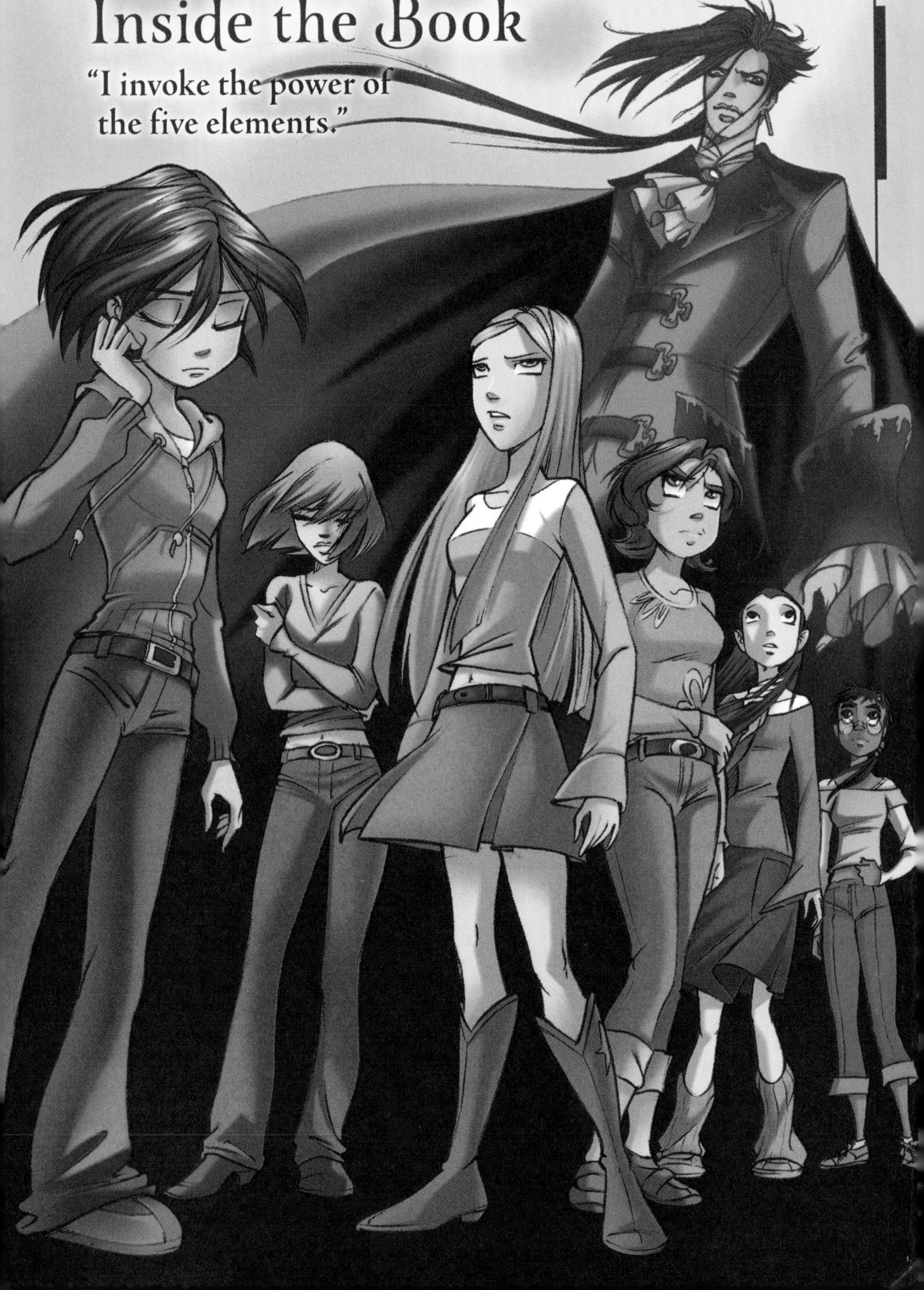

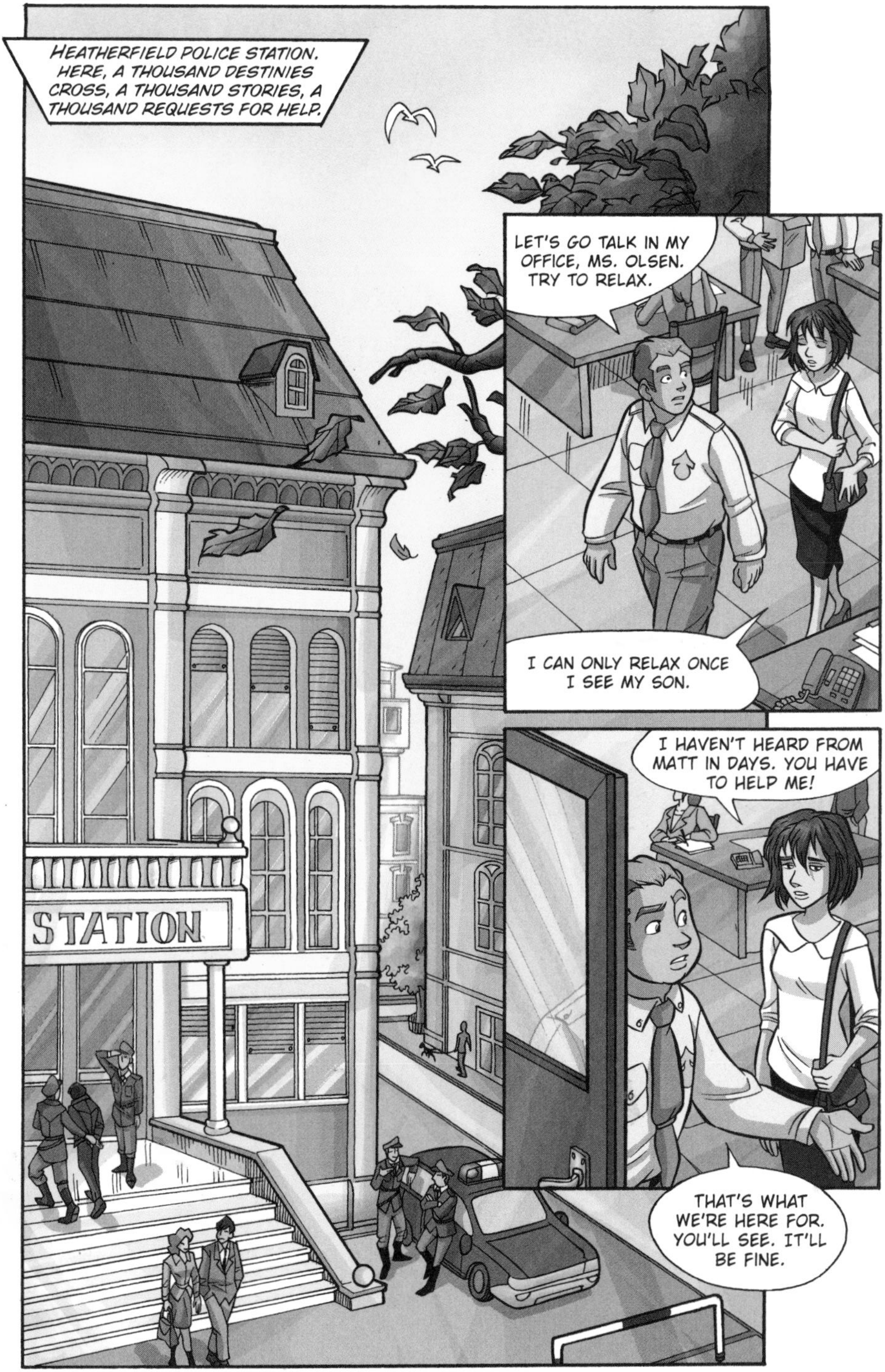
HEATHERFIELD POLICE STATION. HERE, A THOUSAND DESTINIES CROSS, A THOUSAND STORIES, A THOUSAND REQUESTS FOR HELP.
STATION
LET'S GO TALK IN MY OFFICE, MS. OLSEN. TRY TO RELAX.
I CAN ONLY RELAX ONCE I SEE MY SON.
I HAVEN'T HEARD FROM MATT IN DAYS. YOU HAVE TO HELP ME!
THAT'S WHAT WE'RE HERE FOR. YOU'LL SEE. IT'LL BE FINE.

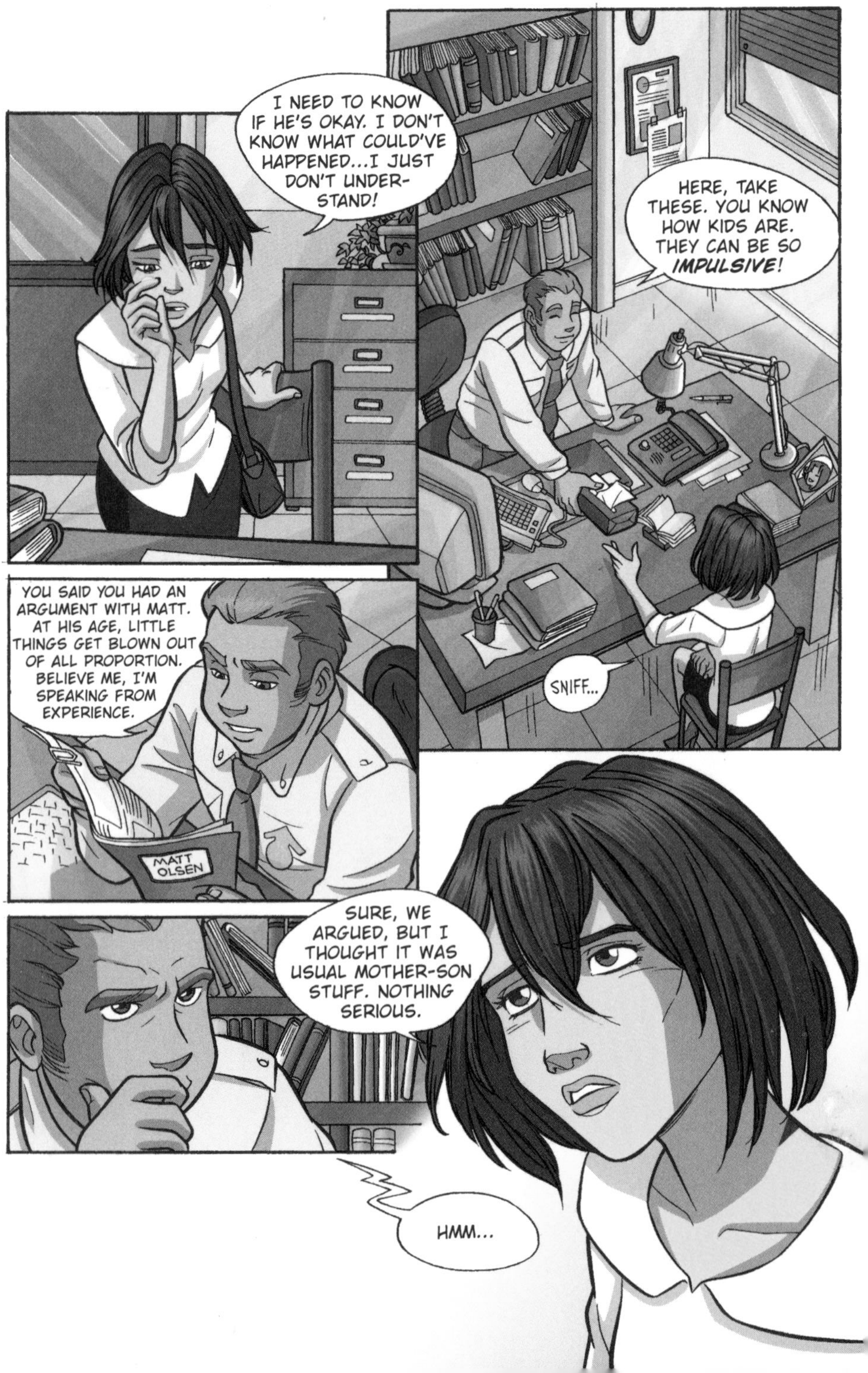
I NEED TO KNOW IF HE'S OKAY. I DON'T KNOW WHAT COULD'VE HAPPENED...I JUST DON'T UNDER-STAND!
HERE, TAKE THESE. YOU KNOW HOW KIDS ARE. THEY CAN BE SO *IMPULSIVE*!
SNIFF...
YOU SAID YOU HAD AN ARGUMENT WITH MATT. AT HIS AGE, LITTLE THINGS GET BLOWN OUT OF ALL PROPORTION. BELIEVE ME, I'M SPEAKING FROM EXPERIENCE.
MATT OLSEN
SURE, WE ARGUED, BUT I THOUGHT IT WAS USUAL MOTHER-SON STUFF. NOTHING SERIOUS.
HMM...
6

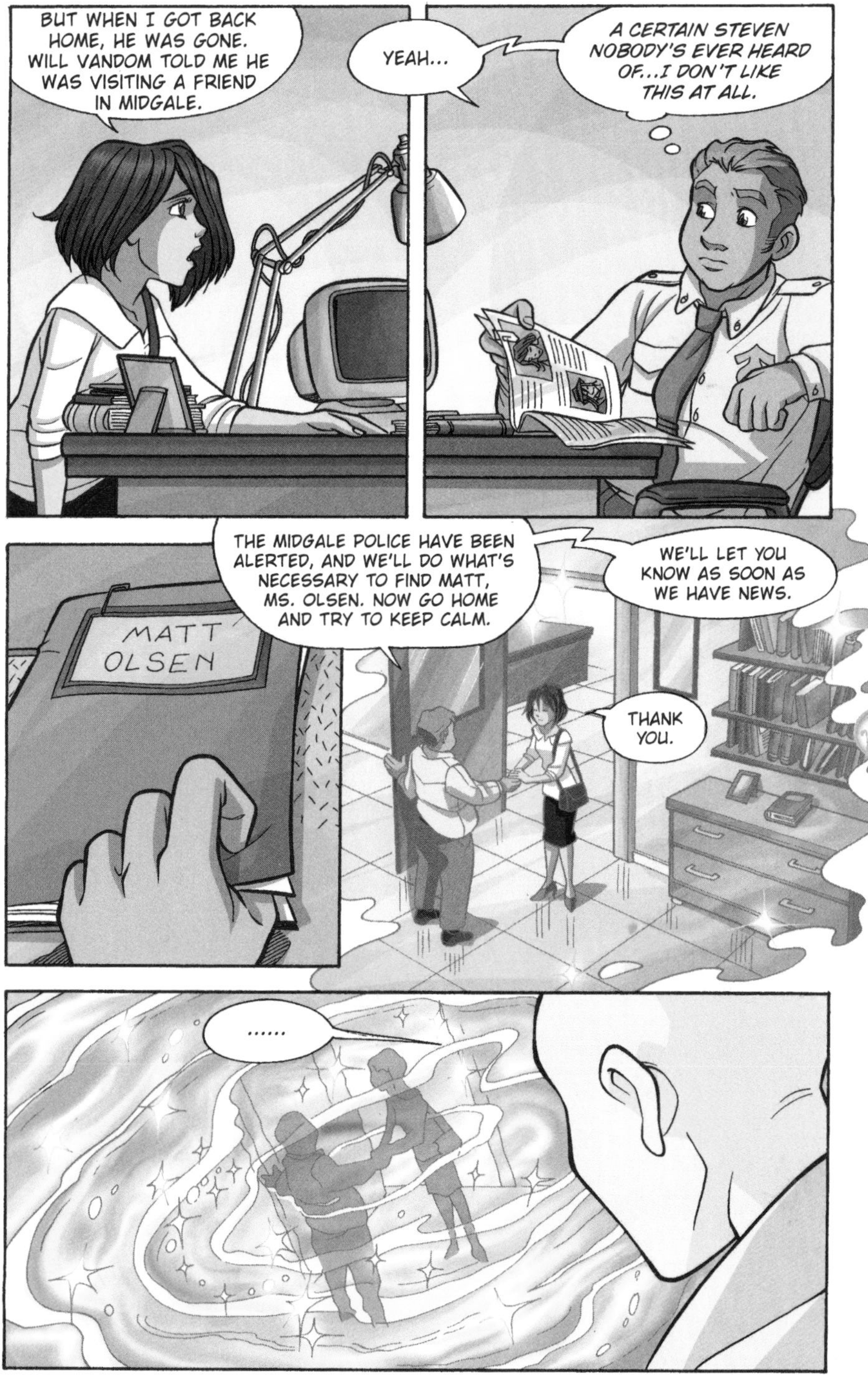
BUT WHEN I GOT BACK HOME, HE WAS GONE. WILL VANDOM TOLD ME HE WAS VISITING A FRIEND IN MIDGALE.
YEAH...
A CERTAIN STEVEN NOBODY'S EVER HEARD OF...I DON'T LIKE THIS AT ALL.
MATT OLSEN
THE MIDGALE POLICE HAVE BEEN ALERTED, AND WE'LL DO WHAT'S NECESSARY TO FIND MATT, MS. OLSEN. NOW GO HOME AND TRY TO KEEP CALM.
WE'LL LET YOU KNOW AS SOON AS WE HAVE NEWS.
THANK YOU.
......

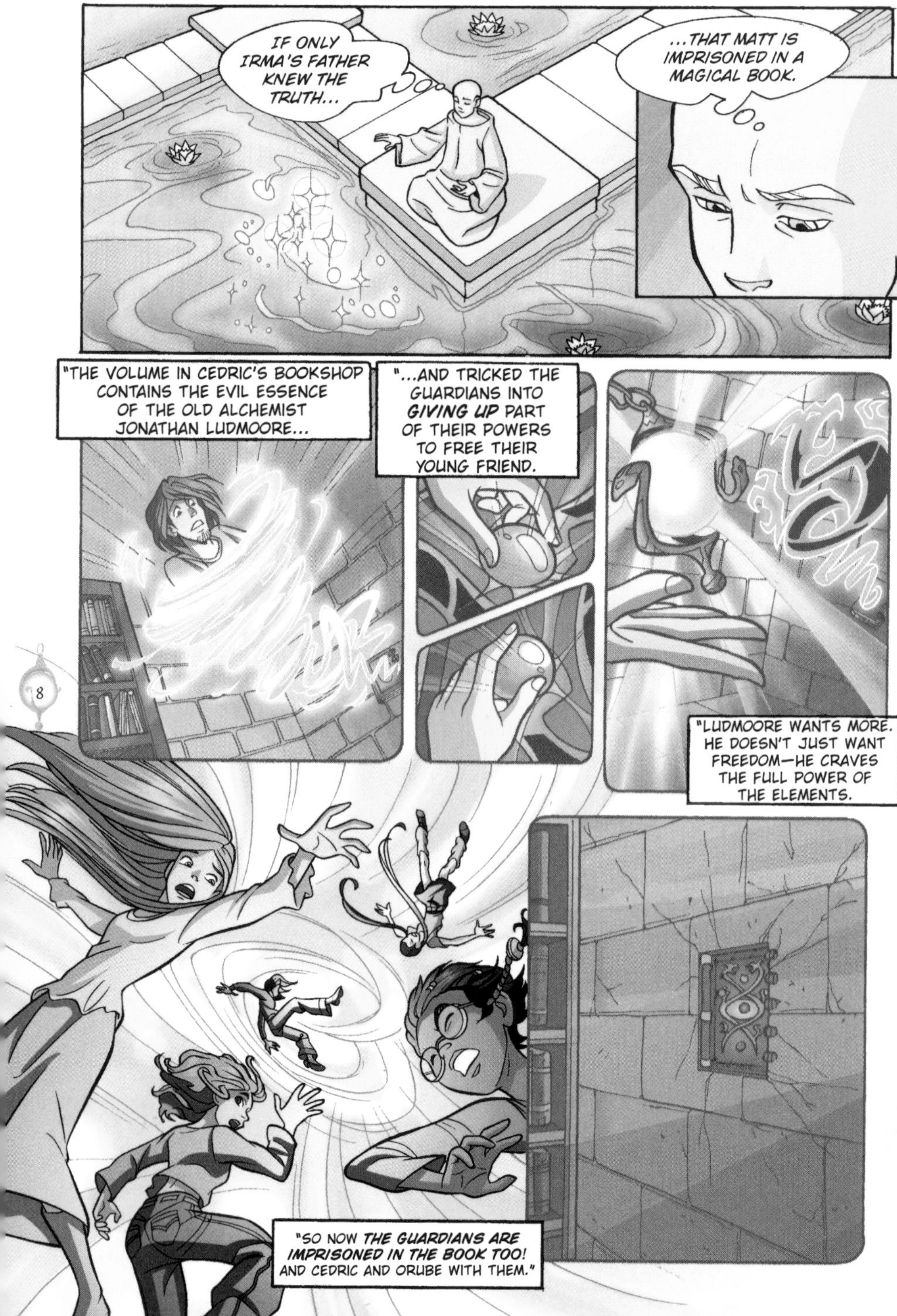

IF ONLY IRMA'S FATHER KNEW THE TRUTH...
...THAT MATT IS IMPRISONED IN A MAGICAL BOOK.
"THE VOLUME IN CEDRIC'S BOOKSHOP CONTAINS THE EVIL ESSENCE OF THE OLD ALCHEMIST JONATHAN LUDMOORE...
"...AND TRICKED THE GUARDIANS INTO GIVING UP PART OF THEIR POWERS TO FREE THEIR YOUNG FRIEND.
"LUDMOORE WANTS MORE. HE DOESN'T JUST WANT FREEDOM—HE CRAVES THE FULL POWER OF THE ELEMENTS.
"SO NOW THE GUARDIANS ARE IMPRISONED IN THE BOOK TOO! AND CEDRIC AND ORUBE WITH THEM."

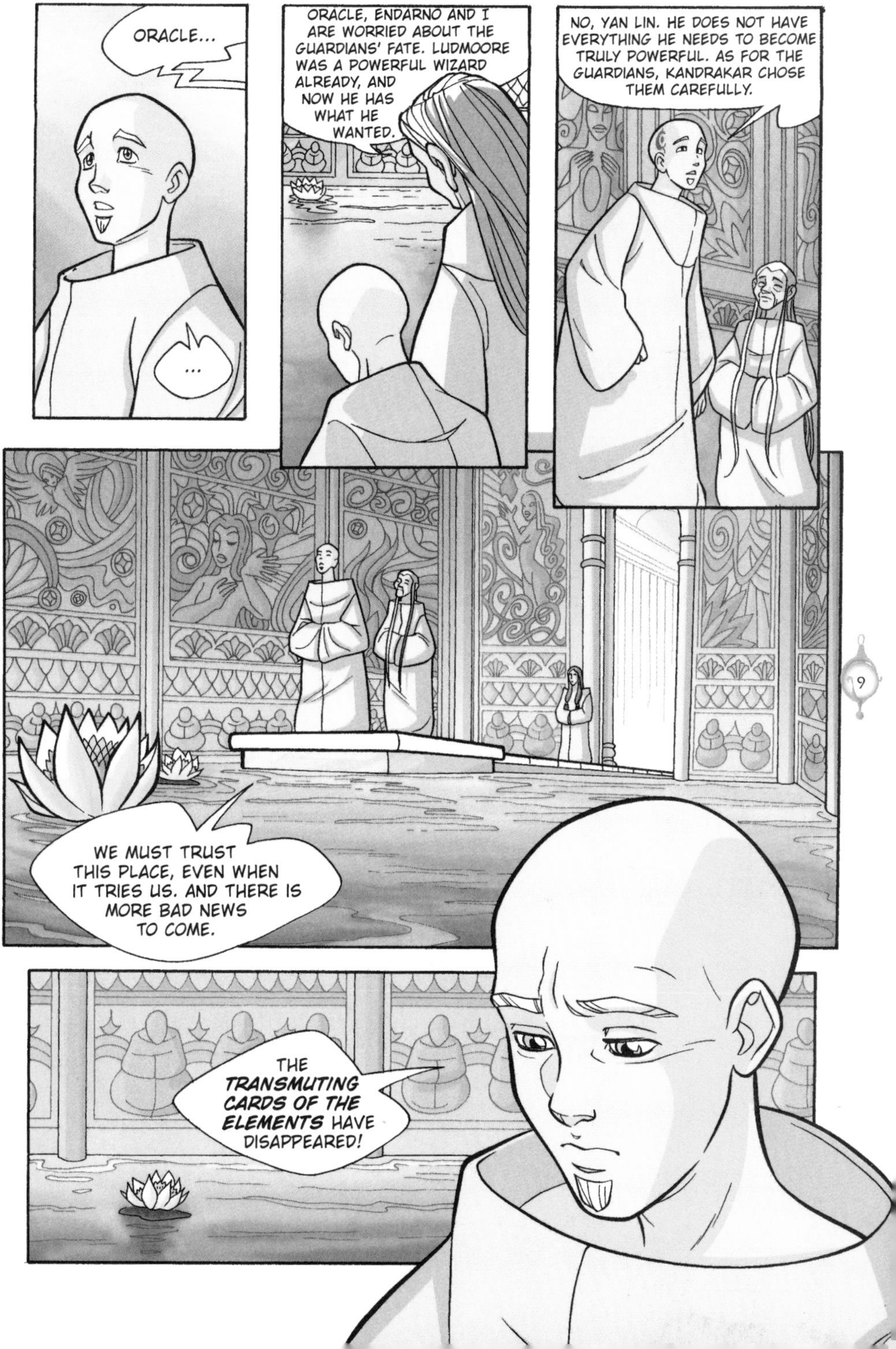
ORACLE...
...
ORACLE, ENDARNO AND I ARE WORRIED ABOUT THE GUARDIANS' FATE. LUDMOORE WAS A POWERFUL WIZARD ALREADY, AND NOW HE HAS WHAT HE WANTED.
NO, YAN LIN. HE DOES NOT HAVE EVERYTHING HE NEEDS TO BECOME TRULY POWERFUL. AS FOR THE GUARDIANS, KANDRAKAR CHOSE THEM CAREFULLY.
WE MUST TRUST THIS PLACE, EVEN WHEN IT TRIES US. AND THERE IS MORE BAD NEWS TO COME.
THE ***TRANSMUTING CARDS OF THE ELEMENTS*** HAVE DISAPPEARED!

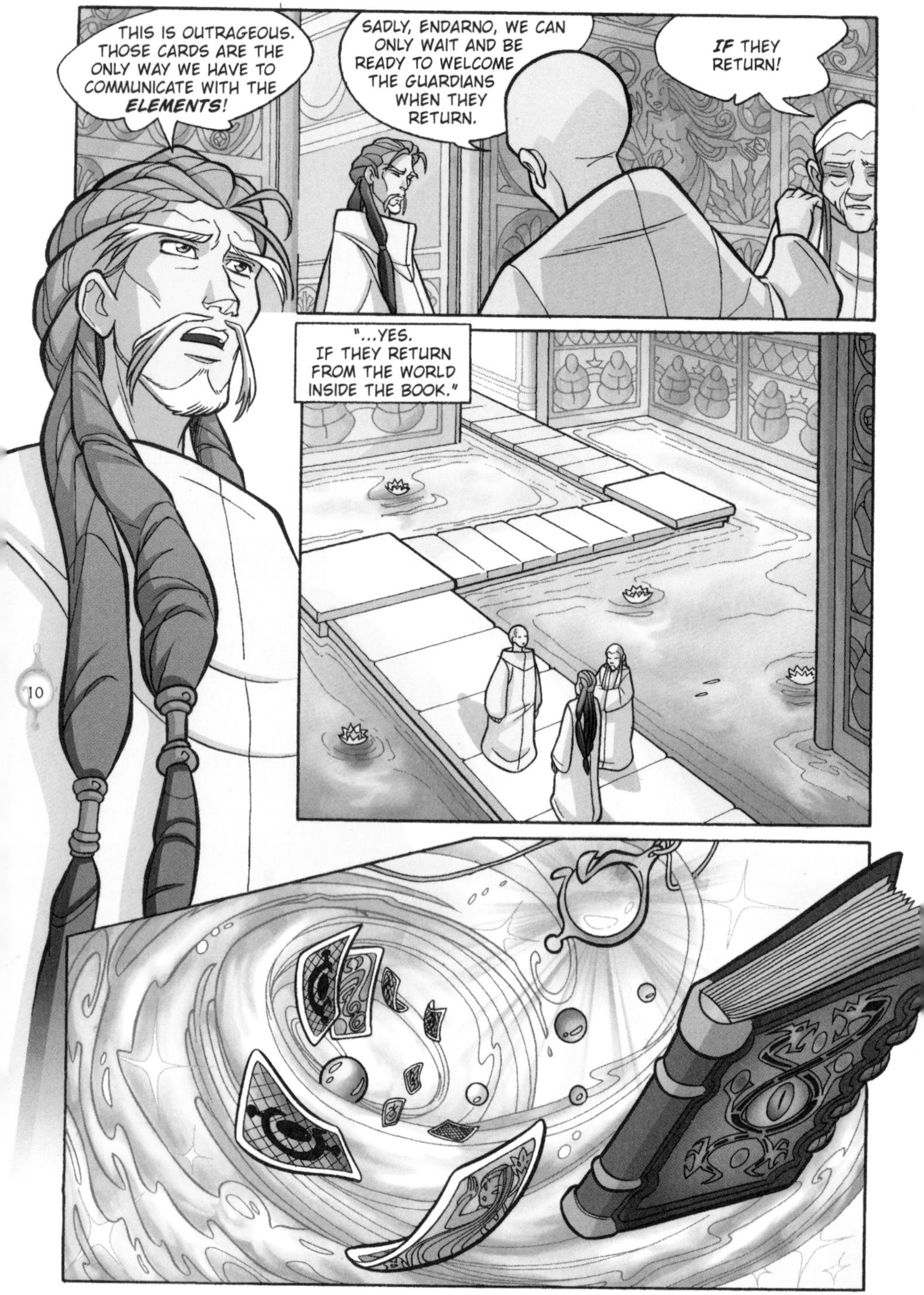
THIS IS OUTRAGEOUS. THOSE CARDS ARE THE ONLY WAY WE HAVE TO COMMUNICATE WITH THE ELEMENTS!
SADLY, ENDARNO, WE CAN ONLY WAIT AND BE READY TO WELCOME THE GUARDIANS WHEN THEY RETURN.
IF THEY RETURN!
"...YES. IF THEY RETURN FROM THE WORLD INSIDE THE BOOK."

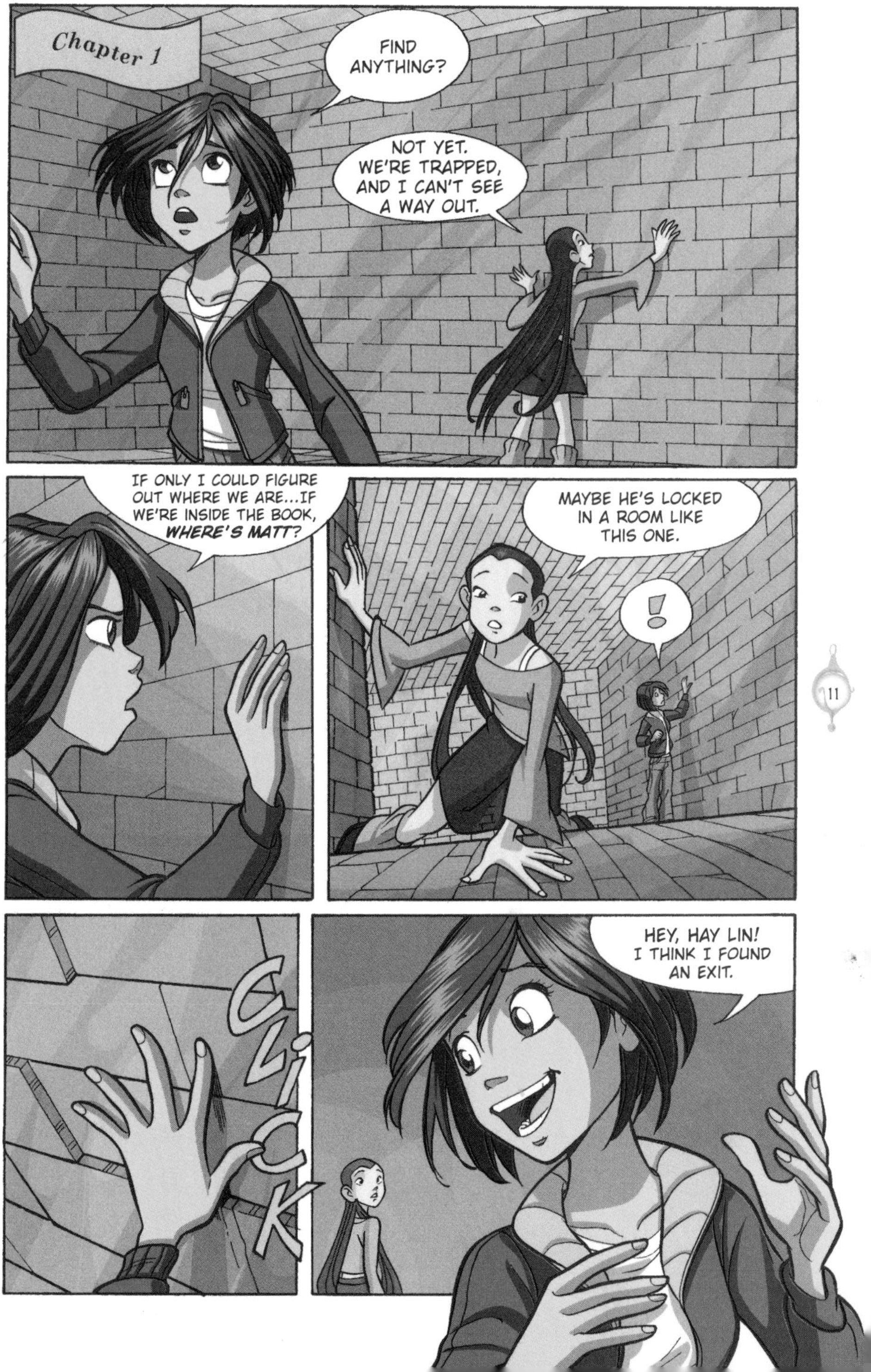
Chapter 1
FIND ANYTHING?
NOT YET. WE'RE TRAPPED, AND I CAN'T SEE A WAY OUT.
IF ONLY I COULD FIGURE OUT WHERE WE ARE...IF WE'RE INSIDE THE BOOK, **WHERE'S MATT?**
MAYBE HE'S LOCKED IN A ROOM LIKE THIS ONE.
!
CLICK
HEY, HAY LIN! I THINK I FOUND AN EXIT.

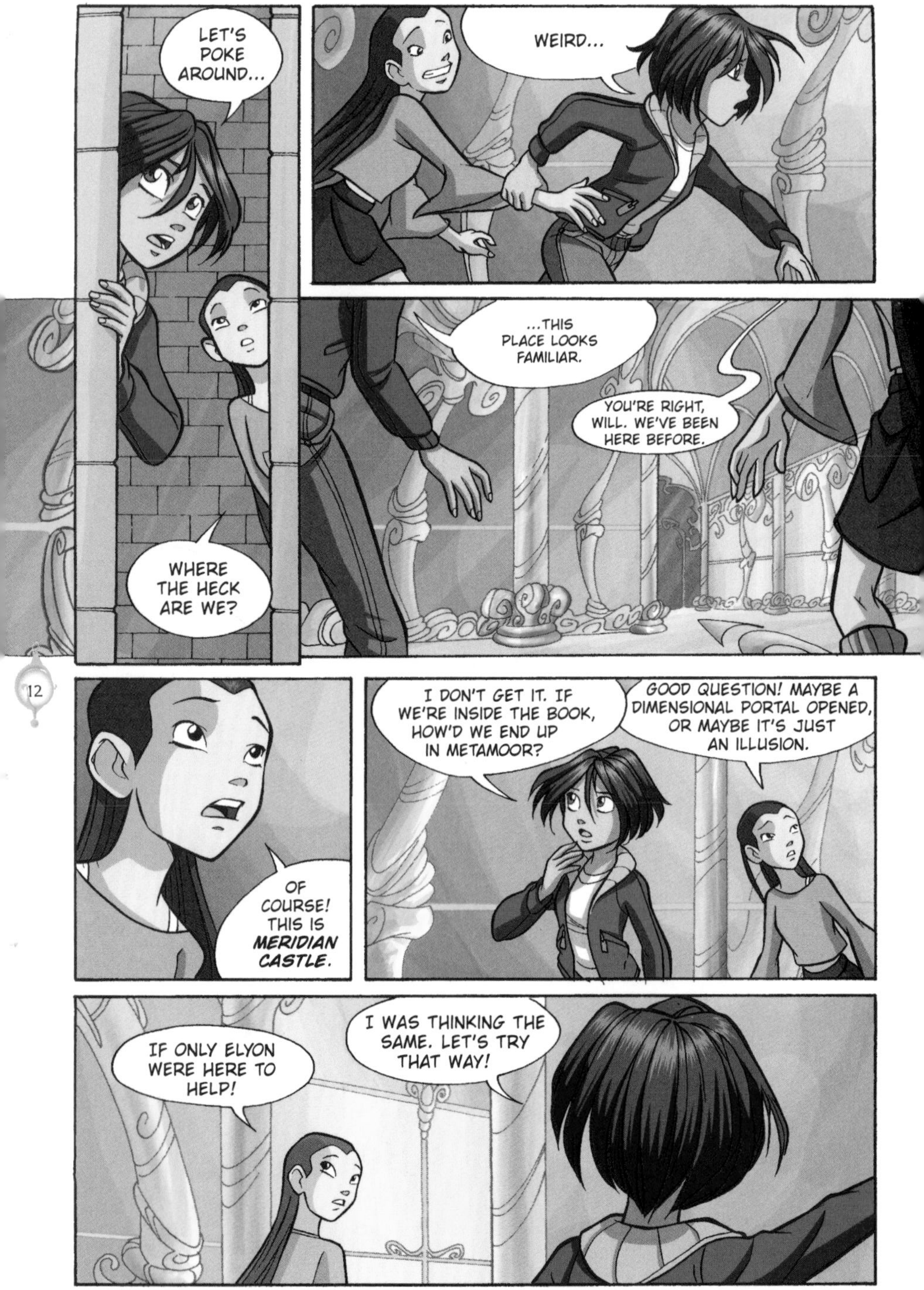
LET'S POKE AROUND...
WEIRD...
WHERE THE HECK ARE WE?
...THIS PLACE LOOKS FAMILIAR.
YOU'RE RIGHT, WILL. WE'VE BEEN HERE BEFORE.
OF COURSE! THIS IS MERIDIAN CASTLE.
I DON'T GET IT. IF WE'RE INSIDE THE BOOK, HOW'D WE END UP IN METAMOOR?
GOOD QUESTION! MAYBE A DIMENSIONAL PORTAL OPENED, OR MAYBE IT'S JUST AN ILLUSION.
IF ONLY ELYON WERE HERE TO HELP!
I WAS THINKING THE SAME. LET'S TRY THAT WAY!

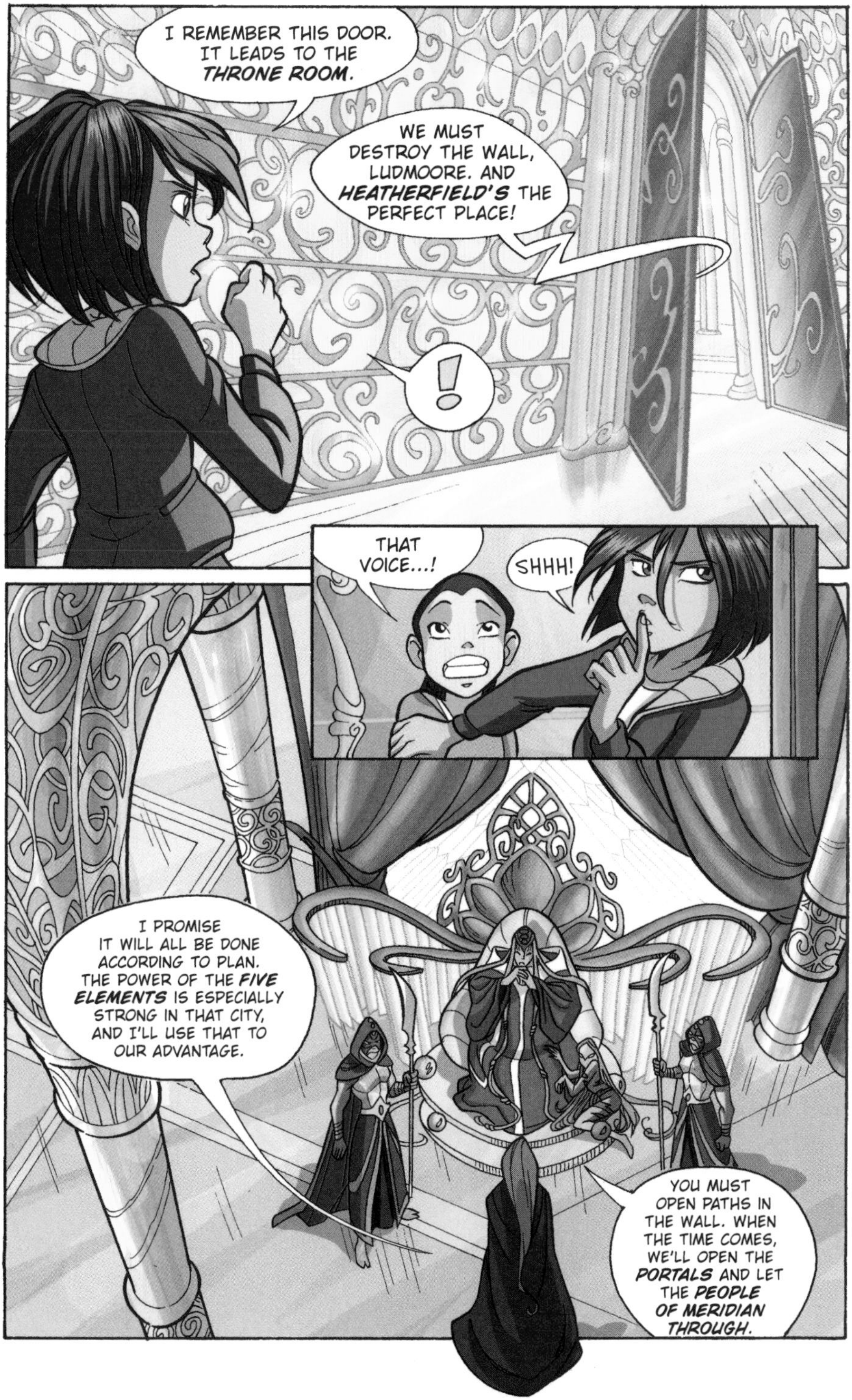
I REMEMBER THIS DOOR. IT LEADS TO THE THRONE ROOM.
WE MUST DESTROY THE WALL, LUDMOORE. AND HEATHERFIELD'S THE PERFECT PLACE!
!
THAT VOICE...!
SHHH!
I PROMISE IT WILL ALL BE DONE ACCORDING TO PLAN. THE POWER OF THE FIVE ELEMENTS IS ESPECIALLY STRONG IN THAT CITY, AND I'LL USE THAT TO OUR ADVANTAGE.
YOU MUST OPEN PATHS IN THE WALL. WHEN THE TIME COMES, WE'LL OPEN THE PORTALS AND LET THE PEOPLE OF MERIDIAN THROUGH.

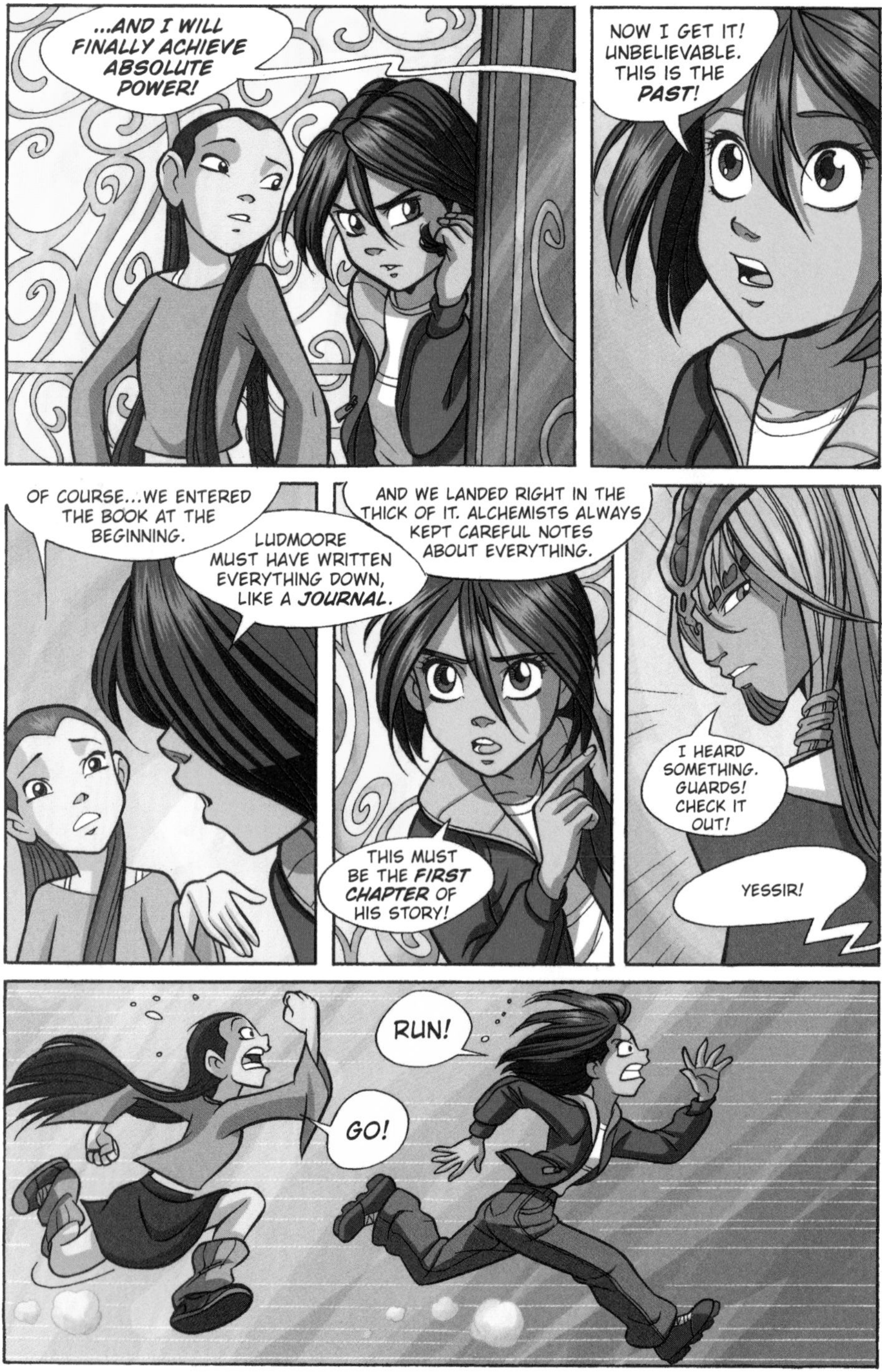
...AND I WILL FINALLY ACHIEVE ABSOLUTE POWER!
NOW I GET IT! UNBELIEVABLE. THIS IS THE PAST!
OF COURSE...WE ENTERED THE BOOK AT THE BEGINNING.
LUDMOORE MUST HAVE WRITTEN EVERYTHING DOWN, LIKE A JOURNAL.
AND WE LANDED RIGHT IN THE THICK OF IT. ALCHEMISTS ALWAYS KEPT CAREFUL NOTES ABOUT EVERYTHING.
THIS MUST BE THE FIRST CHAPTER OF HIS STORY!
I HEARD SOMETHING. GUARDS! CHECK IT OUT!
YESSIR!
RUN!
GO!

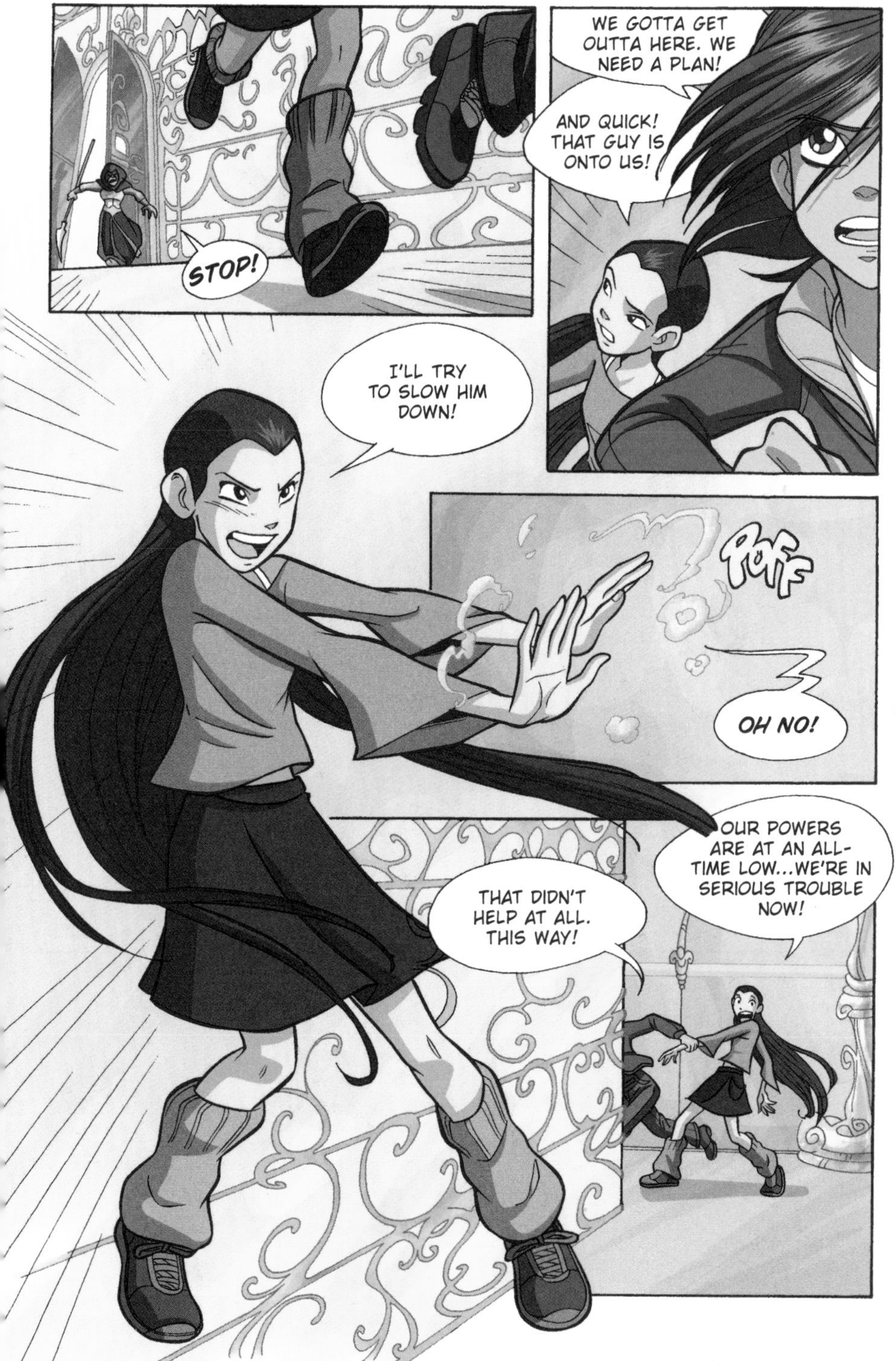
STOP!
WE GOTTA GET OUTTA HERE. WE NEED A PLAN!
AND QUICK! THAT GUY IS ONTO US!
I'LL TRY TO SLOW HIM DOWN!
POFF
OH NO!
THAT DIDN'T HELP AT ALL. THIS WAY!
OUR POWERS ARE AT AN ALL-TIME LOW...WE'RE IN SERIOUS TROUBLE NOW!

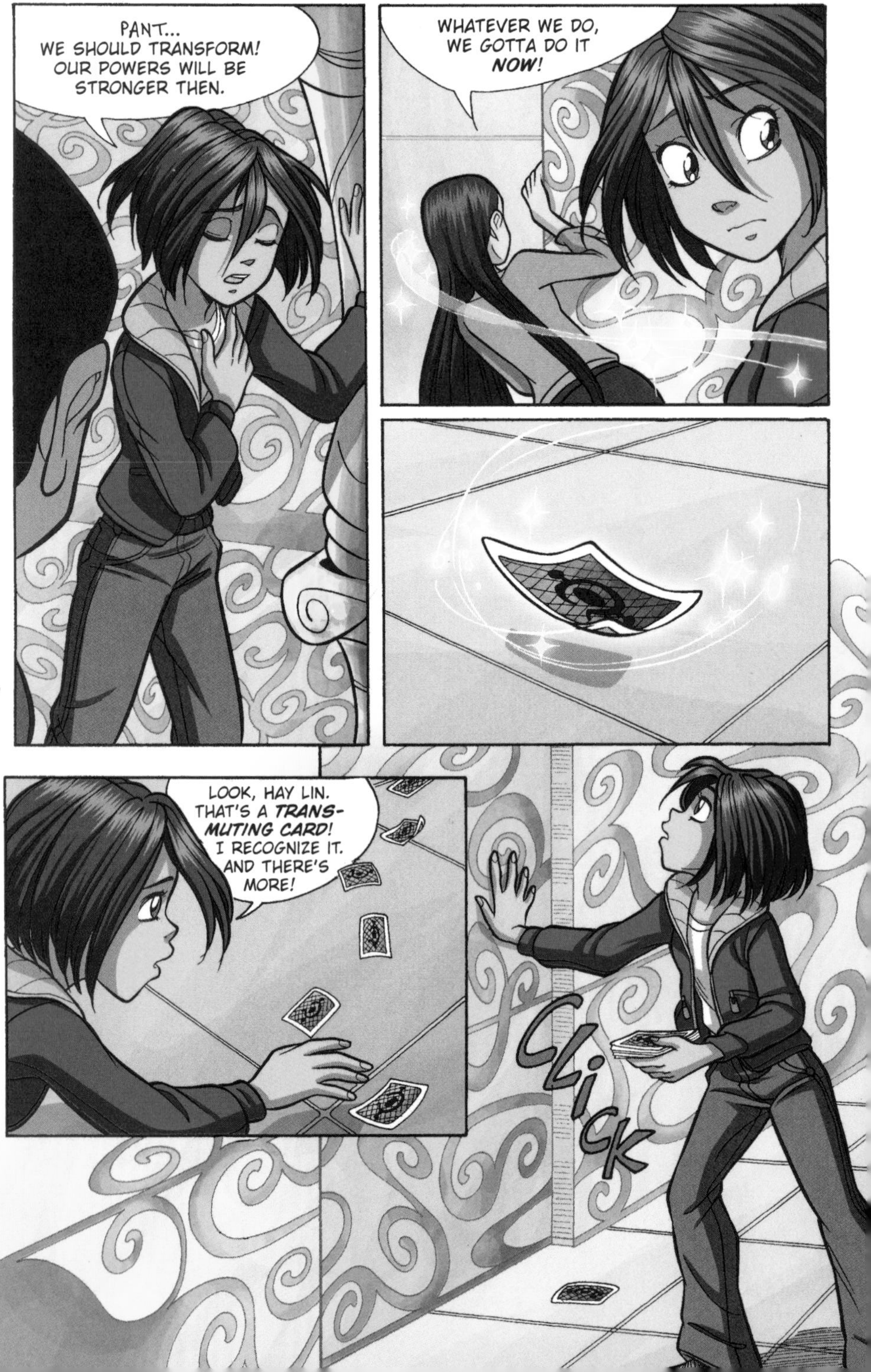
PANT...
WE SHOULD TRANSFORM!
OUR POWERS WILL BE
STRONGER THEN.
WHATEVER WE DO,
WE GOTTA DO IT
NOW!
LOOK, HAY LIN.
THAT'S A ***TRANSMUTING CARD!***
I RECOGNIZE IT.
AND THERE'S
MORE!
CLICK

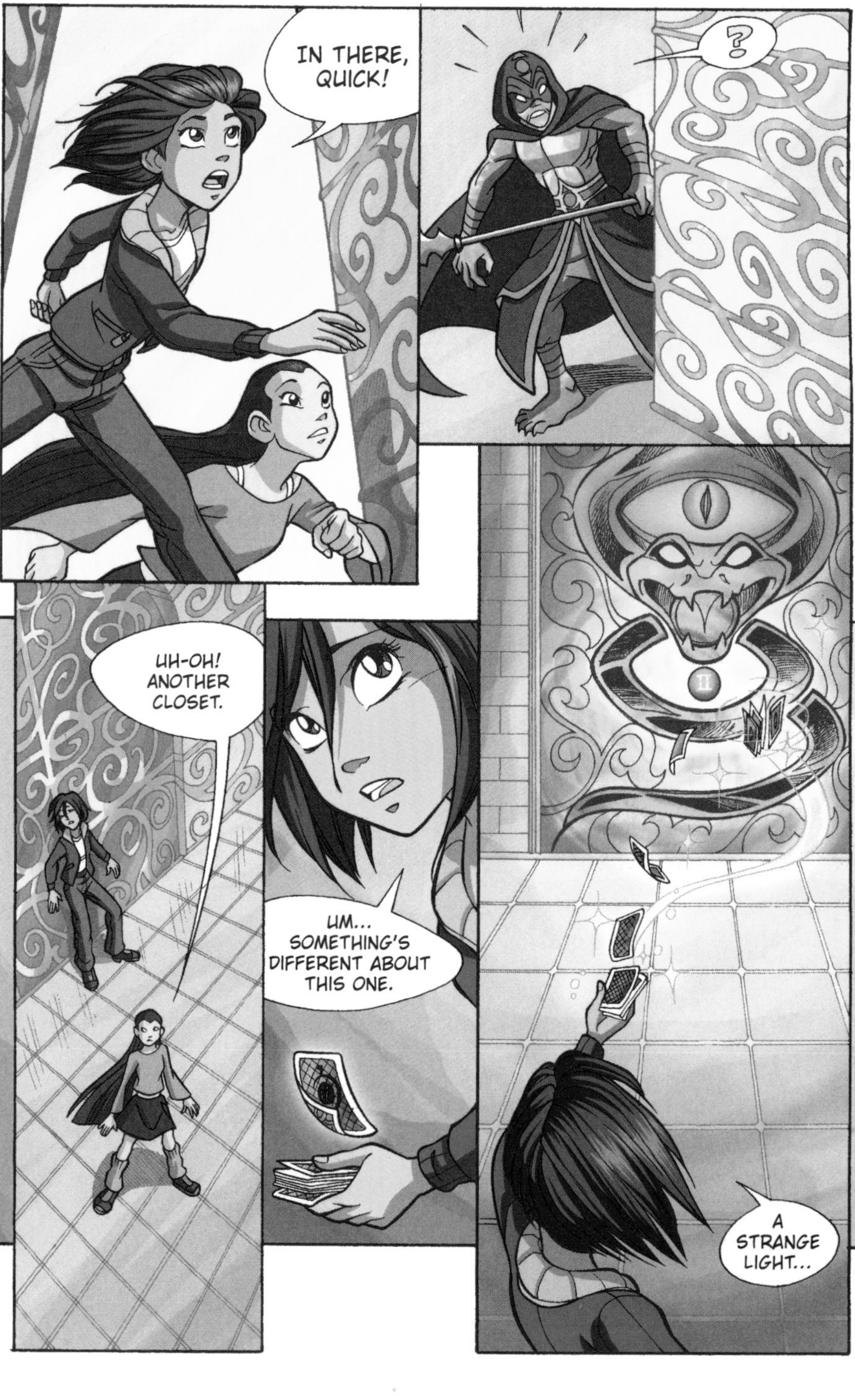
IN THERE, QUICK!
?
UH-OH! ANOTHER CLOSET.
UM... SOMETHING'S DIFFERENT ABOUT THIS ONE.
A STRANGE LIGHT...

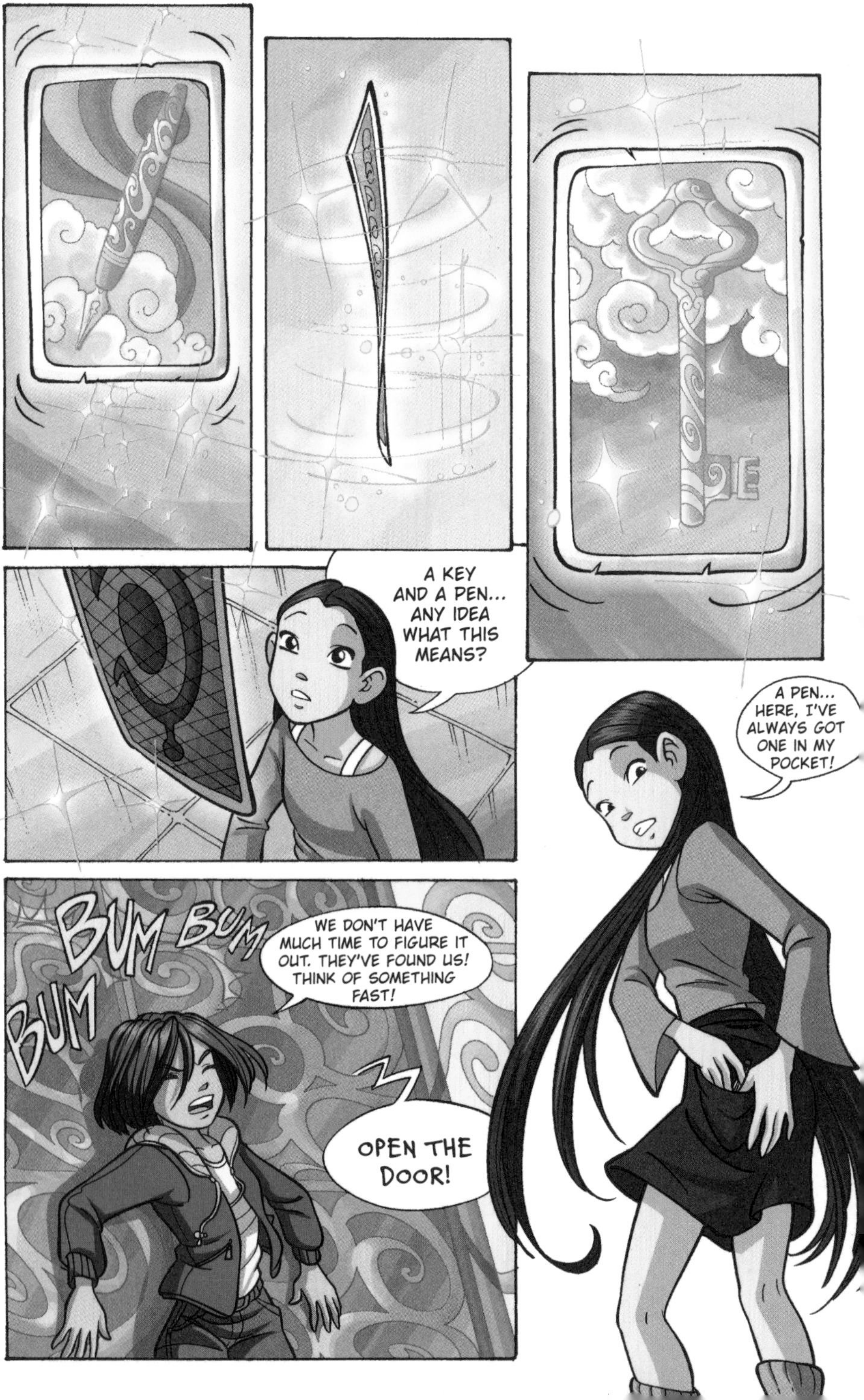
E
A KEY AND A PEN... ANY IDEA WHAT THIS MEANS?
A PEN... HERE, I'VE ALWAYS GOT ONE IN MY POCKET!
BUM BUM BUM BUM
WE DON'T HAVE MUCH TIME TO FIGURE IT OUT. THEY'VE FOUND US! THINK OF SOMETHING FAST!
OPEN THE DOOR!

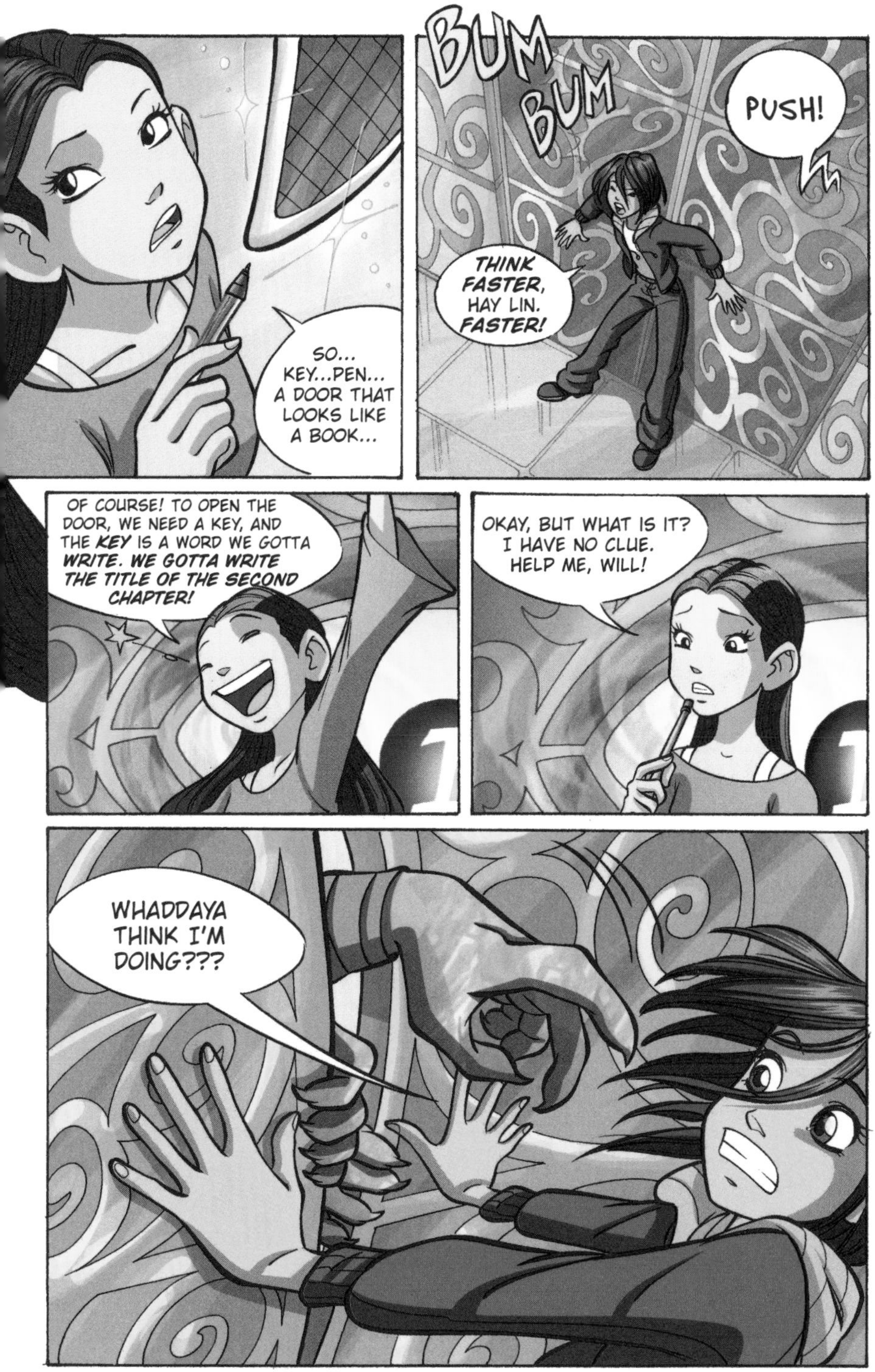
SO... KEY...PEN... A DOOR THAT LOOKS LIKE A BOOK...
BUM BUM
PUSH!
THINK FASTER, HAY LIN. FASTER!
OF COURSE! TO OPEN THE DOOR, WE NEED A KEY, AND THE KEY IS A WORD WE GOTTA WRITE. WE GOTTA WRITE THE TITLE OF THE SECOND CHAPTER!
OKAY, BUT WHAT IS IT? I HAVE NO CLUE. HELP ME, WILL!
WHADDAYA THINK I'M DOING???

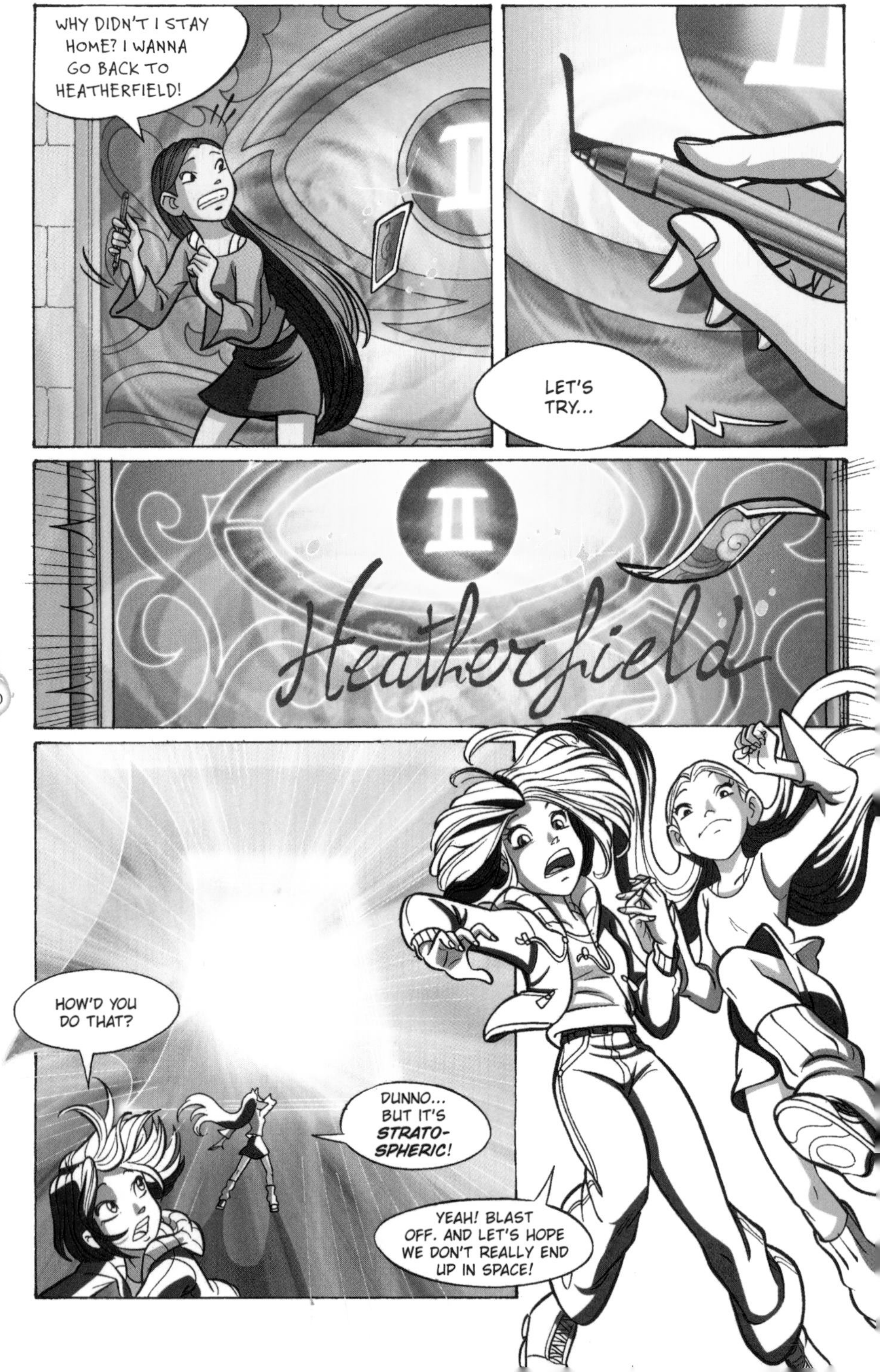
WHY DIDN'T I STAY HOME? I WANNA GO BACK TO HEATHERFIELD!
LET'S TRY...
Heatherfield
HOW'D YOU DO THAT?
DUNNO... BUT IT'S **STRATO-SPHERIC!**
YEAH! BLAST OFF. AND LET'S HOPE WE DON'T REALLY END UP IN SPACE!

Chapter 2

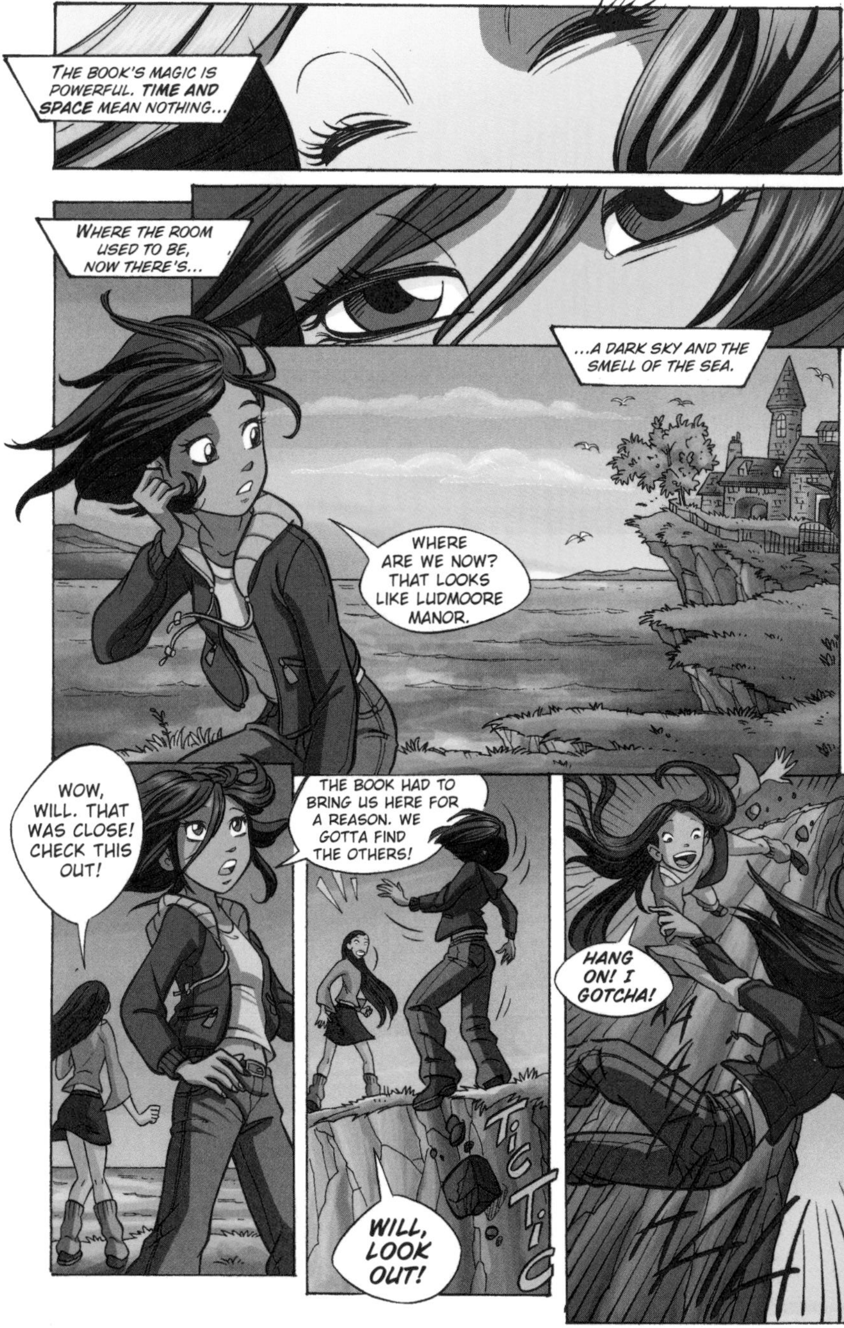
THE BOOK'S MAGIC IS POWERFUL. TIME AND SPACE MEAN NOTHING...
WHERE THE ROOM USED TO BE, NOW THERE'S...
...A DARK SKY AND THE SMELL OF THE SEA.
WHERE ARE WE NOW? THAT LOOKS LIKE LUDMOORE MANOR.
WOW, WILL. THAT WAS CLOSE! CHECK THIS OUT!
THE BOOK HAD TO BRING US HERE FOR A REASON. WE GOTTA FIND THE OTHERS!
TIC TIC
WILL, LOOK OUT!
HANG ON! I GOTCHA!

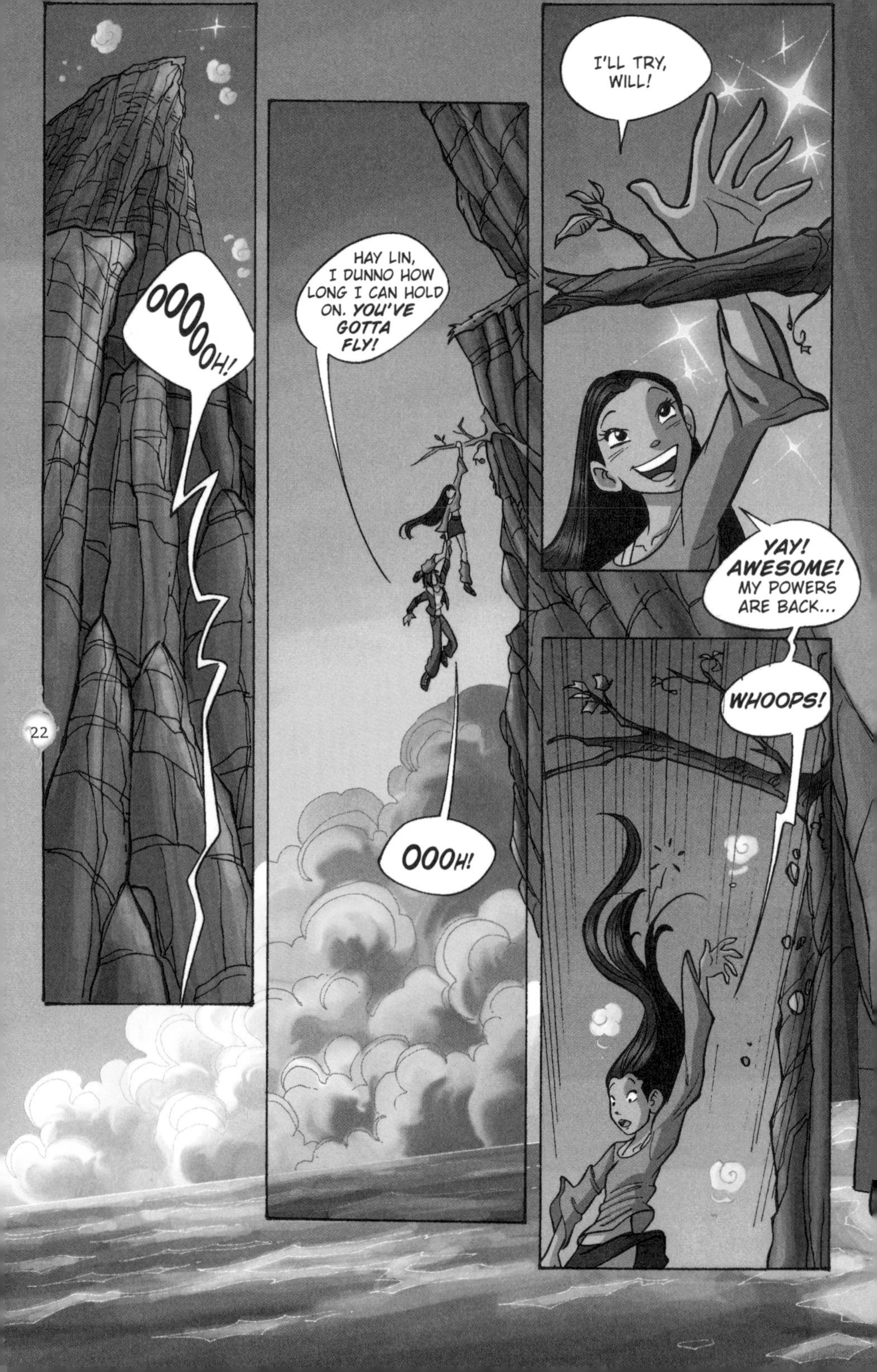
OOOOOH!
HAY LIN, I DUNNO HOW LONG I CAN HOLD ON. YOU'VE GOTTA FLY!
OOOH!
I'LL TRY, WILL!
YAY! AWESOME! MY POWERS ARE BACK...
WHOOPS!

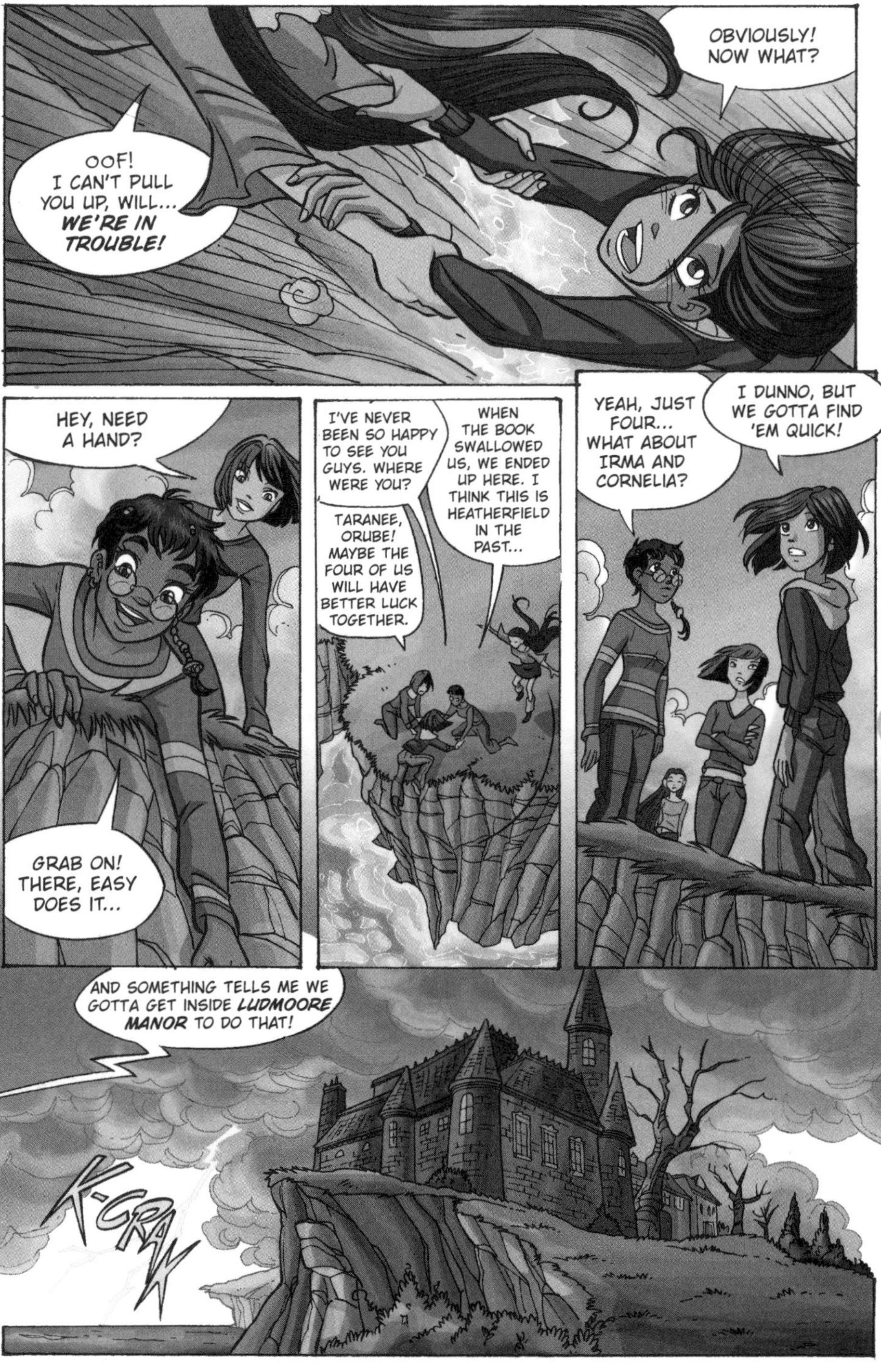
OBVIOUSLY! NOW WHAT?
OOF! I CAN'T PULL YOU UP, WILL... WE'RE IN TROUBLE!
HEY, NEED A HAND?
GRAB ON! THERE, EASY DOES IT...
I'VE NEVER BEEN SO HAPPY TO SEE YOU GUYS. WHERE WERE YOU?
TARANEE, ORUBE! MAYBE THE FOUR OF US WILL HAVE BETTER LUCK TOGETHER.
WHEN THE BOOK SWALLOWED US, WE ENDED UP HERE. I THINK THIS IS HEATHERFIELD IN THE PAST...
YEAH, JUST FOUR... WHAT ABOUT IRMA AND CORNELIA?
I DUNNO, BUT WE GOTTA FIND 'EM QUICK!
AND SOMETHING TELLS ME WE GOTTA GET INSIDE LUDMOORE MANOR TO DO THAT!
K-GRAK

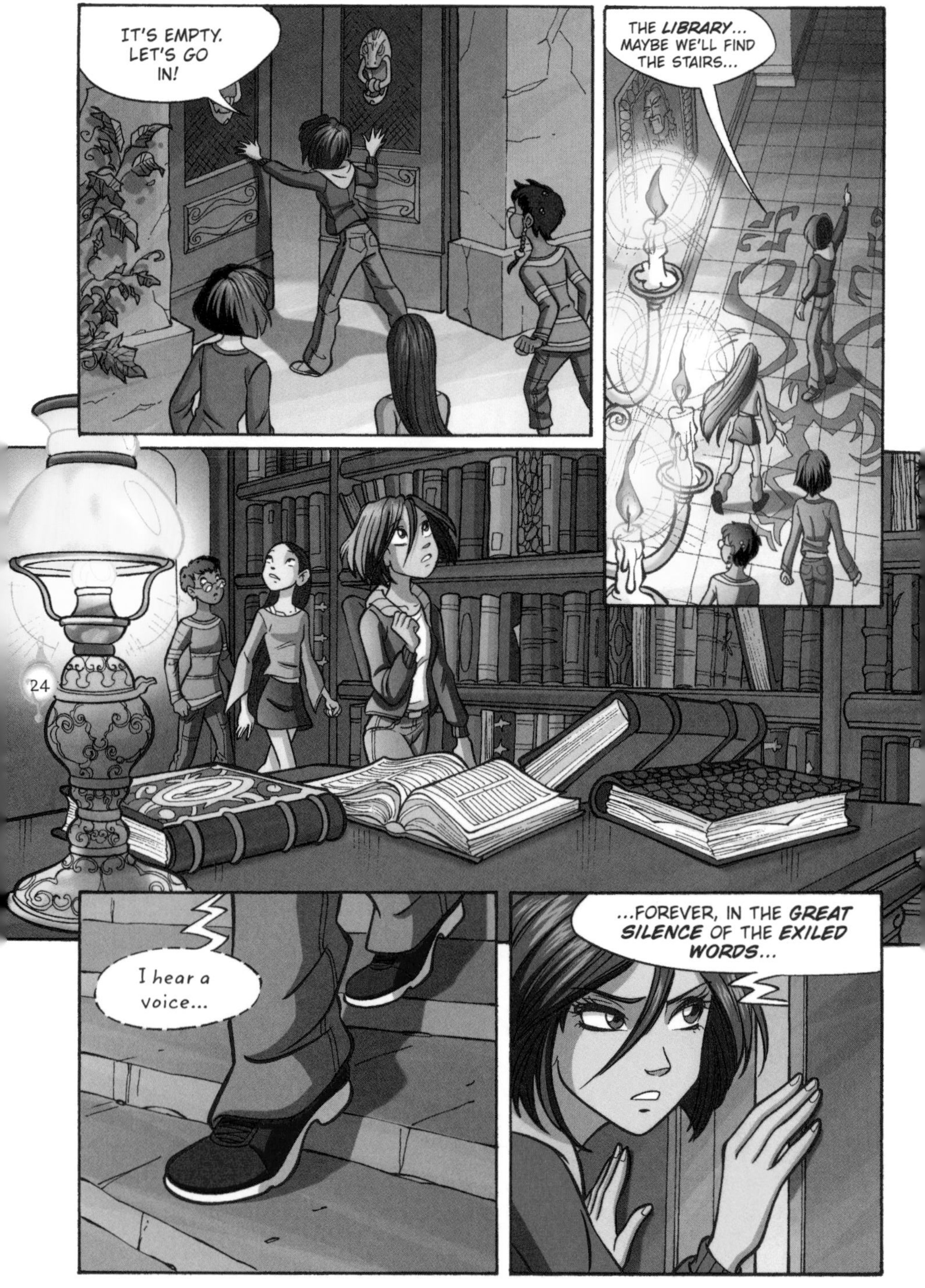
IT'S EMPTY. LET'S GO IN!
THE LIBRARY... MAYBE WE'LL FIND THE STAIRS...
I hear a voice...
...FOREVER, IN THE GREAT SILENCE OF THE EXILED WORDS...

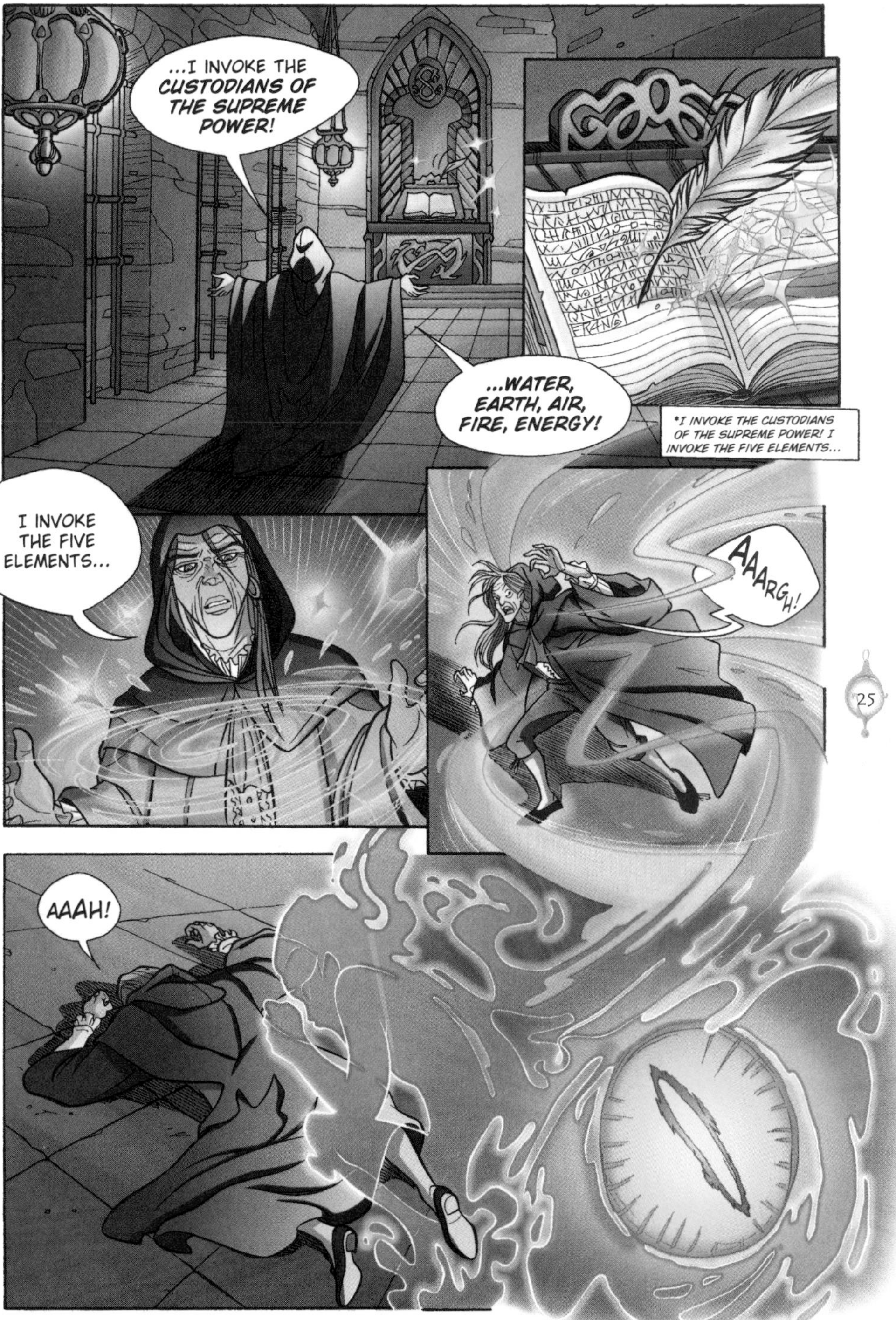

...I INVOKE THE CUSTODIANS OF THE SUPREME POWER!
...WATER, EARTH, AIR, FIRE, ENERGY!
*I INVOKE THE CUSTODIANS OF THE SUPREME POWER! I INVOKE THE FIVE ELEMENTS...
I INVOKE THE FIVE ELEMENTS...
AAARGH!
AAAH!

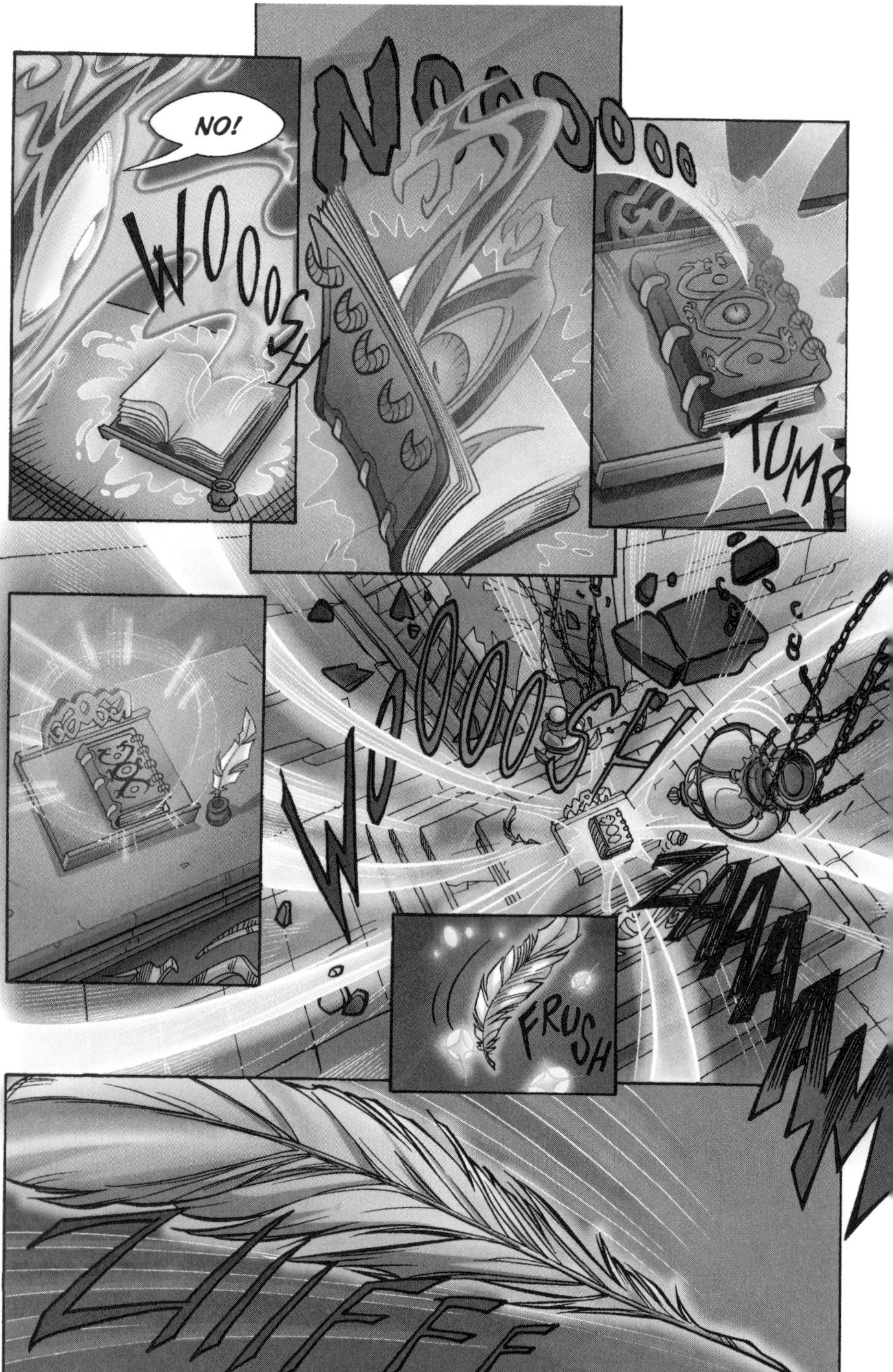
NO!
WOOOSH
NOOOOOOO
TUMP
WOOOOOOSH
ZAAAAAM
FRUSH
ZHIFFF

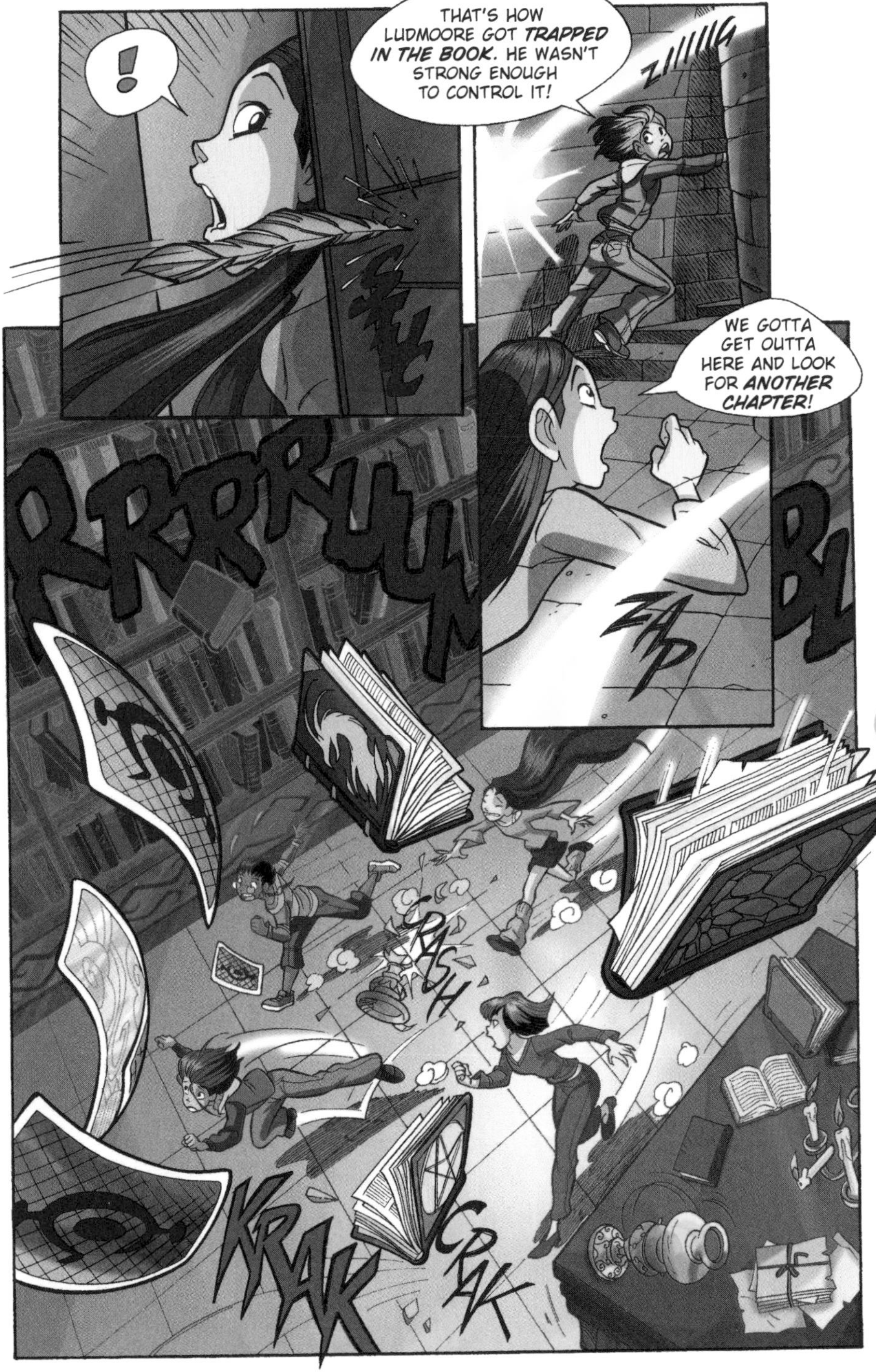
!
THAT'S HOW LUDMOORE GOT TRAPPED IN THE BOOK. HE WASN'T STRONG ENOUGH TO CONTROL IT!
ZIIIIIG
WE GOTTA GET OUTTA HERE AND LOOK FOR ANOTHER CHAPTER!
RRRRUUUMBL
ZAP
CRASH
KRAK
CRAK

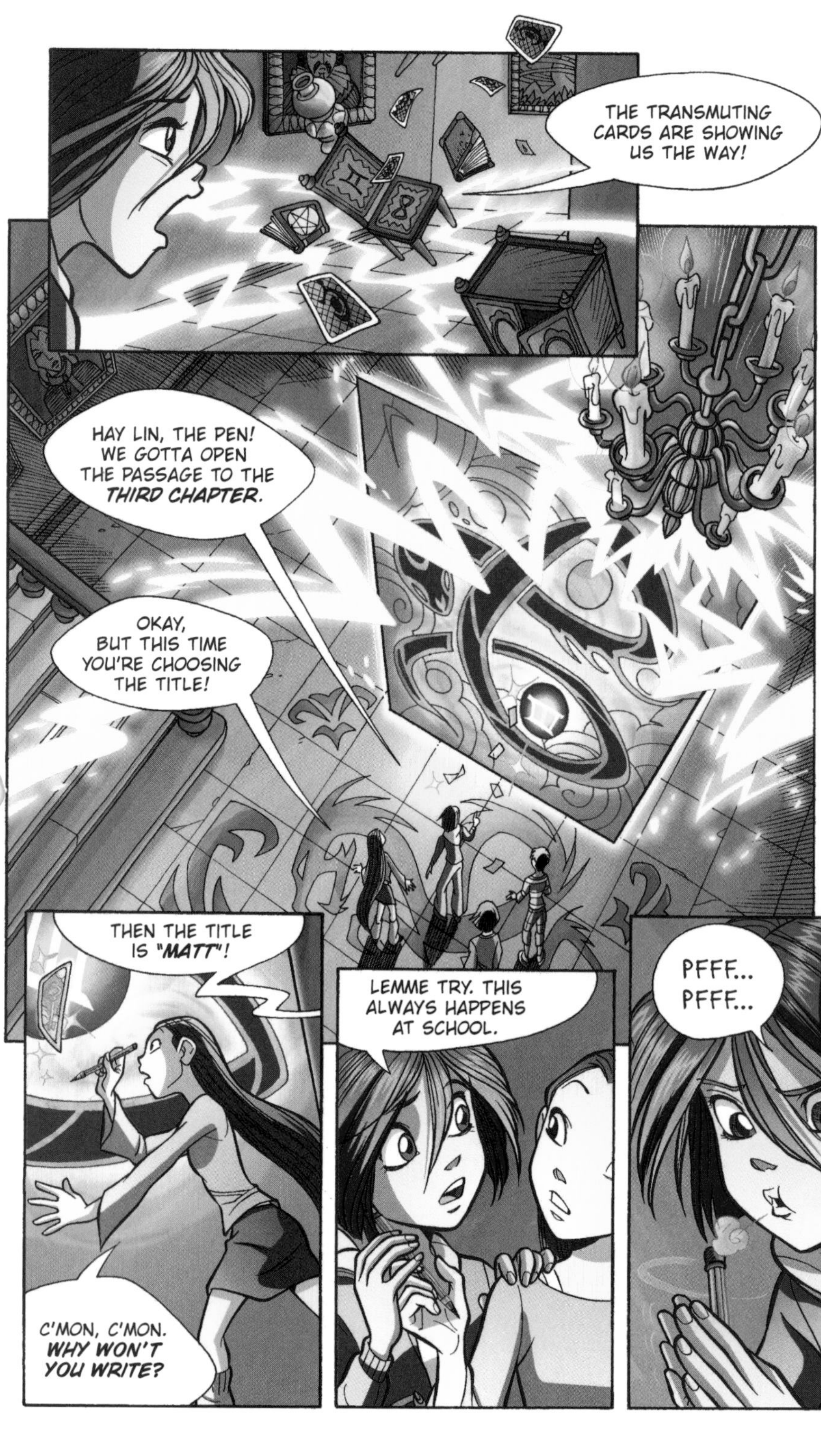
THE TRANSMUTING CARDS ARE SHOWING US THE WAY!
HAY LIN, THE PEN! WE GOTTA OPEN THE PASSAGE TO THE ***THIRD CHAPTER***.
OKAY, BUT THIS TIME YOU'RE CHOOSING THE TITLE!
THEN THE TITLE IS "***MATT***"!
C'MON, C'MON. ***WHY WON'T YOU WRITE?***
LEMME TRY. THIS ALWAYS HAPPENS AT SCHOOL.
PFFF... PFFF...

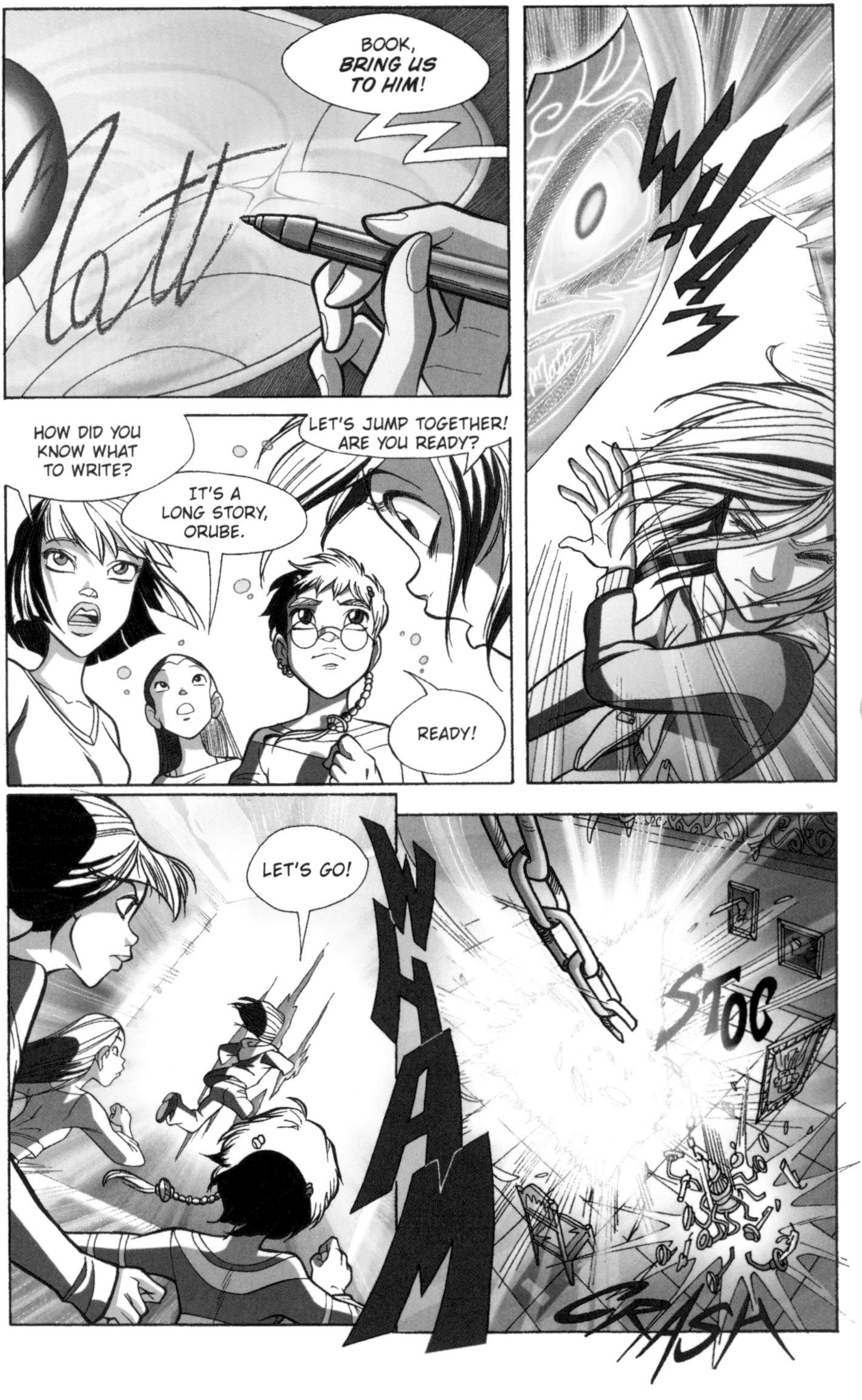
BOOK, BRING US TO HIM!
Matt
WHAM
HOW DID YOU KNOW WHAT TO WRITE?
LET'S JUMP TOGETHER! ARE YOU READY?
IT'S A LONG STORY, ORUBE.
READY!
LET'S GO!
WHAM
STOC
CRASH

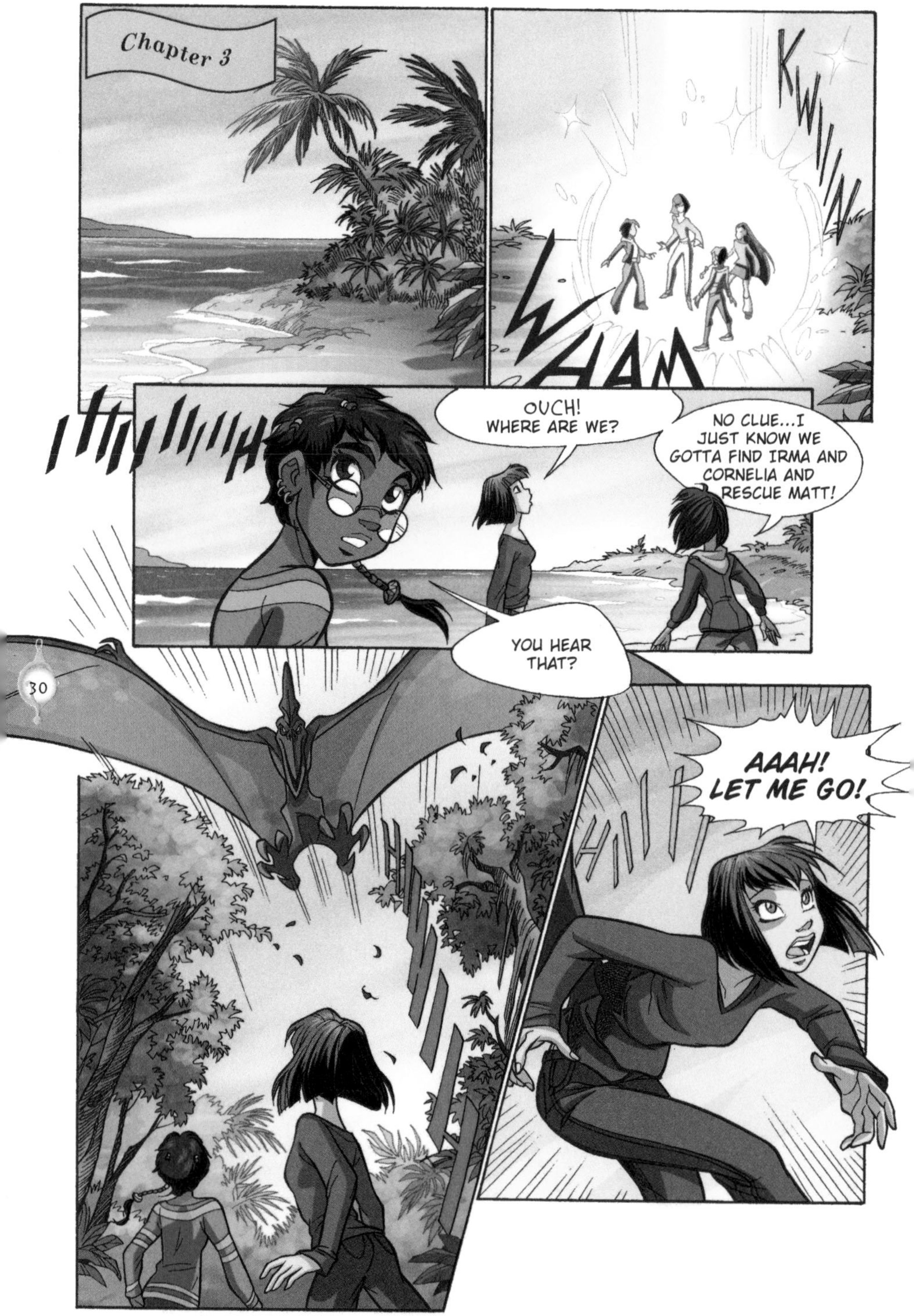
Chapter 3
KWIIIN
WHAM
HHH
OUCH! WHERE ARE WE?
NO CLUE...I JUST KNOW WE GOTTA FIND IRMA AND CORNELIA AND RESCUE MATT!
YOU HEAR THAT?
AAAH! LET ME GO!

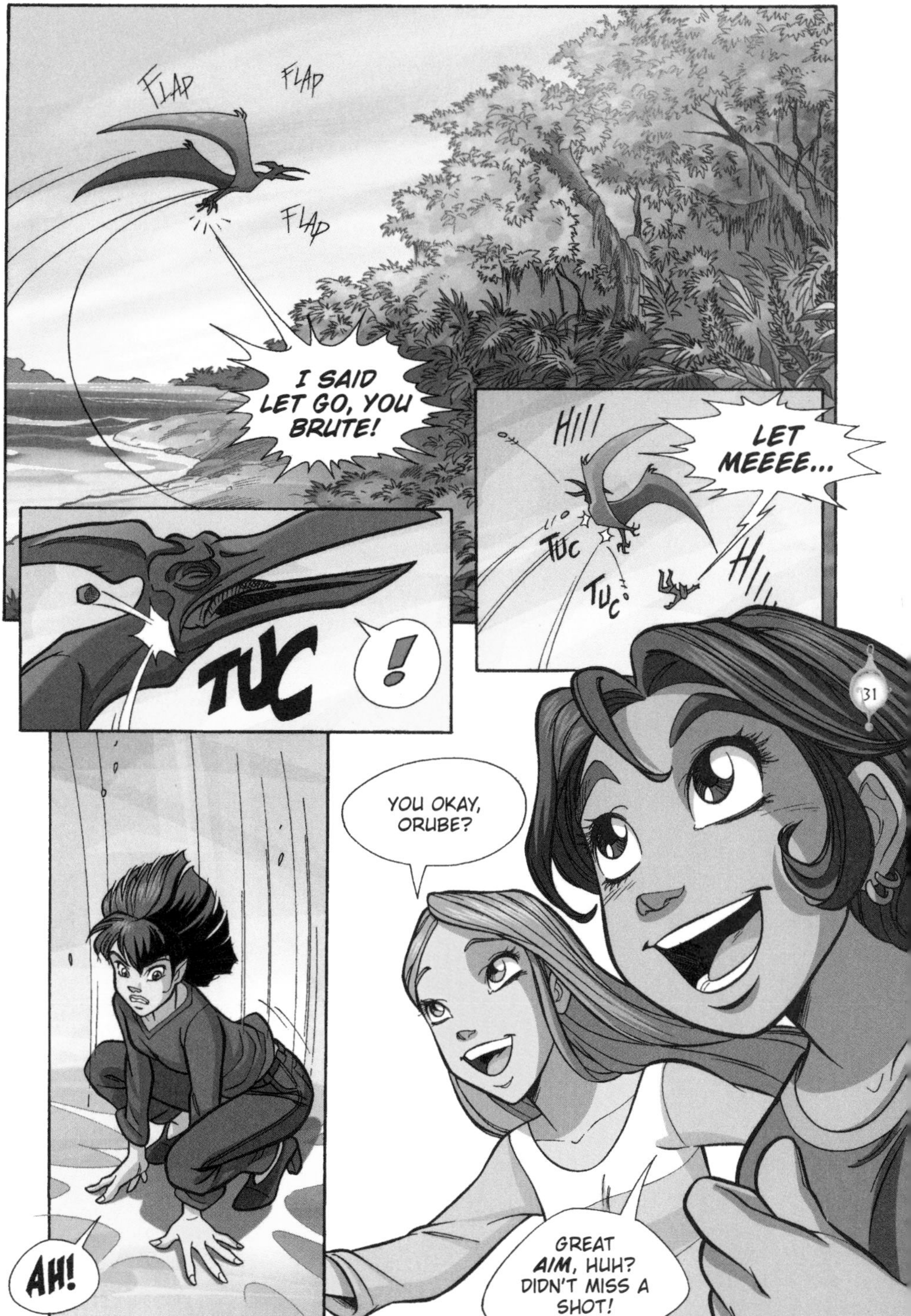
FLAP
FLAP
FLAP
I SAID LET GO, YOU BRUTE!
TUC
!
HI!!
TUC
TUC
LET MEEEE...
HI!!
YOU OKAY, ORUBE?
AH!
GREAT **AIM**, HUH? DIDN'T MISS A SHOT!

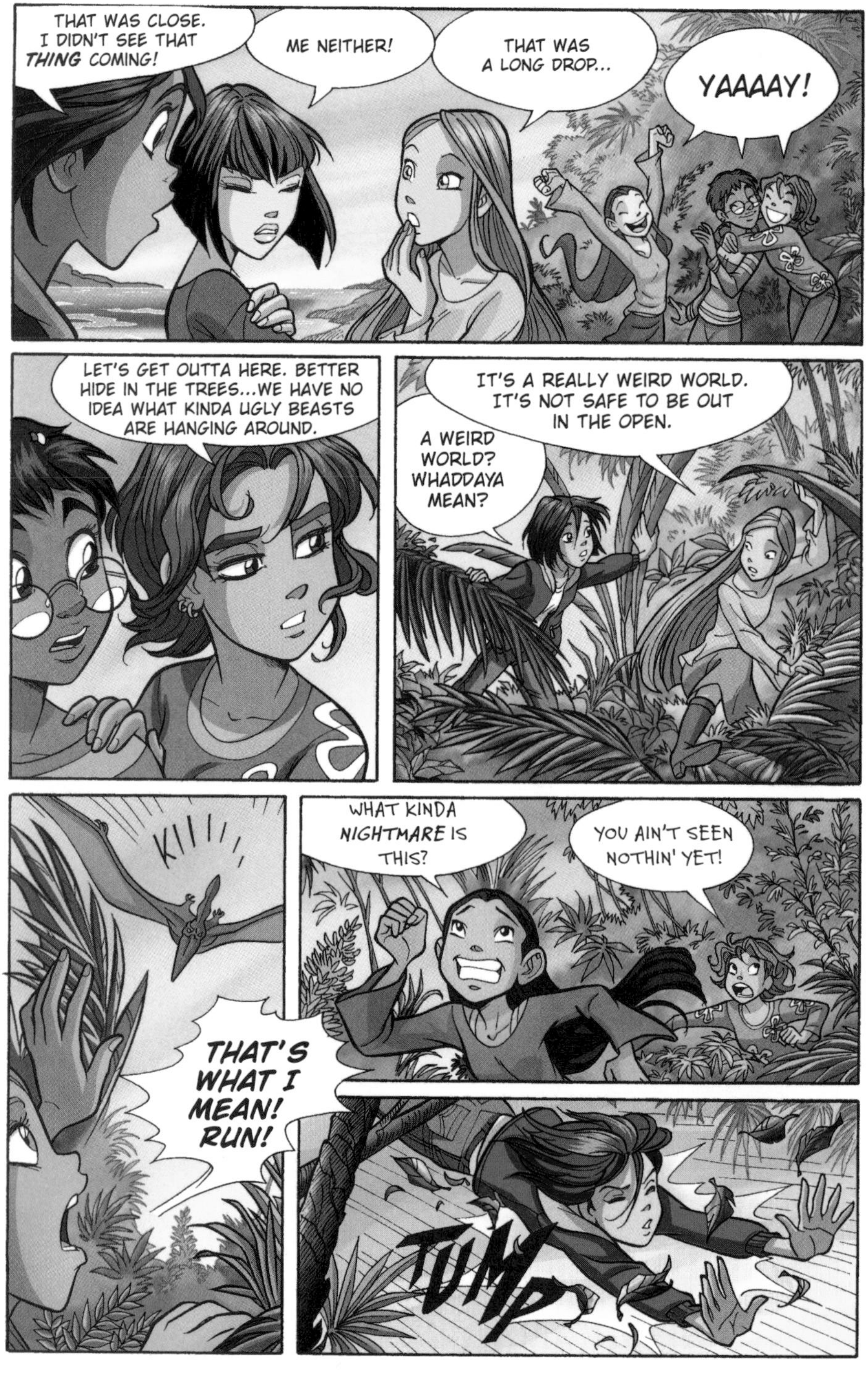

THAT WAS CLOSE. I DIDN'T SEE THAT *THING* COMING!
ME NEITHER!
THAT WAS A LONG DROP...
YAAAAY!
LET'S GET OUTTA HERE. BETTER HIDE IN THE TREES...WE HAVE NO IDEA WHAT KINDA UGLY BEASTS ARE HANGING AROUND.
IT'S A REALLY WEIRD WORLD. IT'S NOT SAFE TO BE OUT IN THE OPEN.
A WEIRD WORLD? WHADDAYA MEAN?
KIII
WHAT KINDA *NIGHTMARE* IS THIS?
YOU AIN'T SEEN NOTHIN' YET!
THAT'S WHAT I MEAN! RUN!
TUMP

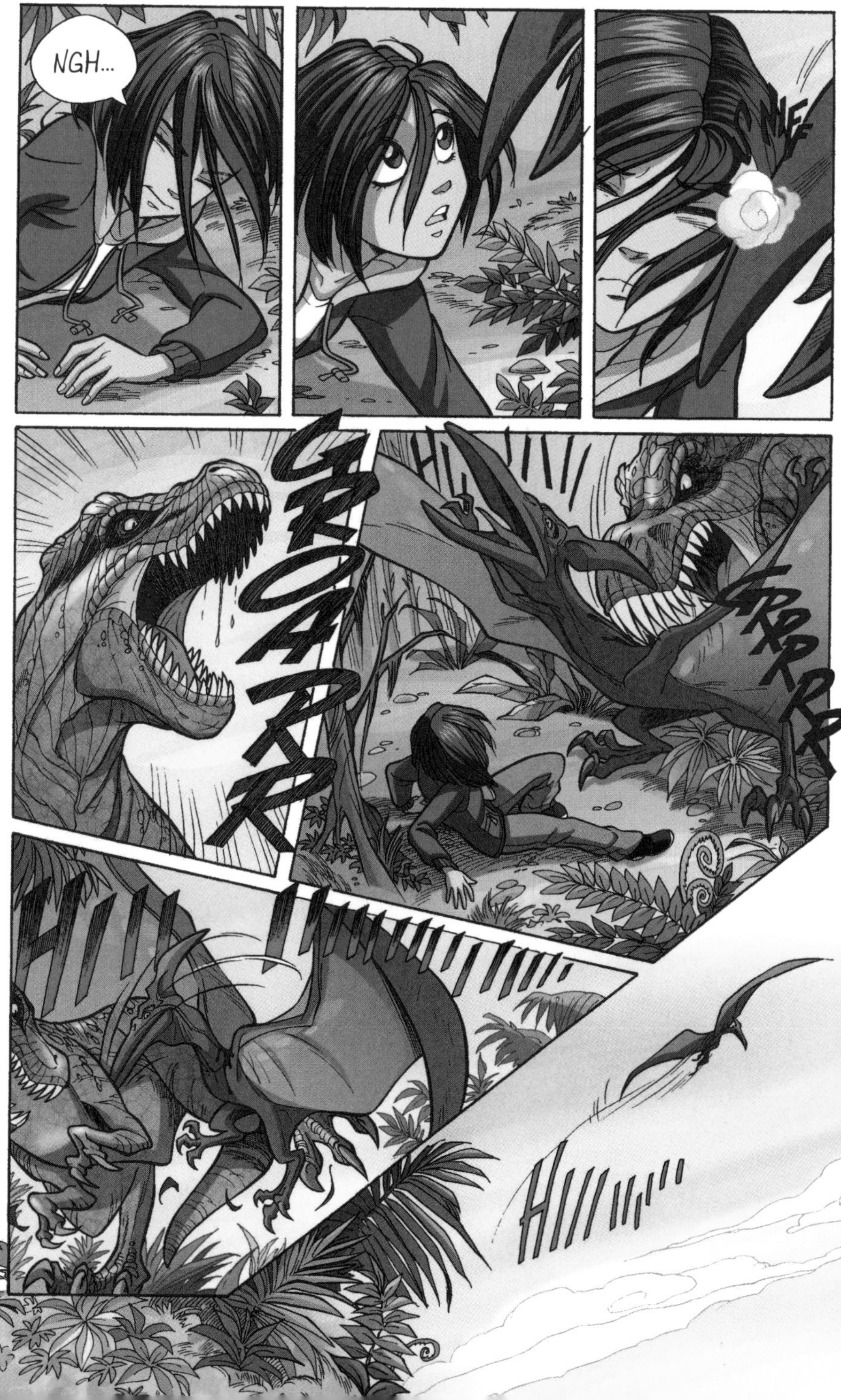
NGH...
SNIFF
GROOAARRR
HU
GRRRRR
HUIIIIIIIII
HUII

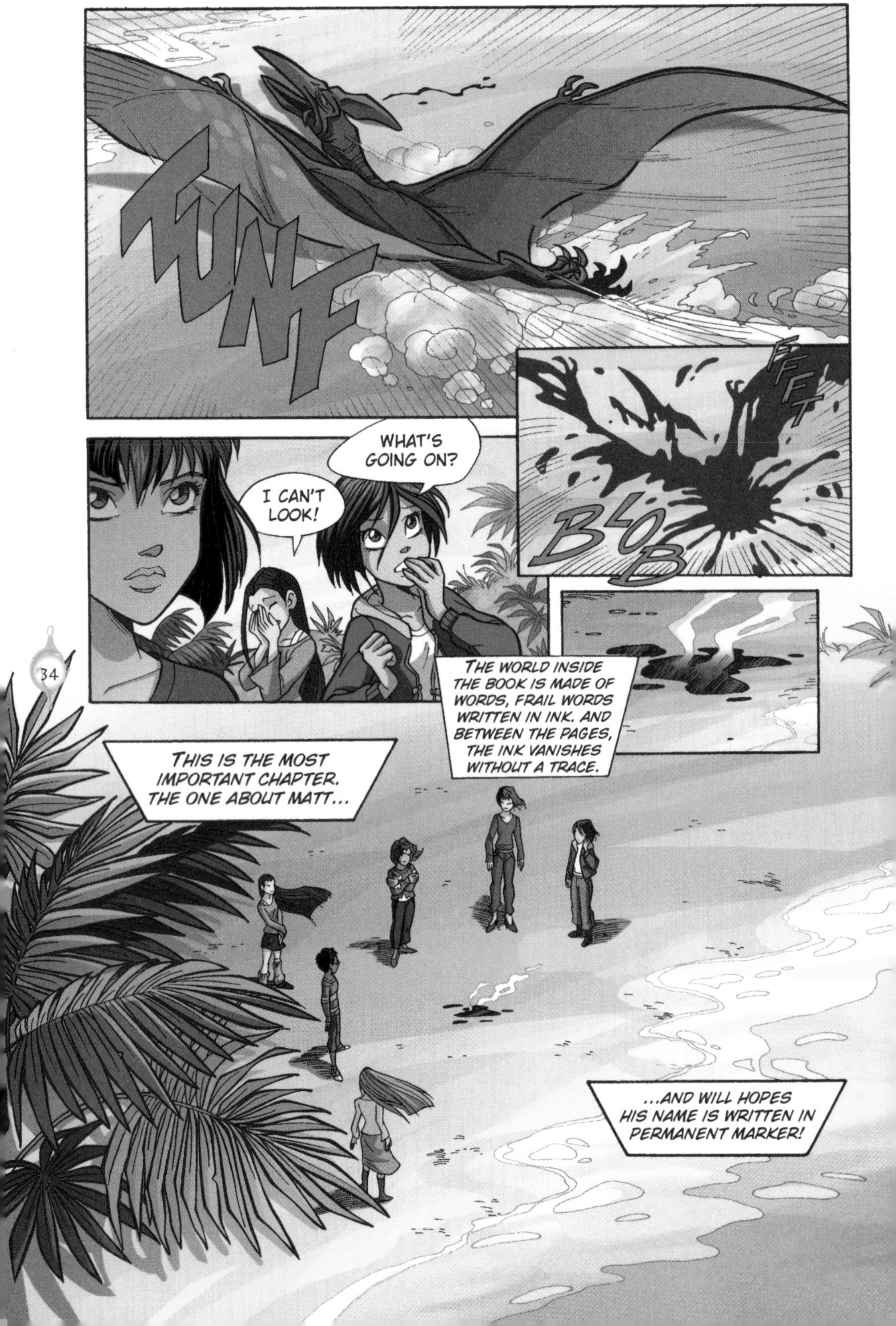

TUNF
FFFT
BLOB
WHAT'S GOING ON?
I CAN'T LOOK!
THE WORLD INSIDE THE BOOK IS MADE OF WORDS, FRAIL WORDS WRITTEN IN INK. AND BETWEEN THE PAGES, THE INK VANISHES WITHOUT A TRACE.
THIS IS THE MOST IMPORTANT CHAPTER. THE ONE ABOUT MATT...
...AND WILL HOPES HIS NAME IS WRITTEN IN PERMANENT MARKER!

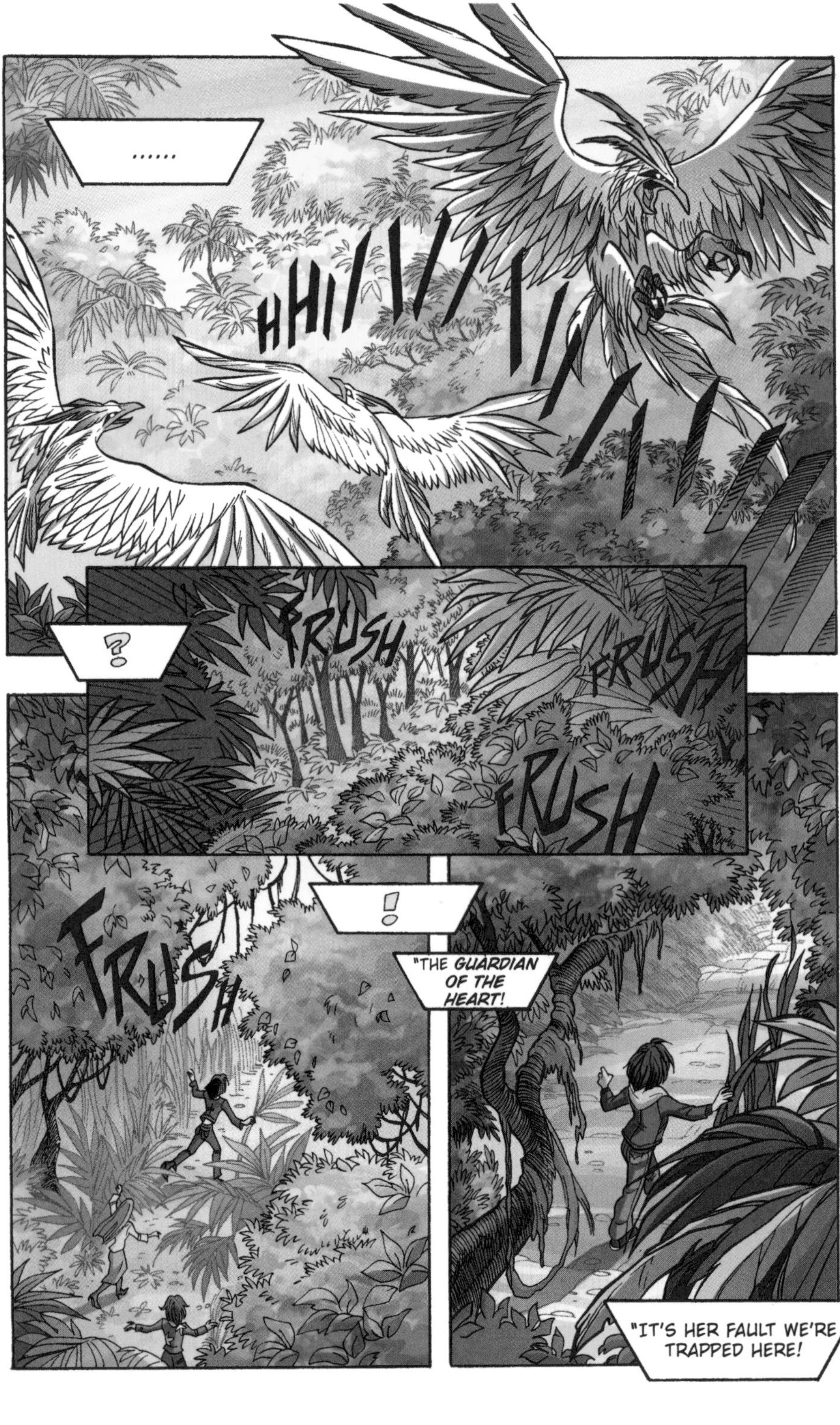

......
HHIIIIIIIIII
?
FRUSH
FRUSH
FRUSH
FRUSH
!
"THE GUARDIAN OF THE HEART!
"IT'S HER FAULT WE'RE TRAPPED HERE!

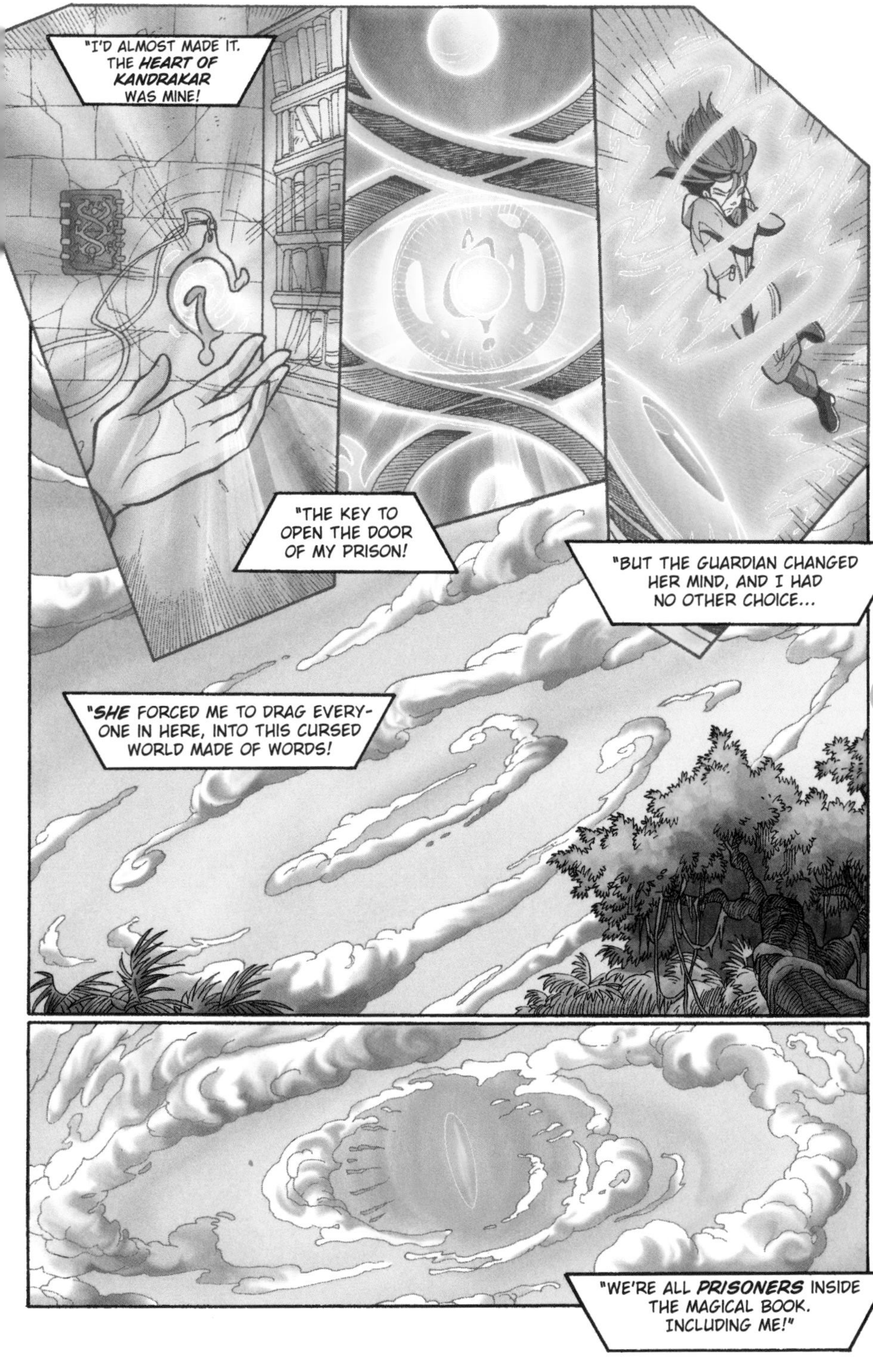
"I'D ALMOST MADE IT. THE HEART OF KANDRAKAR WAS MINE!
"THE KEY TO OPEN THE DOOR OF MY PRISON!
"BUT THE GUARDIAN CHANGED HER MIND, AND I HAD NO OTHER CHOICE...
"SHE FORCED ME TO DRAG EVERY-ONE IN HERE, INTO THIS CURSED WORLD MADE OF WORDS!
"WE'RE ALL PRISONERS INSIDE THE MAGICAL BOOK. INCLUDING ME!"

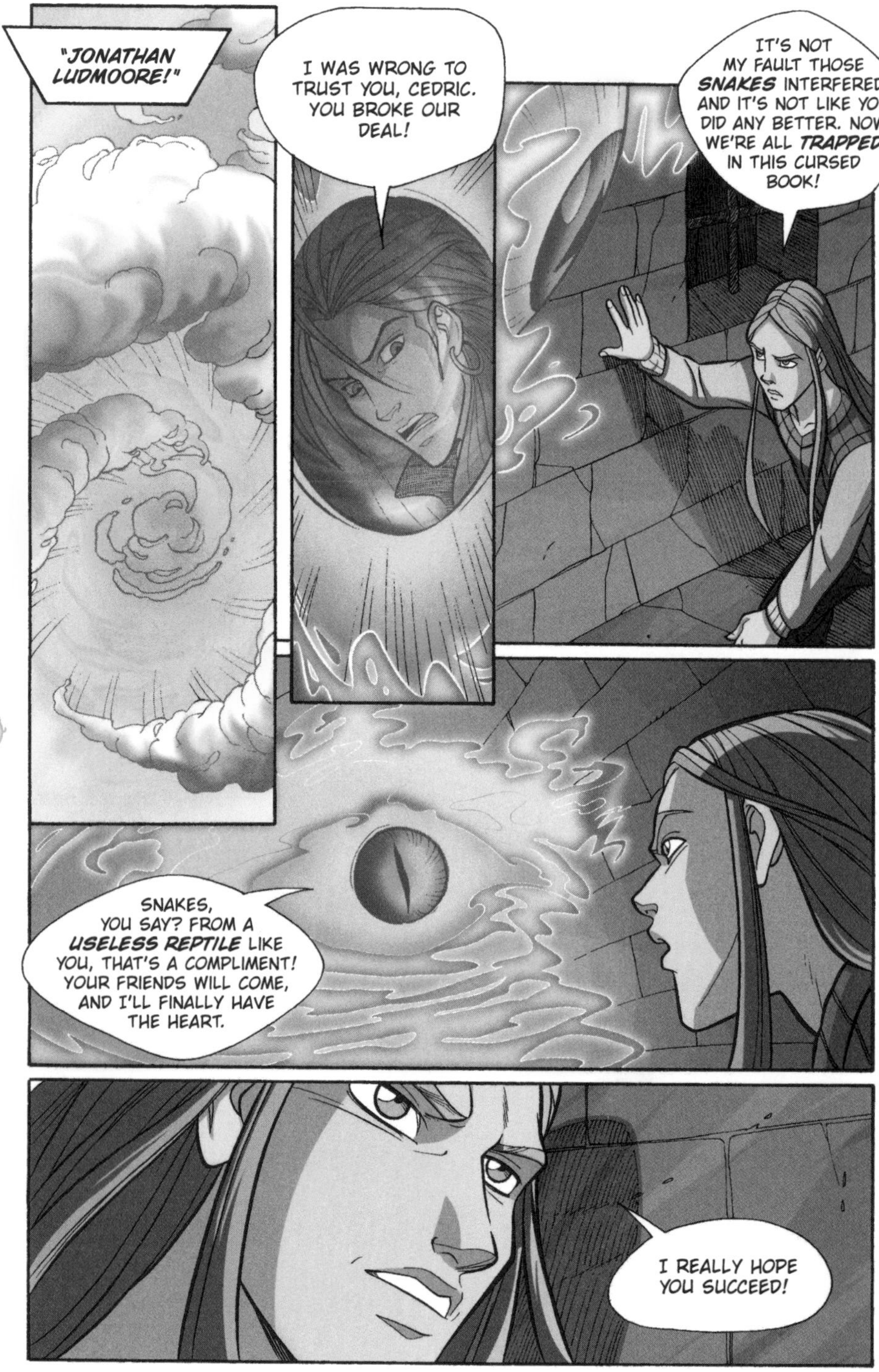
"JONATHAN LUDMOORE!"
I WAS WRONG TO TRUST YOU, CEDRIC. YOU BROKE OUR DEAL!
IT'S NOT MY FAULT THOSE SNAKES INTERFERED, AND IT'S NOT LIKE YOU DID ANY BETTER. NOW WE'RE ALL TRAPPED IN THIS CURSED BOOK!
SNAKES, YOU SAY? FROM A USELESS REPTILE LIKE YOU, THAT'S A COMPLIMENT! YOUR FRIENDS WILL COME, AND I'LL FINALLY HAVE THE HEART.
I REALLY HOPE YOU SUCCEED!

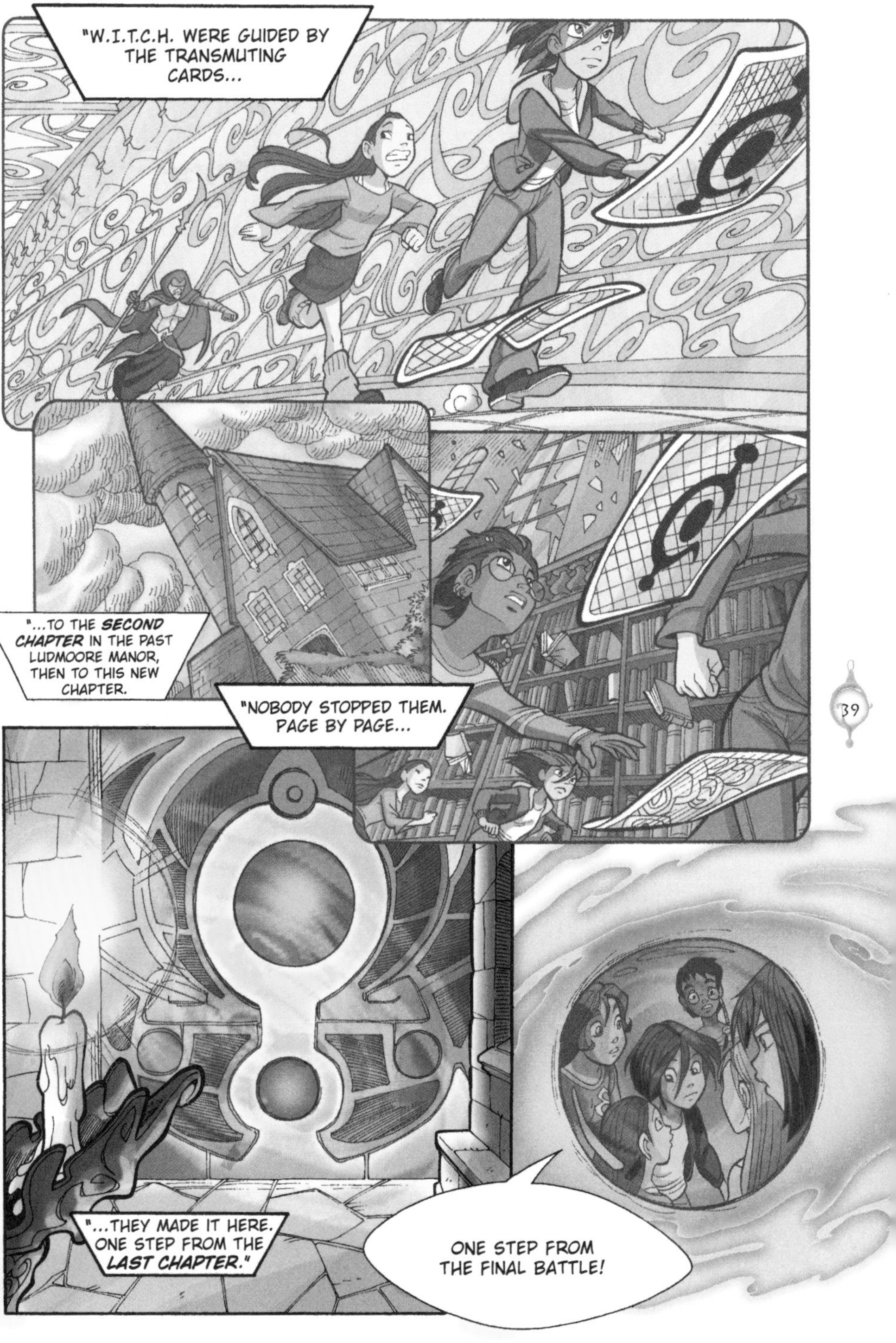
"W.I.T.C.H. WERE GUIDED BY THE TRANSMUTING CARDS...
"...TO THE **SECOND CHAPTER** IN THE PAST LUDMOORE MANOR, THEN TO THIS NEW CHAPTER.
"NOBODY STOPPED THEM. PAGE BY PAGE...
"...THEY MADE IT HERE. ONE STEP FROM THE **LAST CHAPTER.**"
ONE STEP FROM THE FINAL BATTLE!

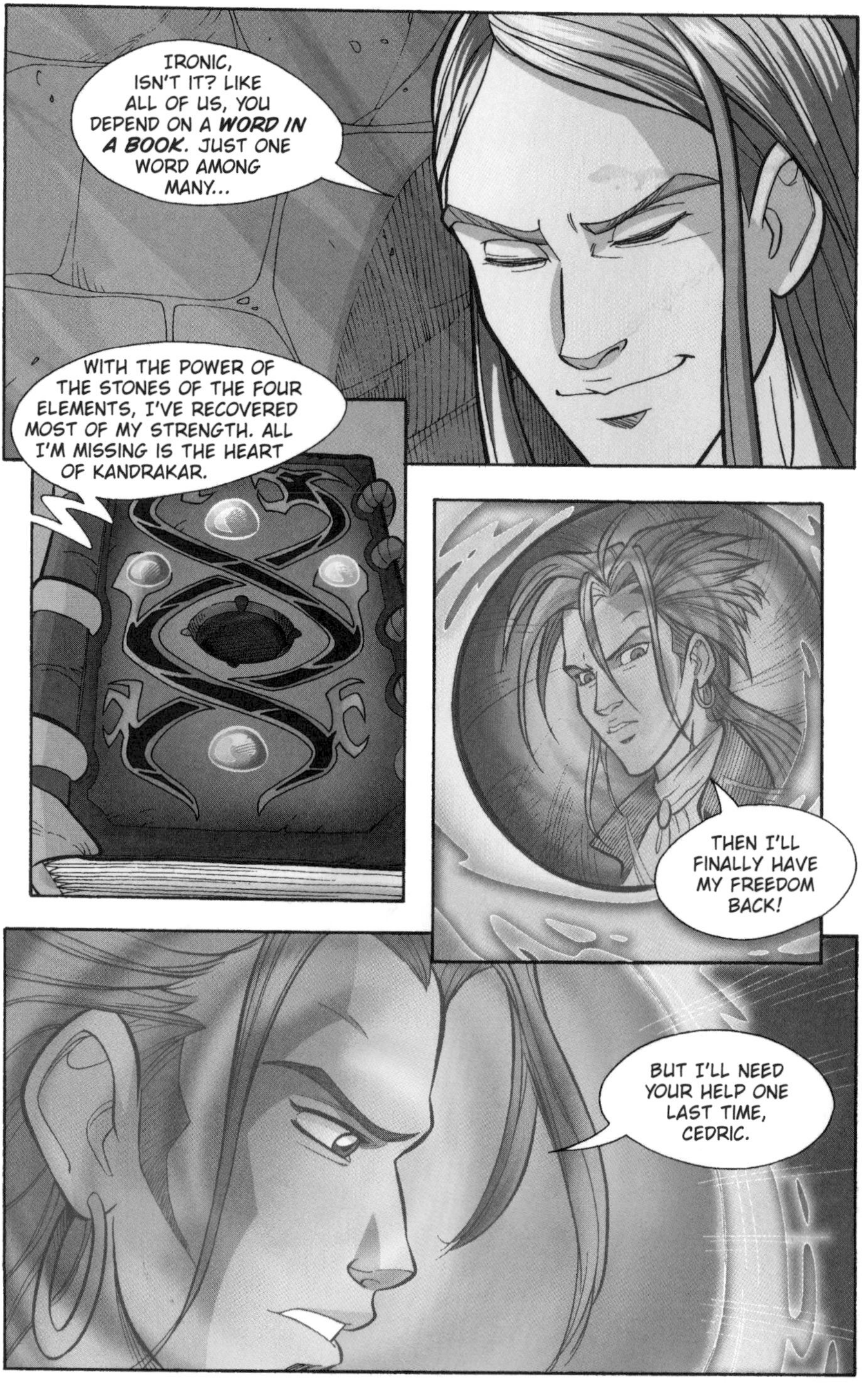
IRONIC, ISN'T IT? LIKE ALL OF US, YOU DEPEND ON A **WORD IN A BOOK**. JUST ONE WORD AMONG MANY...
WITH THE POWER OF THE STONES OF THE FOUR ELEMENTS, I'VE RECOVERED MOST OF MY STRENGTH. ALL I'M MISSING IS THE HEART OF KANDRAKAR.
THEN I'LL FINALLY HAVE MY FREEDOM BACK!
BUT I'LL NEED YOUR HELP ONE LAST TIME, CEDRIC.

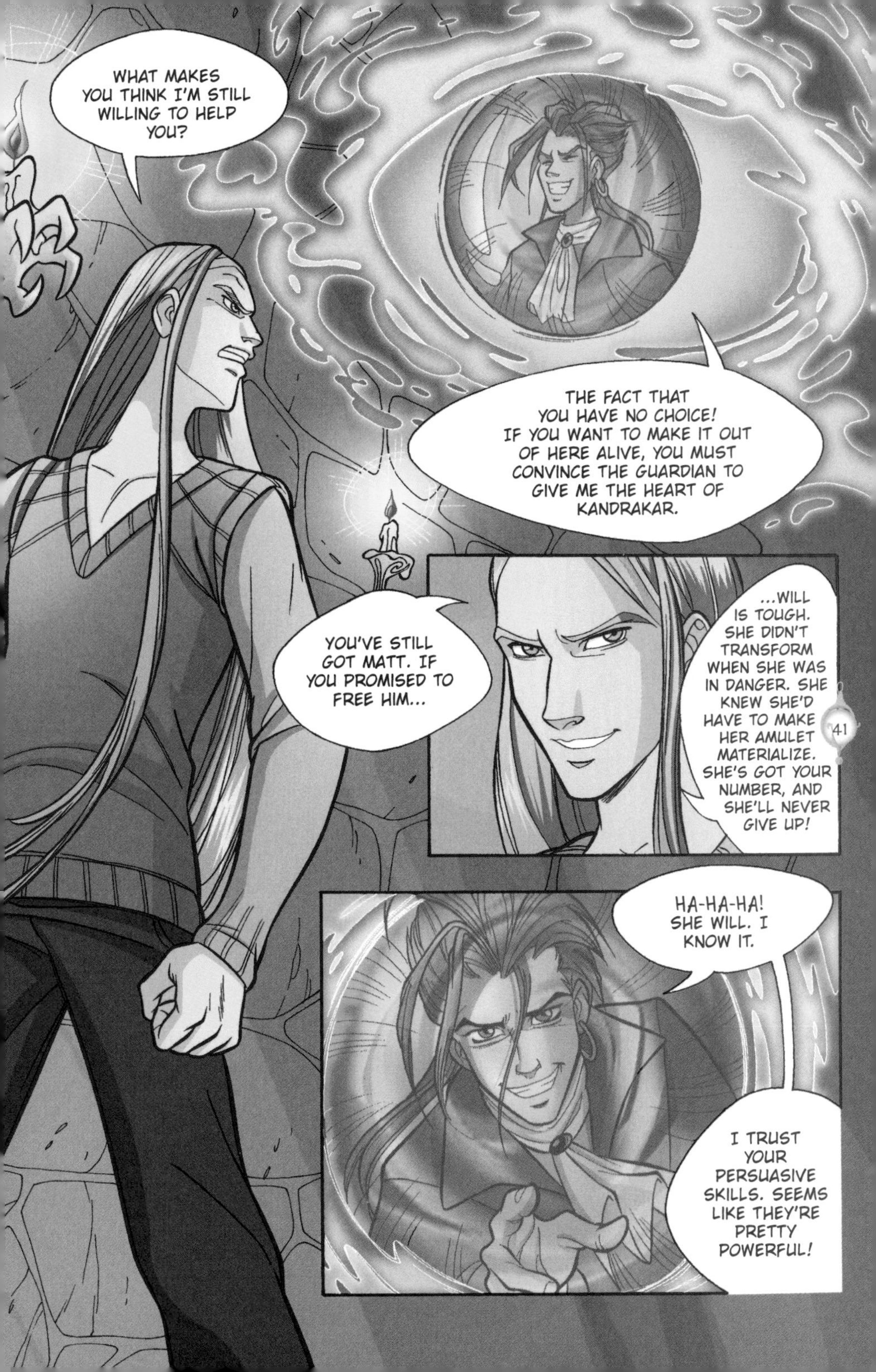
WHAT MAKES YOU THINK I'M STILL WILLING TO HELP YOU?
THE FACT THAT YOU HAVE NO CHOICE! IF YOU WANT TO MAKE IT OUT OF HERE ALIVE, YOU MUST CONVINCE THE GUARDIAN TO GIVE ME THE HEART OF KANDRAKAR.
YOU'VE STILL GOT MATT. IF YOU PROMISED TO FREE HIM...
...WILL IS TOUGH. SHE DIDN'T TRANSFORM WHEN SHE WAS IN DANGER. SHE KNEW SHE'D HAVE TO MAKE HER AMULET MATERIALIZE. SHE'S GOT YOUR NUMBER, AND SHE'LL NEVER GIVE UP!
HA-HA-HA! SHE WILL. I KNOW IT.
I TRUST YOUR PERSUASIVE SKILLS. SEEMS LIKE THEY'RE PRETTY POWERFUL!

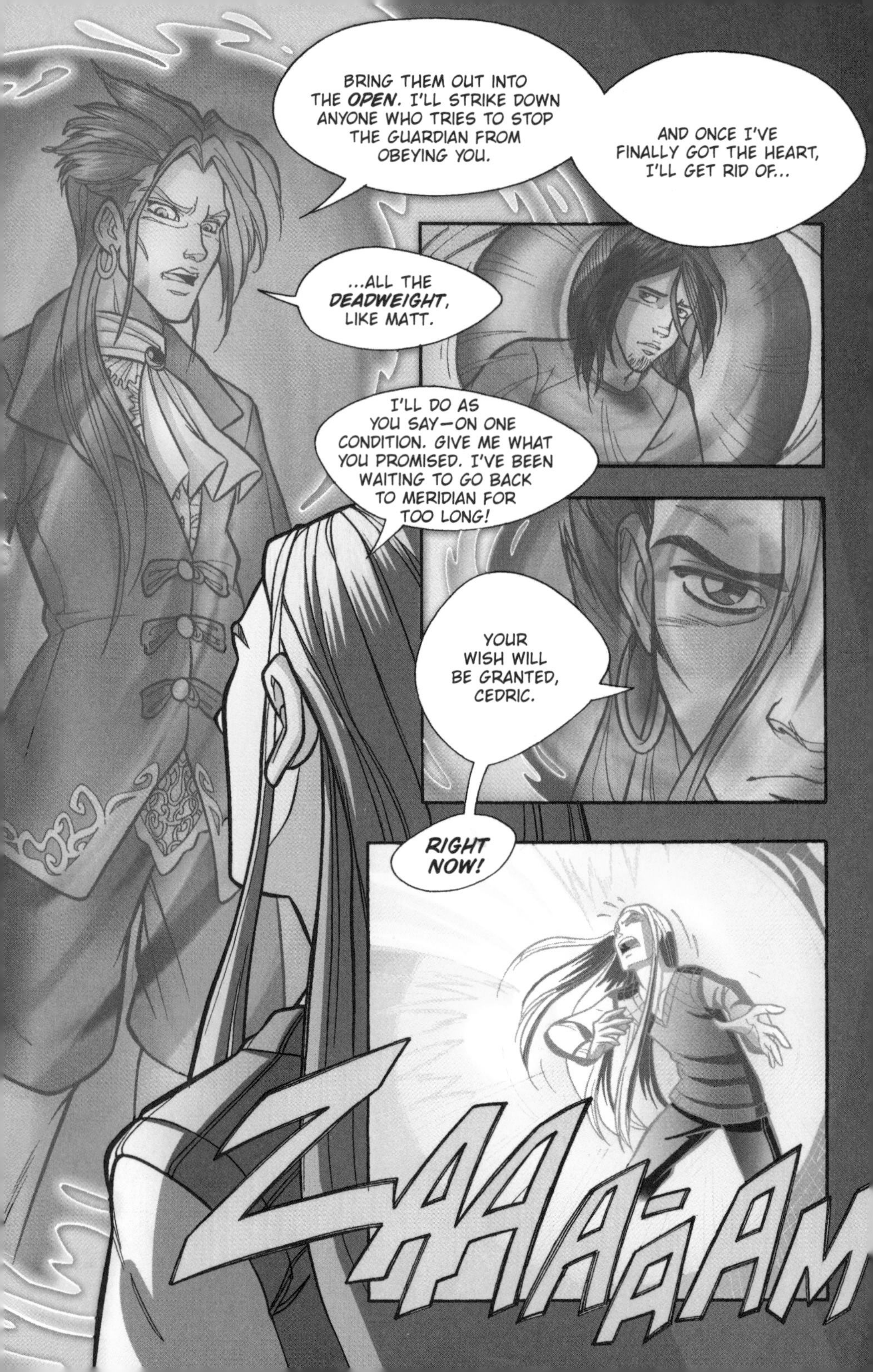
BRING THEM OUT INTO THE *OPEN*. I'LL STRIKE DOWN ANYONE WHO TRIES TO STOP THE GUARDIAN FROM OBEYING YOU.
AND ONCE I'VE FINALLY GOT THE HEART, I'LL GET RID OF...
...ALL THE *DEADWEIGHT*, LIKE MATT.
I'LL DO AS YOU SAY—ON ONE CONDITION. GIVE ME WHAT YOU PROMISED. I'VE BEEN WAITING TO GO BACK TO MERIDIAN FOR TOO LONG!
YOUR WISH WILL BE GRANTED, CEDRIC.
RIGHT NOW!
ZAAAAAM

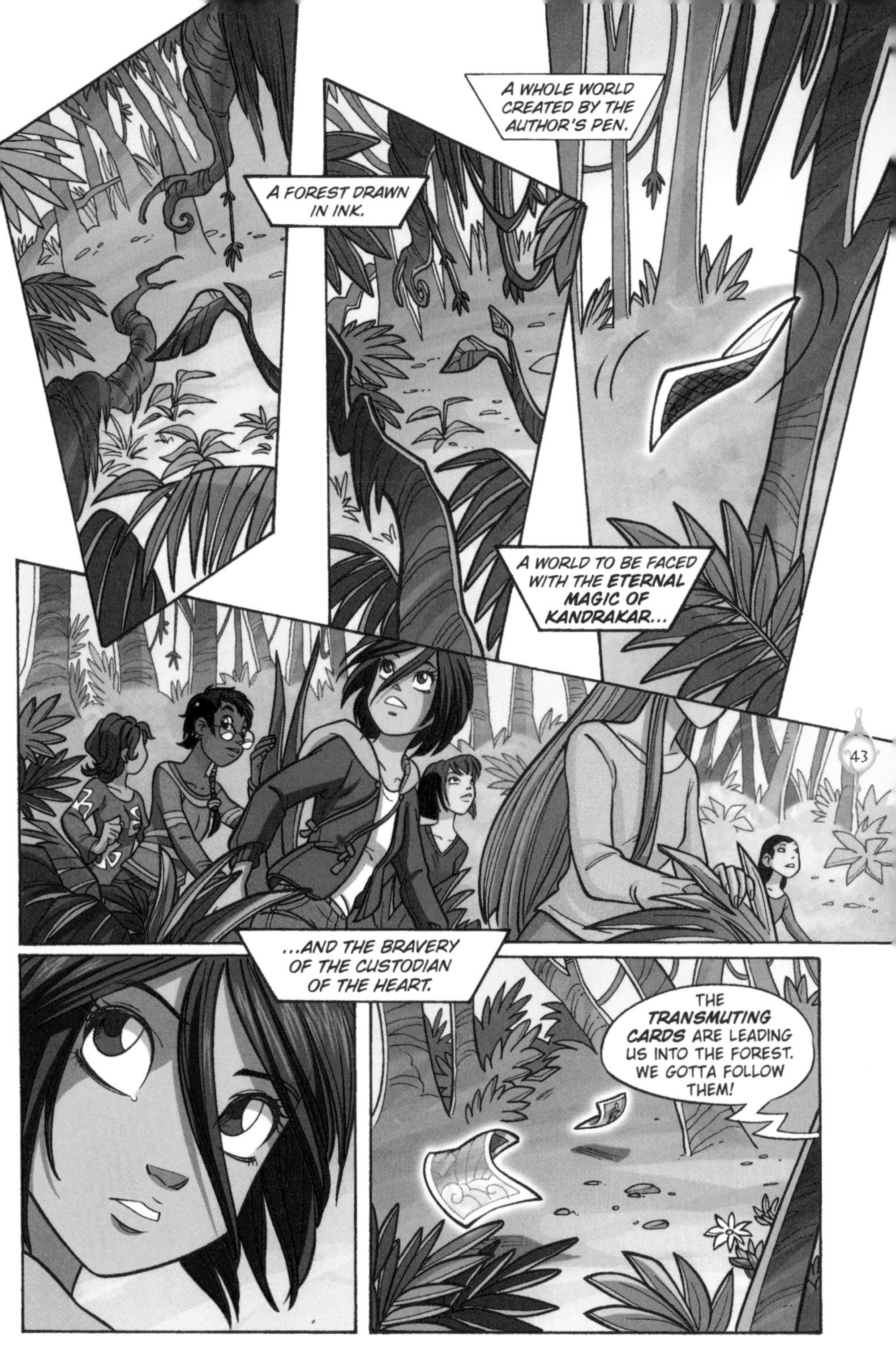

A FOREST DRAWN IN INK.
A WHOLE WORLD CREATED BY THE AUTHOR'S PEN.
A WORLD TO BE FACED WITH THE ETERNAL MAGIC OF KANDRAKAR...
...AND THE BRAVERY OF THE CUSTODIAN OF THE HEART.
THE TRANSMUTING CARDS ARE LEADING US INTO THE FOREST. WE GOTTA FOLLOW THEM!

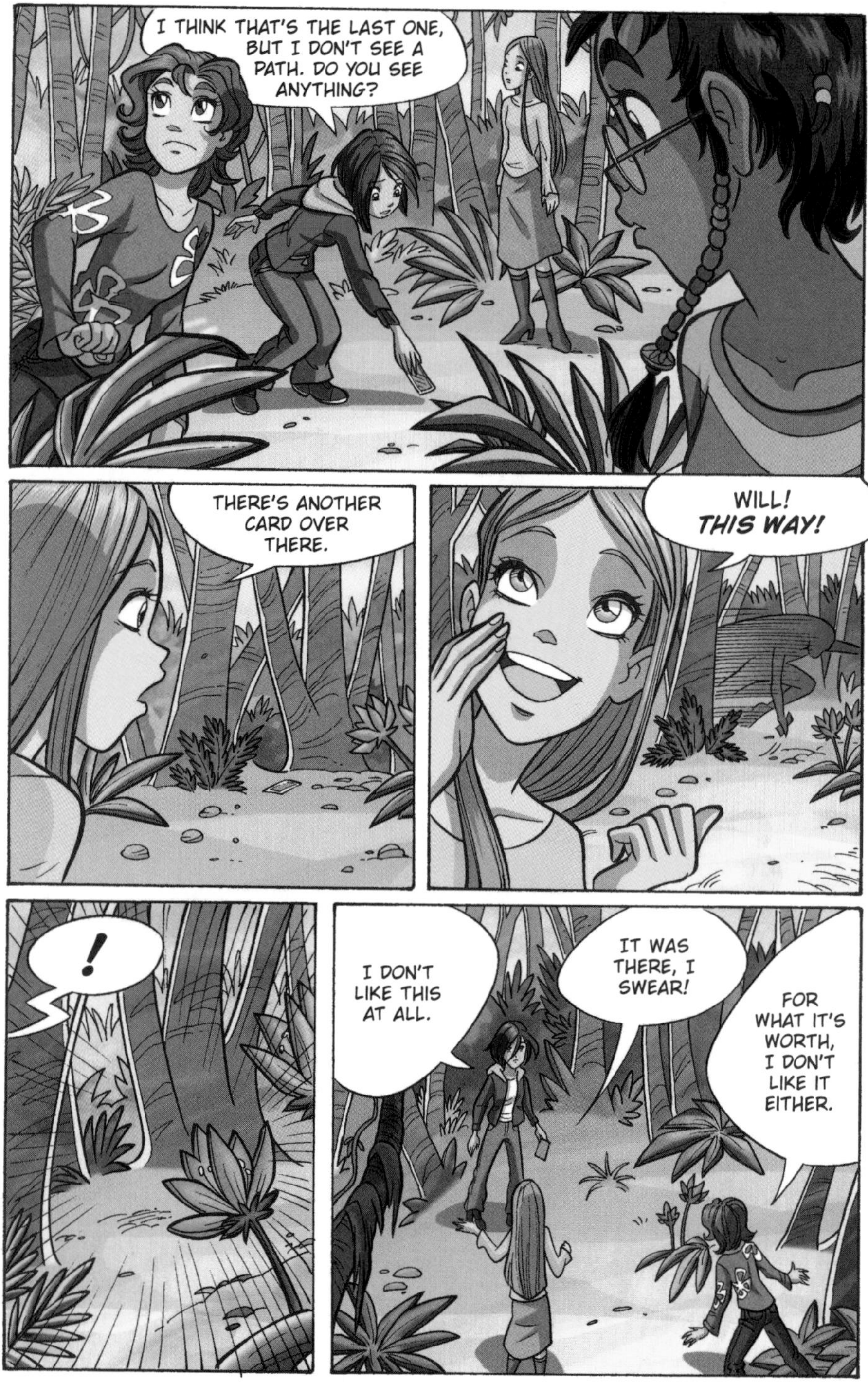
I THINK THAT'S THE LAST ONE, BUT I DON'T SEE A PATH. DO YOU SEE ANYTHING?
THERE'S ANOTHER CARD OVER THERE.
WILL! THIS WAY!
!
I DON'T LIKE THIS AT ALL.
IT WAS THERE, I SWEAR!
FOR WHAT IT'S WORTH, I DON'T LIKE IT EITHER.

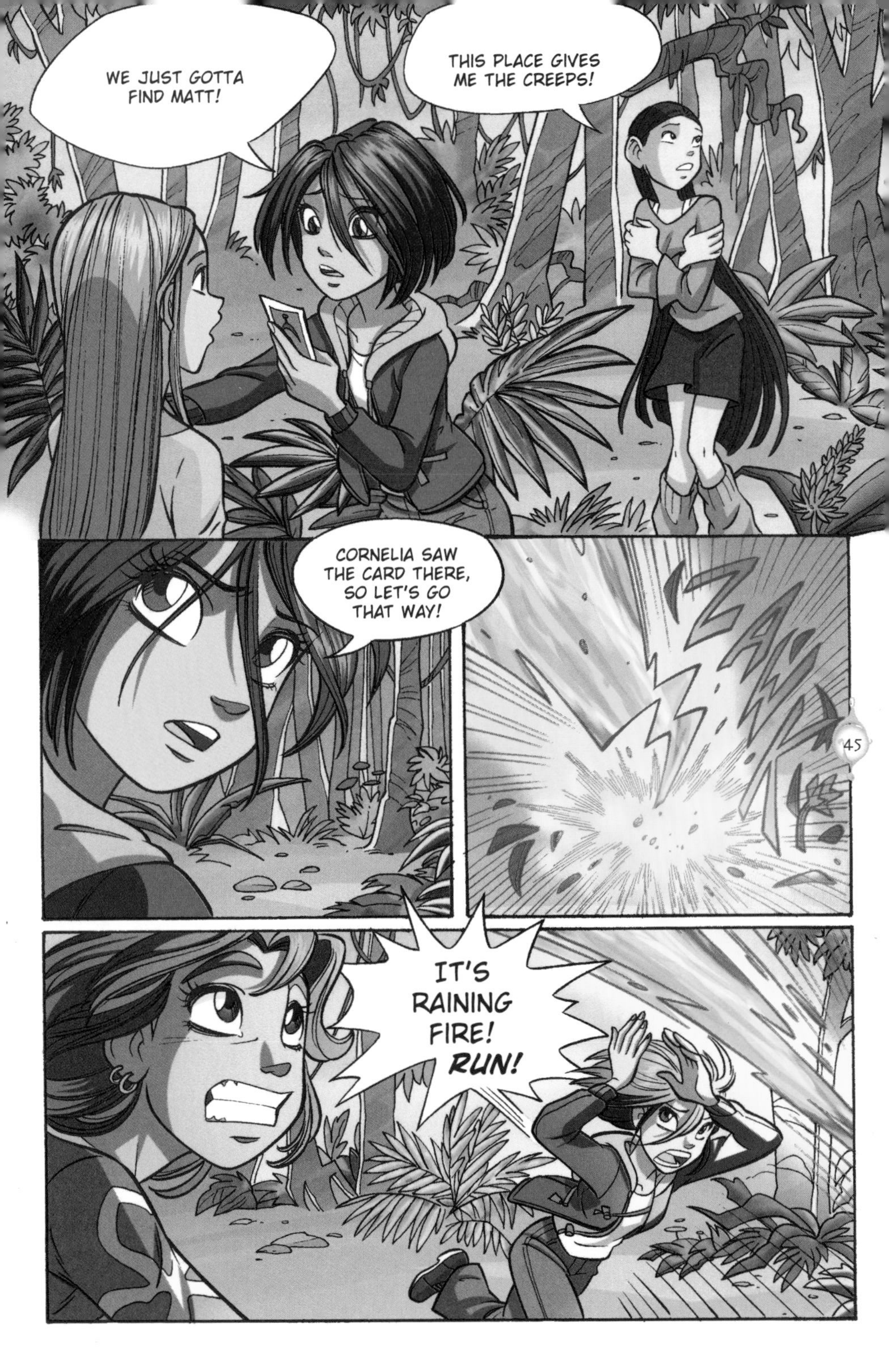
WE JUST GOTTA FIND MATT!
THIS PLACE GIVES ME THE CREEPS!
CORNELIA SAW THE CARD THERE, SO LET'S GO THAT WAY!
IT'S RAINING FIRE! RUN!

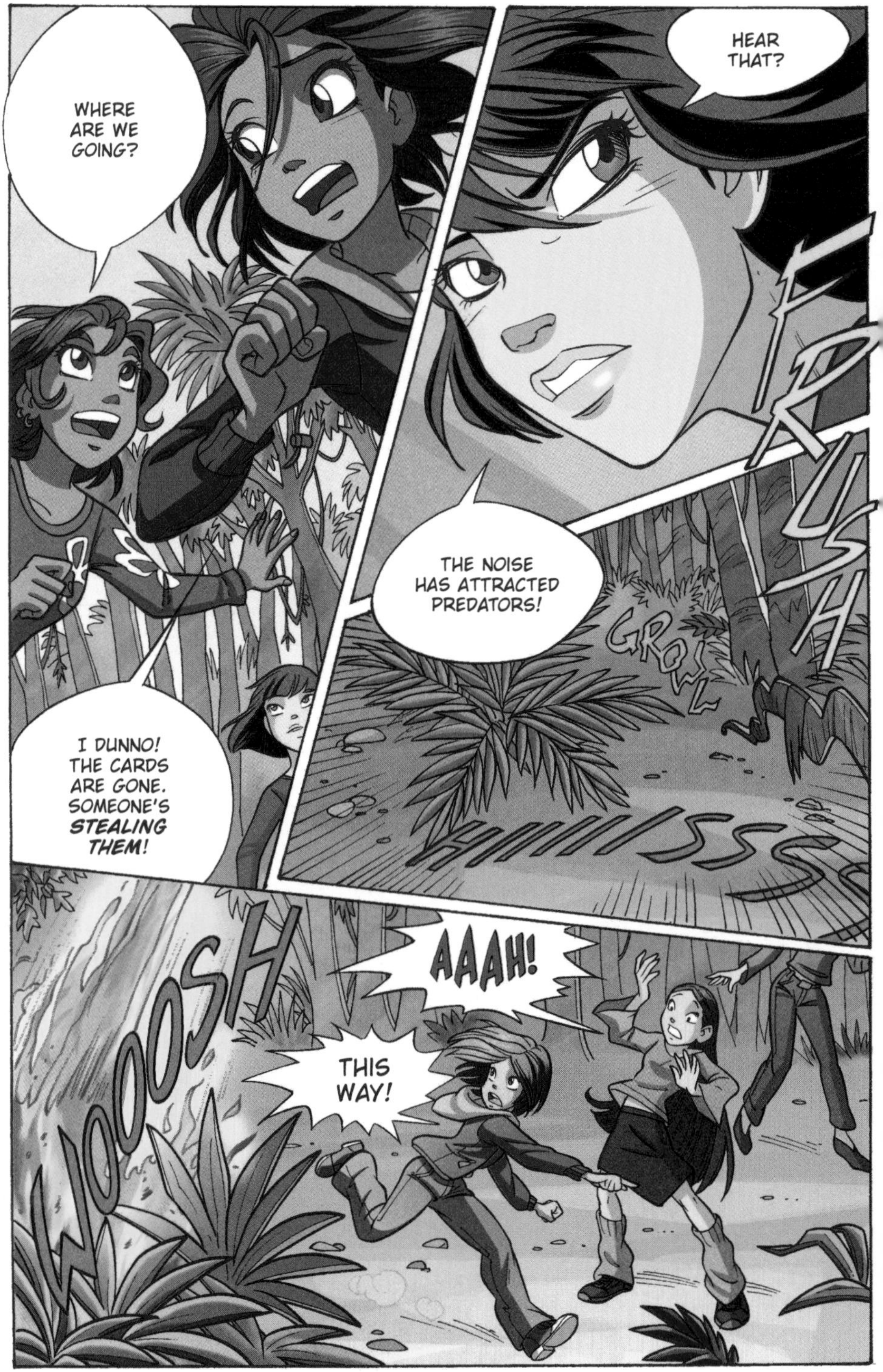
WHERE ARE WE GOING?
HEAR THAT?
FRRUSH
I DUNNO! THE CARDS ARE GONE. SOMEONE'S STEALING THEM!
THE NOISE HAS ATTRACTED PREDATORS!
GROWL
HIIIISSSS
WOOOSH
AAAH!
THIS WAY!

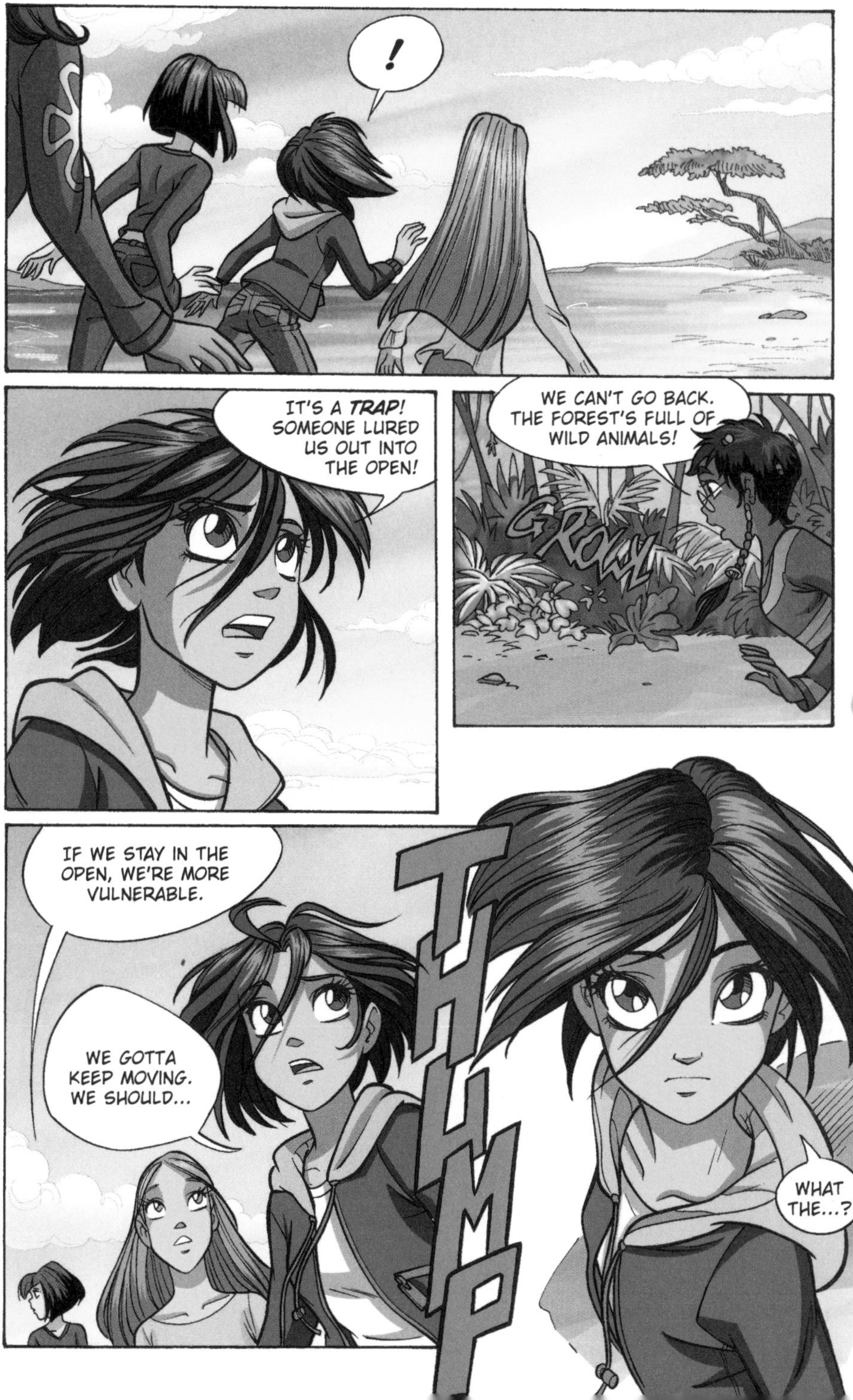
!
IT'S A *TRAP*! SOMEONE LURED US OUT INTO THE OPEN!
WE CAN'T GO BACK. THE FOREST'S FULL OF WILD ANIMALS!
GROWL
IF WE STAY IN THE OPEN, WE'RE MORE VULNERABLE.
WE GOTTA KEEP MOVING. WE SHOULD...
THUMP
WHAT THE...?

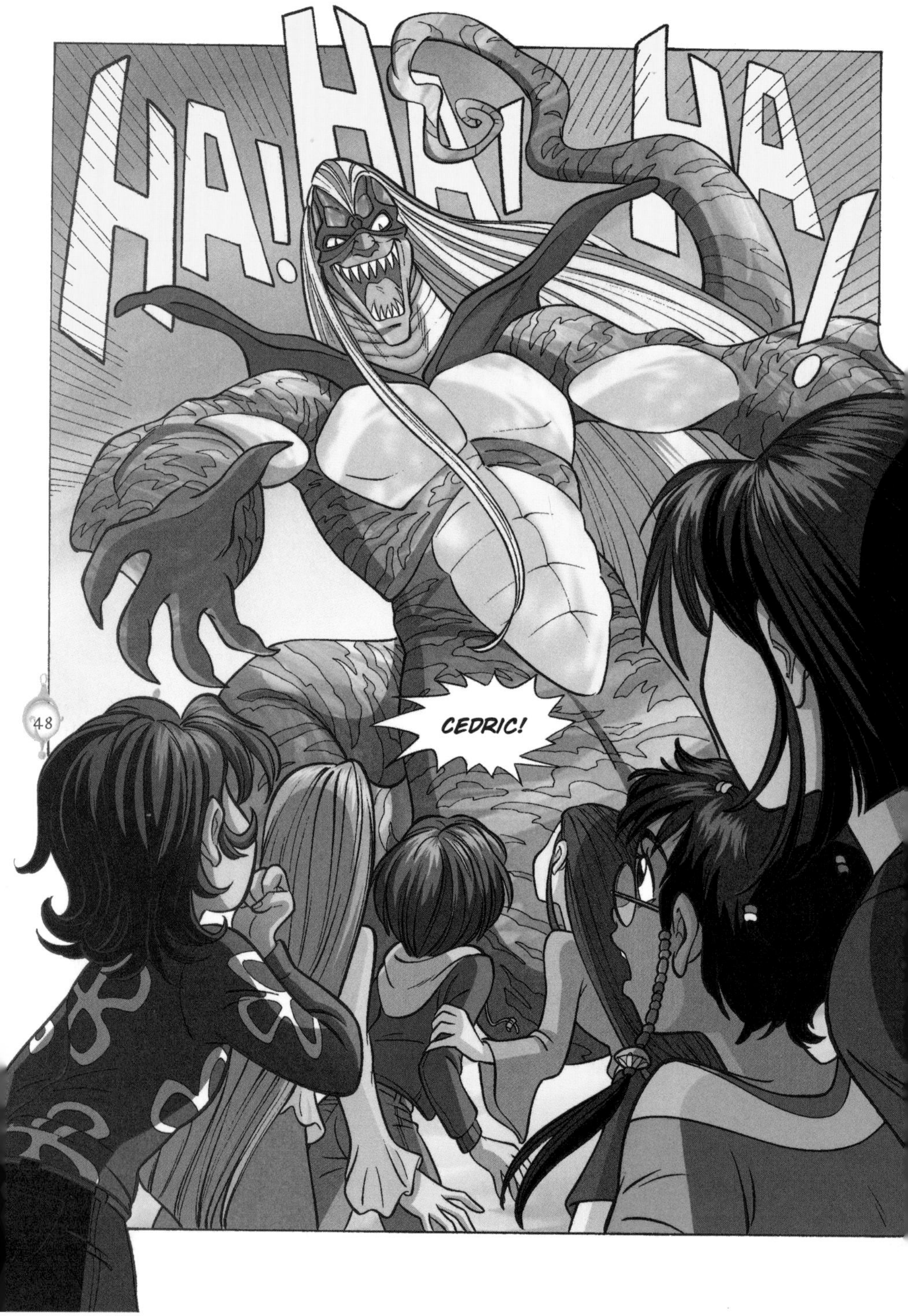

HA! HA! HA! HA!
CEDRIC!

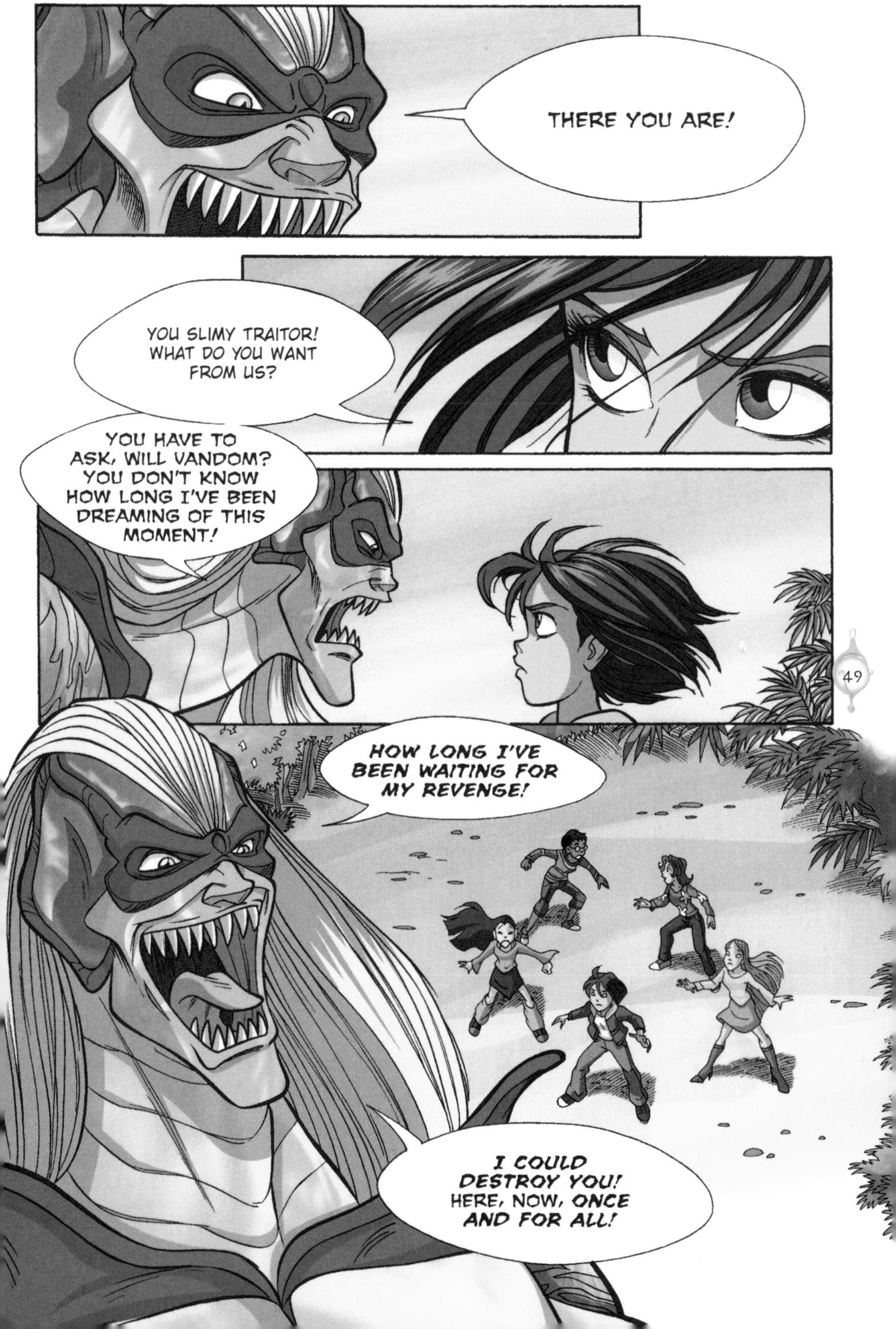

THERE YOU ARE!
YOU SLIMY TRAITOR! WHAT DO YOU WANT FROM US?
YOU HAVE TO ASK, WILL VANDOM? YOU DON'T KNOW HOW LONG I'VE BEEN DREAMING OF THIS MOMENT!
HOW LONG I'VE BEEN WAITING FOR MY REVENGE!
I COULD DESTROY YOU! HERE, NOW, ONCE AND FOR ALL!

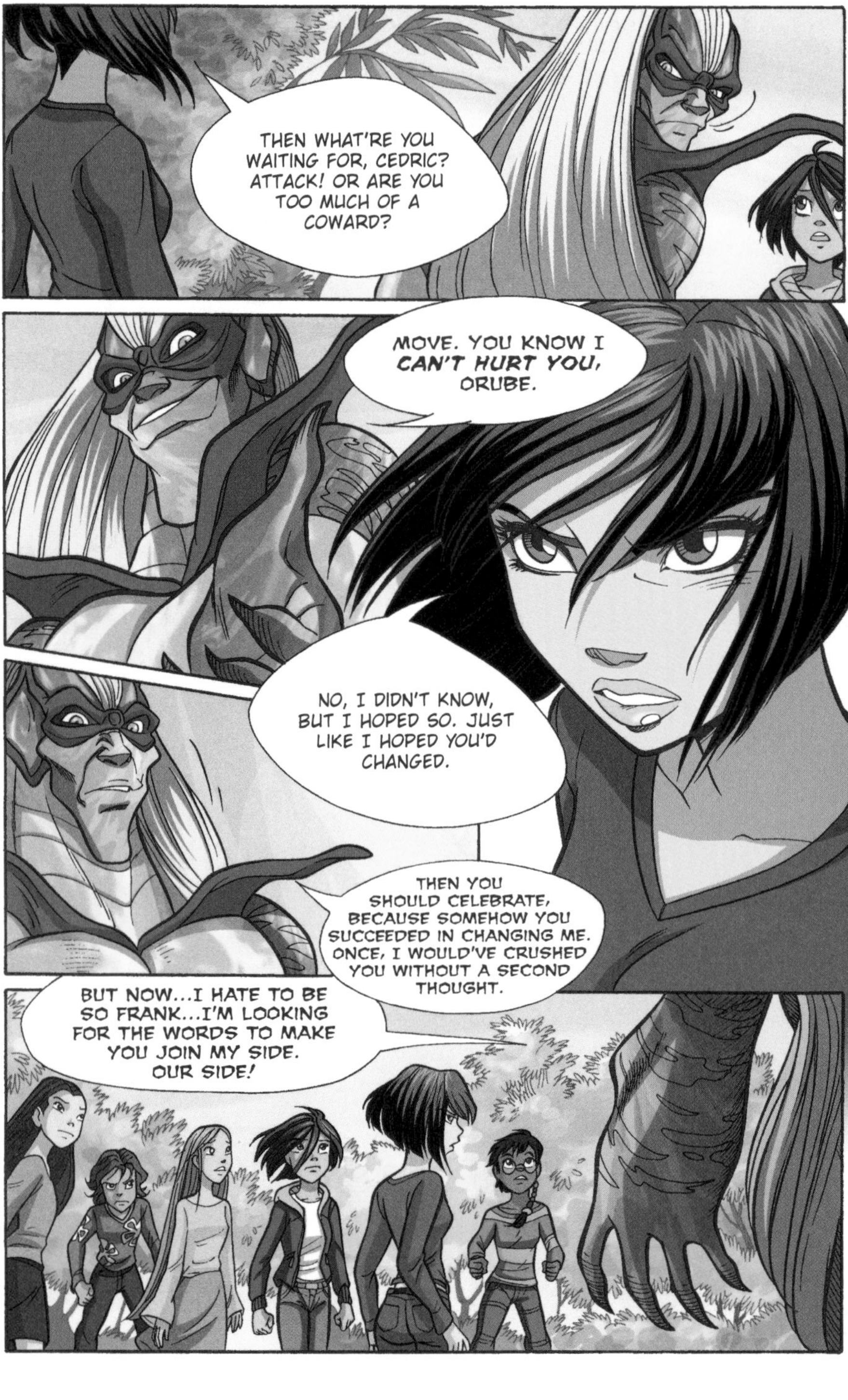
THEN WHAT'RE YOU WAITING FOR, CEDRIC? ATTACK! OR ARE YOU TOO MUCH OF A COWARD?
MOVE. YOU KNOW I **CAN'T HURT YOU,** ORUBE.
NO, I DIDN'T KNOW, BUT I HOPED SO. JUST LIKE I HOPED YOU'D CHANGED.
THEN YOU SHOULD CELEBRATE, BECAUSE SOMEHOW YOU SUCCEEDED IN CHANGING ME. ONCE, I WOULD'VE CRUSHED YOU WITHOUT A SECOND THOUGHT.
BUT NOW...I HATE TO BE SO FRANK...I'M LOOKING FOR THE WORDS TO MAKE YOU JOIN MY SIDE. OUR SIDE!

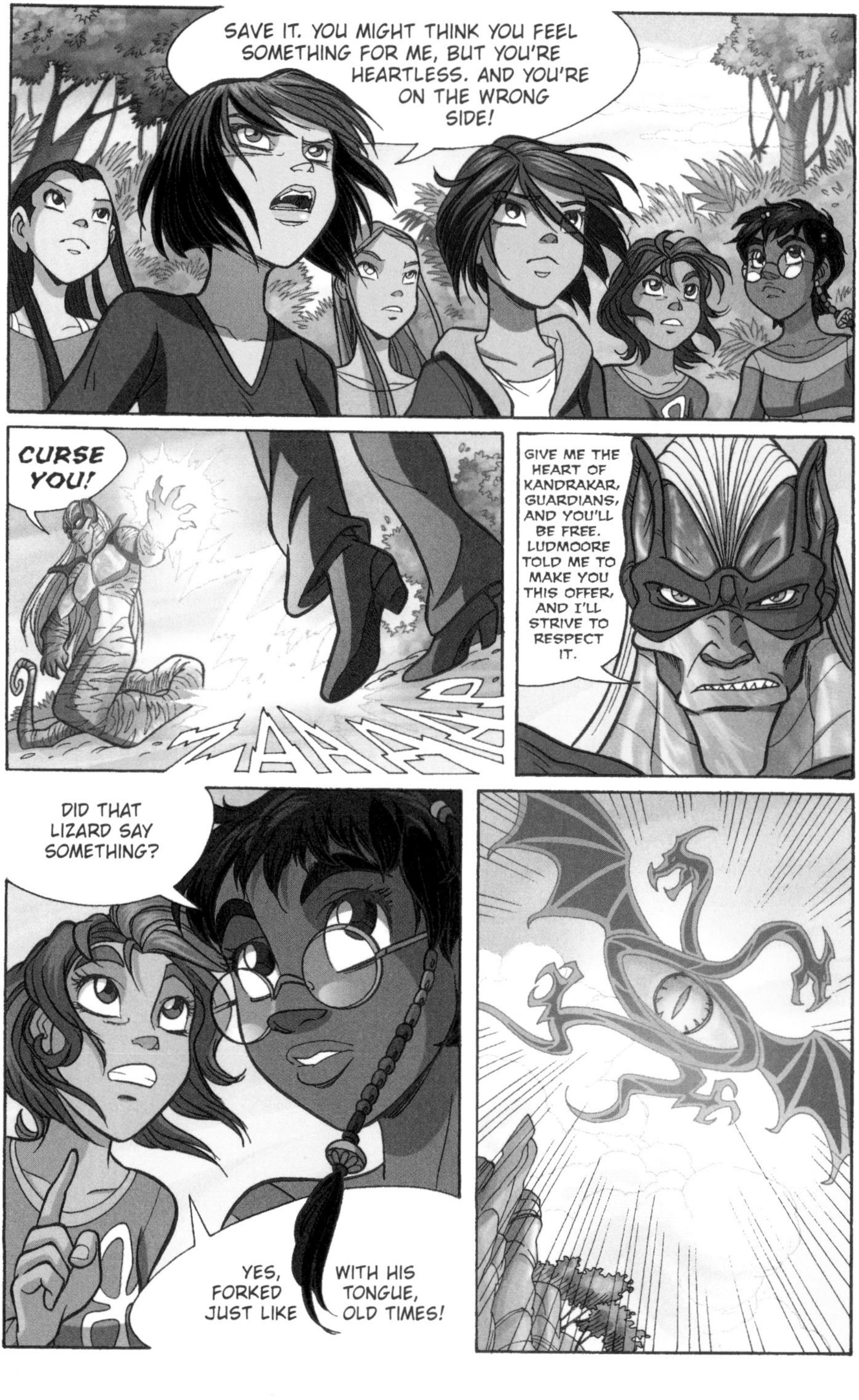
SAVE IT. YOU MIGHT THINK YOU FEEL SOMETHING FOR ME, BUT YOU'RE HEARTLESS. AND YOU'RE ON THE WRONG SIDE!
CURSE YOU!
GIVE ME THE HEART OF KANDRAKAR, GUARDIANS, AND YOU'LL BE FREE. LUDMOORE TOLD ME TO MAKE YOU THIS OFFER, AND I'LL STRIVE TO RESPECT IT.
DID THAT LIZARD SAY SOMETHING?
YES, FORKED JUST LIKE
WITH HIS TONGUE, OLD TIMES!

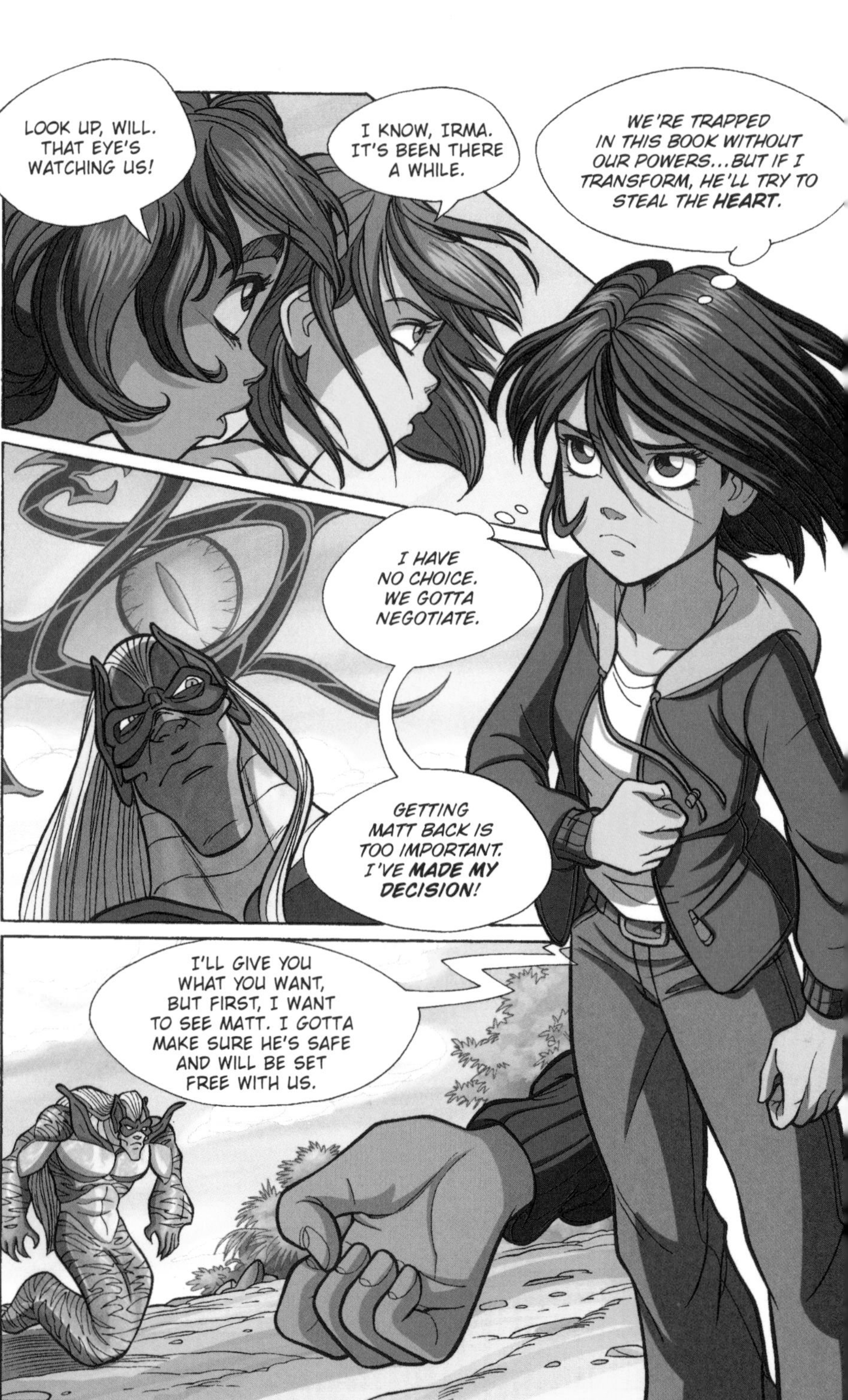
LOOK UP, WILL. THAT EYE'S WATCHING US!
I KNOW, IRMA. IT'S BEEN THERE A WHILE.
WE'RE TRAPPED IN THIS BOOK WITHOUT OUR POWERS...BUT IF I TRANSFORM, HE'LL TRY TO STEAL THE HEART.
I HAVE NO CHOICE. WE GOTTA NEGOTIATE.
GETTING MATT BACK IS TOO IMPORTANT. I'VE MADE MY DECISION!
I'LL GIVE YOU WHAT YOU WANT, BUT FIRST, I WANT TO SEE MATT. I GOTTA MAKE SURE HE'S SAFE AND WILL BE SET FREE WITH US.

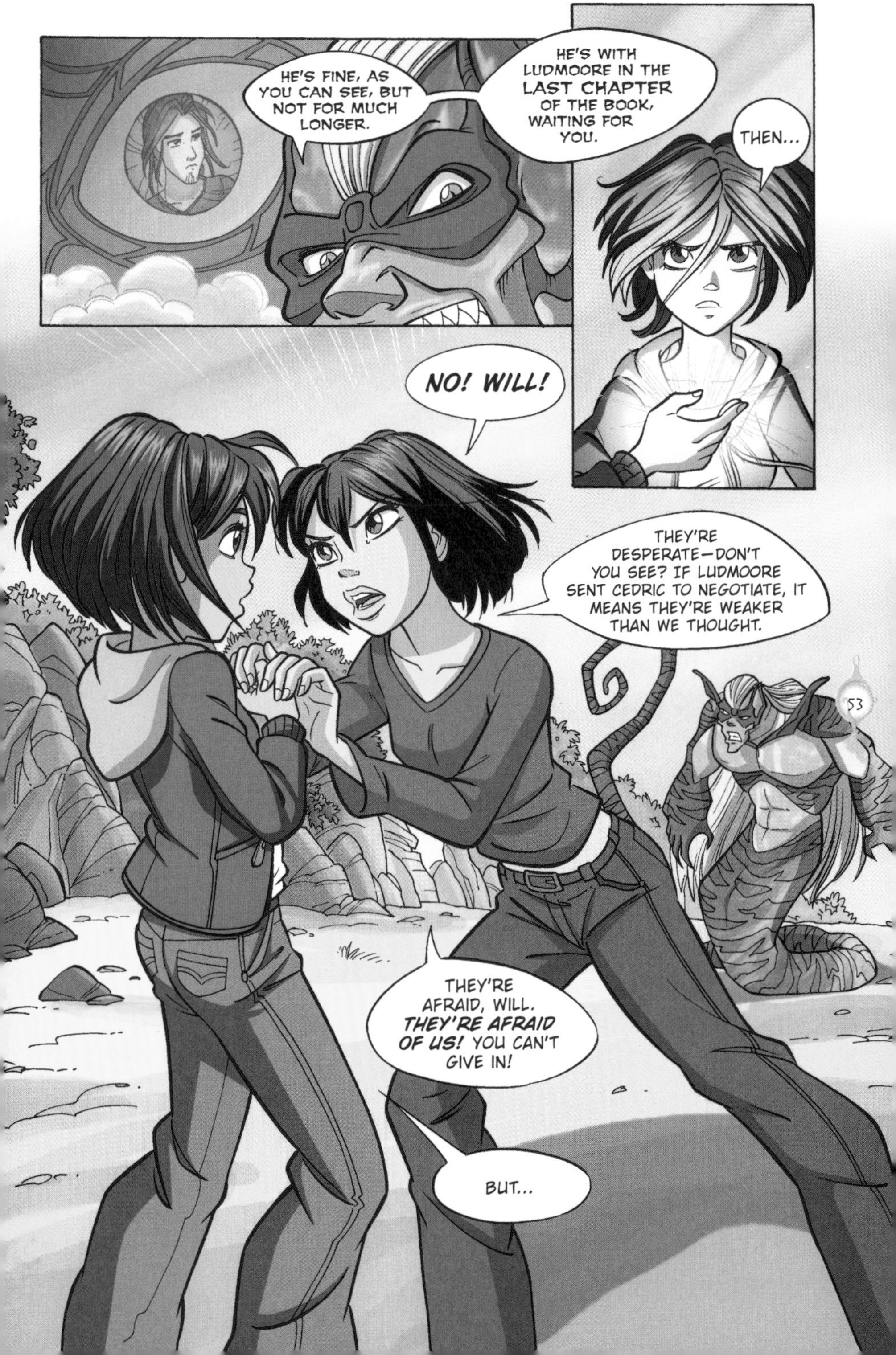
HE'S FINE, AS YOU CAN SEE, BUT NOT FOR MUCH LONGER.
HE'S WITH LUDMOORE IN THE LAST CHAPTER OF THE BOOK, WAITING FOR YOU.
THEN...
NO! WILL!
THEY'RE DESPERATE—DON'T YOU SEE? IF LUDMOORE SENT CEDRIC TO NEGOTIATE, IT MEANS THEY'RE WEAKER THAN WE THOUGHT.
THEY'RE AFRAID, WILL. THEY'RE AFRAID OF US! YOU CAN'T GIVE IN!
BUT...

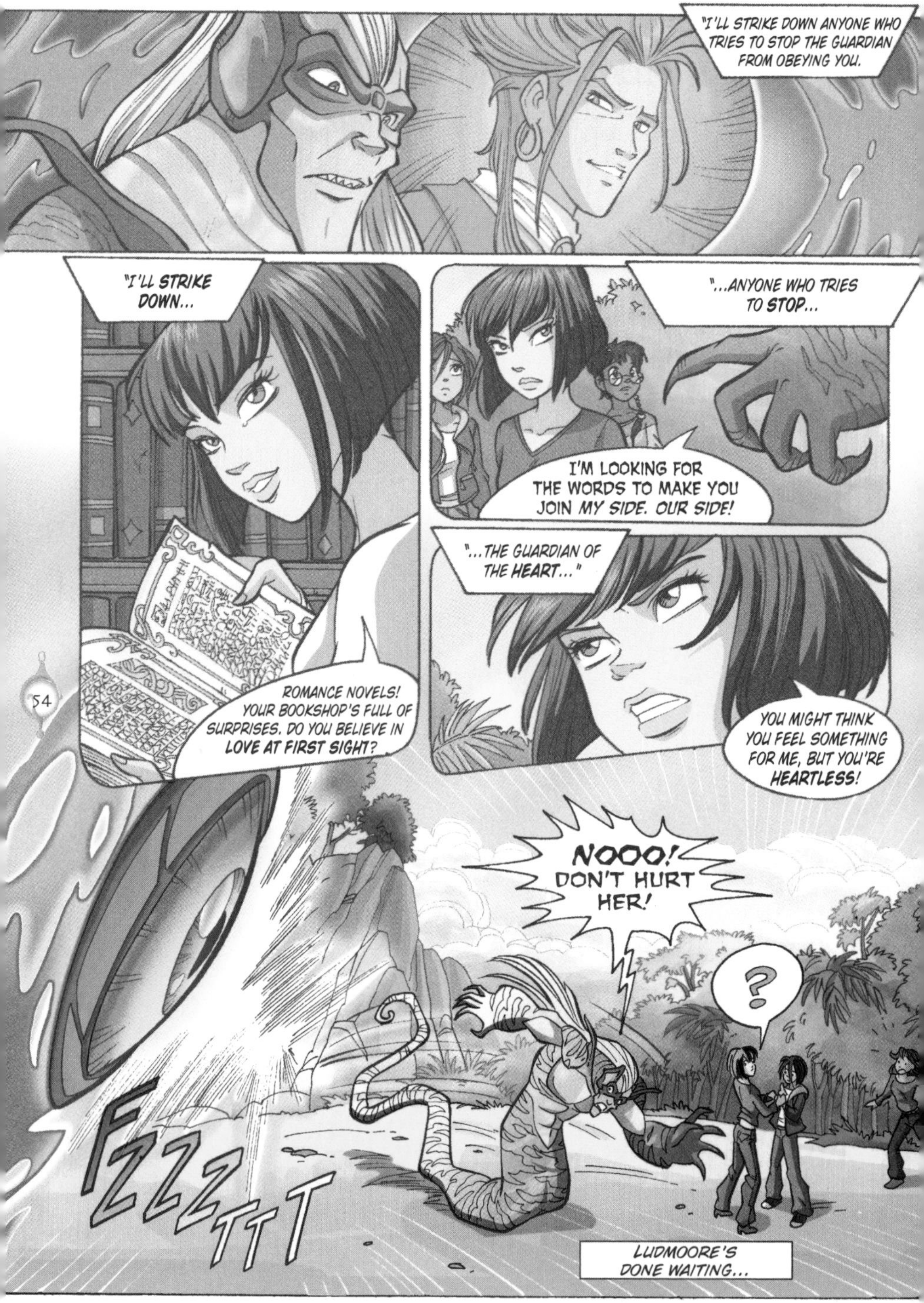
"I'LL STRIKE DOWN ANYONE WHO TRIES TO STOP THE GUARDIAN FROM OBEYING YOU.
"I'LL STRIKE DOWN...
ROMANCE NOVELS! YOUR BOOKSHOP'S FULL OF SURPRISES. DO YOU BELIEVE IN LOVE AT FIRST SIGHT?
"...ANYONE WHO TRIES TO STOP...
I'M LOOKING FOR THE WORDS TO MAKE YOU JOIN MY SIDE. OUR SIDE!
"...THE GUARDIAN OF THE HEART..."
YOU MIGHT THINK YOU FEEL SOMETHING FOR ME, BUT YOU'RE HEARTLESS!
NOOO! DON'T HURT HER!
?
FZZZTTT
LUDMOORE'S DONE WAITING...

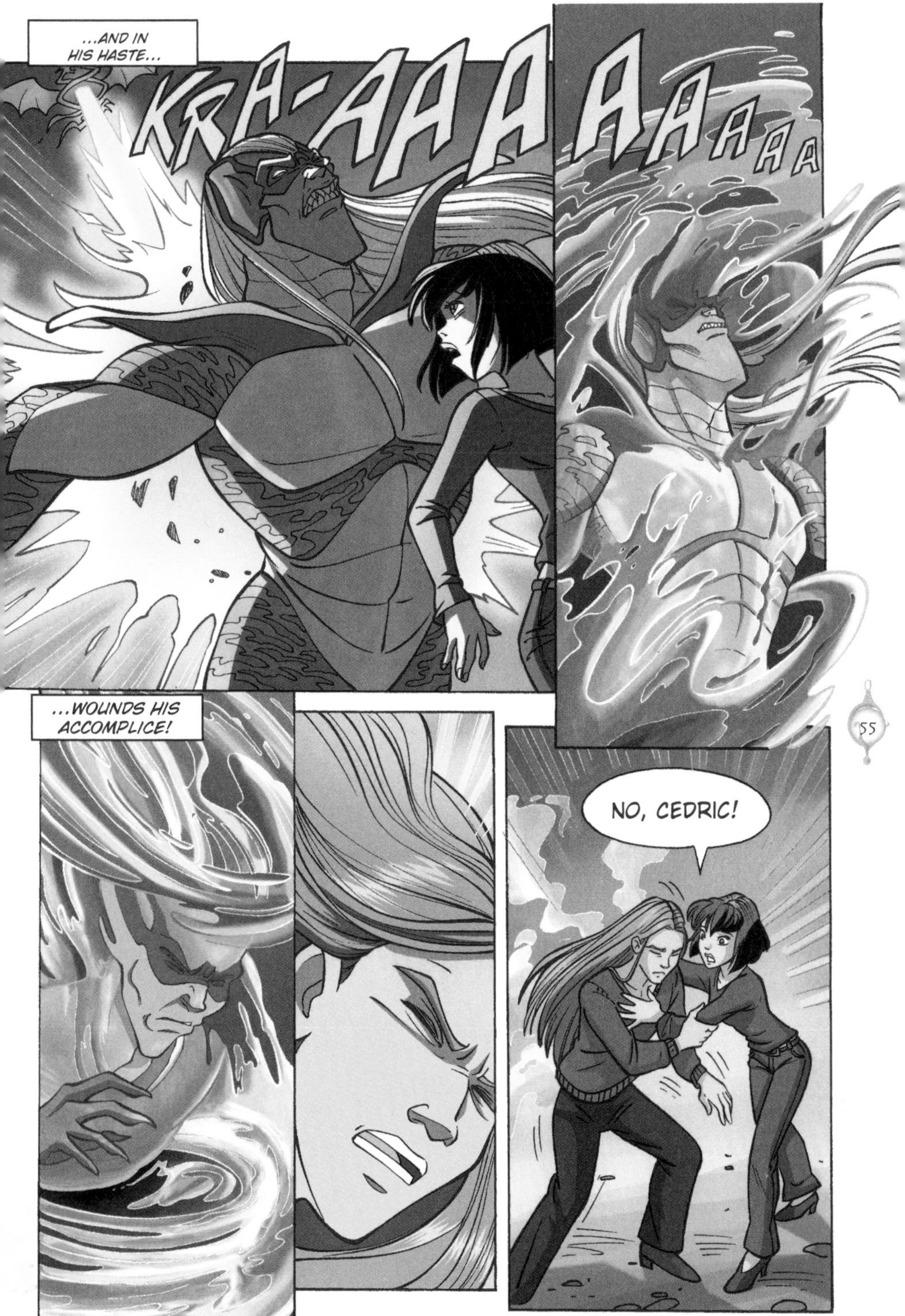
...AND IN HIS HASTE...
KRA-AAAAAAAAA
...WOUNDS HIS ACCOMPLICE!
NO, CEDRIC!

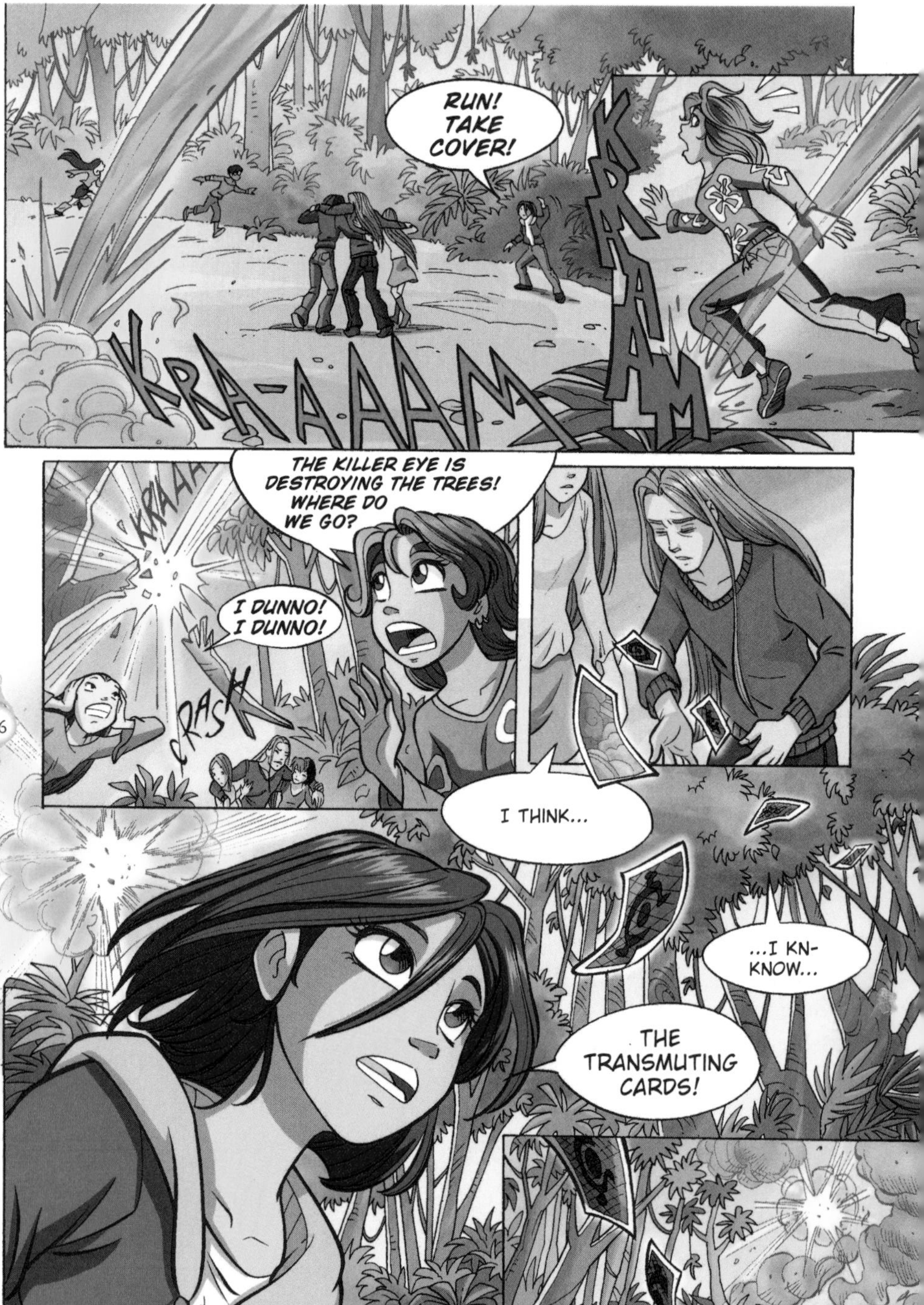
RUN! TAKE COVER!
KRA-AAAM
KRAAAM
THE KILLER EYE IS DESTROYING THE TREES! WHERE DO WE GO?
KRAAA
I DUNNO! I DUNNO!
CRASH
I THINK...
...I KN-KNOW...
THE TRANSMUTING CARDS!

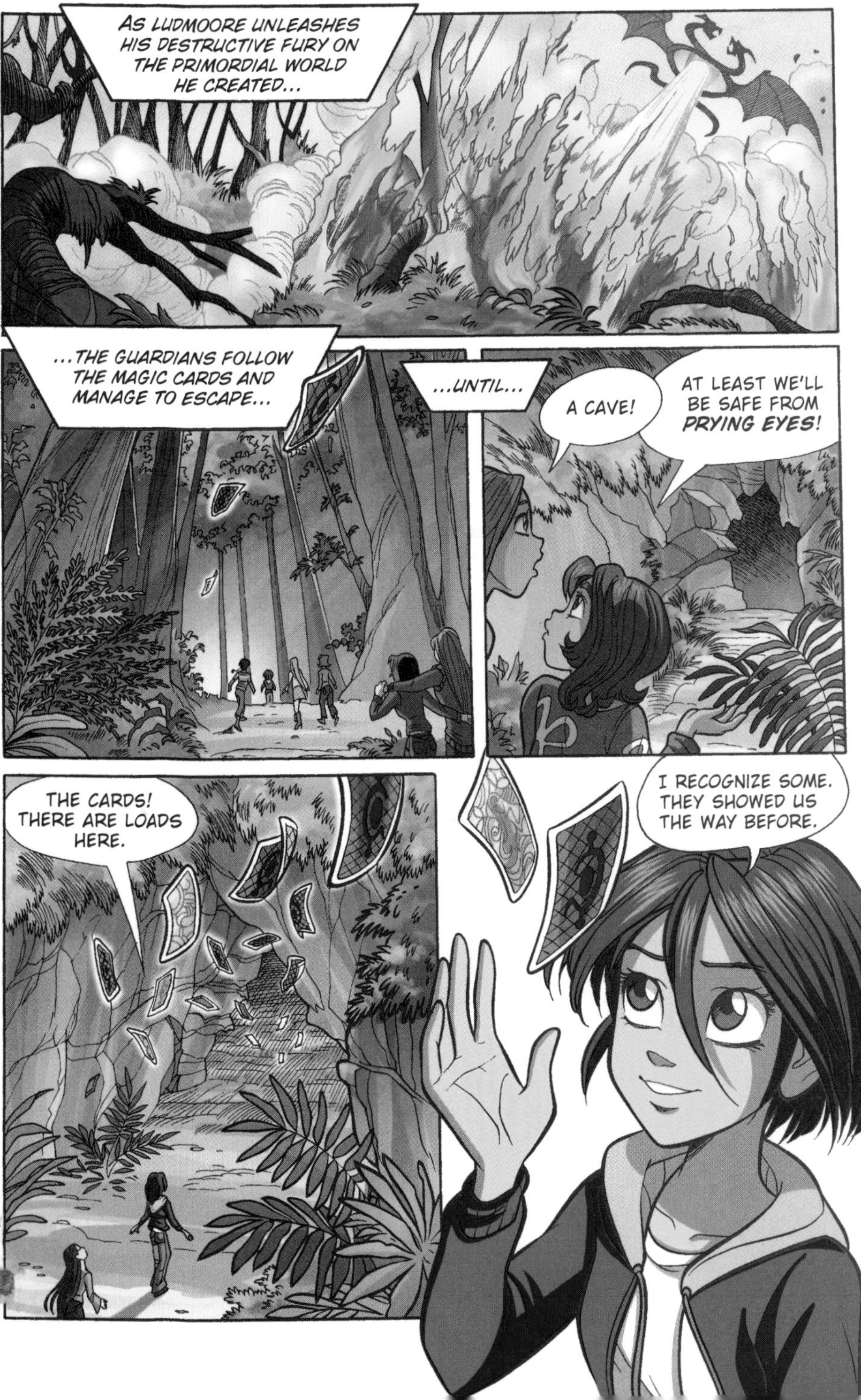
AS LUDMOORE UNLEASHES HIS DESTRUCTIVE FURY ON THE PRIMORDIAL WORLD HE CREATED...
...THE GUARDIANS FOLLOW THE MAGIC CARDS AND MANAGE TO ESCAPE...
...UNTIL...
A CAVE!
AT LEAST WE'LL BE SAFE FROM PRYING EYES!
THE CARDS! THERE ARE LOADS HERE.
I RECOGNIZE SOME. THEY SHOWED US THE WAY BEFORE.

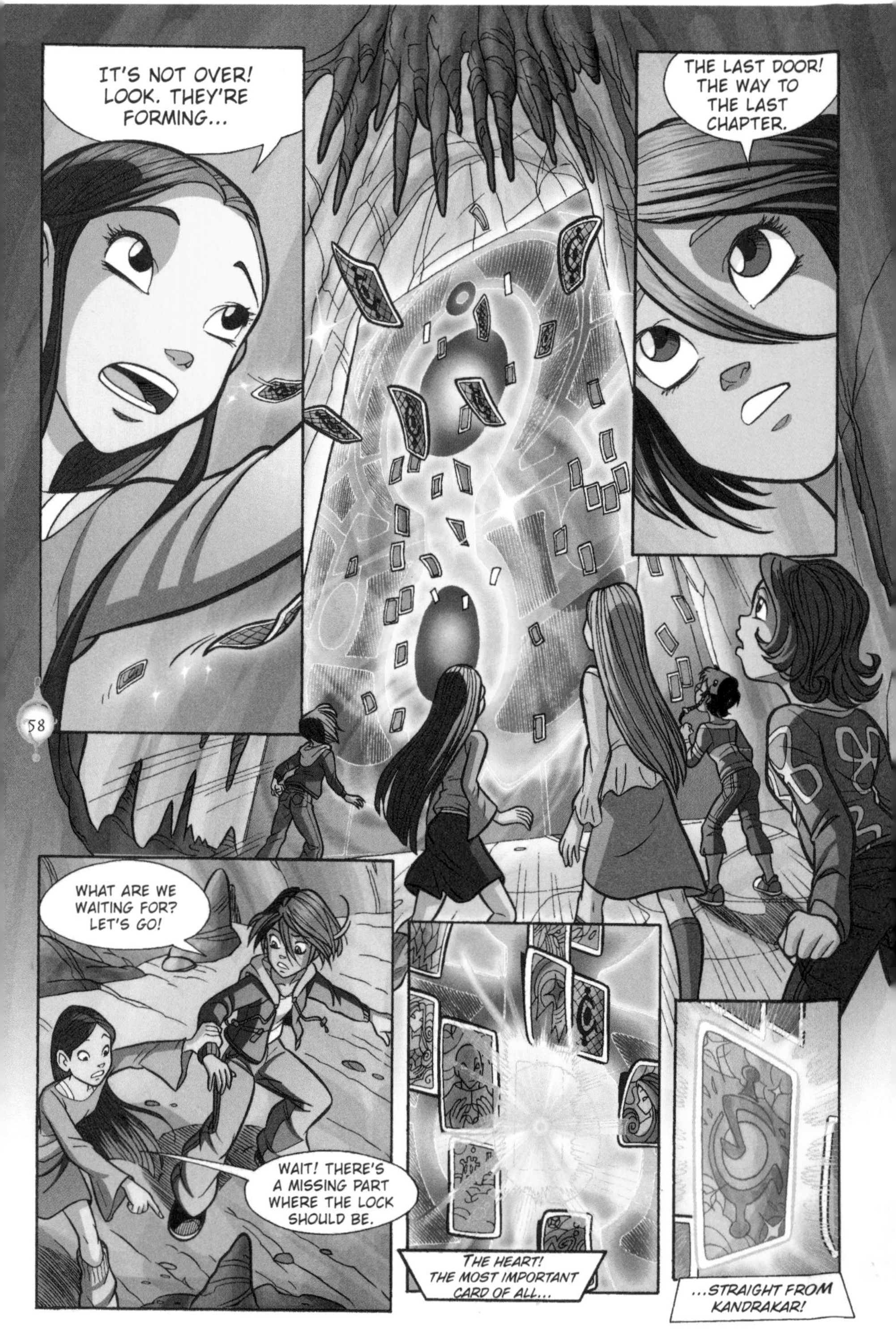
IT'S NOT OVER! LOOK. THEY'RE FORMING...
THE LAST DOOR! THE WAY TO THE LAST CHAPTER.
WHAT ARE WE WAITING FOR? LET'S GO!
WAIT! THERE'S A MISSING PART WHERE THE LOCK SHOULD BE.
THE HEART! THE MOST IMPORTANT CARD OF ALL...
...STRAIGHT FROM KANDRAKAR!

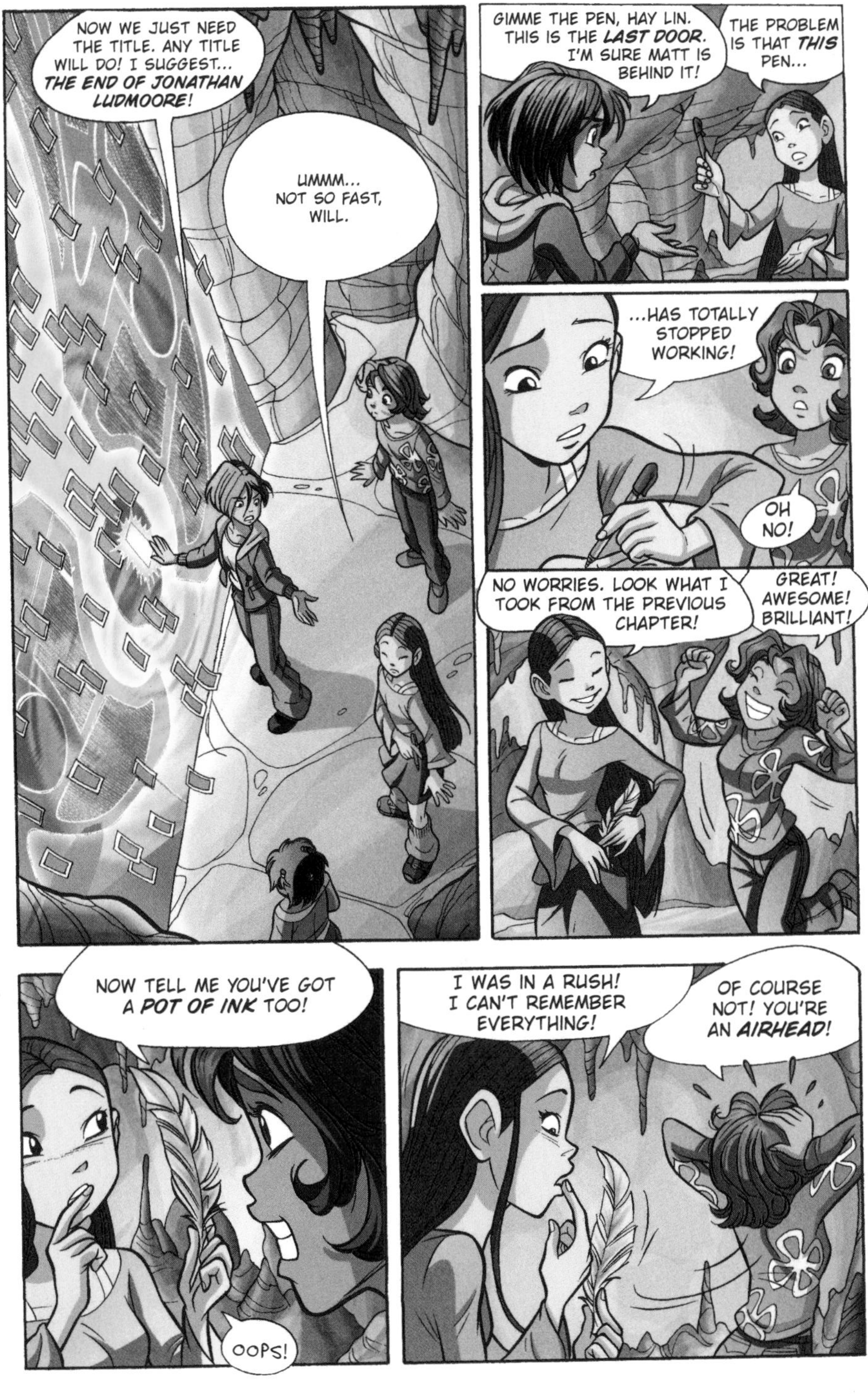
NOW WE JUST NEED THE TITLE. ANY TITLE WILL DO! I SUGGEST... THE END OF JONATHAN LUDMOORE!
UMMM... NOT SO FAST, WILL.
GIMME THE PEN, HAY LIN. THIS IS THE LAST DOOR. I'M SURE MATT IS BEHIND IT!
THE PROBLEM IS THAT THIS PEN...
...HAS TOTALLY STOPPED WORKING!
OH NO!
NO WORRIES. LOOK WHAT I TOOK FROM THE PREVIOUS CHAPTER!
GREAT! AWESOME! BRILLIANT!
NOW TELL ME YOU'VE GOT A POT OF INK TOO!
OOPS!
I WAS IN A RUSH! I CAN'T REMEMBER EVERYTHING!
OF COURSE NOT! YOU'RE AN AIRHEAD!

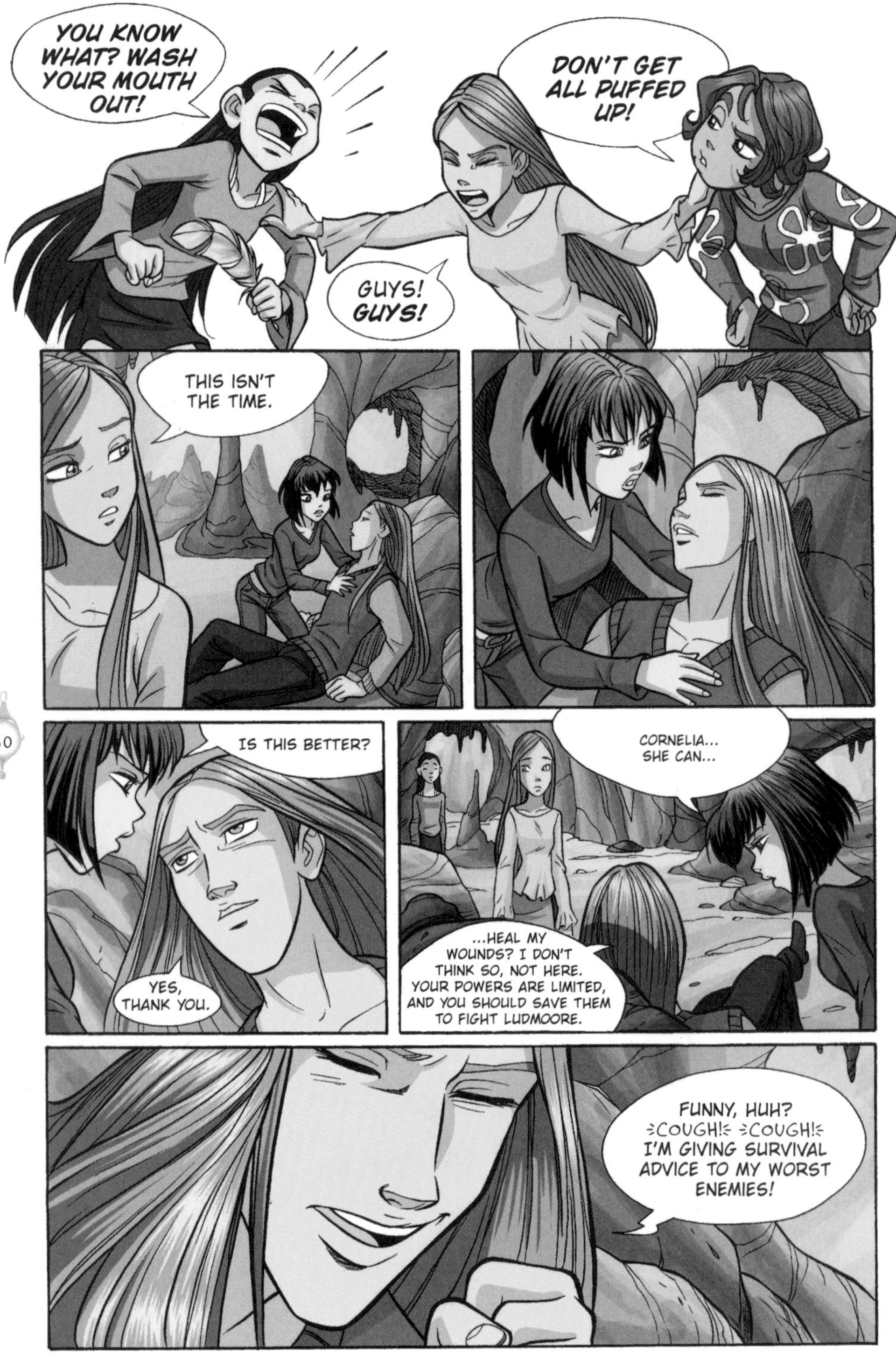
YOU KNOW WHAT? WASH YOUR MOUTH OUT!
DON'T GET ALL PUFFED UP!
GUYS! GUYS!
THIS ISN'T THE TIME.
IS THIS BETTER?
YES, THANK YOU.
CORNELIA... SHE CAN...
...HEAL MY WOUNDS? I DON'T THINK SO, NOT HERE. YOUR POWERS ARE LIMITED, AND YOU SHOULD SAVE THEM TO FIGHT LUDMOORE.
FUNNY, HUH? COUGH! COUGH! I'M GIVING SURVIVAL ADVICE TO MY WORST ENEMIES!

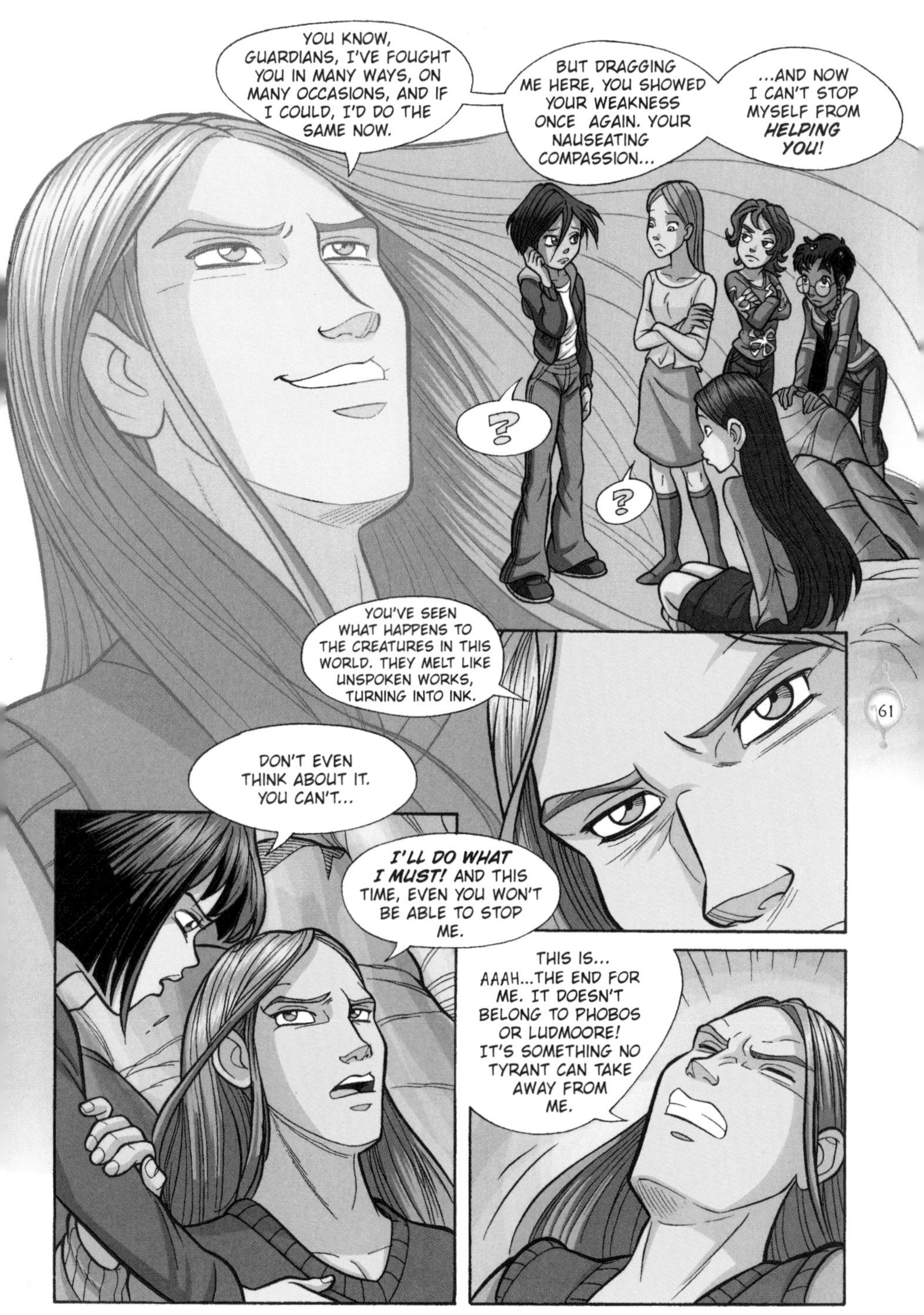
YOU KNOW, GUARDIANS, I'VE FOUGHT YOU IN MANY WAYS, ON MANY OCCASIONS, AND IF I COULD, I'D DO THE SAME NOW.
BUT DRAGGING ME HERE, YOU SHOWED YOUR WEAKNESS ONCE AGAIN. YOUR NAUSEATING COMPASSION...
...AND NOW I CAN'T STOP MYSELF FROM ***HELPING YOU!***
?
?
YOU'VE SEEN WHAT HAPPENS TO THE CREATURES IN THIS WORLD. THEY MELT LIKE UNSPOKEN WORKS, TURNING INTO INK.
DON'T EVEN THINK ABOUT IT. YOU CAN'T...
I'LL DO WHAT I MUST! AND THIS TIME, EVEN YOU WON'T BE ABLE TO STOP ME.
THIS IS... AAAH...THE END FOR ME. IT DOESN'T BELONG TO PHOBOS OR LUDMOORE! IT'S SOMETHING NO TYRANT CAN TAKE AWAY FROM ME.

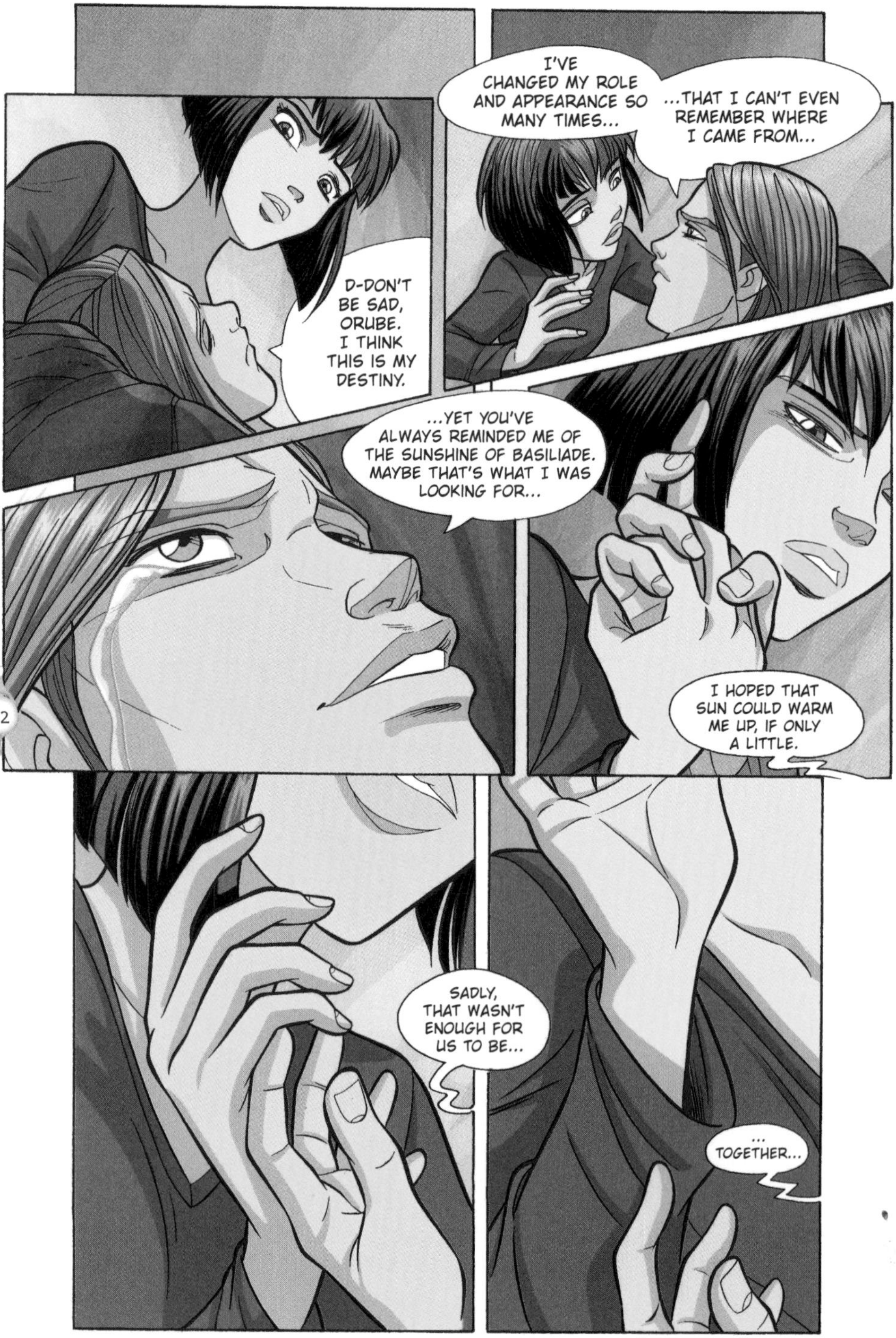
I'VE CHANGED MY ROLE AND APPEARANCE SO MANY TIMES...
...THAT I CAN'T EVEN REMEMBER WHERE I CAME FROM...
D-DON'T BE SAD, ORUBE. I THINK THIS IS MY DESTINY.
...YET YOU'VE ALWAYS REMINDED ME OF THE SUNSHINE OF BASILIADE. MAYBE THAT'S WHAT I WAS LOOKING FOR...
I HOPED THAT SUN COULD WARM ME UP, IF ONLY A LITTLE.
SADLY, THAT WASN'T ENOUGH FOR US TO BE...
... TOGETHER...

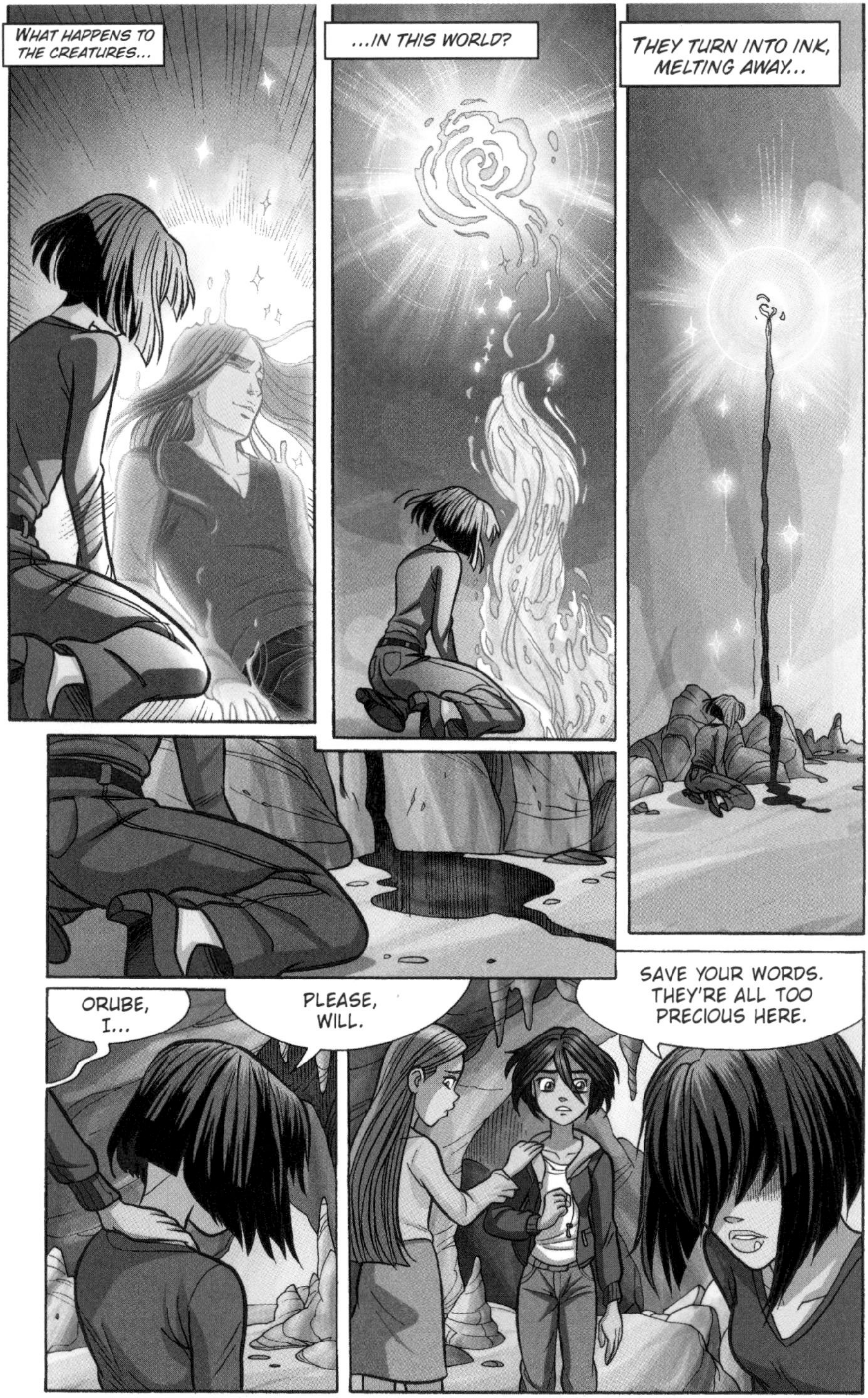
WHAT HAPPENS TO THE CREATURES...
...IN THIS WORLD?
THEY TURN INTO INK, MELTING AWAY...
ORUBE, I...
PLEASE, WILL.
SAVE YOUR WORDS. THEY'RE ALL TOO PRECIOUS HERE.

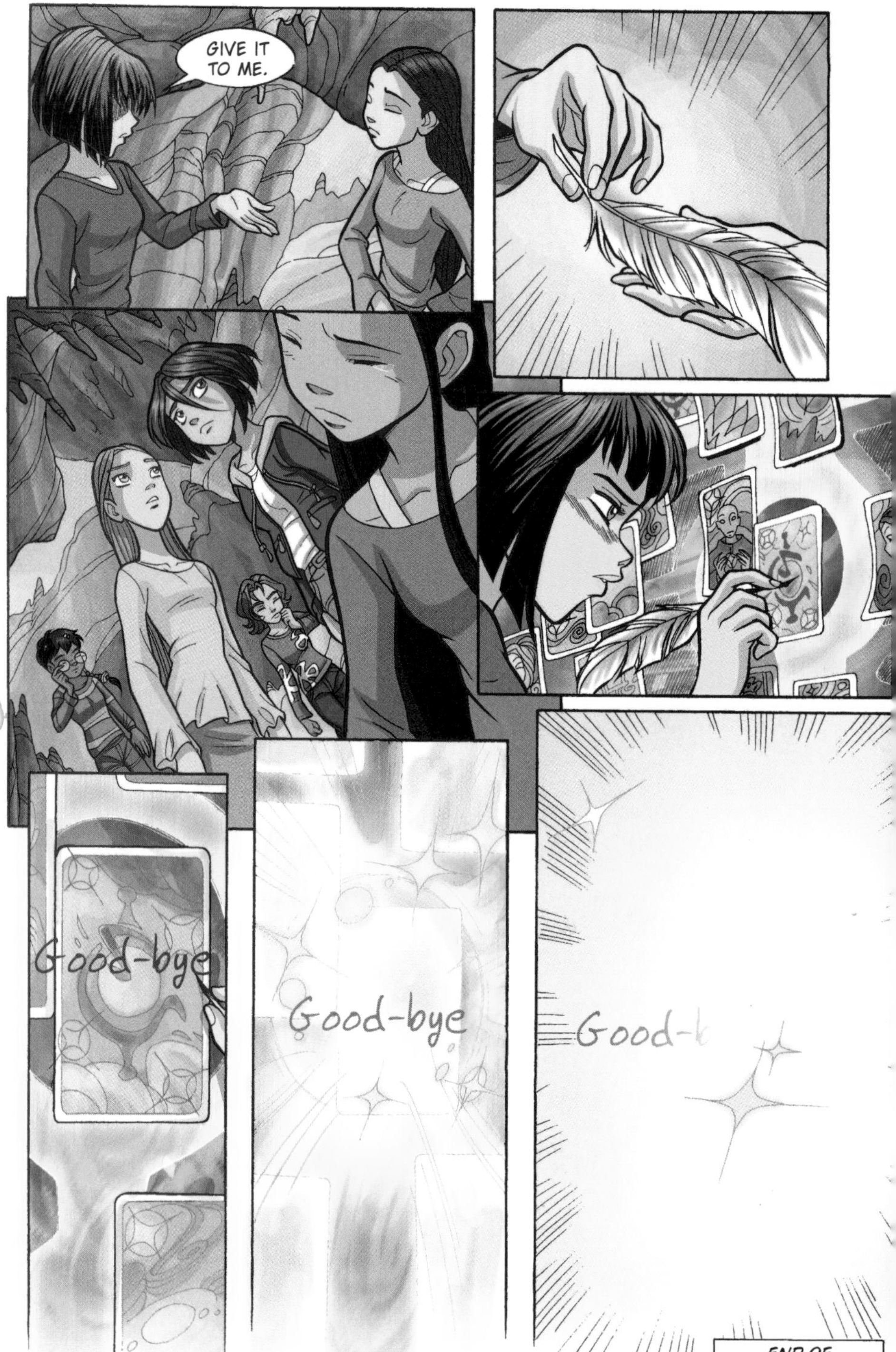
GIVE IT TO ME.
Good-bye
Good-bye
Good-
END OF CHAPTER 61

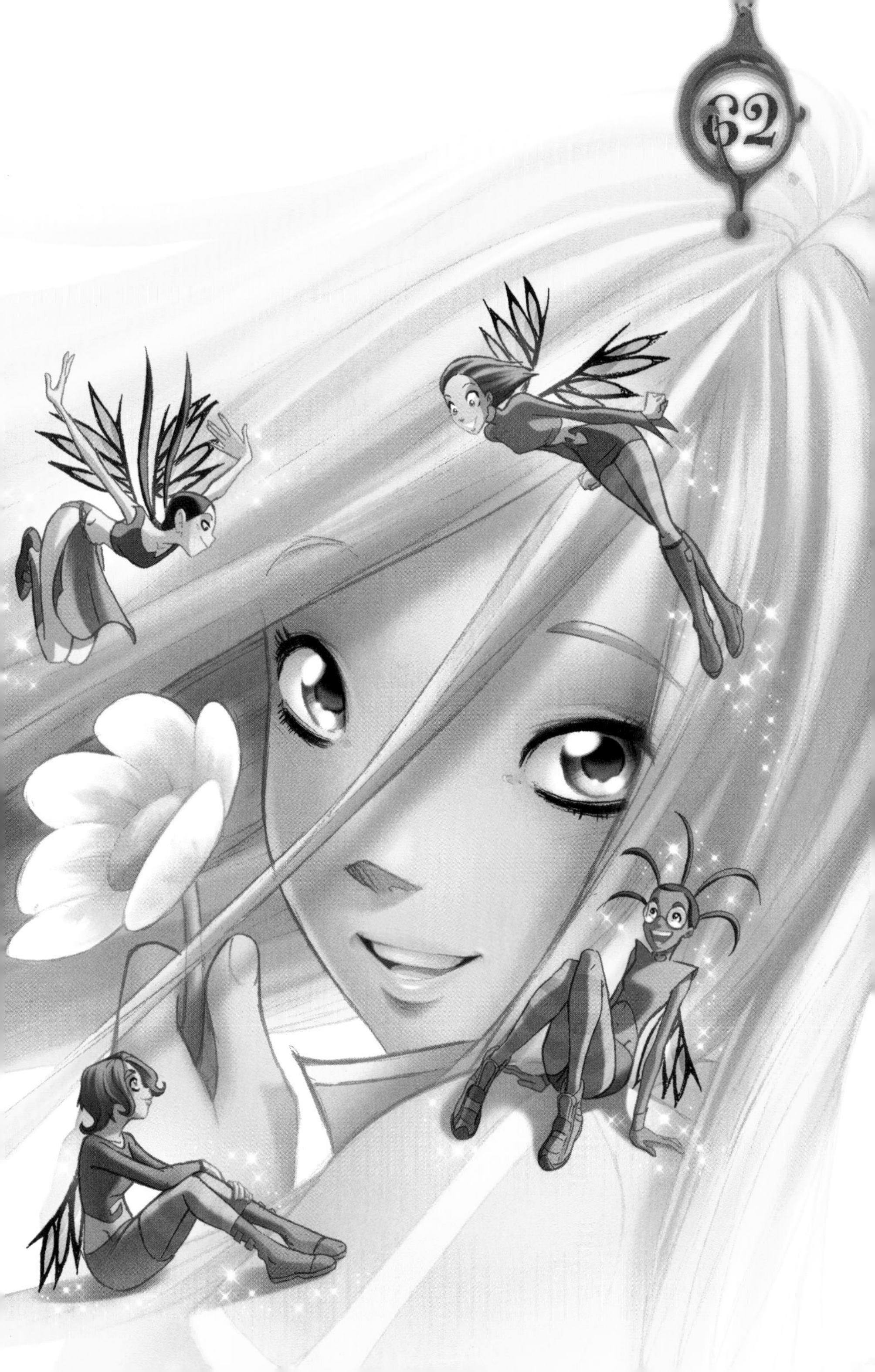
62

Between the Pages

"Kandrakar bows in gratitude to the Guardians."

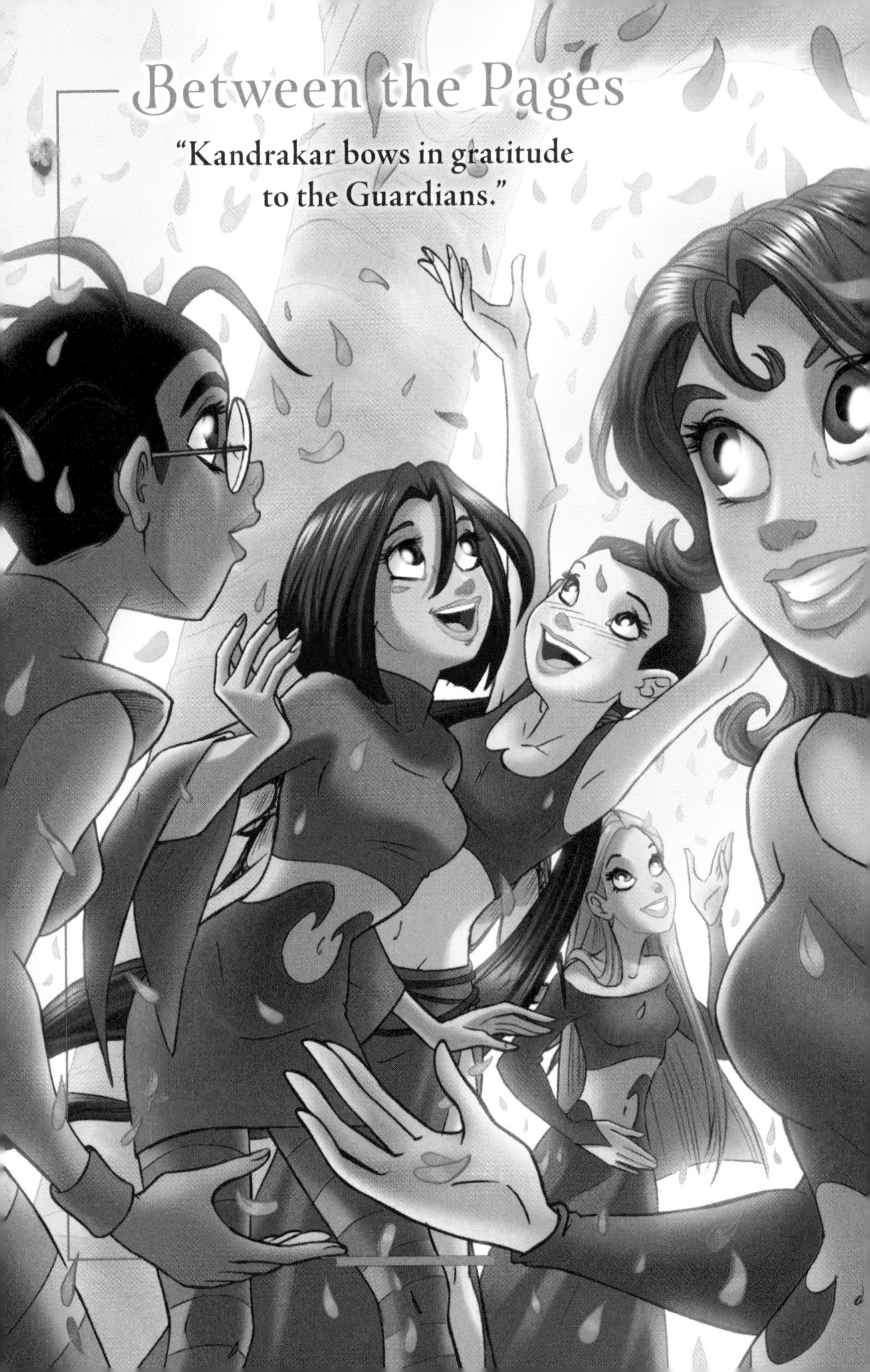

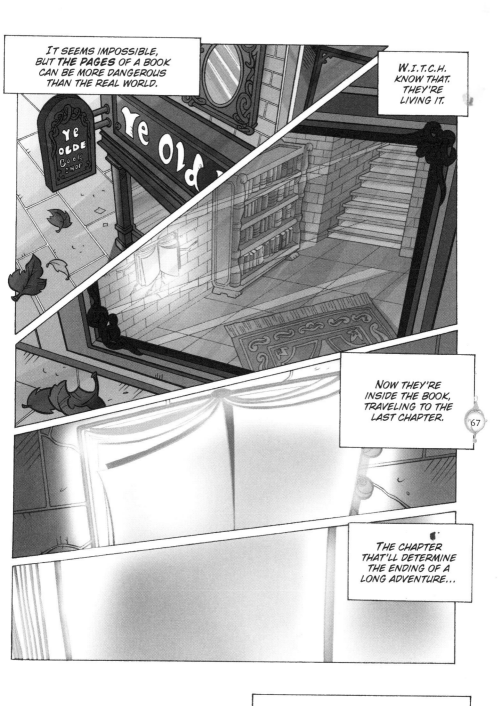

IT SEEMS IMPOSSIBLE, BUT **THE PAGES** OF A BOOK CAN BE MORE DANGEROUS THAN THE REAL WORLD.

W.I.T.C.H. KNOW THAT. THEY'RE LIVING IT.

NOW THEY'RE INSIDE THE BOOK, TRAVELING TO THE LAST CHAPTER.

THE CHAPTER THAT'LL DETERMINE THE ENDING OF A LONG ADVENTURE...

...FULL OF INTENSE EMOTIONS.

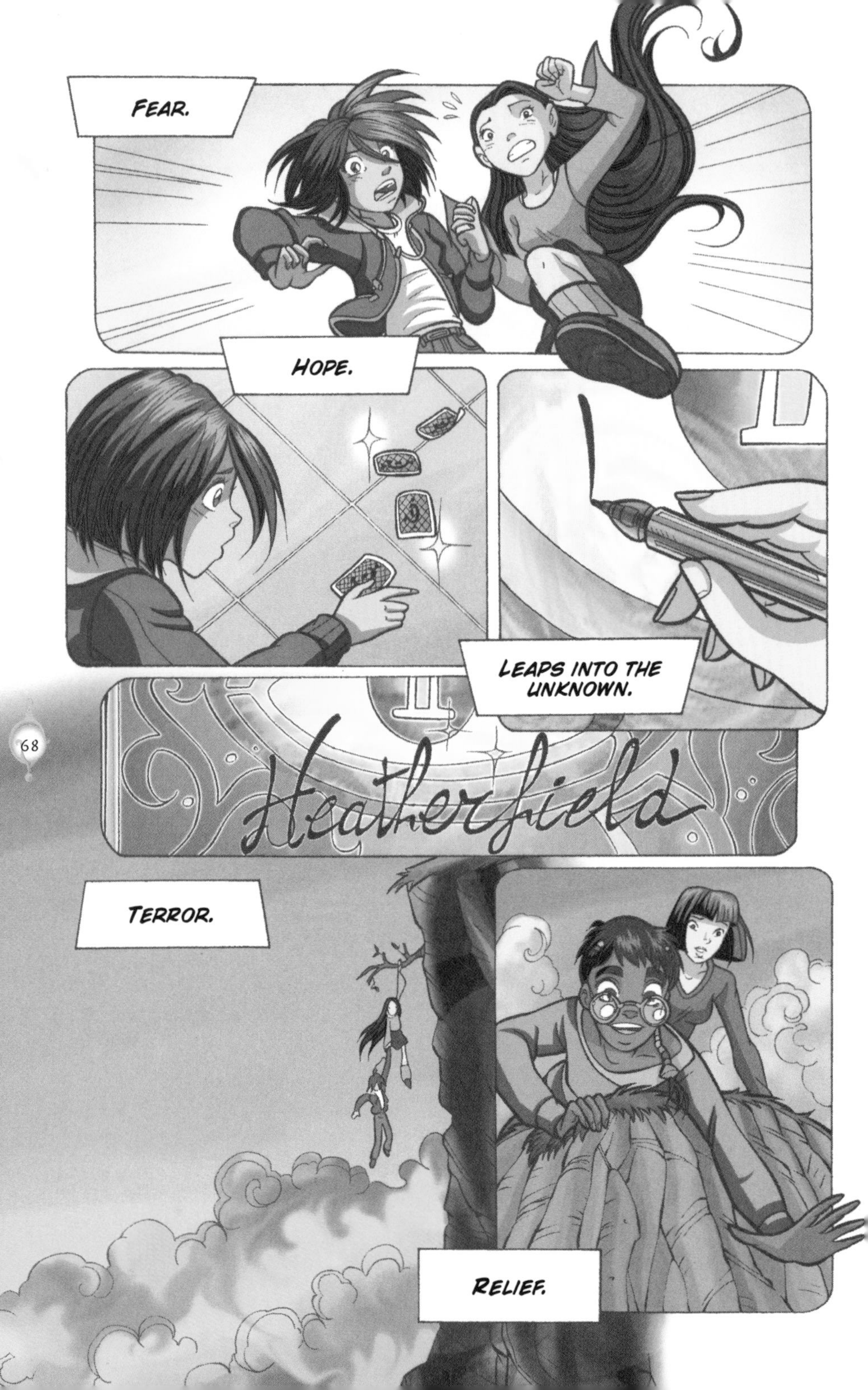
FEAR.
HOPE.
LEAPS INTO THE UNKNOWN.
Heatherfield
TERROR.
RELIEF.

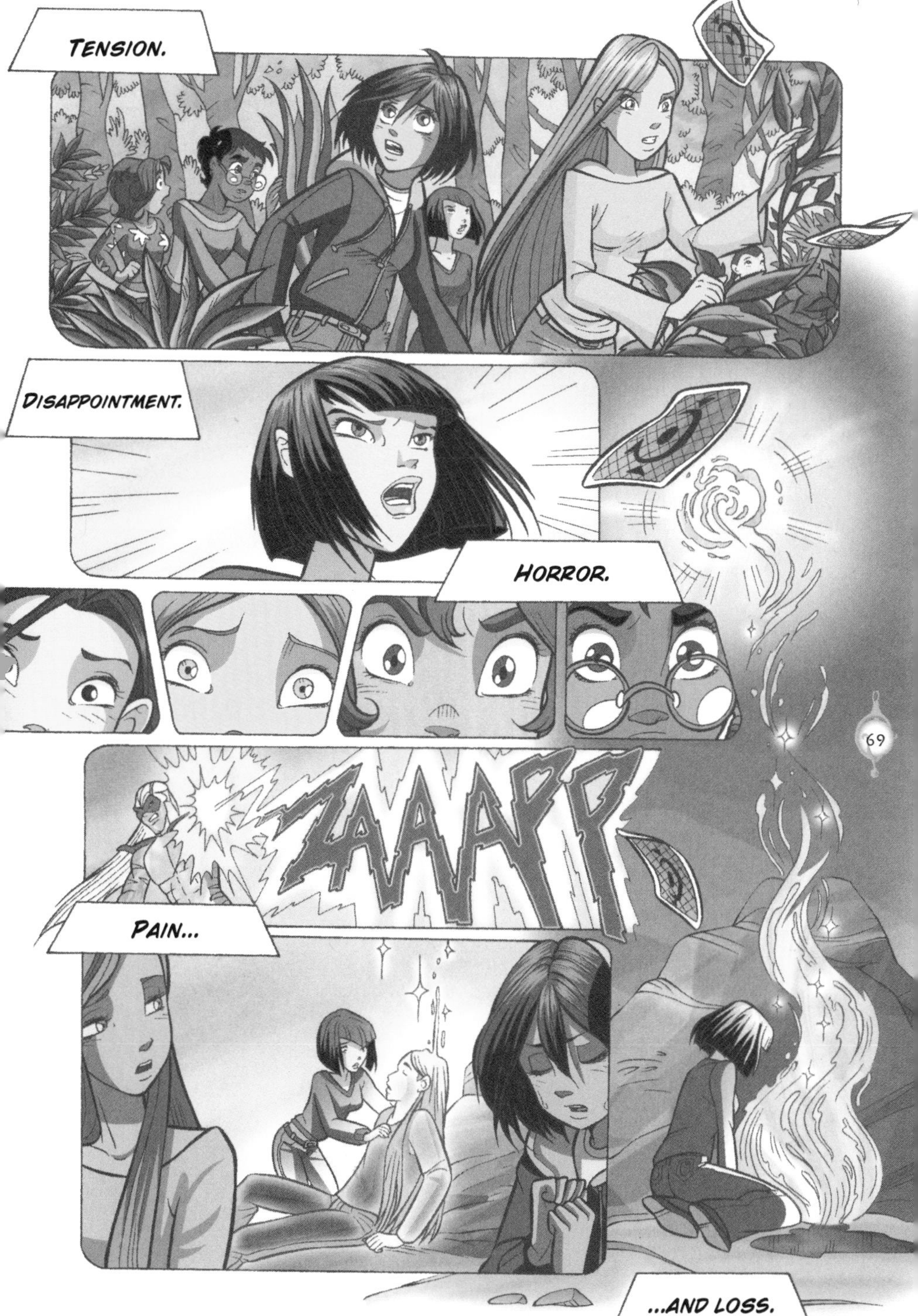

TENSION.
DISAPPOINTMENT.
HORROR.
ZAAAPP
PAIN...
...AND LOSS.

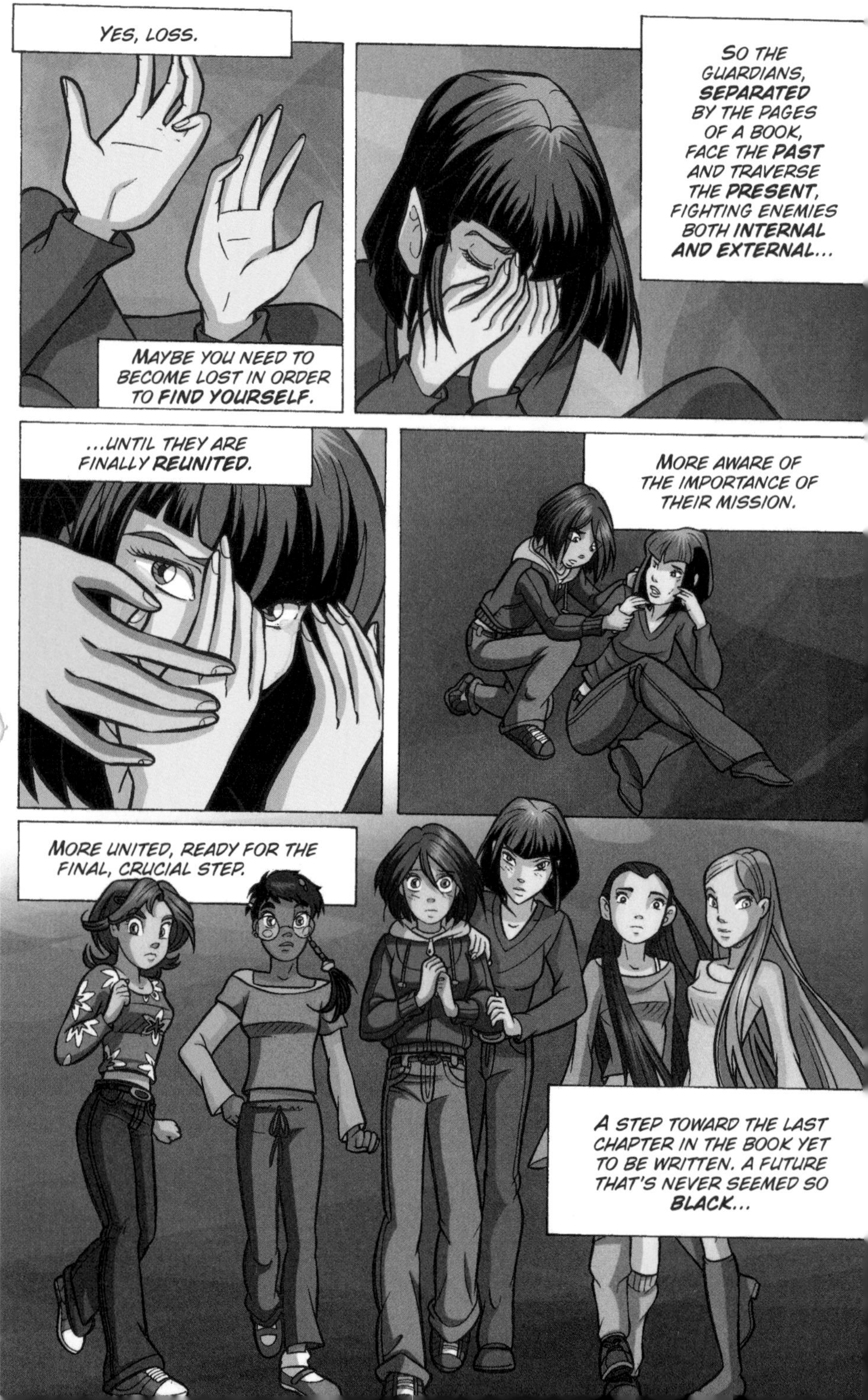
YES, LOSS.
MAYBE YOU NEED TO BECOME LOST IN ORDER TO FIND YOURSELF.
SO THE GUARDIANS, SEPARATED BY THE PAGES OF A BOOK, FACE THE PAST AND TRAVERSE THE PRESENT, FIGHTING ENEMIES BOTH INTERNAL AND EXTERNAL...
...UNTIL THEY ARE FINALLY REUNITED.
MORE AWARE OF THE IMPORTANCE OF THEIR MISSION.
MORE UNITED, READY FOR THE FINAL, CRUCIAL STEP.
A STEP TOWARD THE LAST CHAPTER IN THE BOOK YET TO BE WRITTEN. A FUTURE THAT'S NEVER SEEMED SO BLACK...

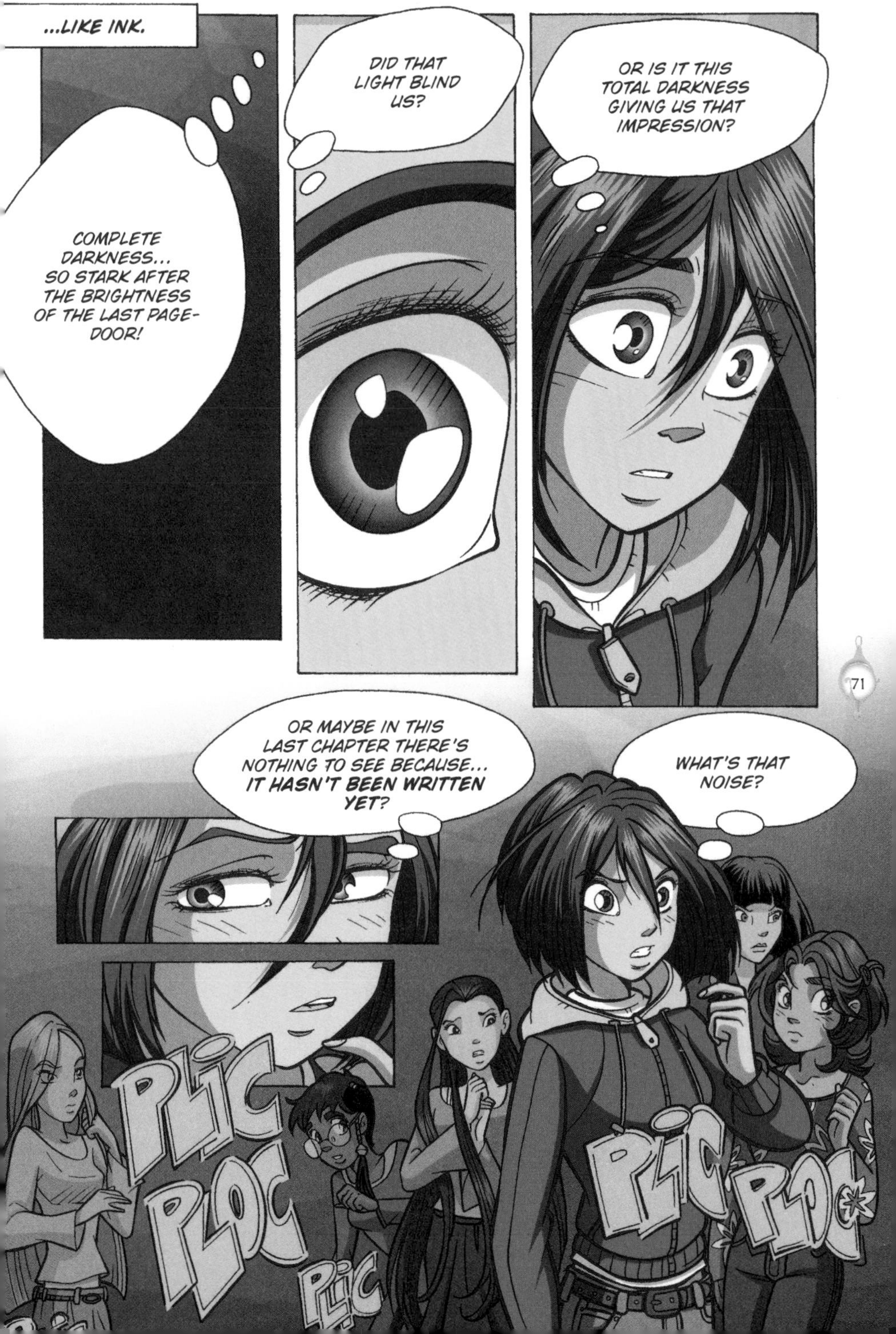
...LIKE INK.
COMPLETE DARKNESS... SO STARK AFTER THE BRIGHTNESS OF THE LAST PAGE-DOOR!
DID THAT LIGHT BLIND US?
OR IS IT THIS TOTAL DARKNESS GIVING US THAT IMPRESSION?
OR MAYBE IN THIS LAST CHAPTER THERE'S NOTHING TO SEE BECAUSE... **IT HASN'T BEEN WRITTEN YET?**
WHAT'S THAT NOISE?
PLIC
PLOC
PLIC
PLIC
PLOC

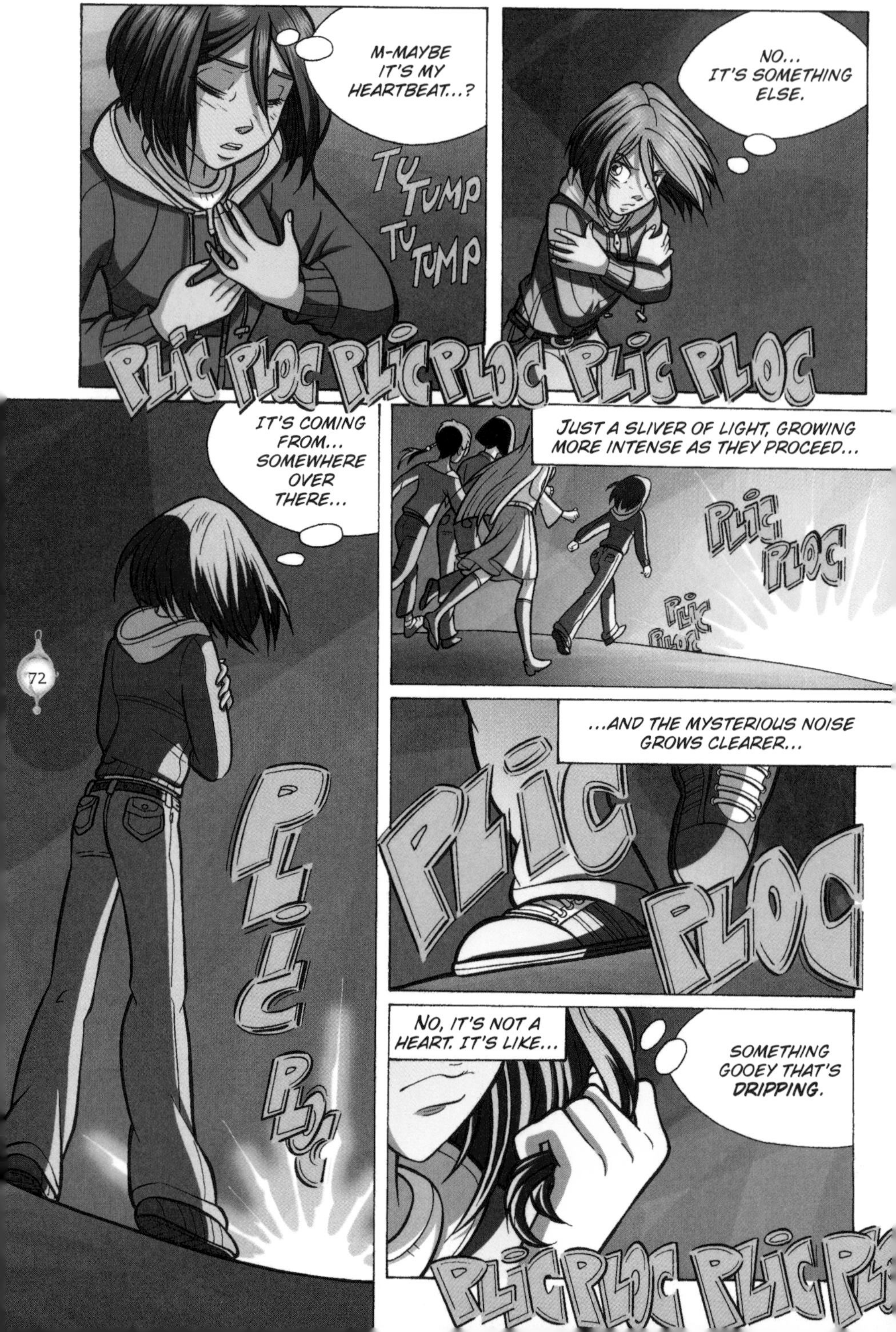
M-MAYBE IT'S MY HEARTBEAT...?
TU TUMP TU TUMP
NO... IT'S SOMETHING ELSE.
PLIC PLOC PLIC PLOC PLIC PLOC
IT'S COMING FROM... SOMEWHERE OVER THERE...
PLIC PLOC
JUST A SLIVER OF LIGHT, GROWING MORE INTENSE AS THEY PROCEED...
PLIC PLOC
PLIC PLOC
...AND THE MYSTERIOUS NOISE GROWS CLEARER...
PLIC PLOC
NO, IT'S NOT A HEART. IT'S LIKE...
SOMETHING GOOEY THAT'S DRIPPING.
PLIC PLOC PLIC

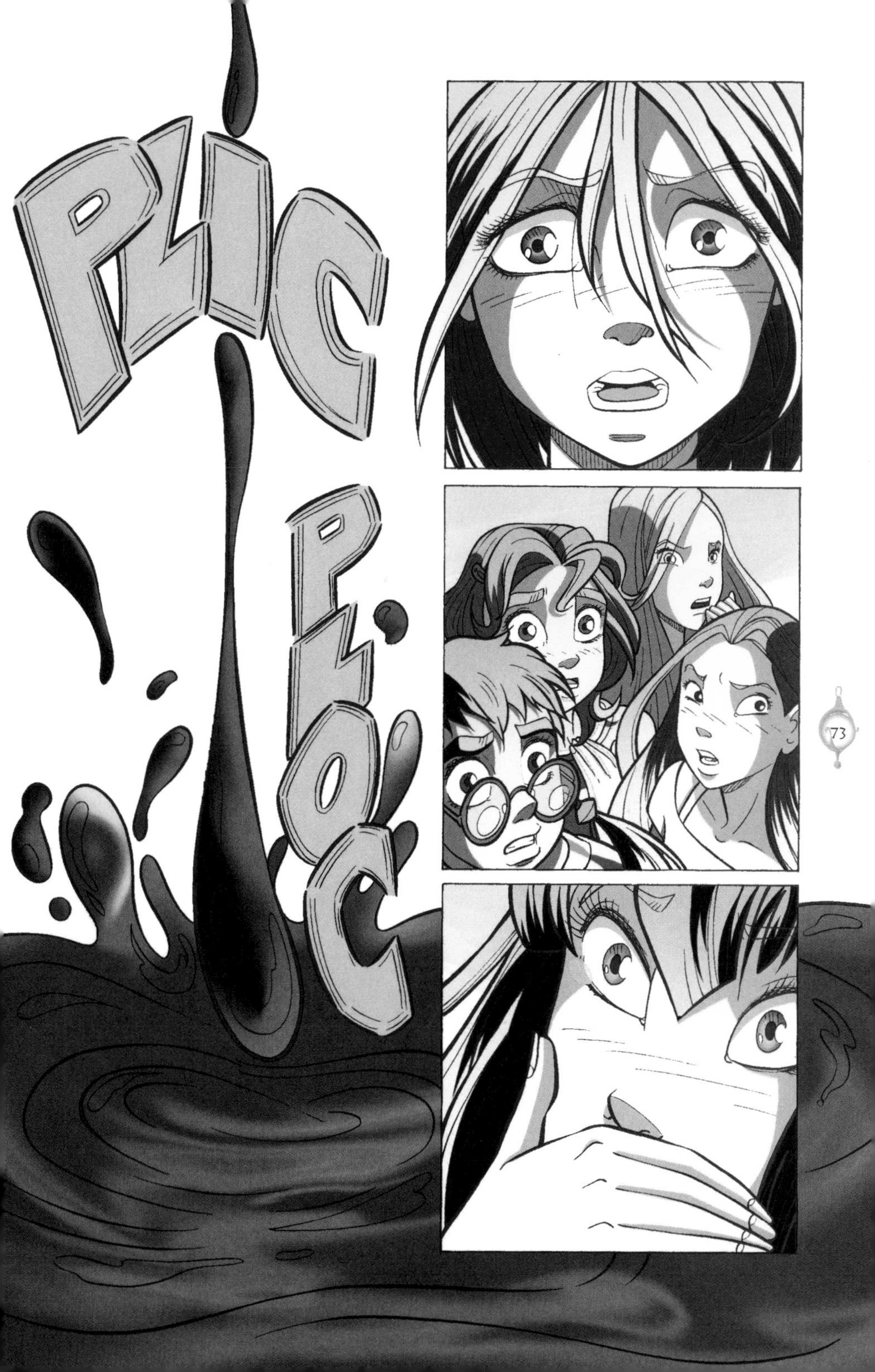
PLIC
PLOC

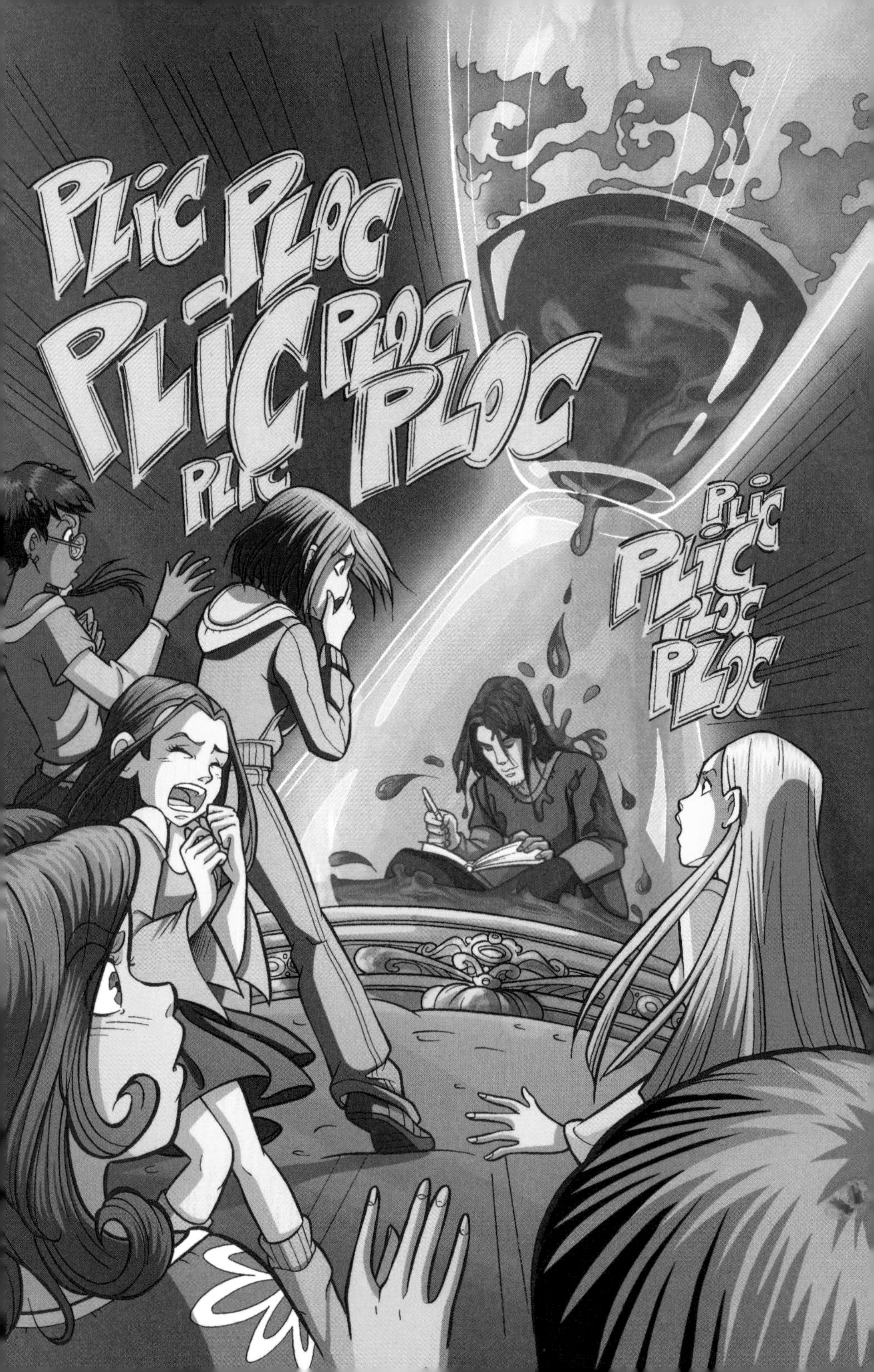
PLIC PLOC
PLIC PLOC
PLOC
PLIC
PLIC
PLIC
PLOC
PLOC

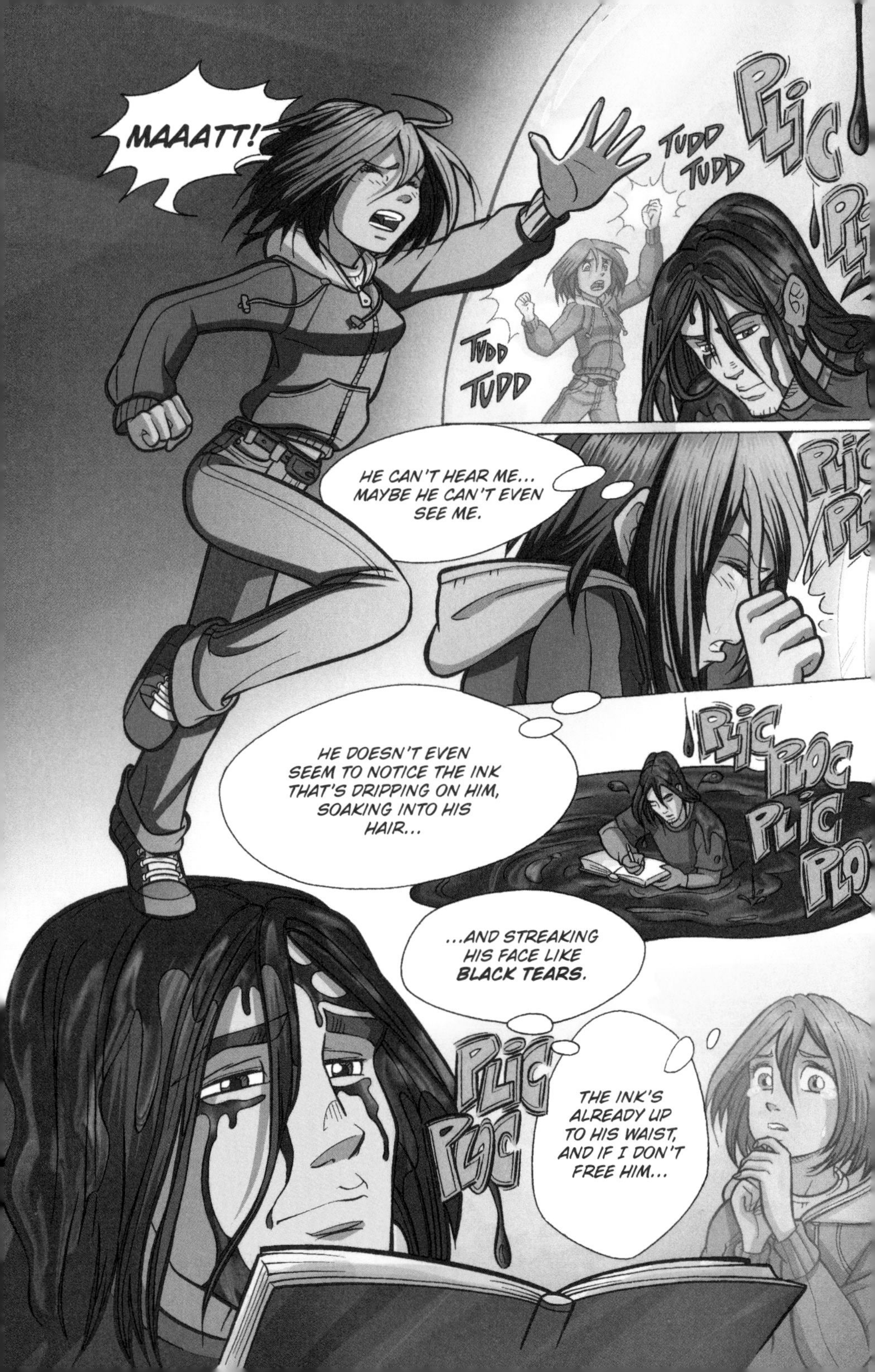
MAAATT!
TUDD TUDD
PLIC
PLIC
TUDD TUDD
HE CAN'T HEAR ME... MAYBE HE CAN'T EVEN SEE ME.
PLIC PLIC
HE DOESN'T EVEN SEEM TO NOTICE THE INK THAT'S DRIPPING ON HIM, SOAKING INTO HIS HAIR...
PLIC PLOC PLIC PLOC
...AND STREAKING HIS FACE LIKE BLACK TEARS.
PLIC PLOC
THE INK'S ALREADY UP TO HIS WAIST, AND IF I DON'T FREE HIM...

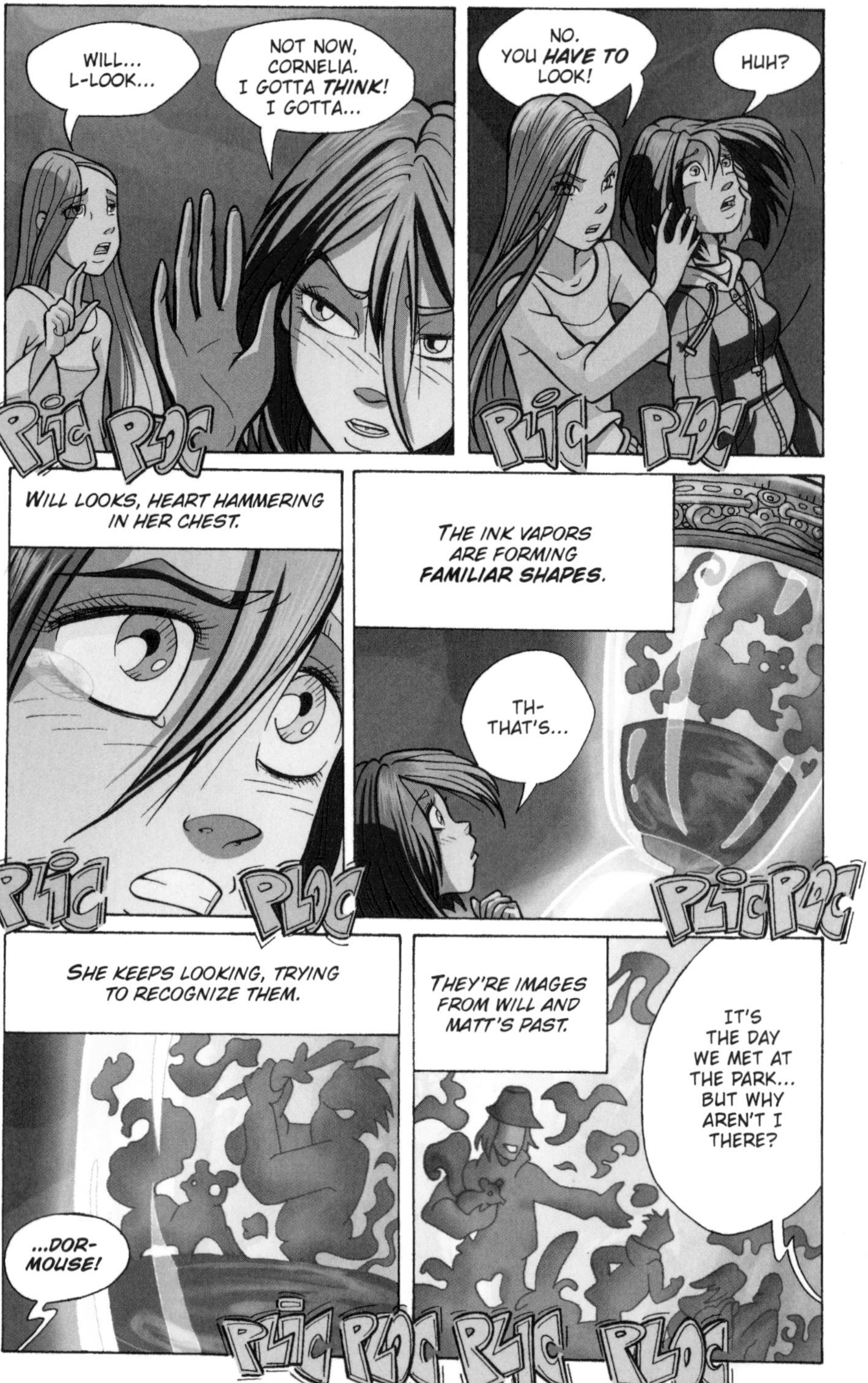
WILL... L-LOOK...
NOT NOW, CORNELIA. I GOTTA THINK! I GOTTA...
PLIC PLOC
NO. YOU HAVE TO LOOK!
HUH?
PLIC PLOC
WILL LOOKS, HEART HAMMERING IN HER CHEST.
PLIC PLOC
THE INK VAPORS ARE FORMING FAMILIAR SHAPES.
TH- THAT'S...
PLIC PLOC
SHE KEEPS LOOKING, TRYING TO RECOGNIZE THEM.
...DOR- MOUSE!
THEY'RE IMAGES FROM WILL AND MATT'S PAST.
IT'S THE DAY WE MET AT THE PARK... BUT WHY AREN'T I THERE?
PLIC PLOC PLIC PLOC

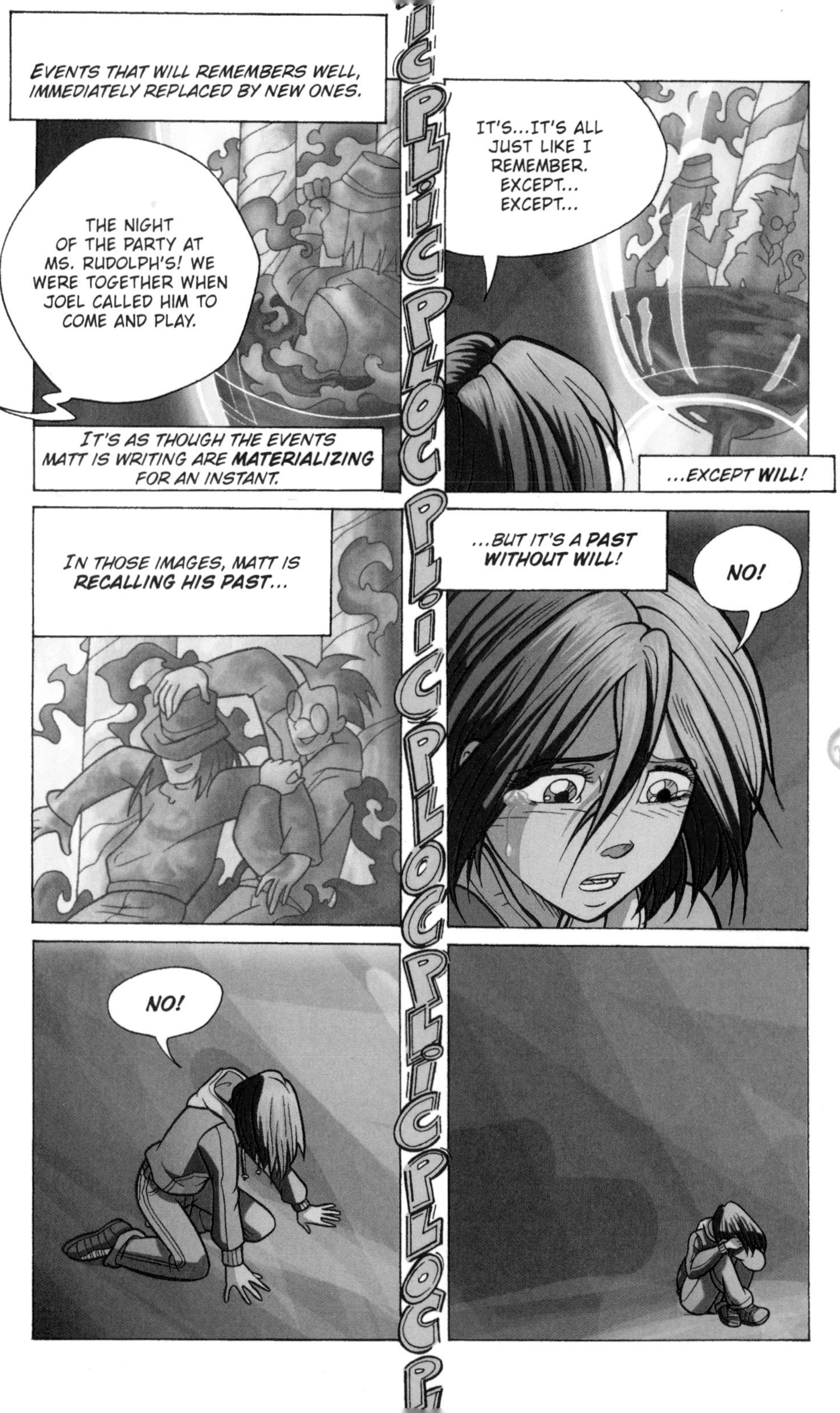
EVENTS THAT WILL REMEMBERS WELL, IMMEDIATELY REPLACED BY NEW ONES.
THE NIGHT OF THE PARTY AT MS. RUDOLPH'S! WE WERE TOGETHER WHEN JOEL CALLED HIM TO COME AND PLAY.
IT'S AS THOUGH THE EVENTS MATT IS WRITING ARE MATERIALIZING FOR AN INSTANT.
IT'S...IT'S ALL JUST LIKE I REMEMBER. EXCEPT... EXCEPT...
...EXCEPT WILL!
IN THOSE IMAGES, MATT IS RECALLING HIS PAST...
...BUT IT'S A PAST WITHOUT WILL!
NO!
NO!
PLIC PLOC PLIC PLOC PLIC PLOC PLIC PLOC PLIC

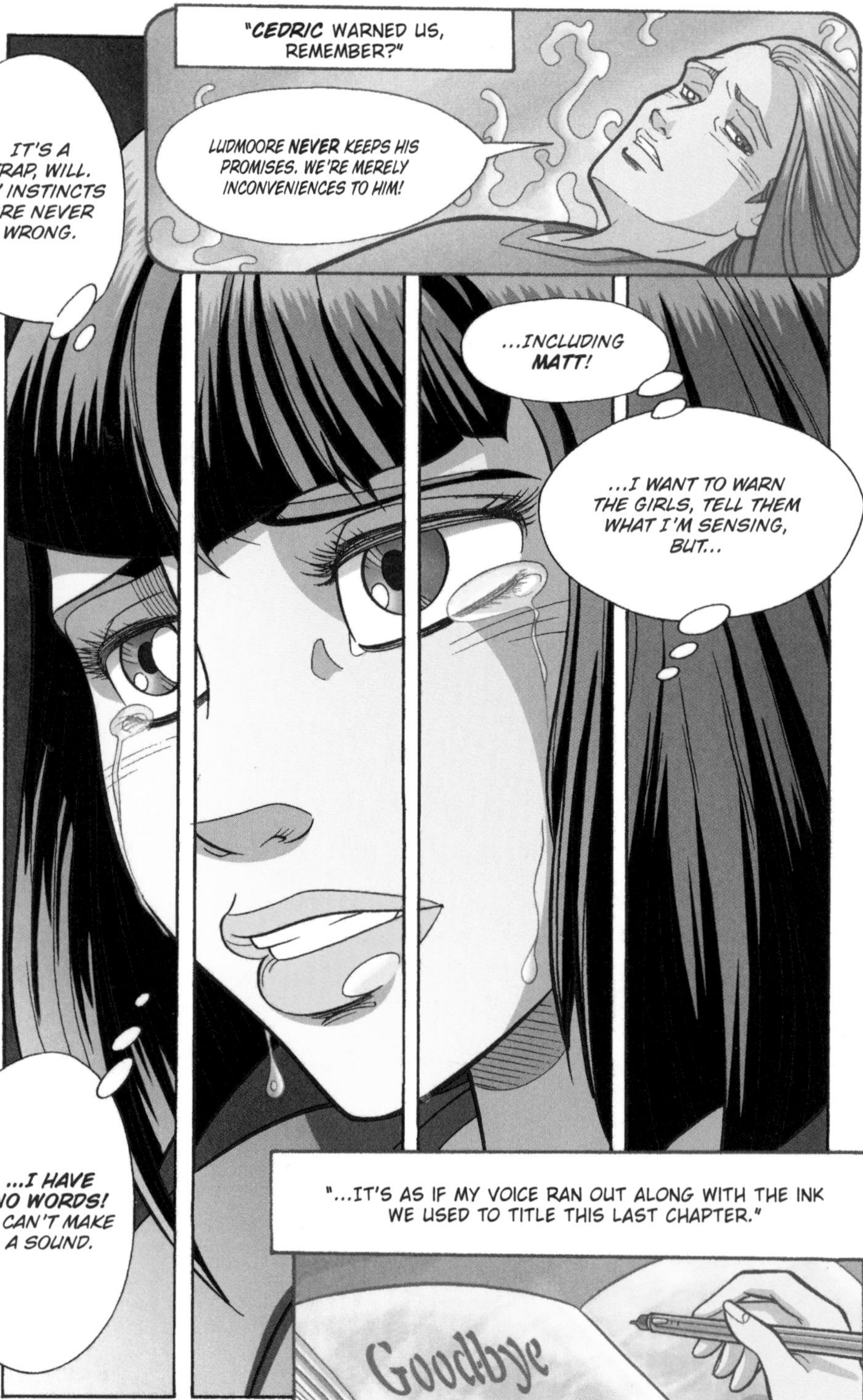
"CEDRIC WARNED US, REMEMBER?"
IT'S A TRAP, WILL. MY INSTINCTS ARE NEVER WRONG.
LUDMOORE NEVER KEEPS HIS PROMISES. WE'RE MERELY INCONVENIENCES TO HIM!
...INCLUDING MATT!
...I WANT TO WARN THE GIRLS, TELL THEM WHAT I'M SENSING, BUT...
...I HAVE NO WORDS! I CAN'T MAKE A SOUND.
"...IT'S AS IF MY VOICE RAN OUT ALONG WITH THE INK WE USED TO TITLE THIS LAST CHAPTER."
Goodbye

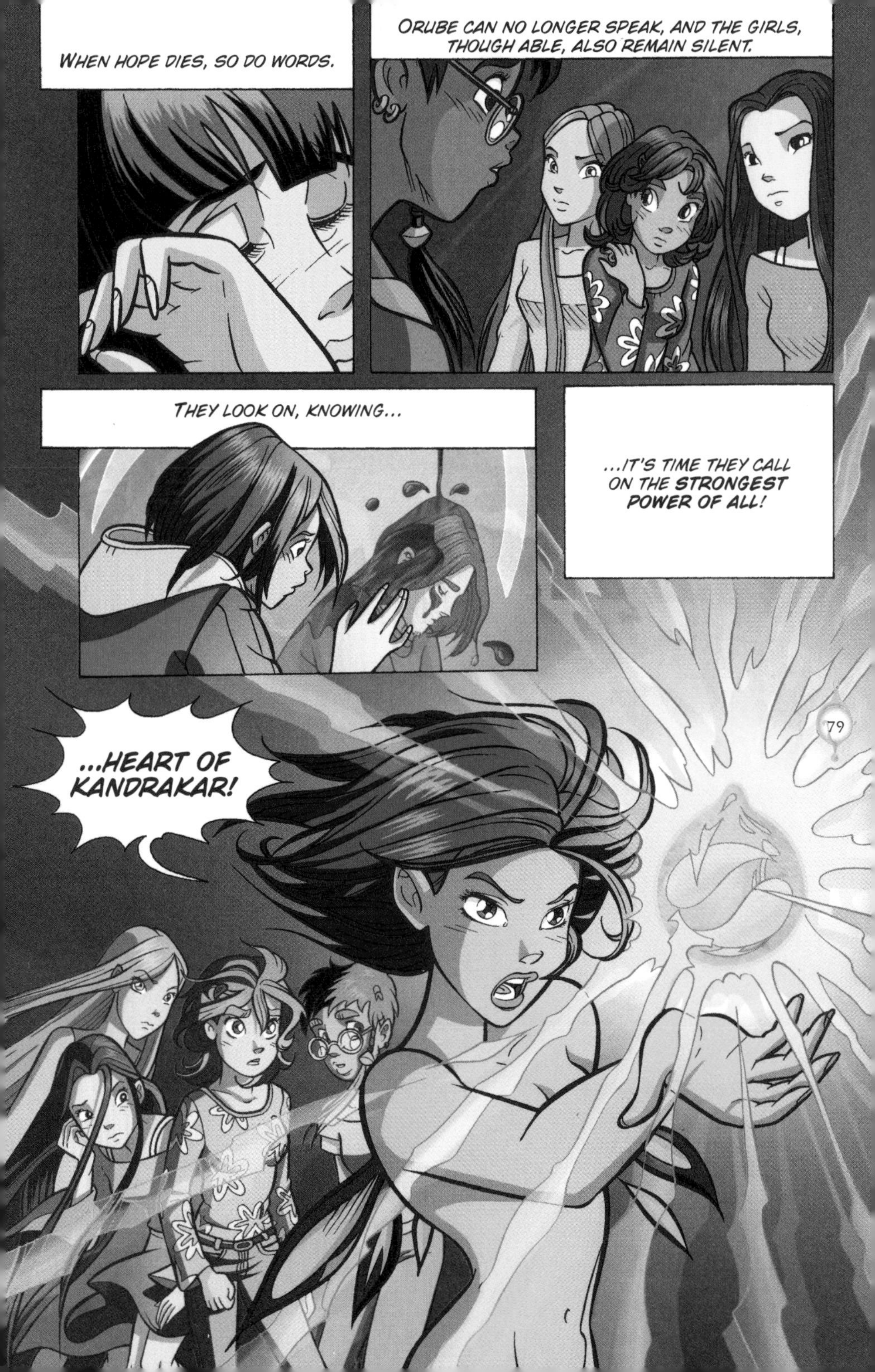

WHEN HOPE DIES, SO DO WORDS.
ORUBE CAN NO LONGER SPEAK, AND THE GIRLS, THOUGH ABLE, ALSO REMAIN SILENT.
THEY LOOK ON, KNOWING...
...IT'S TIME THEY CALL ON THE STRONGEST POWER OF ALL!
...HEART OF KANDRAKAR!

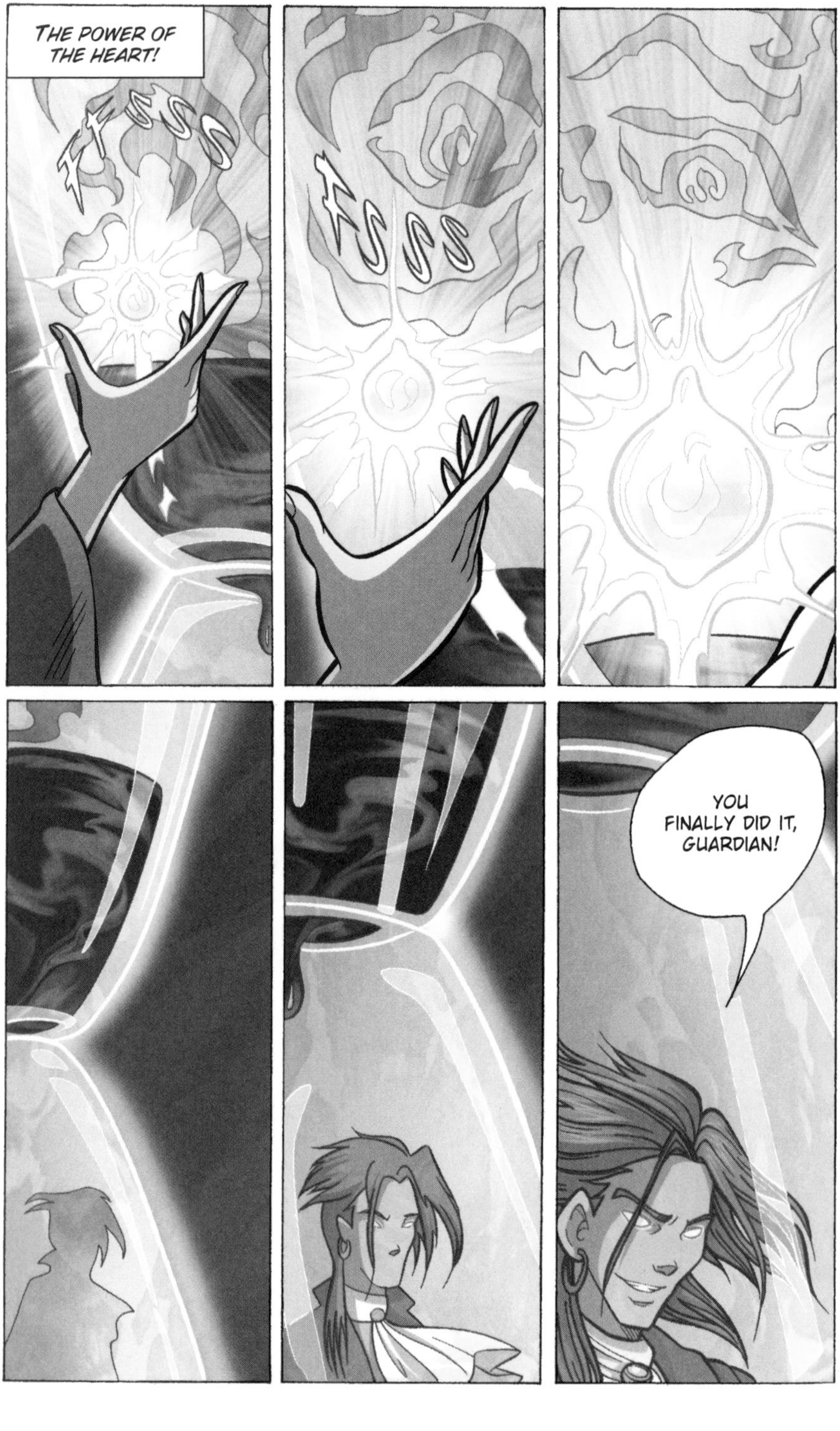
THE POWER OF THE HEART!
FFSSS
FSSS
YOU FINALLY DID IT, GUARDIAN!

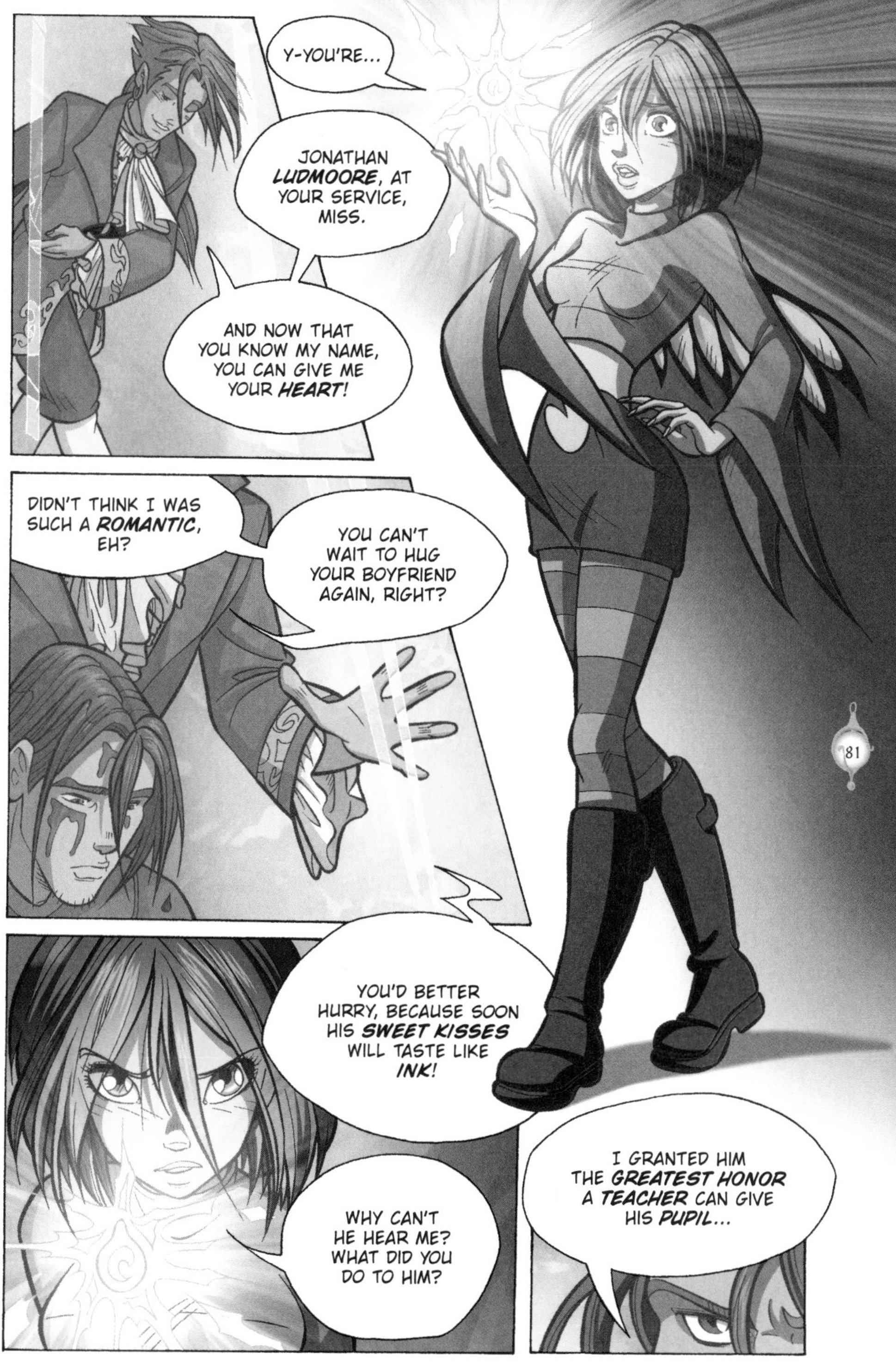
Y-YOU'RE...
JONATHAN LUDMOORE, AT YOUR SERVICE, MISS.
AND NOW THAT YOU KNOW MY NAME, YOU CAN GIVE ME YOUR HEART!
DIDN'T THINK I WAS SUCH A ROMANTIC, EH?
YOU CAN'T WAIT TO HUG YOUR BOYFRIEND AGAIN, RIGHT?
YOU'D BETTER HURRY, BECAUSE SOON HIS SWEET KISSES WILL TASTE LIKE INK!
WHY CAN'T HE HEAR ME? WHAT DID YOU DO TO HIM?
I GRANTED HIM THE GREATEST HONOR A TEACHER CAN GIVE HIS PUPIL...

"I GAVE HIM *MY JOB!*

"THAT OF THE *SCRIBE*, AN ESSENTIAL FIGURE FOR A BOOK THAT WRITES ITSELF...

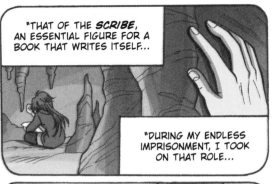

"DURING MY ENDLESS IMPRISONMENT, I TOOK ON THAT ROLE...

"...UNTIL MATT OLSEN ARRIVED.

"EXHAUSTED, HE FOUND SHELTER IN THIS *CAVE*, WHICH HAS ALWAYS BEEN MY REFUGE.

TUMP

"HE RECOGNIZED MY GAZE AS THE ONE THAT HAD FOLLOWED HIM THROUGH THE PAGES, THE ONLY PRESENCE *KEEPING HIM COMPANY...*"

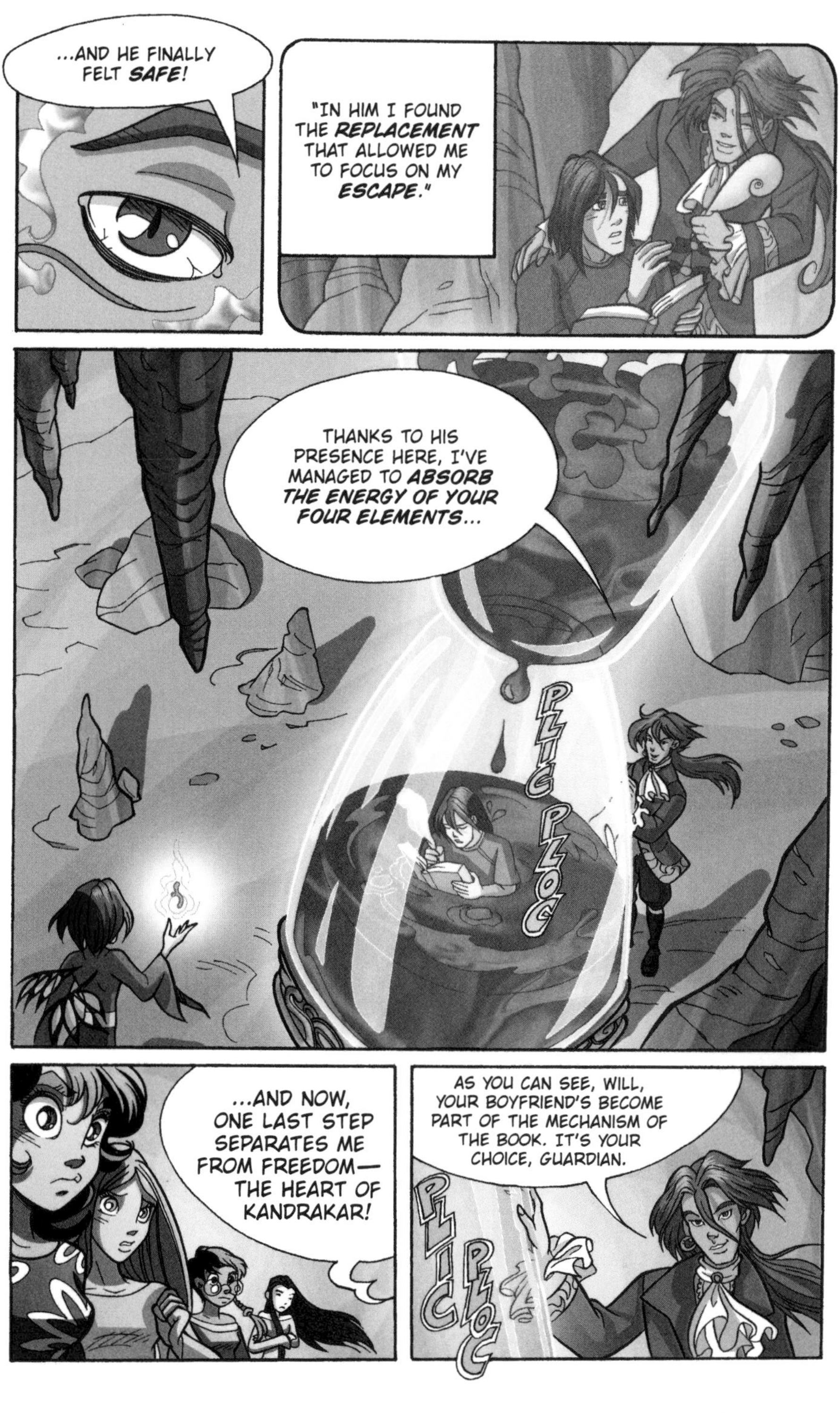
...AND HE FINALLY FELT **SAFE**!
"IN HIM I FOUND THE **REPLACEMENT** THAT ALLOWED ME TO FOCUS ON MY **ESCAPE**."
THANKS TO HIS PRESENCE HERE, I'VE MANAGED TO **ABSORB THE ENERGY OF YOUR FOUR ELEMENTS**...
PLIC PLOG
...AND NOW, ONE LAST STEP SEPARATES ME FROM FREEDOM— THE HEART OF KANDRAKAR!
AS YOU CAN SEE, WILL, YOUR BOYFRIEND'S BECOME PART OF THE MECHANISM OF THE BOOK. IT'S YOUR CHOICE, GUARDIAN.
PLIC PLOC

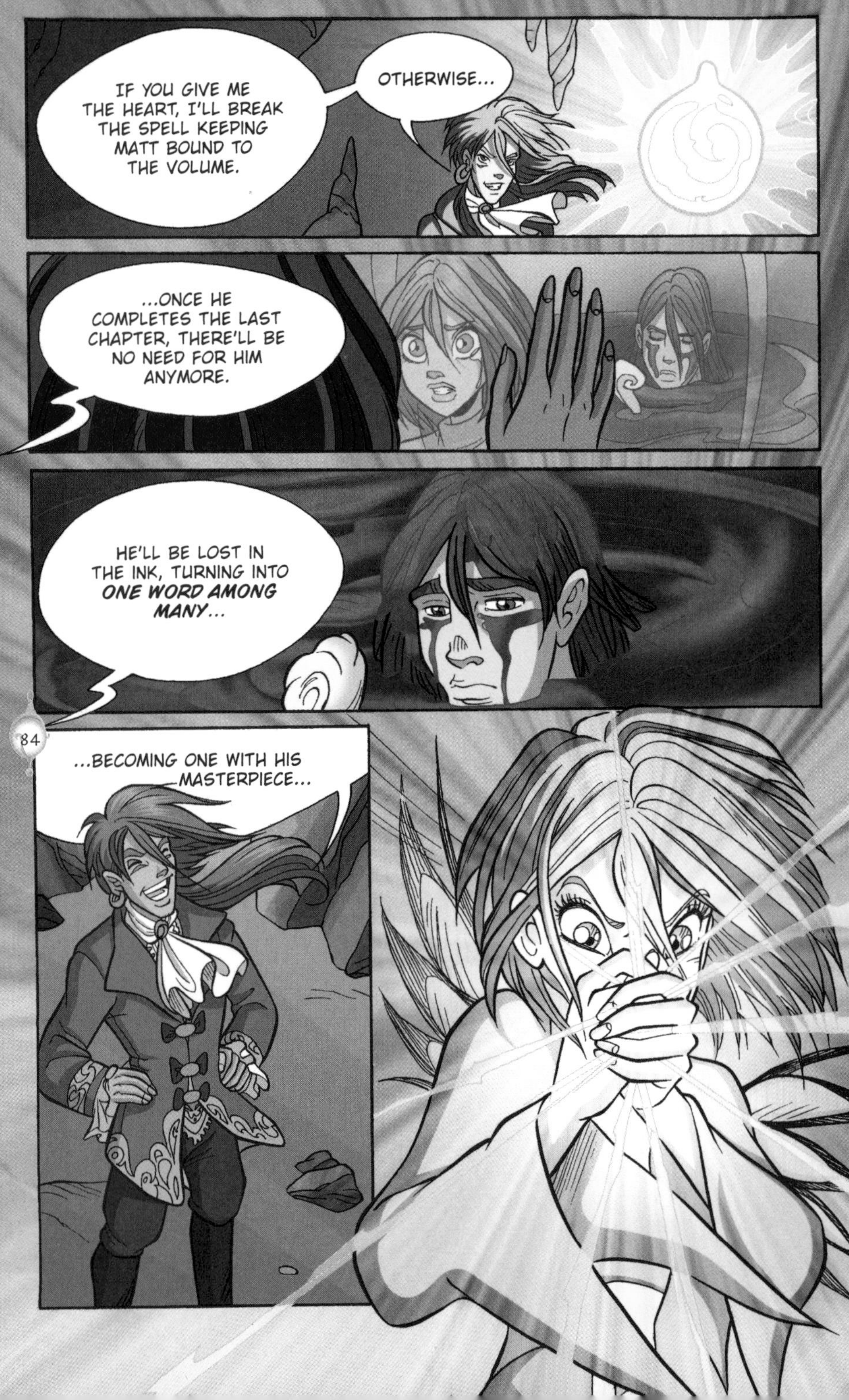
IF YOU GIVE ME THE HEART, I'LL BREAK THE SPELL KEEPING MATT BOUND TO THE VOLUME.
OTHERWISE...
...ONCE HE COMPLETES THE LAST CHAPTER, THERE'LL BE NO NEED FOR HIM ANYMORE.
HE'LL BE LOST IN THE INK, TURNING INTO ***ONE WORD AMONG MANY***...
...BECOMING ONE WITH HIS MASTERPIECE...

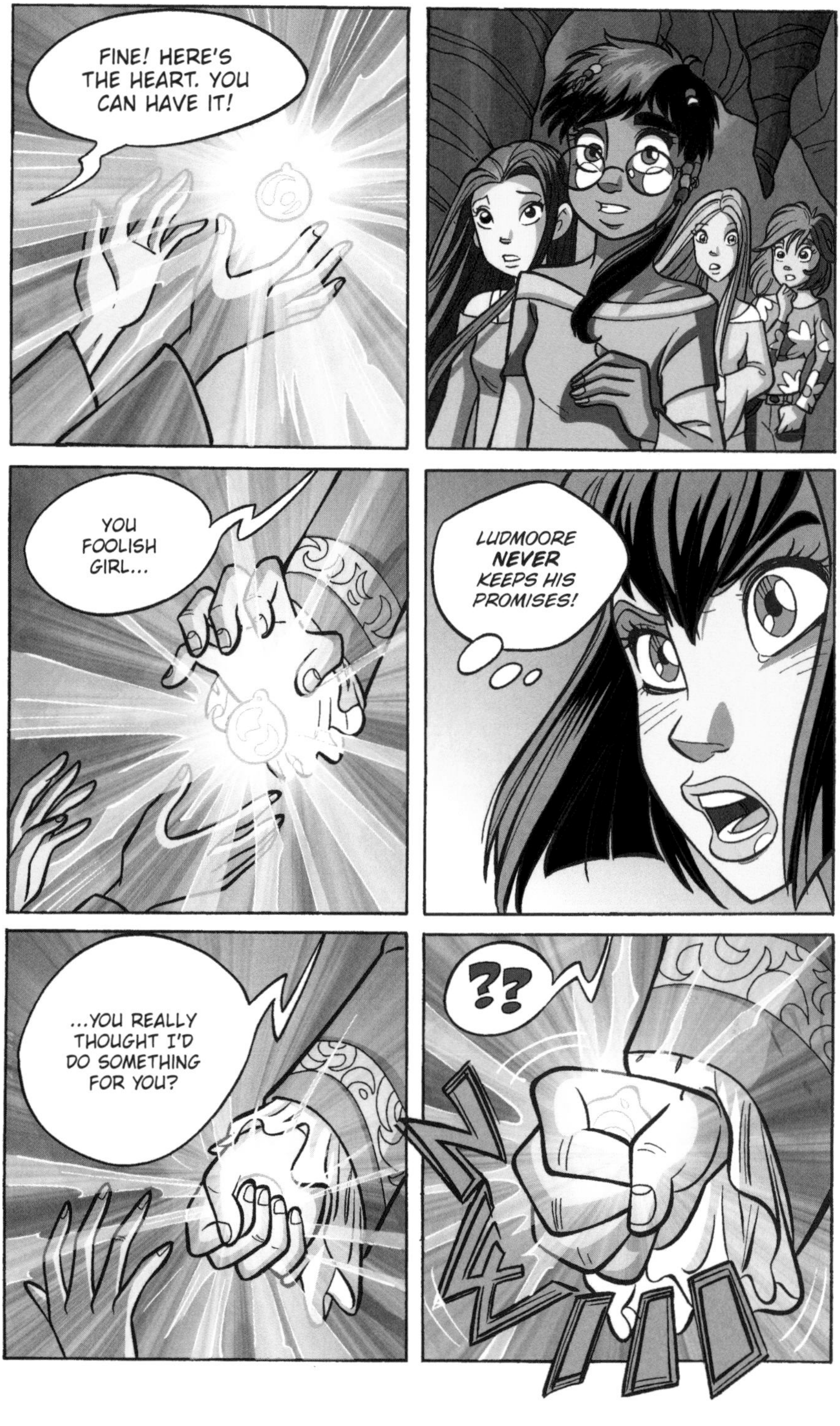
FINE! HERE'S THE HEART. YOU CAN HAVE IT!
YOU FOOLISH GIRL...
LUDMOORE NEVER KEEPS HIS PROMISES!
...YOU REALLY THOUGHT I'D DO SOMETHING FOR YOU?
??
ZWIIIII

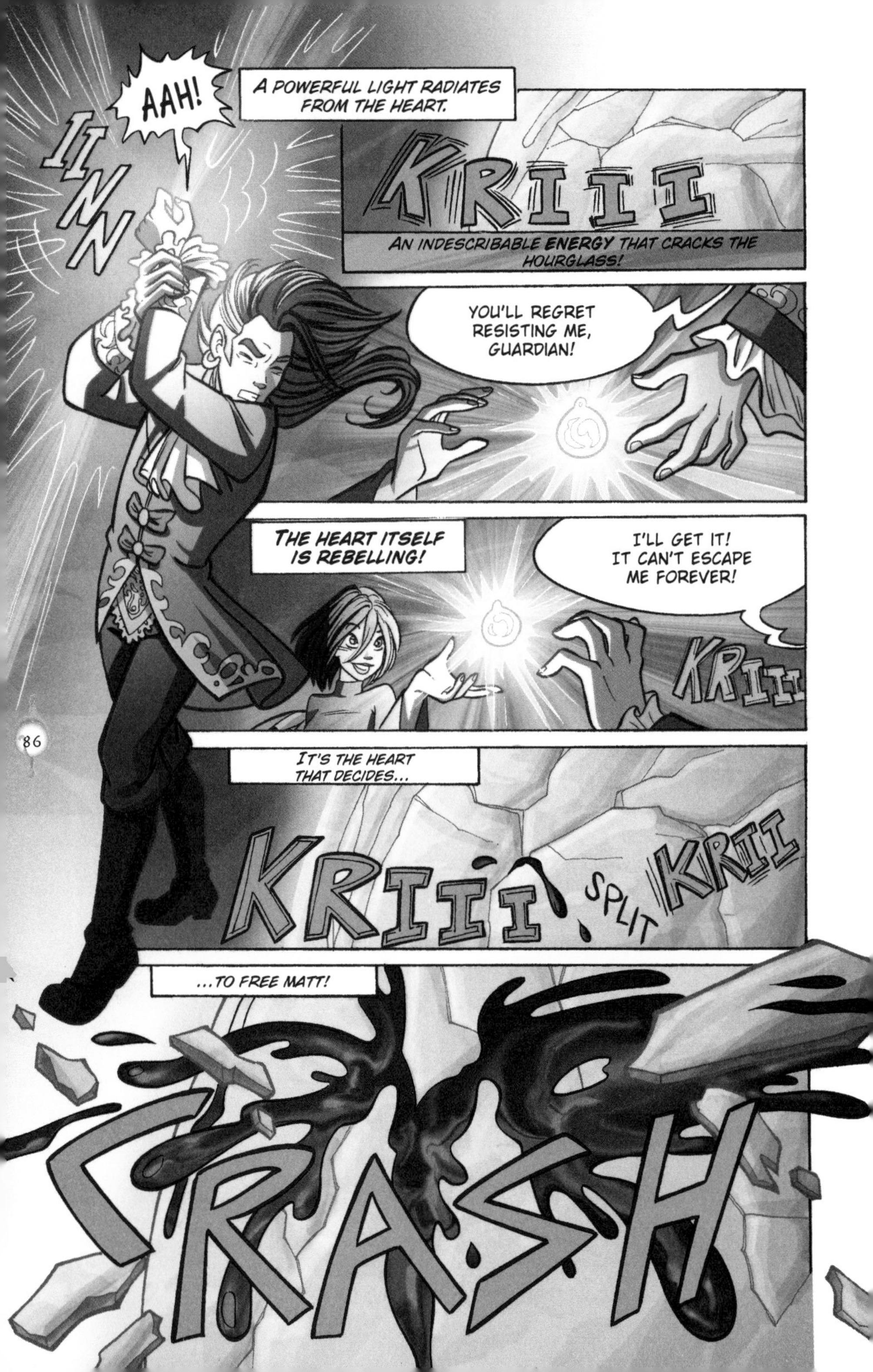

AAH!
A POWERFUL LIGHT RADIATES FROM THE HEART.
IINN
KRIII
AN INDESCRIBABLE ENERGY THAT CRACKS THE HOURGLASS!
YOU'LL REGRET RESISTING ME, GUARDIAN!
THE HEART ITSELF IS REBELLING!
I'LL GET IT! IT CAN'T ESCAPE ME FOREVER!
KRIII
IT'S THE HEART THAT DECIDES...
KRIII
SPLIT
KRII
...TO FREE MATT!
CRASH

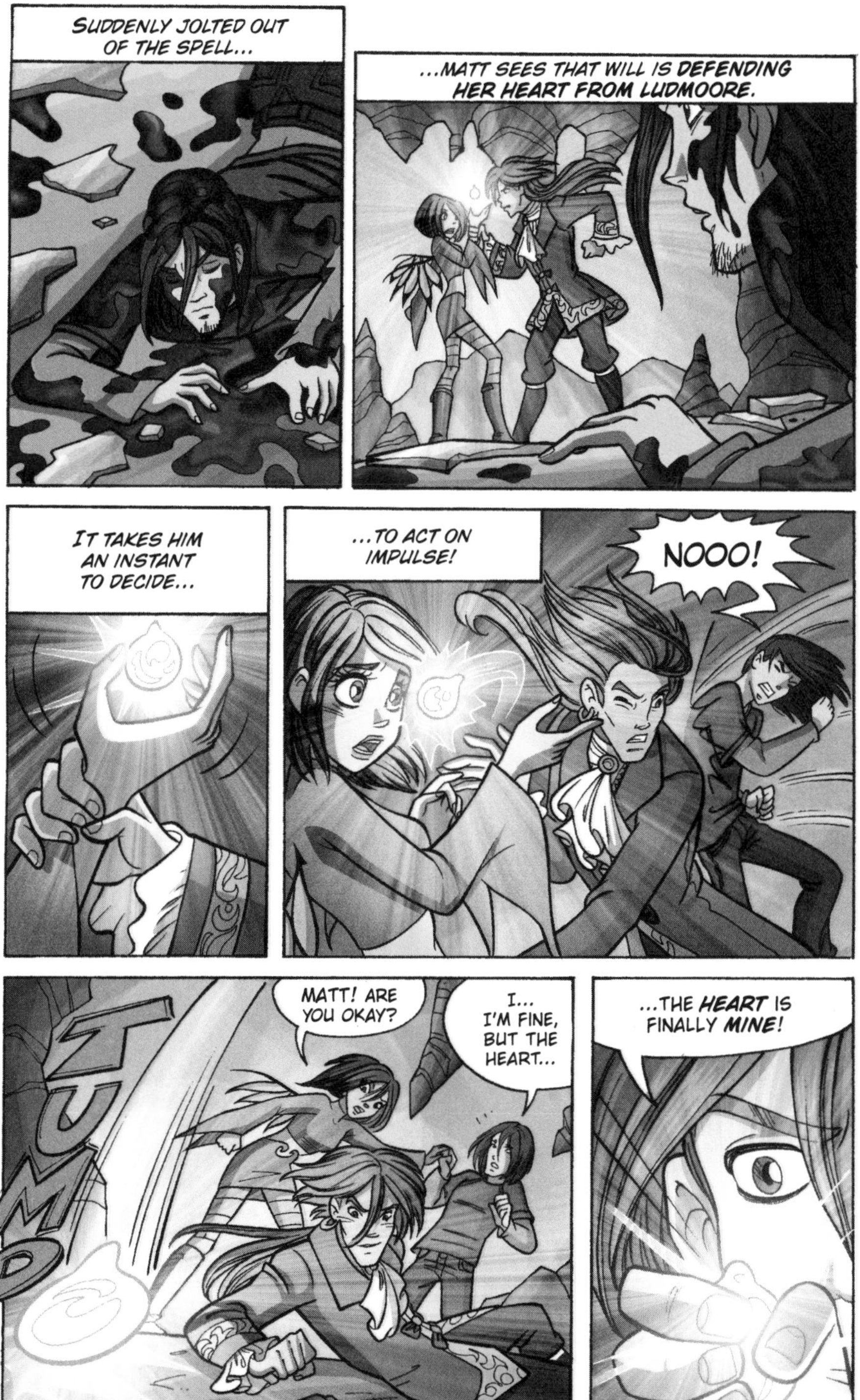
SUDDENLY JOLTED OUT OF THE SPELL...
...MATT SEES THAT WILL IS DEFENDING HER HEART FROM LUDMOORE.
IT TAKES HIM AN INSTANT TO DECIDE...
...TO ACT ON IMPULSE!
NOOO!
TUMP
MATT! ARE YOU OKAY?
I... I'M FINE, BUT THE HEART...
...THE HEART IS FINALLY MINE!

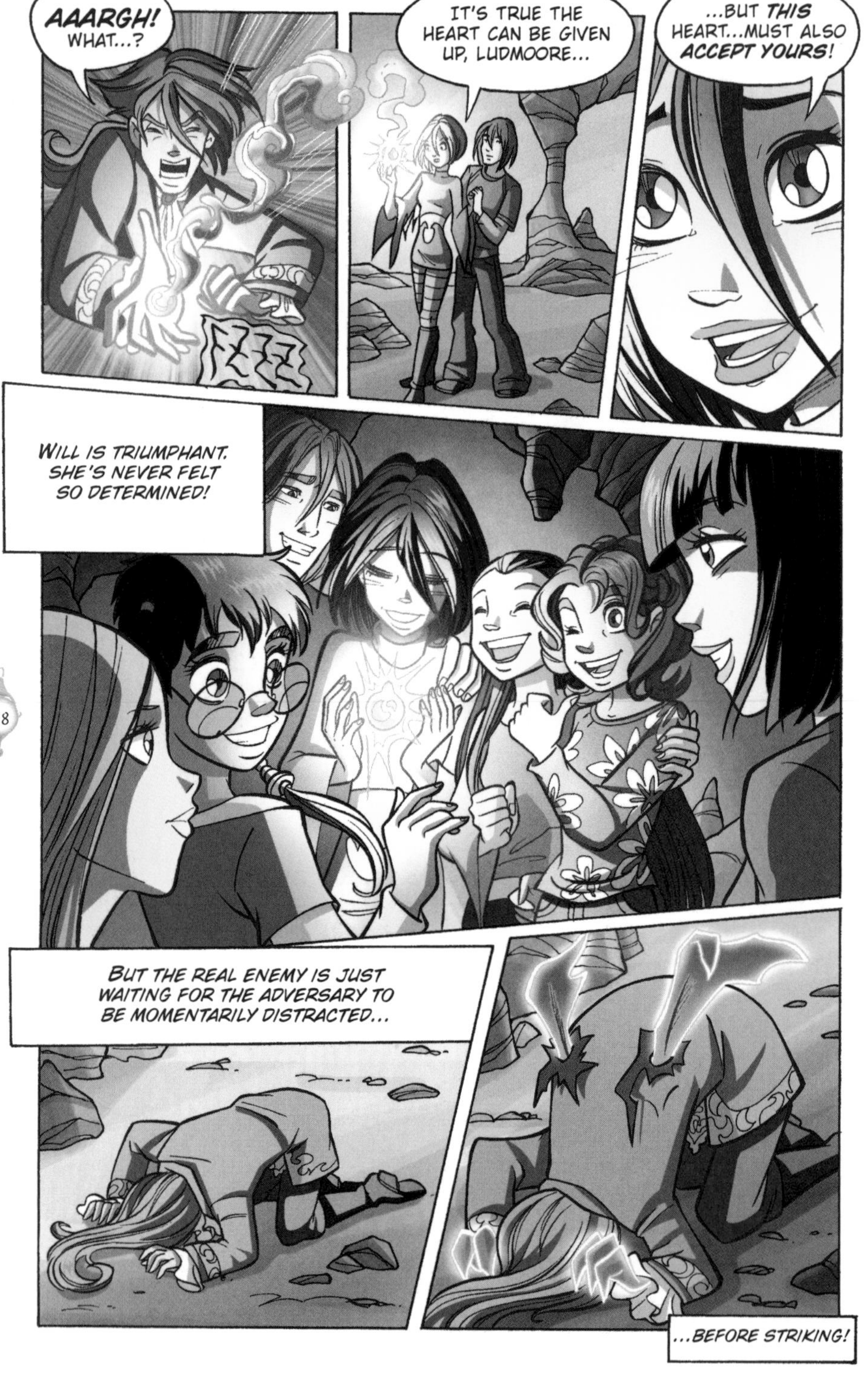

AAARGH! WHAT...?
FZZZ
IT'S TRUE THE HEART CAN BE GIVEN UP, LUDMOORE...
...BUT THIS HEART...MUST ALSO ACCEPT YOURS!
WILL IS TRIUMPHANT. SHE'S NEVER FELT SO DETERMINED!
BUT THE REAL ENEMY IS JUST WAITING FOR THE ADVERSARY TO BE MOMENTARILY DISTRACTED...
...BEFORE STRIKING!

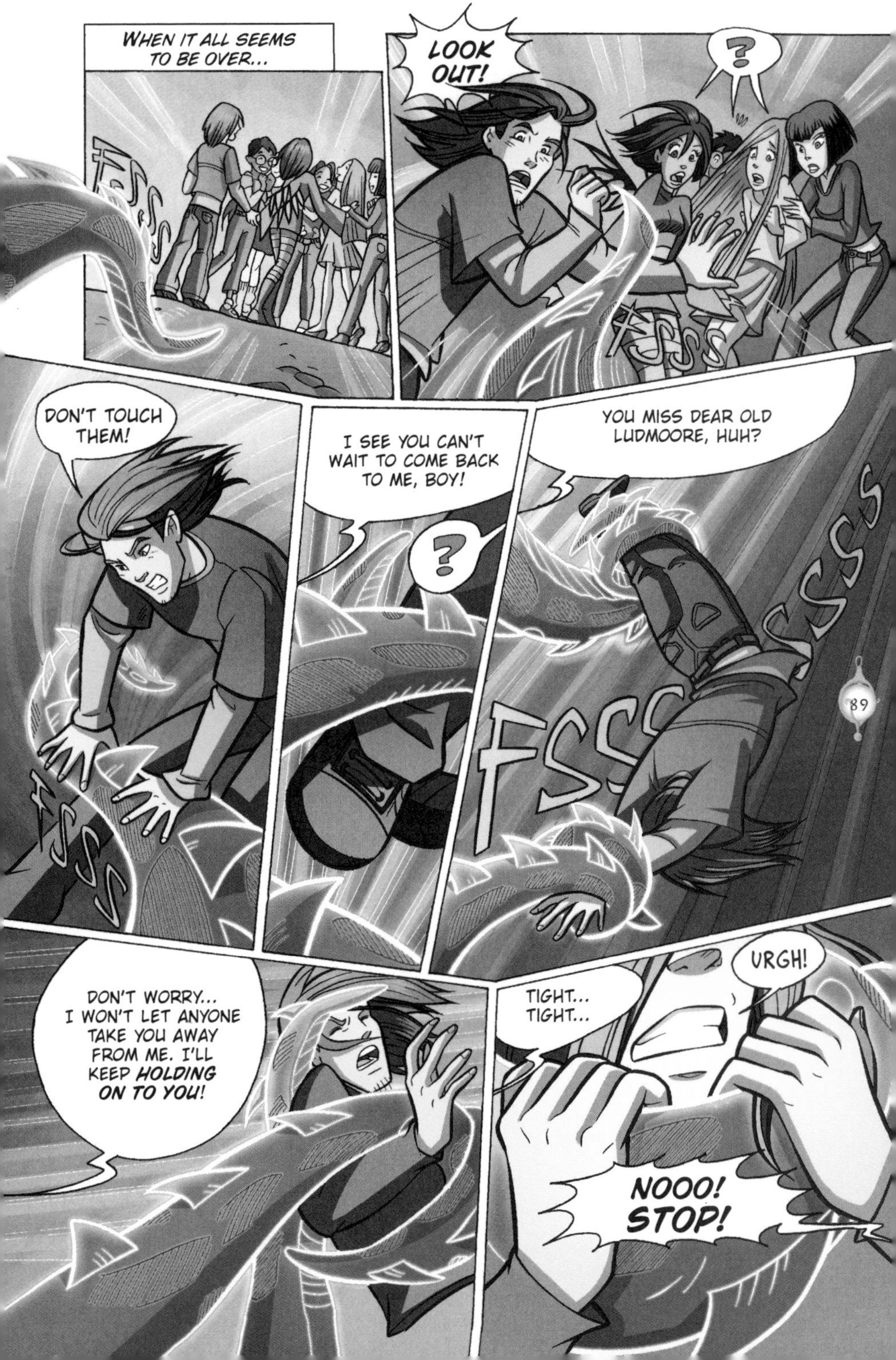
WHEN IT ALL SEEMS TO BE OVER...
FSSS
LOOK OUT!
?
FSSS
DON'T TOUCH THEM!
I SEE YOU CAN'T WAIT TO COME BACK TO ME, BOY!
?
YOU MISS DEAR OLD LUDMOORE, HUH?
FSSSSS
FSSS
FSSS
DON'T WORRY... I WON'T LET ANYONE TAKE YOU AWAY FROM ME. I'LL KEEP HOLDING ON TO YOU!
TIGHT... TIGHT...
URGH!
NOOO! STOP!

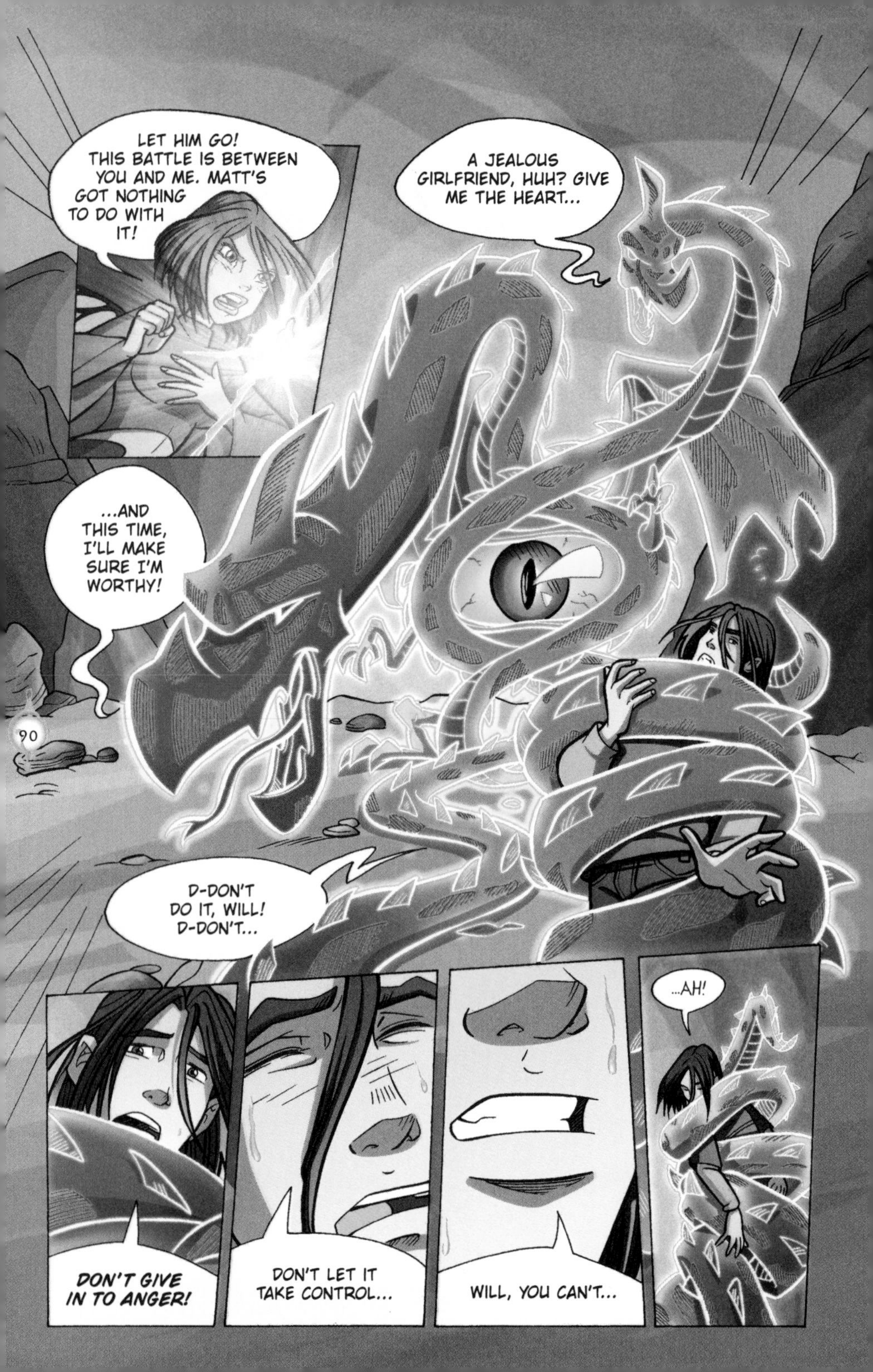

LET HIM GO! THIS BATTLE IS BETWEEN YOU AND ME. MATT'S GOT NOTHING TO DO WITH IT!
A JEALOUS GIRLFRIEND, HUH? GIVE ME THE HEART...
...AND THIS TIME, I'LL MAKE SURE I'M WORTHY!
D-DON'T DO IT, WILL! D-DON'T...
DON'T GIVE IN TO ANGER!
DON'T LET IT TAKE CONTROL...
WILL, YOU CAN'T...
...AH!

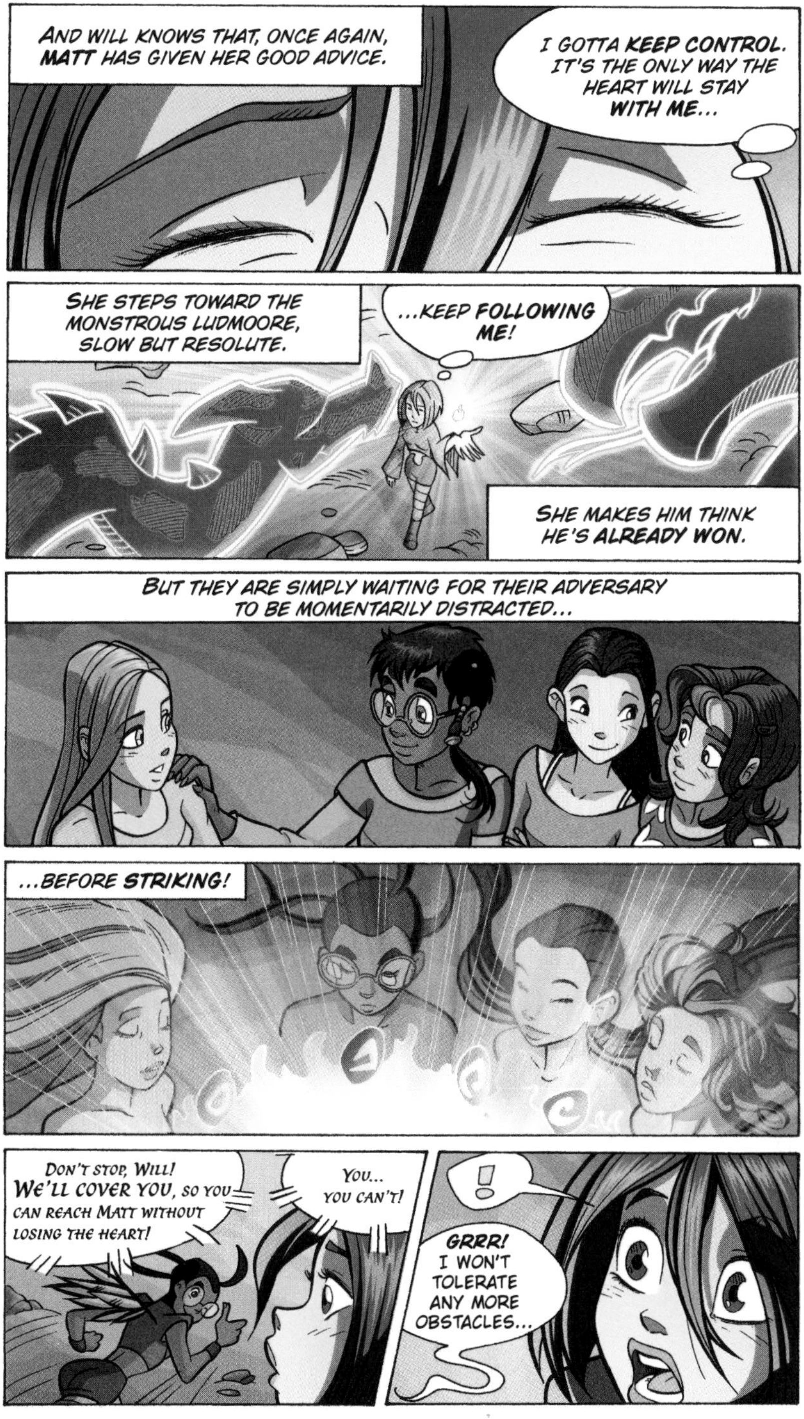
AND WILL KNOWS THAT, ONCE AGAIN, MATT HAS GIVEN HER GOOD ADVICE.
I GOTTA KEEP CONTROL. IT'S THE ONLY WAY THE HEART WILL STAY WITH ME...
SHE STEPS TOWARD THE MONSTROUS LUDMOORE, SLOW BUT RESOLUTE.
...KEEP FOLLOWING ME!
SHE MAKES HIM THINK HE'S ALREADY WON.
BUT THEY ARE SIMPLY WAITING FOR THEIR ADVERSARY TO BE MOMENTARILY DISTRACTED...
...BEFORE STRIKING!
DON'T STOP, WILL! WE'LL COVER YOU, SO YOU CAN REACH MATT WITHOUT LOSING THE HEART!
YOU... YOU CAN'T!
!
GRRR! I WON'T TOLERATE ANY MORE OBSTACLES...

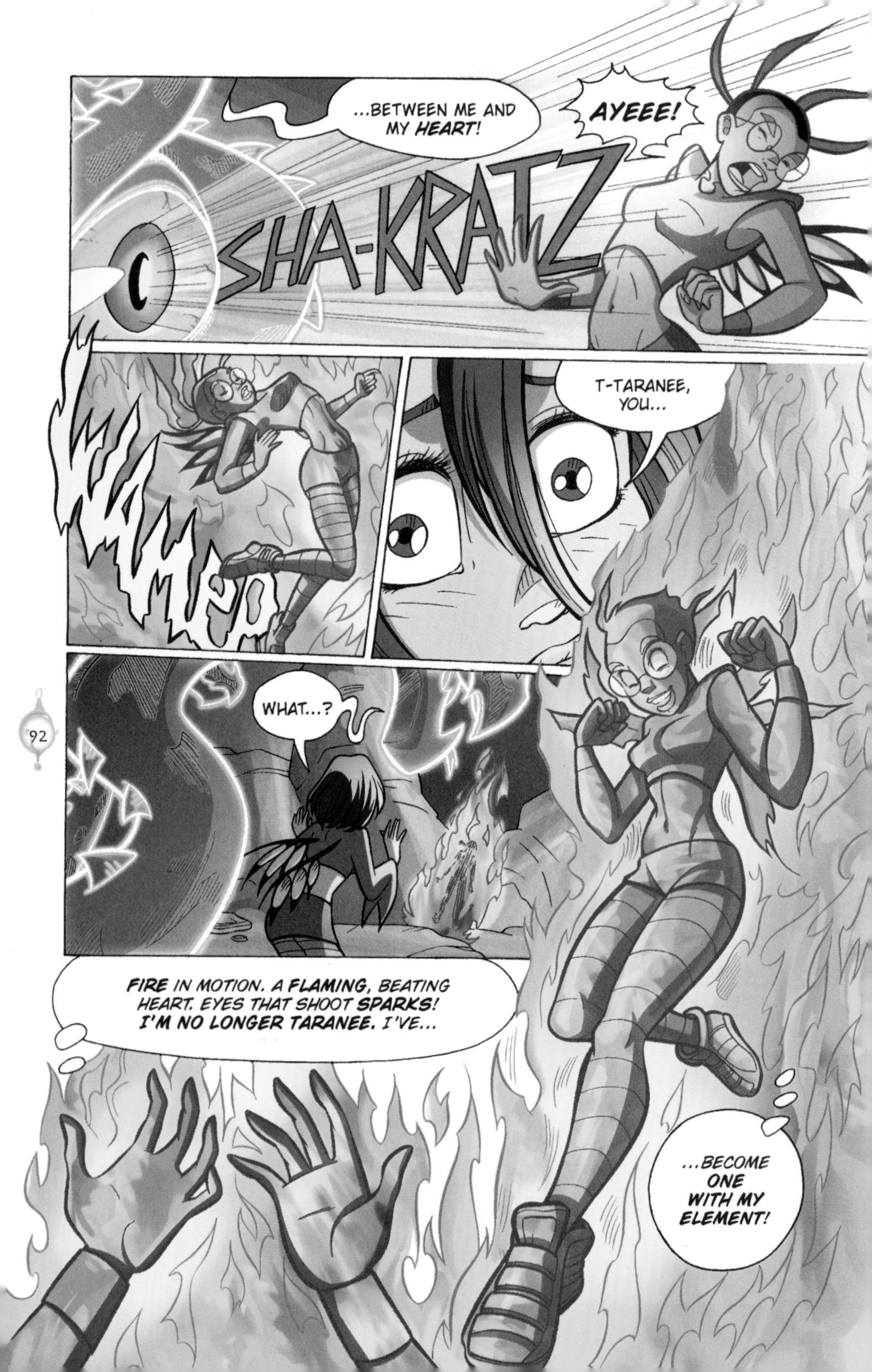

...BETWEEN ME AND MY HEART!
AYEEE!
SHA-KRATZ
T-TARANEE, YOU...
WHAT...?
FIRE IN MOTION. A FLAMING, BEATING HEART. EYES THAT SHOOT SPARKS! I'M NO LONGER TARANEE. I'VE...
...BECOME ONE WITH MY ELEMENT!

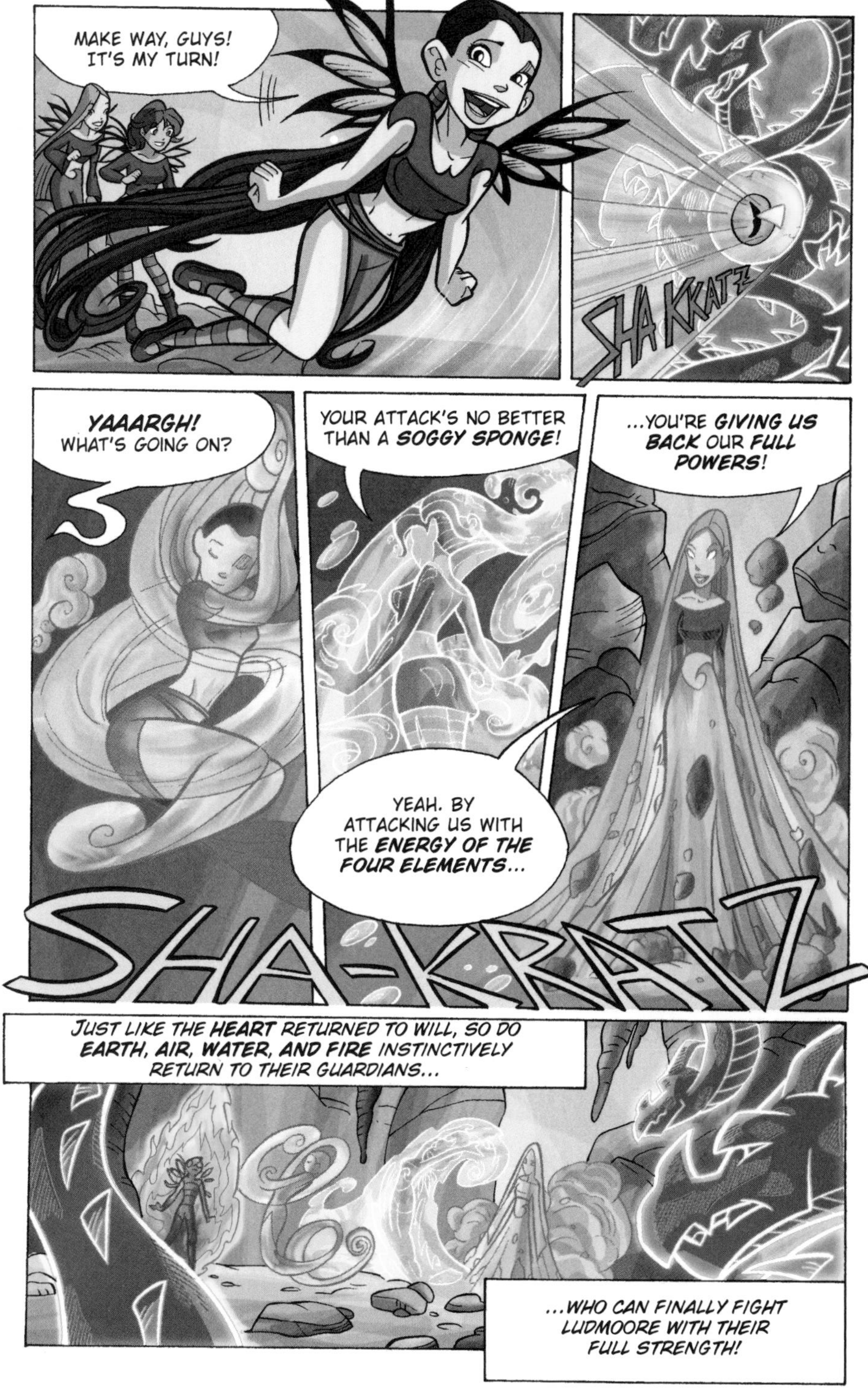
MAKE WAY, GUYS! IT'S MY TURN!
SHA KKATZ
YAAARGH! WHAT'S GOING ON?
YOUR ATTACK'S NO BETTER THAN A SOGGY SPONGE!
...YOU'RE GIVING US BACK OUR FULL POWERS!
YEAH. BY ATTACKING US WITH THE ENERGY OF THE FOUR ELEMENTS...
SHA-KRATZ
JUST LIKE THE HEART RETURNED TO WILL, SO DO EARTH, AIR, WATER, AND FIRE INSTINCTIVELY RETURN TO THEIR GUARDIANS...
...WHO CAN FINALLY FIGHT LUDMOORE WITH THEIR FULL STRENGTH!

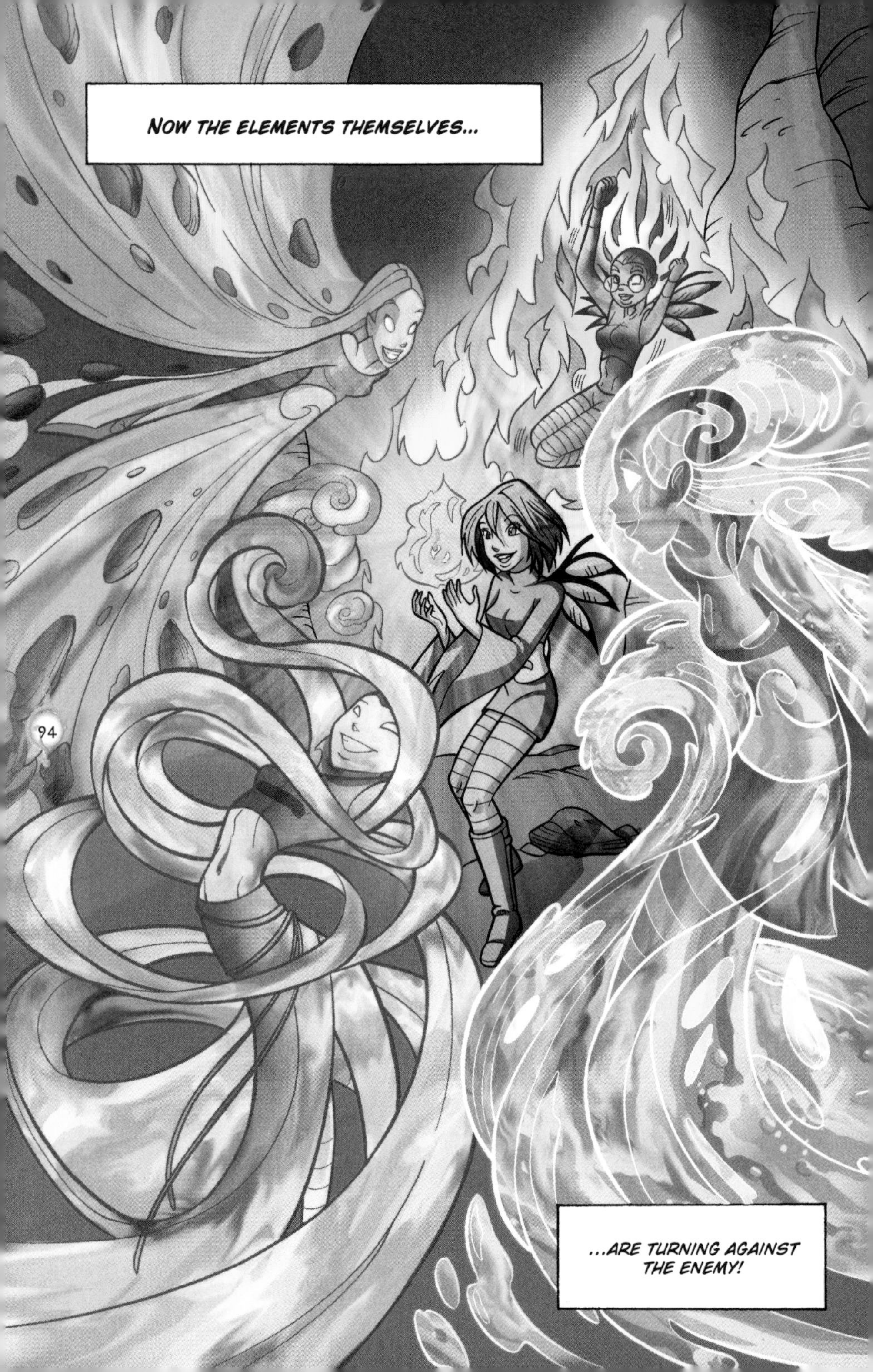
NOW THE ELEMENTS THEMSELVES...
...ARE TURNING AGAINST THE ENEMY!

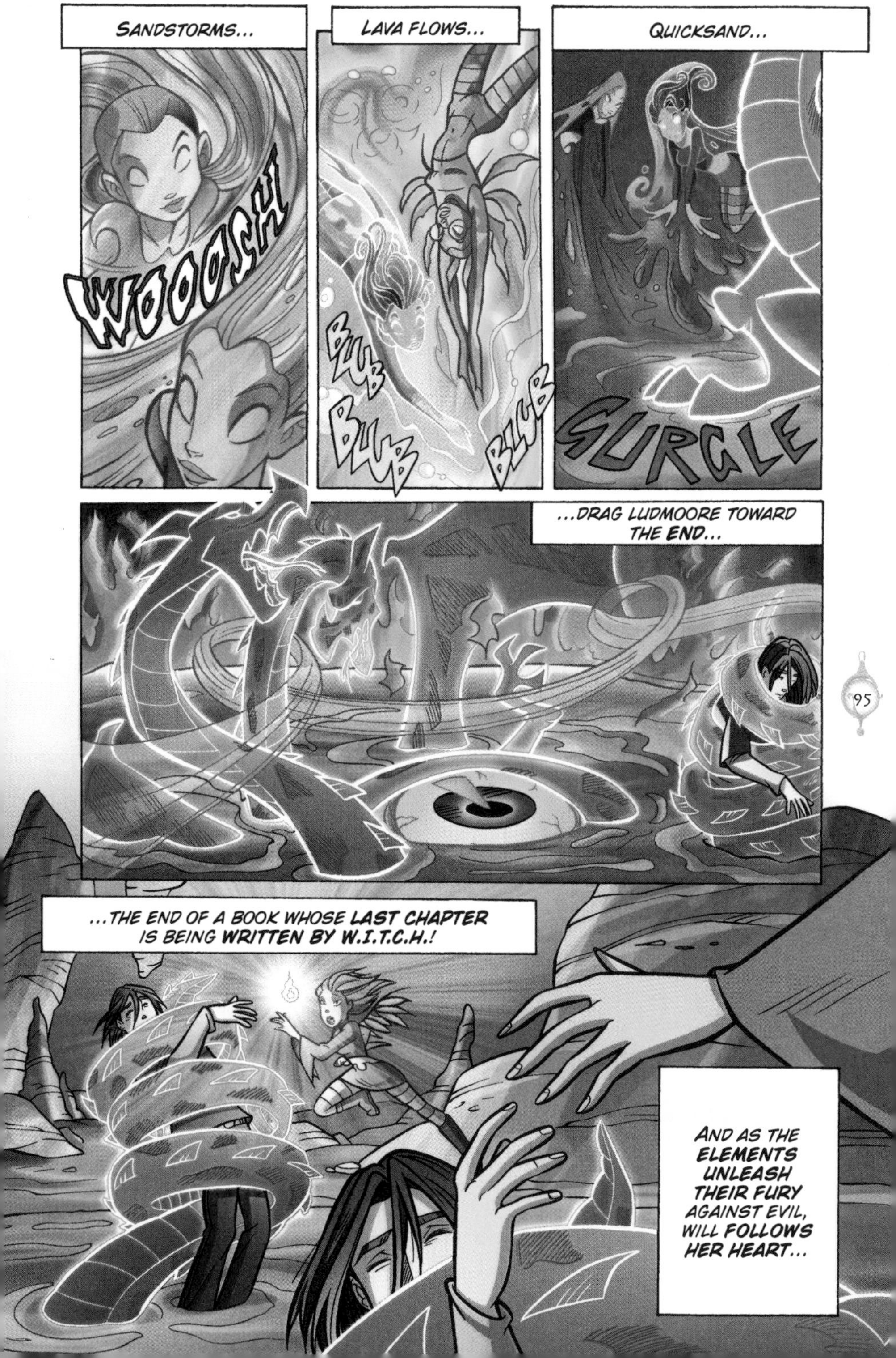
SANDSTORMS...
WOOOSH
LAVA FLOWS...
BLUB
BLUB
BLUB
QUICKSAND...
GURGLE
...DRAG LUDMOORE TOWARD THE END...
...THE END OF A BOOK WHOSE LAST CHAPTER IS BEING WRITTEN BY W.I.T.C.H.!
AND AS THE ELEMENTS UNLEASH THEIR FURY AGAINST EVIL, WILL FOLLOWS HER HEART...

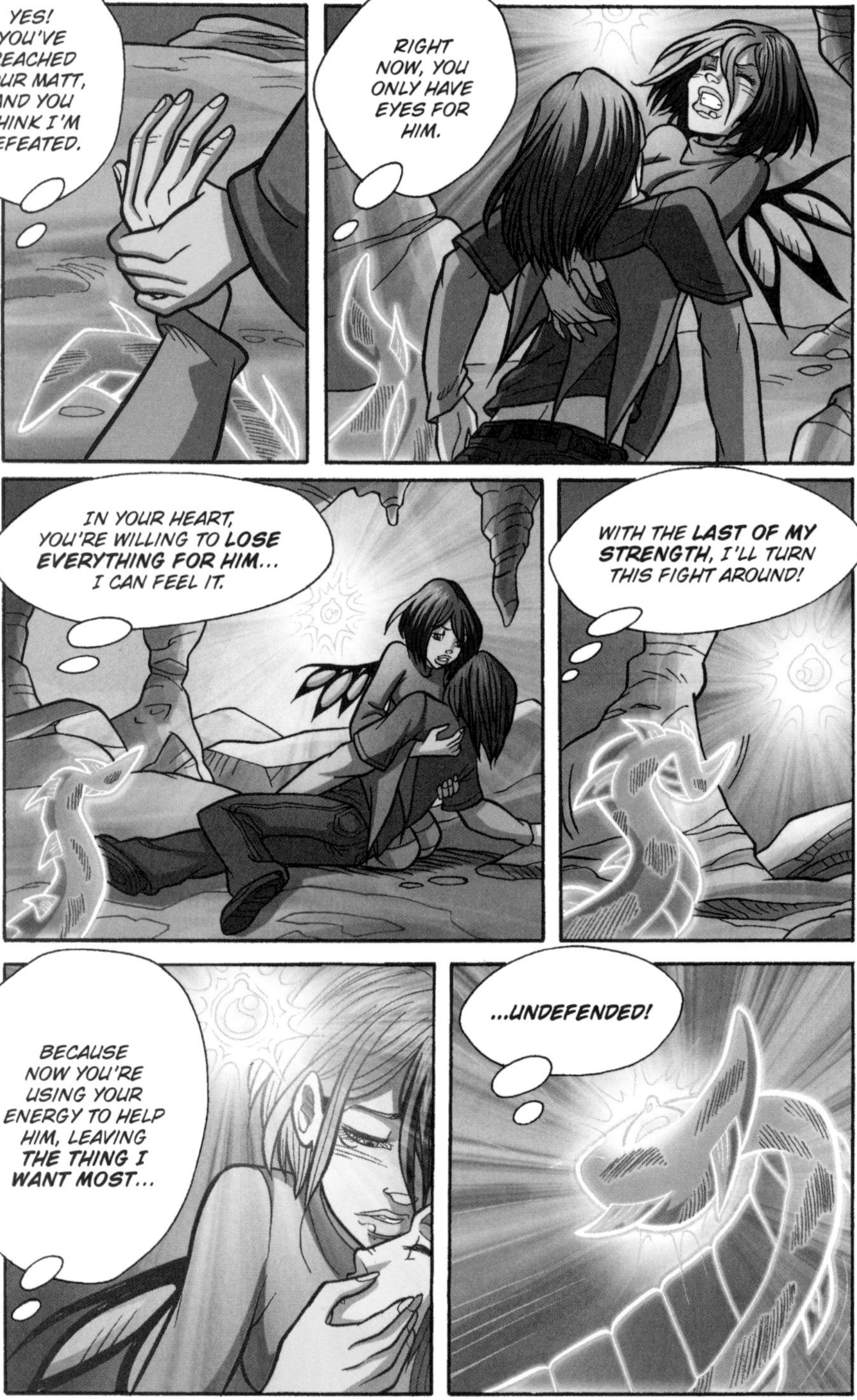
YES! YOU'VE REACHED YOUR MATT, AND YOU THINK I'M DEFEATED.
RIGHT NOW, YOU ONLY HAVE EYES FOR HIM.
IN YOUR HEART, YOU'RE WILLING TO **LOSE EVERYTHING FOR HIM**... I CAN FEEL IT.
WITH THE **LAST OF MY STRENGTH**, I'LL TURN THIS FIGHT AROUND!
BECAUSE NOW YOU'RE USING YOUR ENERGY TO HELP HIM, LEAVING **THE THING I WANT MOST**...
...UNDEFENDED!

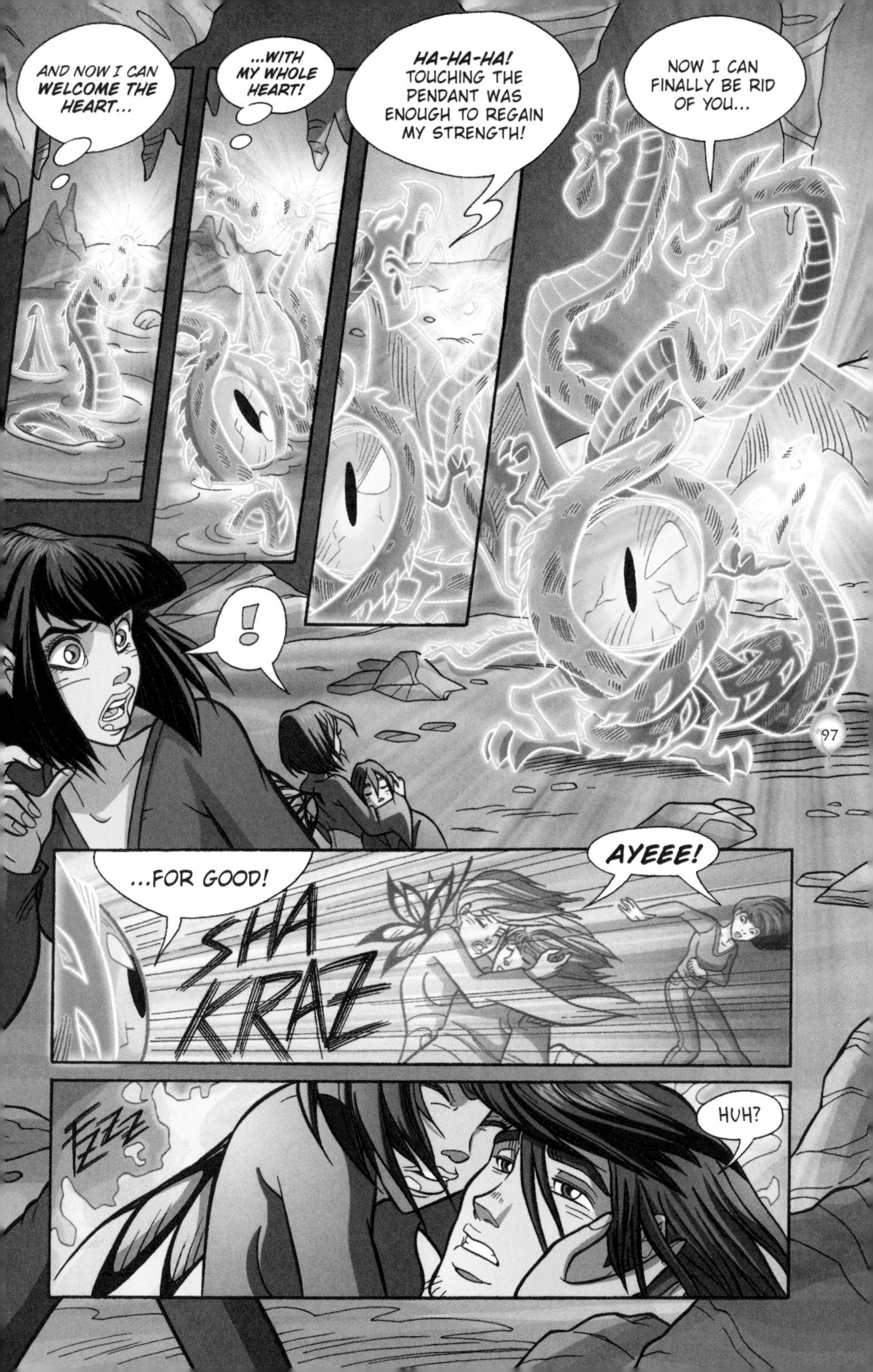
AND NOW I CAN WELCOME THE HEART...
...WITH MY WHOLE HEART!
HA-HA-HA! TOUCHING THE PENDANT WAS ENOUGH TO REGAIN MY STRENGTH!
NOW I CAN FINALLY BE RID OF YOU...
!
...FOR GOOD!
SHA KRAZ
AYEEE!
FZZZ
HUH?

I KNEW MY *PATIENCE* WOULD BE REWARDED!

SHA KRAE

!!

AND NOW, AS IS FAIR, I'LL RECLAIM ALL THE POWERS...

...YOU TOOK FROM ME!

SHAKRAZZ

HE DIDN'T NOTICE ME.

TUMP

ONCE AND FOR ALL, I'LL DESTROY YOU FOR GOOD, SO THAT *THE ELEMENTS HAVE NO ONE ELSE TO RETURN TO!*

I GOTTA DO SOME-THING!

I'LL FINALLY BE MY OWN MASTER. *I WON'T BE ANYONE'S SLAVE!*

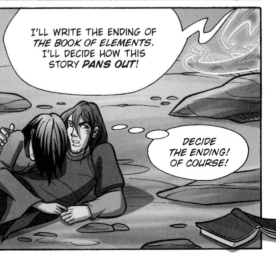

I'LL WRITE THE ENDING OF *THE BOOK OF ELEMENTS.* I'LL DECIDE HOW THIS STORY *PANS OUT!*

DECIDE THE ENDING! OF COURSE!

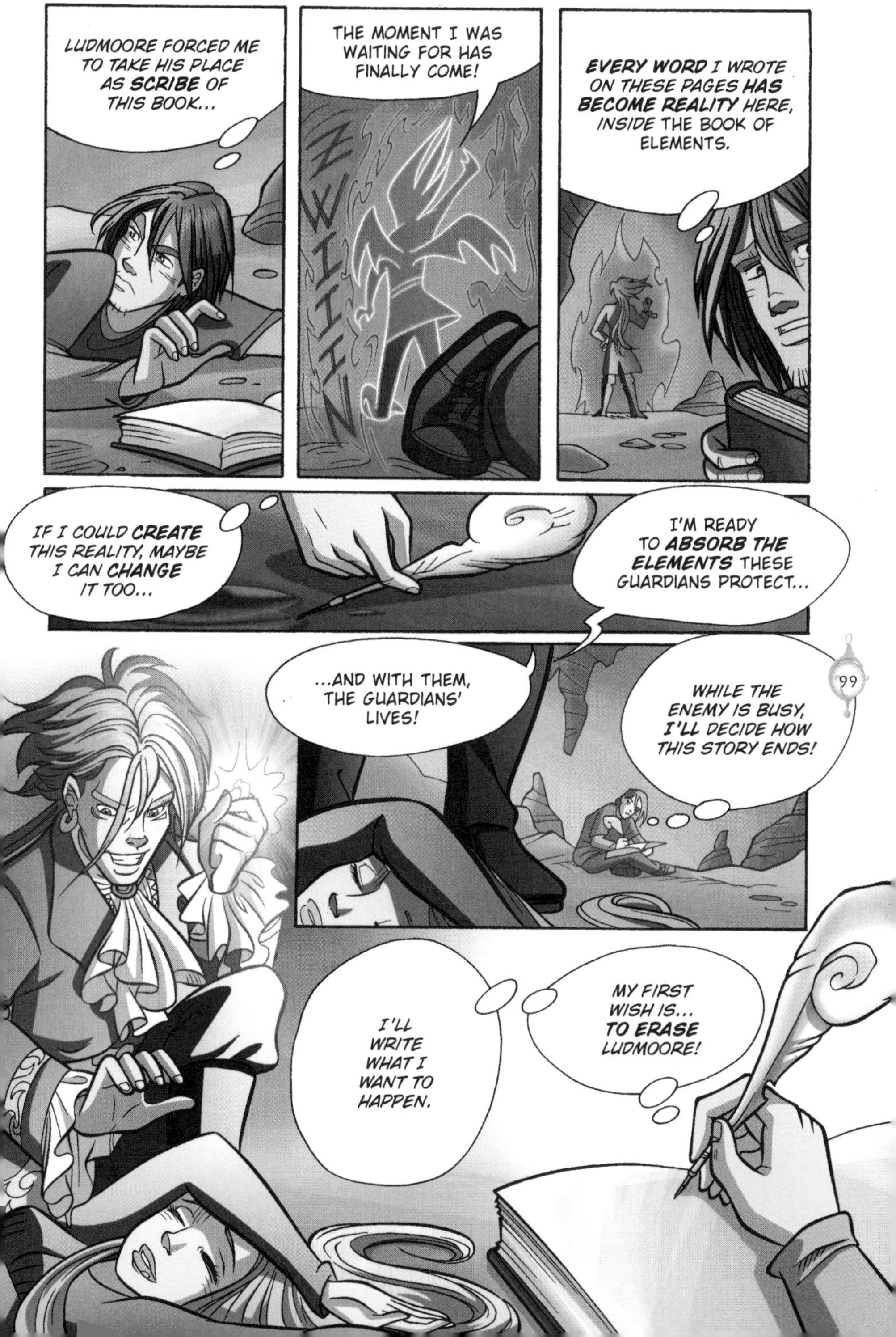
LUDMOORE FORCED ME TO TAKE HIS PLACE AS SCRIBE OF THIS BOOK...
THE MOMENT I WAS WAITING FOR HAS FINALLY COME!
ZWIIIIN
EVERY WORD I WROTE ON THESE PAGES HAS BECOME REALITY HERE, INSIDE THE BOOK OF ELEMENTS.
IF I COULD CREATE THIS REALITY, MAYBE I CAN CHANGE IT TOO...
I'M READY TO ABSORB THE ELEMENTS THESE GUARDIANS PROTECT...
...AND WITH THEM, THE GUARDIANS' LIVES!
WHILE THE ENEMY IS BUSY, I'LL DECIDE HOW THIS STORY ENDS!
I'LL WRITE WHAT I WANT TO HAPPEN.
MY FIRST WISH IS... TO ERASE LUDMOORE!

MATT CROSSES OUT THE **VERY FIRST INSTANCE** OF THEIR ENEMY'S NAME AS IT APPEARS IN THE BOOK...

Ludmoore

...AND WITH THAT, AS HIS NAME IS AUTOMATICALLY ERASED FROM THE FOLLOWING PAGES...

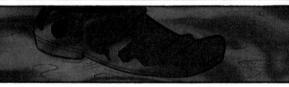

!!

...THE REAL LUDMOORE BEGINS TO **FADE AWAY** TOO.

JONATHAN LUDMOORE'S NAME NO LONGER APPEARS IN THE BOOK OF ELEMENTS. **AS IF HE'D NEVER EXISTED.**

!!

HE RETURNS TO HIS FORM FROM BEFORE THIS ALL BEGAN.

AAH...

A VAGUE ENTITY. SHAPELESS MATTER. A GOOEY, DRIPPING SUBSTANCE THAT CAN'T HOLD THE **WEIGHT OF THE HEART** OF KANDRAKAR...

...WHICH, IN HIS HANDS, WAS **A BLACK HEART.**

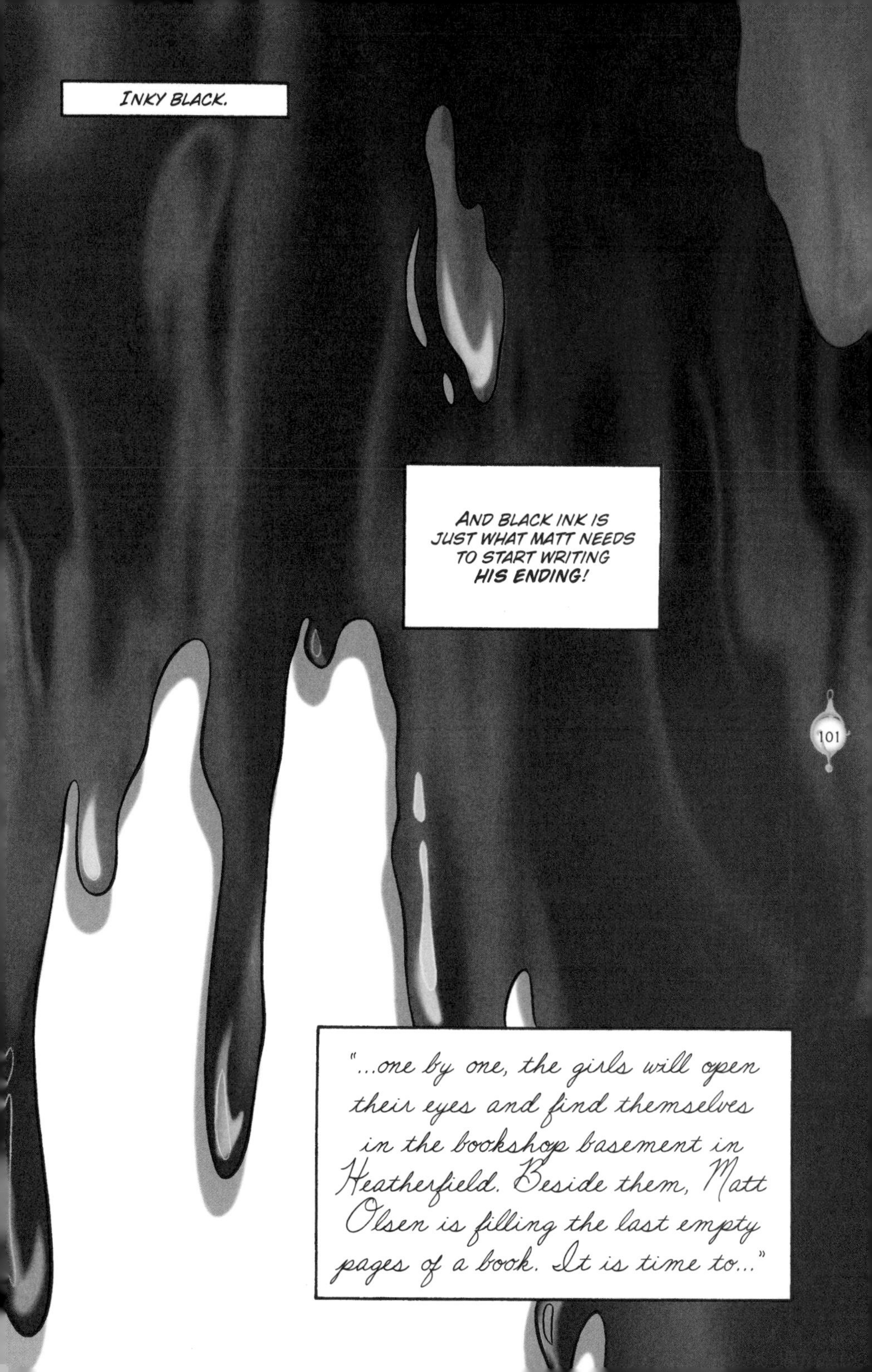
INKY BLACK.
AND BLACK INK IS JUST WHAT MATT NEEDS TO START WRITING HIS ENDING!
"...one by one, the girls will open their eyes and find themselves in the bookshop basement in Heatherfield. Beside them, Matt Olsen is filling the last empty pages of a book. It is time to..."

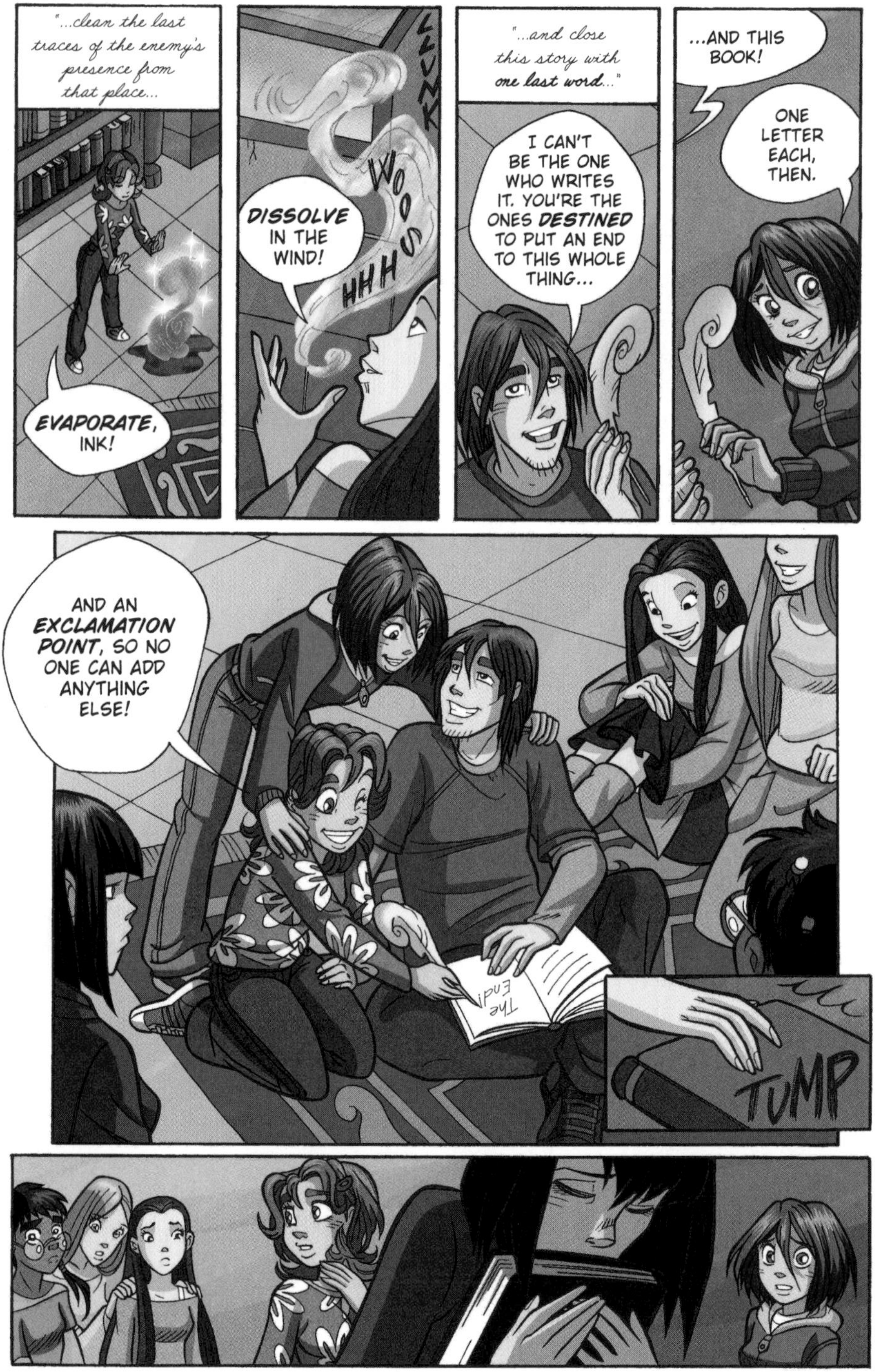
"...clean the last traces of the enemy's presence from that place...
EVAPORATE, INK!
CLUNK
WOOSHHH
DISSOLVE IN THE WIND!
"...and close this story with one last word..."
I CAN'T BE THE ONE WHO WRITES IT. YOU'RE THE ONES DESTINED TO PUT AN END TO THIS WHOLE THING...
...AND THIS BOOK!
ONE LETTER EACH, THEN.
AND AN EXCLAMATION POINT, SO NO ONE CAN ADD ANYTHING ELSE!
The End!
TUMP

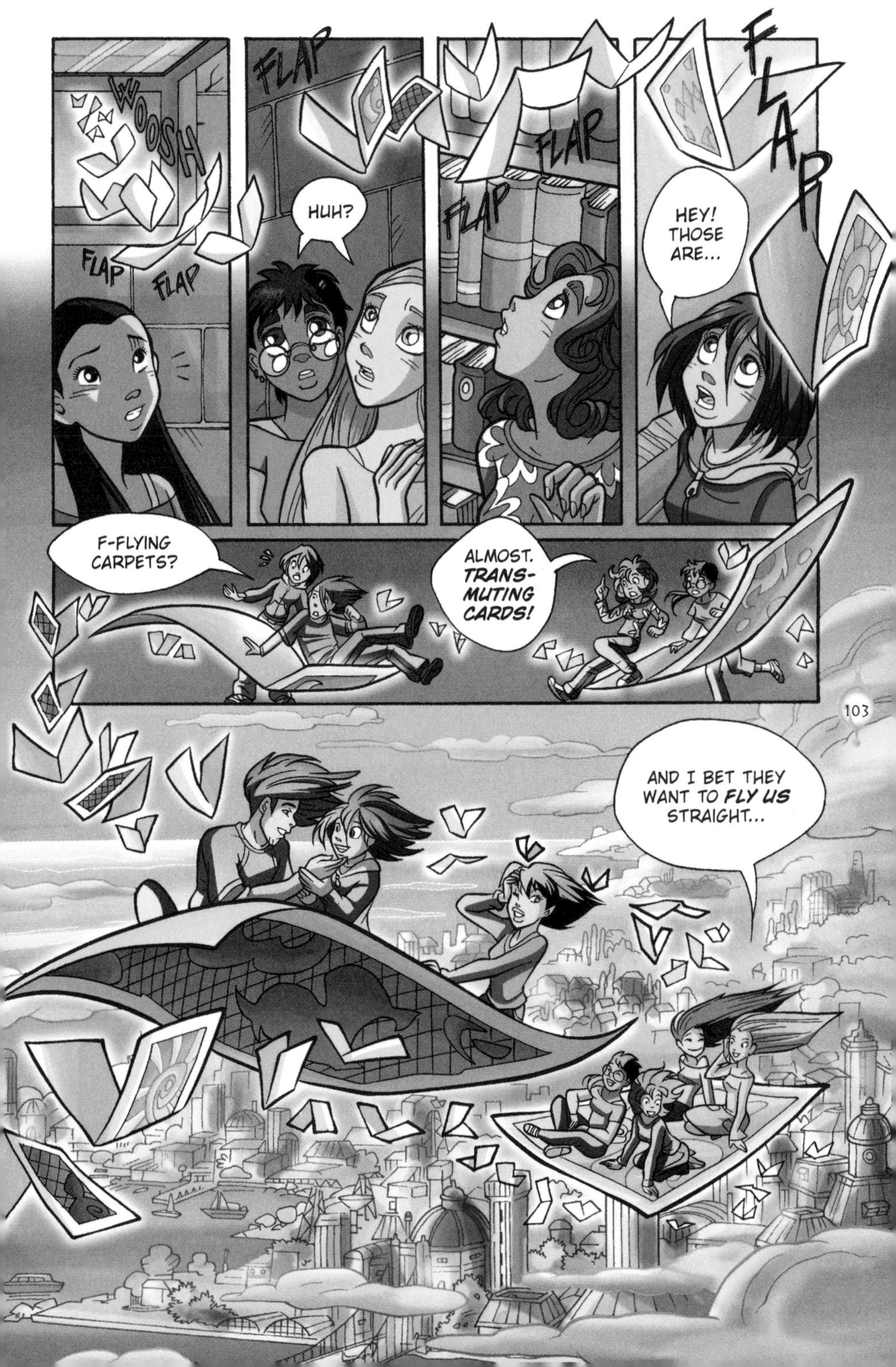
WOOSH
FLAP
FLAP
FLAP
HUH?
FLAP
FLAP
FLAP
HEY! THOSE ARE...
F-FLYING CARPETS?
ALMOST. TRANS-MUTING CARDS!
AND I BET THEY WANT TO FLY US STRAIGHT...

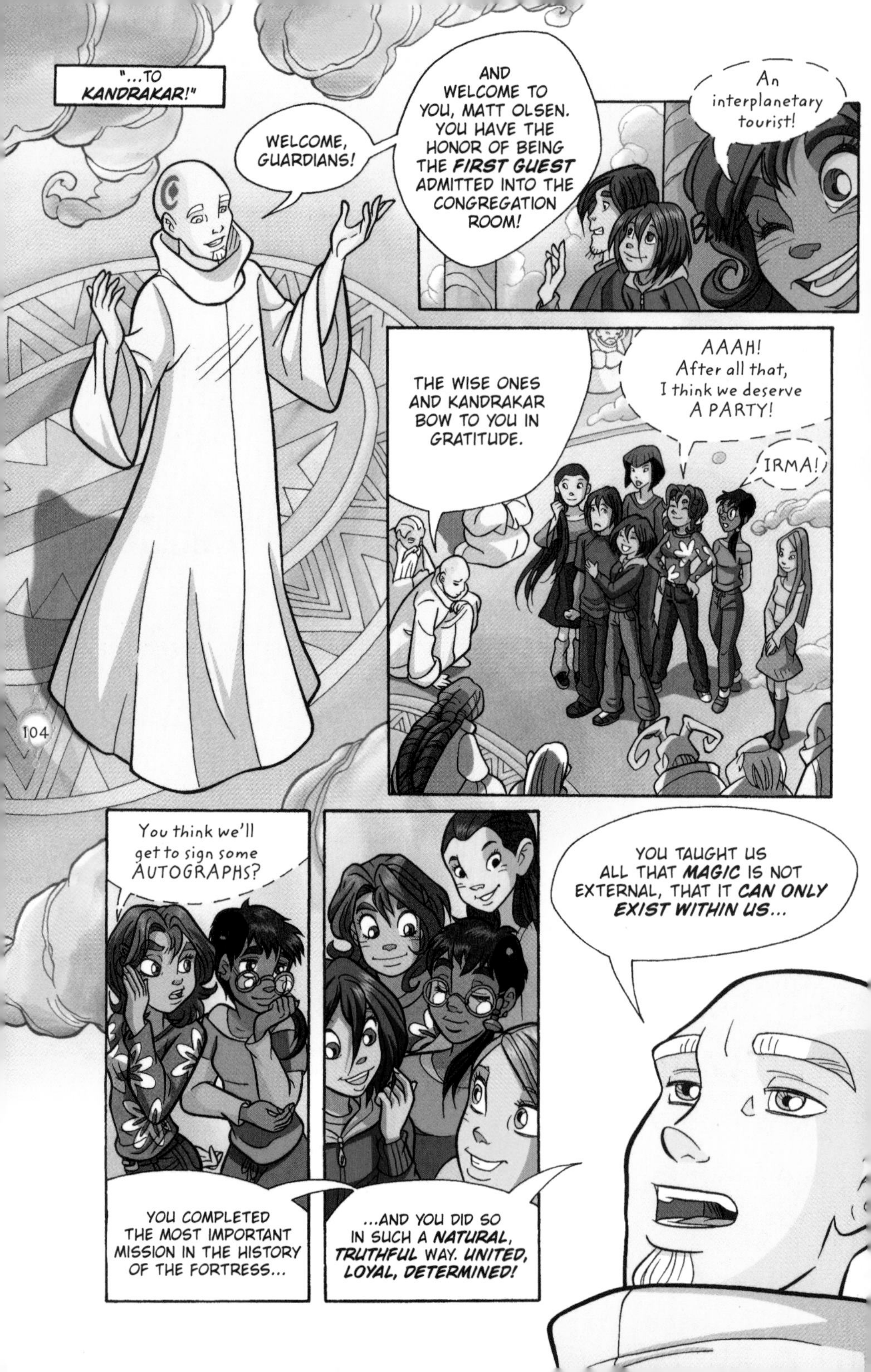
"...TO KANDRAKAR!"
WELCOME, GUARDIANS!
AND WELCOME TO YOU, MATT OLSEN. YOU HAVE THE HONOR OF BEING THE FIRST GUEST ADMITTED INTO THE CONGREGATION ROOM!
An interplanetary tourist!
BLINK
THE WISE ONES AND KANDRAKAR BOW TO YOU IN GRATITUDE.
AAAH! After all that, I think we deserve A PARTY!
IRMA!
You think we'll get to sign some AUTOGRAPHS?
YOU COMPLETED THE MOST IMPORTANT MISSION IN THE HISTORY OF THE FORTRESS...
...AND YOU DID SO IN SUCH A NATURAL, TRUTHFUL WAY. UNITED, LOYAL, DETERMINED!
YOU TAUGHT US ALL THAT MAGIC IS NOT EXTERNAL, THAT IT CAN ONLY EXIST WITHIN US...

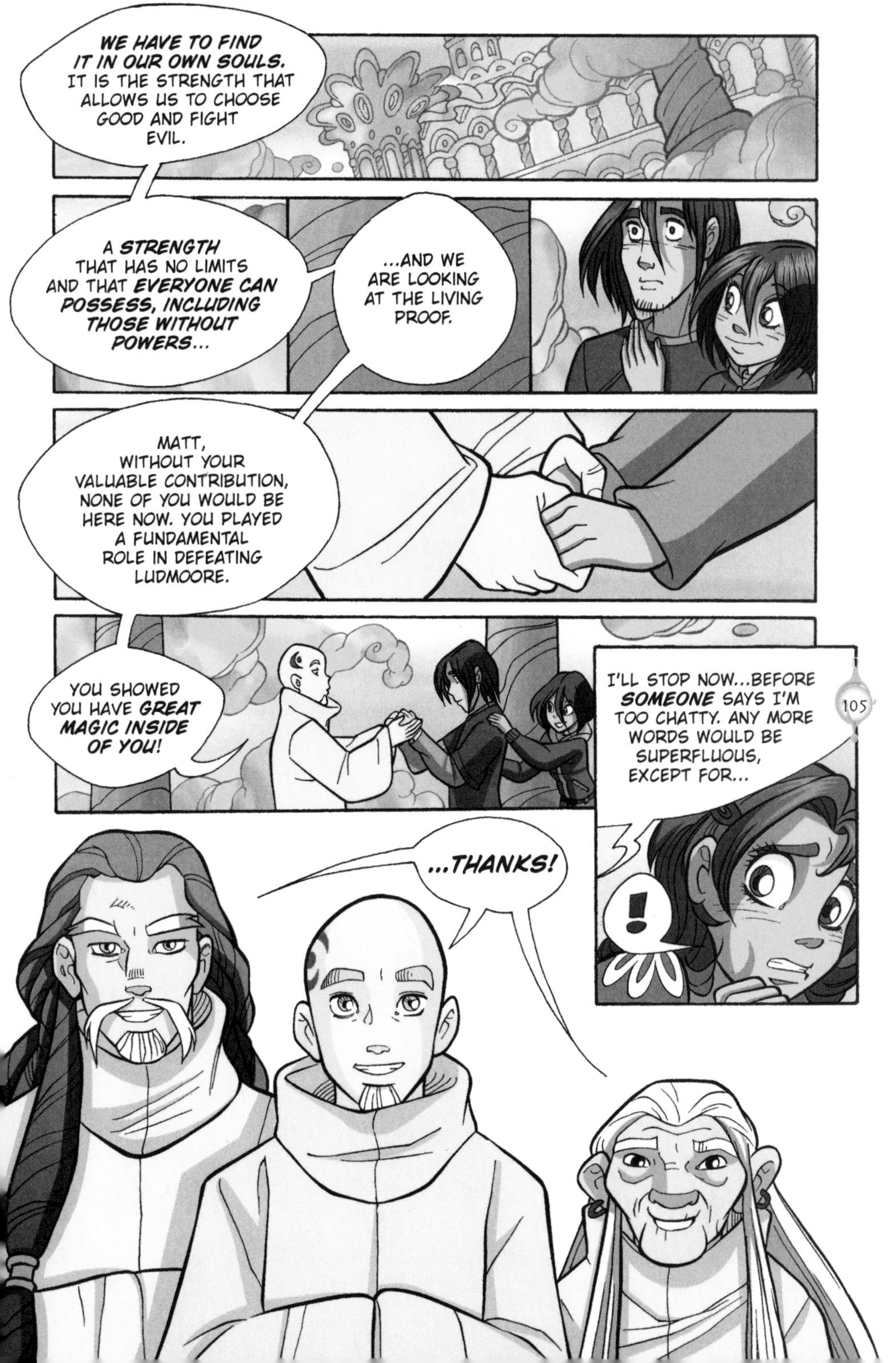
WE HAVE TO FIND IT IN OUR OWN SOULS. IT IS THE STRENGTH THAT ALLOWS US TO CHOOSE GOOD AND FIGHT EVIL.
A STRENGTH THAT HAS NO LIMITS AND THAT EVERYONE CAN POSSESS, INCLUDING THOSE WITHOUT POWERS...
...AND WE ARE LOOKING AT THE LIVING PROOF.
MATT, WITHOUT YOUR VALUABLE CONTRIBUTION, NONE OF YOU WOULD BE HERE NOW. YOU PLAYED A FUNDAMENTAL ROLE IN DEFEATING LUDMOORE.
YOU SHOWED YOU HAVE GREAT MAGIC INSIDE OF YOU!
I'LL STOP NOW...BEFORE SOMEONE SAYS I'M TOO CHATTY. ANY MORE WORDS WOULD BE SUPERFLUOUS, EXCEPT FOR...
!
...THANKS!

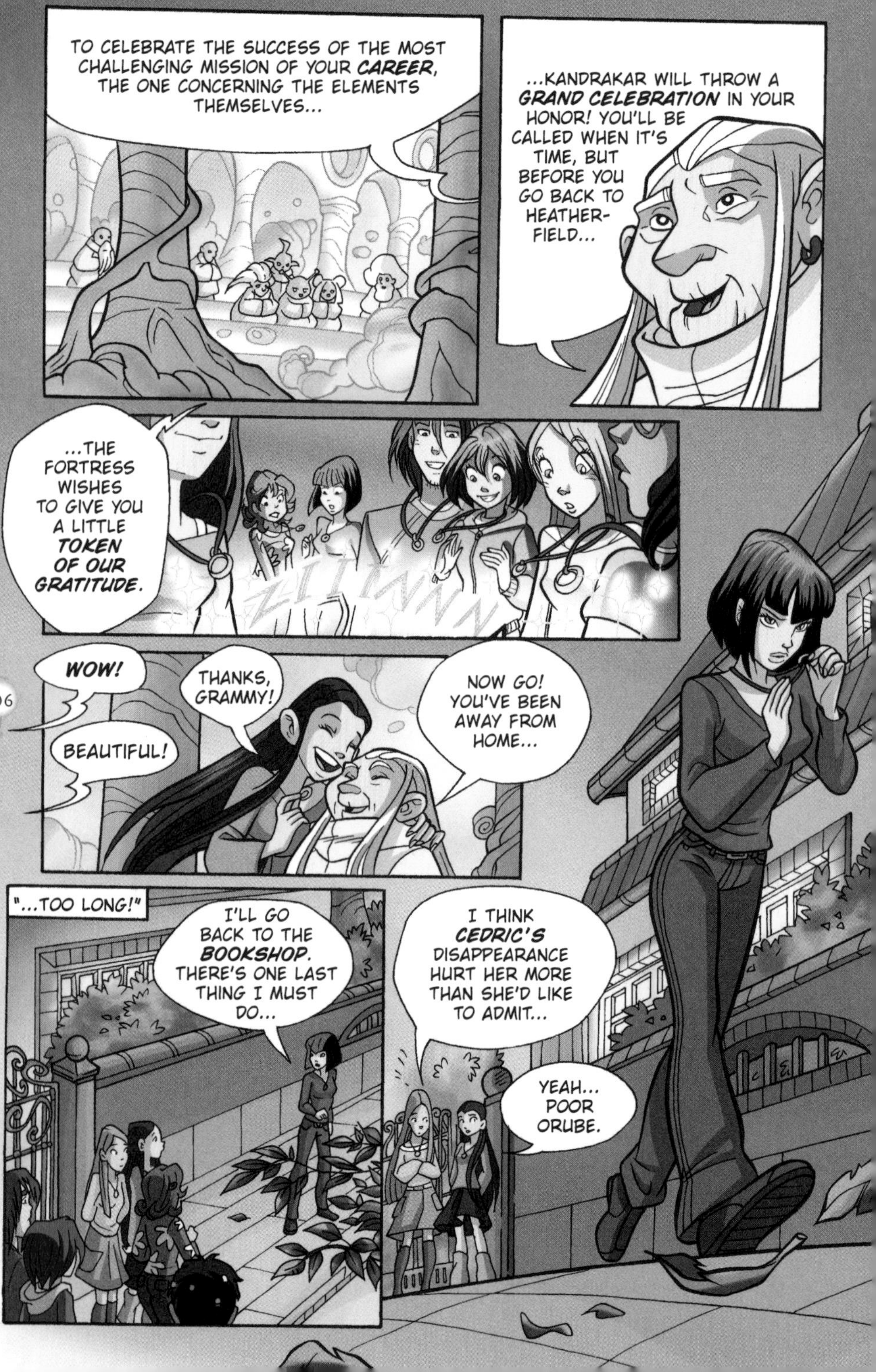
TO CELEBRATE THE SUCCESS OF THE MOST CHALLENGING MISSION OF YOUR CAREER, THE ONE CONCERNING THE ELEMENTS THEMSELVES...
...KANDRAKAR WILL THROW A GRAND CELEBRATION IN YOUR HONOR! YOU'LL BE CALLED WHEN IT'S TIME, BUT BEFORE YOU GO BACK TO HEATHER-FIELD...
...THE FORTRESS WISHES TO GIVE YOU A LITTLE TOKEN OF OUR GRATITUDE.
ZIIINNN
WOW!
BEAUTIFUL!
THANKS, GRAMMY!
NOW GO! YOU'VE BEEN AWAY FROM HOME...
"...TOO LONG!"
I'LL GO BACK TO THE BOOKSHOP. THERE'S ONE LAST THING I MUST DO...
I THINK CEDRIC'S DISAPPEARANCE HURT HER MORE THAN SHE'D LIKE TO ADMIT...
YEAH... POOR ORUBE.

106

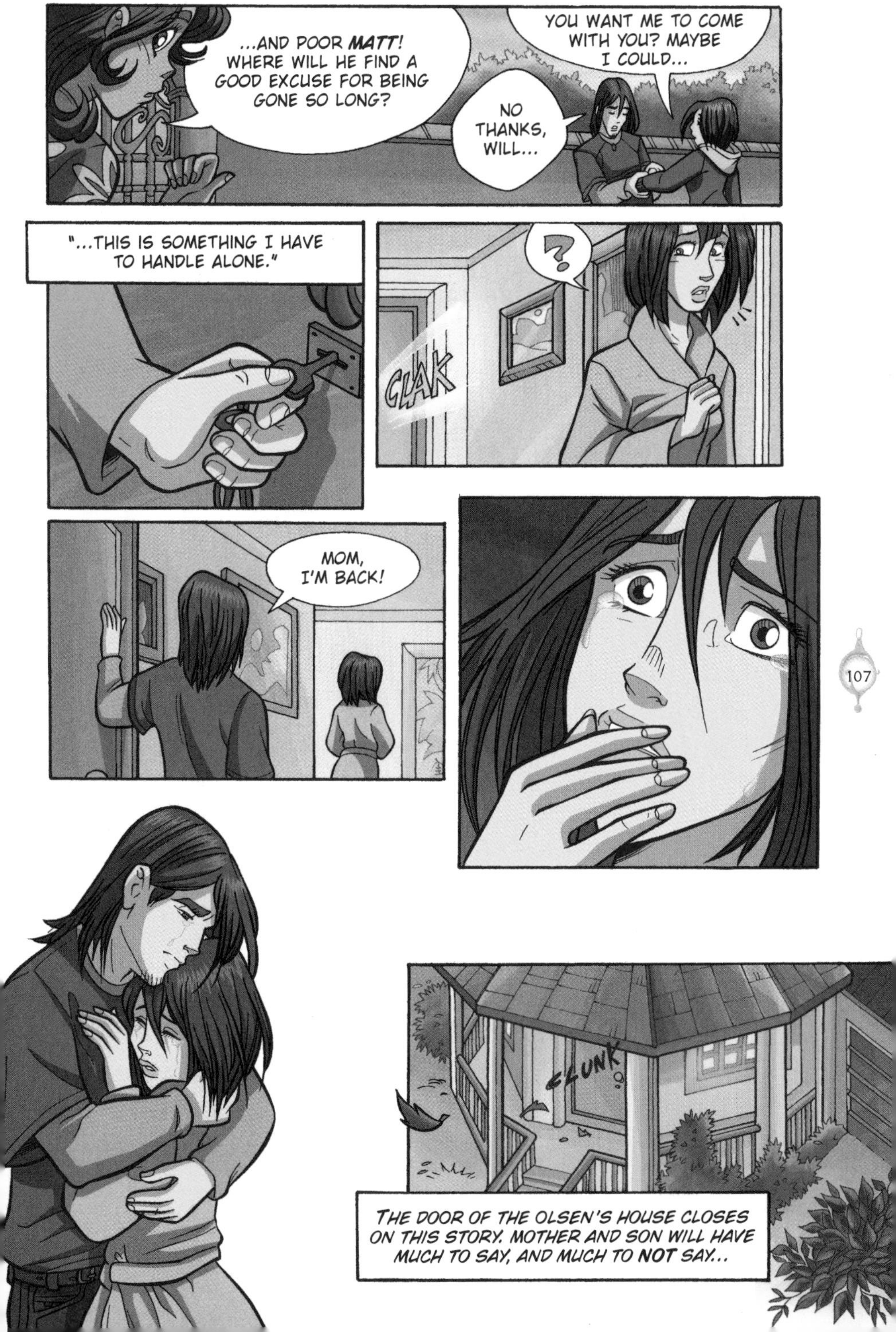
...AND POOR MATT! WHERE WILL HE FIND A GOOD EXCUSE FOR BEING GONE SO LONG?
YOU WANT ME TO COME WITH YOU? MAYBE I COULD...
NO THANKS, WILL...
"...THIS IS SOMETHING I HAVE TO HANDLE ALONE."
?
CLAK
MOM, I'M BACK!
CLUNK
THE DOOR OF THE OLSEN'S HOUSE CLOSES ON THIS STORY. MOTHER AND SON WILL HAVE MUCH TO SAY, AND MUCH TO NOT SAY...

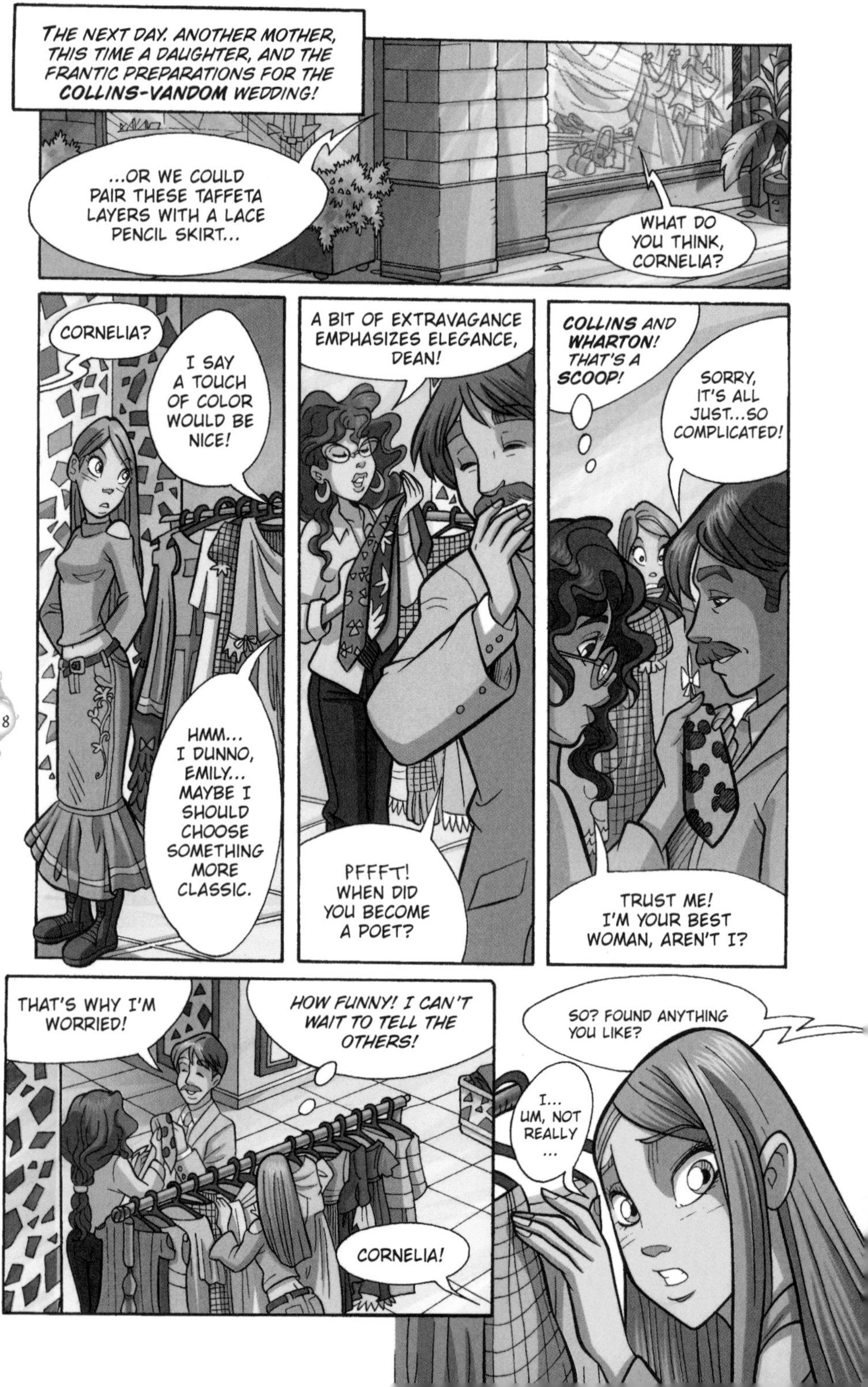
THE NEXT DAY. ANOTHER MOTHER, THIS TIME A DAUGHTER, AND THE FRANTIC PREPARATIONS FOR THE COLLINS-VANDOM WEDDING!
...OR WE COULD PAIR THESE TAFFETA LAYERS WITH A LACE PENCIL SKIRT...
WHAT DO YOU THINK, CORNELIA?
CORNELIA?
I SAY A TOUCH OF COLOR WOULD BE NICE!
HMM... I DUNNO, EMILY... MAYBE I SHOULD CHOOSE SOMETHING MORE CLASSIC.
A BIT OF EXTRAVAGANCE EMPHASIZES ELEGANCE, DEAN!
PFFFT! WHEN DID YOU BECOME A POET?
COLLINS AND WHARTON! THAT'S A SCOOP!
SORRY, IT'S ALL JUST...SO COMPLICATED!
TRUST ME! I'M YOUR BEST WOMAN, AREN'T I?
THAT'S WHY I'M WORRIED!
HOW FUNNY! I CAN'T WAIT TO TELL THE OTHERS!
CORNELIA!
SO? FOUND ANYTHING YOU LIKE?
I... UM, NOT REALLY ...

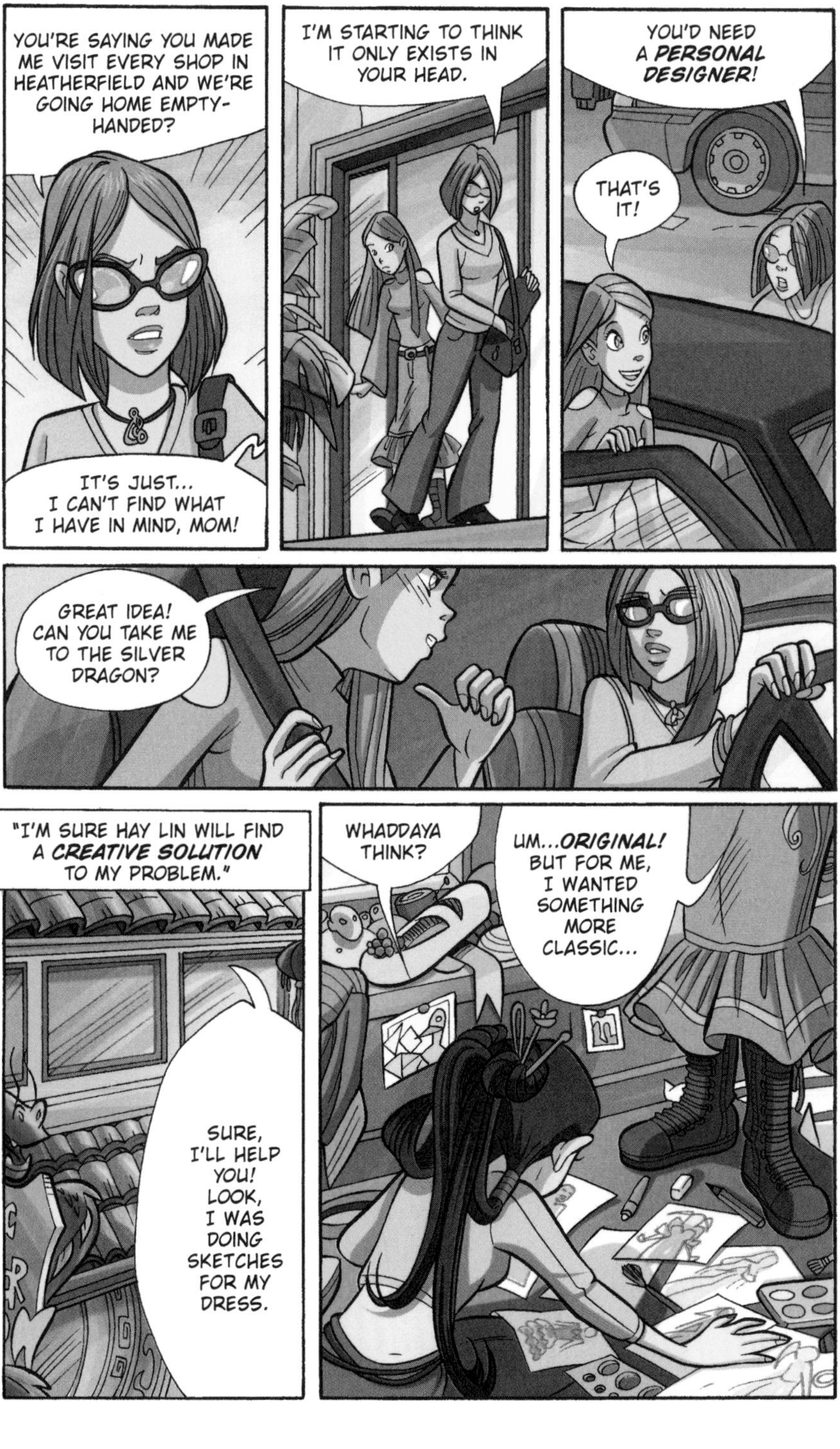
YOU'RE SAYING YOU MADE ME VISIT EVERY SHOP IN HEATHERFIELD AND WE'RE GOING HOME EMPTY-HANDED?
IT'S JUST... I CAN'T FIND WHAT I HAVE IN MIND, MOM!
I'M STARTING TO THINK IT ONLY EXISTS IN YOUR HEAD.
YOU'D NEED A *PERSONAL DESIGNER*!
THAT'S IT!
GREAT IDEA! CAN YOU TAKE ME TO THE SILVER DRAGON?
"I'M SURE HAY LIN WILL FIND A *CREATIVE SOLUTION* TO MY PROBLEM."
SURE, I'LL HELP YOU! LOOK, I WAS DOING SKETCHES FOR MY DRESS.
WHADDAYA THINK?
UM...*ORIGINAL!* BUT FOR ME, I WANTED SOMETHING MORE CLASSIC...

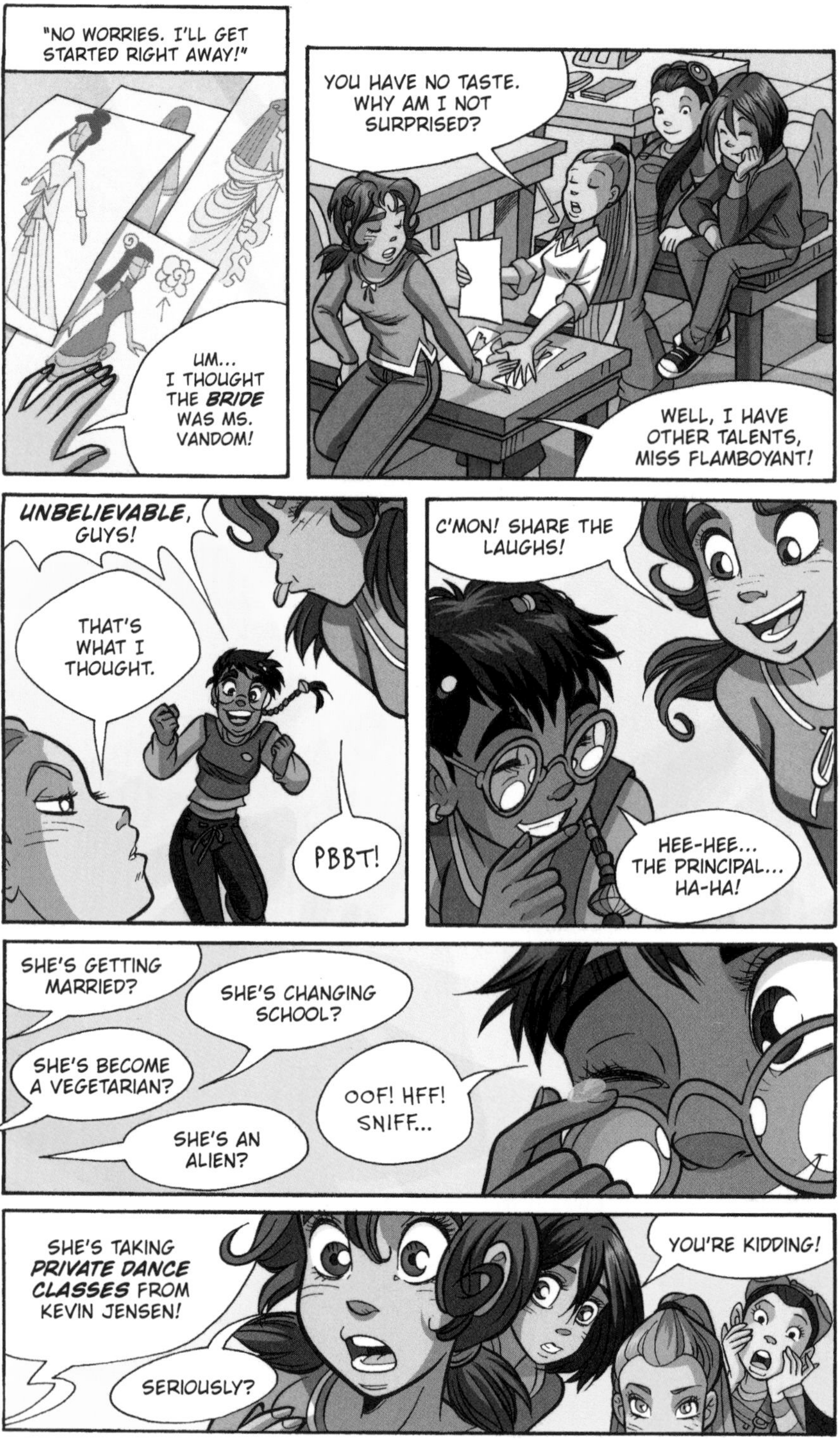
"NO WORRIES. I'LL GET STARTED RIGHT AWAY!"
UM... I THOUGHT THE BRIDE WAS MS. VANDOM!
YOU HAVE NO TASTE. WHY AM I NOT SURPRISED?
WELL, I HAVE OTHER TALENTS, MISS FLAMBOYANT!
UNBELIEVABLE, GUYS!
THAT'S WHAT I THOUGHT.
PBBT!
C'MON! SHARE THE LAUGHS!
HEE-HEE... THE PRINCIPAL... HA-HA!
SHE'S GETTING MARRIED?
SHE'S CHANGING SCHOOL?
SHE'S BECOME A VEGETARIAN?
SHE'S AN ALIEN?
OOF! HFF! SNIFF...
SHE'S TAKING PRIVATE DANCE CLASSES FROM KEVIN JENSEN!
SERIOUSLY?
YOU'RE KIDDING!

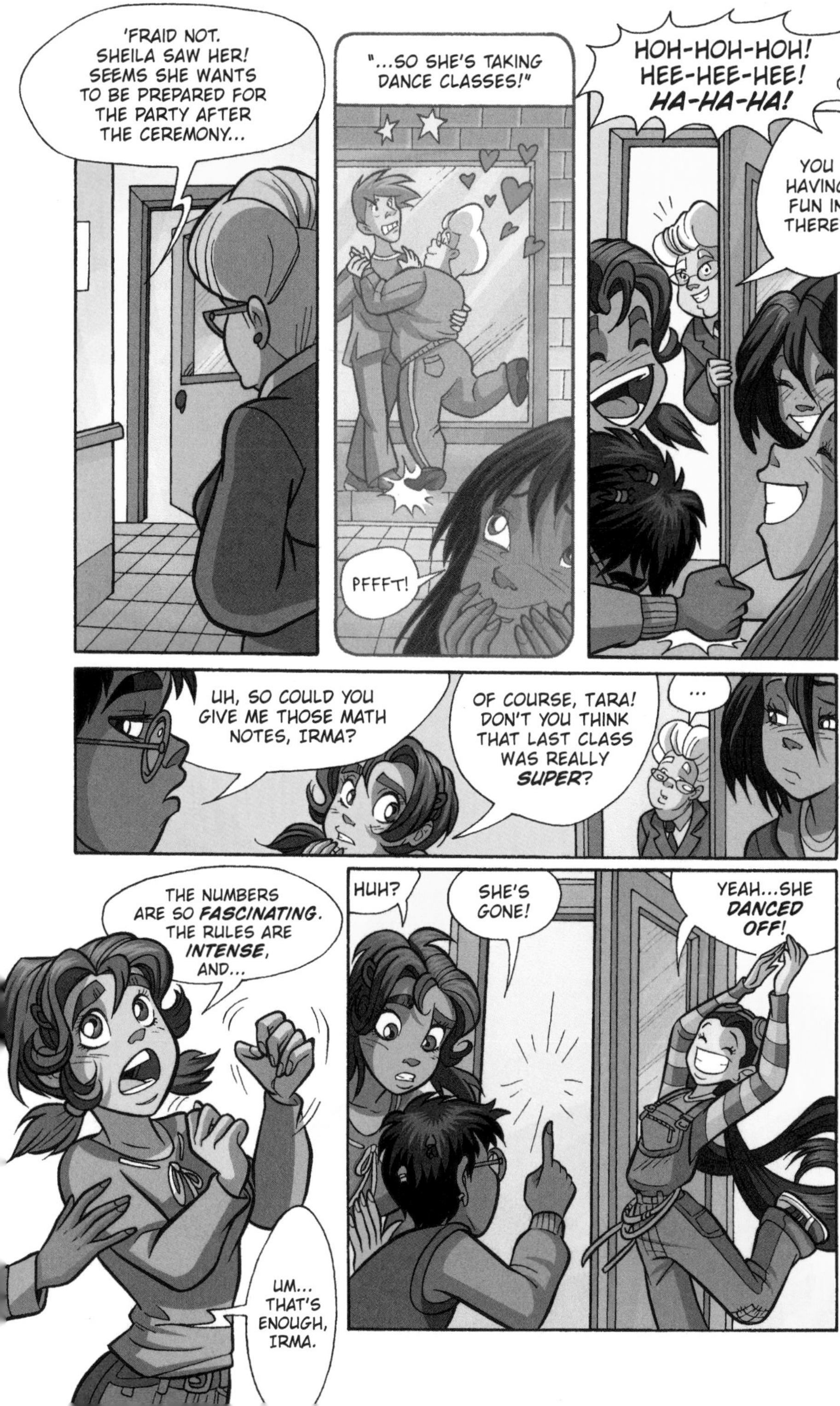

'FRAID NOT. SHEILA SAW HER! SEEMS SHE WANTS TO BE PREPARED FOR THE PARTY AFTER THE CEREMONY...
"...SO SHE'S TAKING DANCE CLASSES!"
PFFFT!
HOH-HOH-HOH! HEE-HEE-HEE! *HA-HA-HA!*
YOU HAVING FUN IN THERE?
UH, SO COULD YOU GIVE ME THOSE MATH NOTES, IRMA?
OF COURSE, TARA! DON'T YOU THINK THAT LAST CLASS WAS REALLY ***SUPER***?
...
THE NUMBERS ARE SO ***FASCINATING***. THE RULES ARE ***INTENSE***, AND...
UM... THAT'S ENOUGH, IRMA.
HUH?
SHE'S GONE!
YEAH...SHE ***DANCED OFF***!

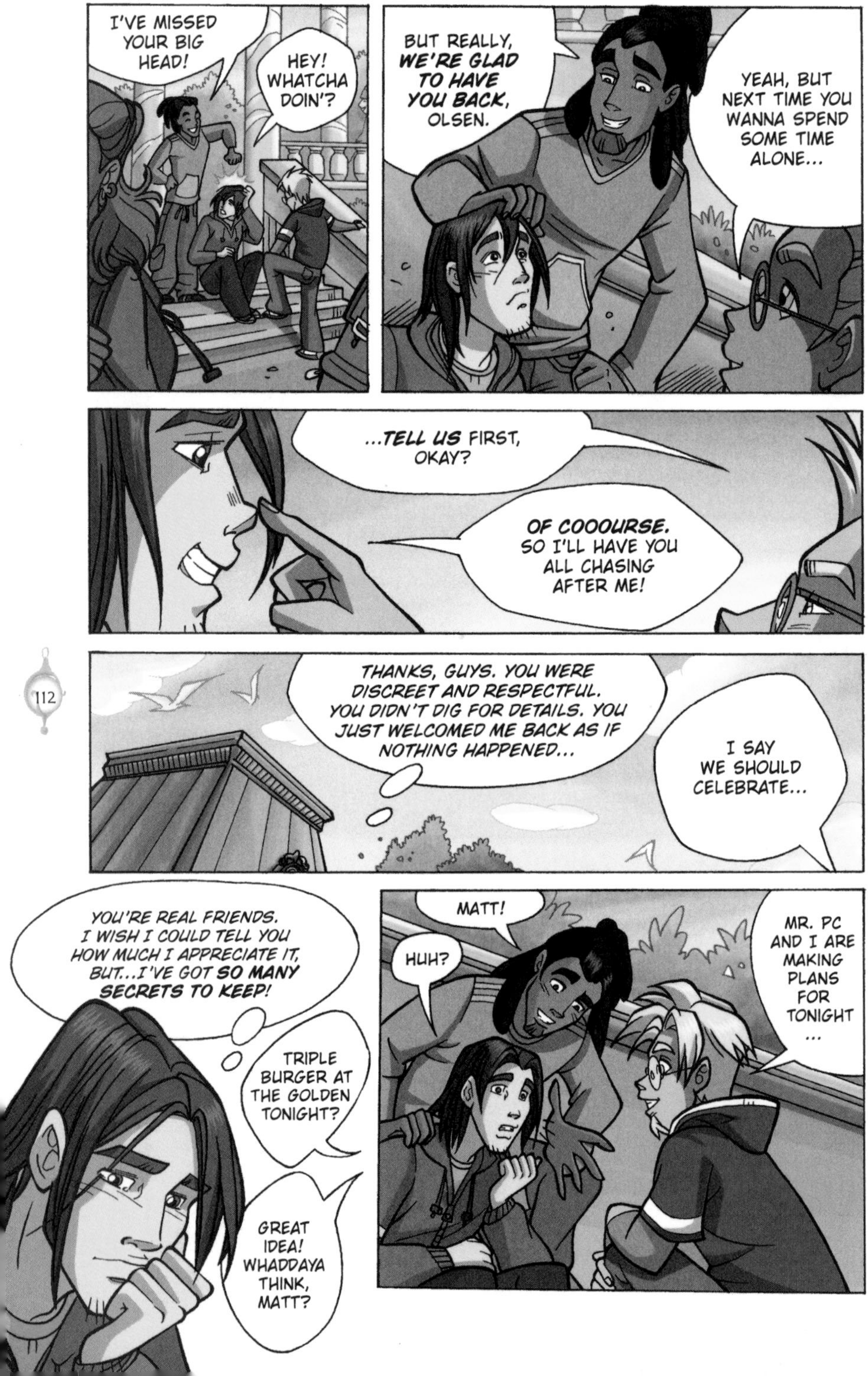
I'VE MISSED YOUR BIG HEAD!
HEY! WHATCHA DOIN'?
BUT REALLY, **WE'RE GLAD TO HAVE YOU BACK,** OLSEN.
YEAH, BUT NEXT TIME YOU WANNA SPEND SOME TIME ALONE...
...**TELL US** FIRST, OKAY?
OF COOOURSE. SO I'LL HAVE YOU ALL CHASING AFTER ME!
THANKS, GUYS. YOU WERE DISCREET AND RESPECTFUL. YOU DIDN'T DIG FOR DETAILS. YOU JUST WELCOMED ME BACK AS IF NOTHING HAPPENED...
I SAY WE SHOULD CELEBRATE...
YOU'RE REAL FRIENDS. I WISH I COULD TELL YOU HOW MUCH I APPRECIATE IT, BUT...I'VE GOT ***SO MANY SECRETS TO KEEP!***
TRIPLE BURGER AT THE GOLDEN TONIGHT?
GREAT IDEA! WHADDAYA THINK, MATT?
MATT!
HUH?
MR. PC AND I ARE MAKING PLANS FOR TONIGHT ...

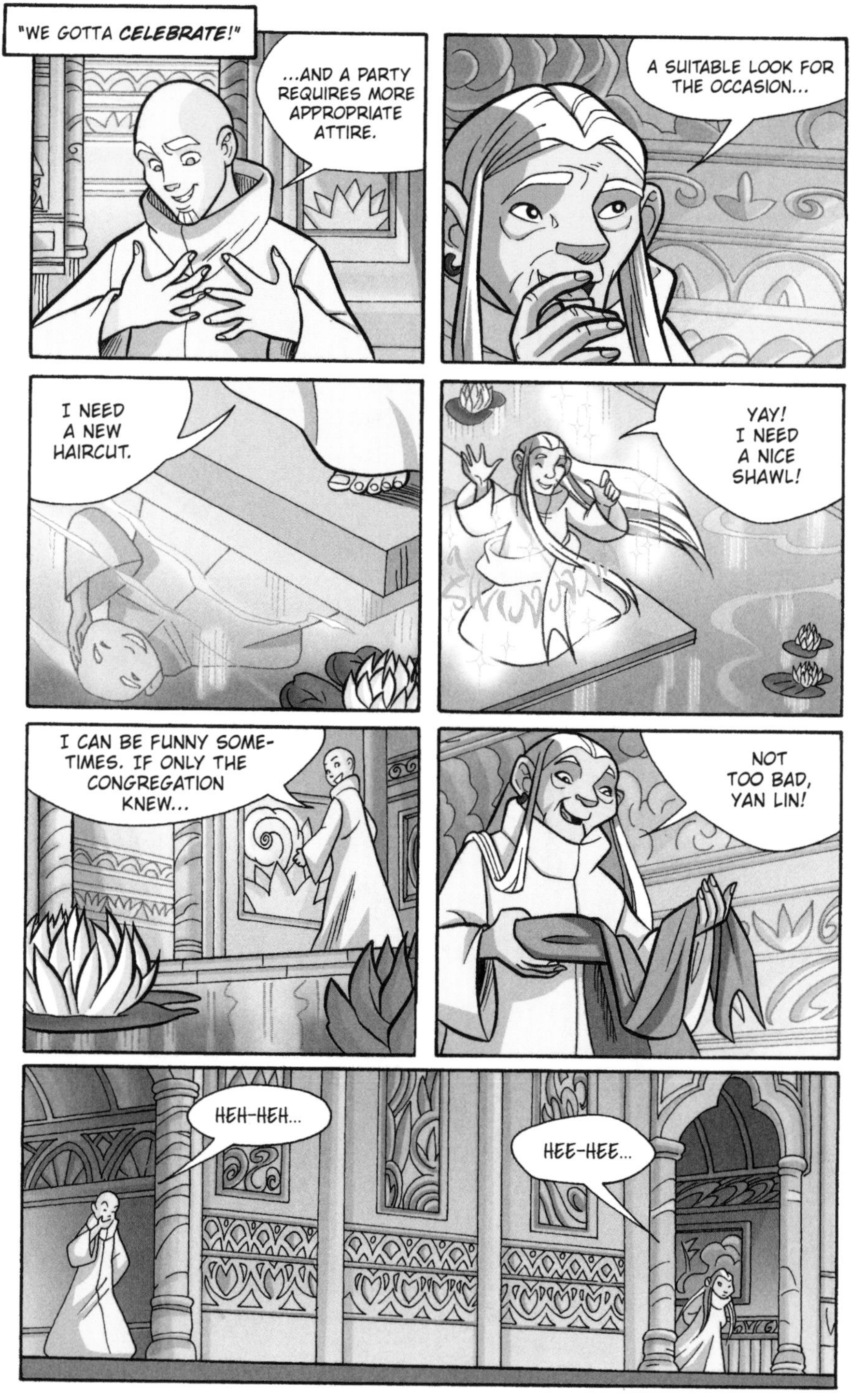
"WE GOTTA CELEBRATE!"
...AND A PARTY REQUIRES MORE APPROPRIATE ATTIRE.
A SUITABLE LOOK FOR THE OCCASION...
I NEED A NEW HAIRCUT.
YAY! I NEED A NICE SHAWL!
I CAN BE FUNNY SOMETIMES. IF ONLY THE CONGREGATION KNEW...
NOT TOO BAD, YAN LIN!
HEH-HEH...
HEE-HEE...

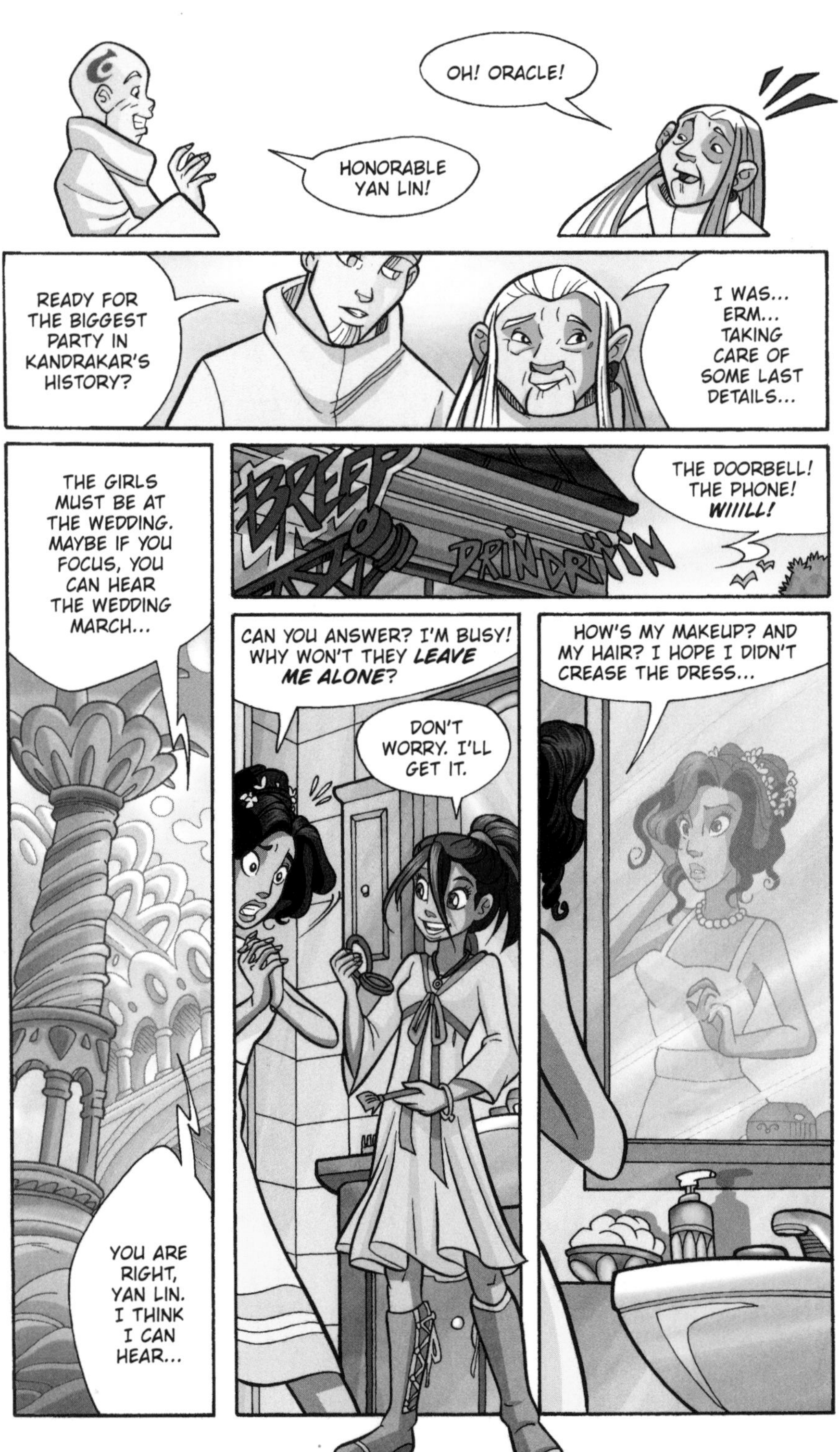

HONORABLE YAN LIN!
OH! ORACLE!
READY FOR THE BIGGEST PARTY IN KANDRAKAR'S HISTORY?
I WAS... ERM... TAKING CARE OF SOME LAST DETAILS...
THE GIRLS MUST BE AT THE WEDDING. MAYBE IF YOU FOCUS, YOU CAN HEAR THE WEDDING MARCH...
YOU ARE RIGHT, YAN LIN. I THINK I CAN HEAR...
BREEP
DRINDRIIIN
THE DOORBELL! THE PHONE! WIIILL!
CAN YOU ANSWER? I'M BUSY! WHY WON'T THEY LEAVE ME ALONE?
DON'T WORRY. I'LL GET IT.
HOW'S MY MAKEUP? AND MY HAIR? I HOPE I DIDN'T CREASE THE DRESS...

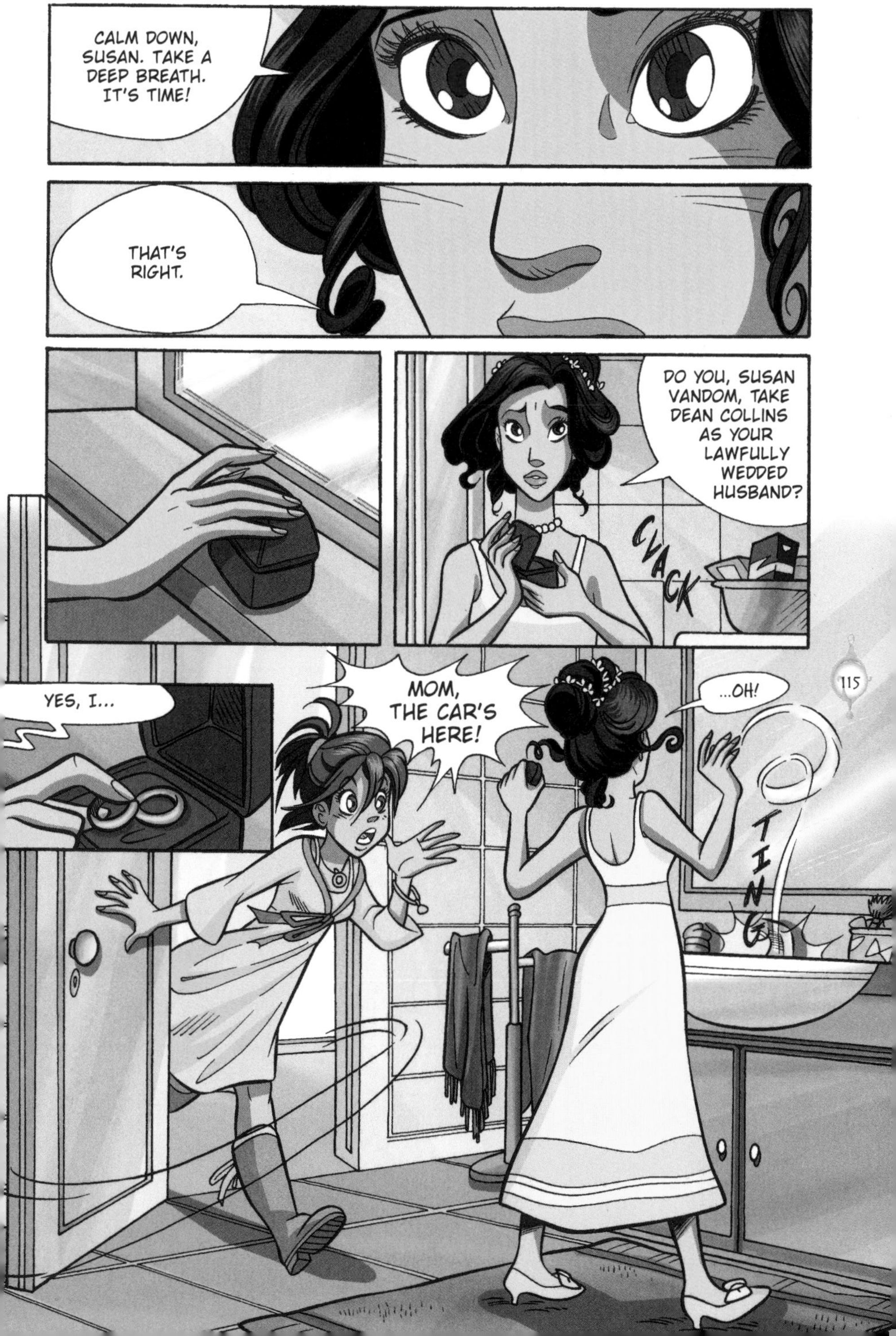
CALM DOWN, SUSAN. TAKE A DEEP BREATH. IT'S TIME!
THAT'S RIGHT.
DO YOU, SUSAN VANDOM, TAKE DEAN COLLINS AS YOUR LAWFULLY WEDDED HUSBAND?
CRACK
YES, I...
MOM, THE CAR'S HERE!
...OH!
TING

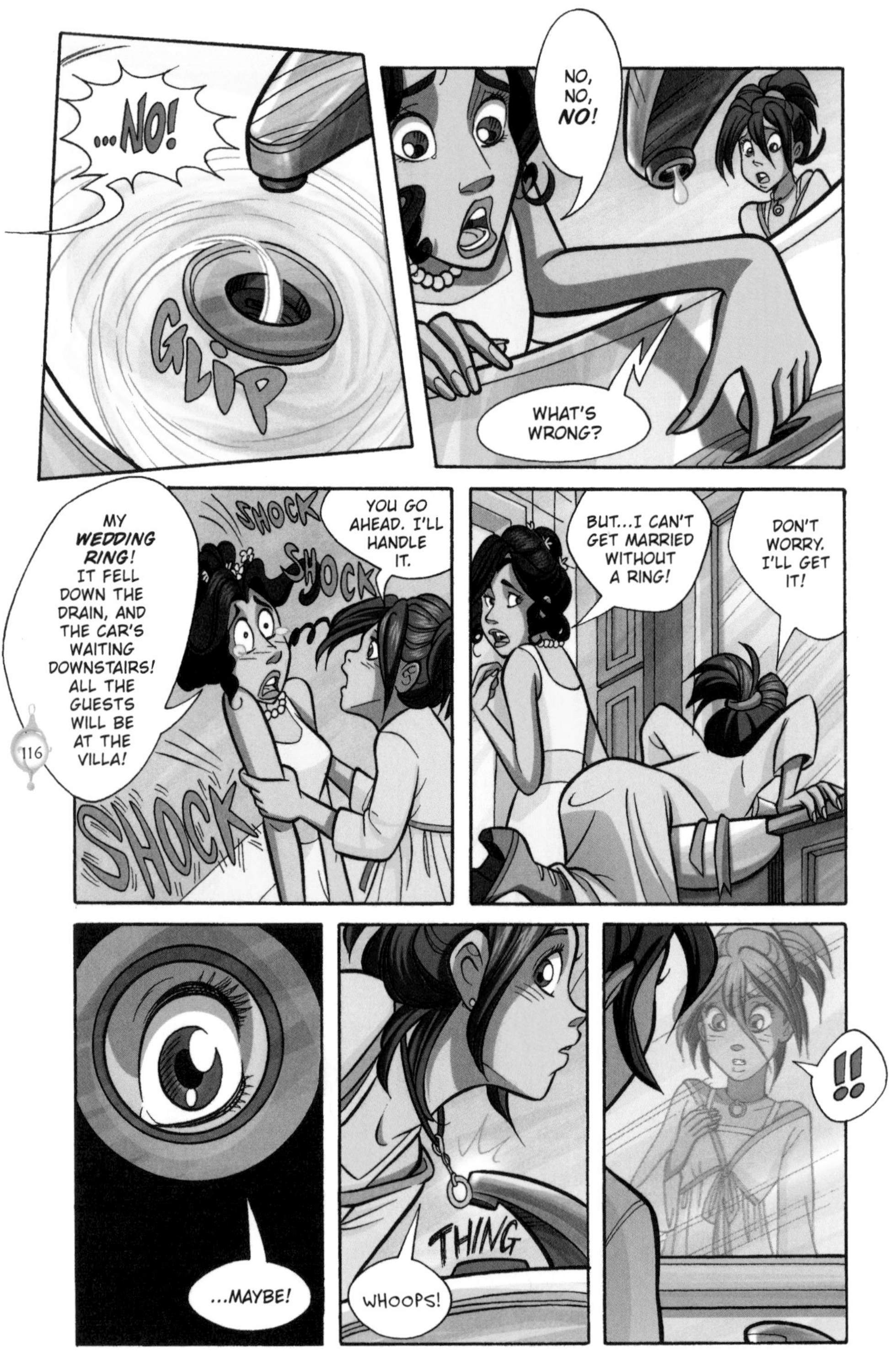
...NO!
GLIP
NO, NO, NO!
WHAT'S WRONG?
MY WEDDING RING! IT FELL DOWN THE DRAIN, AND THE CAR'S WAITING DOWNSTAIRS! ALL THE GUESTS WILL BE AT THE VILLA!
SHOCK
SHOCK
YOU GO AHEAD. I'LL HANDLE IT.
SHOCK
BUT...I CAN'T GET MARRIED WITHOUT A RING!
DON'T WORRY. I'LL GET IT!
...MAYBE!
THING
WHOOPS!
!!

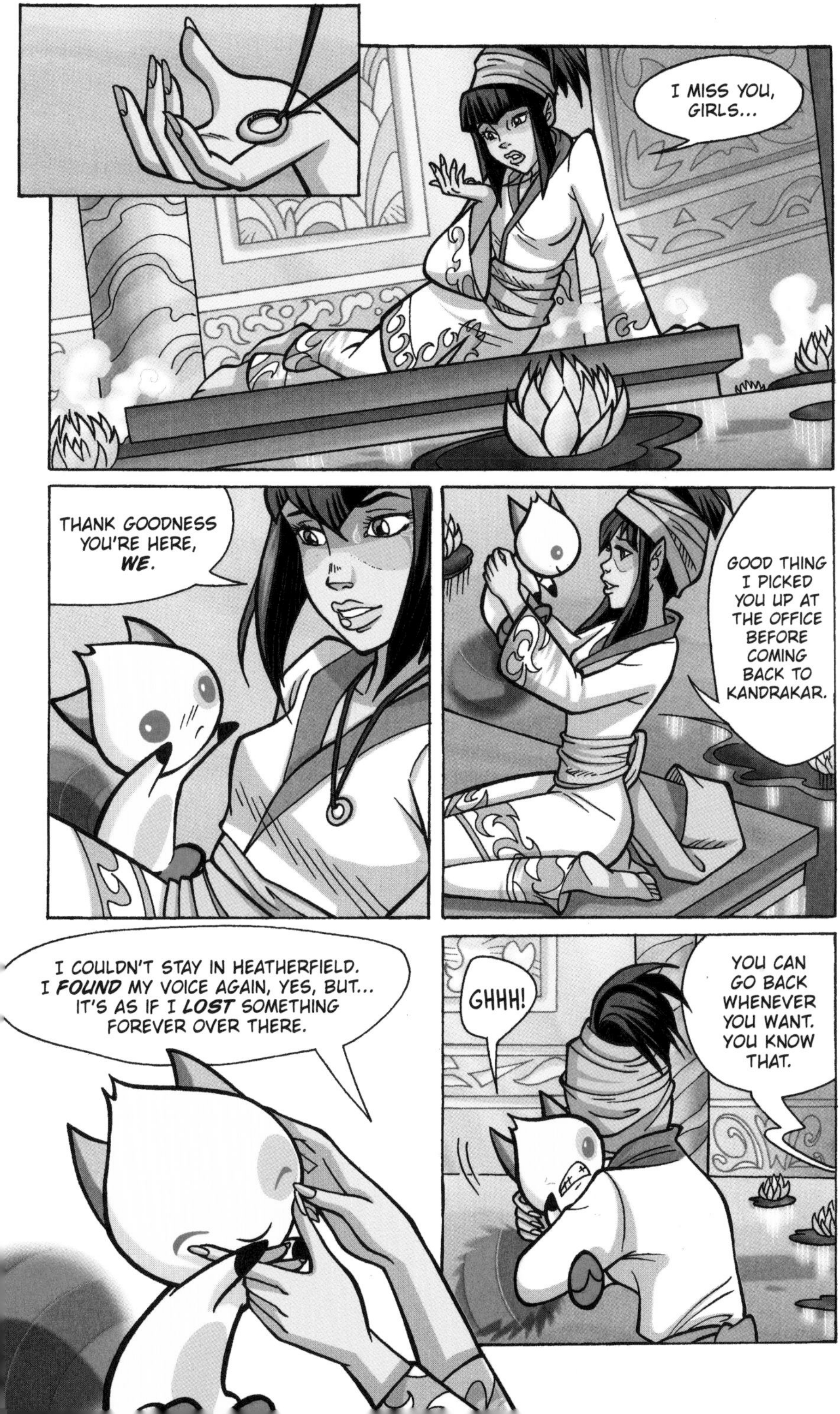

I MISS YOU, GIRLS...
THANK GOODNESS YOU'RE HERE, WE.
GOOD THING I PICKED YOU UP AT THE OFFICE BEFORE COMING BACK TO KANDRAKAR.
I COULDN'T STAY IN HEATHERFIELD. I FOUND MY VOICE AGAIN, YES, BUT... IT'S AS IF I LOST SOMETHING FOREVER OVER THERE.
GHHH!
YOU CAN GO BACK WHENEVER YOU WANT. YOU KNOW THAT.

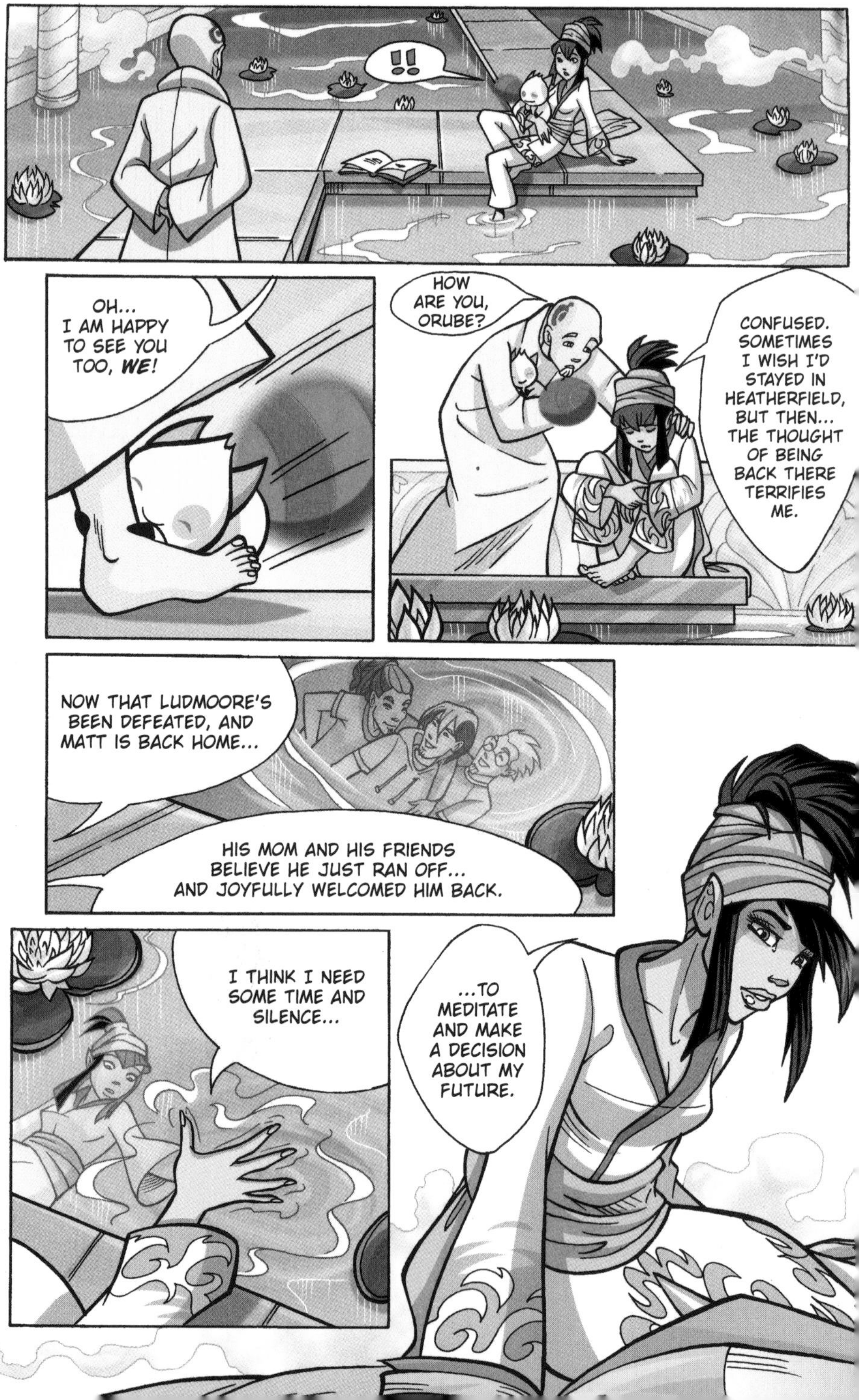
!!
OH... I AM HAPPY TO SEE YOU TOO, ***WE***!
HOW ARE YOU, ORUBE?
CONFUSED. SOMETIMES I WISH I'D STAYED IN HEATHERFIELD, BUT THEN... THE THOUGHT OF BEING BACK THERE TERRIFIES ME.
NOW THAT LUDMOORE'S BEEN DEFEATED, AND MATT IS BACK HOME...
HIS MOM AND HIS FRIENDS BELIEVE HE JUST RAN OFF... AND JOYFULLY WELCOMED HIM BACK.
I THINK I NEED SOME TIME AND SILENCE...
...TO MEDITATE AND MAKE A DECISION ABOUT MY FUTURE.

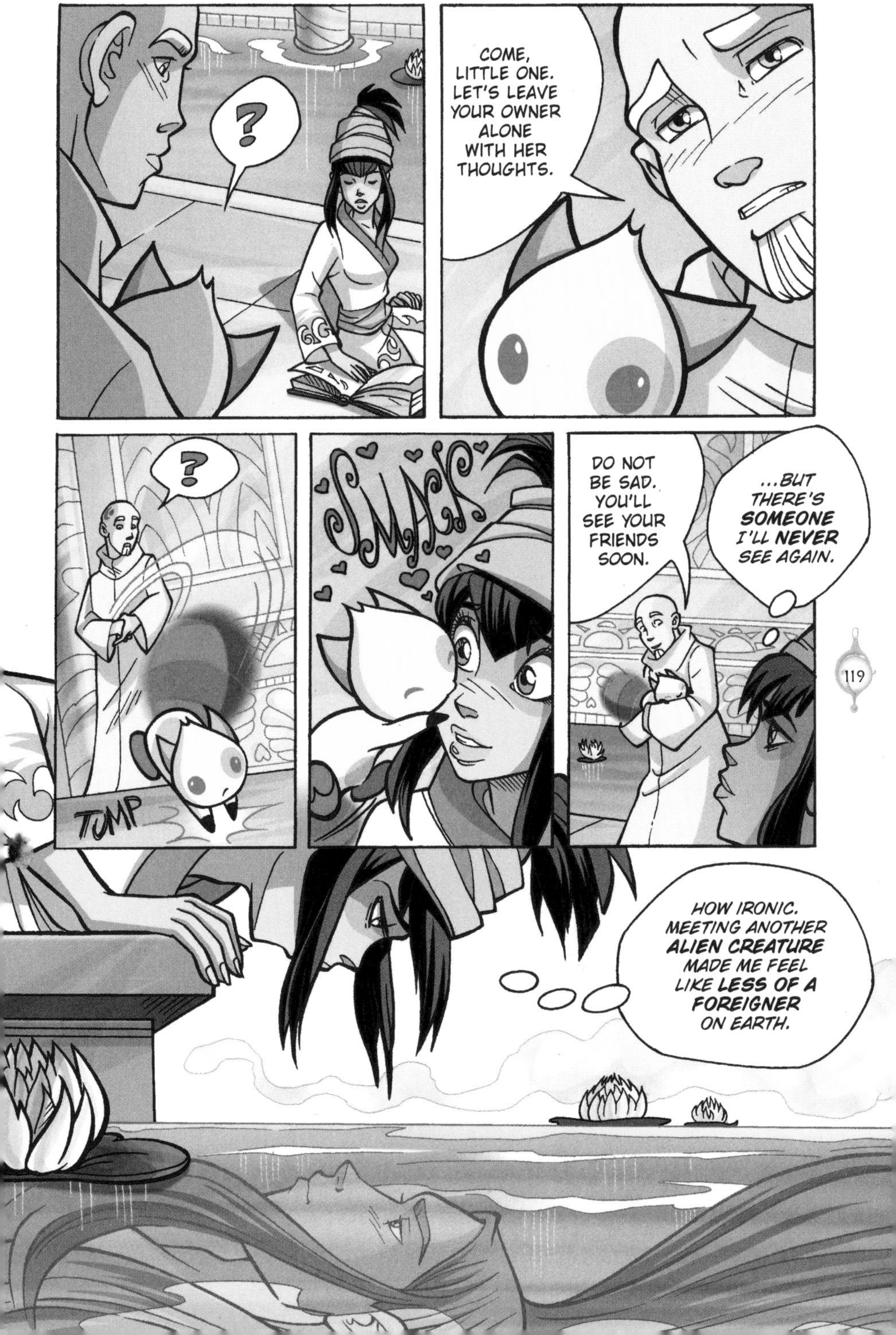
?
COME, LITTLE ONE. LET'S LEAVE YOUR OWNER ALONE WITH HER THOUGHTS.
?
TUMP
SMACK
DO NOT BE SAD. YOU'LL SEE YOUR FRIENDS SOON.
...BUT THERE'S **SOMEONE** I'LL **NEVER** SEE AGAIN.
HOW IRONIC. MEETING ANOTHER **ALIEN CREATURE** MADE ME FEEL LIKE **LESS OF A FOREIGNER** ON EARTH.

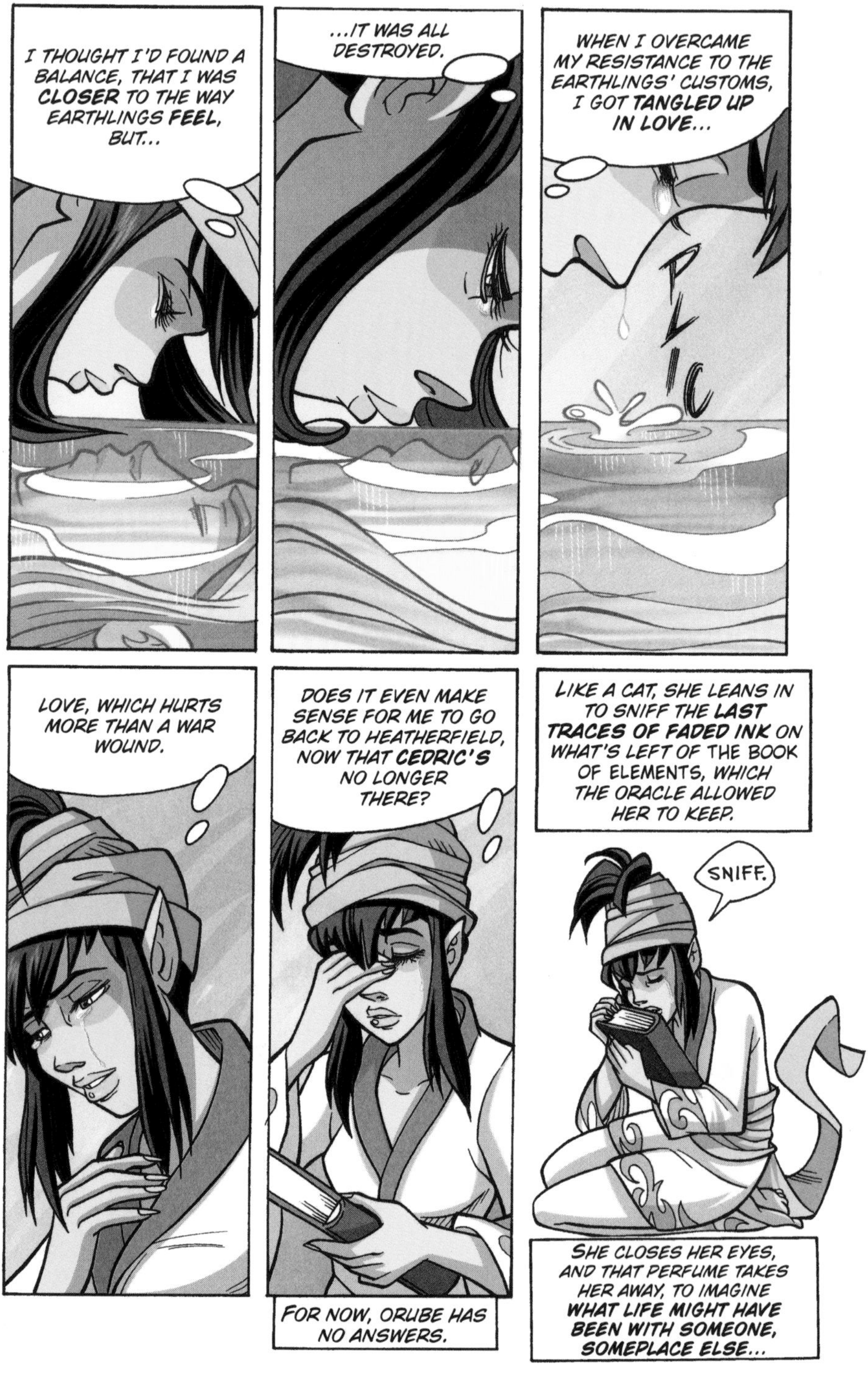
I THOUGHT I'D FOUND A BALANCE, THAT I WAS CLOSER TO THE WAY EARTHLINGS FEEL, BUT...
...IT WAS ALL DESTROYED.
WHEN I OVERCAME MY RESISTANCE TO THE EARTHLINGS' CUSTOMS, I GOT TANGLED UP IN LOVE...
PLIC
LOVE, WHICH HURTS MORE THAN A WAR WOUND.
DOES IT EVEN MAKE SENSE FOR ME TO GO BACK TO HEATHERFIELD, NOW THAT CEDRIC'S NO LONGER THERE?
FOR NOW, ORUBE HAS NO ANSWERS.
LIKE A CAT, SHE LEANS IN TO SNIFF THE LAST TRACES OF FADED INK ON WHAT'S LEFT OF THE BOOK OF ELEMENTS, WHICH THE ORACLE ALLOWED HER TO KEEP.
SNIFF.
SHE CLOSES HER EYES, AND THAT PERFUME TAKES HER AWAY, TO IMAGINE WHAT LIFE MIGHT HAVE BEEN WITH SOMEONE, SOMEPLACE ELSE...

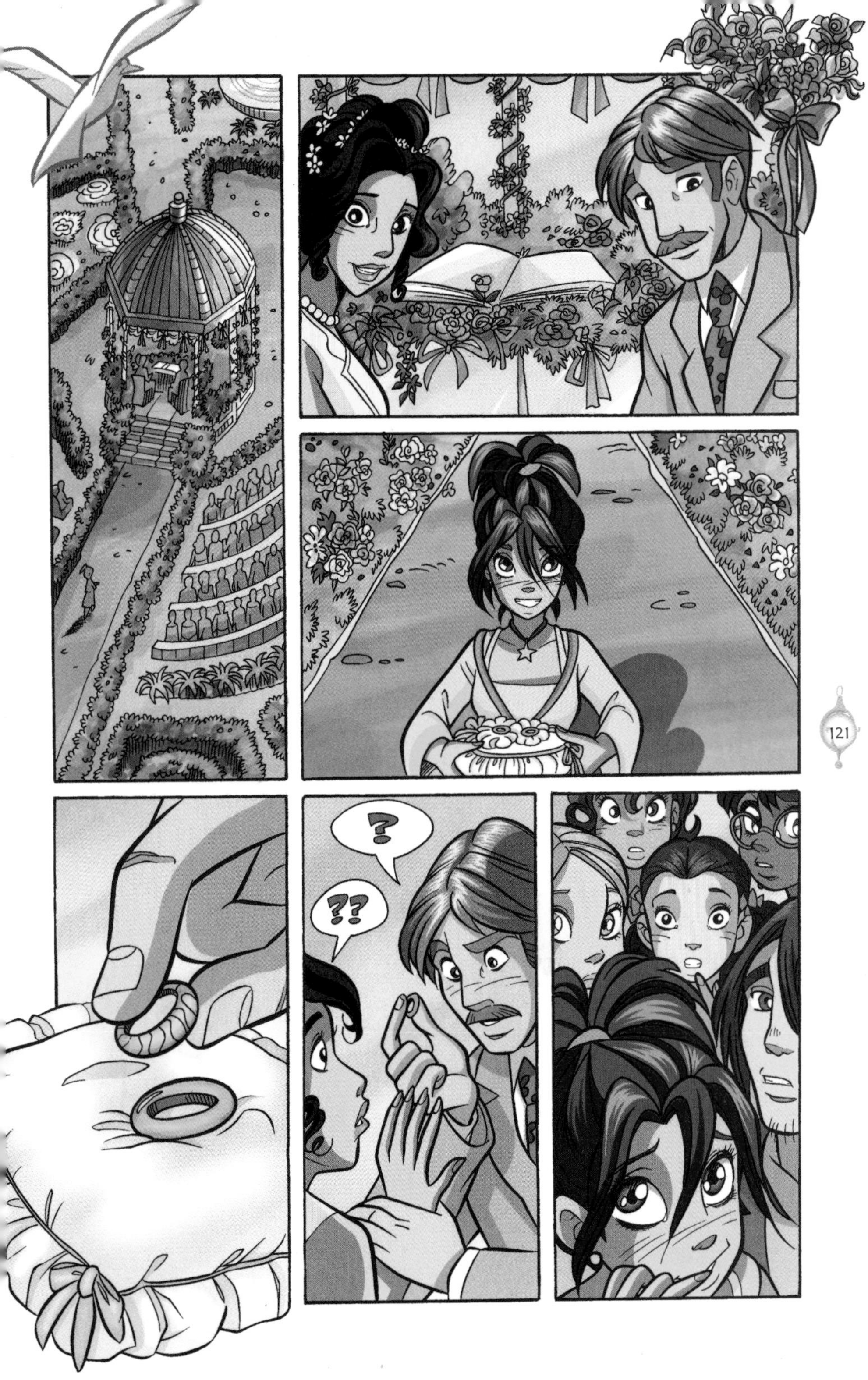
?
??

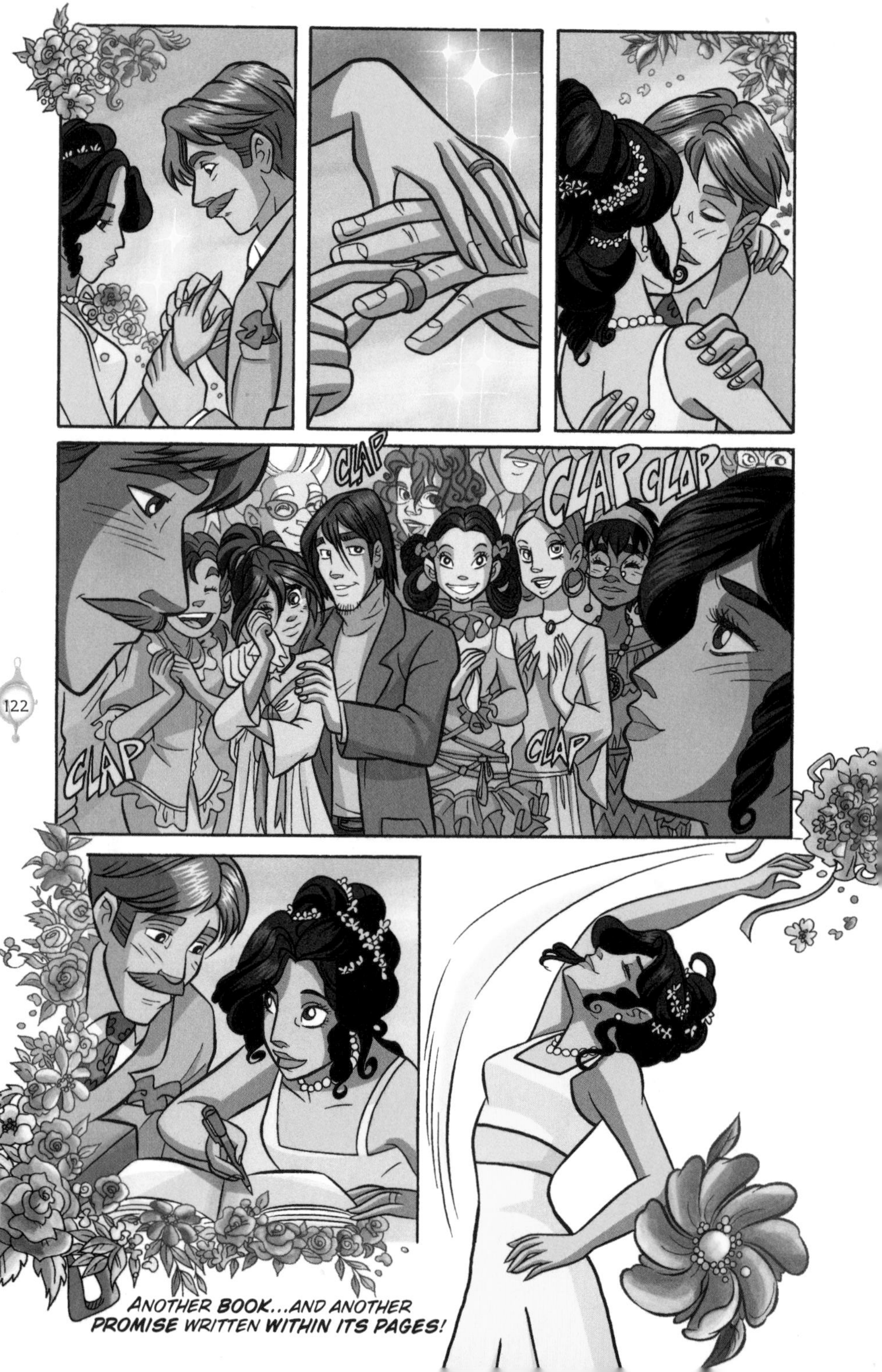

CLAP
CLAP CLAP
CLAP
CLAP
ANOTHER BOOK...AND ANOTHER PROMISE WRITTEN WITHIN ITS PAGES!

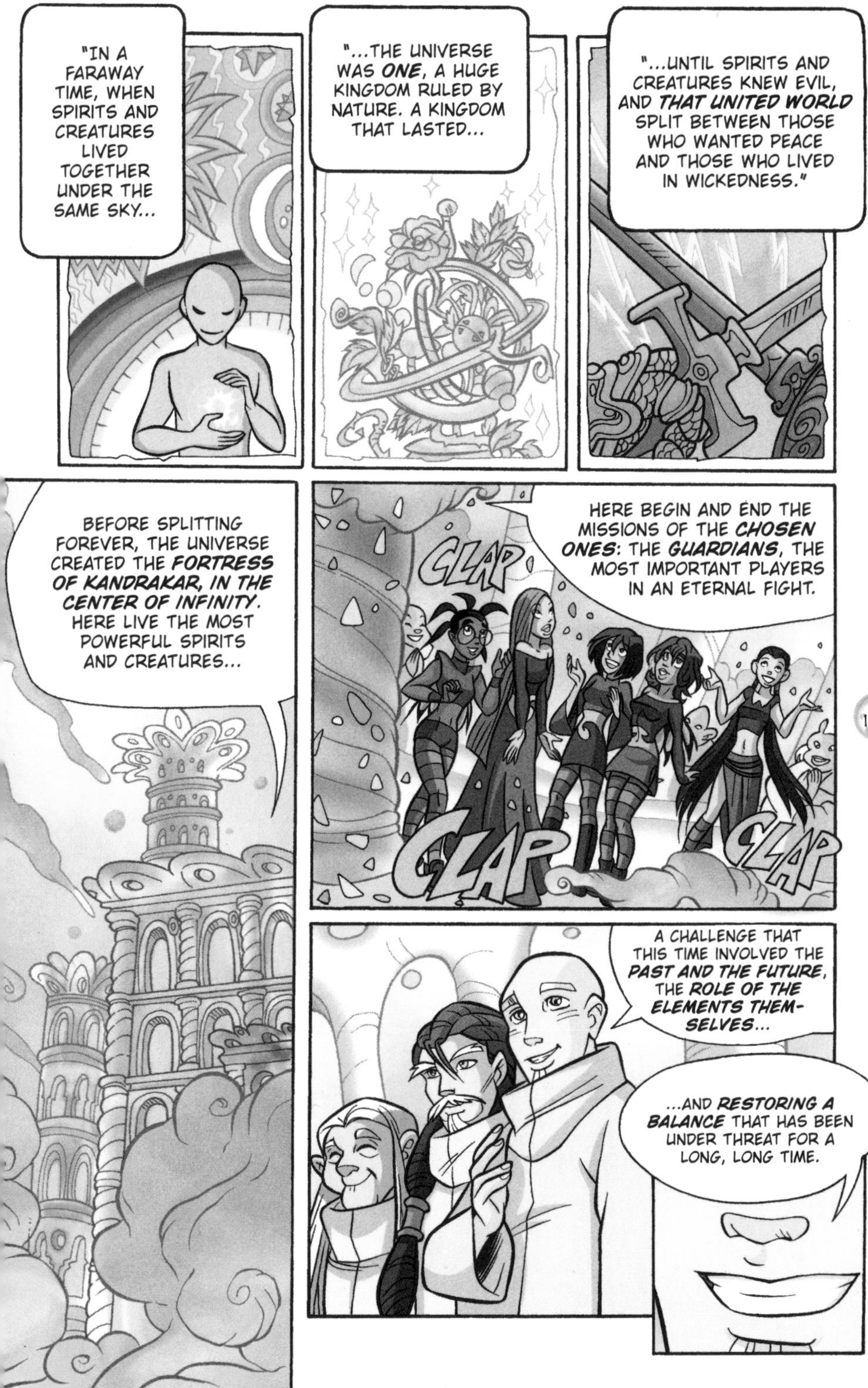
"IN A FARAWAY TIME, WHEN SPIRITS AND CREATURES LIVED TOGETHER UNDER THE SAME SKY...
"...THE UNIVERSE WAS *ONE*, A HUGE KINGDOM RULED BY NATURE. A KINGDOM THAT LASTED...
"...UNTIL SPIRITS AND CREATURES KNEW EVIL, AND *THAT UNITED WORLD* SPLIT BETWEEN THOSE WHO WANTED PEACE AND THOSE WHO LIVED IN WICKEDNESS."
BEFORE SPLITTING FOREVER, THE UNIVERSE CREATED THE *FORTRESS OF KANDRAKAR, IN THE CENTER OF INFINITY*. HERE LIVE THE MOST POWERFUL SPIRITS AND CREATURES...
HERE BEGIN AND END THE MISSIONS OF THE *CHOSEN ONES*: THE *GUARDIANS*, THE MOST IMPORTANT PLAYERS IN AN ETERNAL FIGHT.
CLAP
CLAP
CLAP
A CHALLENGE THAT THIS TIME INVOLVED THE *PAST AND THE FUTURE*, THE *ROLE OF THE ELEMENTS THEMSELVES*...
...AND *RESTORING A BALANCE* THAT HAS BEEN UNDER THREAT FOR A LONG, LONG TIME.

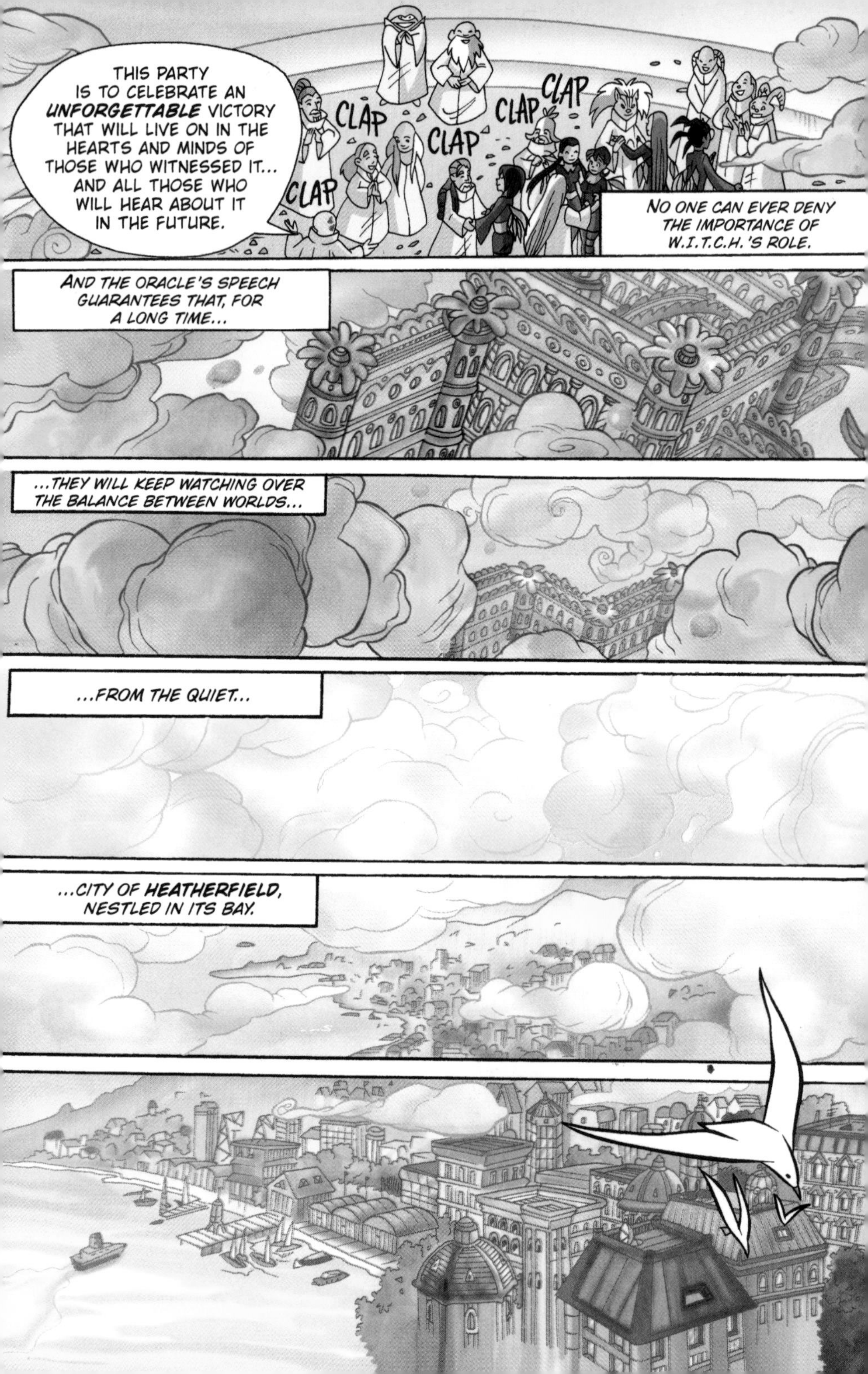

THIS PARTY IS TO CELEBRATE AN UNFORGETTABLE VICTORY THAT WILL LIVE ON IN THE HEARTS AND MINDS OF THOSE WHO WITNESSED IT... AND ALL THOSE WHO WILL HEAR ABOUT IT IN THE FUTURE.
CLAP
CLAP
CLAP
CLAP
CLAP
NO ONE CAN EVER DENY THE IMPORTANCE OF W.I.T.C.H.'S ROLE.
AND THE ORACLE'S SPEECH GUARANTEES THAT, FOR A LONG TIME...
...THEY WILL KEEP WATCHING OVER THE BALANCE BETWEEN WORLDS...
...FROM THE QUIET...
...CITY OF HEATHERFIELD, NESTLED IN ITS BAY.

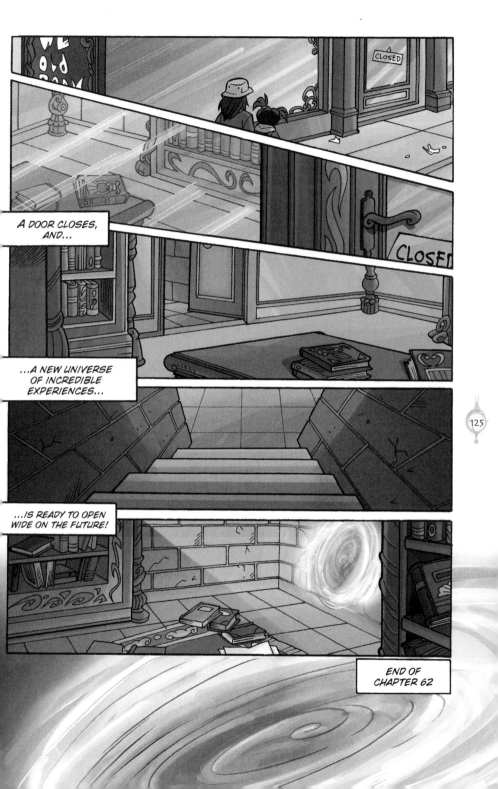

CLOSED

A DOOR CLOSES,
AND...

CLOSED

...A NEW UNIVERSE
OF INCREDIBLE
EXPERIENCES...

125

...IS READY TO OPEN
WIDE ON THE FUTURE!

END OF
CHAPTER 62

W.i.t.c.h.

Will Irma Taranee Cornelia Hay Lin

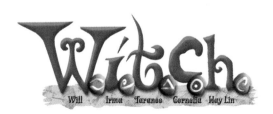

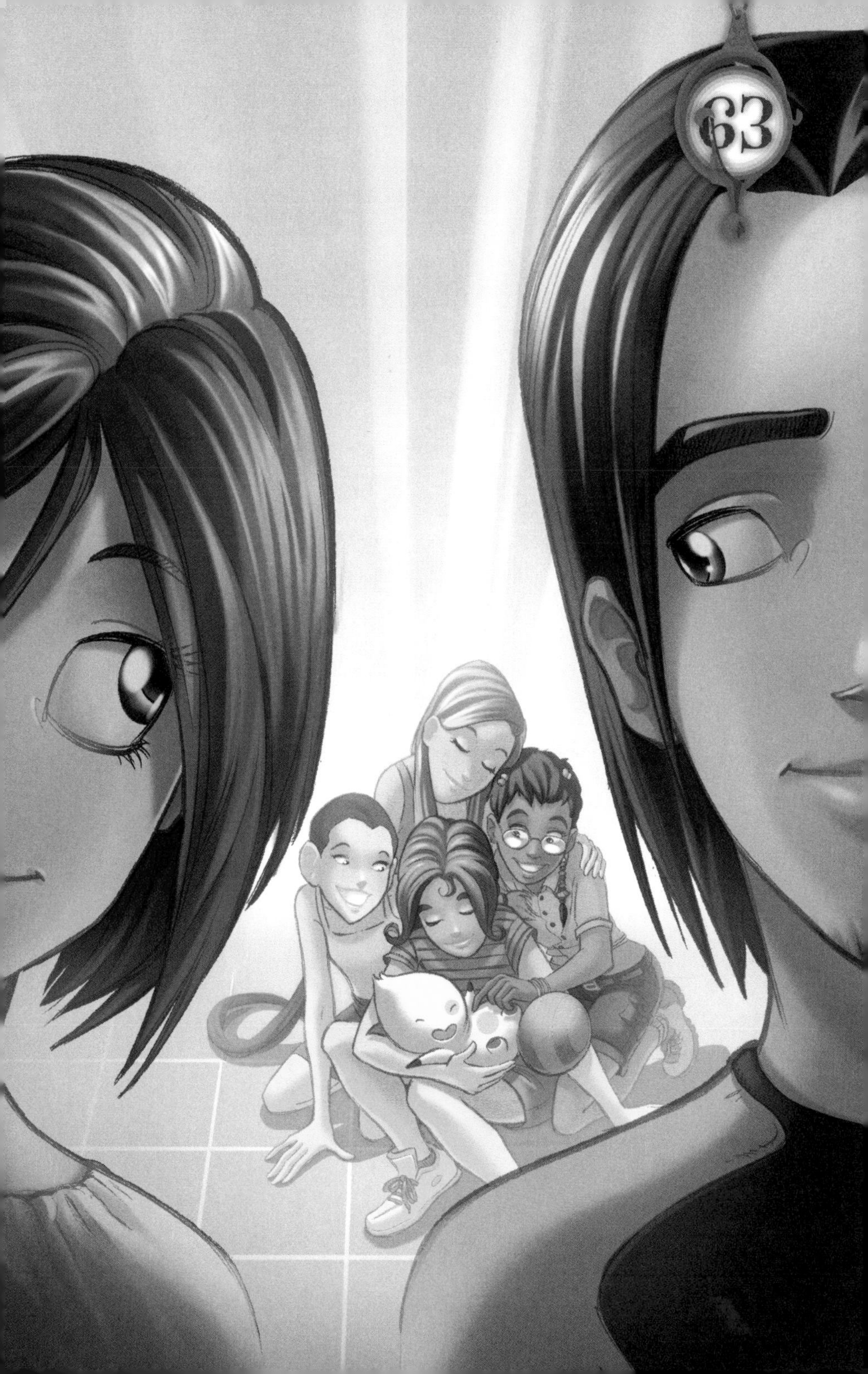
63

Arrivals and Departures

"This isn't farewell... just see you later!"

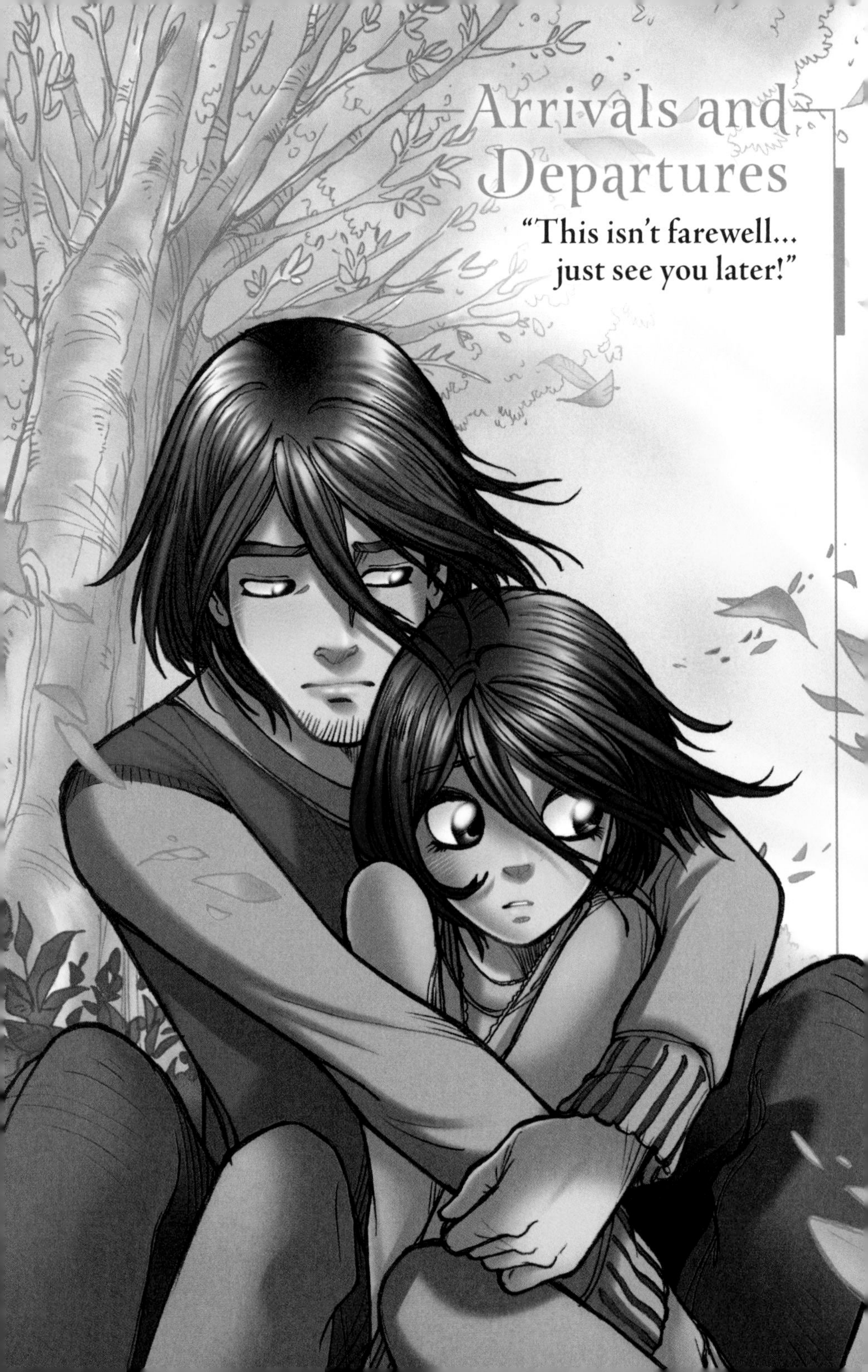

W.i.t.c.h.

Will Irma Taranee Cornelia Hay Lin

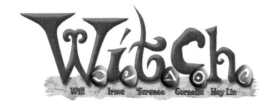

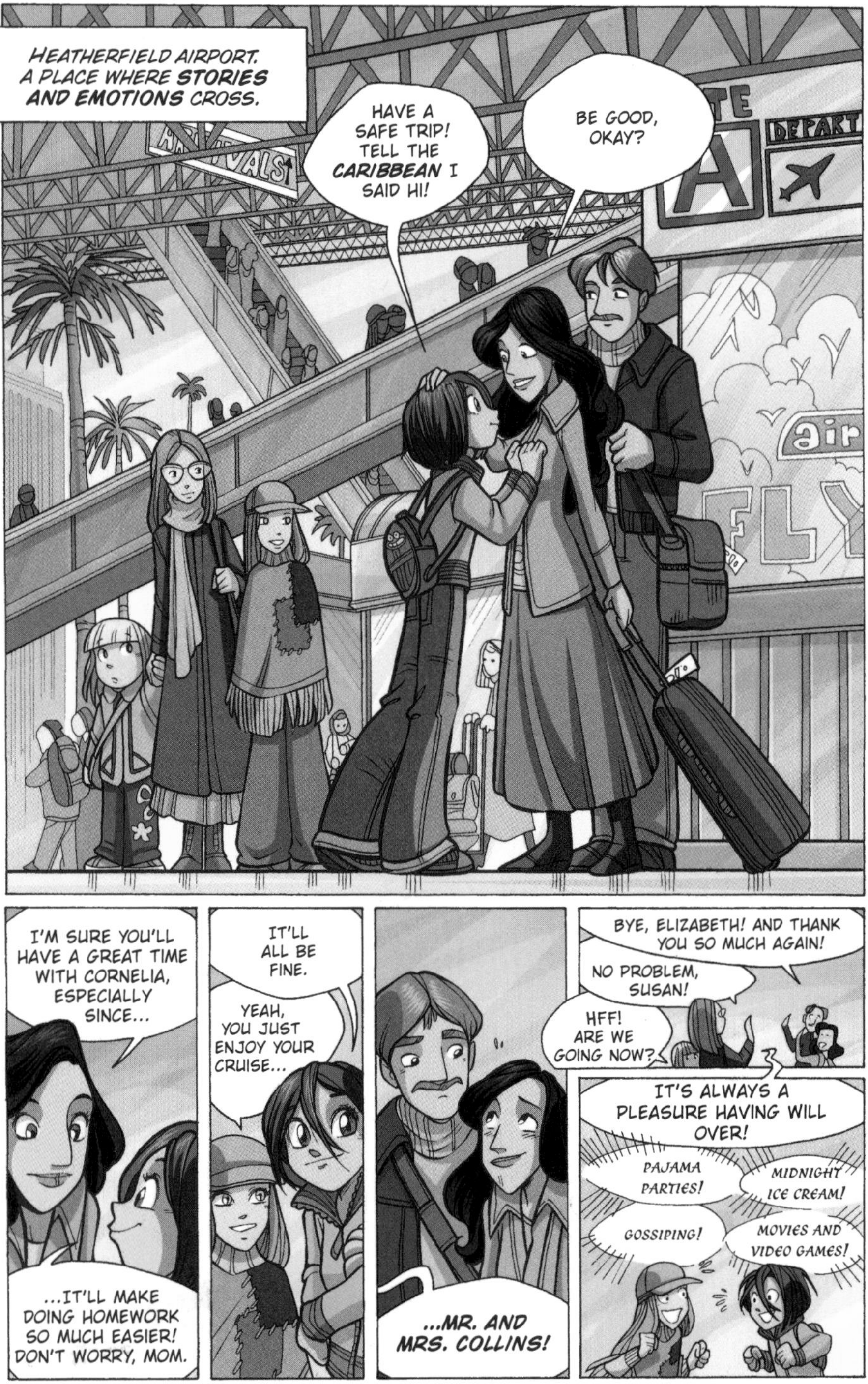

HEATHERFIELD AIRPORT. A PLACE WHERE **STORIES AND EMOTIONS** CROSS.
HAVE A SAFE TRIP! TELL THE **CARIBBEAN** I SAID HI!
BE GOOD, OKAY?
ARRIVALS
DEPART
A
air
FLY
I'M SURE YOU'LL HAVE A GREAT TIME WITH CORNELIA, ESPECIALLY SINCE...
...IT'LL MAKE DOING HOMEWORK SO MUCH EASIER! DON'T WORRY, MOM.
IT'LL ALL BE FINE.
YEAH, YOU JUST ENJOY YOUR CRUISE...
...MR. AND MRS. COLLINS!
BYE, ELIZABETH! AND THANK YOU SO MUCH AGAIN!
NO PROBLEM, SUSAN!
HFF! ARE WE GOING NOW?
IT'S ALWAYS A PLEASURE HAVING WILL OVER!
PAJAMA PARTIES!
MIDNIGHT ICE CREAM!
GOSSIPING!
MOVIES AND VIDEO GAMES!

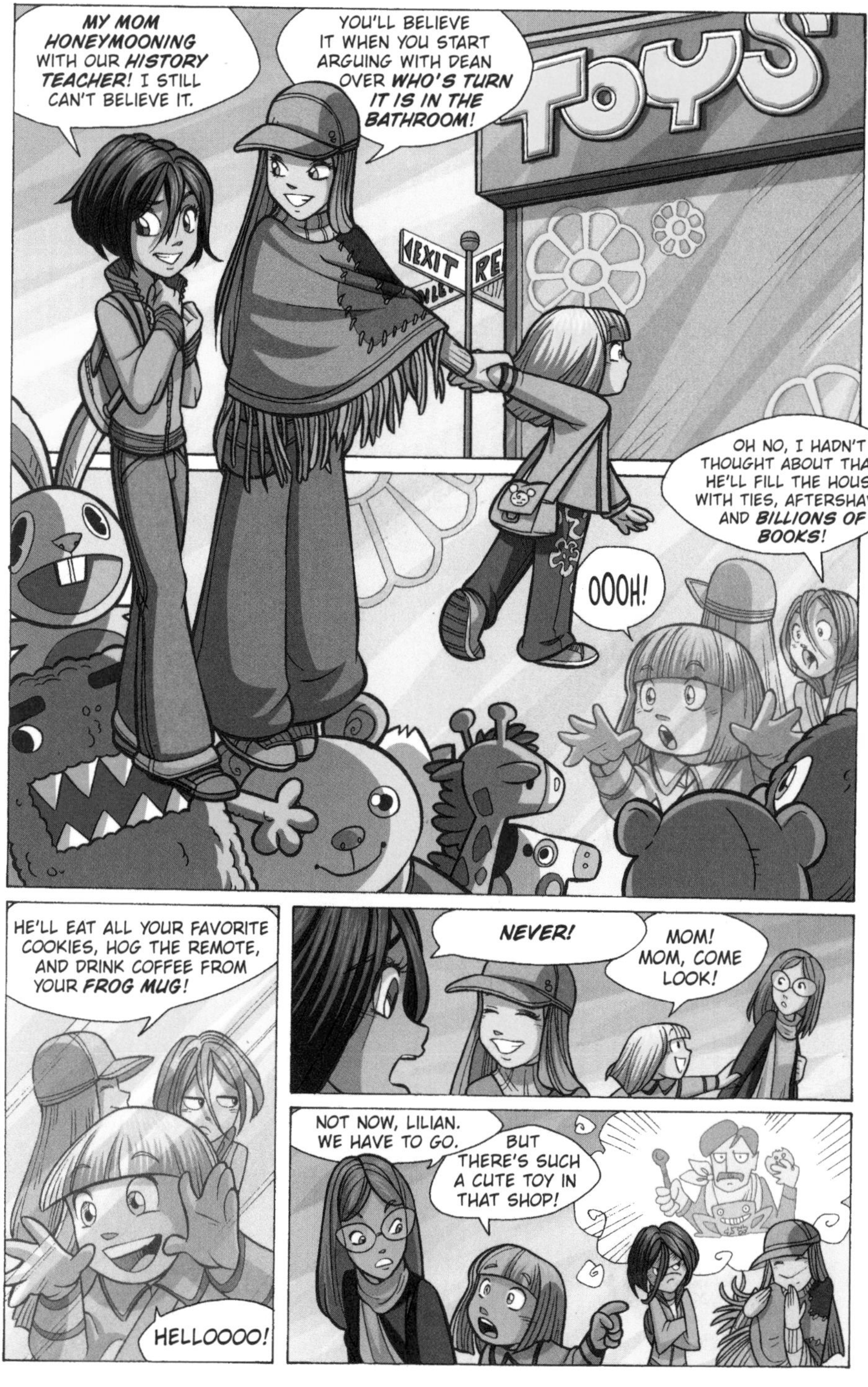
MY MOM HONEYMOONING WITH OUR HISTORY TEACHER! I STILL CAN'T BELIEVE IT.
YOU'LL BELIEVE IT WHEN YOU START ARGUING WITH DEAN OVER WHO'S TURN IT IS IN THE BATHROOM!
TOYS
EXIT
OH NO, I HADN'T THOUGHT ABOUT THAT! HE'LL FILL THE HOUSE WITH TIES, AFTERSHAVE, AND BILLIONS OF BOOKS!
OOOH!
HE'LL EAT ALL YOUR FAVORITE COOKIES, HOG THE REMOTE, AND DRINK COFFEE FROM YOUR FROG MUG!
HELLOOOO!
NEVER!
MOM! MOM, COME LOOK!
NOT NOW, LILIAN. WE HAVE TO GO.
BUT THERE'S SUCH A CUTE TOY IN THAT SHOP!

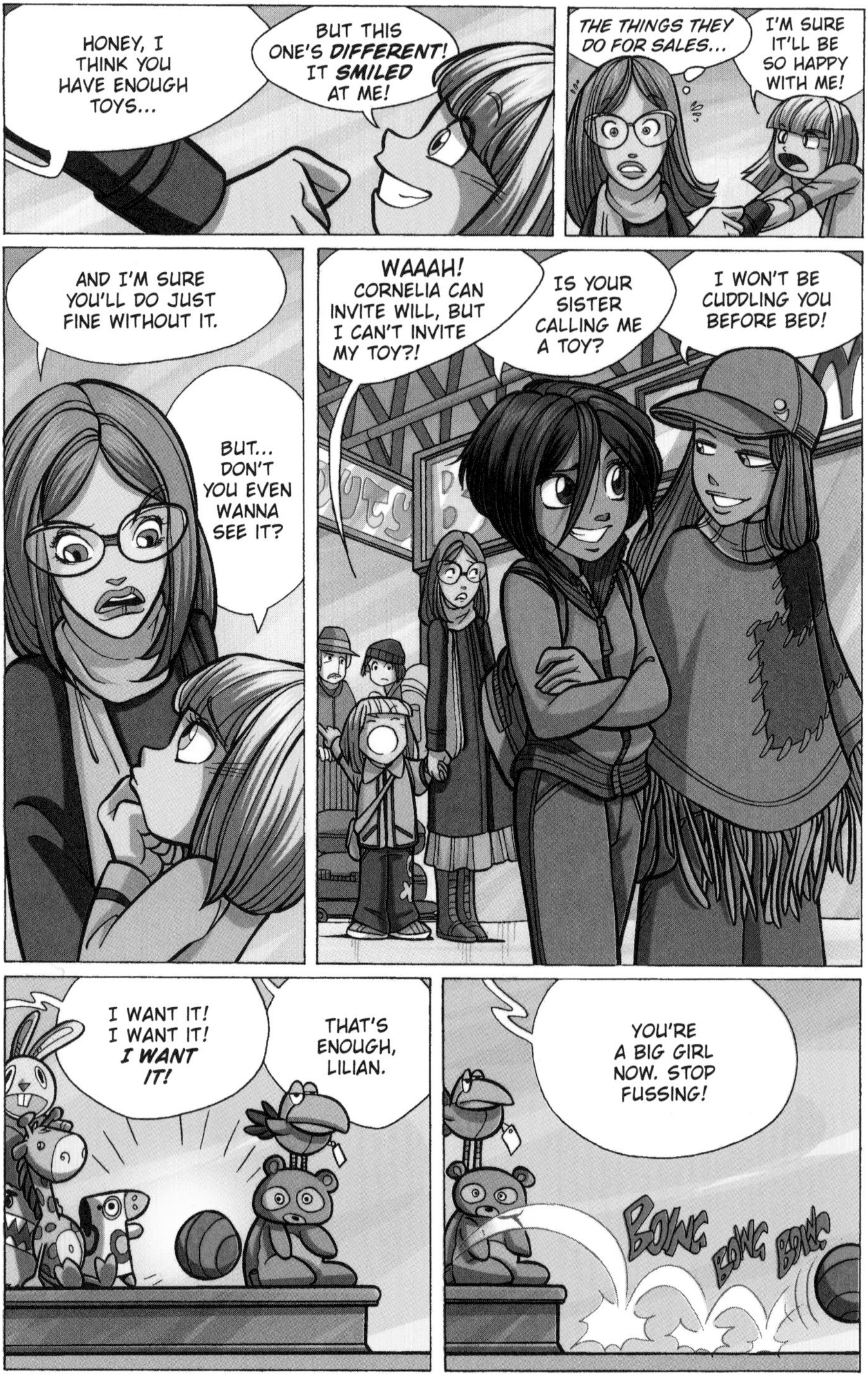

HONEY, I THINK YOU HAVE ENOUGH TOYS...
BUT THIS ONE'S ***DIFFERENT***! IT ***SMILED*** AT ME!
THE THINGS THEY DO FOR SALES...
I'M SURE IT'LL BE SO HAPPY WITH ME!
AND I'M SURE YOU'LL DO JUST FINE WITHOUT IT.
BUT... DON'T YOU EVEN WANNA SEE IT?
WAAAH! CORNELIA CAN INVITE WILL, BUT I CAN'T INVITE MY TOY?!
IS YOUR SISTER CALLING ME A TOY?
I WON'T BE CUDDLING YOU BEFORE BED!
I WANT IT! I WANT IT! ***I WANT IT!***
THAT'S ENOUGH, LILIAN.
YOU'RE A BIG GIRL NOW. STOP FUSSING!
BOING
BOING
BOING

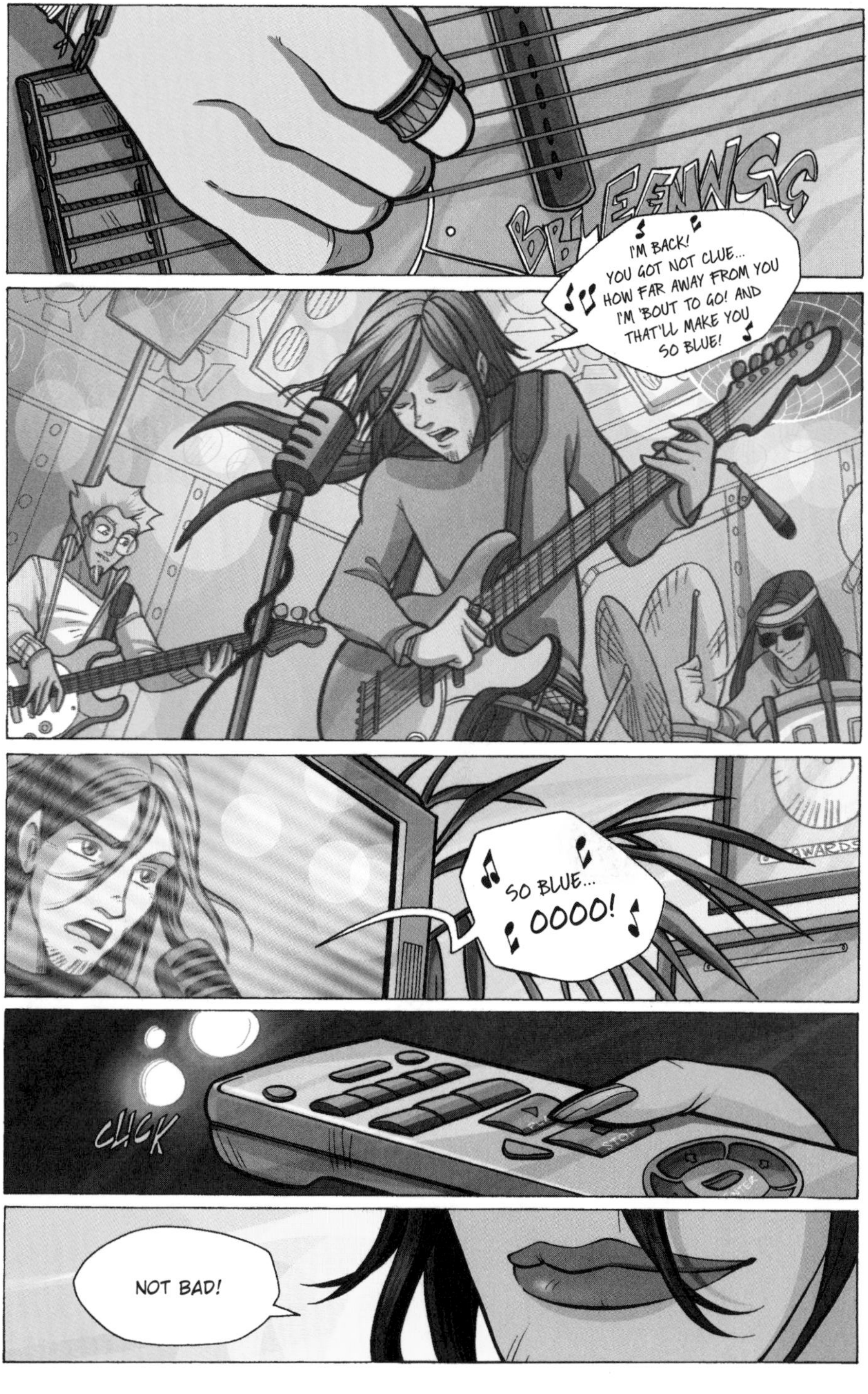
BBLEENNGG
I'M BACK! YOU GOT NOT CLUE... HOW FAR AWAY FROM YOU I'M 'BOUT TO GO! AND THAT'LL MAKE YOU SO BLUE!
SO BLUE... OOOO!
AWARDS
CLICK
STOP
NOT BAD!

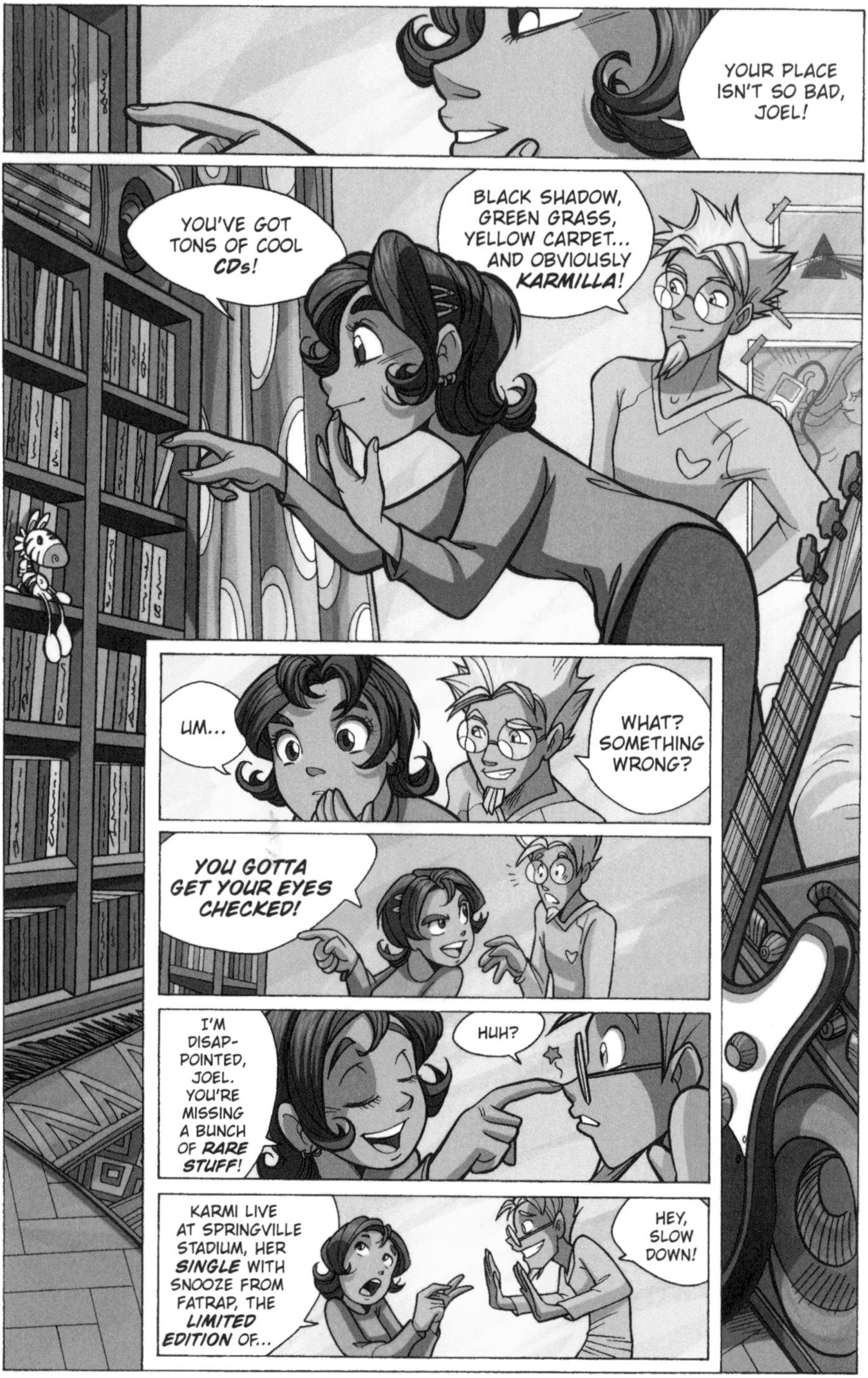
YOUR PLACE ISN'T SO BAD, JOEL!
YOU'VE GOT TONS OF COOL CDs!
BLACK SHADOW, GREEN GRASS, YELLOW CARPET... AND OBVIOUSLY KARMILLA!
UM...
WHAT? SOMETHING WRONG?
YOU GOTTA GET YOUR EYES CHECKED!
I'M DISAPPOINTED, JOEL. YOU'RE MISSING A BUNCH OF RARE STUFF!
HUH?
KARMI LIVE AT SPRINGVILLE STADIUM, HER SINGLE WITH SNOOZE FROM FATRAP, THE LIMITED EDITION OF...
HEY, SLOW DOWN!

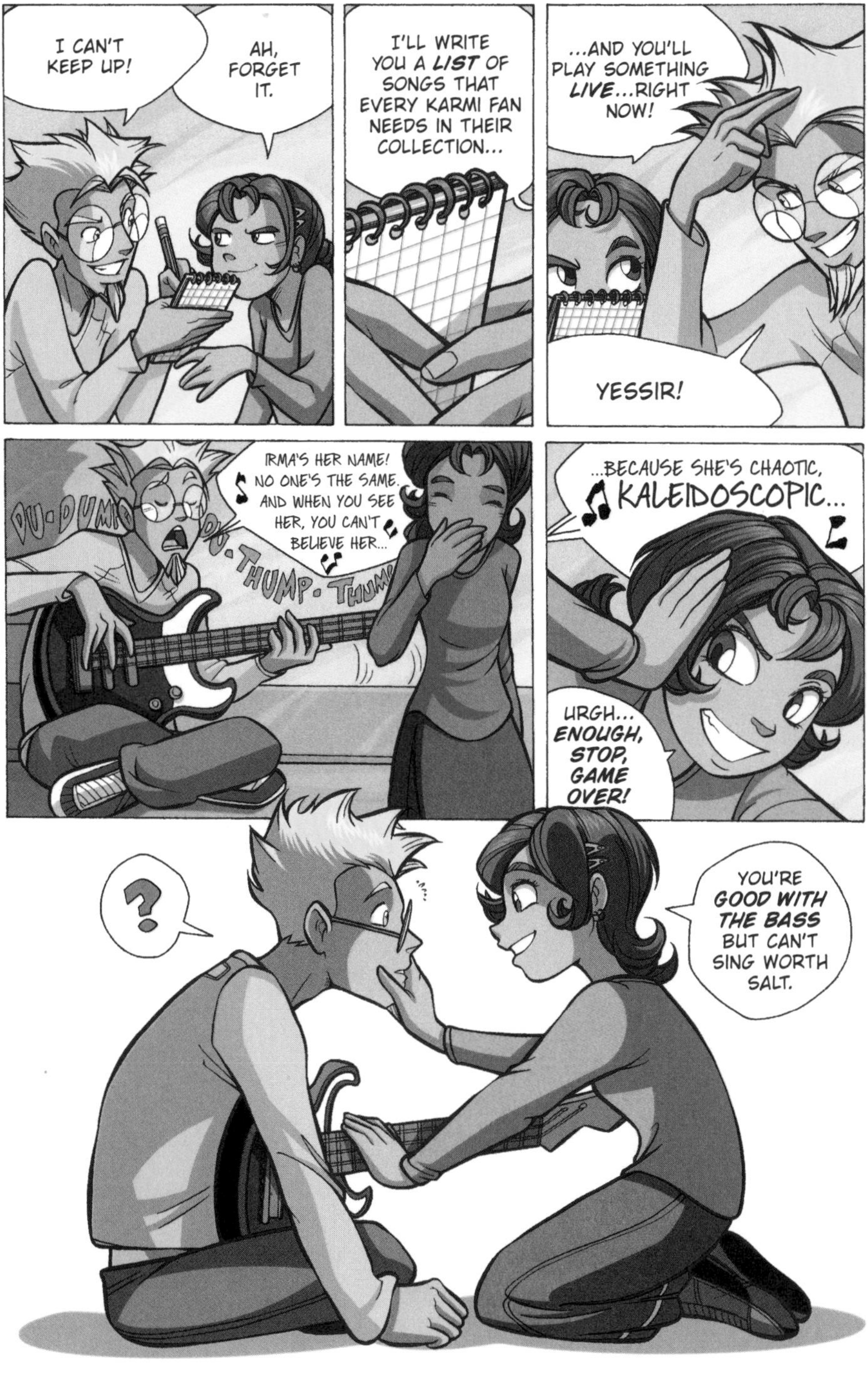

I CAN'T KEEP UP!
AH, FORGET IT.
I'LL WRITE YOU A LIST OF SONGS THAT EVERY KARMI FAN NEEDS IN THEIR COLLECTION...
...AND YOU'LL PLAY SOMETHING LIVE...RIGHT NOW!
YESSIR!
DU-DUM
DU-THUMP-THUMP-THUMP
IRMA'S HER NAME! NO ONE'S THE SAME. AND WHEN YOU SEE HER, YOU CAN'T BELIEVE HER...
...BECAUSE SHE'S CHAOTIC, KALEIDOSCOPIC...
URGH... ENOUGH, STOP, GAME OVER!
?
YOU'RE GOOD WITH THE BASS BUT CAN'T SING WORTH SALT.

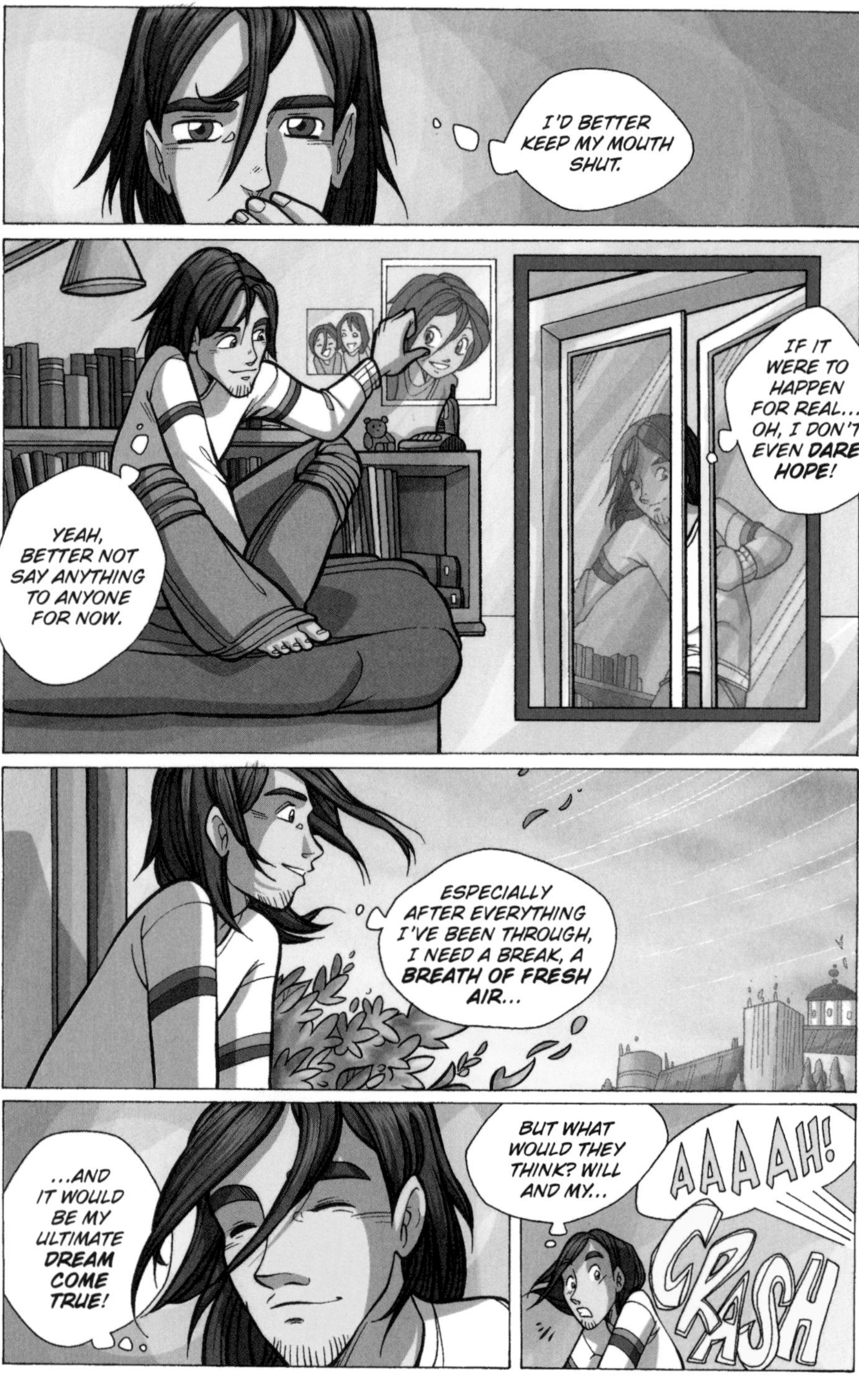

I'D BETTER KEEP MY MOUTH SHUT.
YEAH, BETTER NOT SAY ANYTHING TO ANYONE FOR NOW.
IF IT WERE TO HAPPEN FOR REAL... OH, I DON'T EVEN DARE HOPE!
ESPECIALLY AFTER EVERYTHING I'VE BEEN THROUGH, I NEED A BREAK, A BREATH OF FRESH AIR...
...AND IT WOULD BE MY ULTIMATE DREAM COME TRUE!
BUT WHAT WOULD THEY THINK? WILL AND MY...
AAAAH!
CRASH

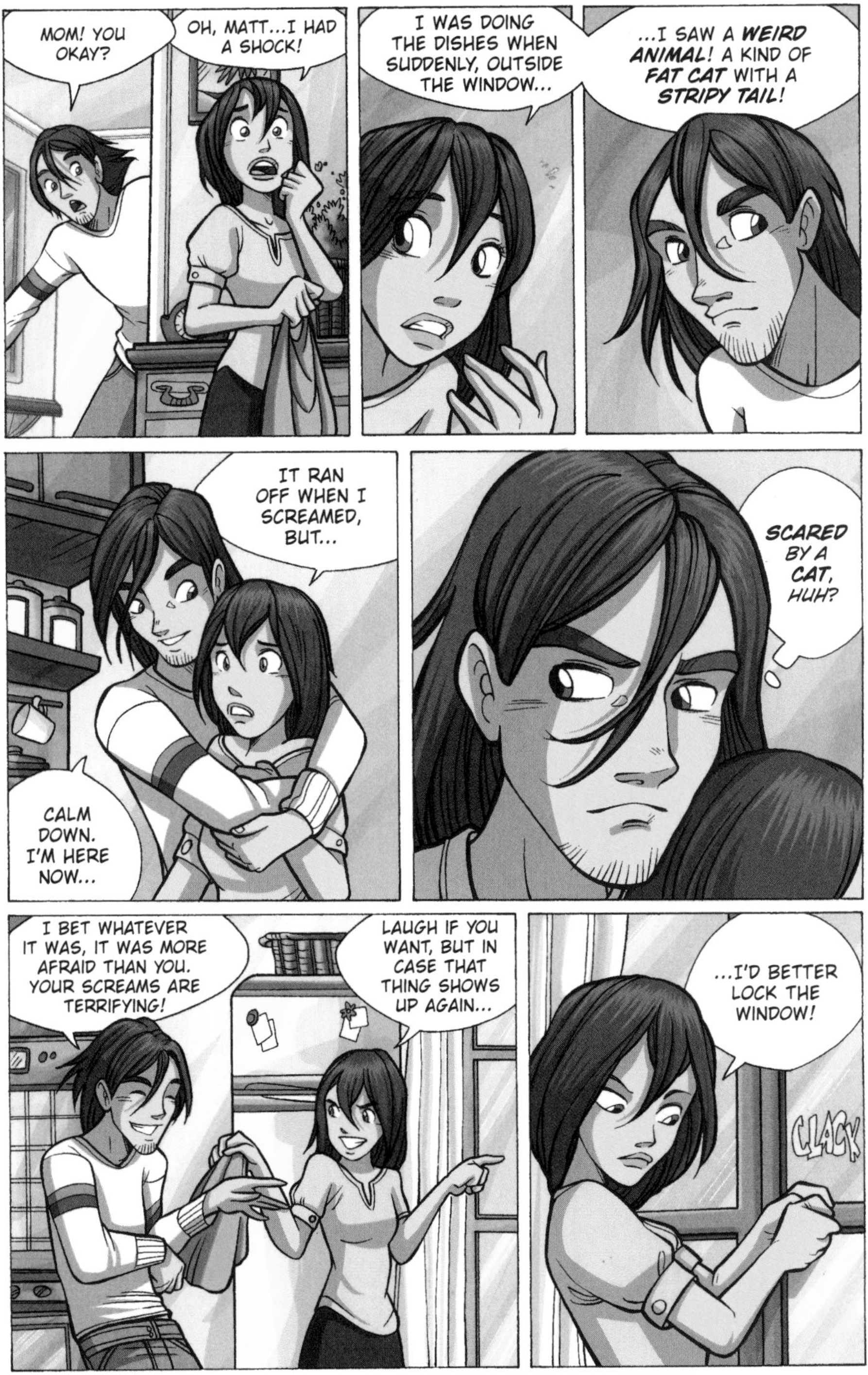
MOM! YOU OKAY?
OH, MATT...I HAD A SHOCK!
I WAS DOING THE DISHES WHEN SUDDENLY, OUTSIDE THE WINDOW...
...I SAW A WEIRD ANIMAL! A KIND OF FAT CAT WITH A STRIPY TAIL!
IT RAN OFF WHEN I SCREAMED, BUT...
CALM DOWN. I'M HERE NOW...
SCARED BY A CAT, HUH?
I BET WHATEVER IT WAS, IT WAS MORE AFRAID THAN YOU. YOUR SCREAMS ARE TERRIFYING!
LAUGH IF YOU WANT, BUT IN CASE THAT THING SHOWS UP AGAIN...
...I'D BETTER LOCK THE WINDOW!
CLACK

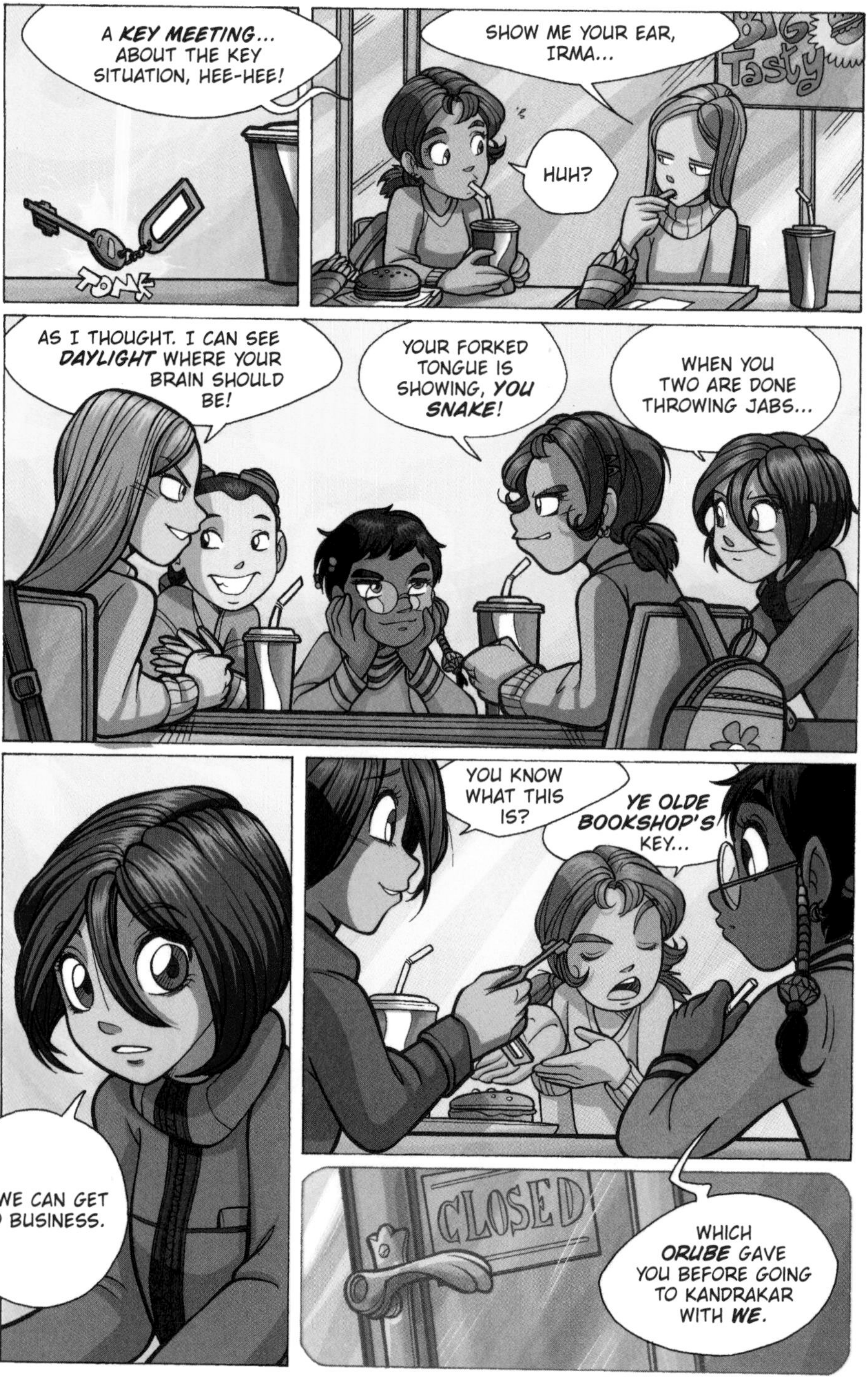
A KEY MEETING... ABOUT THE KEY SITUATION, HEE-HEE!
TONK
SHOW ME YOUR EAR, IRMA...
HUH?
AS I THOUGHT. I CAN SEE DAYLIGHT WHERE YOUR BRAIN SHOULD BE!
YOUR FORKED TONGUE IS SHOWING, YOU SNAKE!
WHEN YOU TWO ARE DONE THROWING JABS...
...WE CAN GET TO BUSINESS.
YOU KNOW WHAT THIS IS?
YE OLDE BOOKSHOP'S KEY...
CLOSED
WHICH ORUBE GAVE YOU BEFORE GOING TO KANDRAKAR WITH WE.

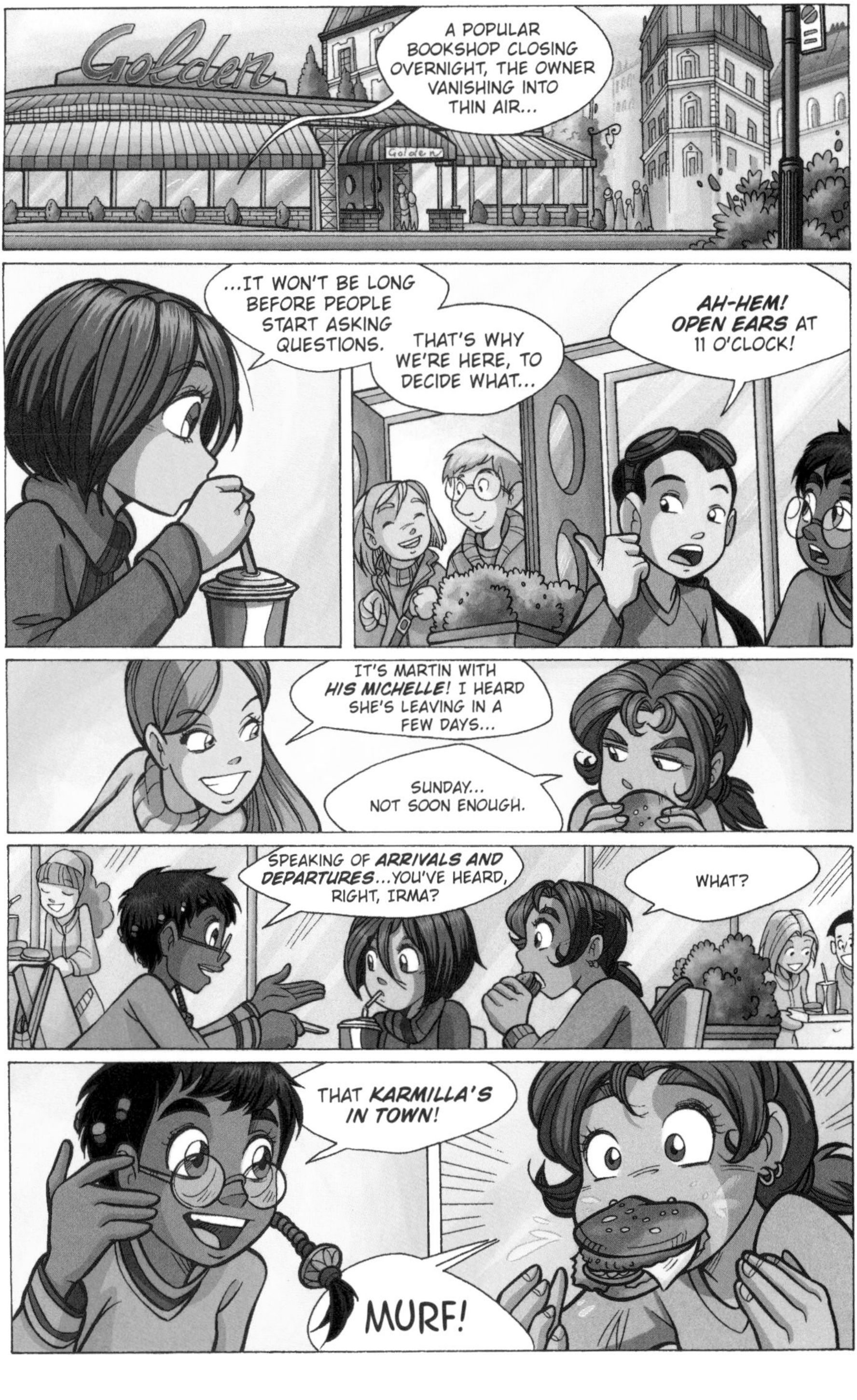
Golden
A POPULAR BOOKSHOP CLOSING OVERNIGHT, THE OWNER VANISHING INTO THIN AIR...
...IT WON'T BE LONG BEFORE PEOPLE START ASKING QUESTIONS.
THAT'S WHY WE'RE HERE, TO DECIDE WHAT...
AH-HEM! OPEN EARS AT 11 O'CLOCK!
IT'S MARTIN WITH HIS MICHELLE! I HEARD SHE'S LEAVING IN A FEW DAYS...
SUNDAY... NOT SOON ENOUGH.
SPEAKING OF ARRIVALS AND DEPARTURES...YOU'VE HEARD, RIGHT, IRMA?
WHAT?
THAT KARMILLA'S IN TOWN!
MURF!

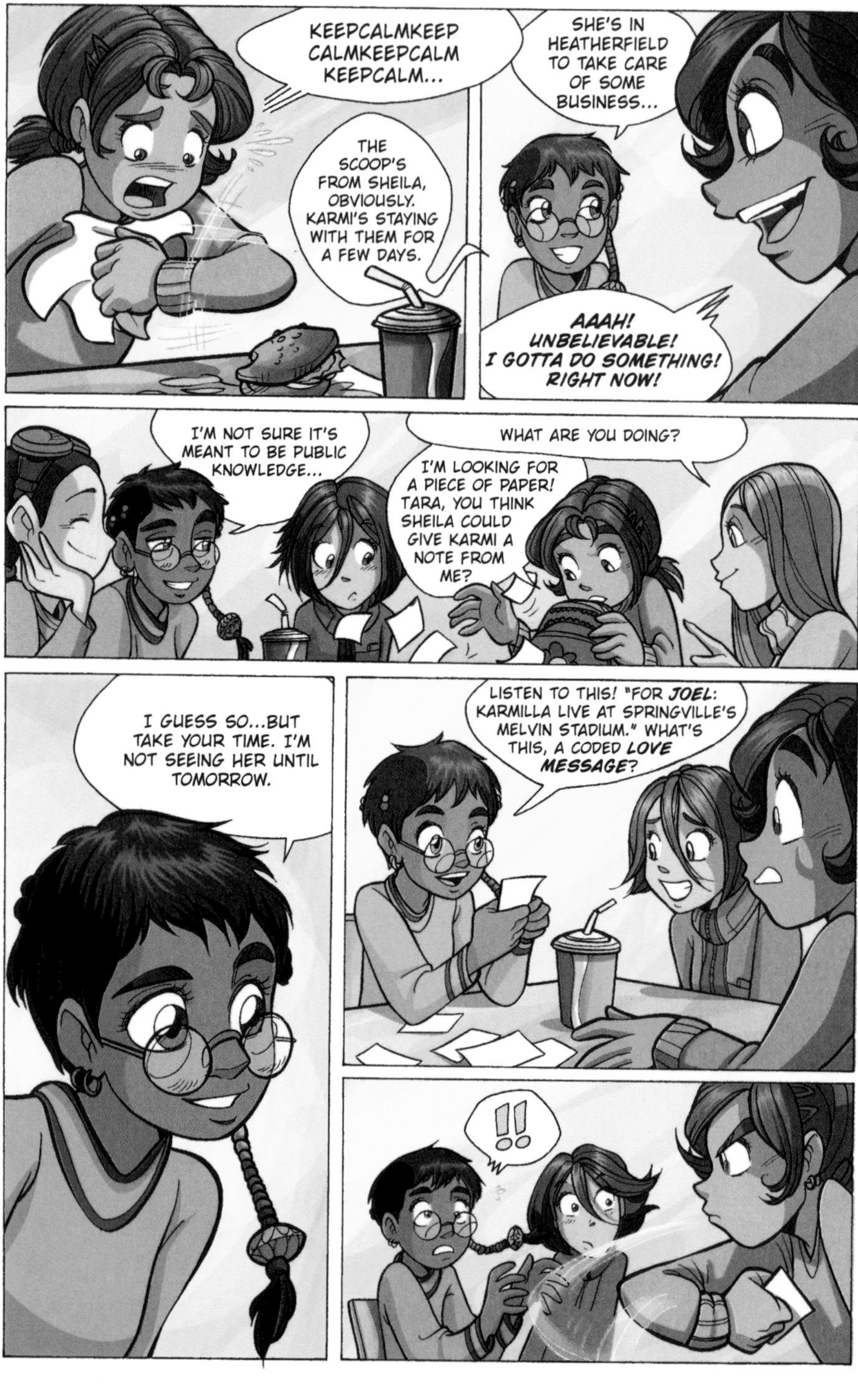
KEEPCALMKEEP CALMKEEPCALM KEEPCALM...
SHE'S IN HEATHERFIELD TO TAKE CARE OF SOME BUSINESS...
THE SCOOP'S FROM SHEILA, OBVIOUSLY. KARMI'S STAYING WITH THEM FOR A FEW DAYS.
AAAH! UNBELIEVABLE! I GOTTA DO SOMETHING! RIGHT NOW!
I'M NOT SURE IT'S MEANT TO BE PUBLIC KNOWLEDGE...
WHAT ARE YOU DOING?
I'M LOOKING FOR A PIECE OF PAPER! TARA, YOU THINK SHEILA COULD GIVE KARMI A NOTE FROM ME?
I GUESS SO...BUT TAKE YOUR TIME. I'M NOT SEEING HER UNTIL TOMORROW.
LISTEN TO THIS! "FOR JOEL: KARMILLA LIVE AT SPRINGVILLE'S MELVIN STADIUM." WHAT'S THIS, A CODED LOVE MESSAGE?
!!

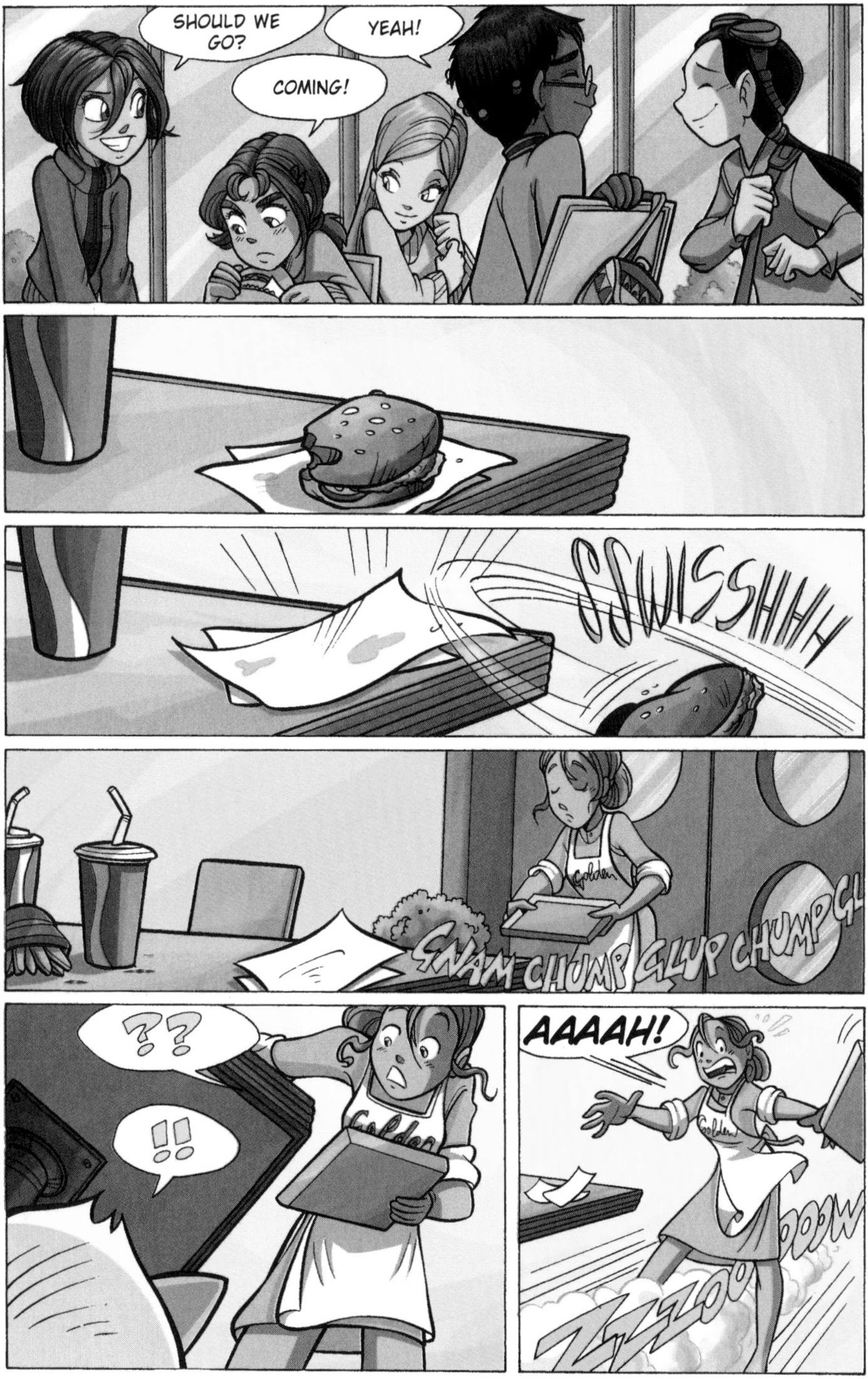

SHOULD WE GO?
COMING!
YEAH!
SSWISSHHH
GNAM CHUMP GLUP CHUMP GL
??
!!
AAAAH!
ZZZZOOOOOW

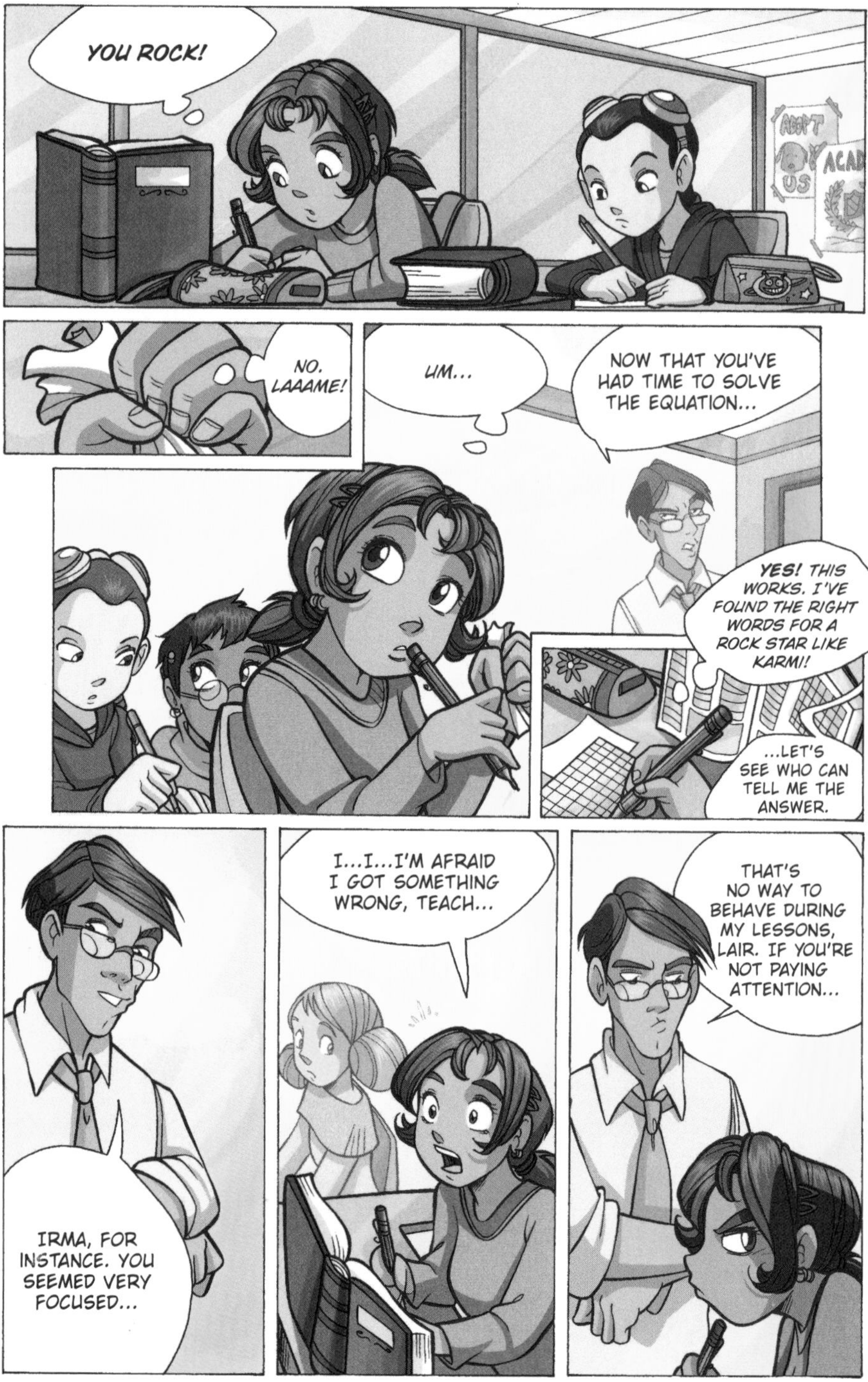
YOU ROCK!
NO. LAAAME!
UM...
NOW THAT YOU'VE HAD TIME TO SOLVE THE EQUATION...
YES! THIS WORKS. I'VE FOUND THE RIGHT WORDS FOR A ROCK STAR LIKE KARMI!
...LET'S SEE WHO CAN TELL ME THE ANSWER.
IRMA, FOR INSTANCE. YOU SEEMED VERY FOCUSED...
I...I...I'M AFRAID I GOT SOMETHING WRONG, TEACH...
THAT'S NO WAY TO BEHAVE DURING MY LESSONS, LAIR. IF YOU'RE NOT PAYING ATTENTION...

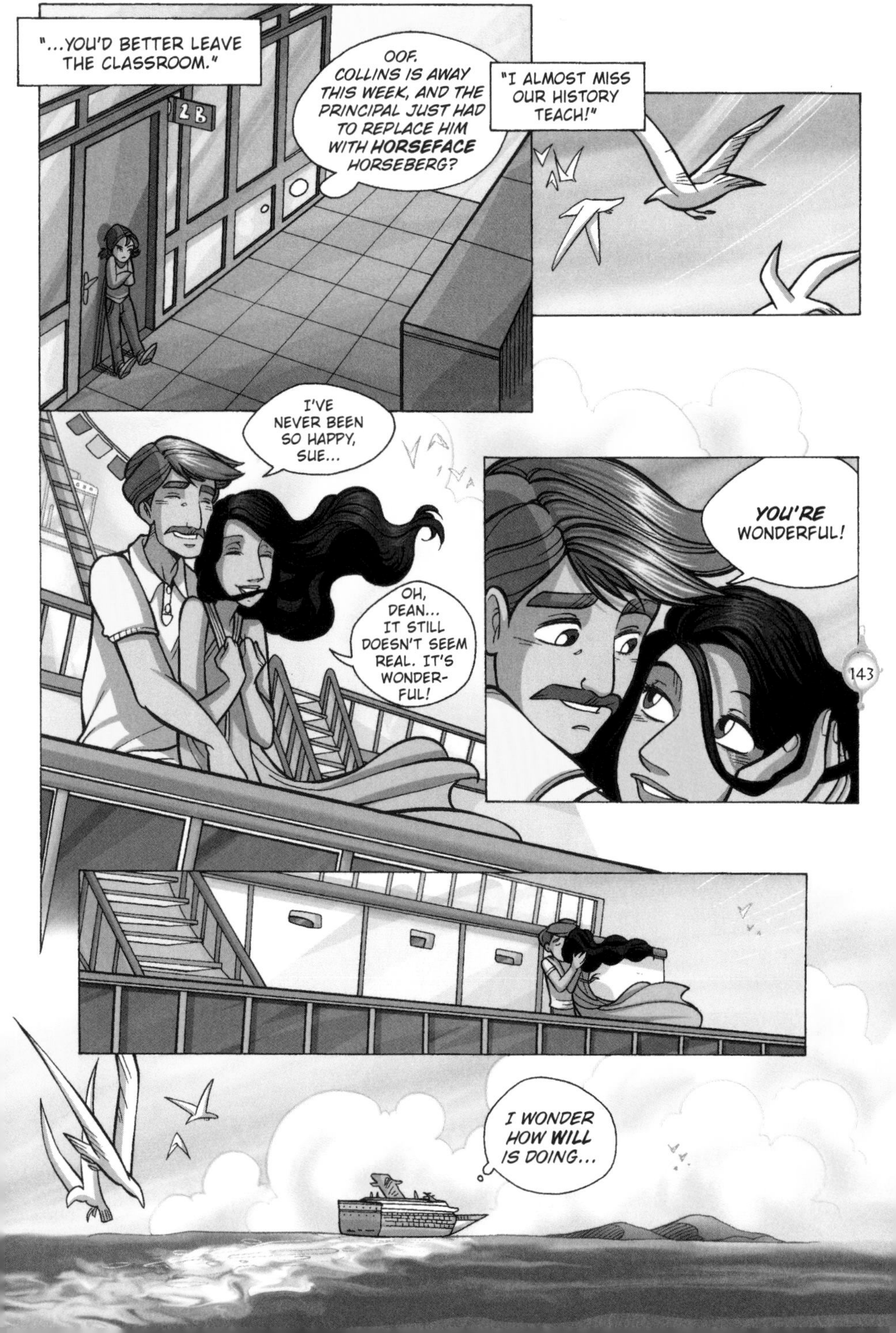
"...YOU'D BETTER LEAVE THE CLASSROOM."
OOF. COLLINS IS AWAY THIS WEEK, AND THE PRINCIPAL JUST HAD TO REPLACE HIM WITH **HORSEFACE** HORSEBERG?
2B
"I ALMOST MISS OUR HISTORY TEACH!"
I'VE NEVER BEEN SO HAPPY, SUE...
OH, DEAN... IT STILL DOESN'T SEEM REAL. IT'S WONDER-FUL!
YOU'RE WONDERFUL!
I WONDER HOW **WILL** IS DOING...

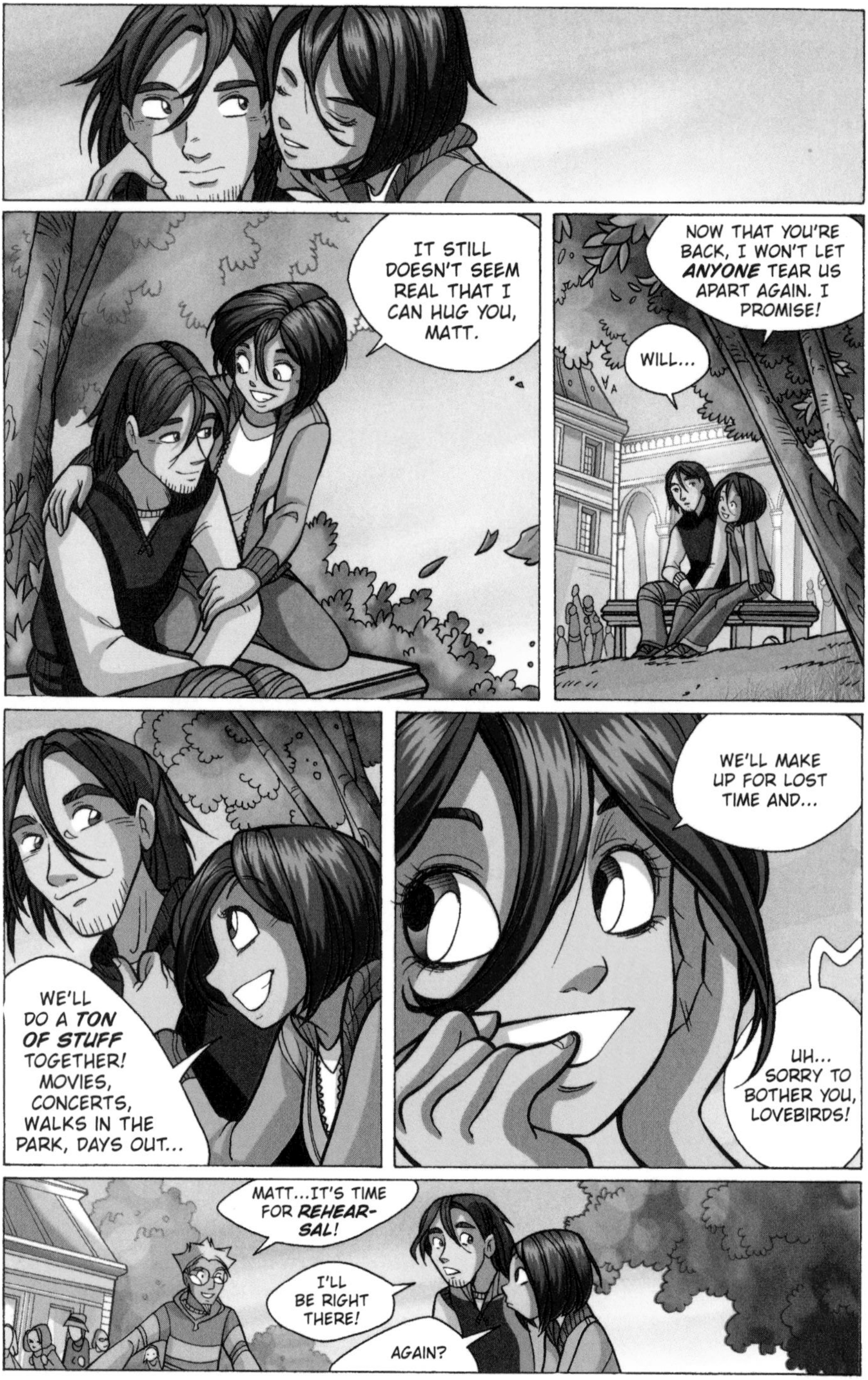

IT STILL DOESN'T SEEM REAL THAT I CAN HUG YOU, MATT.
NOW THAT YOU'RE BACK, I WON'T LET **ANYONE** TEAR US APART AGAIN. I PROMISE!
WILL...
WE'LL DO A **TON OF STUFF** TOGETHER! MOVIES, CONCERTS, WALKS IN THE PARK, DAYS OUT...
WE'LL MAKE UP FOR LOST TIME AND...
UH... SORRY TO BOTHER YOU, LOVEBIRDS!
MATT...IT'S TIME FOR **REHEAR-SAL**!
I'LL BE RIGHT THERE!
AGAIN?

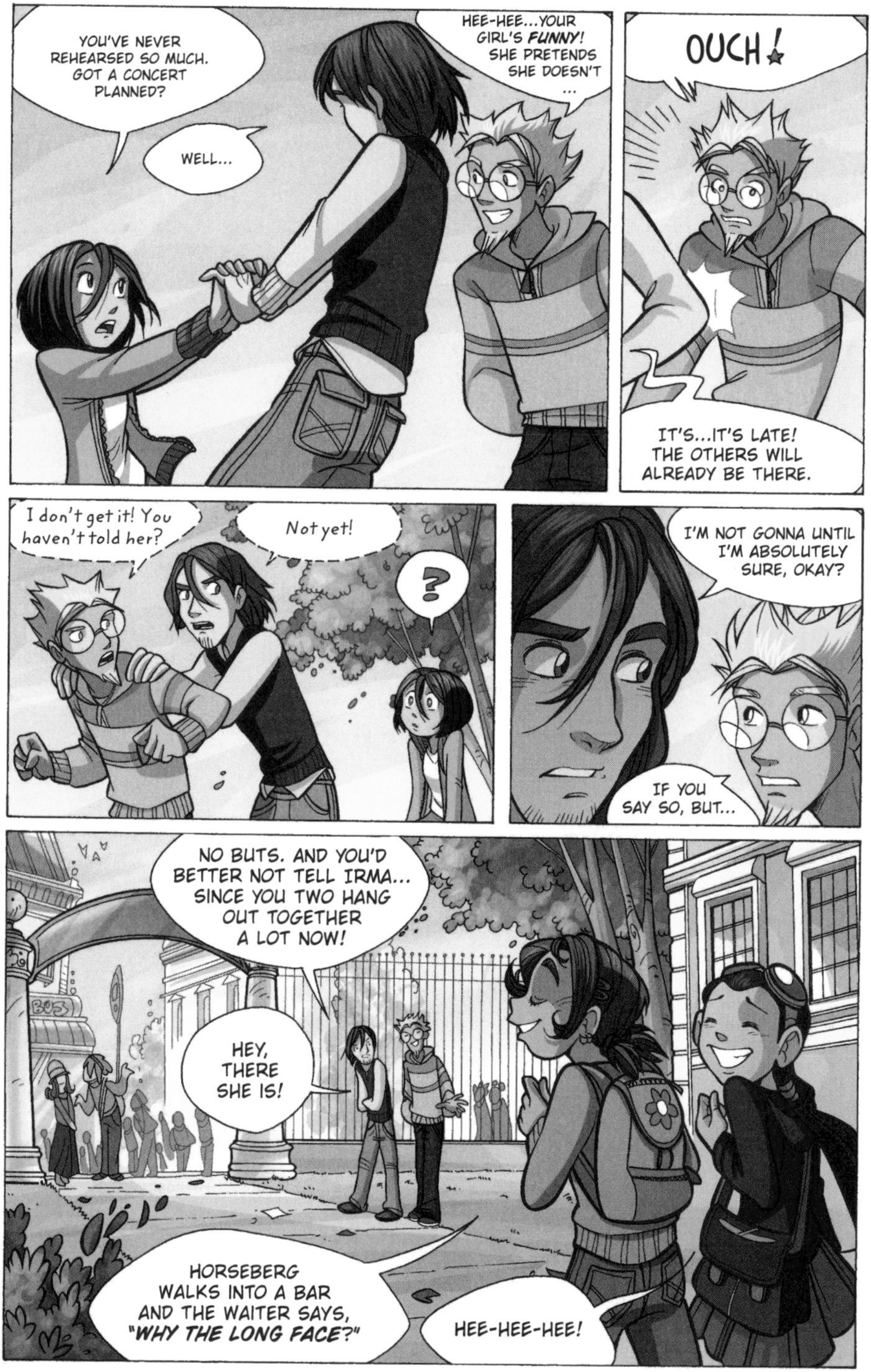
YOU'VE NEVER REHEARSED SO MUCH. GOT A CONCERT PLANNED?
WELL...
HEE-HEE...YOUR GIRL'S *FUNNY*! SHE PRETENDS SHE DOESN'T ...
OUCH!
IT'S...IT'S LATE! THE OTHERS WILL ALREADY BE THERE.
I don't get it! You haven't told her?
Not yet!
?
I'M NOT GONNA UNTIL I'M ABSOLUTELY SURE, OKAY?
IF YOU SAY SO, BUT...
NO BUTS. AND YOU'D BETTER NOT TELL IRMA... SINCE YOU TWO HANG OUT TOGETHER A LOT NOW!
HEY, THERE SHE IS!
HORSEBERG WALKS INTO A BAR AND THE WAITER SAYS, "*WHY THE LONG FACE*?"
HEE-HEE-HEE!

145

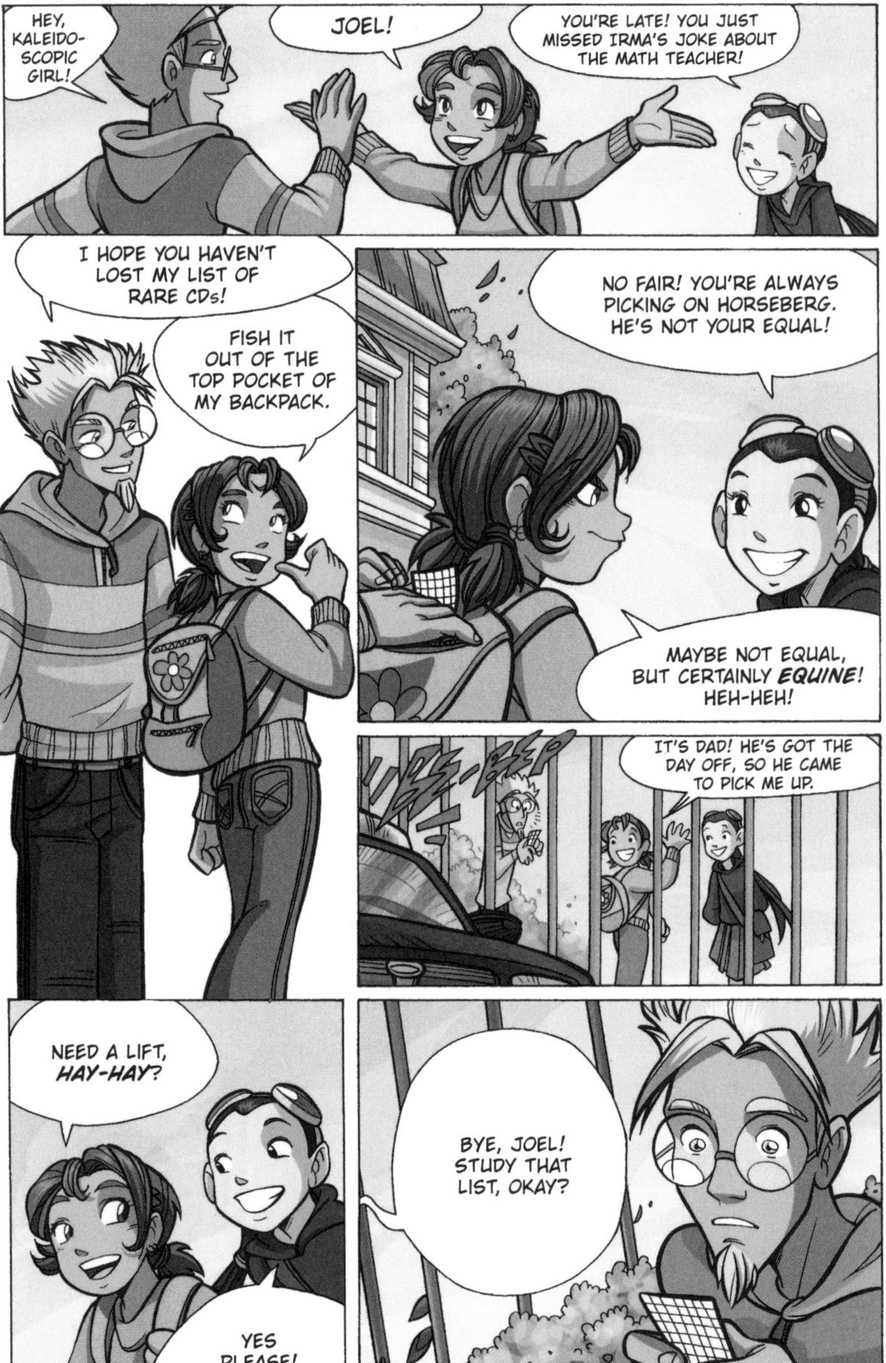
HEY, KALEIDO-SCOPIC GIRL!
JOEL!
YOU'RE LATE! YOU JUST MISSED IRMA'S JOKE ABOUT THE MATH TEACHER!
I HOPE YOU HAVEN'T LOST MY LIST OF RARE CDs!
FISH IT OUT OF THE TOP POCKET OF MY BACKPACK.
NO FAIR! YOU'RE ALWAYS PICKING ON HORSEBERG. HE'S NOT YOUR EQUAL!
MAYBE NOT EQUAL, BUT CERTAINLY *EQUINE*! HEH-HEH!
BEEP-BEEP
IT'S DAD! HE'S GOT THE DAY OFF, SO HE CAME TO PICK ME UP.
NEED A LIFT, *HAY-HAY*?
YES PLEASE!
BYE, JOEL! STUDY THAT LIST, OKAY?

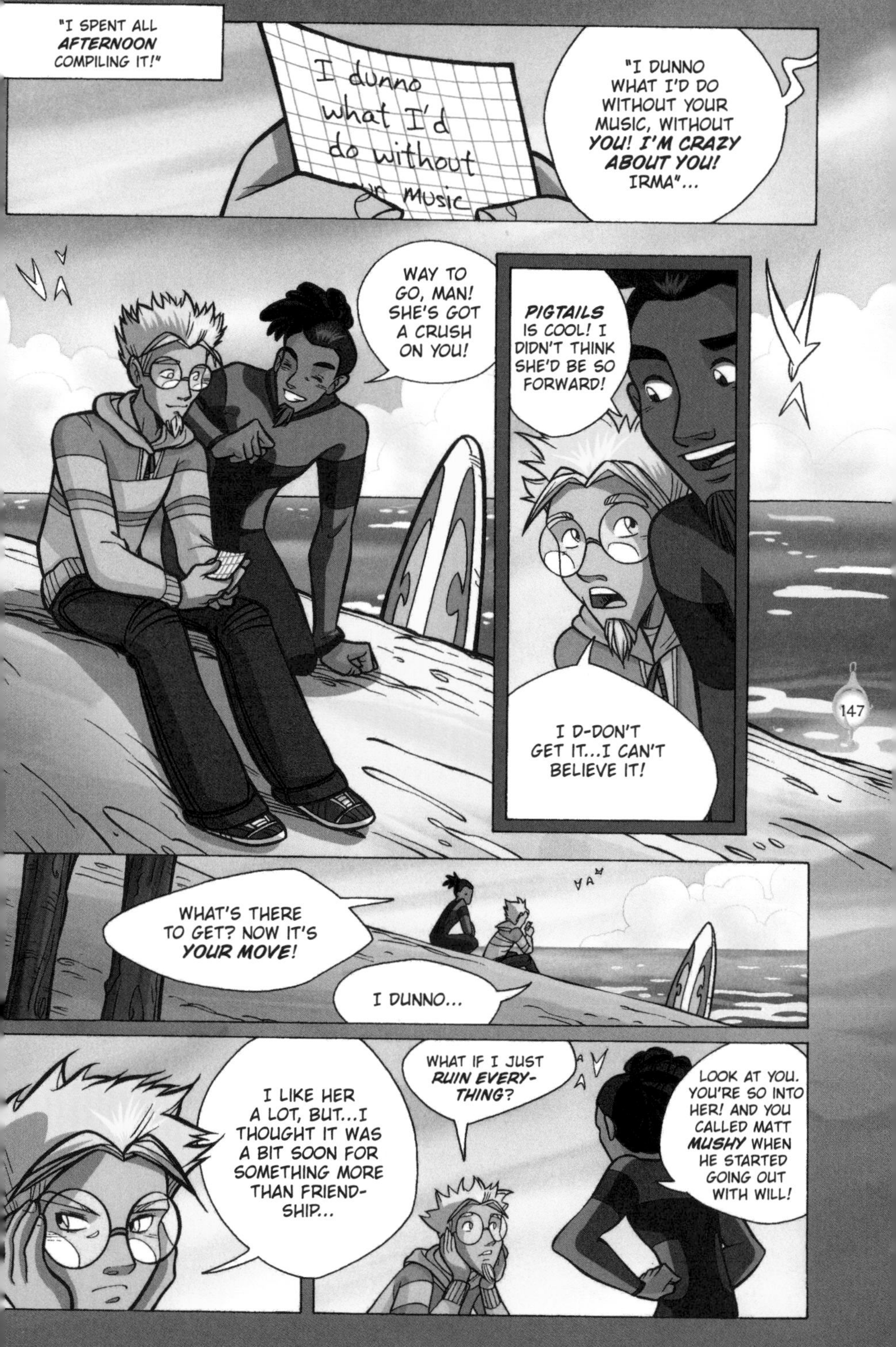
"I SPENT ALL AFTERNOON COMPILING IT!"
I dunno what I'd do without your music
"I DUNNO WHAT I'D DO WITHOUT YOUR MUSIC, WITHOUT YOU! I'M CRAZY ABOUT YOU! IRMA"...
WAY TO GO, MAN! SHE'S GOT A CRUSH ON YOU!
PIGTAILS IS COOL! I DIDN'T THINK SHE'D BE SO FORWARD!
I D-DON'T GET IT...I CAN'T BELIEVE IT!
WHAT'S THERE TO GET? NOW IT'S YOUR MOVE!
I DUNNO...
I LIKE HER A LOT, BUT...I THOUGHT IT WAS A BIT SOON FOR SOMETHING MORE THAN FRIEND-SHIP...
WHAT IF I JUST RUIN EVERY-THING?
LOOK AT YOU. YOU'RE SO INTO HER! AND YOU CALLED MATT MUSHY WHEN HE STARTED GOING OUT WITH WILL!

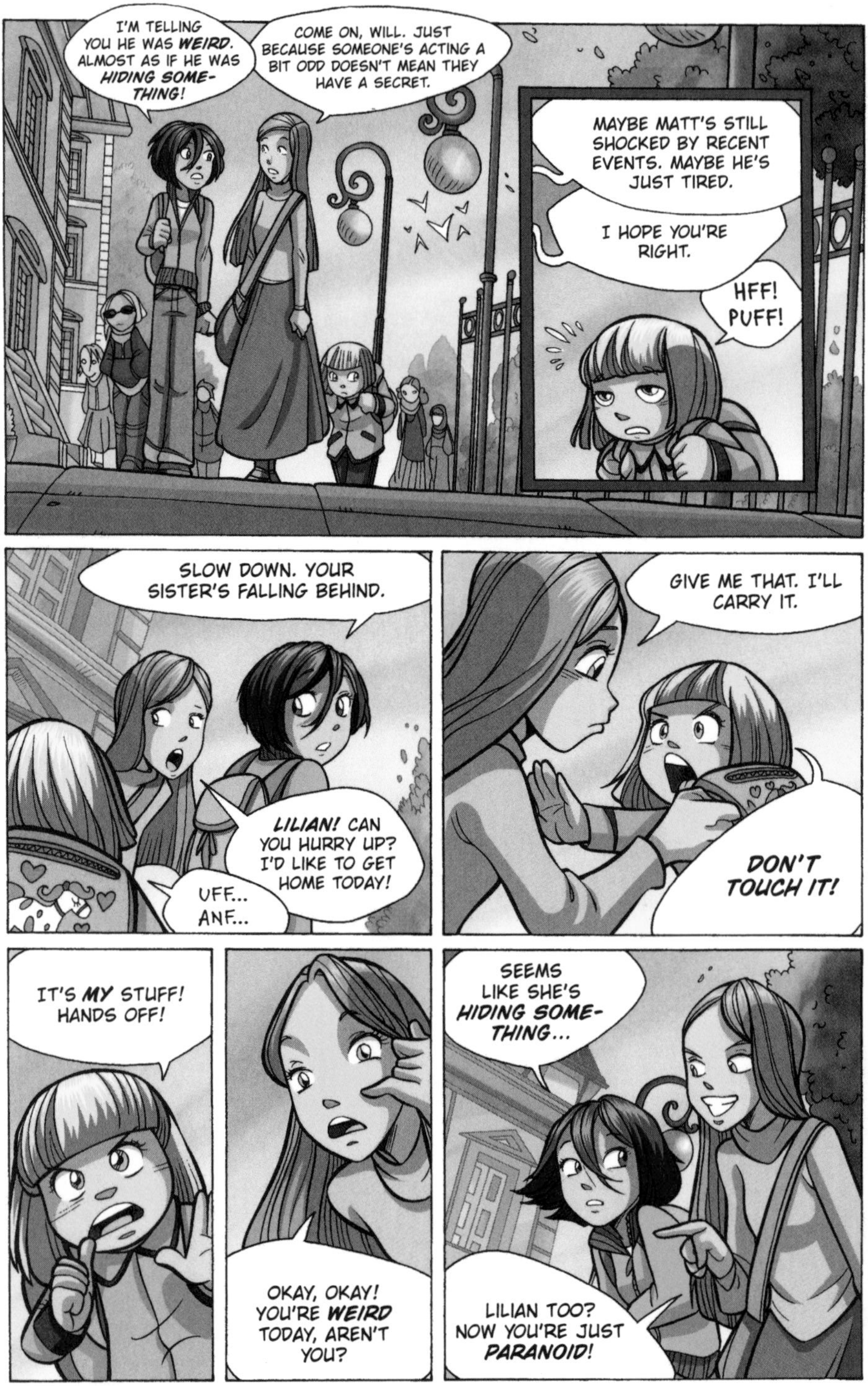
I'M TELLING YOU HE WAS WEIRD. ALMOST AS IF HE WAS HIDING SOMETHING!
COME ON, WILL. JUST BECAUSE SOMEONE'S ACTING A BIT ODD DOESN'T MEAN THEY HAVE A SECRET.
MAYBE MATT'S STILL SHOCKED BY RECENT EVENTS. MAYBE HE'S JUST TIRED.
I HOPE YOU'RE RIGHT.
HFF! PUFF!
SLOW DOWN. YOUR SISTER'S FALLING BEHIND.
LILIAN! CAN YOU HURRY UP? I'D LIKE TO GET HOME TODAY!
UFF... ANF...
GIVE ME THAT. I'LL CARRY IT.
DON'T TOUCH IT!
IT'S MY STUFF! HANDS OFF!
OKAY, OKAY! YOU'RE WEIRD TODAY, AREN'T YOU?
SEEMS LIKE SHE'S HIDING SOMETHING...
LILIAN TOO? NOW YOU'RE JUST PARANOID!

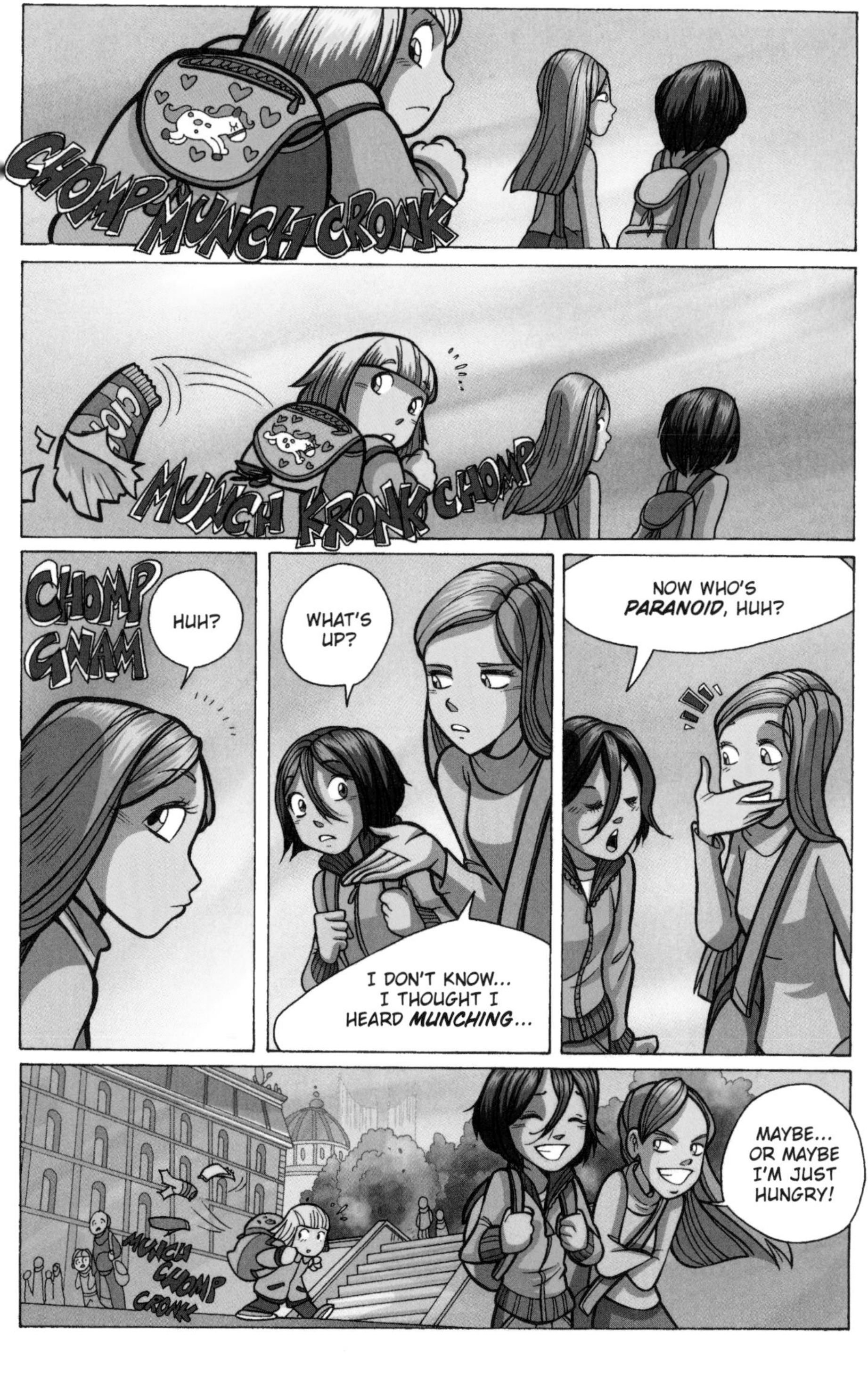
CHOMP MUNCH CRONK
MUNCH KRONK CHOMP
CHOMP GNAM
HUH?
WHAT'S UP?
I DON'T KNOW... I THOUGHT I HEARD MUNCHING...
NOW WHO'S PARANOID, HUH?
MAYBE... OR MAYBE I'M JUST HUNGRY!
MUNCH CHOMP CRONK

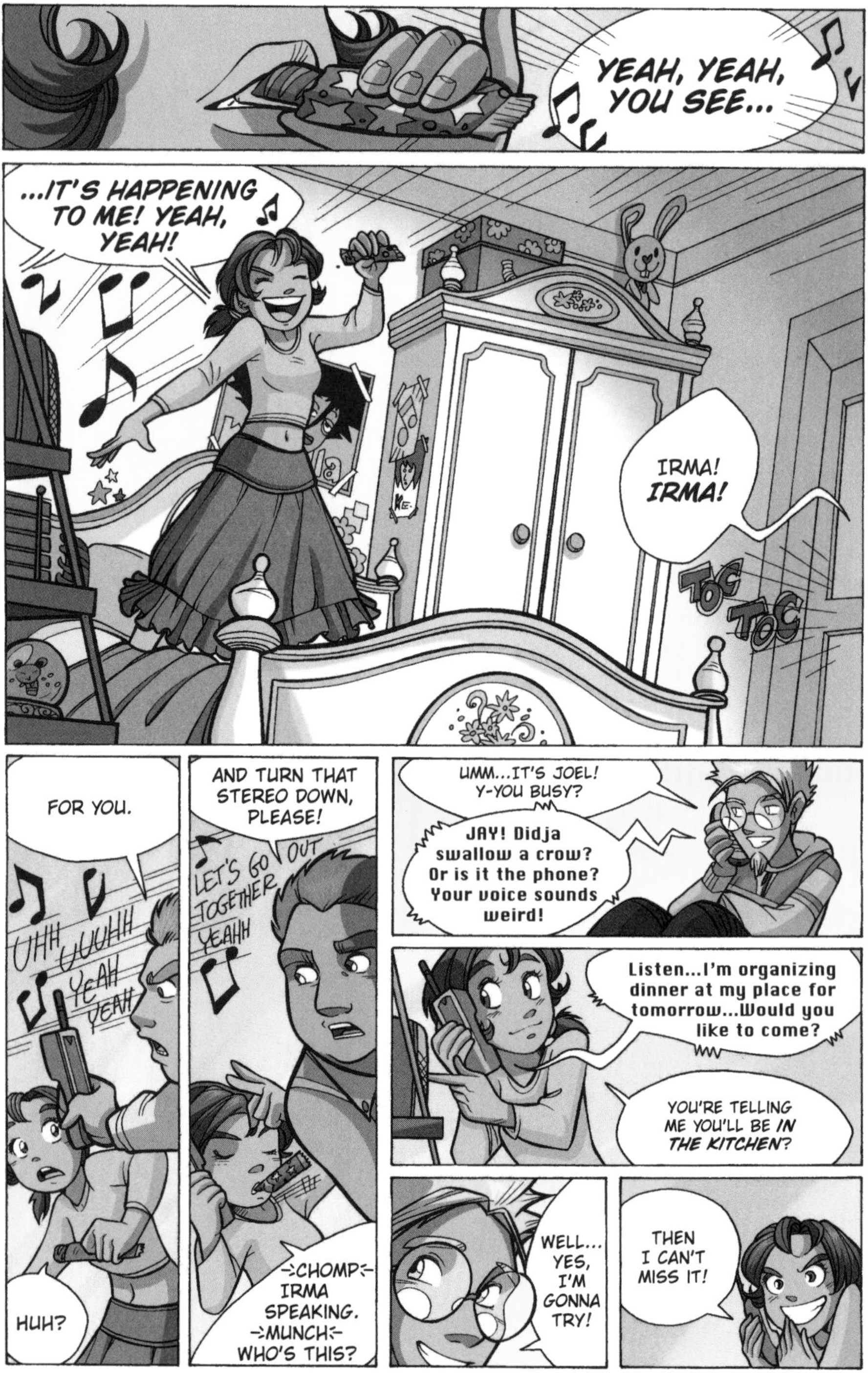

YEAH, YEAH, YOU SEE...
...IT'S HAPPENING TO ME! YEAH, YEAH!
IRMA! IRMA!
TOC TOC
FOR YOU.
UHH UUUHH YEAH YEAH
HUH?
AND TURN THAT STEREO DOWN, PLEASE!
LET'S GO OUT TOGETHER YEAHH
CHOMP
IRMA SPEAKING.
MUNCH
WHO'S THIS?
UMM...IT'S JOEL! Y-YOU BUSY?
JAY! Didja swallow a crow? Or is it the phone? Your voice sounds weird!
Listen...I'm organizing dinner at my place for tomorrow...Would you like to come?
YOU'RE TELLING ME YOU'LL BE IN THE KITCHEN?
WELL... YES, I'M GONNA TRY!
THEN I CAN'T MISS IT!

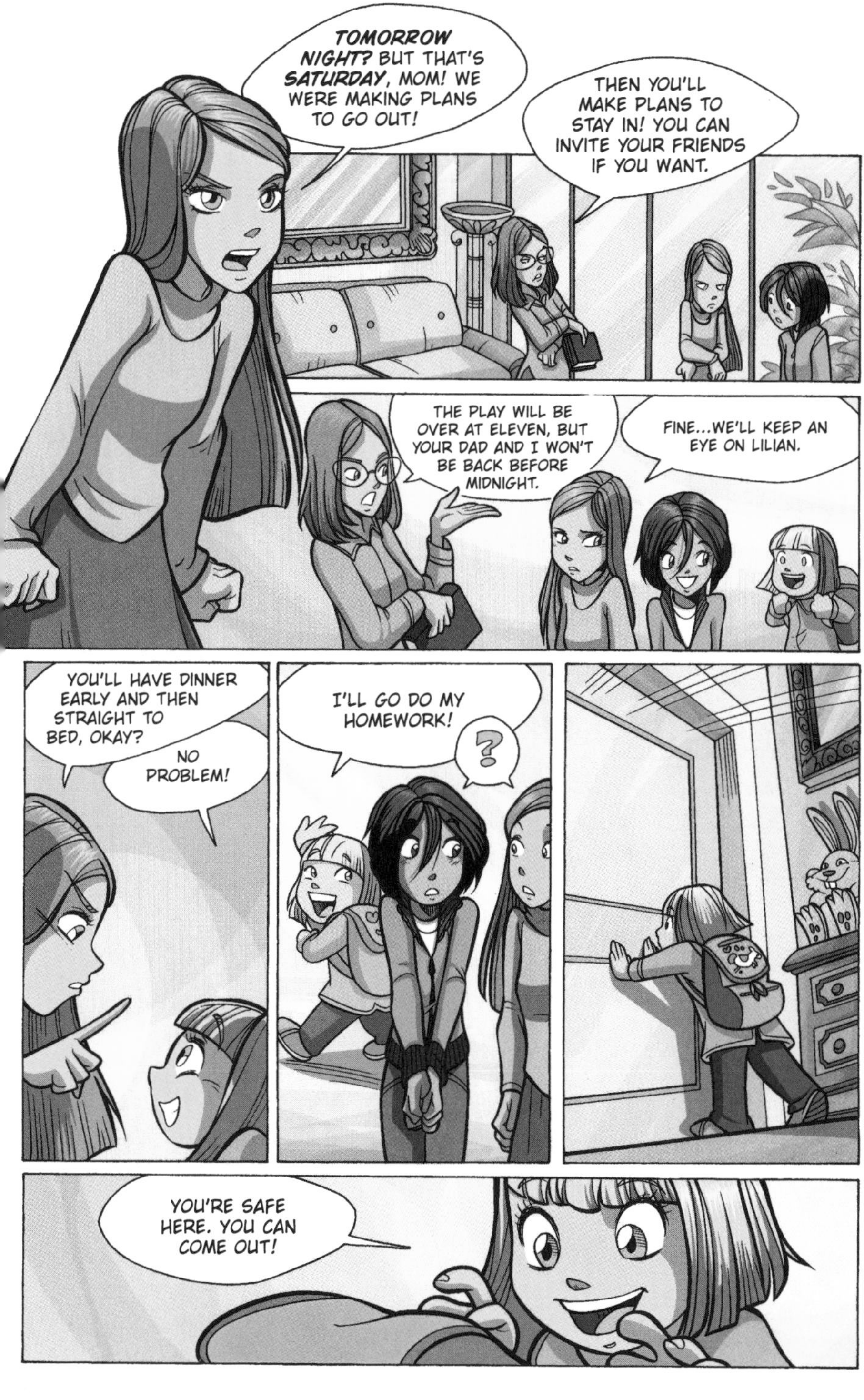
TOMORROW NIGHT? BUT THAT'S SATURDAY, MOM! WE WERE MAKING PLANS TO GO OUT!
THEN YOU'LL MAKE PLANS TO STAY IN! YOU CAN INVITE YOUR FRIENDS IF YOU WANT.
THE PLAY WILL BE OVER AT ELEVEN, BUT YOUR DAD AND I WON'T BE BACK BEFORE MIDNIGHT.
FINE...WE'LL KEEP AN EYE ON LILIAN.
YOU'LL HAVE DINNER EARLY AND THEN STRAIGHT TO BED, OKAY?
NO PROBLEM!
I'LL GO DO MY HOMEWORK!
?
YOU'RE SAFE HERE. YOU CAN COME OUT!

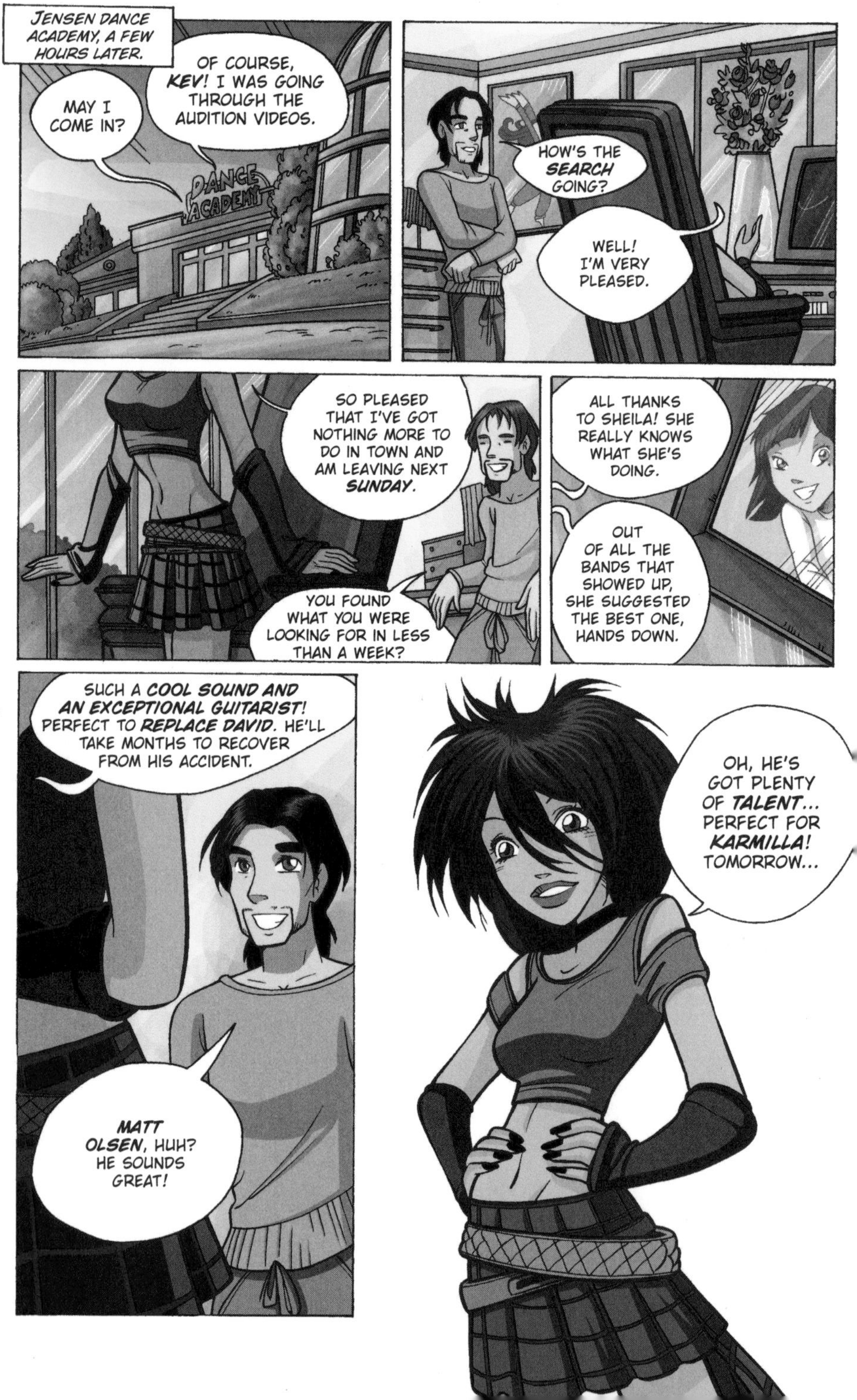
JENSEN DANCE ACADEMY, A FEW HOURS LATER.
MAY I COME IN?
OF COURSE, KEV! I WAS GOING THROUGH THE AUDITION VIDEOS.
DANCE ACADEMY
HOW'S THE SEARCH GOING?
WELL! I'M VERY PLEASED.
SO PLEASED THAT I'VE GOT NOTHING MORE TO DO IN TOWN AND AM LEAVING NEXT SUNDAY.
YOU FOUND WHAT YOU WERE LOOKING FOR IN LESS THAN A WEEK?
ALL THANKS TO SHEILA! SHE REALLY KNOWS WHAT SHE'S DOING.
OUT OF ALL THE BANDS THAT SHOWED UP, SHE SUGGESTED THE BEST ONE, HANDS DOWN.
SUCH A COOL SOUND AND AN EXCEPTIONAL GUITARIST! PERFECT TO REPLACE DAVID. HE'LL TAKE MONTHS TO RECOVER FROM HIS ACCIDENT.
MATT OLSEN, HUH? HE SOUNDS GREAT!
OH, HE'S GOT PLENTY OF TALENT... PERFECT FOR KARMILLA! TOMORROW...

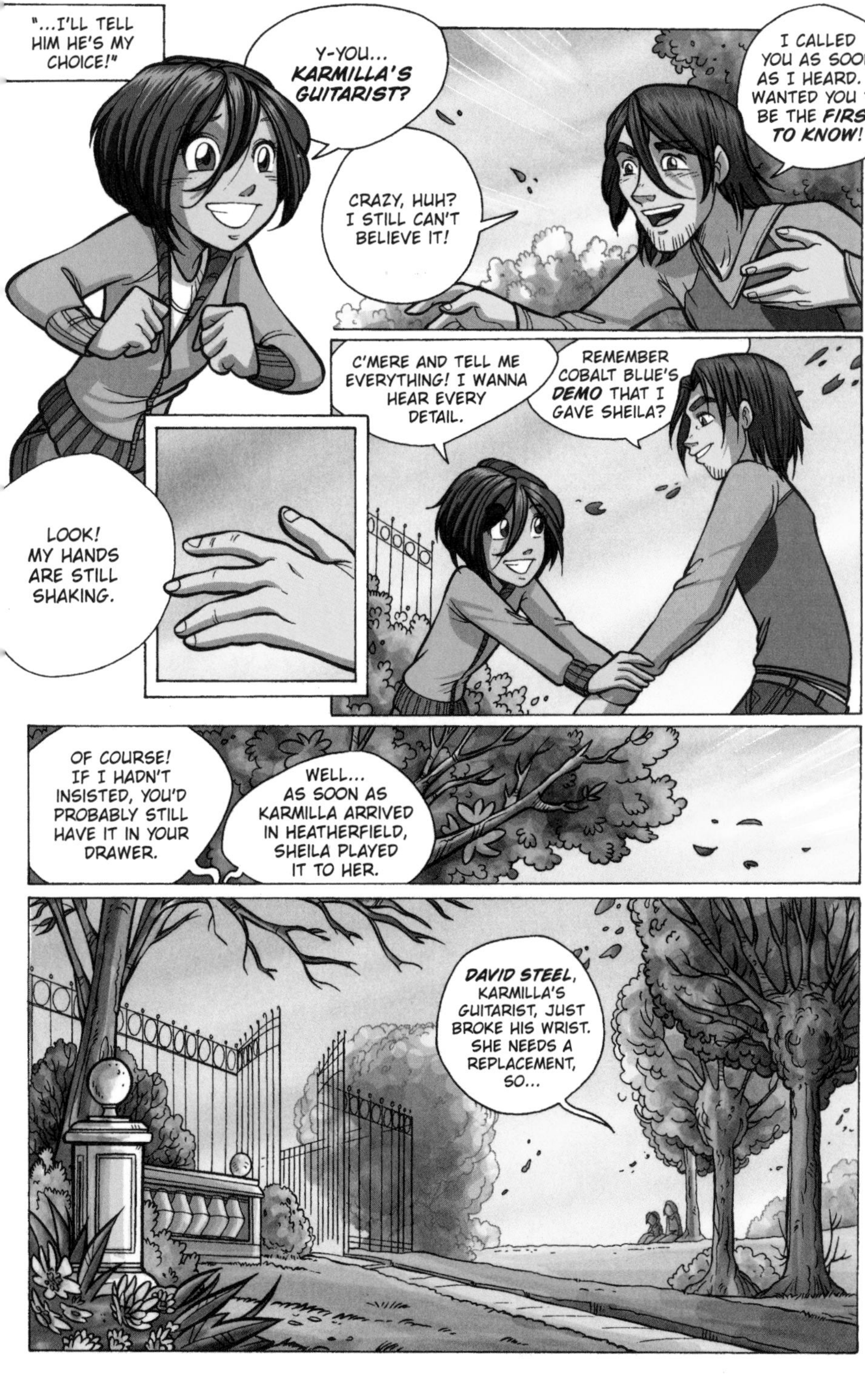
"...I'LL TELL HIM HE'S MY CHOICE!"
Y-YOU... KARMILLA'S GUITARIST?
I CALLED YOU AS SOON AS I HEARD. I WANTED YOU TO BE THE FIRST TO KNOW!
CRAZY, HUH? I STILL CAN'T BELIEVE IT!
C'MERE AND TELL ME EVERYTHING! I WANNA HEAR EVERY DETAIL.
LOOK! MY HANDS ARE STILL SHAKING.
REMEMBER COBALT BLUE'S DEMO THAT I GAVE SHEILA?
OF COURSE! IF I HADN'T INSISTED, YOU'D PROBABLY STILL HAVE IT IN YOUR DRAWER.
WELL... AS SOON AS KARMILLA ARRIVED IN HEATHERFIELD, SHEILA PLAYED IT TO HER.
DAVID STEEL, KARMILLA'S GUITARIST, JUST BROKE HIS WRIST. SHE NEEDS A REPLACEMENT, SO...

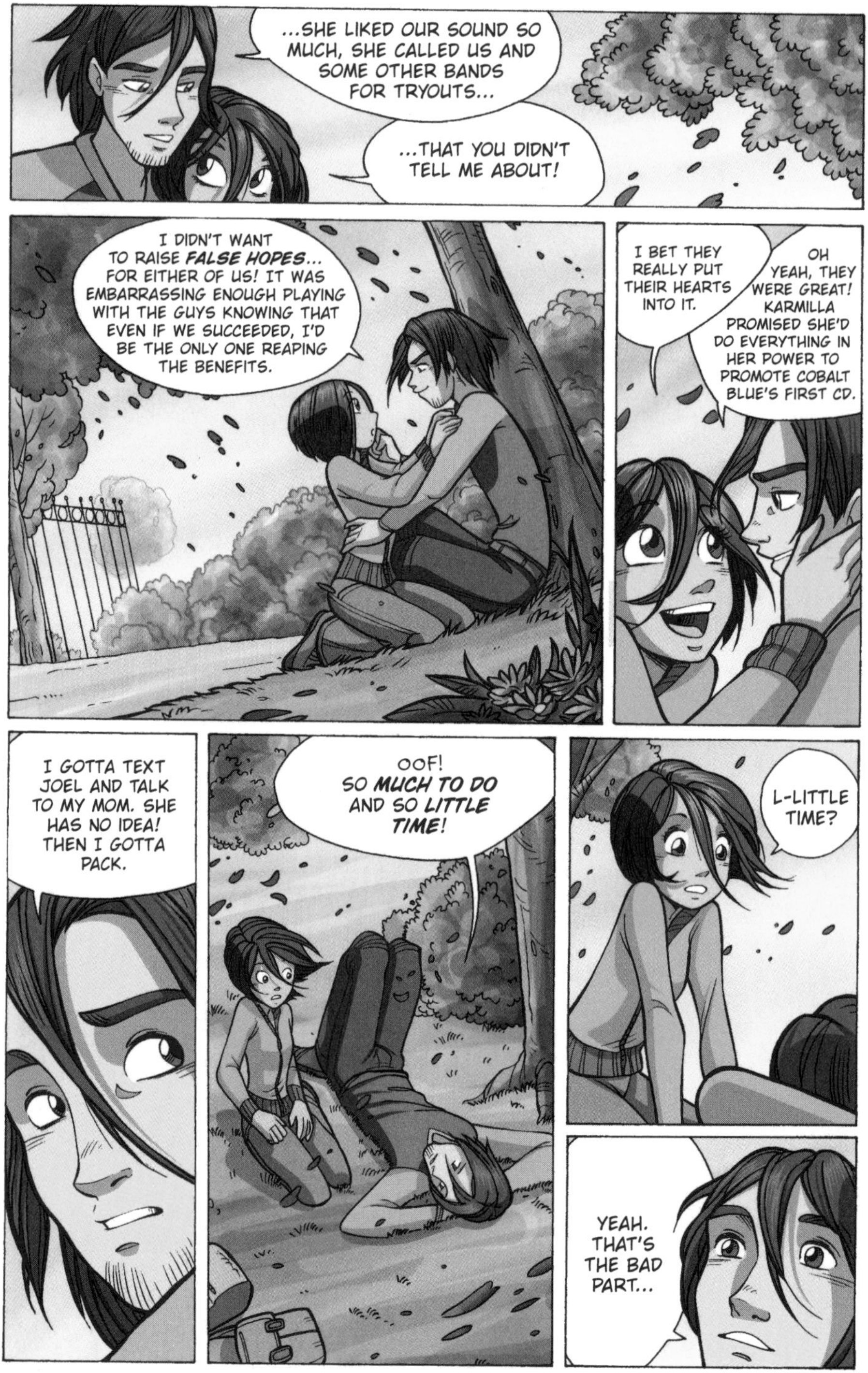
...SHE LIKED OUR SOUND SO MUCH, SHE CALLED US AND SOME OTHER BANDS FOR TRYOUTS...
...THAT YOU DIDN'T TELL ME ABOUT!
I DIDN'T WANT TO RAISE FALSE HOPES... FOR EITHER OF US! IT WAS EMBARRASSING ENOUGH PLAYING WITH THE GUYS KNOWING THAT EVEN IF WE SUCCEEDED, I'D BE THE ONLY ONE REAPING THE BENEFITS.
I BET THEY REALLY PUT THEIR HEARTS INTO IT.
OH YEAH, THEY WERE GREAT! KARMILLA PROMISED SHE'D DO EVERYTHING IN HER POWER TO PROMOTE COBALT BLUE'S FIRST CD.
I GOTTA TEXT JOEL AND TALK TO MY MOM. SHE HAS NO IDEA! THEN I GOTTA PACK.
OOF! SO MUCH TO DO AND SO LITTLE TIME!
L-LITTLE TIME?
YEAH. THAT'S THE BAD PART...

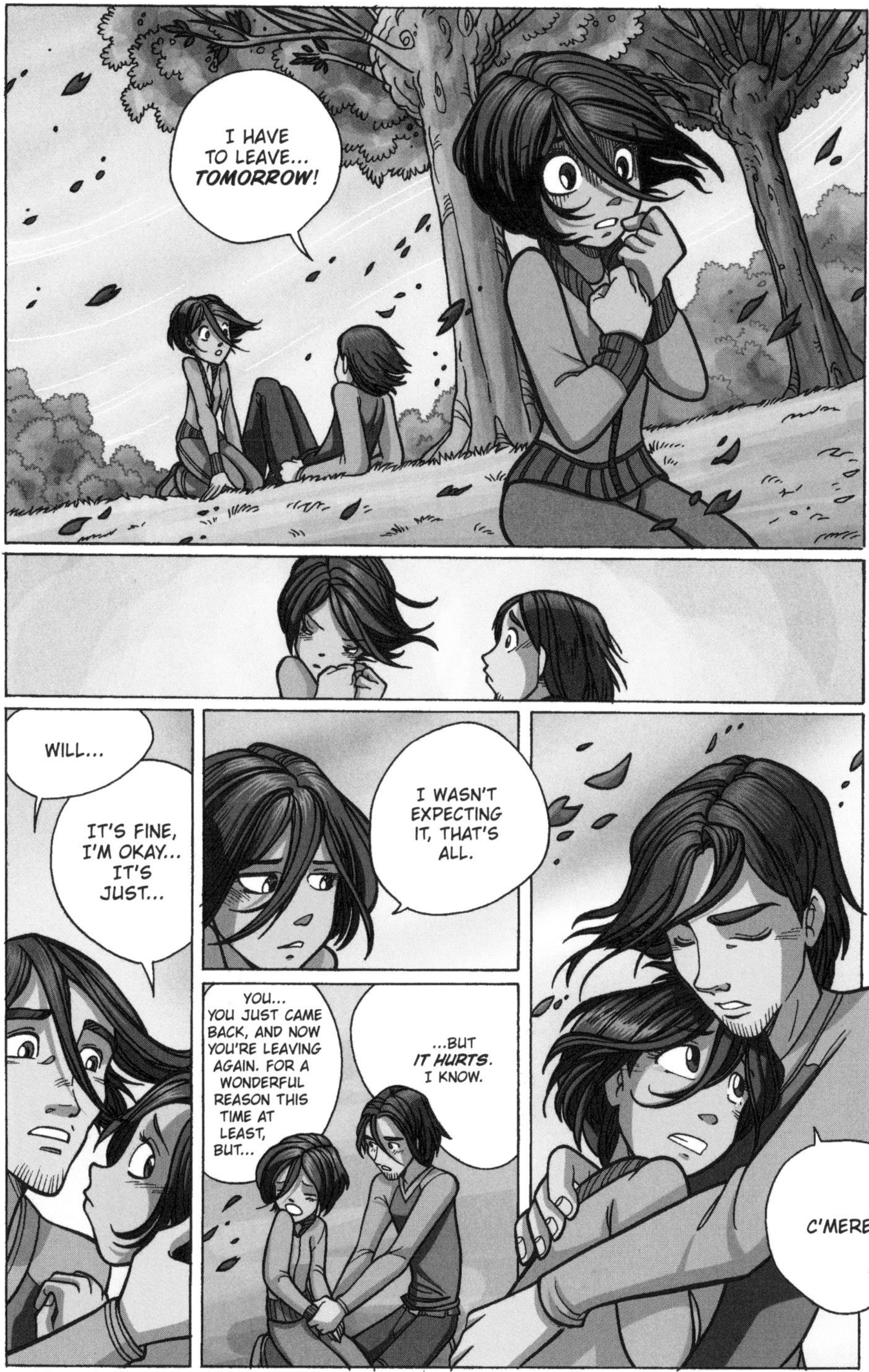
I HAVE TO LEAVE... *TOMORROW*!
WILL...
IT'S FINE, I'M OKAY... IT'S JUST...
I WASN'T EXPECTING IT, THAT'S ALL.
YOU... YOU JUST CAME BACK, AND NOW YOU'RE LEAVING AGAIN. FOR A WONDERFUL REASON THIS TIME AT LEAST, BUT...
...BUT *IT HURTS*. I KNOW.
C'MERE!

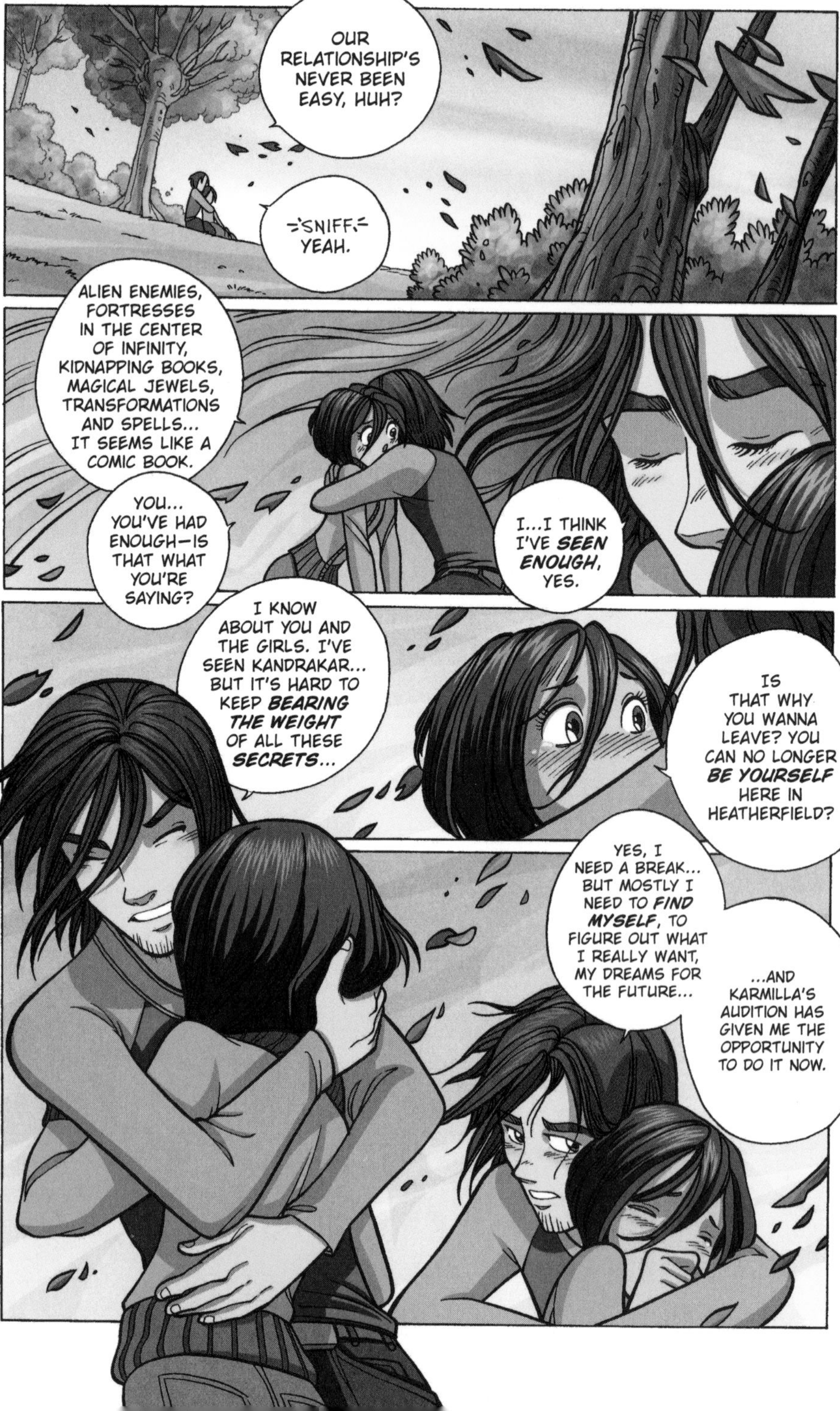
OUR RELATIONSHIP'S NEVER BEEN EASY, HUH?
=SNIFF= YEAH.
ALIEN ENEMIES, FORTRESSES IN THE CENTER OF INFINITY, KIDNAPPING BOOKS, MAGICAL JEWELS, TRANSFORMATIONS AND SPELLS... IT SEEMS LIKE A COMIC BOOK.
YOU... YOU'VE HAD ENOUGH—IS THAT WHAT YOU'RE SAYING?
I...I THINK I'VE ***SEEN ENOUGH***, YES.
I KNOW ABOUT YOU AND THE GIRLS. I'VE SEEN KANDRAKAR... BUT IT'S HARD TO KEEP ***BEARING THE WEIGHT*** OF ALL THESE ***SECRETS***...
IS THAT WHY YOU WANNA LEAVE? YOU CAN NO LONGER ***BE YOURSELF*** HERE IN HEATHERFIELD?
YES, I NEED A BREAK... BUT MOSTLY I NEED TO ***FIND MYSELF***, TO FIGURE OUT WHAT I REALLY WANT, MY DREAMS FOR THE FUTURE...
...AND KARMILLA'S AUDITION HAS GIVEN ME THE OPPORTUNITY TO DO IT NOW.

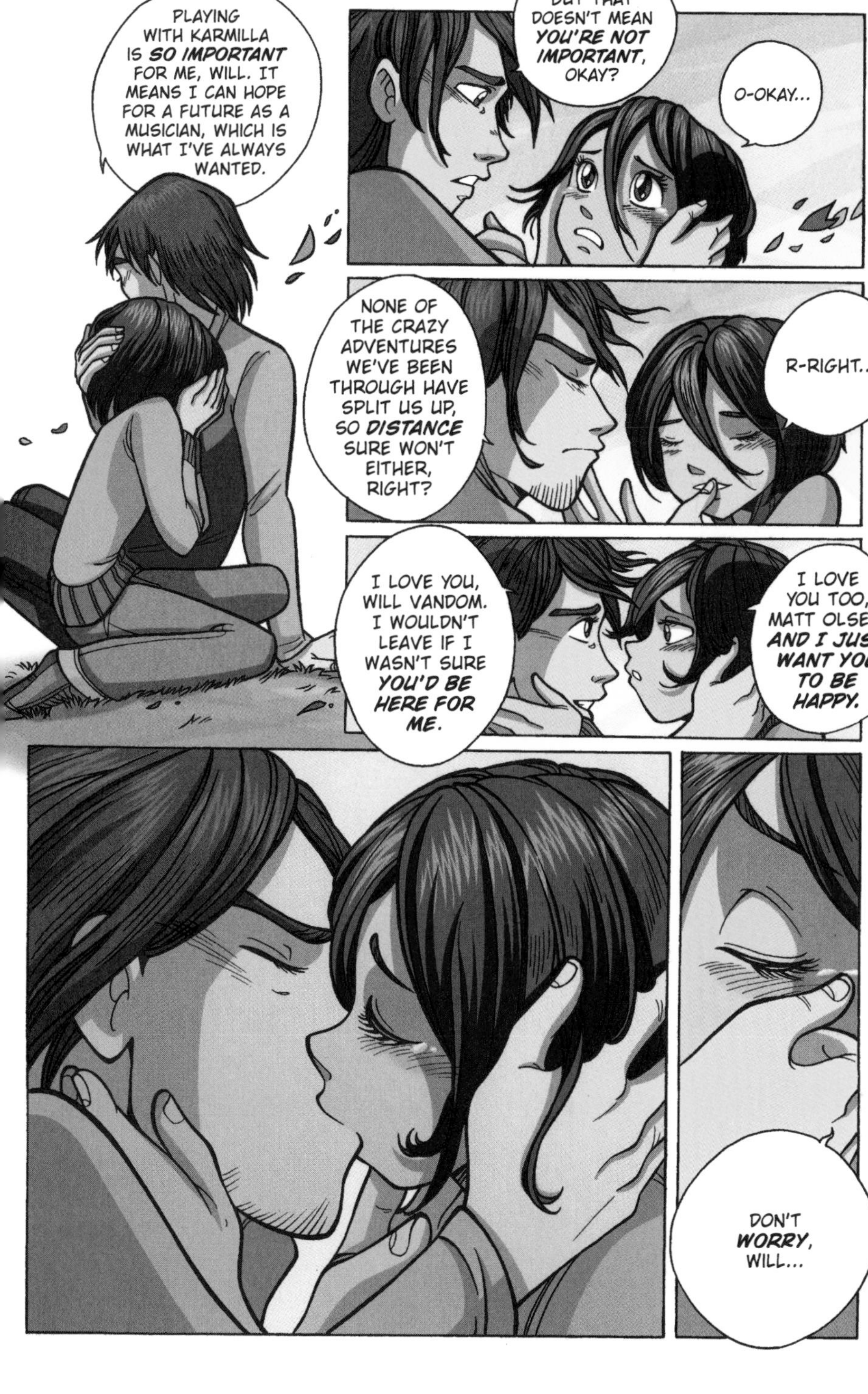
PLAYING WITH KARMILLA IS **SO IMPORTANT** FOR ME, WILL. IT MEANS I CAN HOPE FOR A FUTURE AS A MUSICIAN, WHICH IS WHAT I'VE ALWAYS WANTED.
BUT THAT DOESN'T MEAN ***YOU'RE NOT IMPORTANT***, OKAY?
O-OKAY...
NONE OF THE CRAZY ADVENTURES WE'VE BEEN THROUGH HAVE SPLIT US UP, SO ***DISTANCE*** SURE WON'T EITHER, RIGHT?
R-RIGHT...
I LOVE YOU, WILL VANDOM. I WOULDN'T LEAVE IF I WASN'T SURE ***YOU'D BE HERE FOR ME***.
I LOVE YOU TOO, MATT OLSEN. ***AND I JUST WANT YOU TO BE HAPPY.***
DON'T ***WORRY***, WILL...

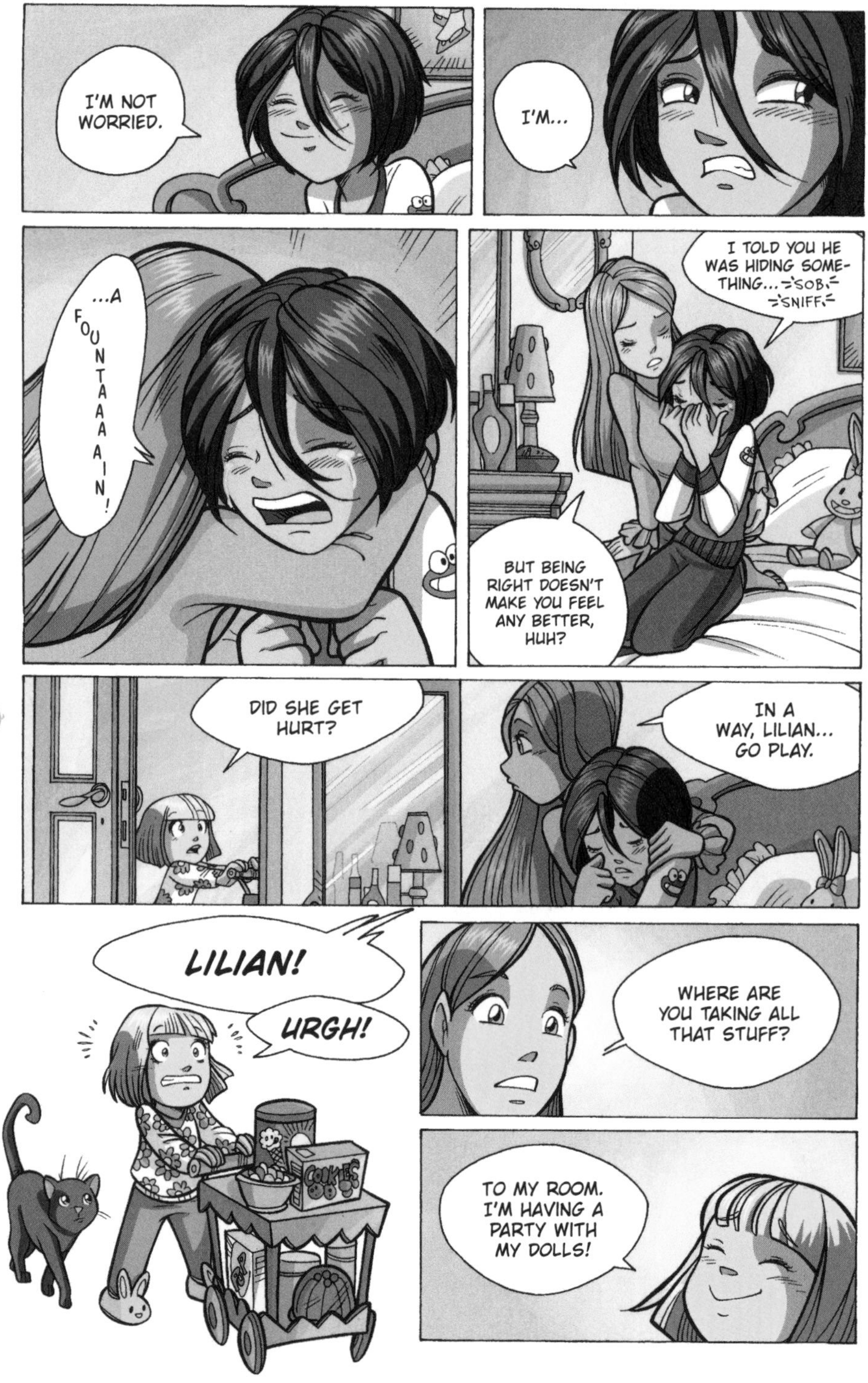

I'M NOT WORRIED.
I'M...
...A FOUNTAAAAAIN!
I TOLD YOU HE WAS HIDING SOME-THING... SOB SNIFF
BUT BEING RIGHT DOESN'T MAKE YOU FEEL ANY BETTER, HUH?
DID SHE GET HURT?
IN A WAY, LILIAN... GO PLAY.
LILIAN!
URGH!
WHERE ARE YOU TAKING ALL THAT STUFF?
TO MY ROOM. I'M HAVING A PARTY WITH MY DOLLS!
COOKIES

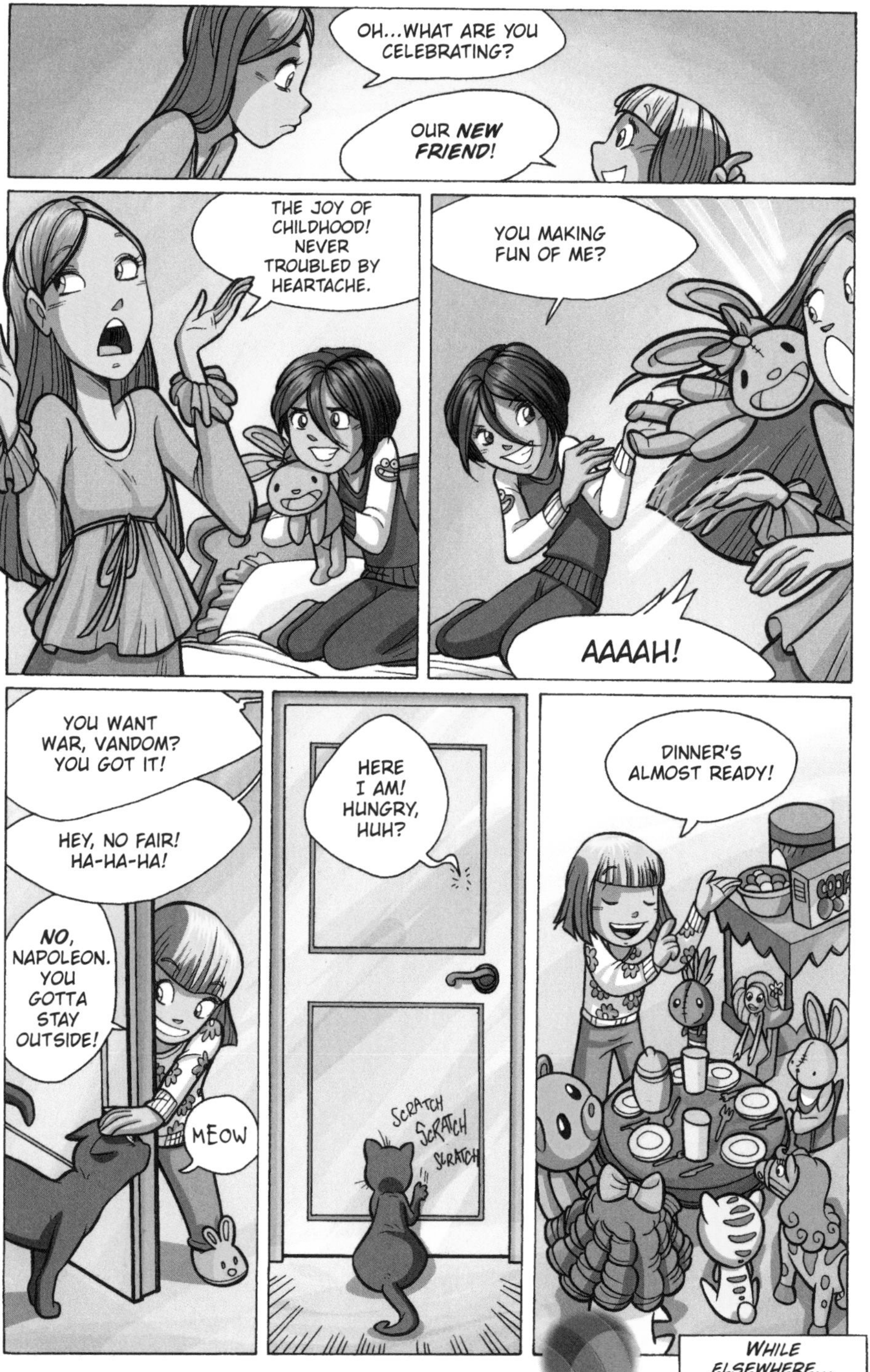
OH...WHAT ARE YOU CELEBRATING?
OUR NEW FRIEND!
THE JOY OF CHILDHOOD! NEVER TROUBLED BY HEARTACHE.
YOU MAKING FUN OF ME?
AAAAH!
YOU WANT WAR, VANDOM? YOU GOT IT!
HEY, NO FAIR! HA-HA-HA!
NO, NAPOLEON. YOU GOTTA STAY OUTSIDE!
MEOW
HERE I AM! HUNGRY, HUH?
SCRATCH SCRATCH SCRATCH
DINNER'S ALMOST READY!
WHILE ELSEWHERE...

W.I.T.C.H.

Will Irma Taranee Cornelia Hay Lin

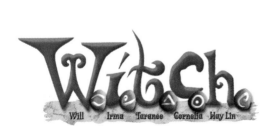

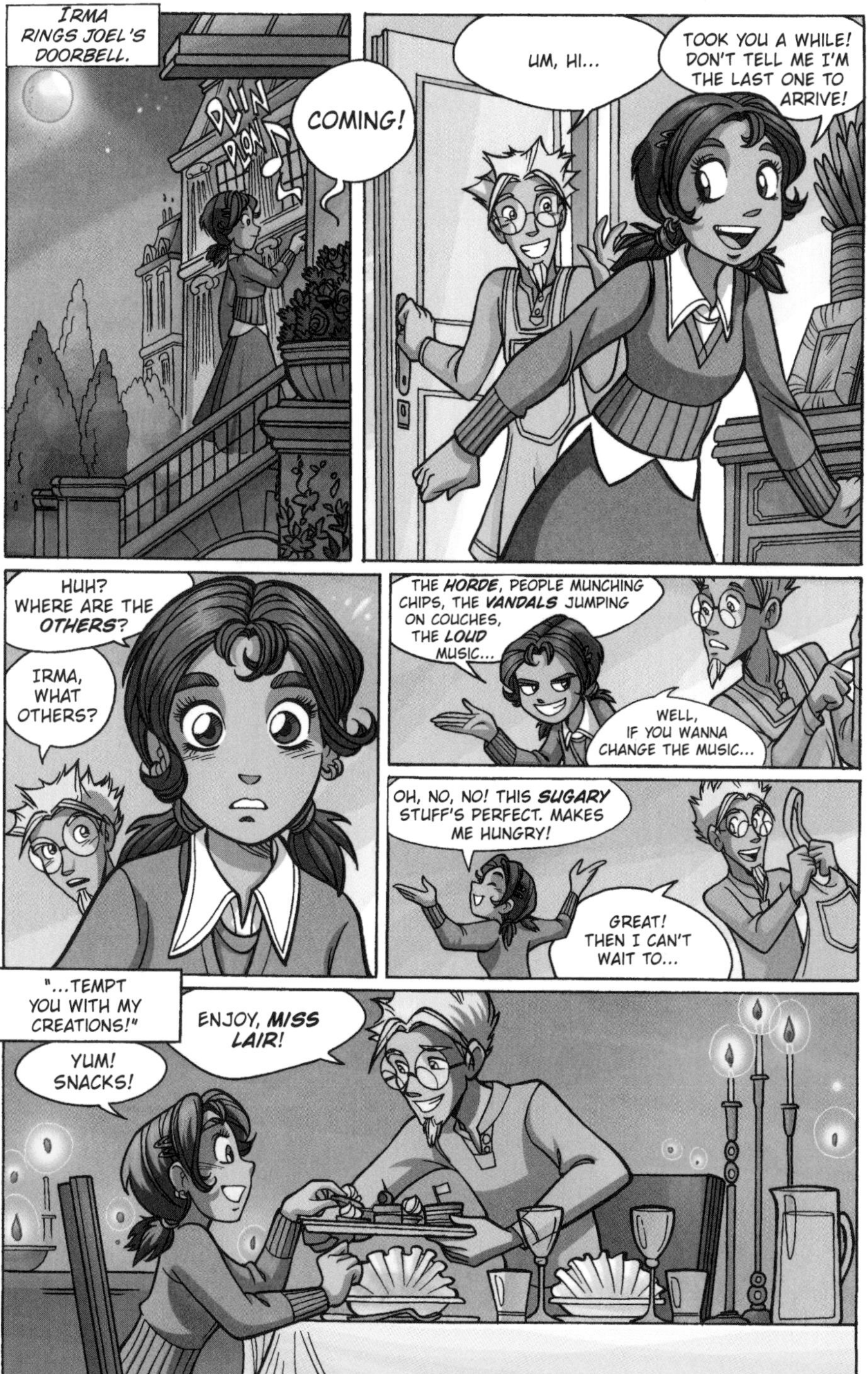
IRMA RINGS JOEL'S DOORBELL.
DLIN DLON
COMING!
UM, HI...
TOOK YOU A WHILE! DON'T TELL ME I'M THE LAST ONE TO ARRIVE!
HUH? WHERE ARE THE **OTHERS**?
IRMA, WHAT OTHERS?
THE **HORDE**, PEOPLE MUNCHING CHIPS, THE **VANDALS** JUMPING ON COUCHES, THE **LOUD** MUSIC...
WELL, IF YOU WANNA CHANGE THE MUSIC...
OH, NO, NO! THIS **SUGARY** STUFF'S PERFECT. MAKES ME HUNGRY!
GREAT! THEN I CAN'T WAIT TO...
"...TEMPT YOU WITH MY CREATIONS!"
ENJOY, **MISS LAIR**!
YUM! SNACKS!

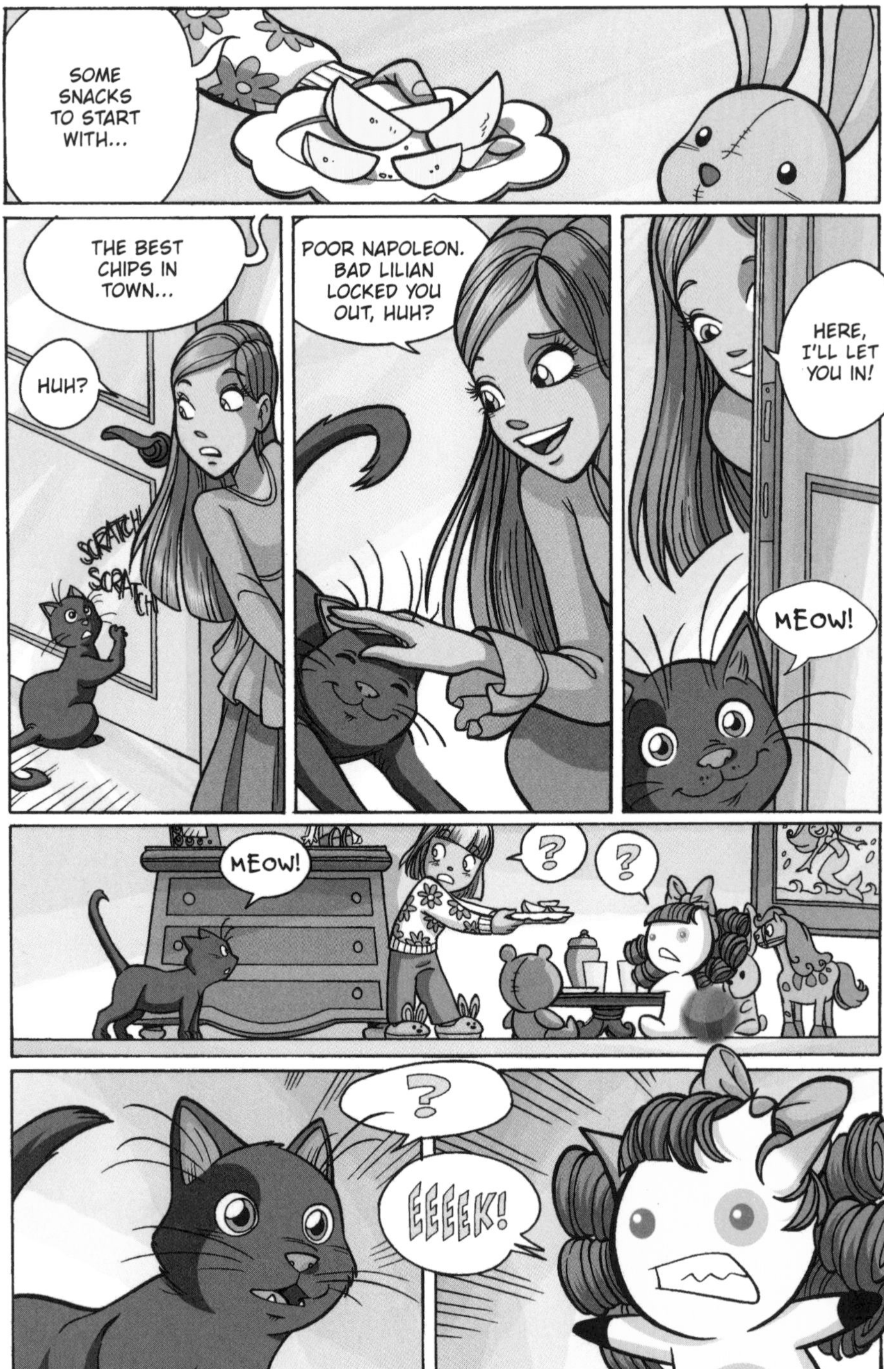
SOME SNACKS TO START WITH...
THE BEST CHIPS IN TOWN...
HUH?
SCRATCH! SCRATCH!
POOR NAPOLEON. BAD LILIAN LOCKED YOU OUT, HUH?
HERE, I'LL LET YOU IN!
MEOW!
MEOW!
?
?
?
EEEEK!

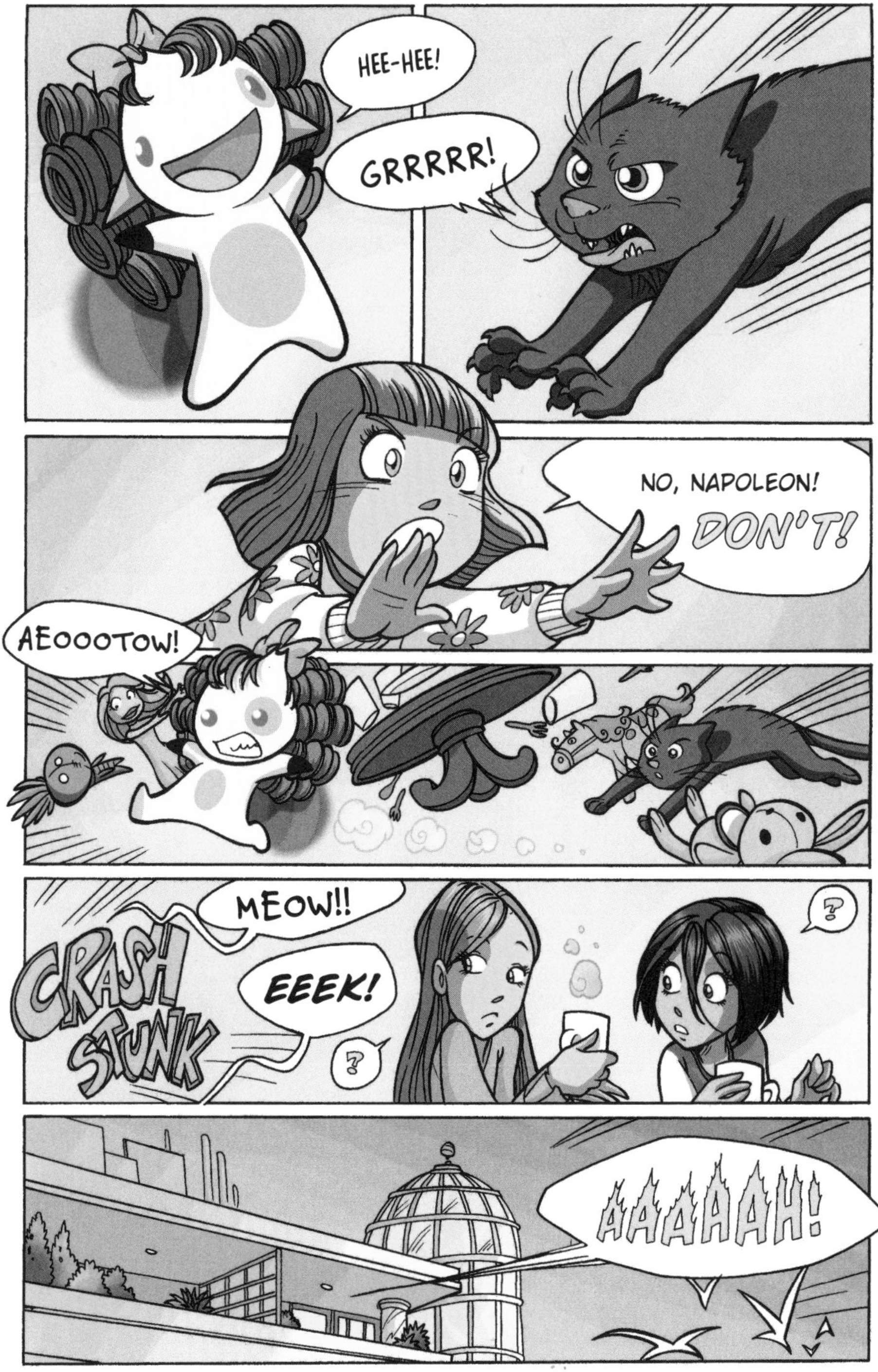
HEE-HEE!
GRRRRR!
NO, NAPOLEON!
DON'T!
AEOOOTOW!
MEOW!!
CRASH
STUNK
EEEK!
?
?
AAAAAH!

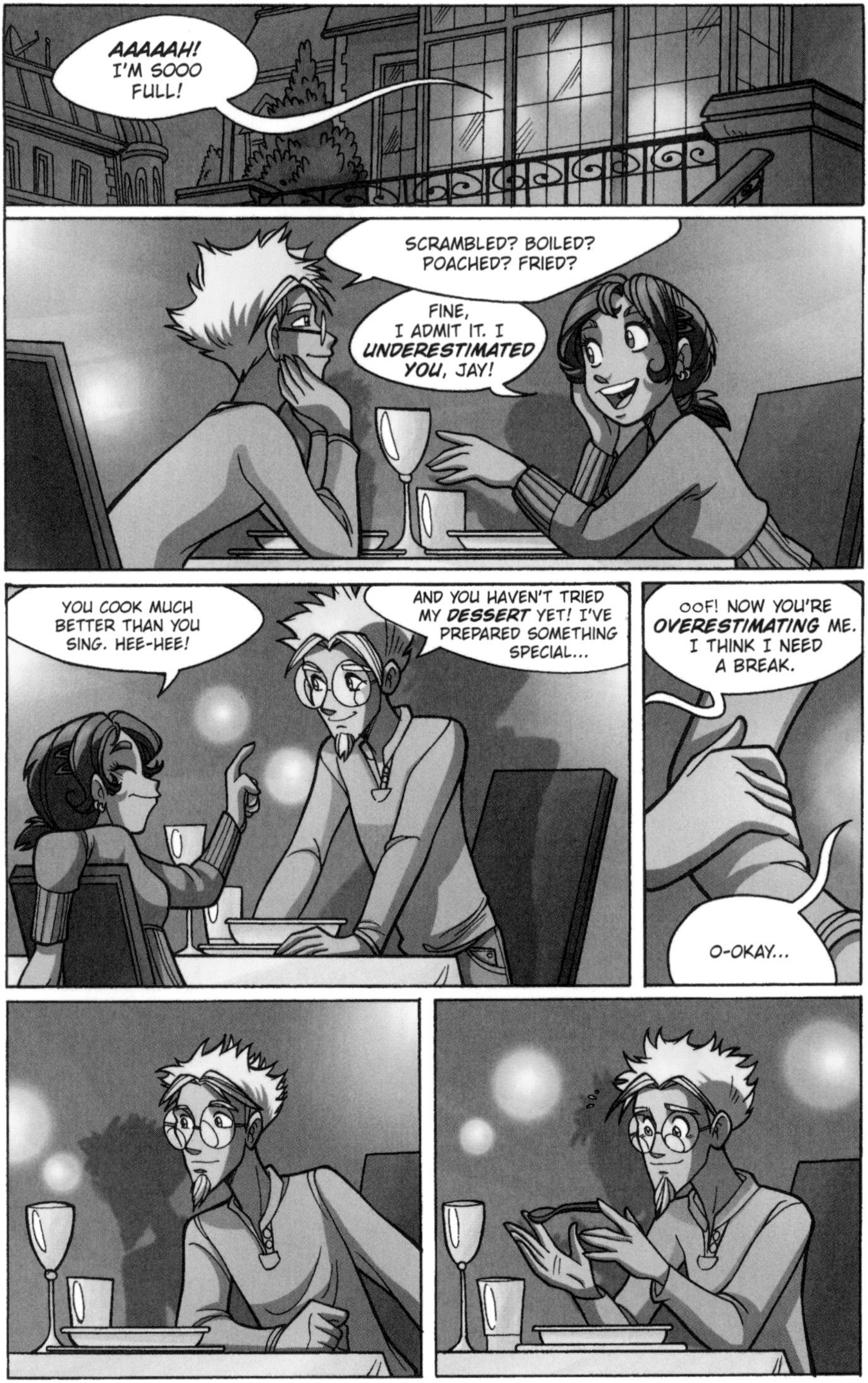

AAAAAH! I'M SOOO FULL!
SCRAMBLED? BOILED? POACHED? FRIED?
FINE, I ADMIT IT. I ***UNDERESTIMATED YOU***, JAY!
YOU COOK MUCH BETTER THAN YOU SING. HEE-HEE!
AND YOU HAVEN'T TRIED MY ***DESSERT*** YET! I'VE PREPARED SOMETHING SPECIAL...
OOF! NOW YOU'RE ***OVERESTIMATING*** ME. I THINK I NEED A BREAK.
O-OKAY...

164

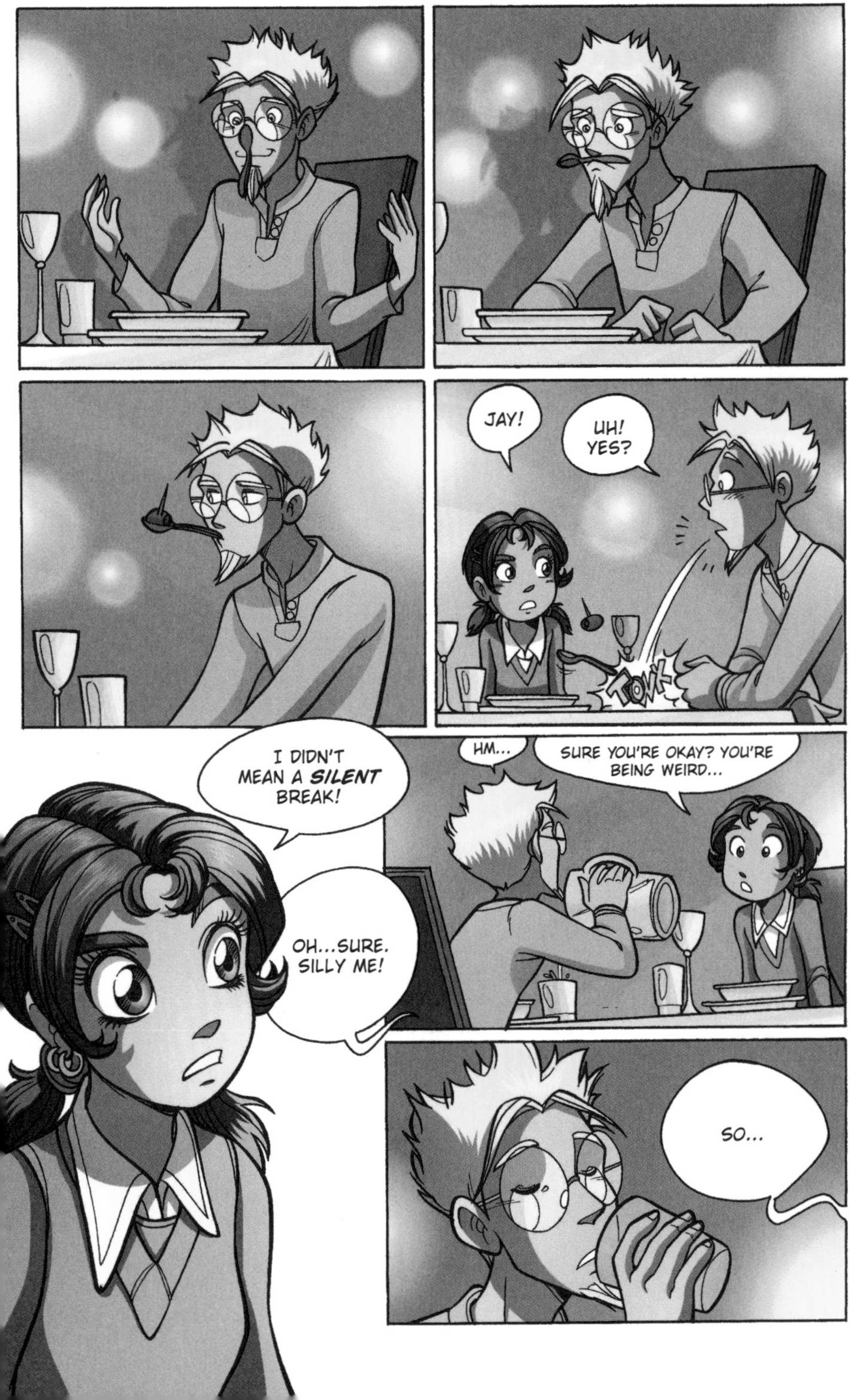
JAY!
UH! YES?
TONK
I DIDN'T MEAN A SILENT BREAK!
OH...SURE. SILLY ME!
HM...
SURE YOU'RE OKAY? YOU'RE BEING WEIRD...
SO...

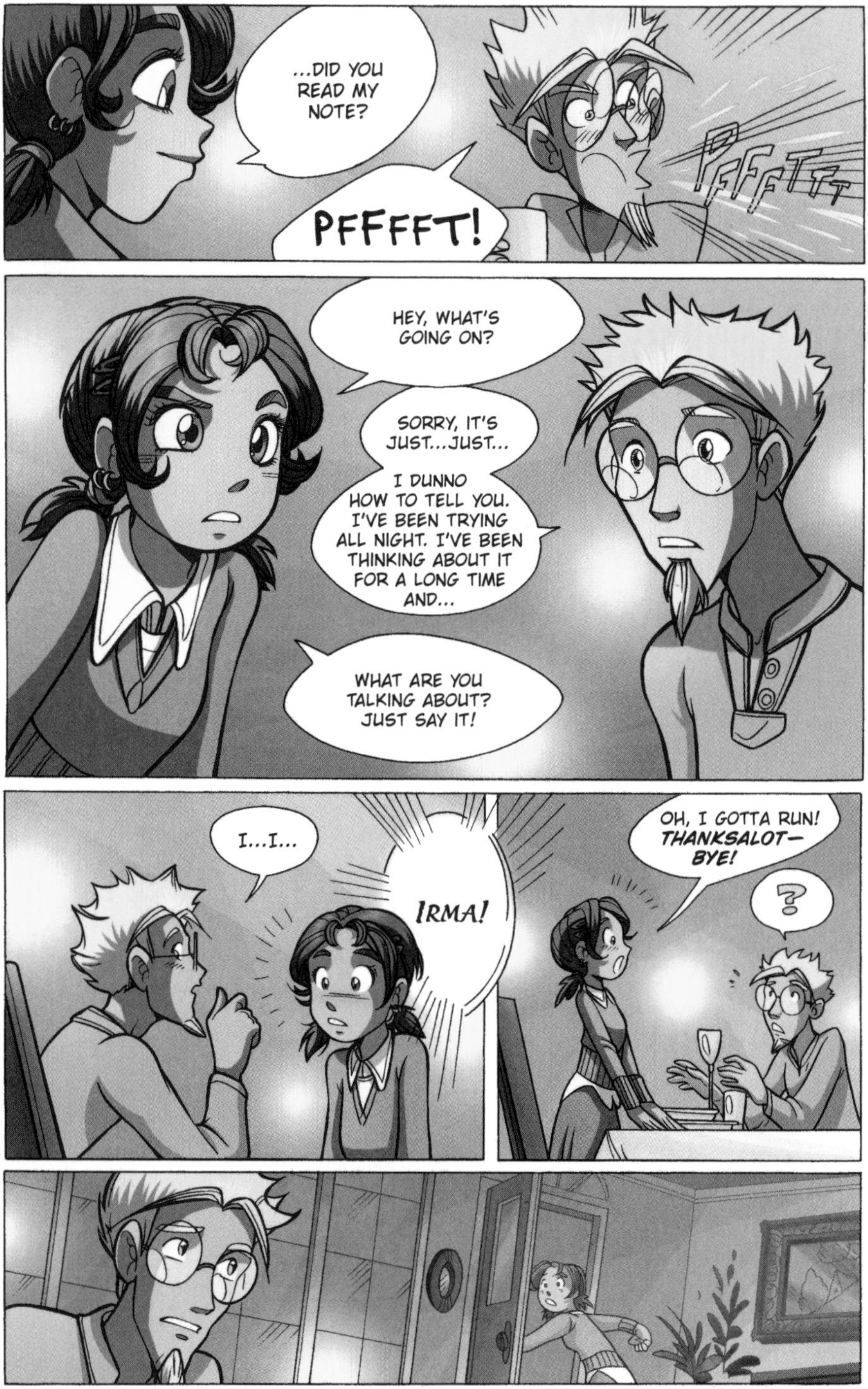
...DID YOU READ MY NOTE?
PFFFFT!
PFFFTTTT
HEY, WHAT'S GOING ON?
SORRY, IT'S JUST...JUST...
I DUNNO HOW TO TELL YOU. I'VE BEEN TRYING ALL NIGHT. I'VE BEEN THINKING ABOUT IT FOR A LONG TIME AND...
WHAT ARE YOU TALKING ABOUT? JUST SAY IT!
I...I...
IRMA!
OH, I GOTTA RUN! THANKSALOT—BYE!
?

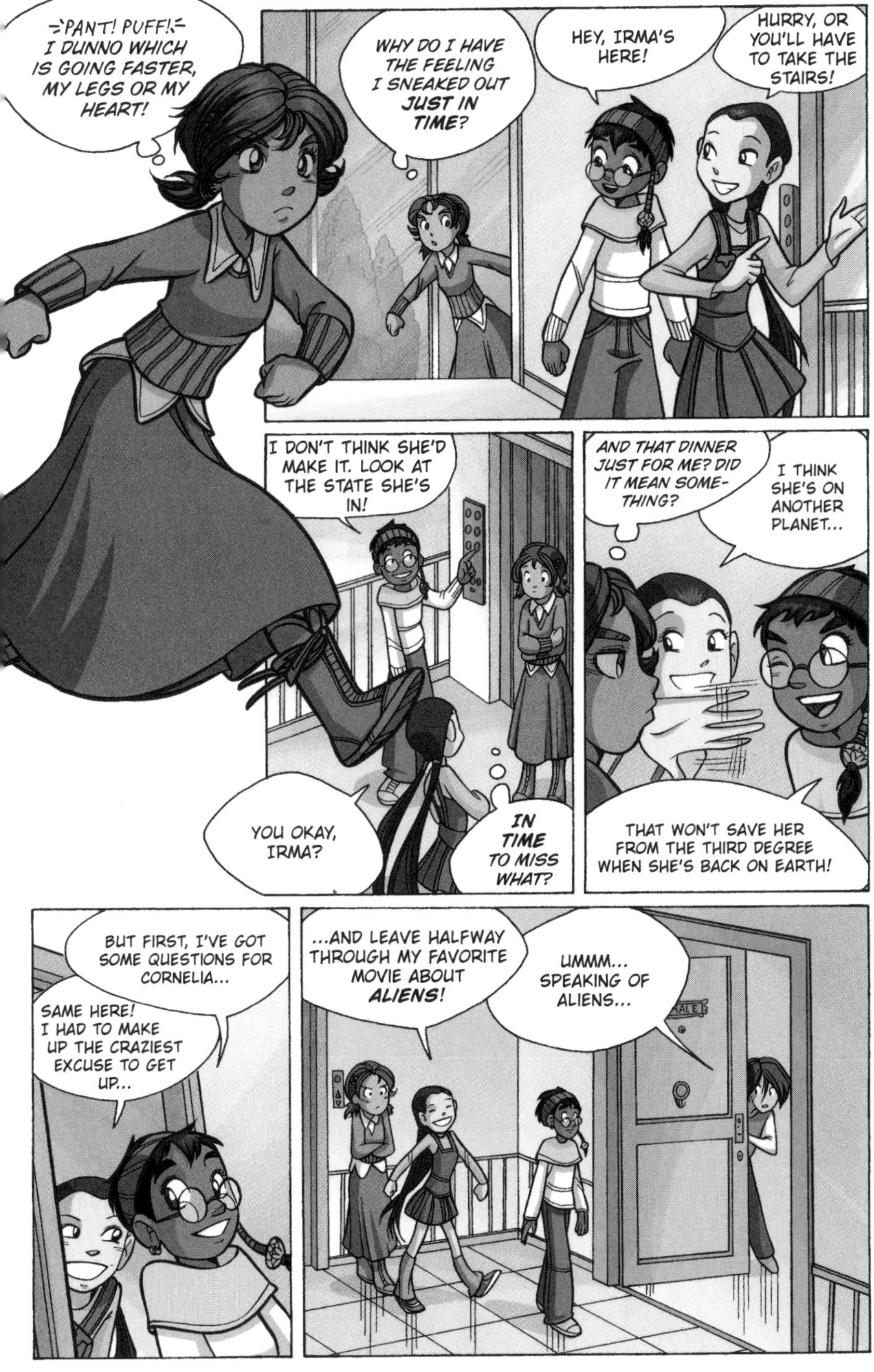
=PANT! PUFF!= I DUNNO WHICH IS GOING FASTER, MY LEGS OR MY HEART!
WHY DO I HAVE THE FEELING I SNEAKED OUT JUST IN TIME?
HEY, IRMA'S HERE!
HURRY, OR YOU'LL HAVE TO TAKE THE STAIRS!
I DON'T THINK SHE'D MAKE IT. LOOK AT THE STATE SHE'S IN!
YOU OKAY, IRMA?
IN TIME TO MISS WHAT?
AND THAT DINNER JUST FOR ME? DID IT MEAN SOME-THING?
I THINK SHE'S ON ANOTHER PLANET...
THAT WON'T SAVE HER FROM THE THIRD DEGREE WHEN SHE'S BACK ON EARTH!
BUT FIRST, I'VE GOT SOME QUESTIONS FOR CORNELIA...
SAME HERE! I HAD TO MAKE UP THE CRAZIEST EXCUSE TO GET UP...
...AND LEAVE HALFWAY THROUGH MY FAVORITE MOVIE ABOUT ALIENS!
UMMM... SPEAKING OF ALIENS...
HALE

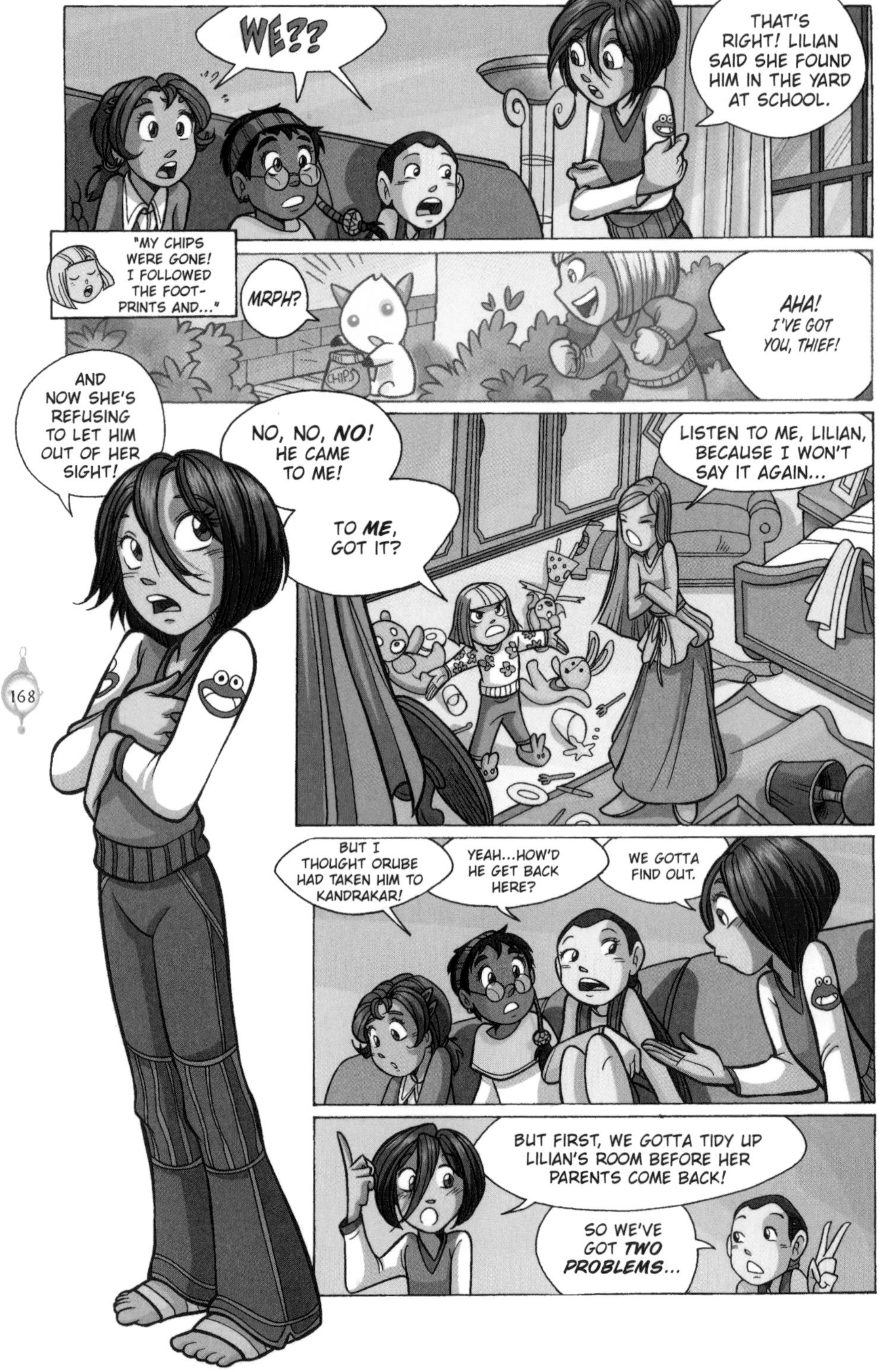
WE??
THAT'S RIGHT! LILIAN SAID SHE FOUND HIM IN THE YARD AT SCHOOL.
"MY CHIPS WERE GONE! I FOLLOWED THE FOOT-PRINTS AND..."
MRPH?
CHIPS
AHA! I'VE GOT YOU, THIEF!
AND NOW SHE'S REFUSING TO LET HIM OUT OF HER SIGHT!
NO, NO, NO! HE CAME TO ME!
TO ME, GOT IT?
LISTEN TO ME, LILIAN, BECAUSE I WON'T SAY IT AGAIN...
BUT I THOUGHT ORUBE HAD TAKEN HIM TO KANDRAKAR!
YEAH...HOW'D HE GET BACK HERE?
WE GOTTA FIND OUT.
BUT FIRST, WE GOTTA TIDY UP LILIAN'S ROOM BEFORE HER PARENTS COME BACK!
SO WE'VE GOT TWO PROBLEMS...

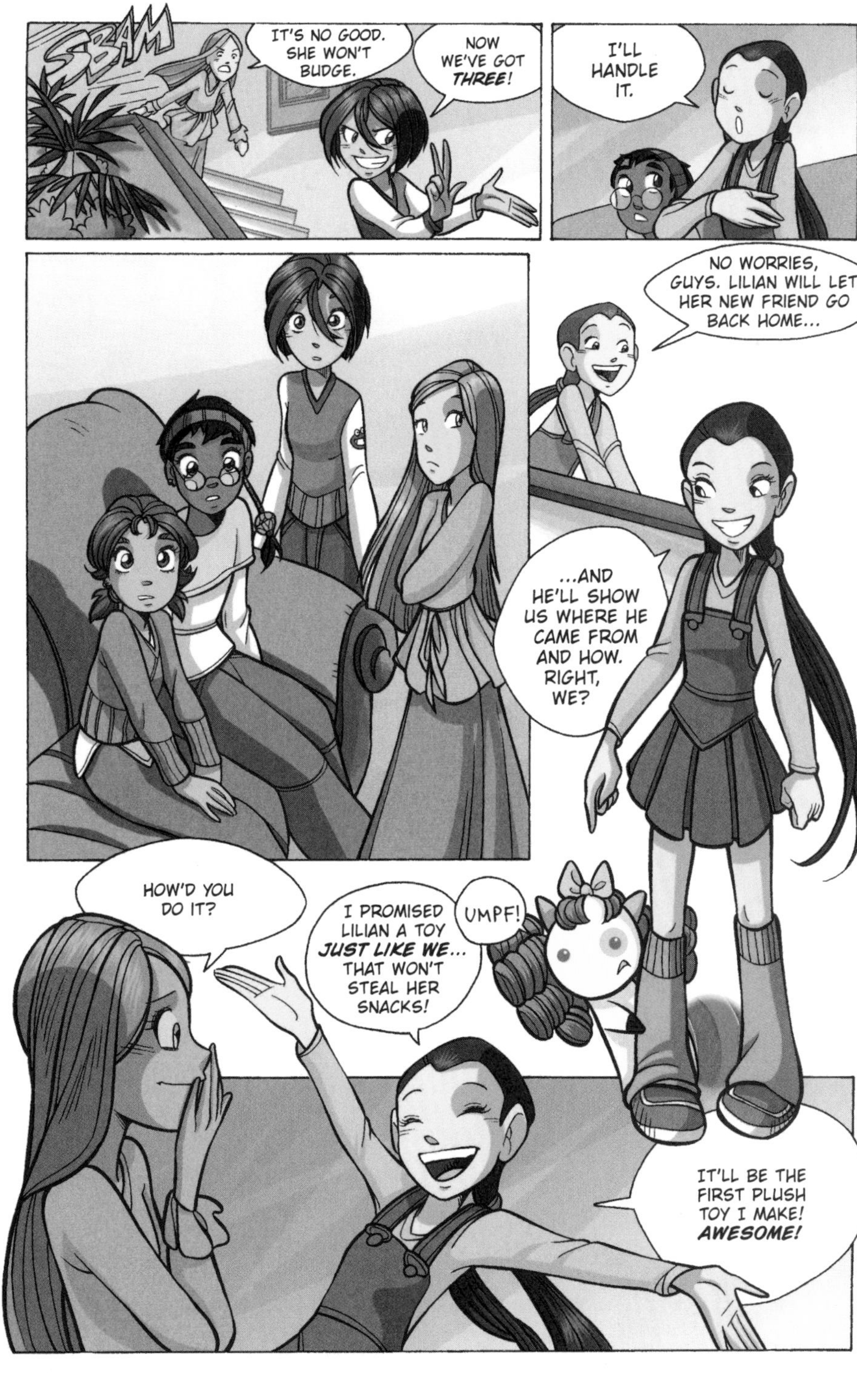
SBAM
IT'S NO GOOD. SHE WON'T BUDGE.
NOW WE'VE GOT ***THREE!***
I'LL HANDLE IT.
NO WORRIES, GUYS. LILIAN WILL LET HER NEW FRIEND GO BACK HOME...
...AND HE'LL SHOW US WHERE HE CAME FROM AND HOW. RIGHT, WE?
HOW'D YOU DO IT?
I PROMISED LILIAN A TOY ***JUST LIKE WE***... THAT WON'T STEAL HER SNACKS!
UMPF!
IT'LL BE THE FIRST PLUSH TOY I MAKE! ***AWESOME!***

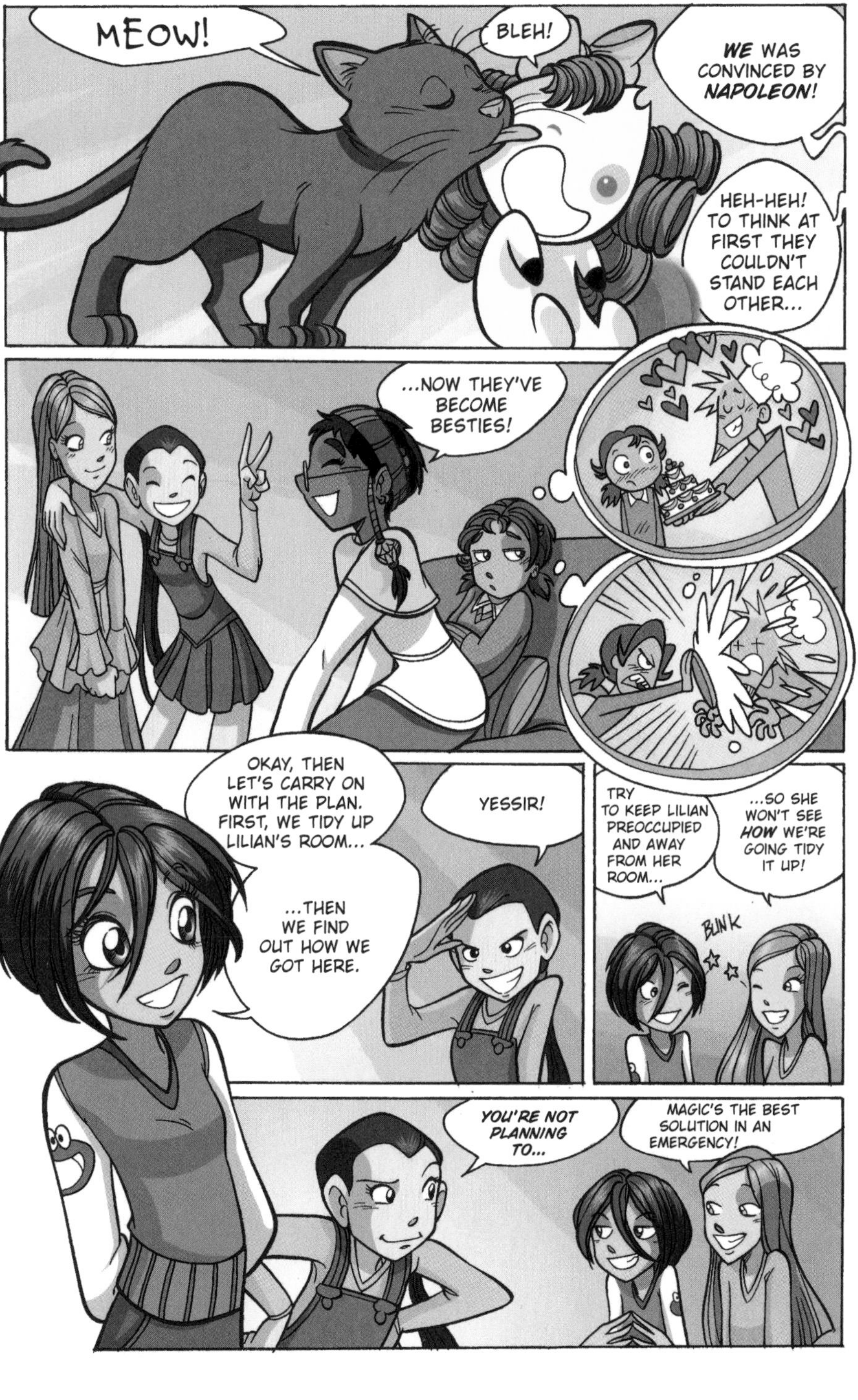
MEOW!
BLEH!
WE WAS CONVINCED BY **NAPOLEON!**
HEH-HEH! TO THINK AT FIRST THEY COULDN'T STAND EACH OTHER...
...NOW THEY'VE BECOME BESTIES!
OKAY, THEN LET'S CARRY ON WITH THE PLAN. FIRST, WE TIDY UP LILIAN'S ROOM...
...THEN WE FIND OUT HOW WE GOT HERE.
YESSIR!
TRY TO KEEP LILIAN PREOCCUPIED AND AWAY FROM HER ROOM...
...SO SHE WON'T SEE **HOW** WE'RE GOING TIDY IT UP!
BLINK
YOU'RE NOT PLANNING TO...
MAGIC'S THE BEST SOLUTION IN AN EMERGENCY!

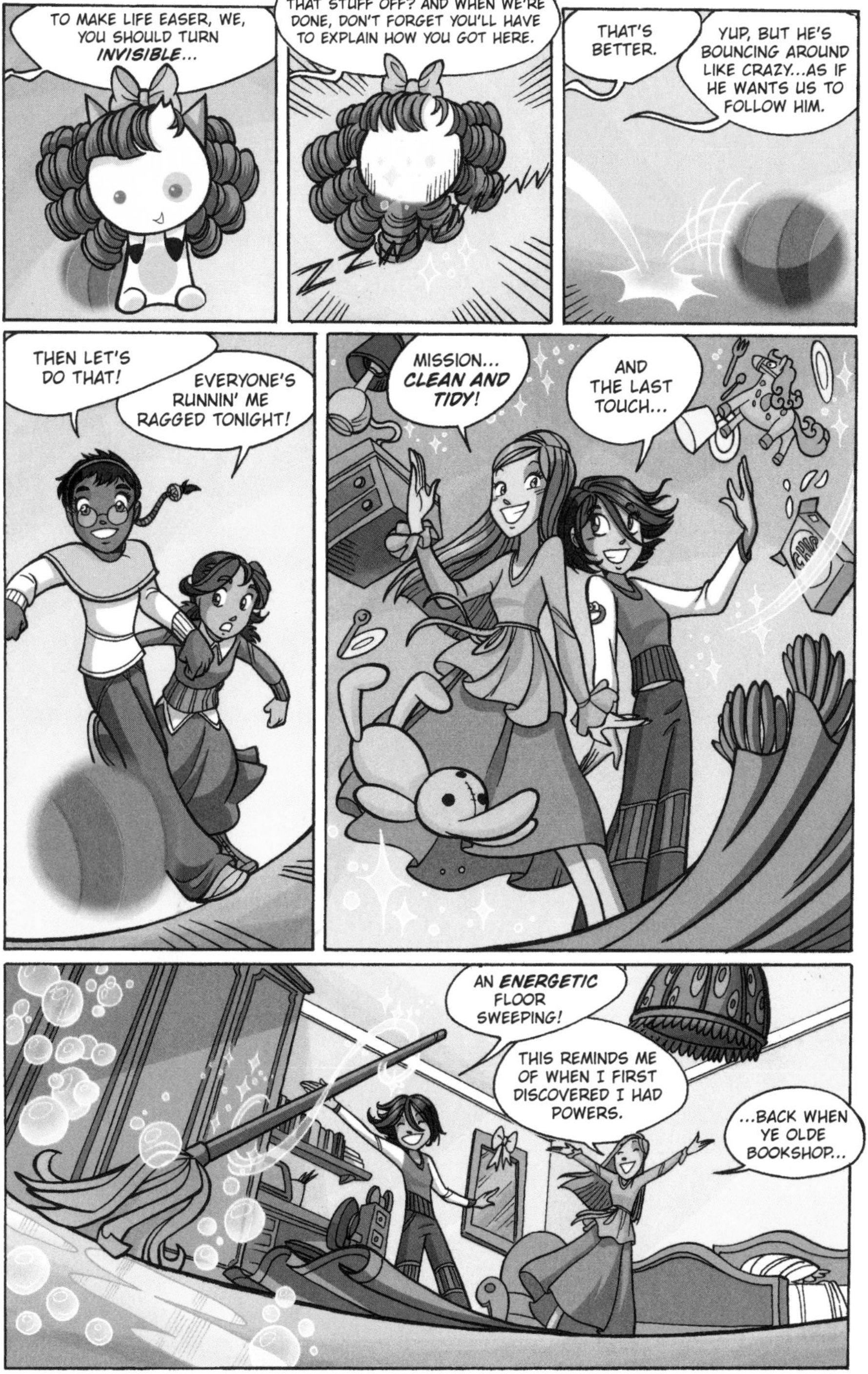
TO MAKE LIFE EASER, WE, YOU SHOULD TURN INVISIBLE...
UM...HOW ABOUT TAKING THAT STUFF OFF? AND WHEN WE'RE DONE, DON'T FORGET YOU'LL HAVE TO EXPLAIN HOW YOU GOT HERE.
THAT'S BETTER.
YUP, BUT HE'S BOUNCING AROUND LIKE CRAZY...AS IF HE WANTS US TO FOLLOW HIM.
THEN LET'S DO THAT!
EVERYONE'S RUNNIN' ME RAGGED TONIGHT!
MISSION... CLEAN AND TIDY!
AND THE LAST TOUCH...
AN ENERGETIC FLOOR SWEEPING!
THIS REMINDS ME OF WHEN I FIRST DISCOVERED I HAD POWERS.
...BACK WHEN YE OLDE BOOKSHOP...

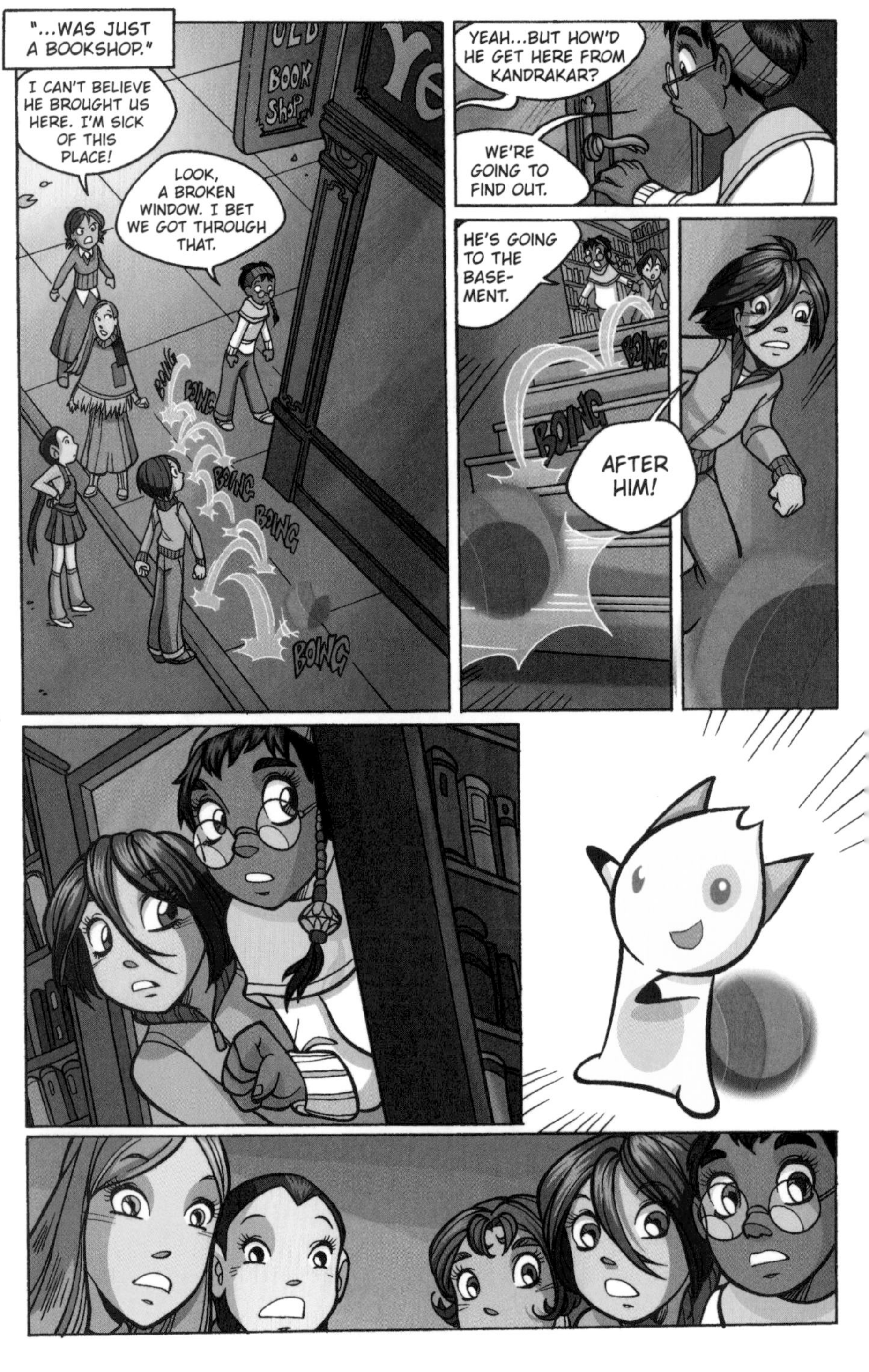
"...WAS JUST A BOOKSHOP."
OLD BOOK Shop
I CAN'T BELIEVE HE BROUGHT US HERE. I'M SICK OF THIS PLACE!
LOOK, A BROKEN WINDOW. I BET WE GOT THROUGH THAT.
BOING
BOING
BOING
BOING
BOING
YEAH...BUT HOW'D HE GET HERE FROM KANDRAKAR?
WE'RE GOING TO FIND OUT.
HE'S GOING TO THE BASE-MENT.
BOING
BOING
AFTER HIM!

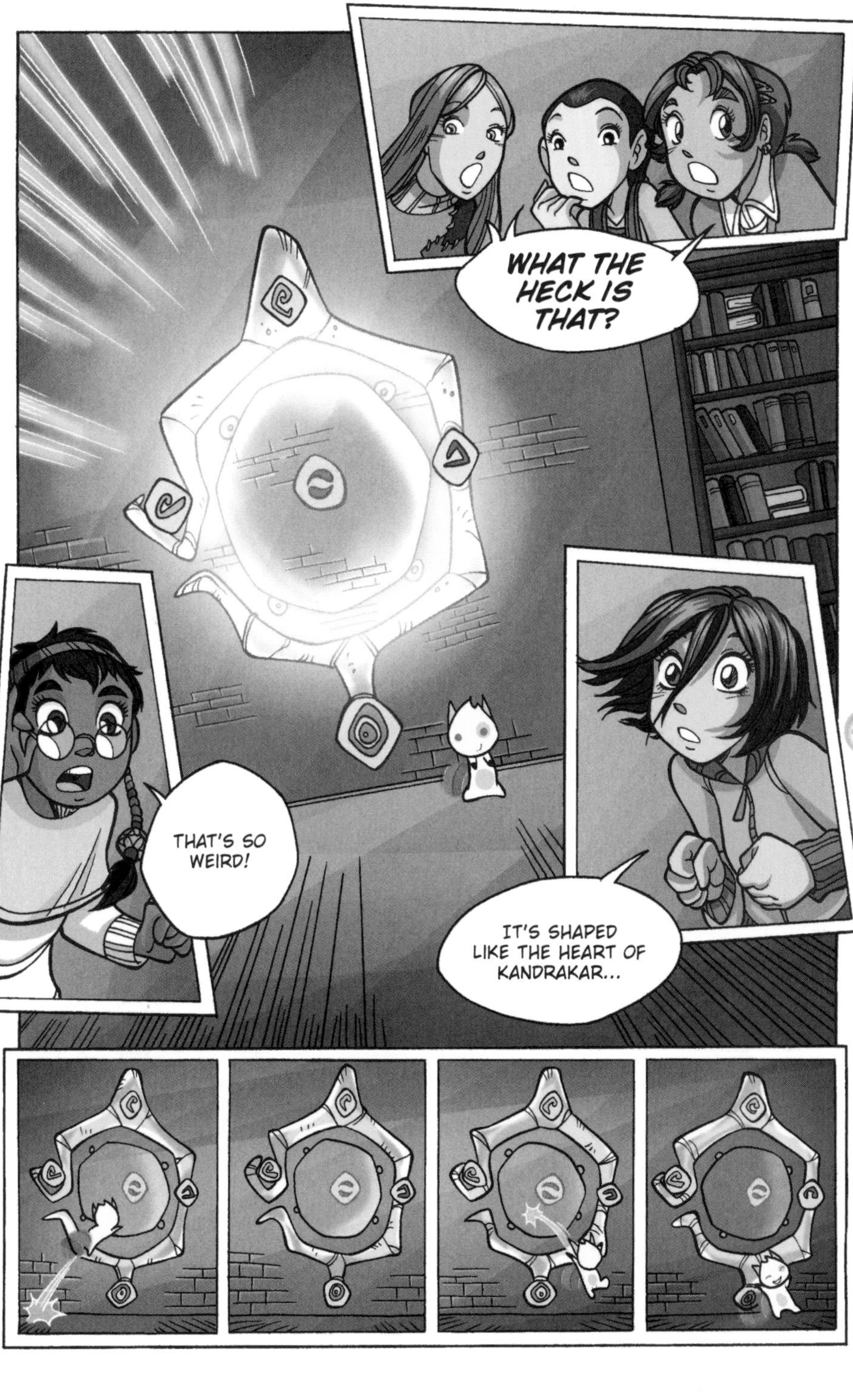

WHAT THE HECK IS THAT?
THAT'S SO WEIRD!
IT'S SHAPED LIKE THE HEART OF KANDRAKAR...

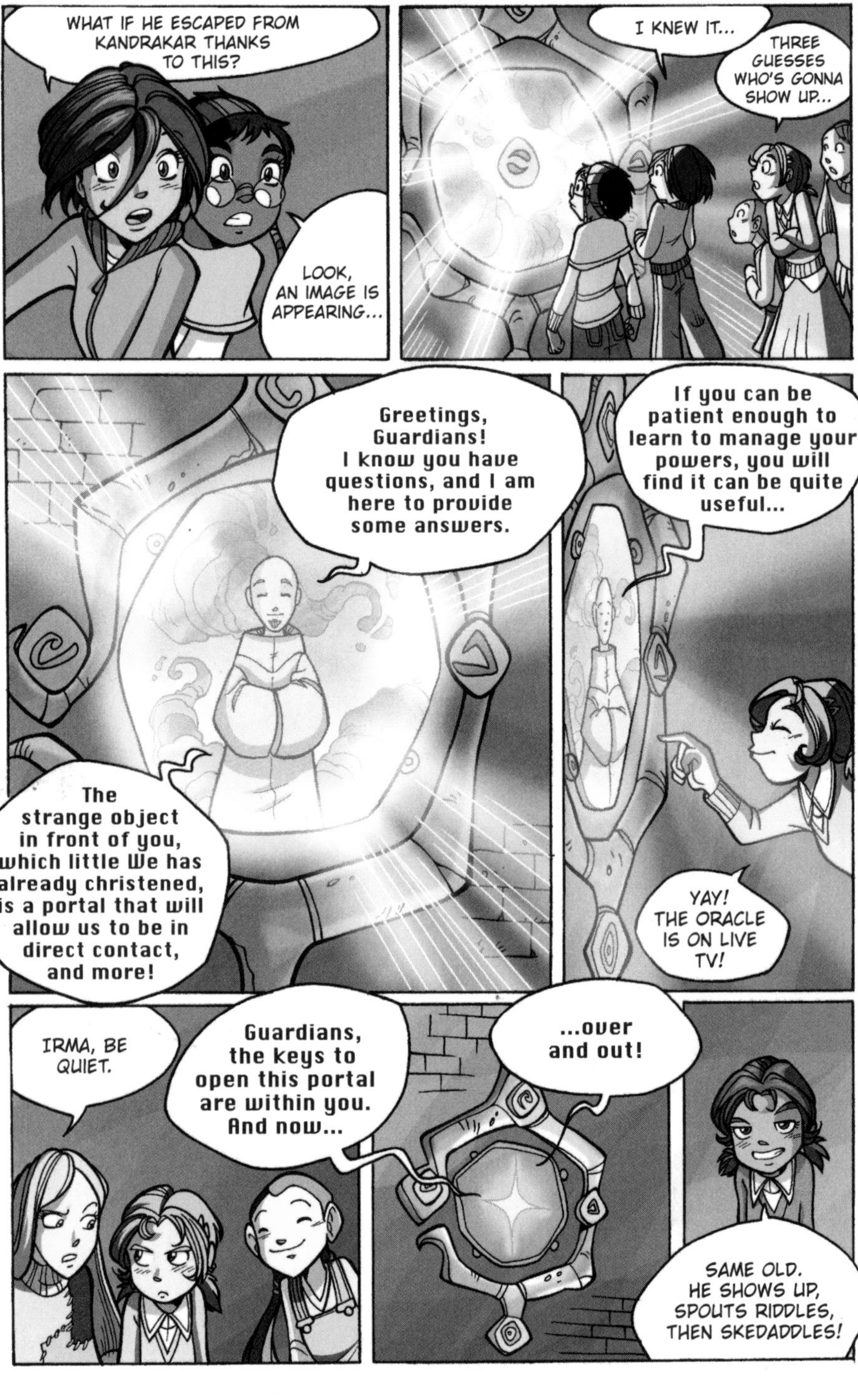
WHAT IF HE ESCAPED FROM KANDRAKAR THANKS TO THIS?
LOOK, AN IMAGE IS APPEARING...
I KNEW IT...
THREE GUESSES WHO'S GONNA SHOW UP...
Greetings, Guardians! I know you have questions, and I am here to provide some answers.
The strange object in front of you, which little We has already christened, is a portal that will allow us to be in direct contact, and more!
If you can be patient enough to learn to manage your powers, you will find it can be quite useful...
YAY! THE ORACLE IS ON LIVE TV!
IRMA, BE QUIET.
Guardians, the keys to open this portal are within you. And now...
...over and out!
SAME OLD. HE SHOWS UP, SPOUTS RIDDLES, THEN SKEDADDLES!

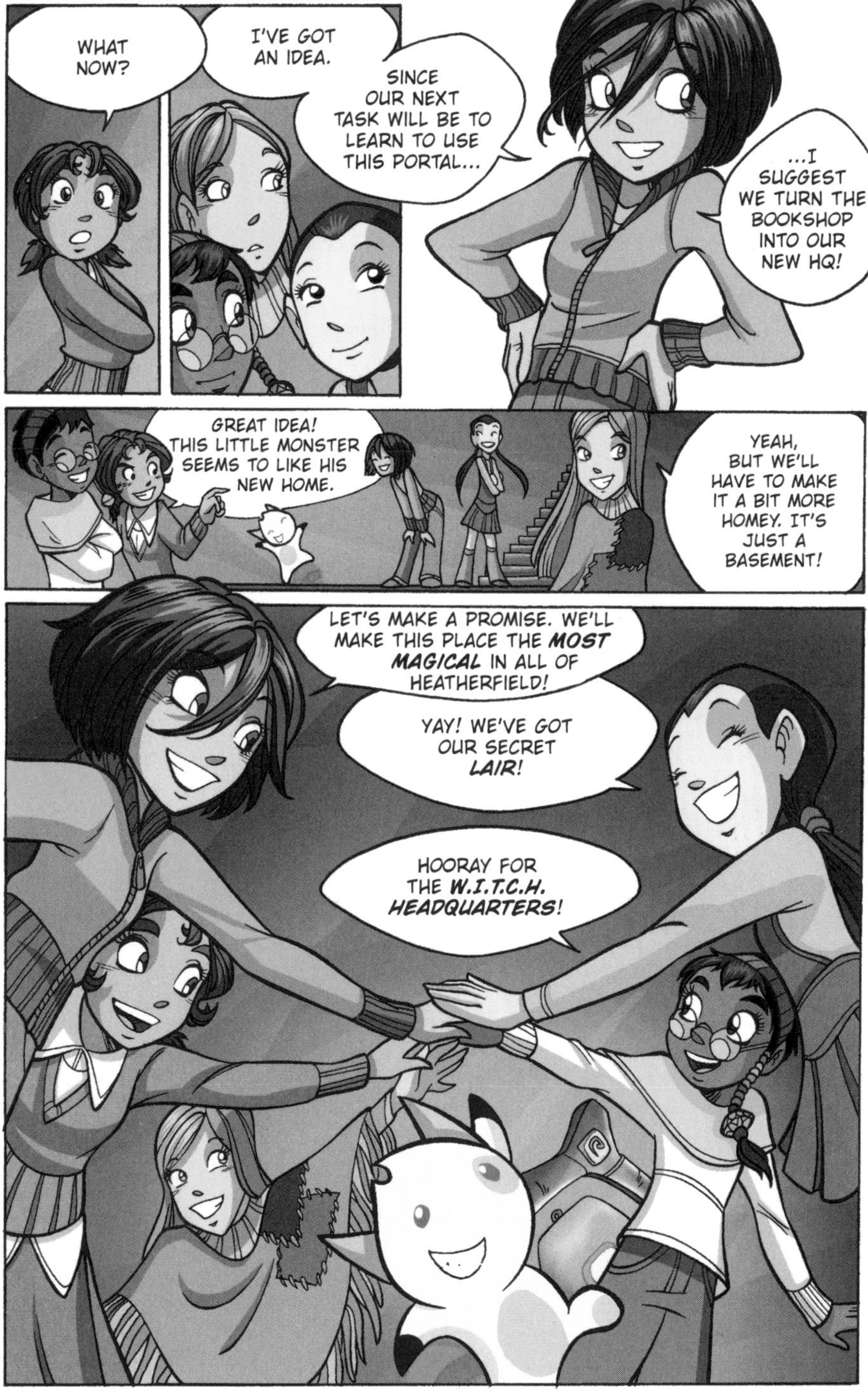
WHAT NOW?
I'VE GOT AN IDEA.
SINCE OUR NEXT TASK WILL BE TO LEARN TO USE THIS PORTAL...
...I SUGGEST WE TURN THE BOOKSHOP INTO OUR NEW HQ!
GREAT IDEA! THIS LITTLE MONSTER SEEMS TO LIKE HIS NEW HOME.
YEAH, BUT WE'LL HAVE TO MAKE IT A BIT MORE HOMEY. IT'S JUST A BASEMENT!
LET'S MAKE A PROMISE. WE'LL MAKE THIS PLACE THE MOST MAGICAL IN ALL OF HEATHERFIELD!
YAY! WE'VE GOT OUR SECRET LAIR!
HOORAY FOR THE W.I.T.C.H. HEADQUARTERS!

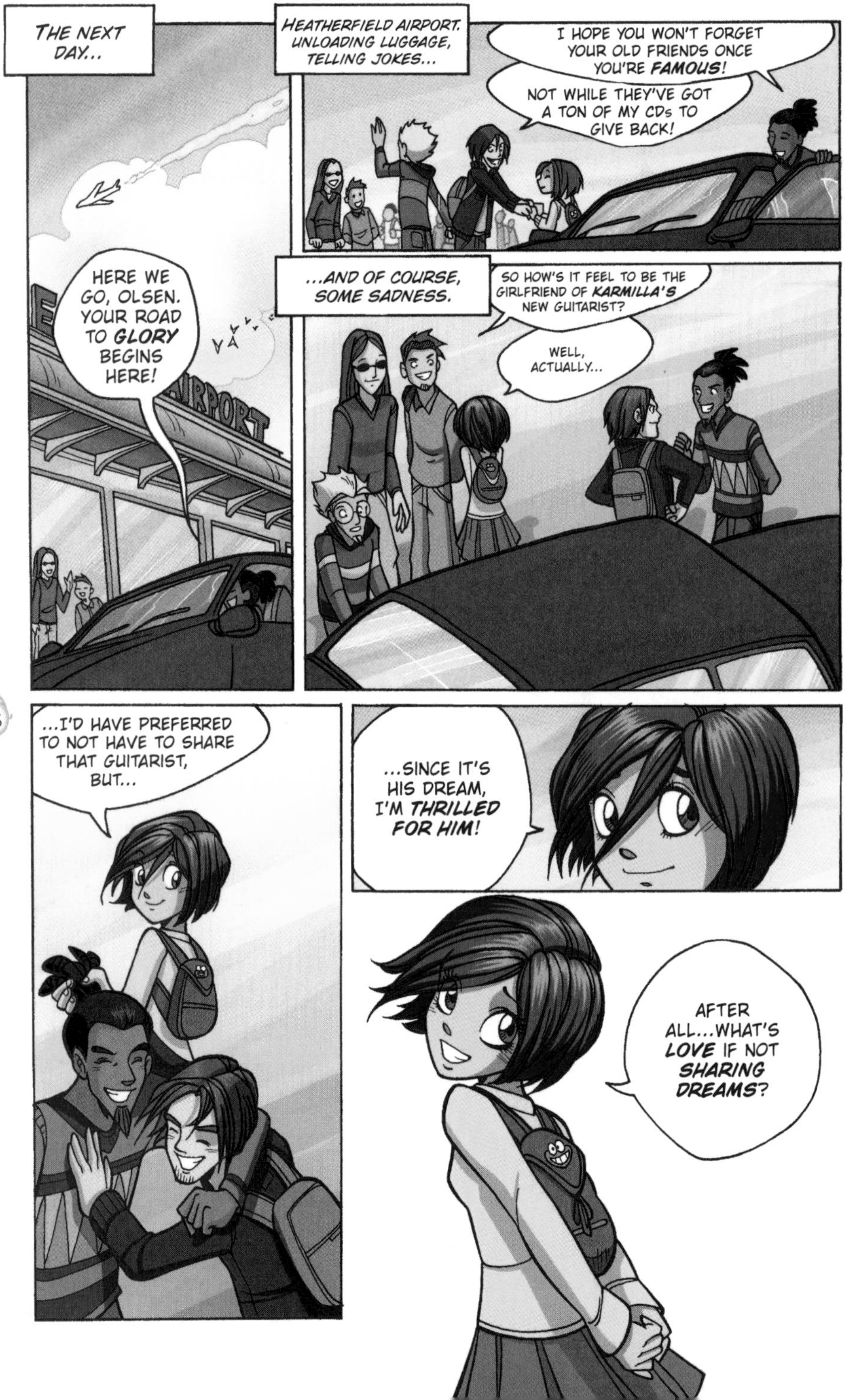
THE NEXT DAY...
HEATHERFIELD AIRPORT. UNLOADING LUGGAGE, TELLING JOKES...
I HOPE YOU WON'T FORGET YOUR OLD FRIENDS ONCE YOU'RE FAMOUS!
NOT WHILE THEY'VE GOT A TON OF MY CDs TO GIVE BACK!
HERE WE GO, OLSEN. YOUR ROAD TO GLORY BEGINS HERE!
AIRPORT
...AND OF COURSE, SOME SADNESS.
SO HOW'S IT FEEL TO BE THE GIRLFRIEND OF KARMILLA'S NEW GUITARIST?
WELL, ACTUALLY...
...I'D HAVE PREFERRED TO NOT HAVE TO SHARE THAT GUITARIST, BUT...
...SINCE IT'S HIS DREAM, I'M THRILLED FOR HIM!
AFTER ALL...WHAT'S LOVE IF NOT SHARING DREAMS?

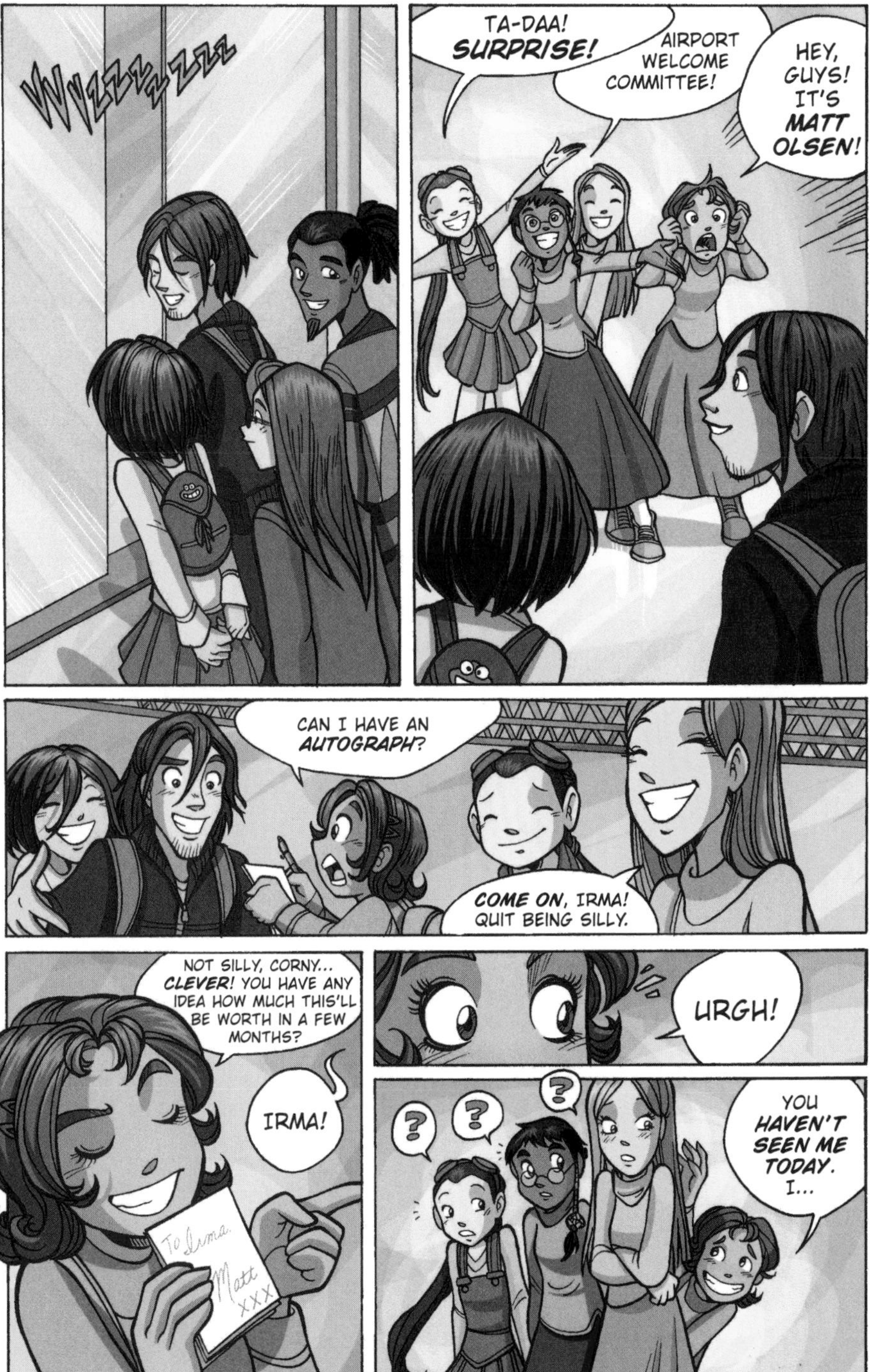
VVVZZZZZZZZ
TA-DAA! SURPRISE!
AIRPORT WELCOME COMMITTEE!
HEY, GUYS! IT'S MATT OLSEN!
CAN I HAVE AN AUTOGRAPH?
COME ON, IRMA! QUIT BEING SILLY.
NOT SILLY, CORNY... CLEVER! YOU HAVE ANY IDEA HOW MUCH THIS'LL BE WORTH IN A FEW MONTHS?
IRMA!
To Irma. Matt XXX
URGH!
?
?
?
YOU HAVEN'T SEEN ME TODAY. I...

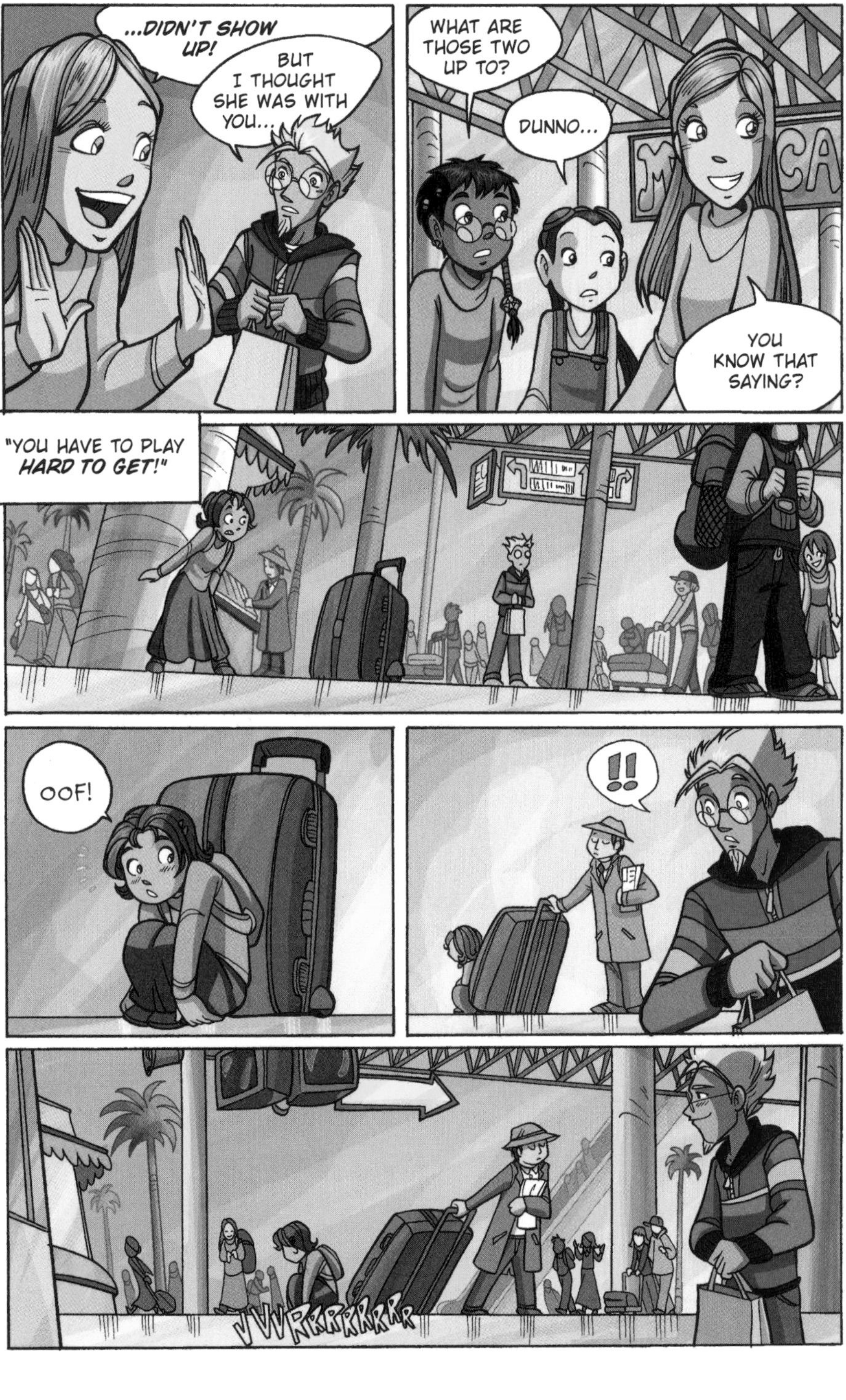
...DIDN'T SHOW UP!
BUT I THOUGHT SHE WAS WITH YOU...
WHAT ARE THOSE TWO UP TO?
DUNNO...
YOU KNOW THAT SAYING?
"YOU HAVE TO PLAY HARD TO GET!"
OOF!
!!
JVVVRRRRRRRRR

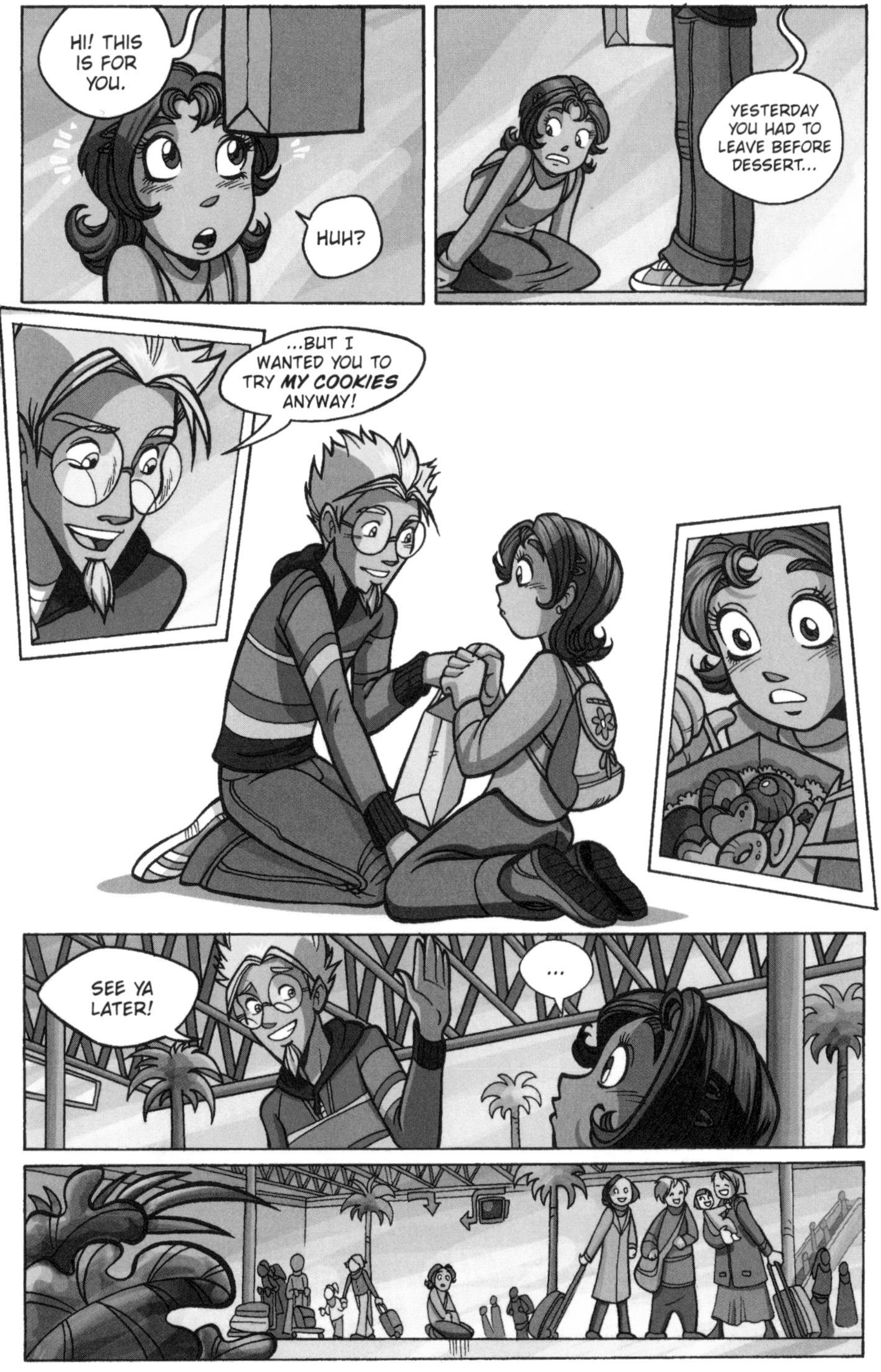
HI! THIS IS FOR YOU.
HUH?
YESTERDAY YOU HAD TO LEAVE BEFORE DESSERT...
...BUT I WANTED YOU TO TRY MY COOKIES ANYWAY!
SEE YA LATER!
...

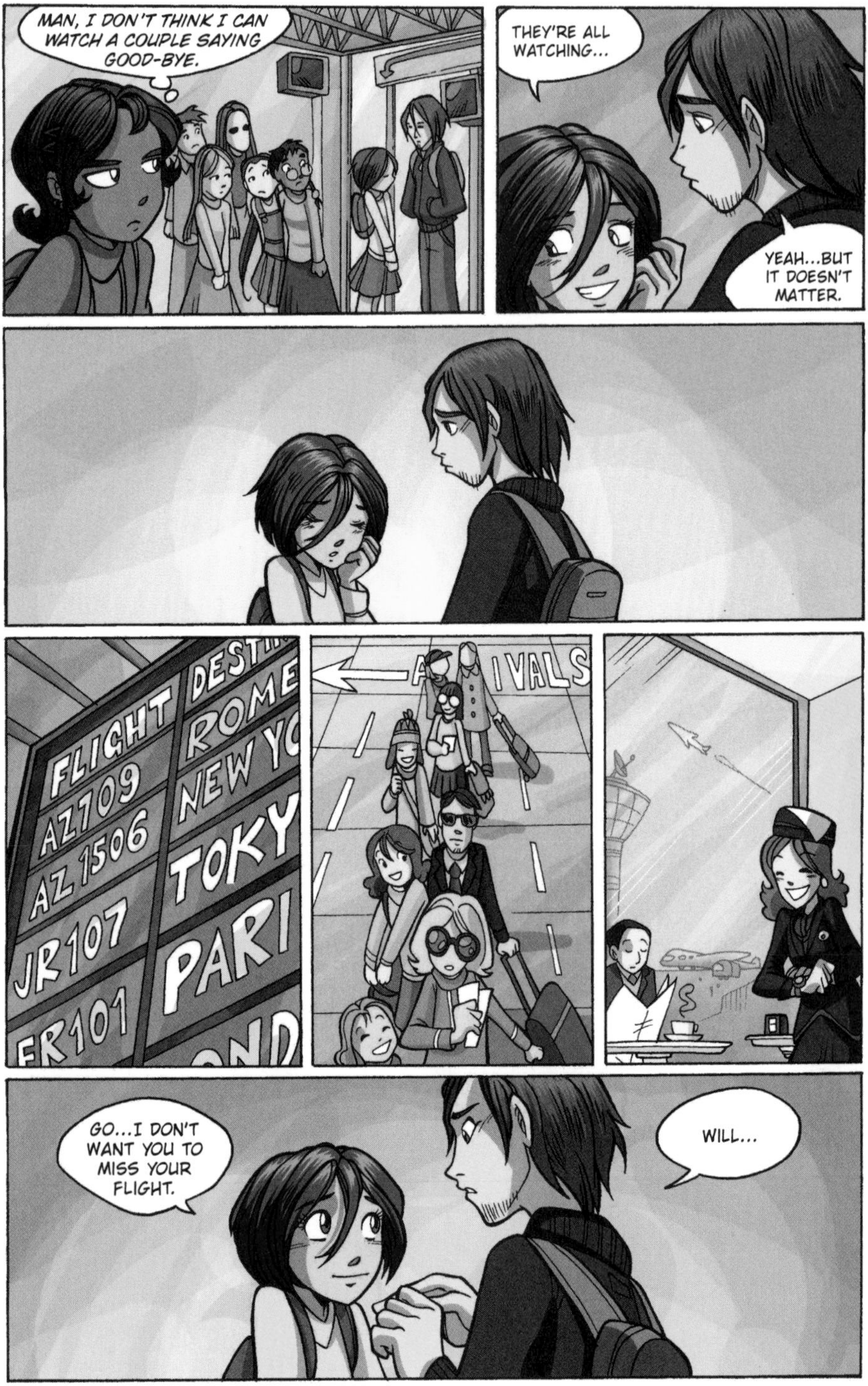
MAN, I DON'T THINK I CAN WATCH A COUPLE SAYING GOOD-BYE.
THEY'RE ALL WATCHING...
YEAH...BUT IT DOESN'T MATTER.
FLIGHT
AZ709
AZ1506
JR107
FR101
ROME
NEW YO
TOKY
PARI
IVALS
GO...I DON'T WANT YOU TO MISS YOUR FLIGHT.
WILL...

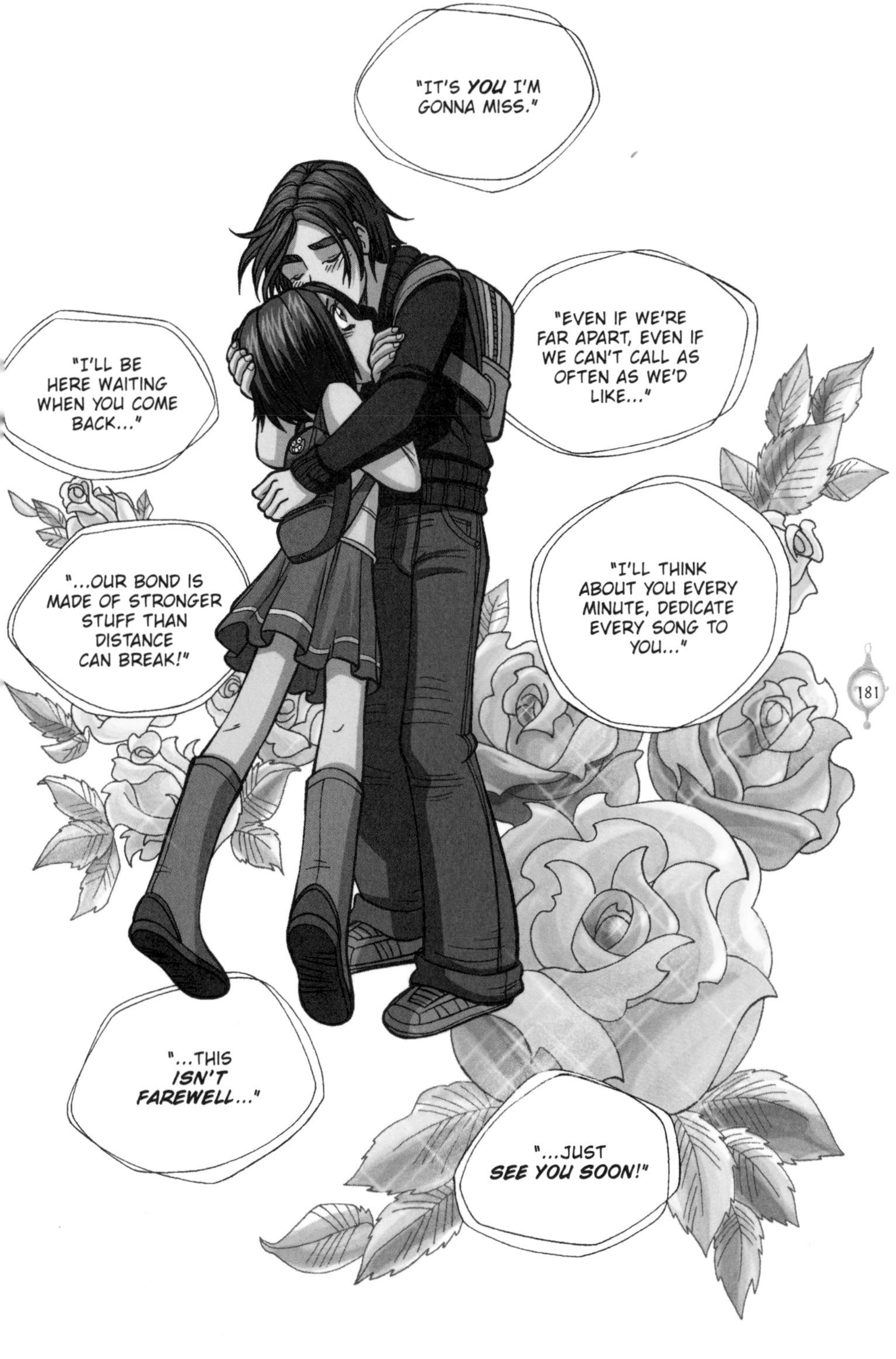
"IT'S YOU I'M GONNA MISS."
"I'LL BE HERE WAITING WHEN YOU COME BACK..."
"EVEN IF WE'RE FAR APART, EVEN IF WE CAN'T CALL AS OFTEN AS WE'D LIKE..."
"...OUR BOND IS MADE OF STRONGER STUFF THAN DISTANCE CAN BREAK!"
"I'LL THINK ABOUT YOU EVERY MINUTE, DEDICATE EVERY SONG TO YOU..."
"...THIS ISN'T FAREWELL..."
"...JUST SEE YOU SOON!"

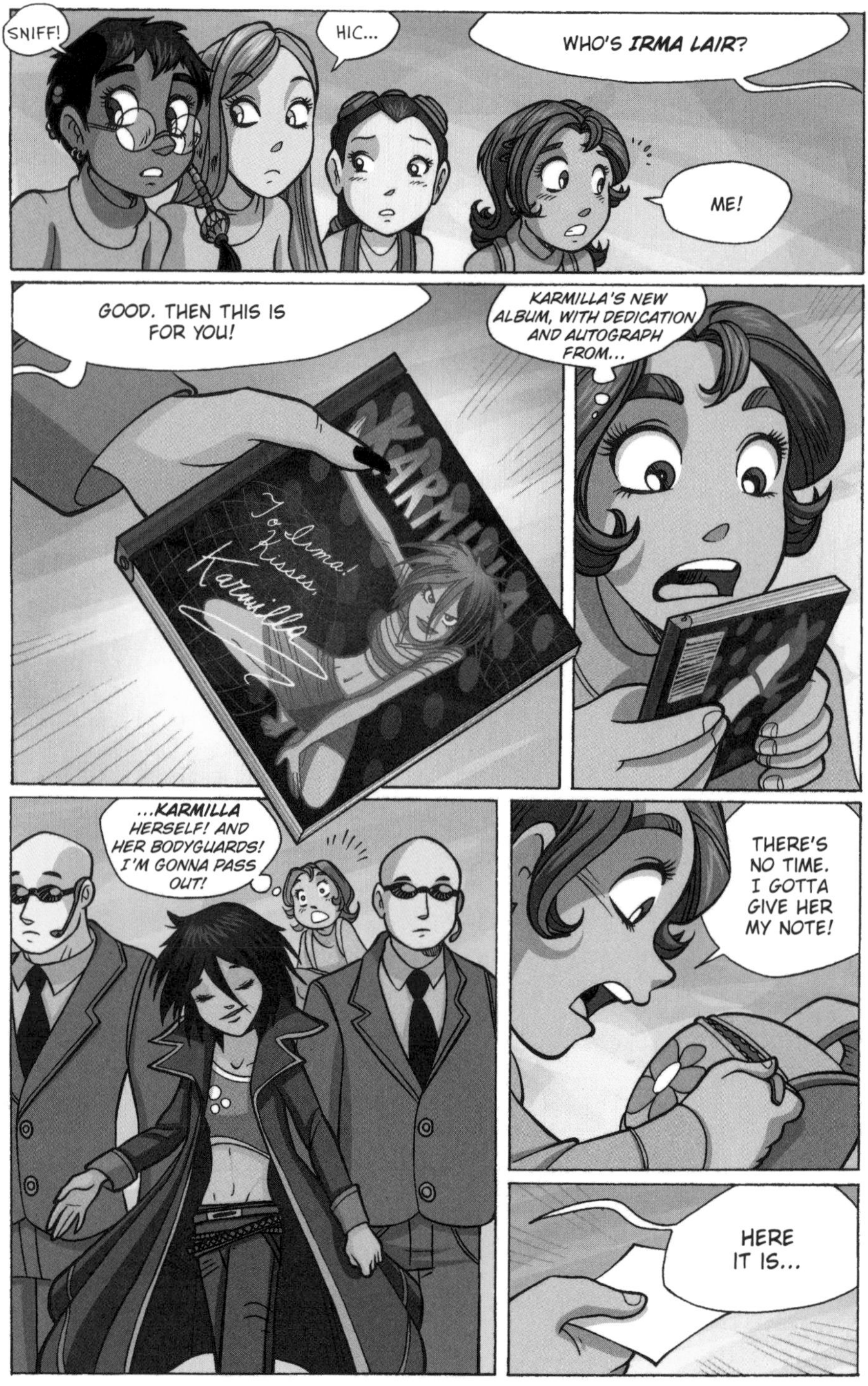
SNIFF!
HIC...
WHO'S IRMA LAIR?
ME!
GOOD. THEN THIS IS FOR YOU!
KARMILLA'S NEW ALBUM, WITH DEDICATION AND AUTOGRAPH FROM...
KARMILLA
To Irma! Kisses, Karmilla
...KARMILLA HERSELF! AND HER BODYGUARDS! I'M GONNA PASS OUT!
THERE'S NO TIME. I GOTTA GIVE HER MY NOTE!
HERE IT IS...

182

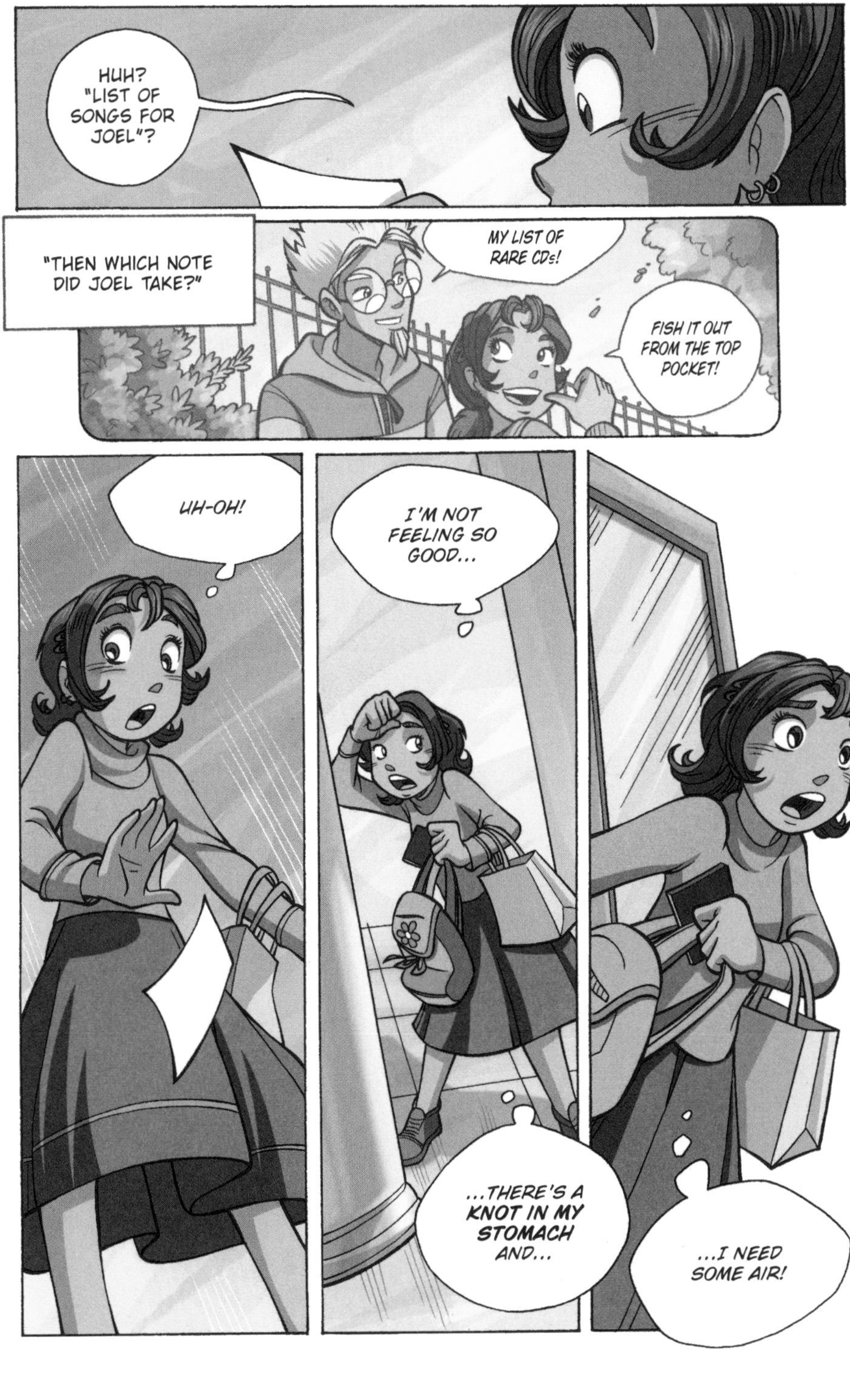

HUH? "LIST OF SONGS FOR JOEL"?
"THEN WHICH NOTE DID JOEL TAKE?"
MY LIST OF RARE CDs!
FISH IT OUT FROM THE TOP POCKET!
UH-OH!
I'M NOT FEELING SO GOOD...
...THERE'S A KNOT IN MY STOMACH AND...
...I NEED SOME AIR!

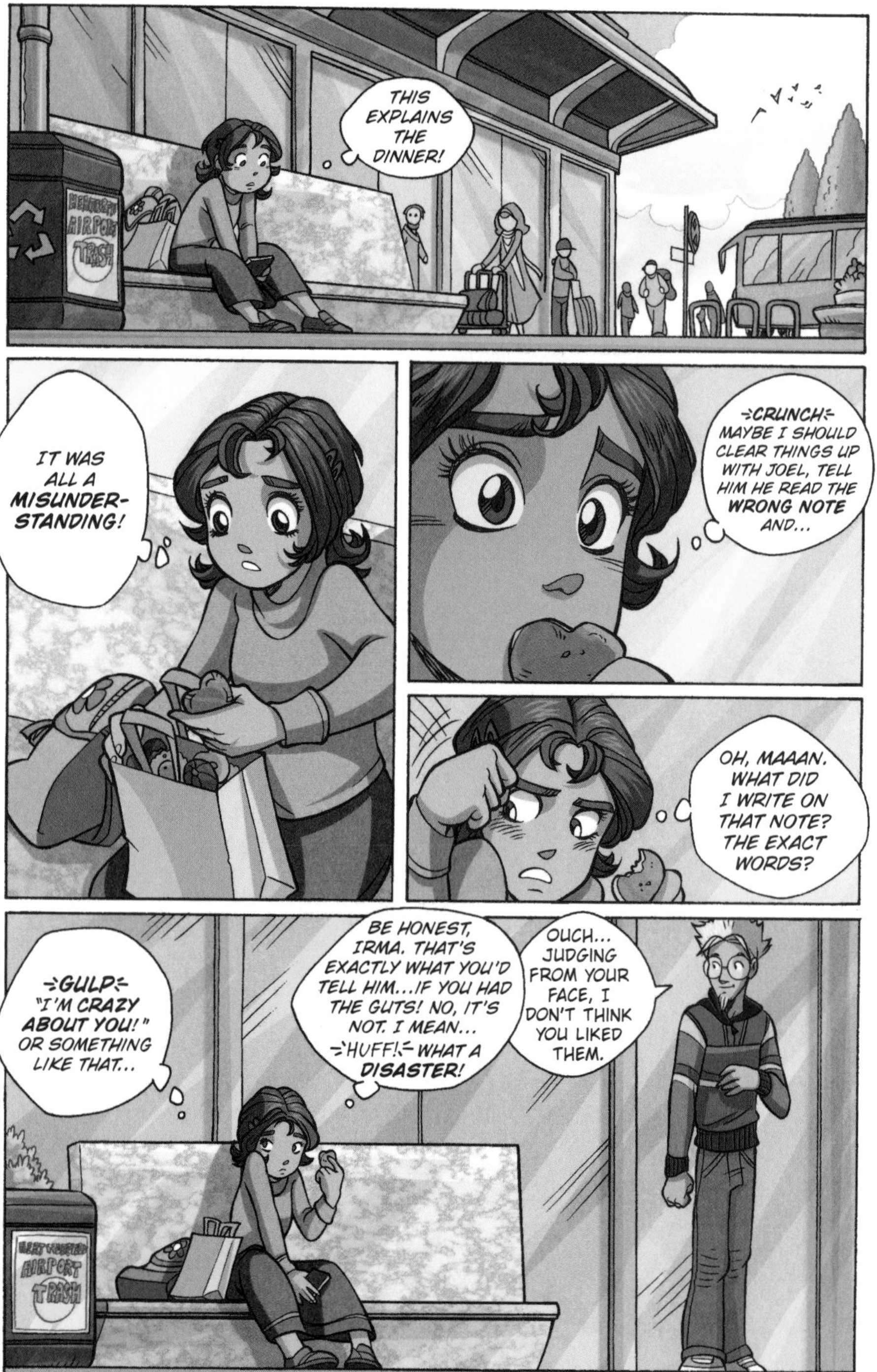

THIS EXPLAINS THE DINNER!
AIRPORT TRASH
IT WAS ALL A MISUNDERSTANDING!
=CRUNCH= MAYBE I SHOULD CLEAR THINGS UP WITH JOEL, TELL HIM HE READ THE WRONG NOTE AND...
OH, MAAAN. WHAT DID I WRITE ON THAT NOTE? THE EXACT WORDS?
=GULP= "I'M CRAZY ABOUT YOU!" OR SOMETHING LIKE THAT...
BE HONEST, IRMA. THAT'S EXACTLY WHAT YOU'D TELL HIM...IF YOU HAD THE GUTS! NO, IT'S NOT. I MEAN... =HUFF!= WHAT A DISASTER!
OUCH... JUDGING FROM YOUR FACE, I DON'T THINK YOU LIKED THEM.
AIRPORT TRASH

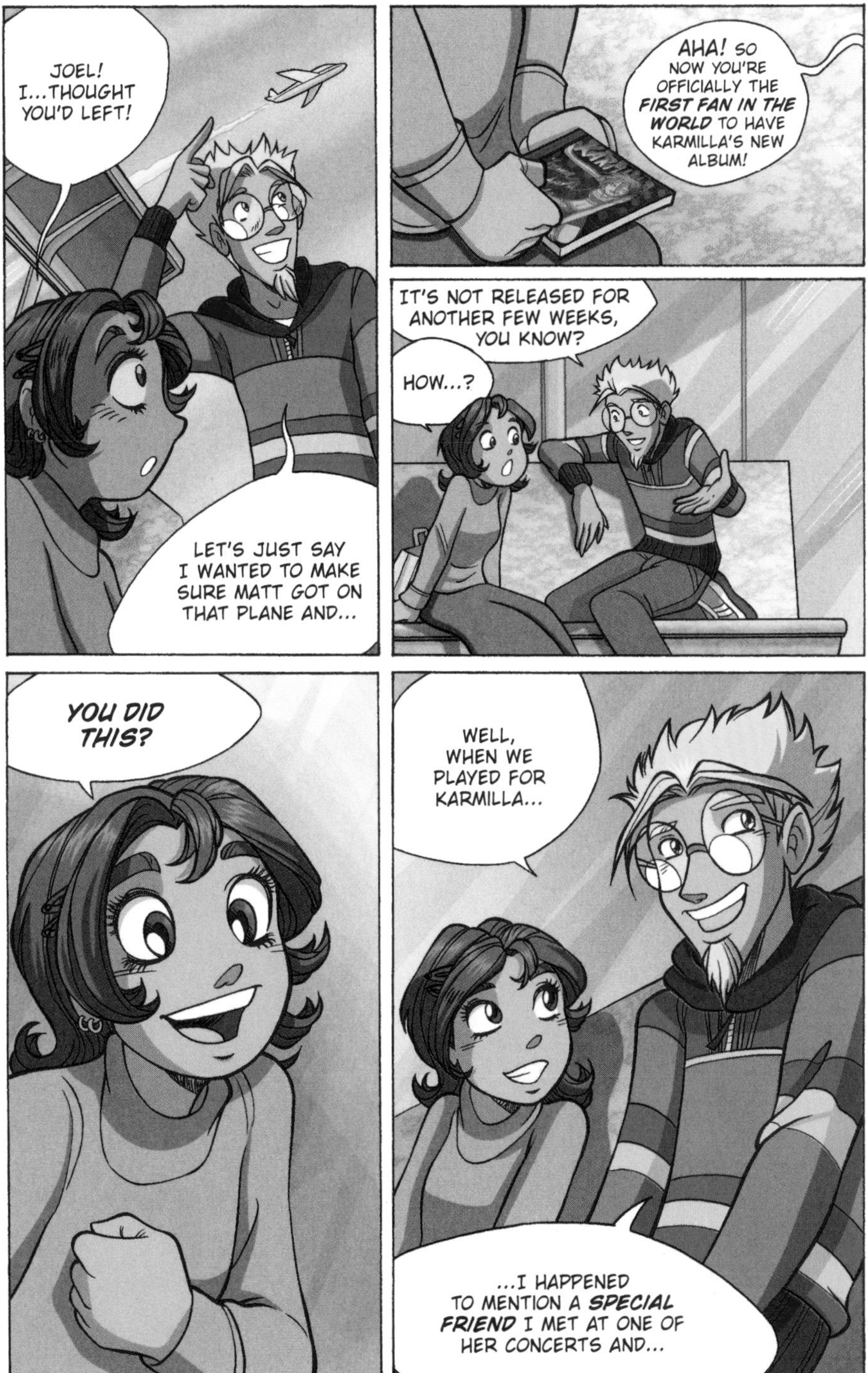
JOEL! I...THOUGHT YOU'D LEFT!
LET'S JUST SAY I WANTED TO MAKE SURE MATT GOT ON THAT PLANE AND...
AHA! SO NOW YOU'RE OFFICIALLY THE FIRST FAN IN THE WORLD TO HAVE KARMILLA'S NEW ALBUM!
IT'S NOT RELEASED FOR ANOTHER FEW WEEKS, YOU KNOW?
HOW...?
YOU DID THIS?
WELL, WHEN WE PLAYED FOR KARMILLA...
...I HAPPENED TO MENTION A SPECIAL FRIEND I MET AT ONE OF HER CONCERTS AND...

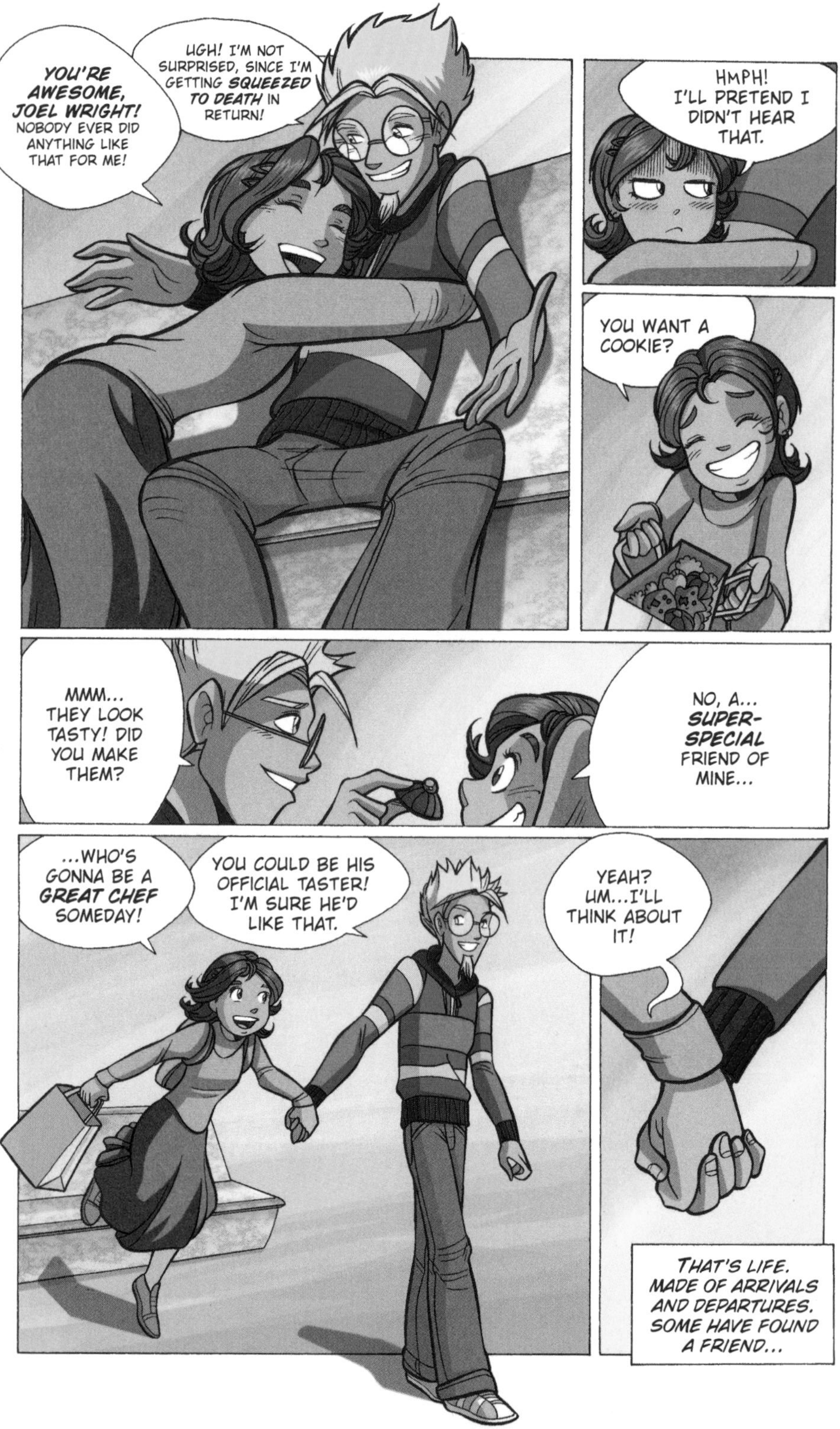
YOU'RE AWESOME, JOEL WRIGHT! NOBODY EVER DID ANYTHING LIKE THAT FOR ME!
UGH! I'M NOT SURPRISED, SINCE I'M GETTING SQUEEZED TO DEATH IN RETURN!
HMPH! I'LL PRETEND I DIDN'T HEAR THAT.
YOU WANT A COOKIE?
MMM... THEY LOOK TASTY! DID YOU MAKE THEM?
NO, A... SUPER-SPECIAL FRIEND OF MINE...
...WHO'S GONNA BE A GREAT CHEF SOMEDAY!
YOU COULD BE HIS OFFICIAL TASTER! I'M SURE HE'D LIKE THAT.
YEAH? UM...I'LL THINK ABOUT IT!
THAT'S LIFE. MADE OF ARRIVALS AND DEPARTURES. SOME HAVE FOUND A FRIEND...

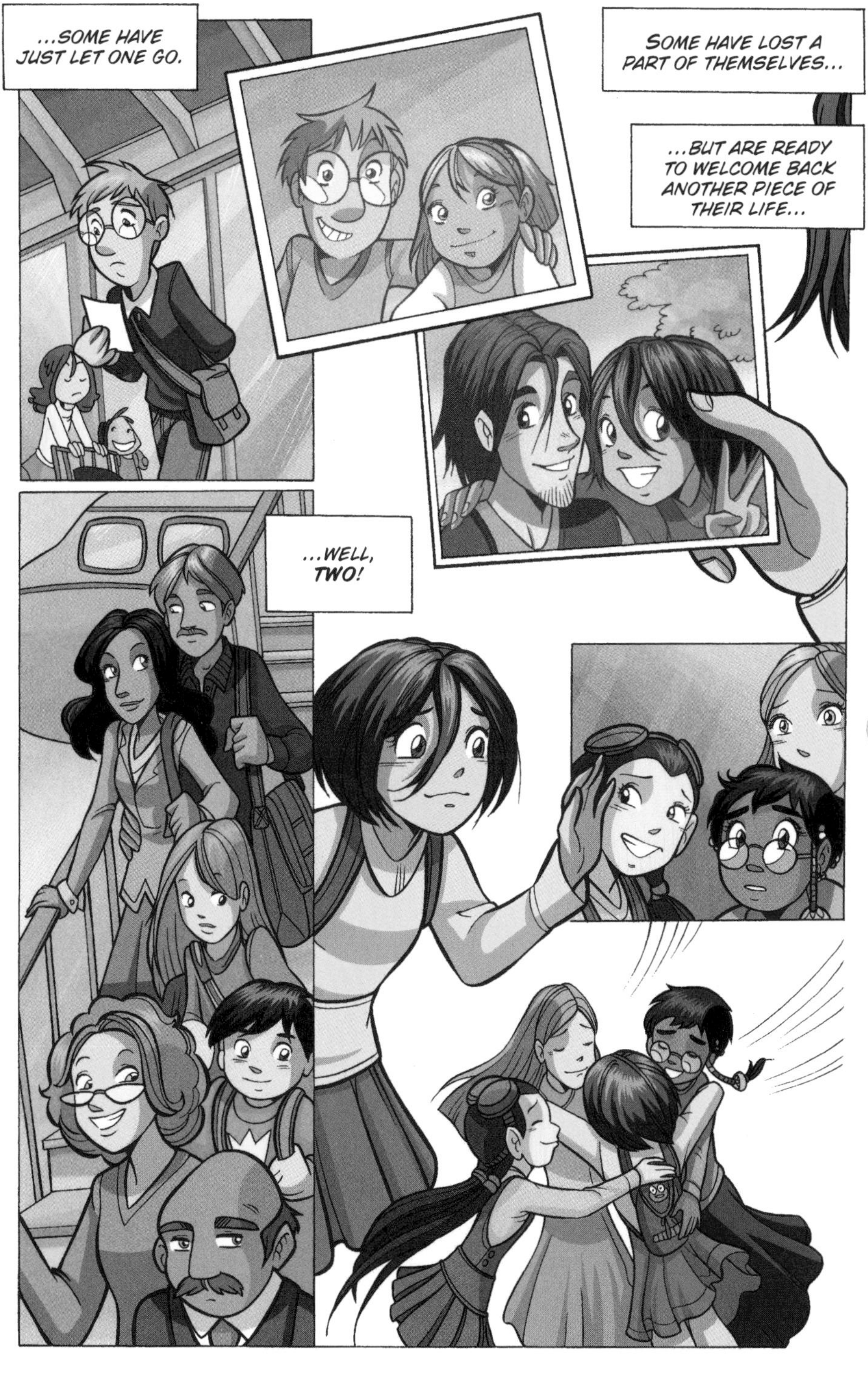
...SOME HAVE JUST LET ONE GO.
SOME HAVE LOST A PART OF THEMSELVES...
...BUT ARE READY TO WELCOME BACK ANOTHER PIECE OF THEIR LIFE...
...WELL, TWO!

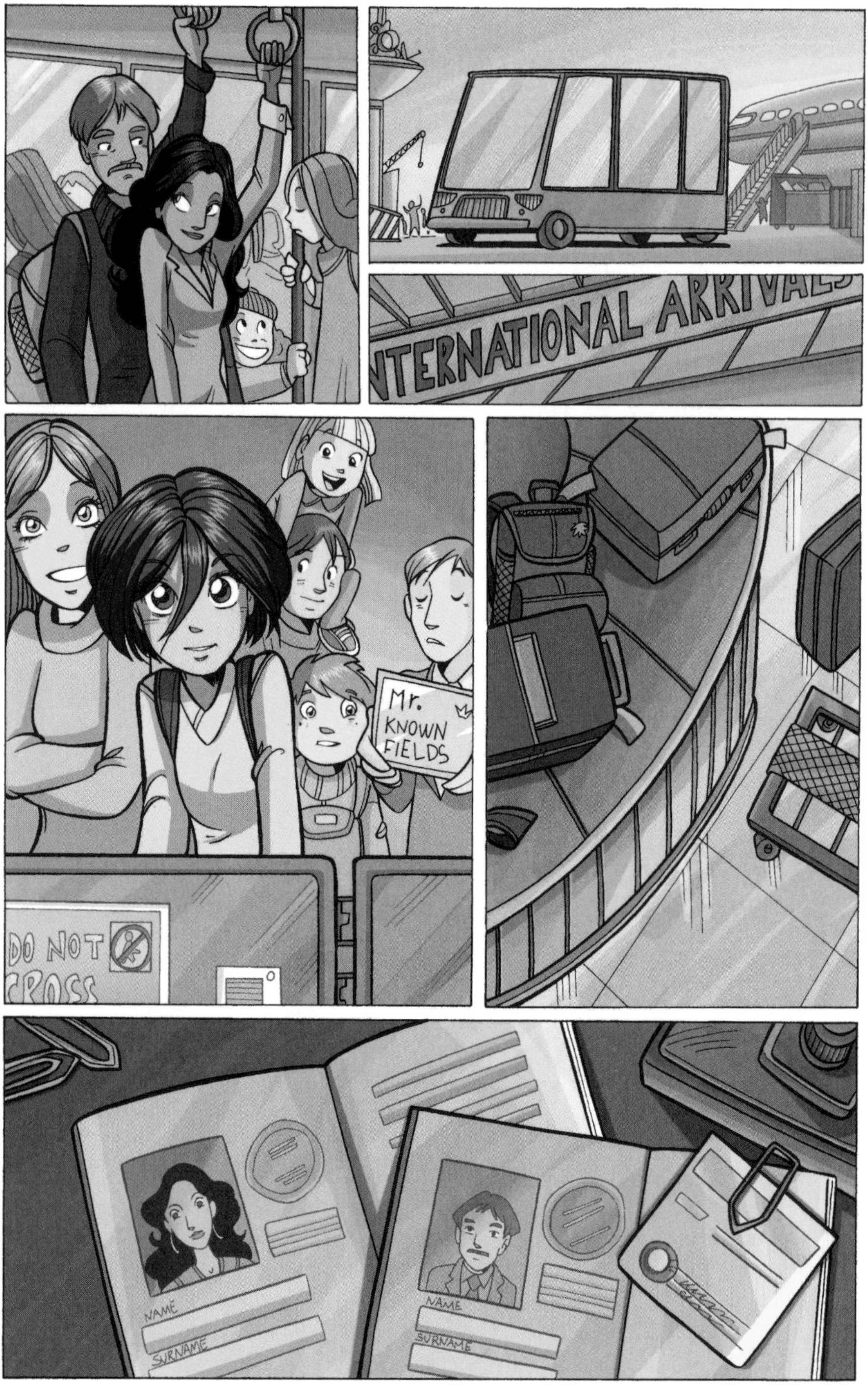
NTERNATIONAL ARRIVAL
Mr. KNOWN FIELDS
DO NOT
NAME
SURNAME
NAME
SURNAME

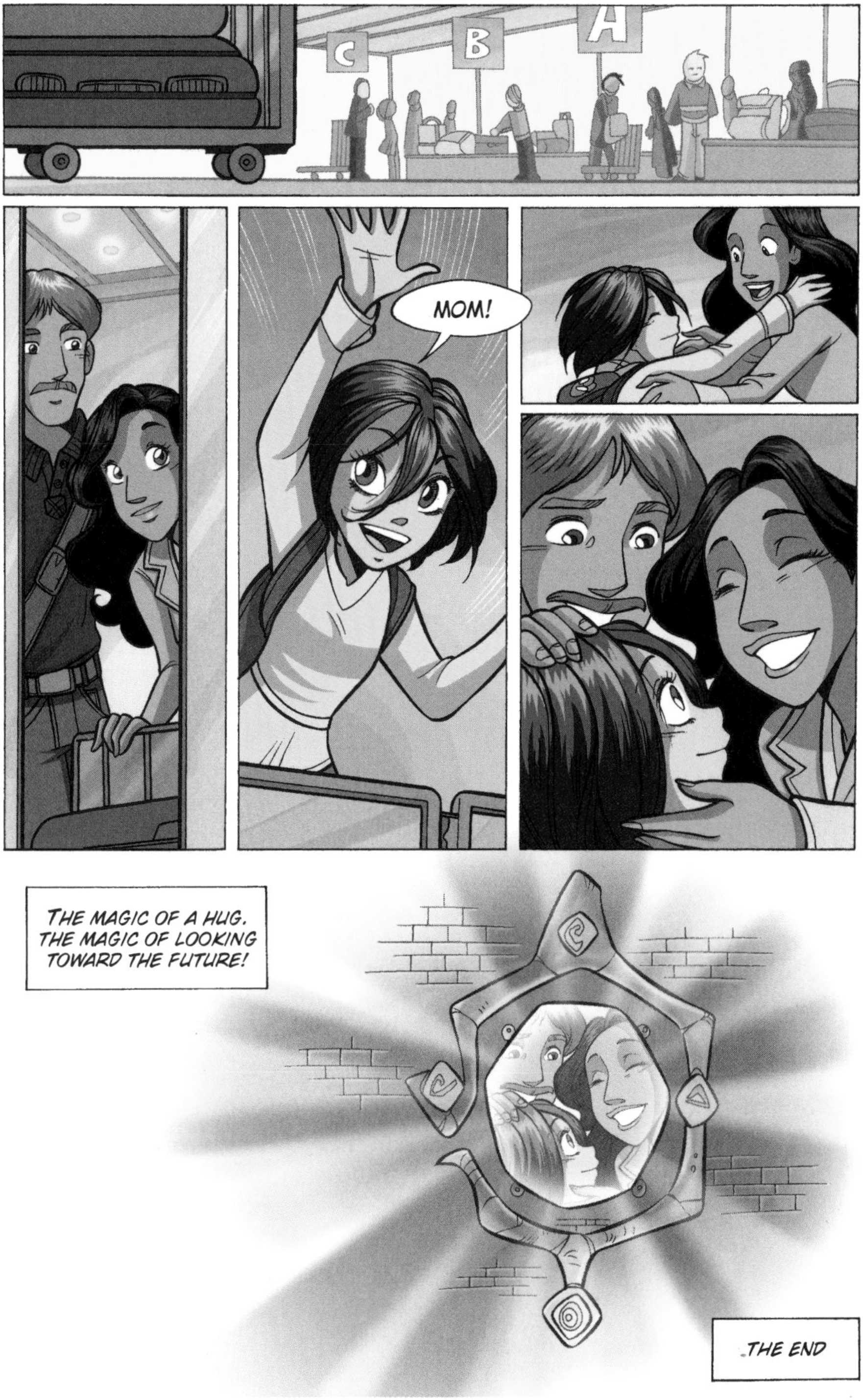
MOM!
THE MAGIC OF A HUG. THE MAGIC OF LOOKING TOWARD THE FUTURE!
THE END

Read on in Volume 17!

Pin Up Gallery

To celebrate the *50th magical issue of W.I.T.C.H.* appearing in *The Book of Elements Arc*, various artists created some special illustrations that you'll discover in the following pages!

A present offered to readers, old and new, as a thank you for keeping *W.I.T.C.H.* alive in your hearts!

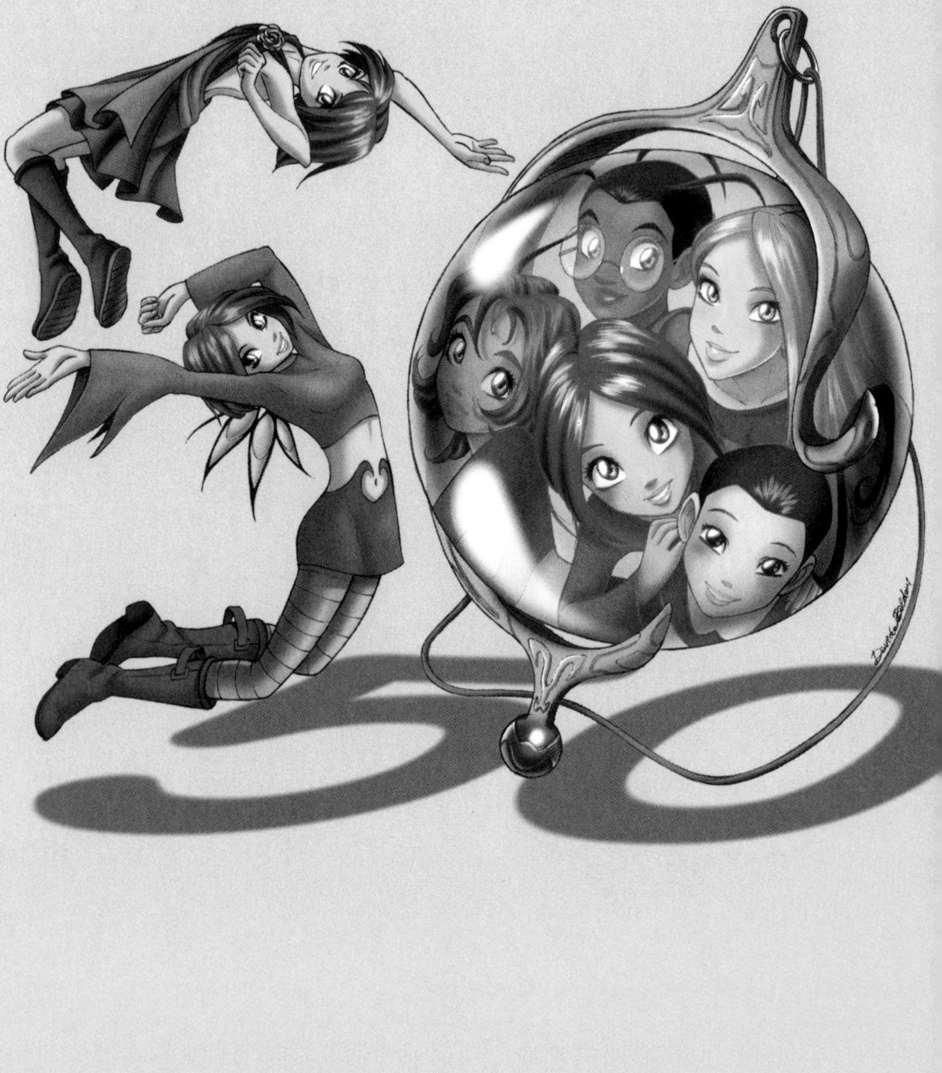

Illustration by: Davide Baldoni – Color by: Stefania Santi

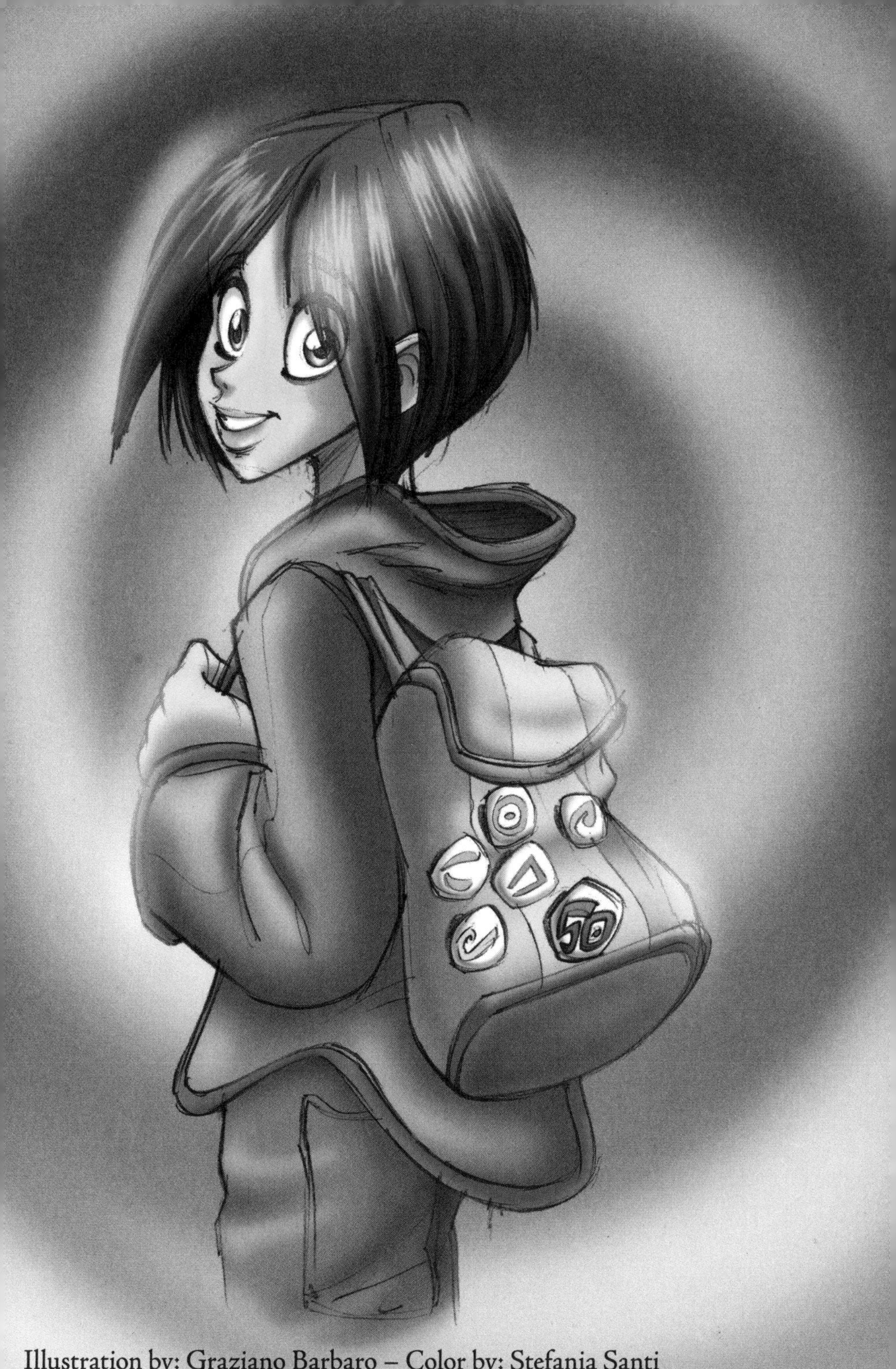

Illustration by: Graziano Barbaro – Color by: Stefania Santi

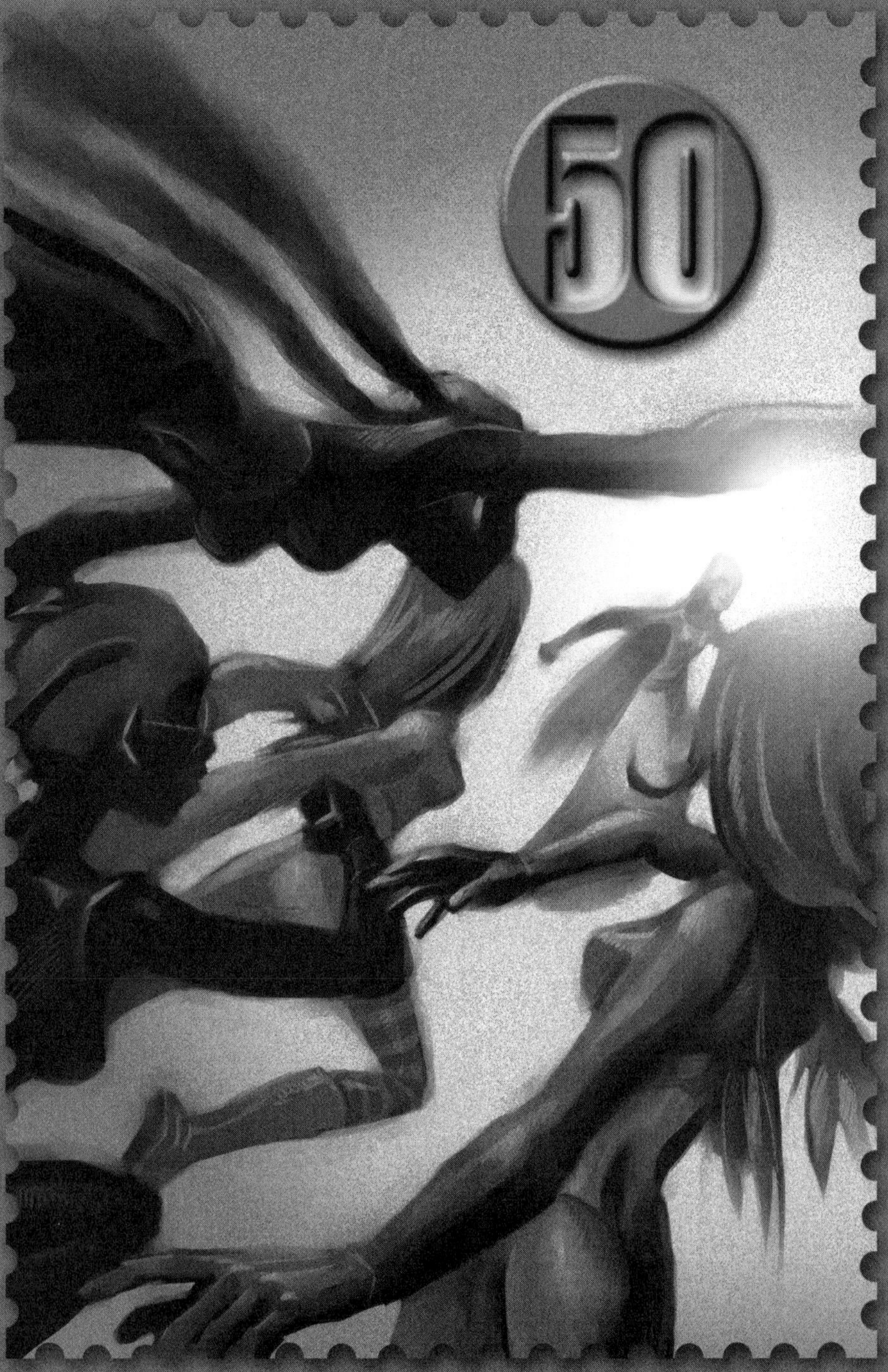
50

FEDERICO BERTOLUCCI 2005

Illustration and color by: Federico Bertolucci

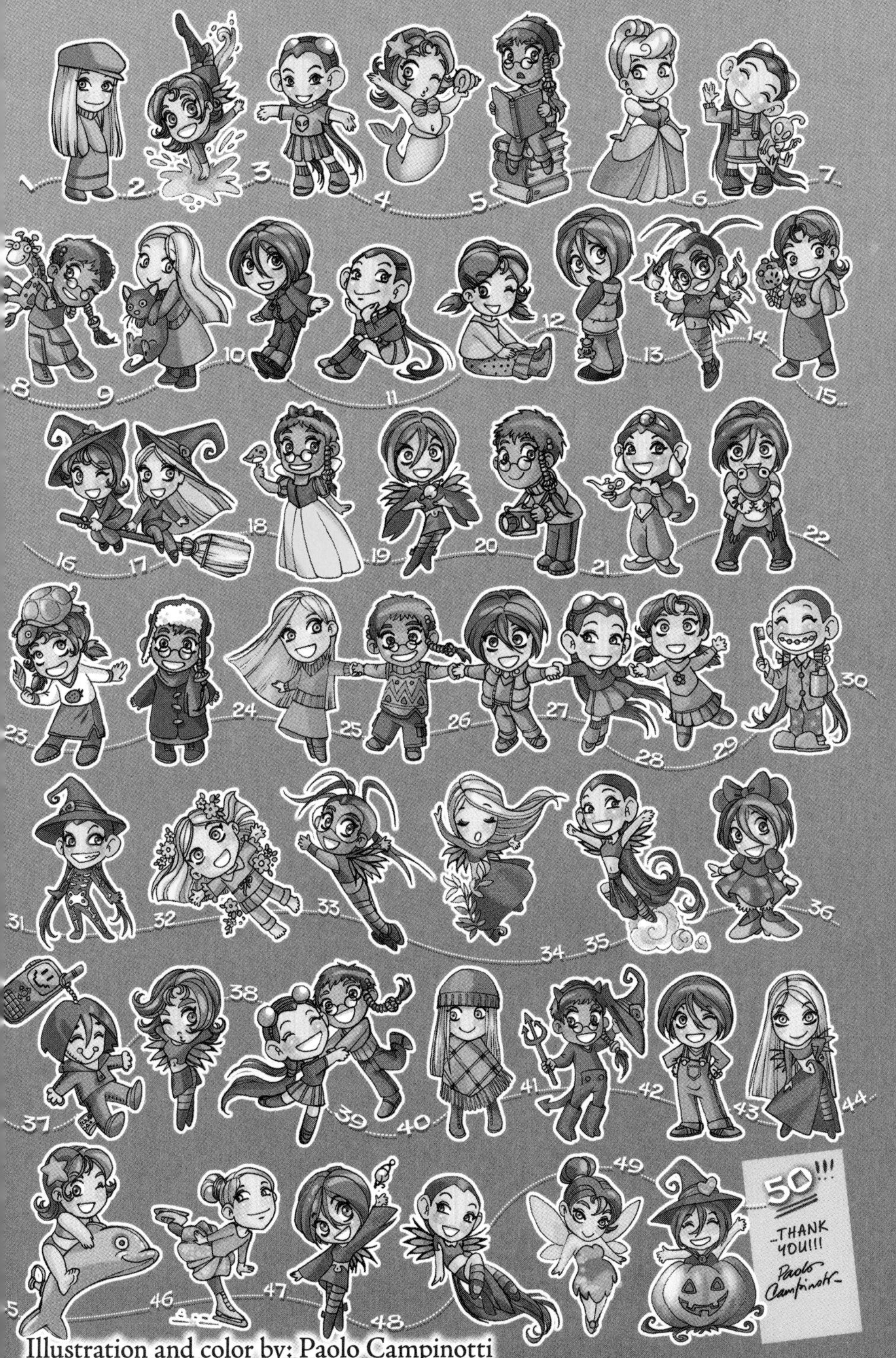
1 2 3 4 5 6 7
8 9 10 11 12 13 14 15
16 17 18 19 20 21 22
23 24 25 26 27 28 29 30
31 32 33 34 35 36
37 38 39 40 41 42 43 44
46 47 48 49
50!!!
...THANK YOU!!!
Paolo Campinotti

Illustration and color by: Paolo Campinotti

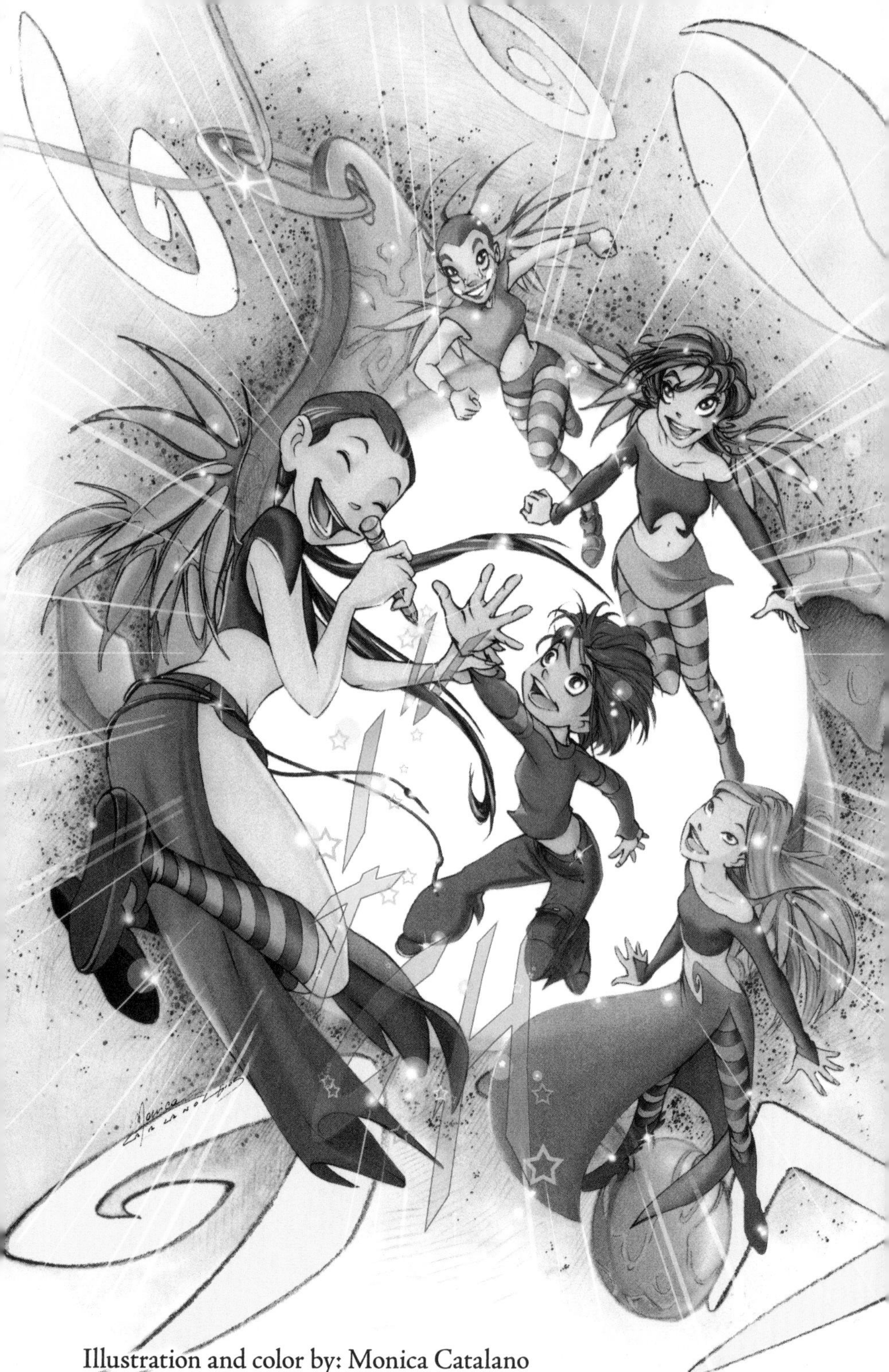

Illustration and color by: Monica Catalano

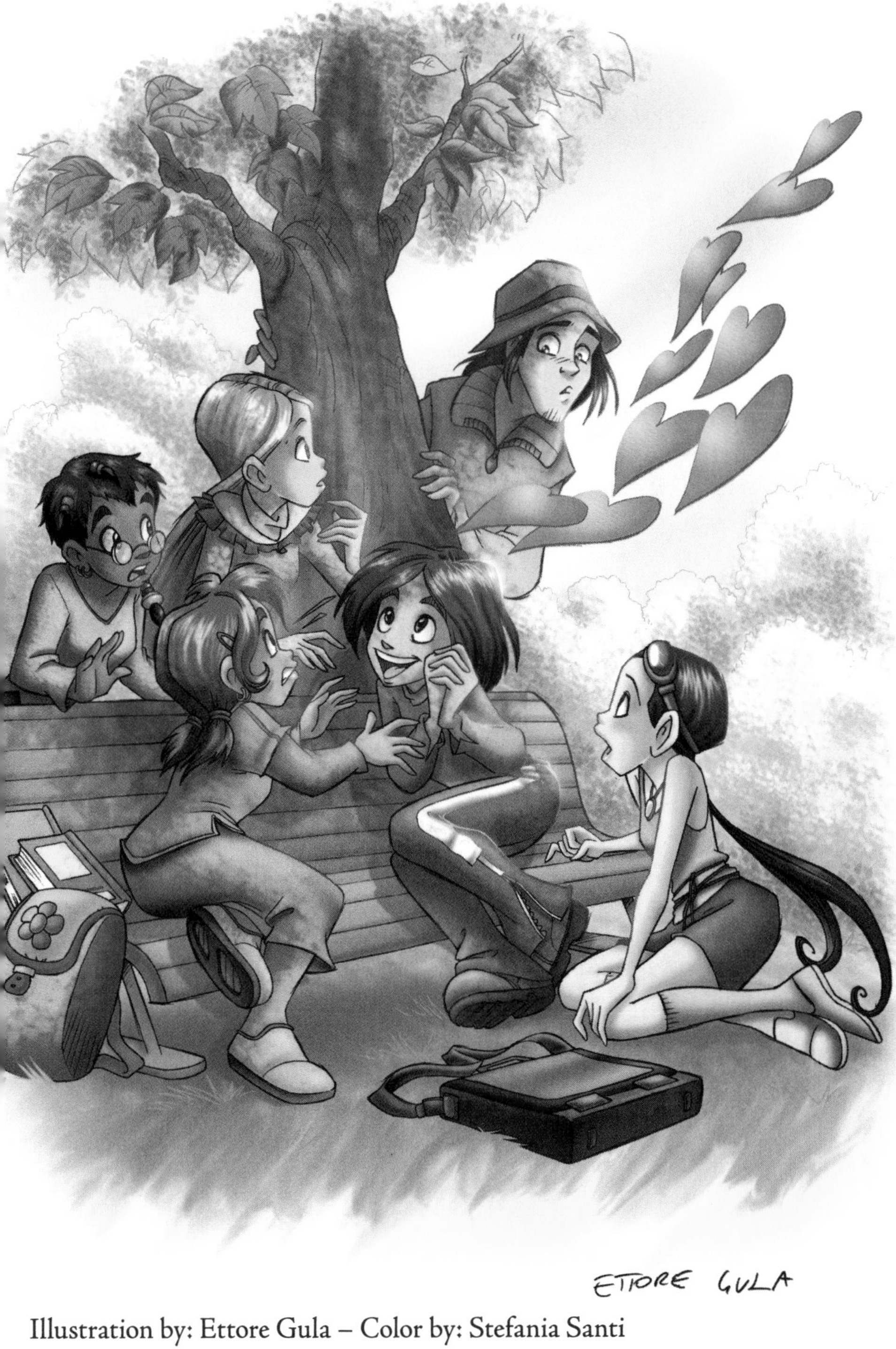
Illustration by: Ettore Gula – Color by: Stefania Santi

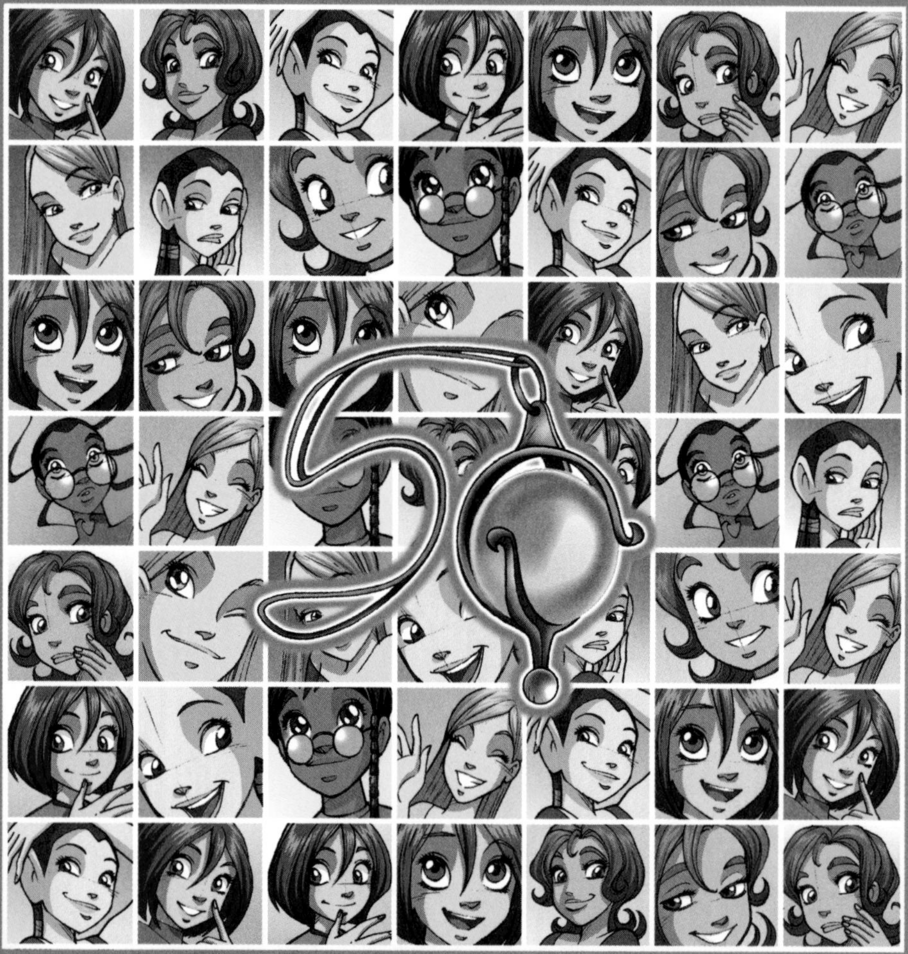

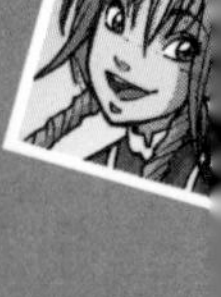

Illustration and color by: Francesco Negramandi

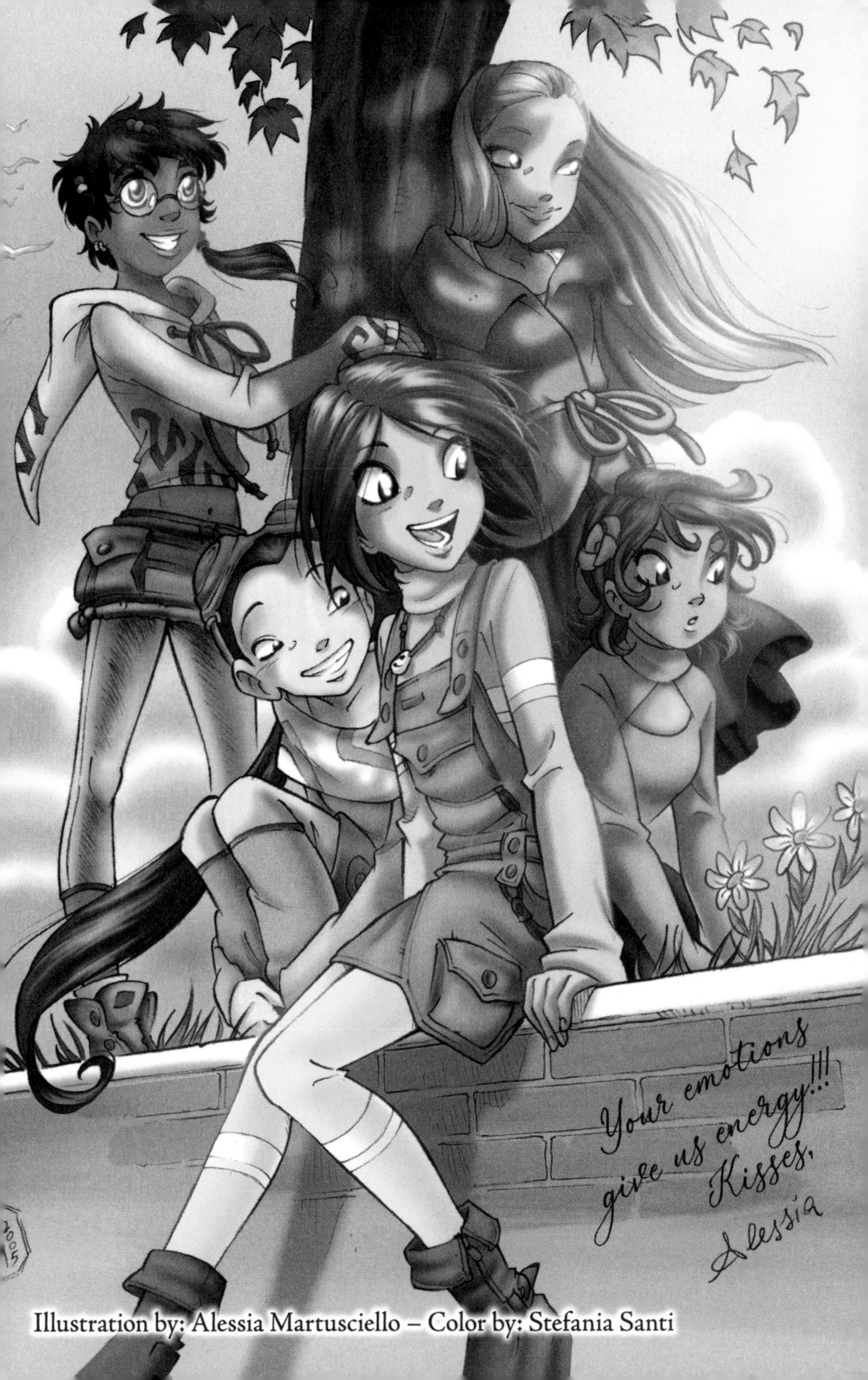
Your emotions
give us energy!!!
Kisses,
Alessia
2005
Illustration by: Alessia Martusciello – Color by: Stefania Santi

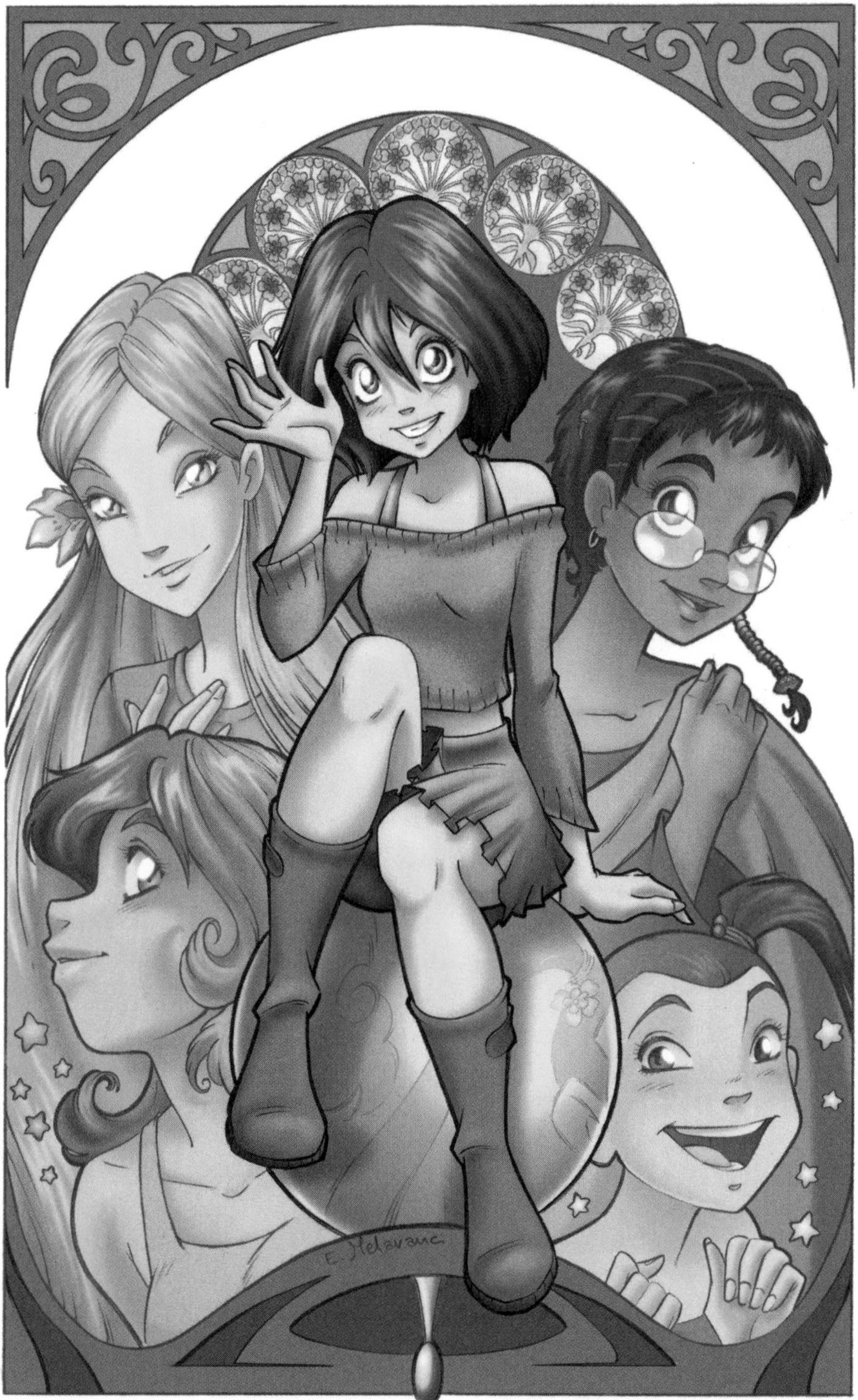

Illustration by: Elisabetta Melaranci – Color by: Stefania Santi

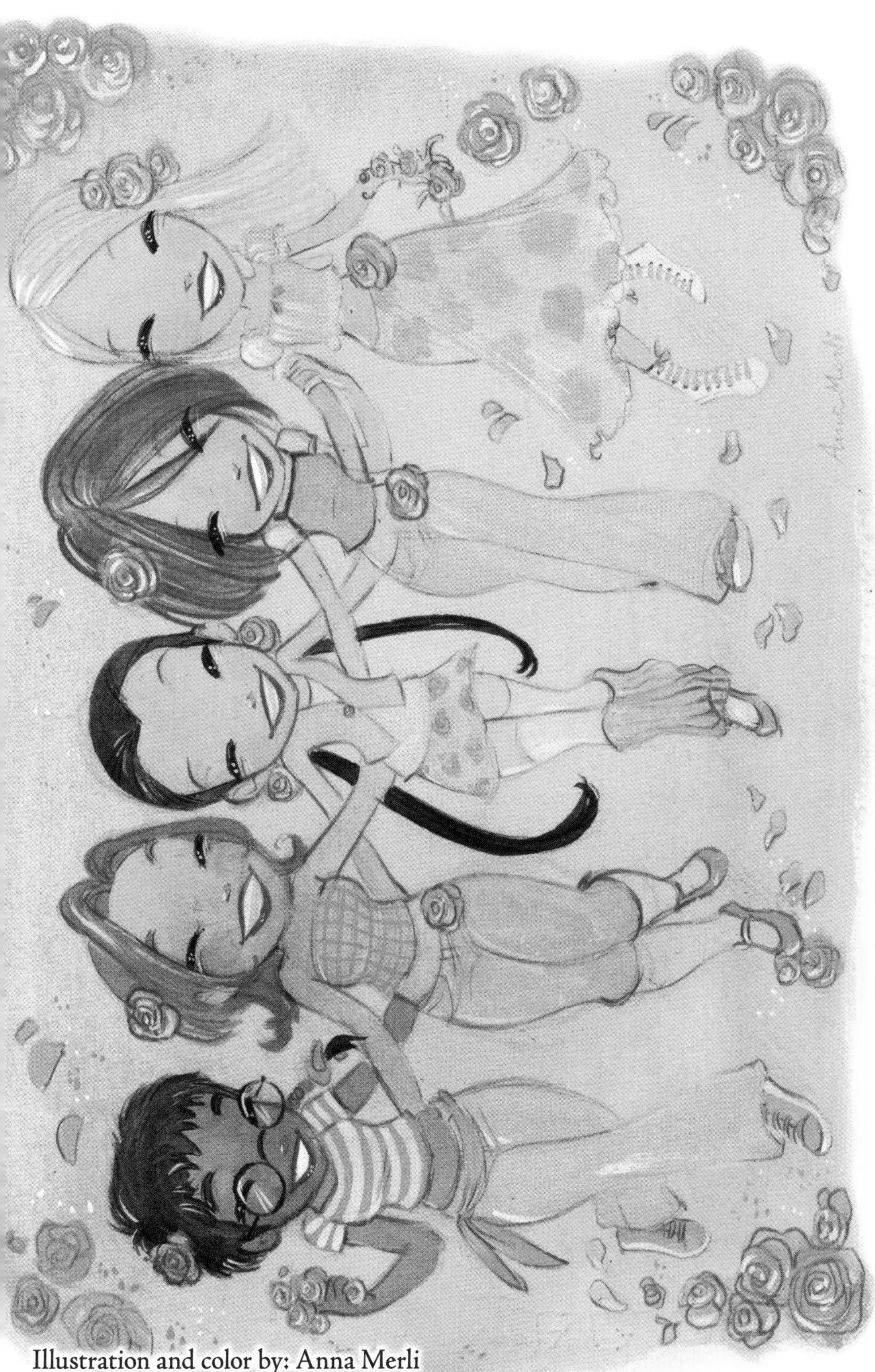

Illustration and color by: Anna Merli

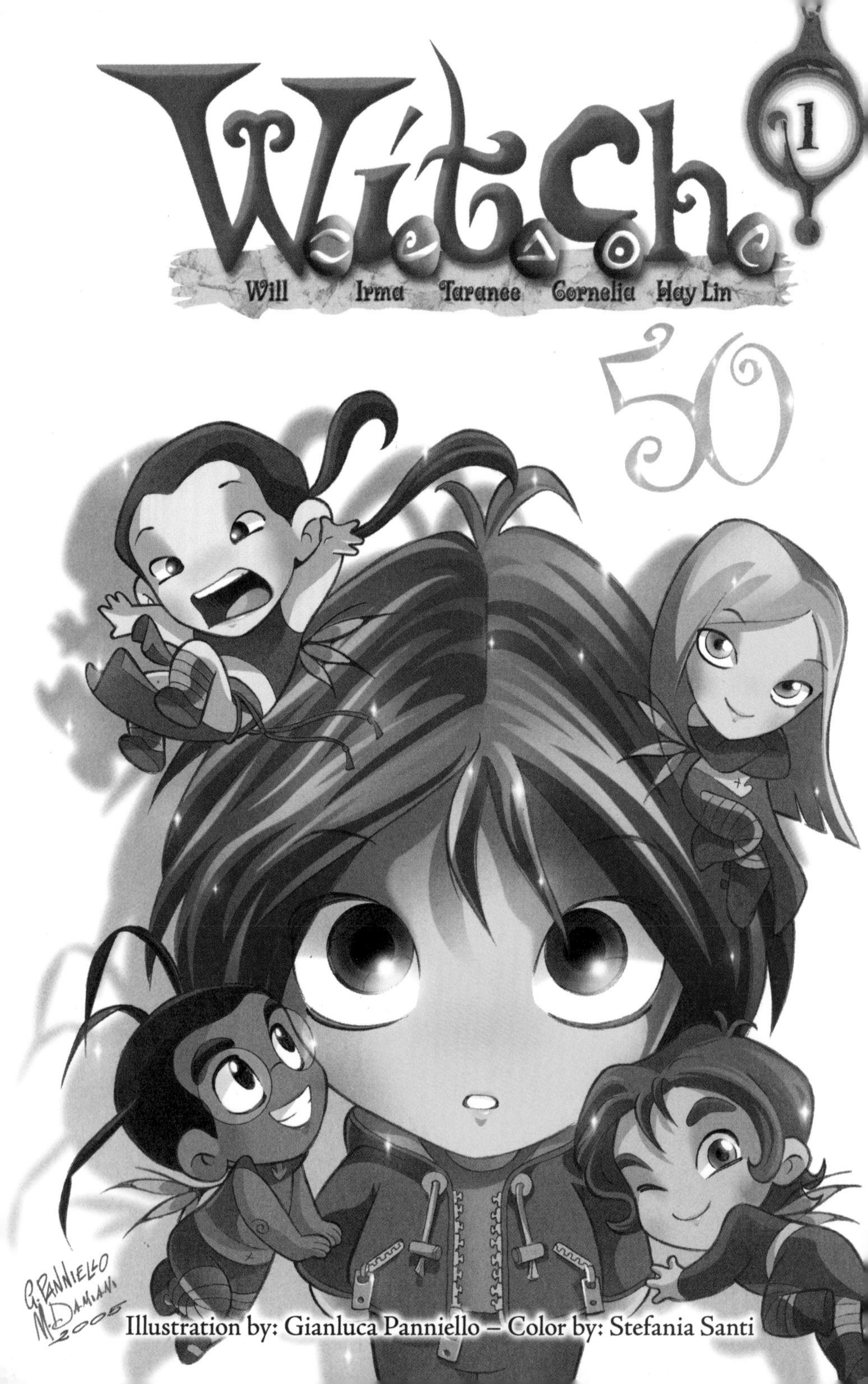
W.i.t.c.h.
1
Will Irma Taranee Cornelia Hay Lin
50
G. PANNIELLO
M. DAMIANI
2005

Illustration by: Gianluca Panniello – Color by: Stefania Santi

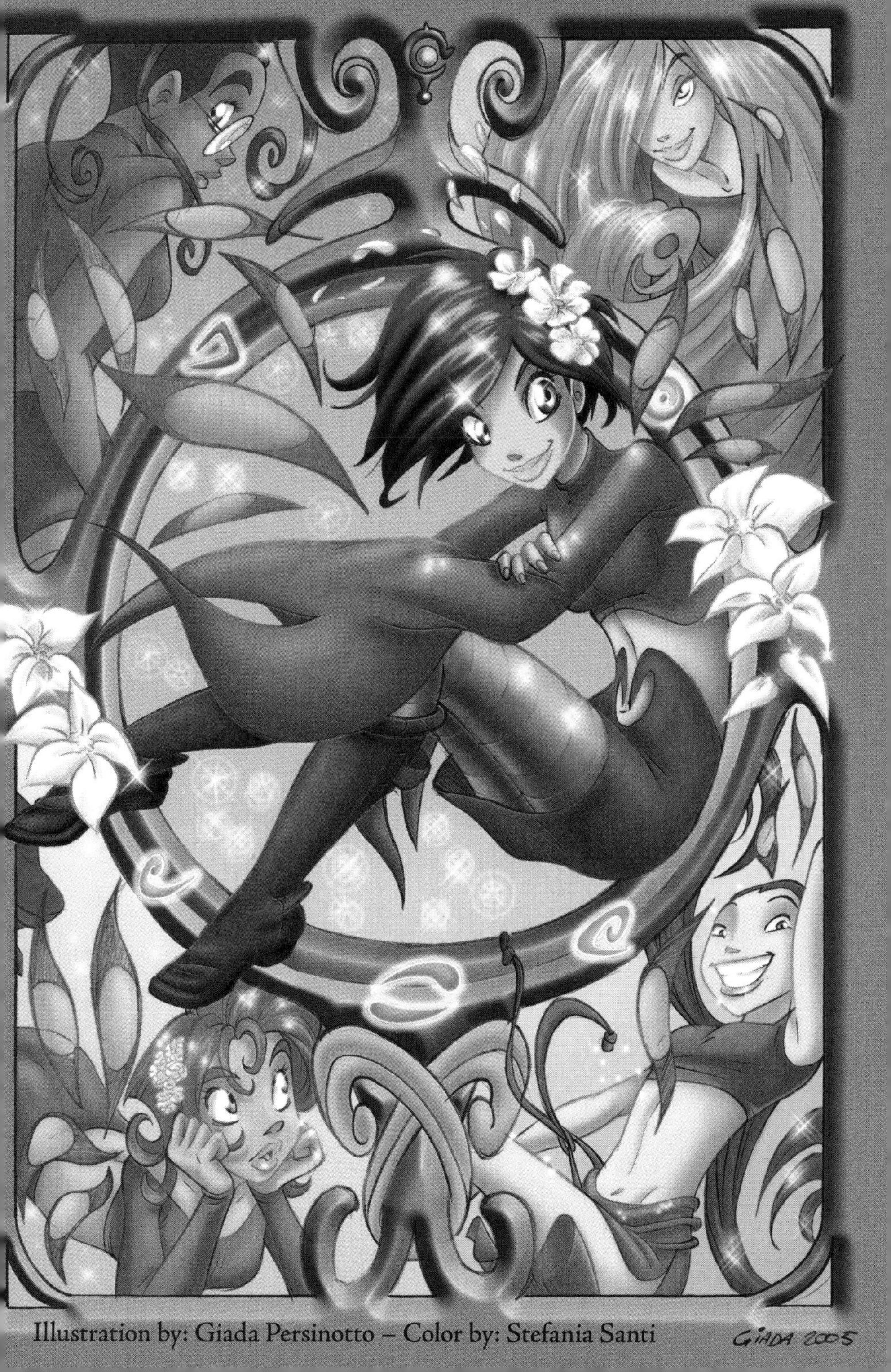

Illustration by: Giada Persinotto – Color by: Stefania Santi

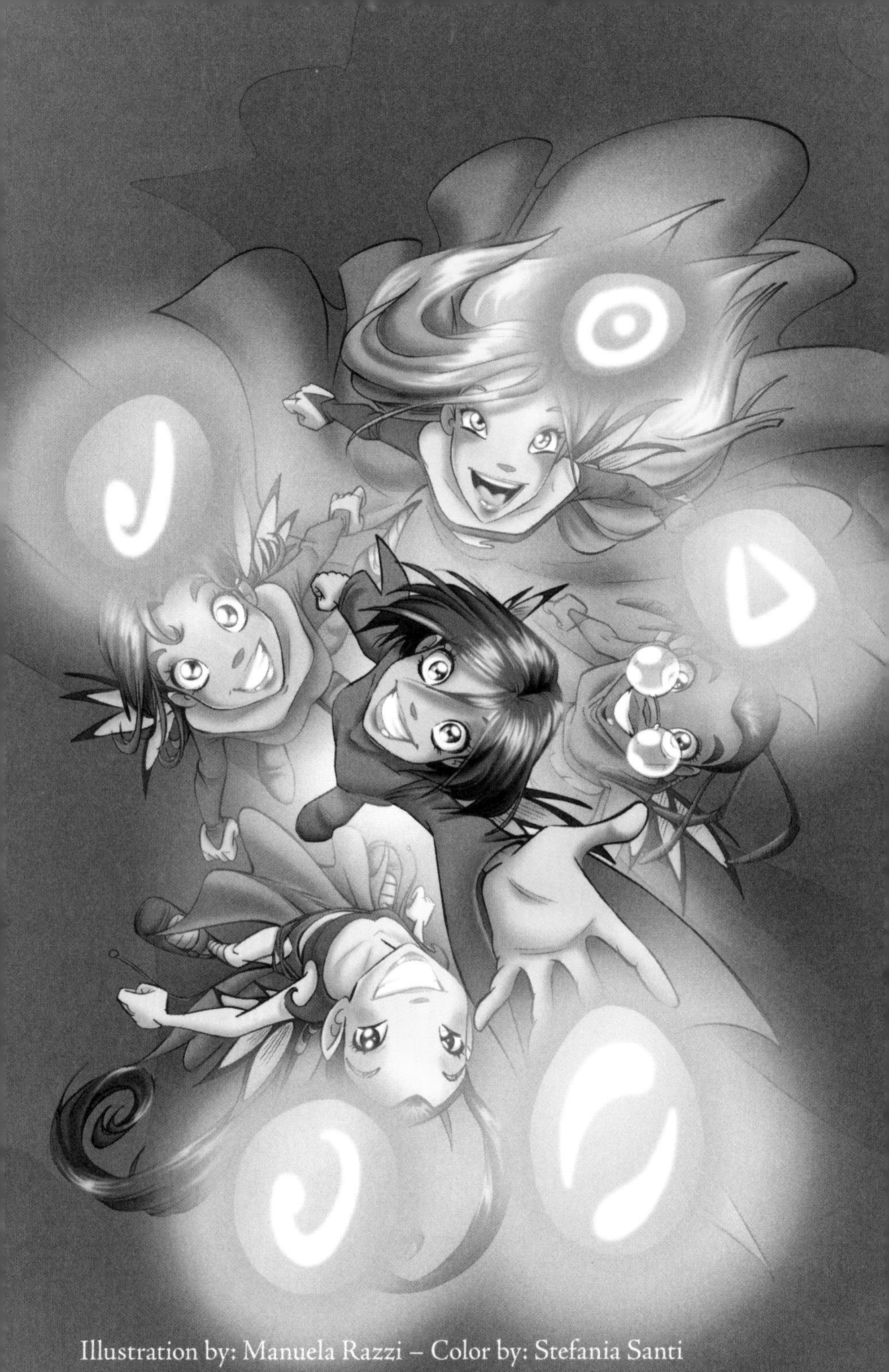

Illustration by: Manuela Razzi – Color by: Stefania Santi

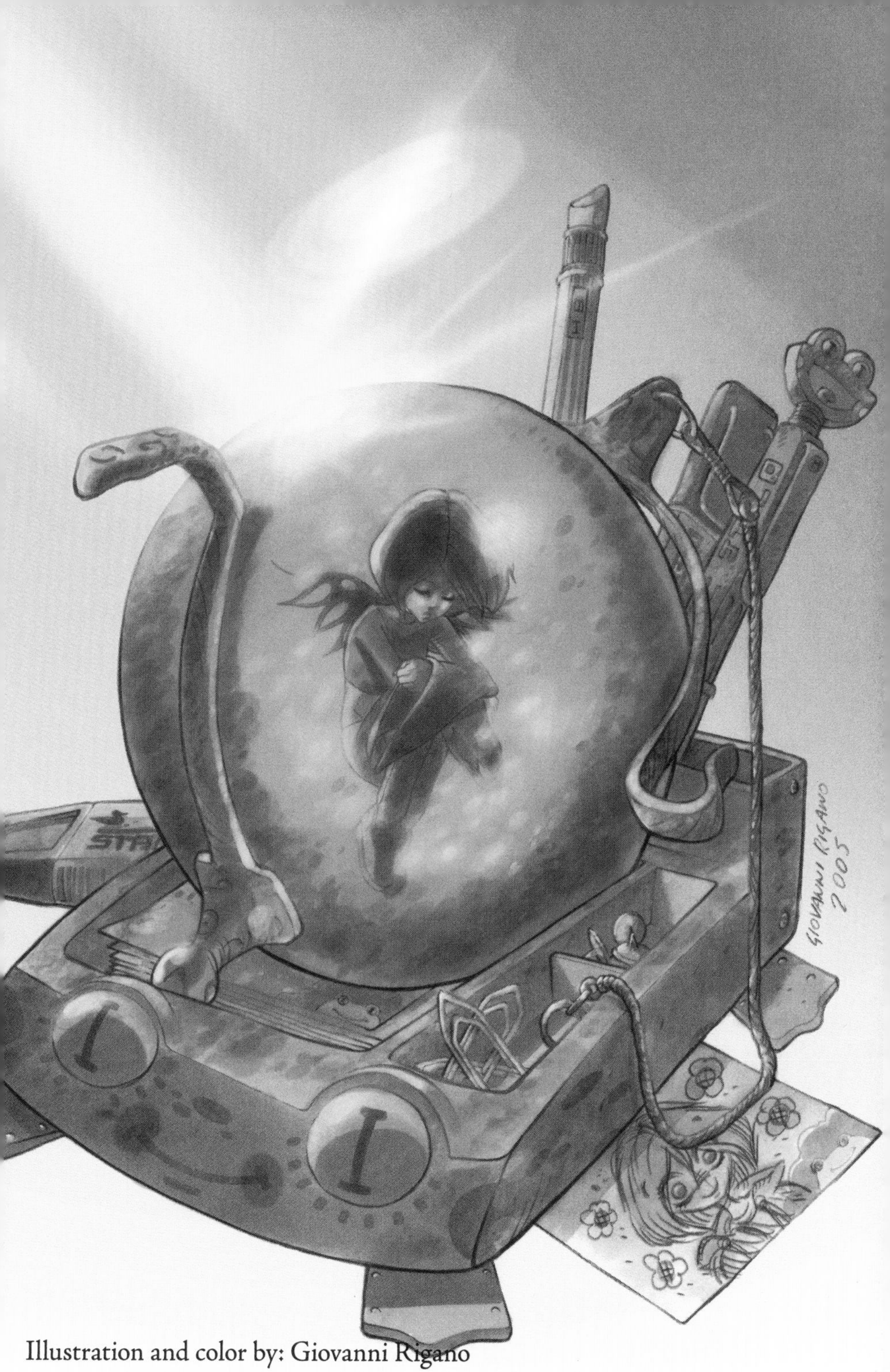
GIOVANNI RIGANO
2005

Illustration and color by: Giovanni Rigano

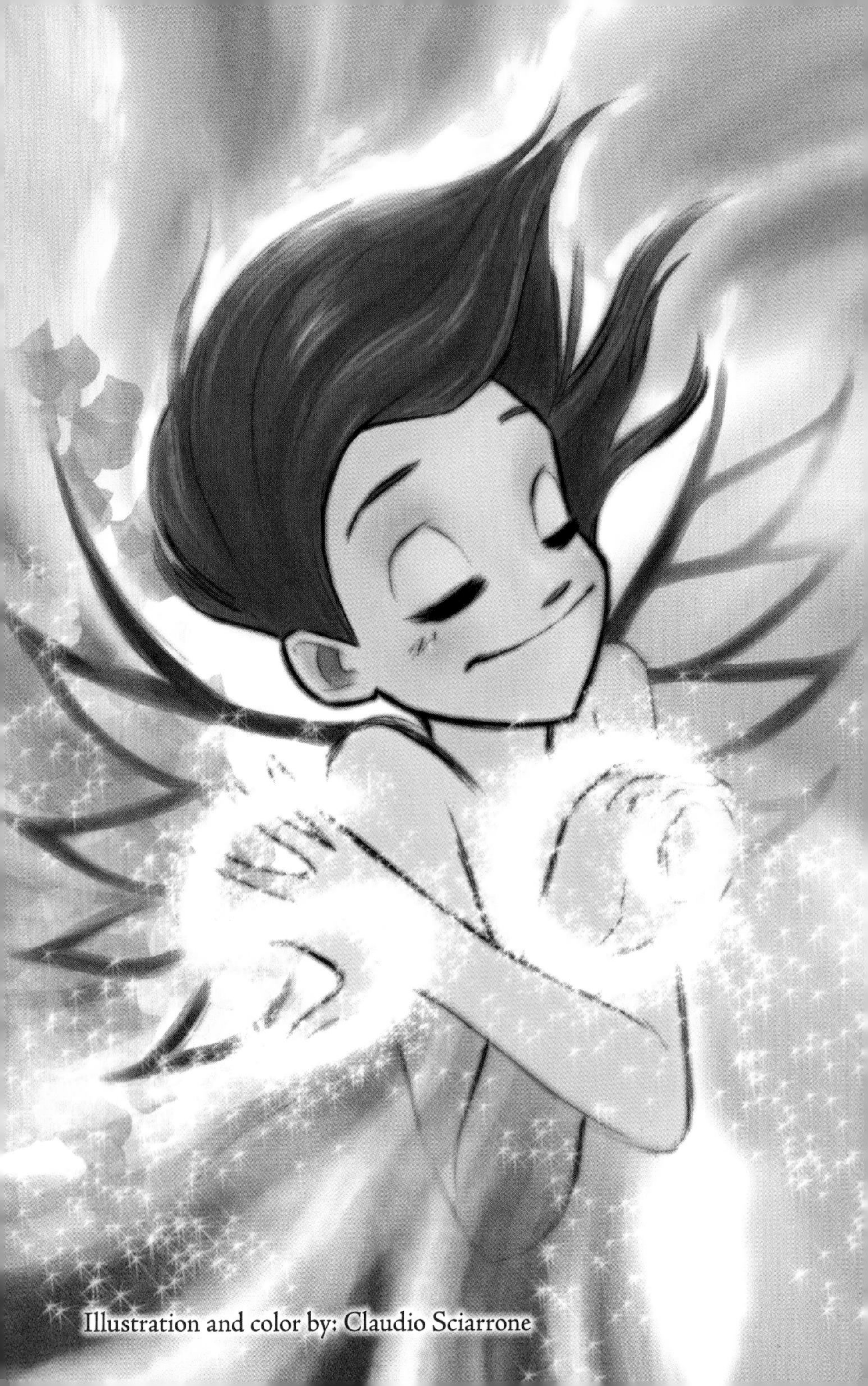

Illustration and color by: Claudio Sciarrone

THANK YOU FOR LETTING US INTO YOUR WORLD

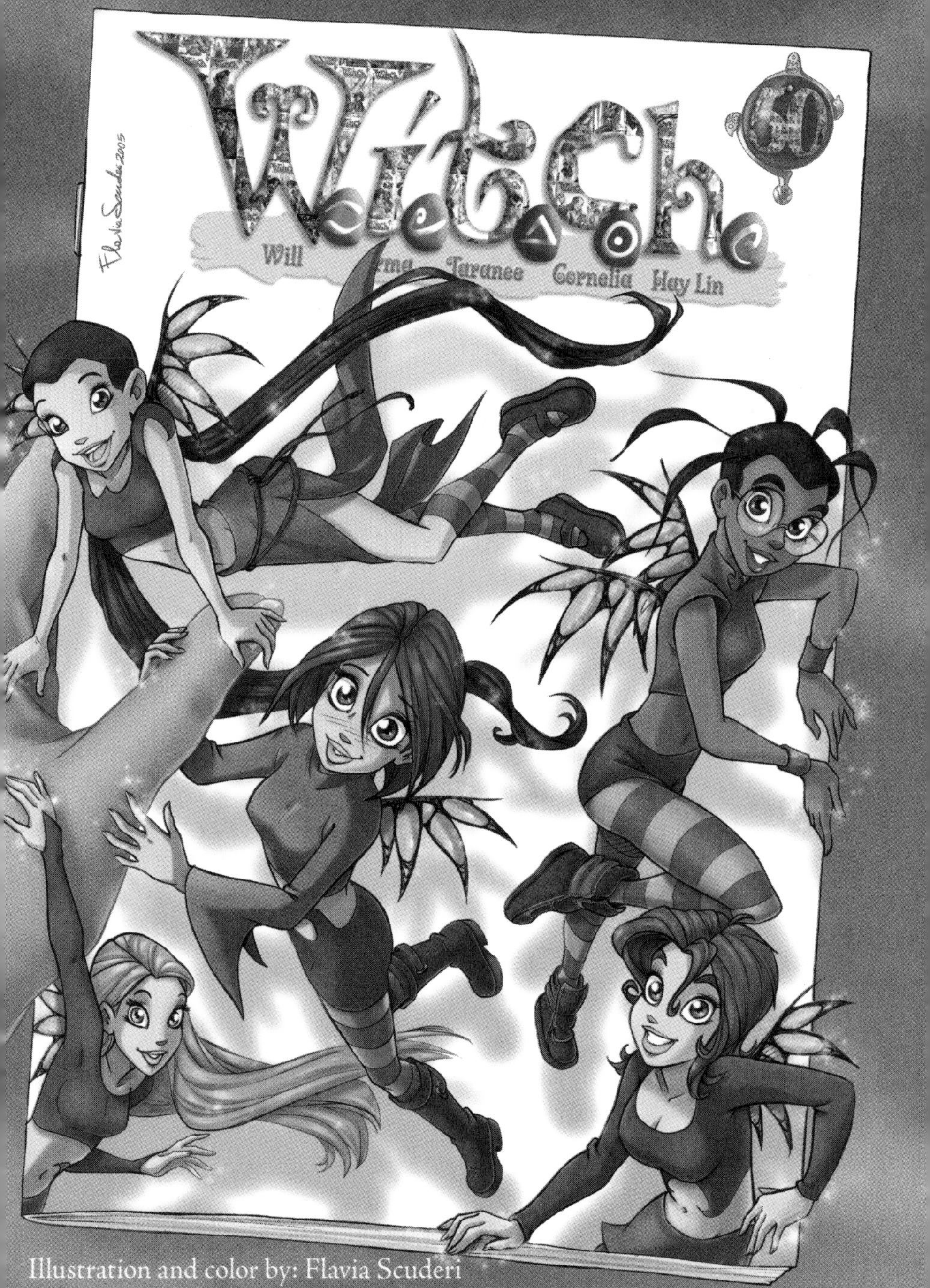
Will
Taranee
Cornelia
Hay Lin

Illustration and color by: Flavia Scuderi

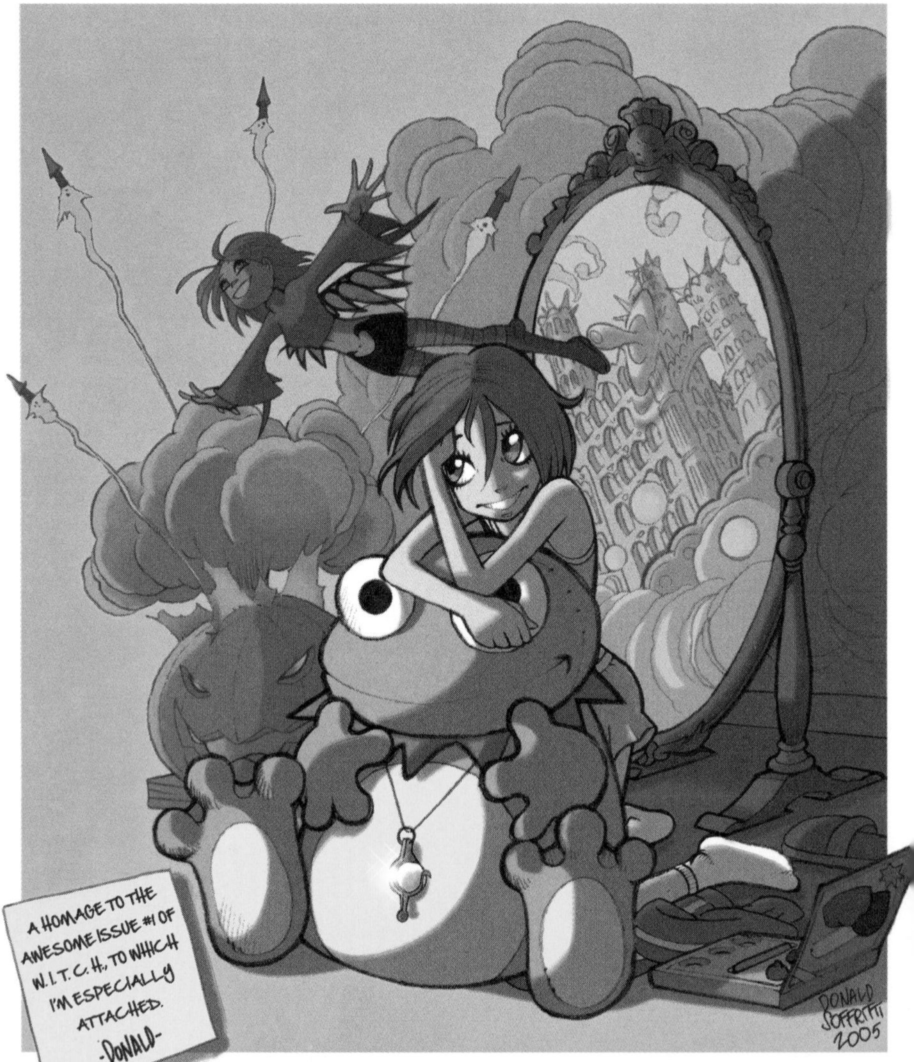
A HOMAGE TO THE AWESOME ISSUE #1 OF W.I.T.C.H., TO WHICH I'M ESPECIALLY ATTACHED.
-DONALD-
DONALD SOFFRITTI 2005

Illustration and color by: Donald Soffritti

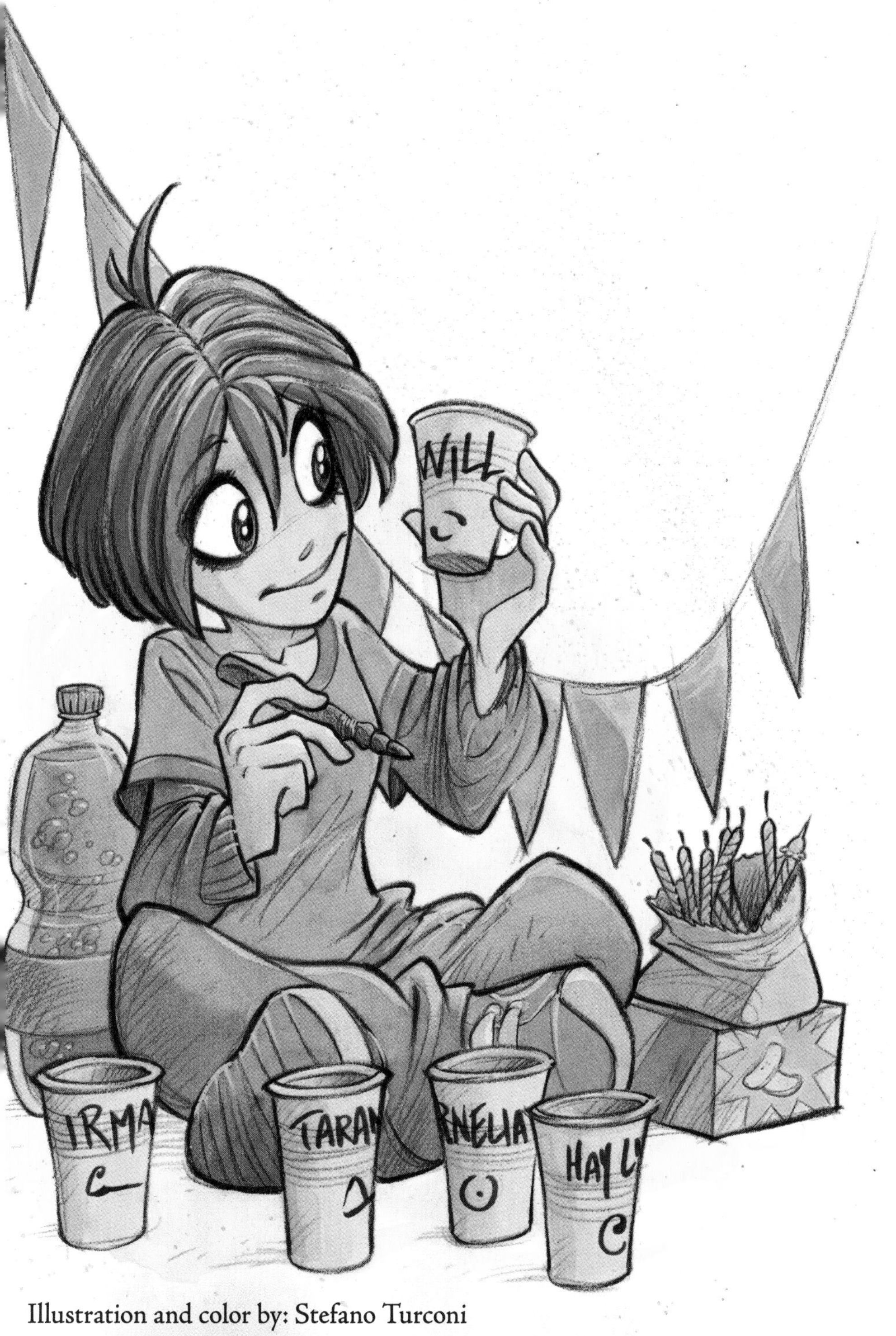
WILL
IRMA

Illustration and color by: Stefano Turconi

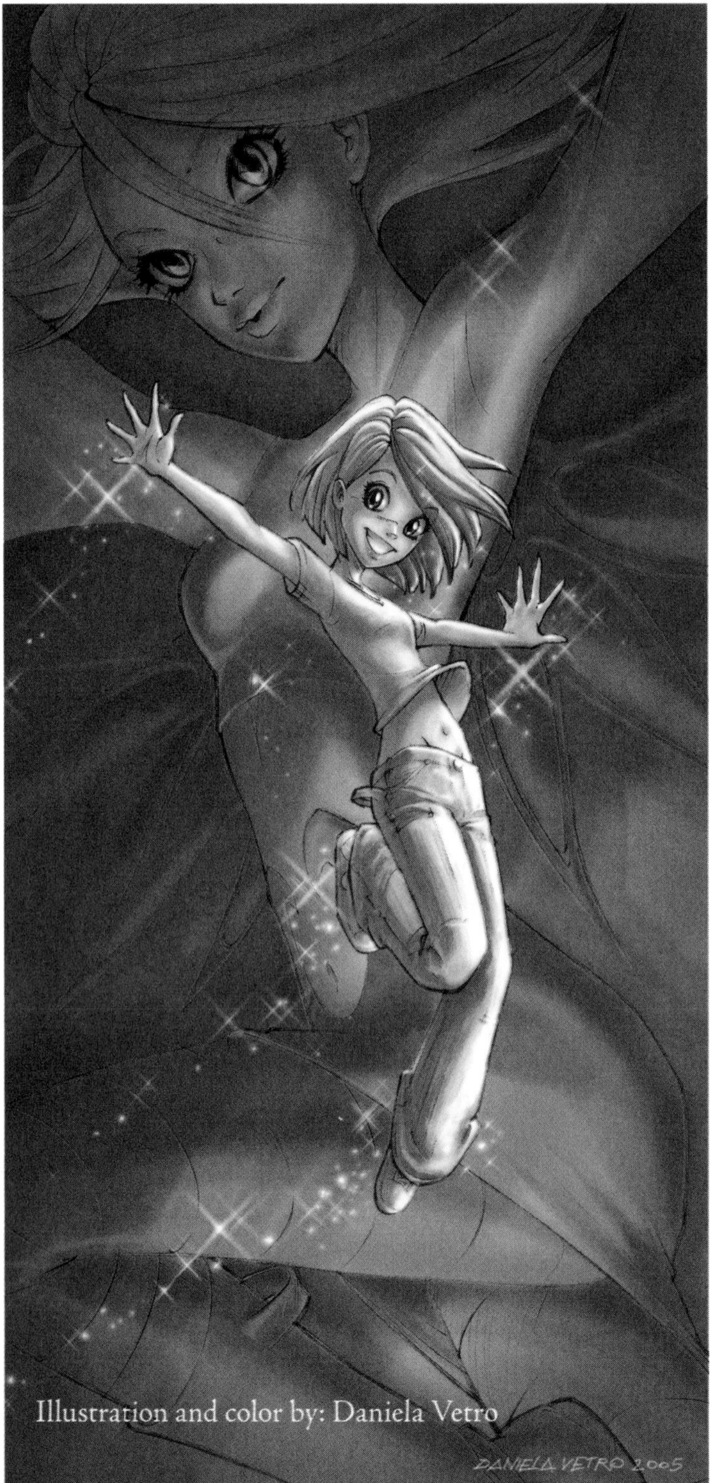
DANIELA VETRO 2005

Illustration and color by: Daniela Vetro

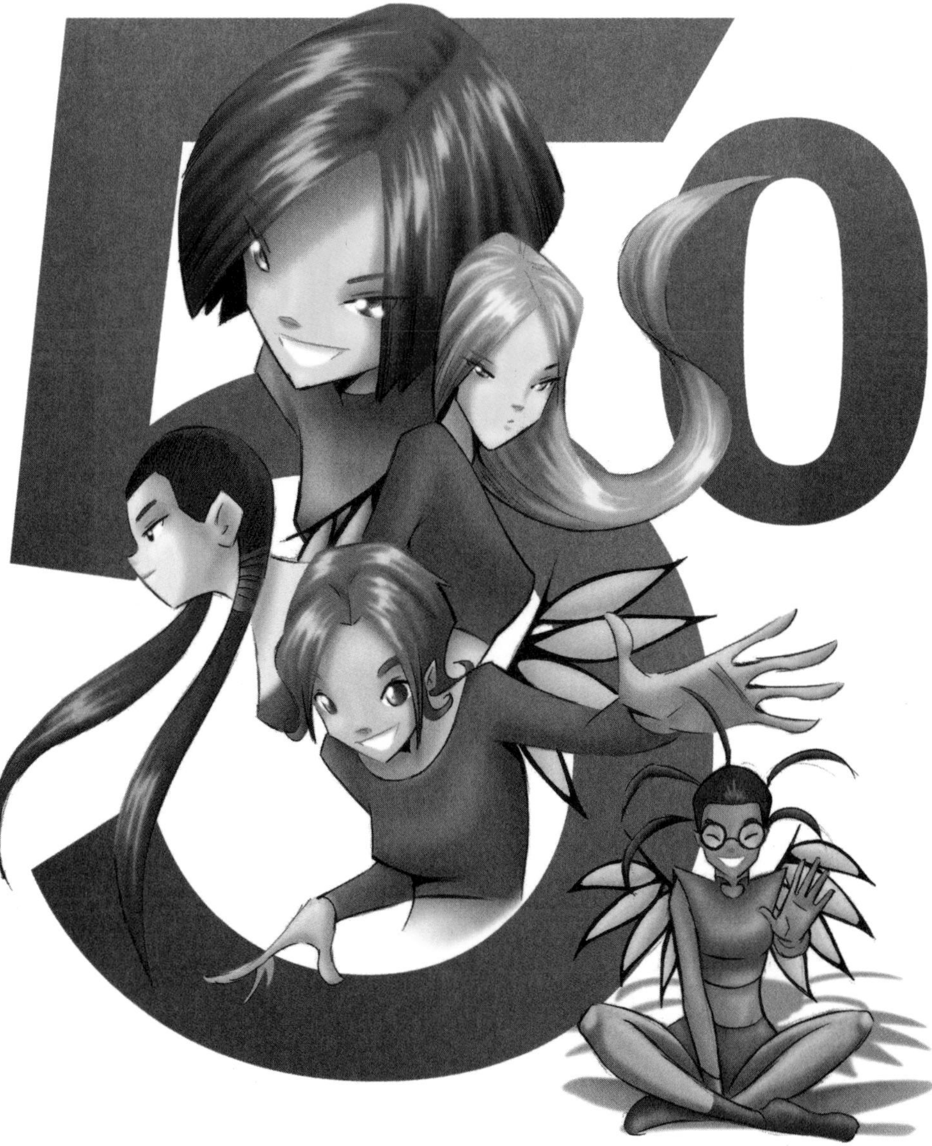

Illustration by: Alberto Zanon – Color by: Stefania Santi

W.i.t.c.h.

Will Irma Taranee Cornelia Hay Lin

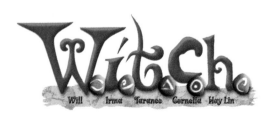

W.I.T.C.H. Art

Let's Draw Will

At last, a lesson on how to draw W.I.T.C.H.!
Grab a pencil and paper and follow the instructions.

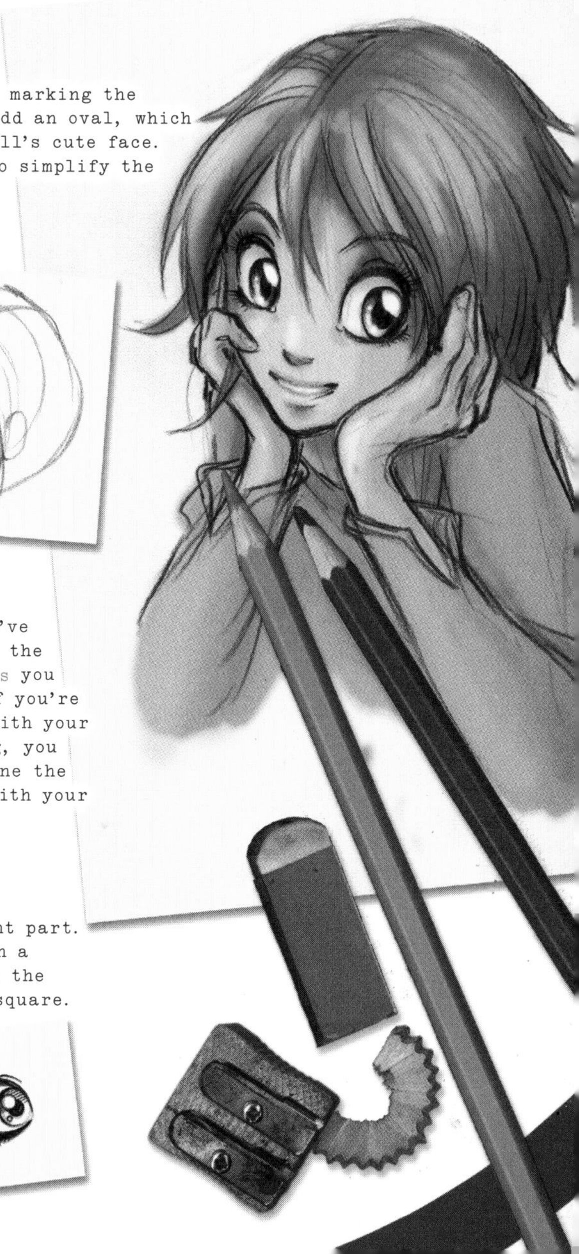

1. Draw a sphere, marking the middle, then add an oval, which will become Will's cute face. The trick is to simplify the shapes!

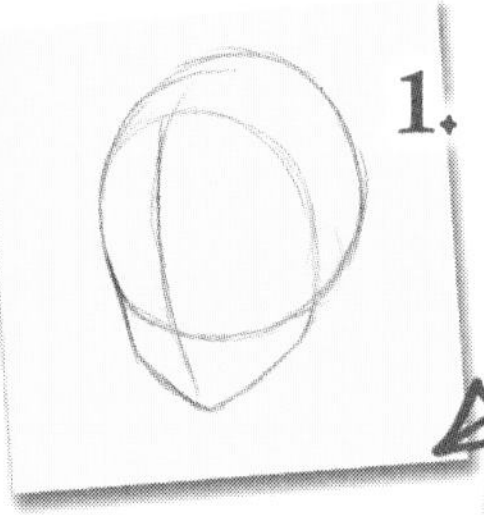

2. Add the shape of the hair, a little above the top of her head. Sketch the eyes, nose, and mouth.

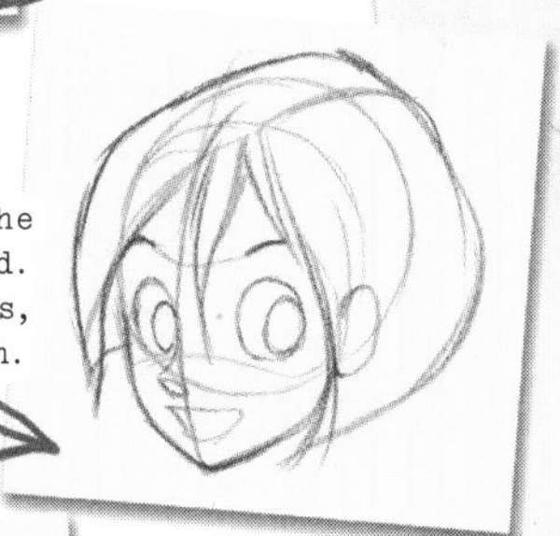

3. Now you've got all the elements you need. If you're happy with your drawing, you can define the lines with your pencil.

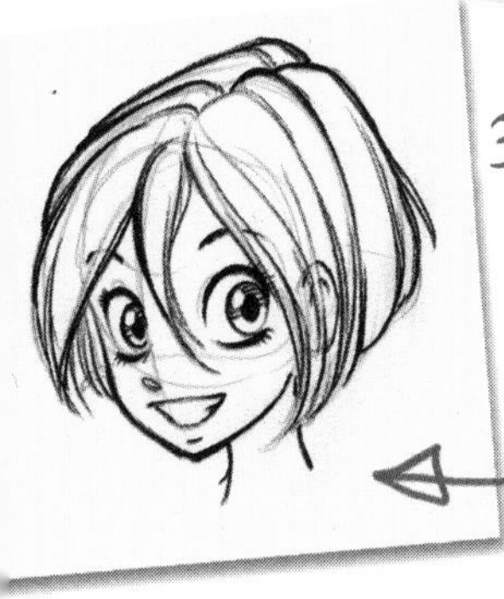

4. The eyes are the most important part. To draw Will's eyes, start with a circle that gets thicker where the lashes are, ending up almost square.

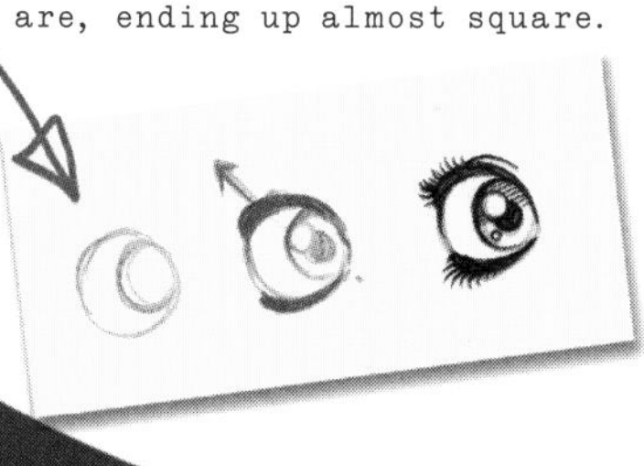

Practice Your Style

W.I.T.C.H. Art

Drawing the full figure is more complicated. Practice by copying these drawings and be careful to keep the head in proportion.

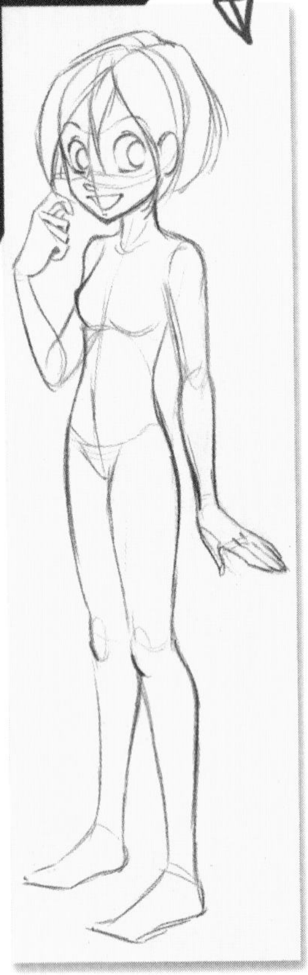

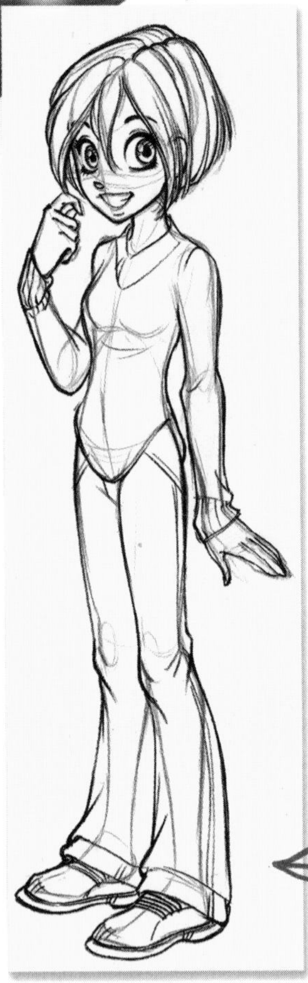

Once you've learned to draw the head and body, you can add clothes. Play with the folds and layers of fabric. Have fun creating a new wardrobe for Will!

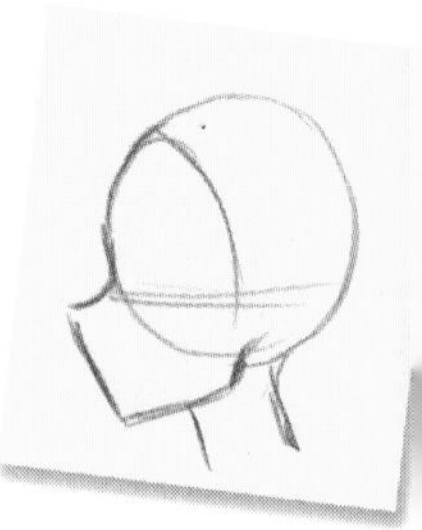

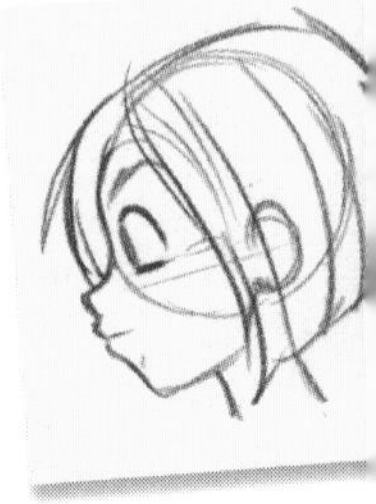

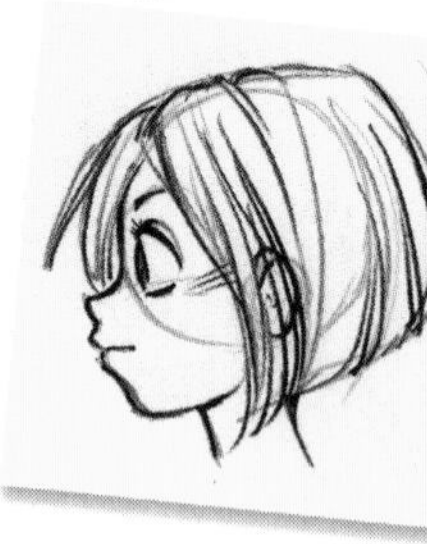

Practice drawing Will from the front and from the side by following the instructions on the previous page.

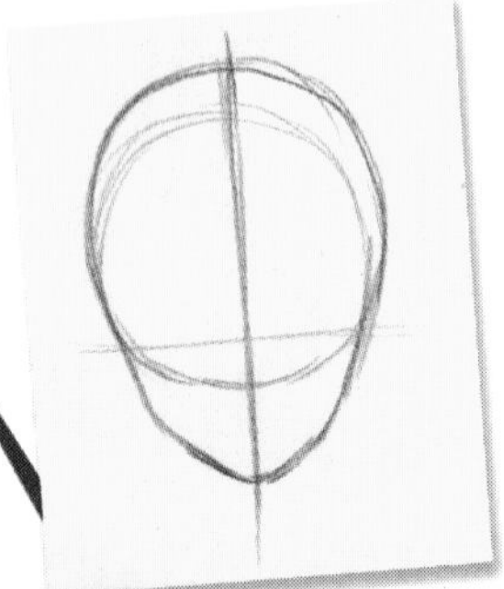

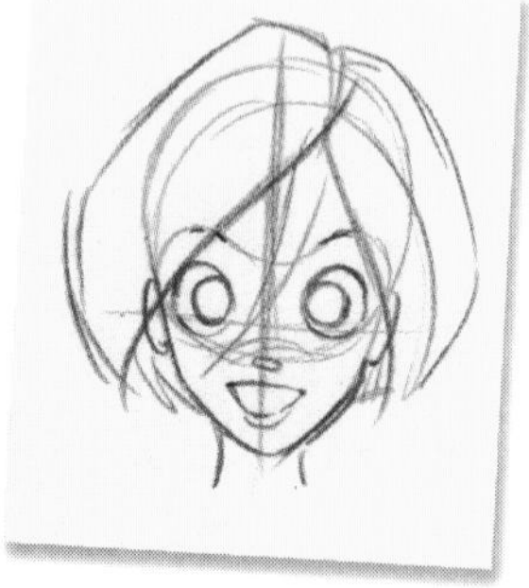

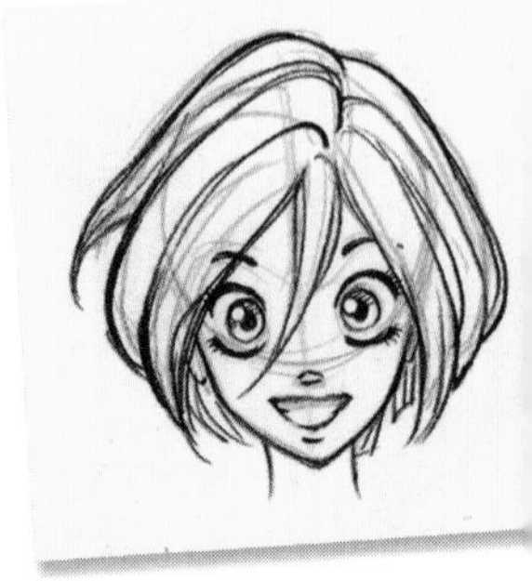

Now you can practice drawing various expressions. Don't be afraid to copy and don't get discouraged if it seems hard at first…

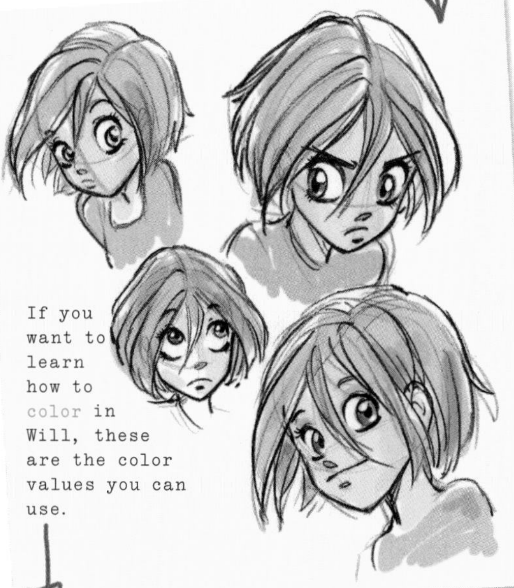

If you want to learn how to color in Will, these are the color values you can use.

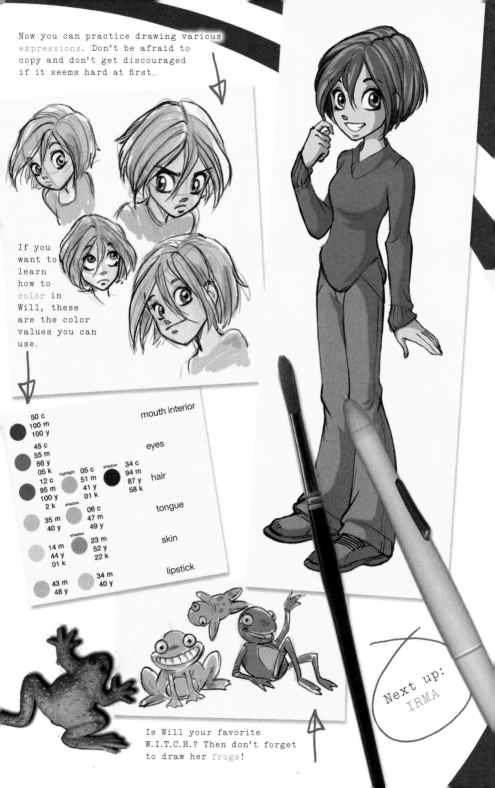

mouth interior	50 c 100 m 100 y		
eyes	45 c 55 m 66 y 05 k		
hair	12 c 95 m 100 y 2 k	highlight: 05 c 51 m 41 y 01 k	shadow: 34 c 94 m 87 y 58 k
tongue	35 m 40 y	shadow: 06 c 47 m 49 y	
skin	14 m 44 y 01 k	shadow: 23 m 52 y 22 k	
lipstick	43 m 48 y	34 m 40 y	

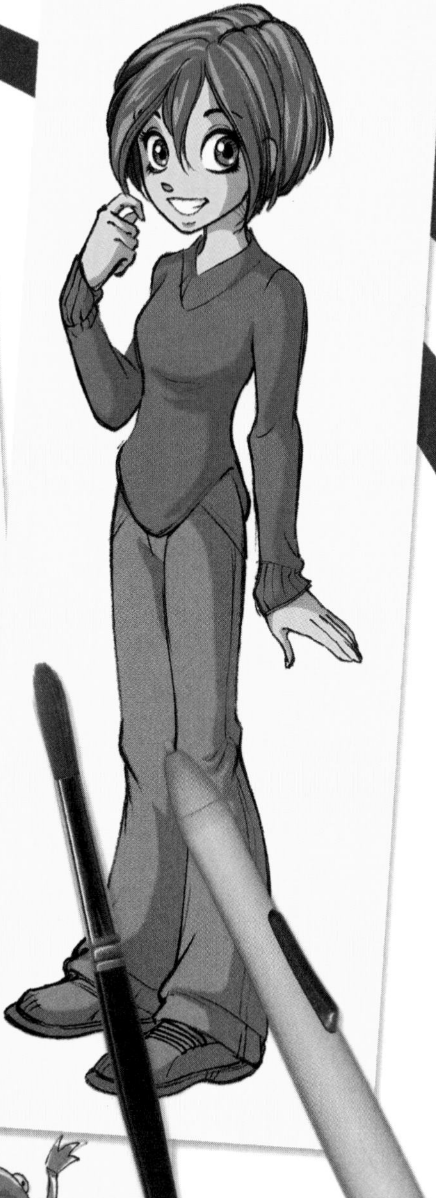

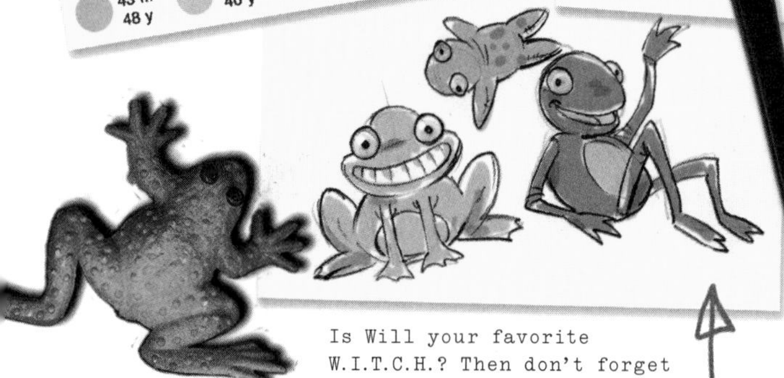

Is Will your favorite W.I.T.C.H.? Then don't forget to draw her frogs!

Next up: IRMA

W.i.t.c.h.

Will Irma Taranee Cornelia Hay Lin

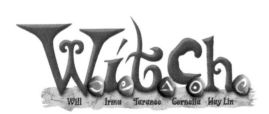

W.I.T.C.H. Art

Let's Draw Irma

After Will, learn to draw awesome Irma—it's easier than you think!

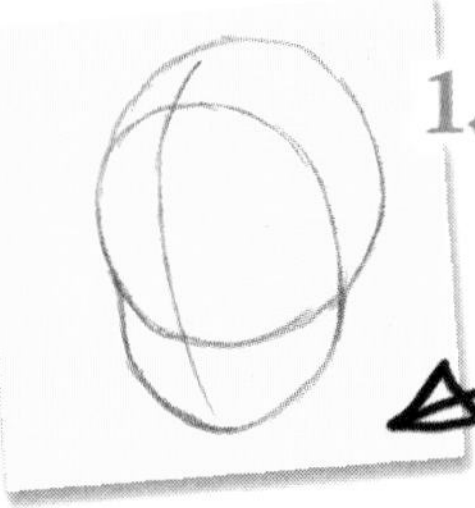

1. Drawing her head is like drawing Will's: You simplify the main shapes, drawing a sphere for the head and a kind of mask for the face.

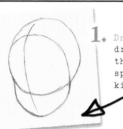

2. Add her hair, sketching Irma's signature bangs. Then add her eyes, nose, mouth, and eyebrows—very important for facial expressions.

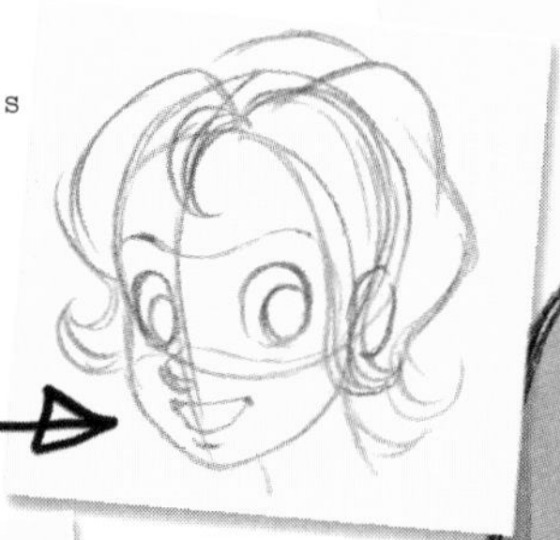

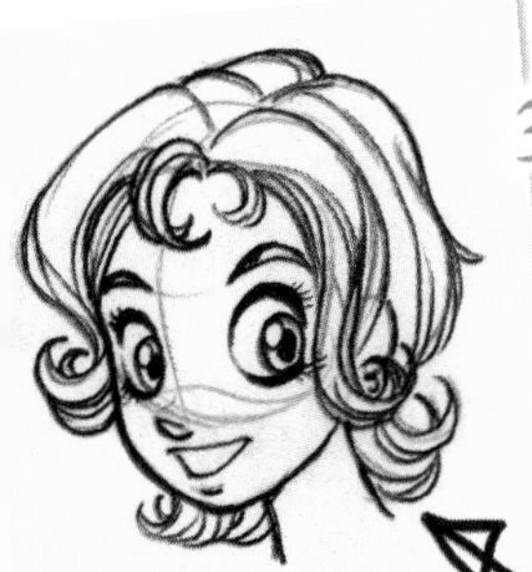

3. Now you can add details to your drawing, paying special attention to the bangs framing Irma's forehead. She changes hairdos often, but the bangs are always there!

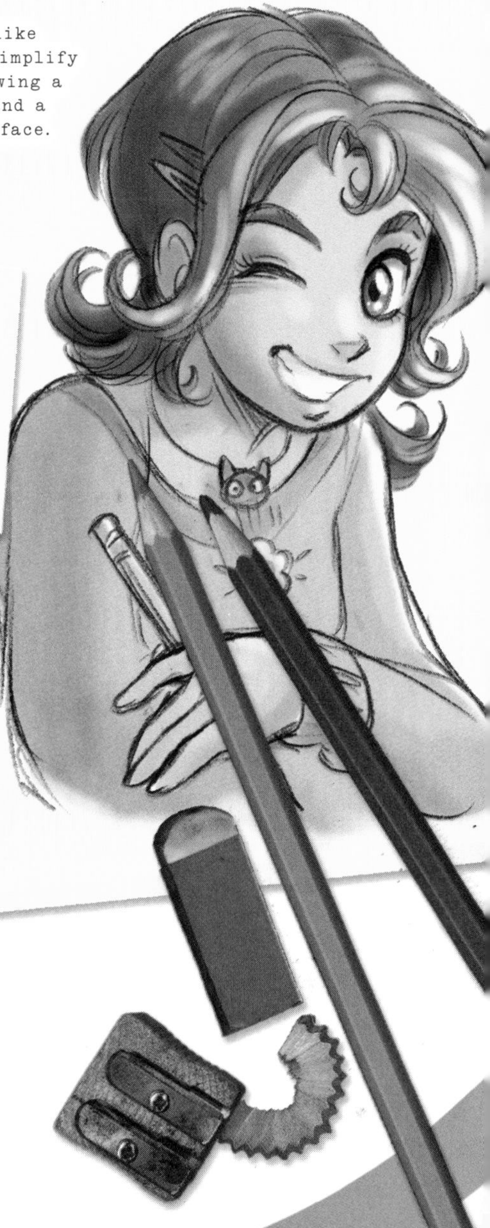

4. Irma's eyes have a similar shape to Will's, but with a little upward slant.

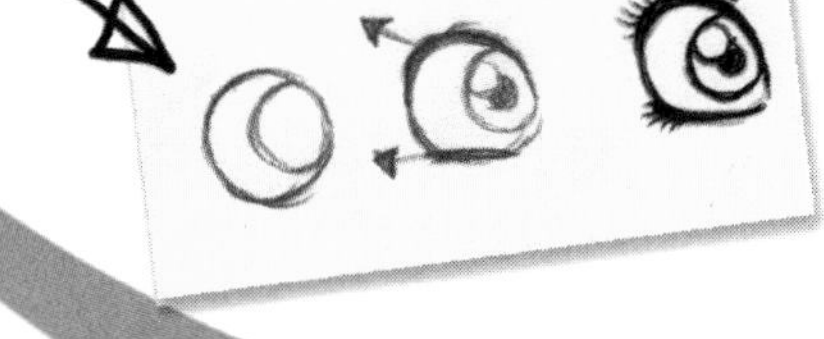

W.I.T.C.H. Art

Practice Your Style

Irma's body has slightly softer and more pronounced contours, since she's a little curvier than the other Guardians. So try to avoid sharp lines and corners.

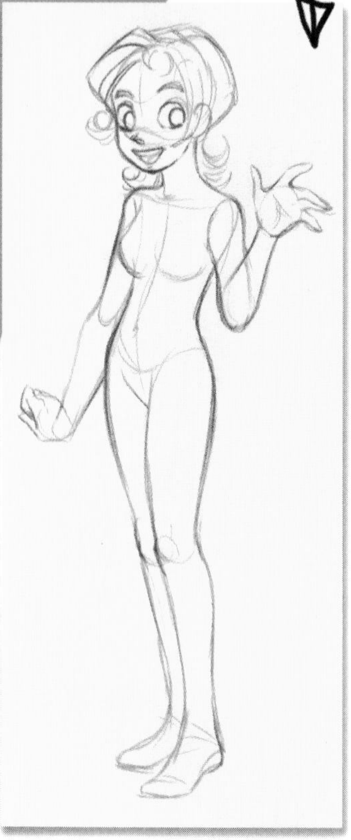

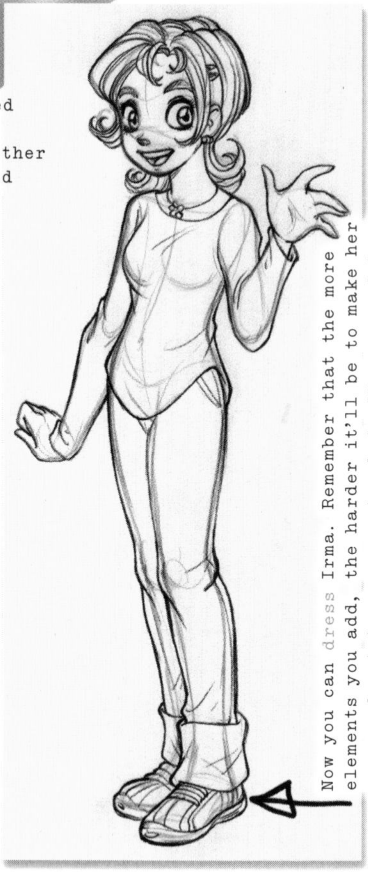

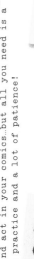

Now you can dress Irma. Remember that the more elements you add, the harder it'll be to make her move and act in your comics…but all you need is a little practice and a lot of patience!

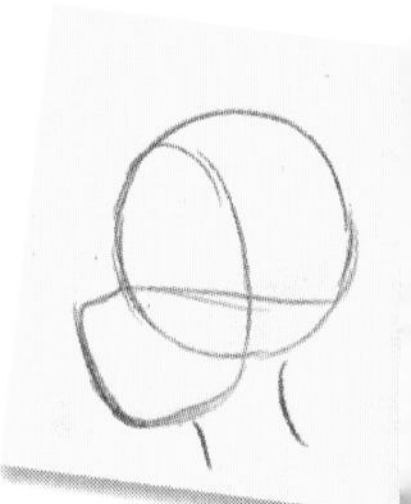

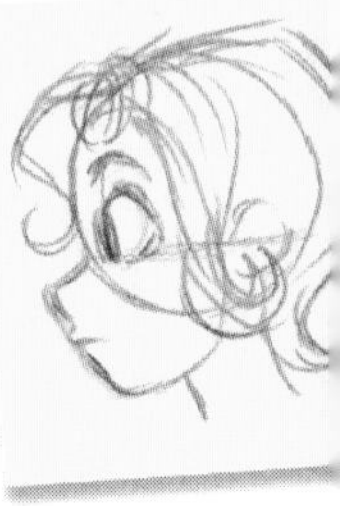

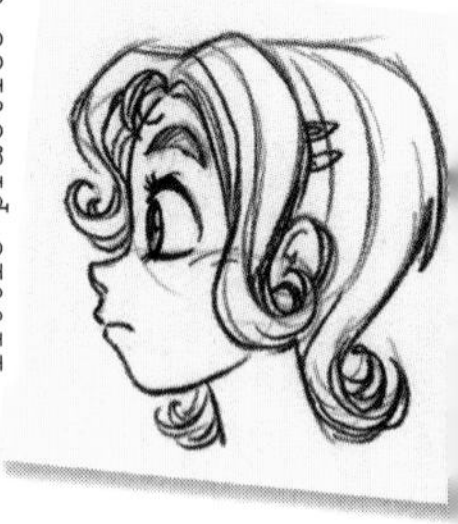

Front and side view: Do what you did for Will. Mind the position of the ears and try to keep the eyes even!

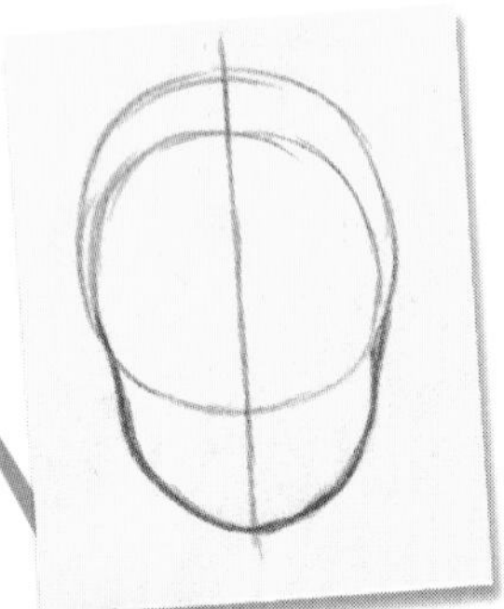

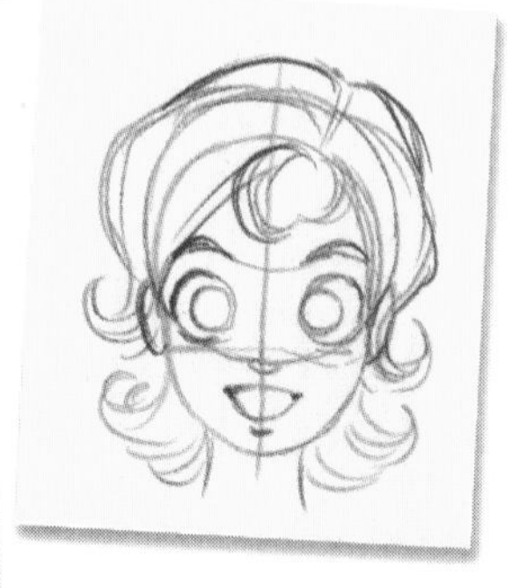

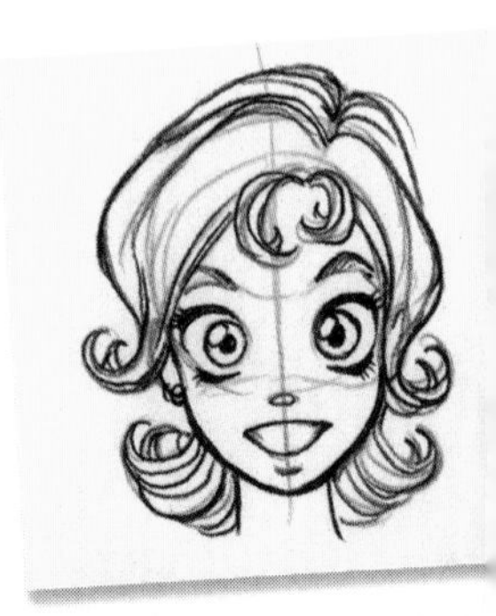

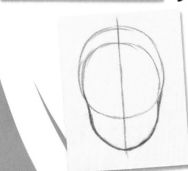

Irma's typical expressions are very intense! After all, she never does anything halfway. Study these expressions and try to copy them, then make up some new ones.

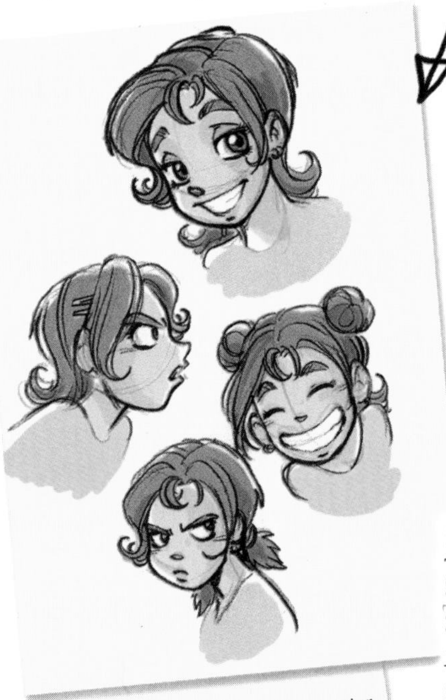

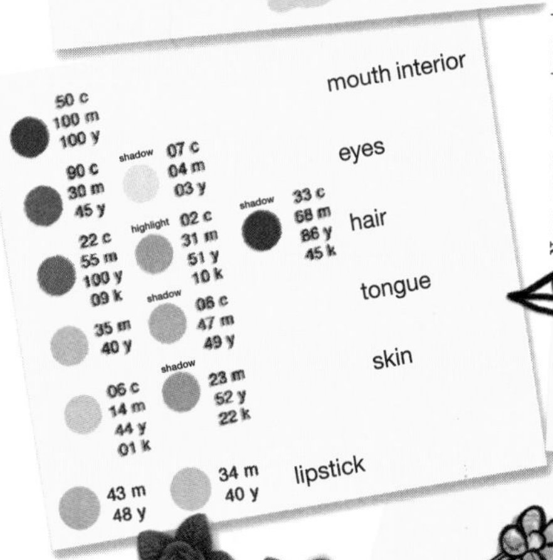
mouth interior
50 c
100 m
100 y
eyes
90 c
30 m
45 y
shadow
07 c
04 m
03 y
hair
22 c
55 m
100 y
09 k
highlight
02 c
31 m
51 y
10 k
shadow
33 c
68 m
86 y
45 k
tongue
35 m
40 y
shadow
06 c
47 m
49 y
skin
06 c
14 m
44 y
01 k
shadow
23 m
52 y
22 k
lipstick
43 m
48 y
34 m
40 y

Now you can try to color her: Remember that Irma loves pastel colors (and all shades of blue).

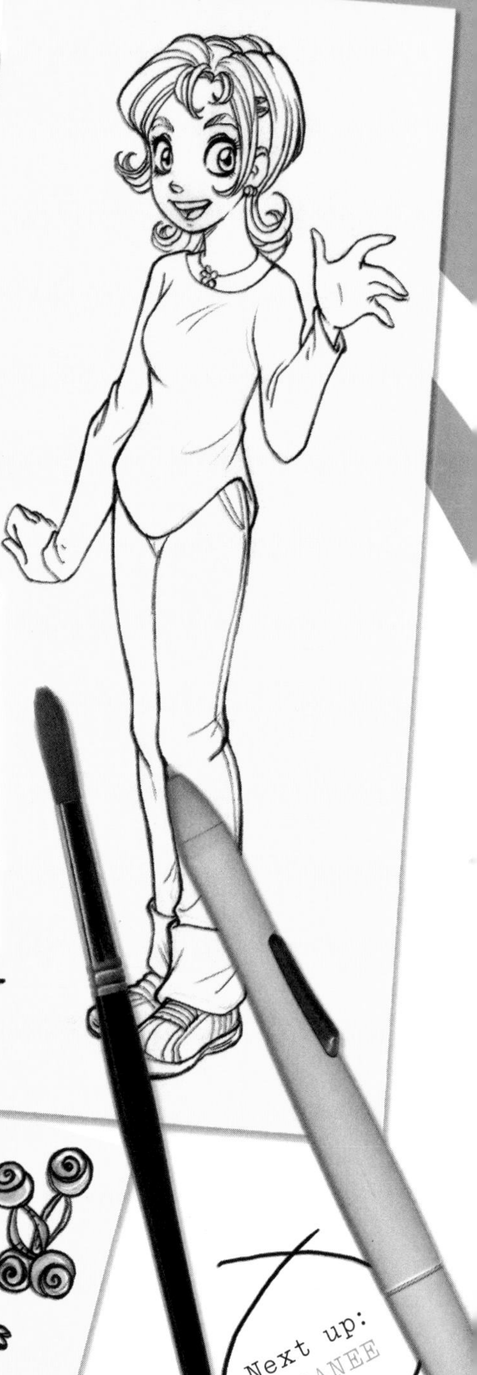

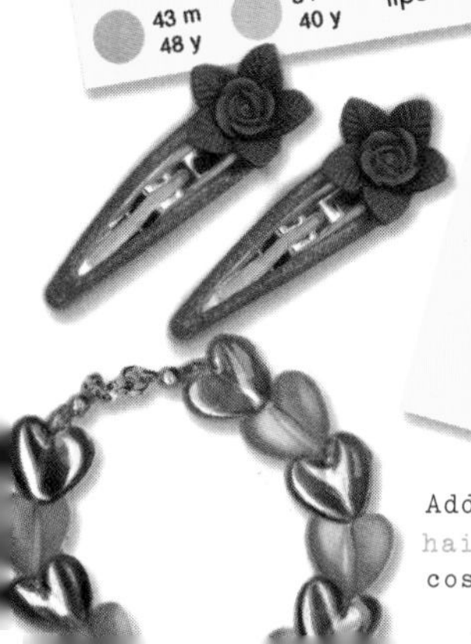

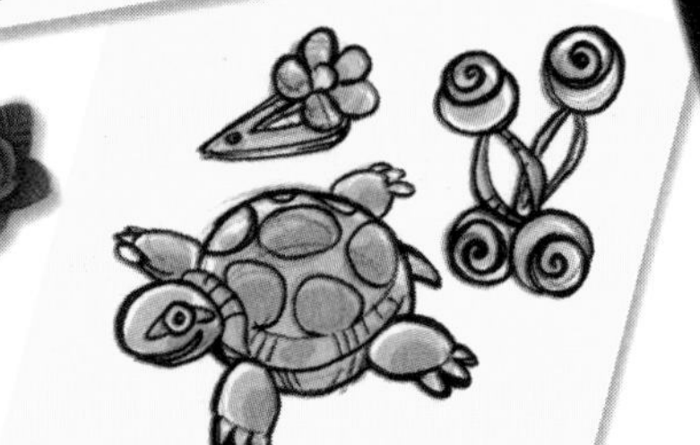

Add the finishing touch with hair clips, plush toys, and costume jewelry!

Next up: TARANEE

In Taranee's Dance Studio

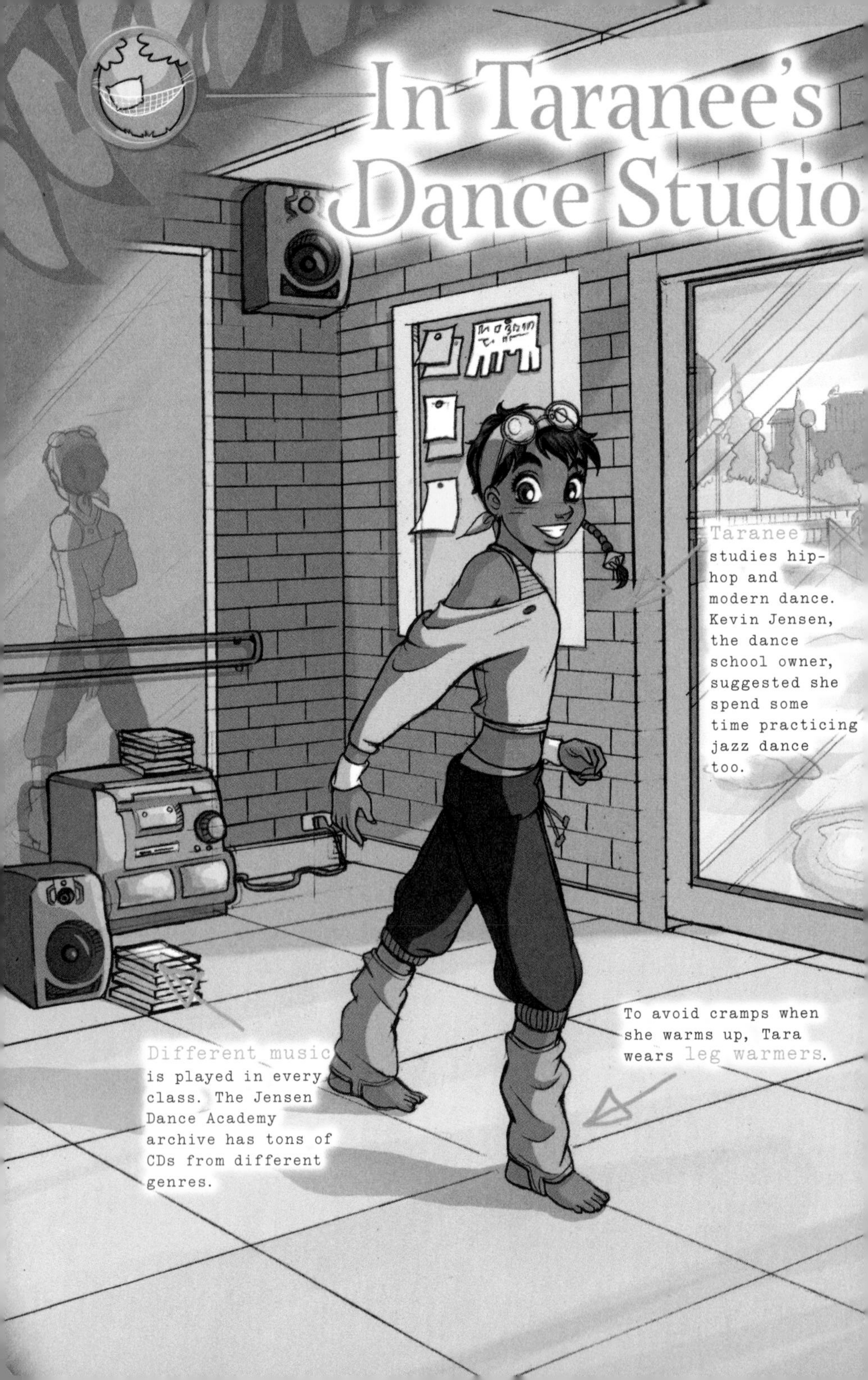
Taranee studies hip-hop and modern dance. Kevin Jensen, the dance school owner, suggested she spend some time practicing jazz dance too.
To avoid cramps when she warms up, Tara wears leg warmers.
Different music is played in every class. The Jensen Dance Academy archive has tons of CDs from different genres.

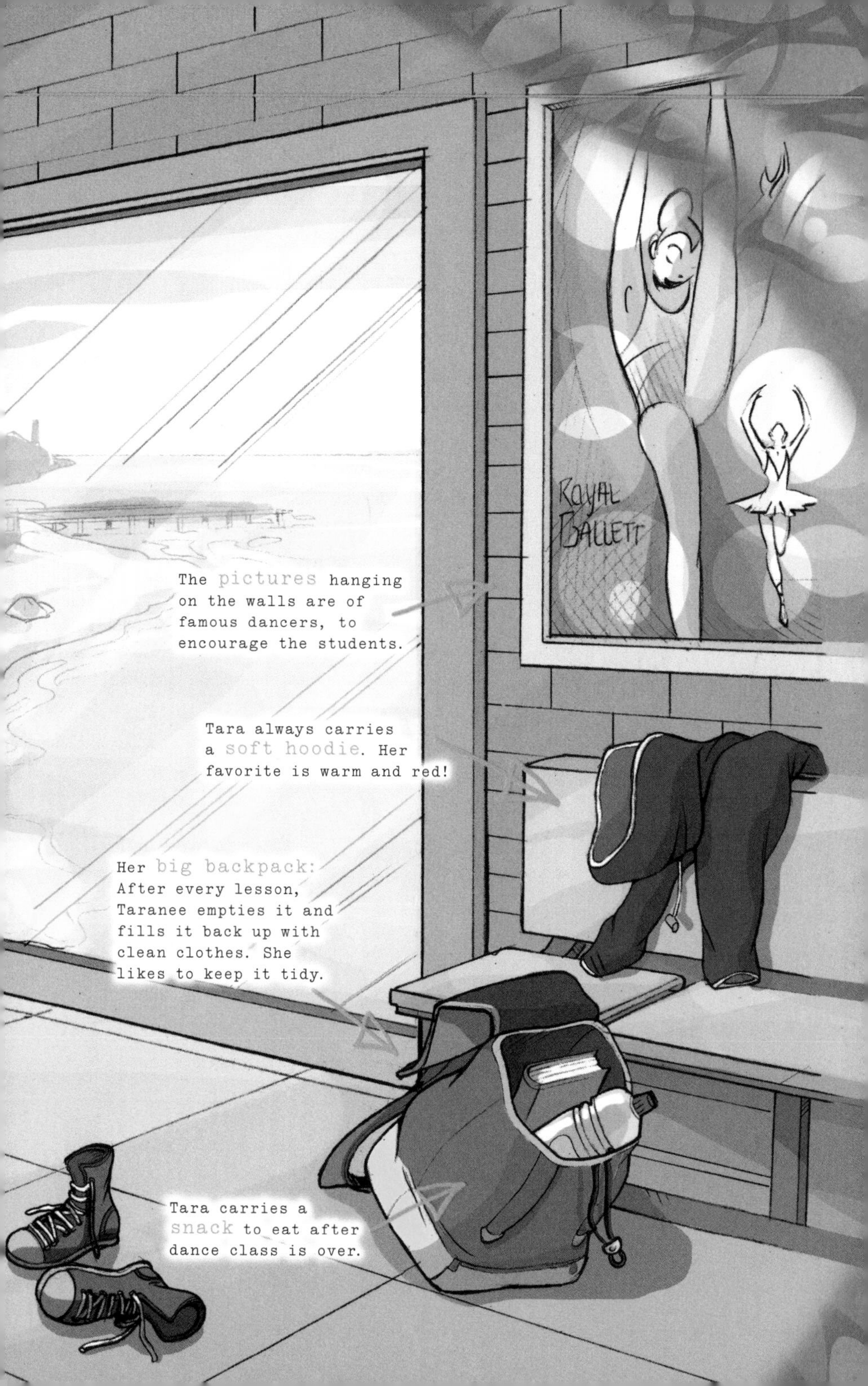
ROYAL BALLETT
The pictures hanging on the walls are of famous dancers, to encourage the students.
Tara always carries a soft hoodie. Her favorite is warm and red!
Her big backpack: After every lesson, Taranee empties it and fills it back up with clean clothes. She likes to keep it tidy.
Tara carries a snack to eat after dance class is over.

W.I.T.C.H.

Will Irma Taranee Cornelia Hay Lin

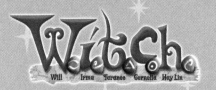

Part V. The Book of Elements • Volume 4

16

Series Created by Elisabetta Gnone
Comic Art Direction: Alessandro Barbucci, Barbara Canepa

This book is a work of fiction. Names, characters, places, and incidents are the product of the author's imagination or are used fictitiously. Any resemblance to actual events, locales, or persons, living or dead, is coincidental.

JY
1290 Avenue of the Americas
New York, NY 10104

Visit us at jyforkids.com
facebook.com/jyforkids
twitter.com/jyforkids
jyforkids.tumblr.com
instagram.com/jyforkids

First JY Edition: May 2019

JY is an imprint of Yen Press, LLC.
The JY name and logo are trademarks of Yen Press, LLC.

The publisher is not responsible for websites (or their content) that are not owned by the publisher.

Library of Congress Control Number: 2017950917

ISBNs:
978-1-9753-8389-3 (paperback)
978-1-9753-8390-9 (ebook)

10 9 8 7 6 5 4 3 2 1

LSC-C

Printed in the United States of America

Cover Art by Federico Bertolucci
Colors by Andrea Cagol

Translation by Linda Ghio and Stephanie Dagg at Editing Zone
Lettering by Katie Blakeslee

THE WORLD INSIDE THE BOOK

Concept by Bruno Enna
Script by Giulia Conti
Layout by Monica Catalano
Pencils by Davide Baldoni
Inks by Marina Baggio and Roberta Zanotta
Color and Light Direction by Francesco Legramandi
Title Page Art by Monica Catalano
with colors by Andrea Cagol

BETWEEN THE PAGES

Concept and Script by Teresa Radice
Layout by Flavia Scuderi
Pencils by Lucia Balletti
Inks by Marina Baggio, Roberta Zanotta, and Santa Zangari
Color and Light Direction by Francesco Legramandi
Title Page Art by Alberta Zanon
with colors by Andrea Cagol

ARRIVALS AND DEPARTURES

Concept and Script by Teresa Radice
Layout and Pencils by Paolo Campinoti
Inks by Santa Zangari, Federica Salfo, and Danilo Loizedda
Color and Light Direction by Francesco Legramandi
Title Page Art by Federico Bertolucci
with colors by Andrea Cagol